TRIANGLE CLASSICS

ILLUMINATING THE GAY AND LESBIAN EXPERIENCE

And the Band Played On
by Randy Shilts

Another Mother Tongue
by Judy Grahn

The Autobiography of Alice B. Toklas
by Gertrude Stein

The Beebo Brinker Chronicles
by Ann Bannon

Before Night Falls
by Reinaldo Arenas

Bertram Cope's Year
by Henry Blake Fuller

Borrowed Time/Love Alone/Becoming a Man
by Paul Monette

A Boy's Own Story/
The Beautiful Room Is Empty
by Edmund White

Brideshead Revisited
by Evelyn Waugh

The Celluloid Closet
by Vito Russo

City of Night
by John Rechy

Dancer from the Dance
by Andrew Holleran

Death in Venice and Seven Other Stories
by Thomas Mann

Family Dancing
by David Leavitt

The Family of Max Desir
by Robert Ferro

The Front Runner
by Patricia Nell Warren

Gay Spirit/Gay Soul
by Mark Thompson

The Gilda Stories/Bones & Ash
by Jewelle Gomez

Giovanni's Room
by James Baldwin

A Home at the End of the World/Flesh and Blood
by Michael Cunningham

I've a Feeling We're Not in Kansas Anymore/
Buddies/Everybody Loves You
by Ethan Mordden

The Lord Won't Mind/One for the Gods
by Gordon Merrick

The Lure
by Felice Picano

The Naked Civil Servant/How to Become a Virgin/
Resident Alien
by Quentin Crisp

Nightwood/Ladies Almanack
by Djuna Barnes

Olivia
by Olivia

Oranges Are Not the Only Fruit
by Jeanette Winterson

Orlando
by Virginia Woolf

The Picture of Dorian Gray
by Oscar Wilde

The Price of Salt
by Patricia Highsmith

Rubyfruit Jungle
by Rita Mae Brown

Sexual Politics/Sita
by Kate Millett

A Single Man
by Christopher Isherwood

Skinflick/Gravedigger/Nightwork
by Joseph Hansen

The Sophie Horowitz Story/Girls, Visions and
Everything/After Dolores
by Sarah Schulman

Stone Butch Blues
by Leslie Feinberg

Surpassing the Love of Men
by Lillian Faderman

The Swimming-Pool Library
by Alan Hollinghurst

The Well of Loneliness
by Radclyffe Hall

What Is Found There/An Atlas of the Difficult World/
The Fact of a Doorframe
by Adrienne Rich

Zami/Sister Outsider/Undersong
by Audre Lorde

I'VE A FEELING WE'RE
NOT IN KANSAS
ANYMORE

BUDDIES

EVERYBODY LOVES YOU

I'VE A FEELING WE'RE NOT IN KANSAS ANYMORE

BUDDIES

EVERYBODY LOVES YOU

ETHAN MORDDEN

InsightOut Books
New York

Introduction

Scotch. Kumquats. Asparagus.

These are the sorts of things I'd always assumed made up that shady realm commonly referred to as "acquired taste." It's stuff that makes most kids spit, but makes lots of adults feel tingly and speak rhapsodically. Many of these adults, of course, are themselves the expectorating tykes of yore.

I'd always thought this whole acquired-taste business was pretty strictly a food thing. Well, food and *New Yorker* cartoons. Then I discovered Ethan Mordden's "Buddies" books. Or, to be more accurate, rediscovered.

In 1997, an editor asked me to review *Some Men Are Lookers*, Mordden's decade-later return to the characters he created in his original threesome of "Buddies" volumes: *I've a Feeling We're Not in Kansas Anymore*, *Buddies*, and *Everybody Loves You*. When I first encountered these bittersweet comic tales of life in Manhattan's gay ghetto, I was mightily put off by their portrayals of free-range sex, gender roleplay, and oddly structured relationships. In taking on the new book for review, I promised myself I would do the requisite homework. I knew that just like that time I was assigned the sequel to a novel about Jesuit missionaries in outer space, I was going to have to bite the bullet and go back to the originals. And to me, reading the "Buddies" books was even more daunting than a double dose of Vatican-sponsored adventures on the planet Rakhat.

Almost ten years earlier, I was a stumbly newcomer to all things gay, living in an underwear and beer can strewn off-campus apartment at the University of Pennsylvania (whose alumni, unbeknownst to me, included one Ethan Mordden). Alongside the futon, plopped amidst the boxer briefs and empty Buds, were the "Buddies" books. They were not mine. They belonged to my first boyfriend, a gay-prideful caterer and fine disco dancer who, in the spirit of Mordden's own true-identity-blurring character nicknames, will here be known as Boy Perky.

I didn't allow myself to really absorb the content of Boy Perky's original editions of the "Buddies" books. I would flip them open now and again and find myself discomforted from the very first story, "Interview with the Drag Queen," in which "Miss Titania soothed Carl's hole with her tongue and slowly worked it open."

Ohmigod and please pass the J. D. Salinger!

"It sounds fun," said Boy Perky, who, I imagined, wore rainbow flag Pampers as a toddler. "Let's try it. Or at least rent a video of it!"

I would sheepishly turn the trilogy's pages, made uneasy by Mordden's clever references to sex in the Fire Island dunes, nights at the opera, cruising on Christopher Street, 1940s movie trivia.

I don't want these cliches to be my life, I grumbled.

"Have you seen Miss Cranky?" called Boy Perky. This was his nickname for the fleshy pink dildo he'd coaxed me into buying him as a Valentine's gift.

In retrospect, I think that while Boy Perky comfortably bought into gay stereotypes, I needed to *grow* into them. As a newly out twenty-year-old, my own taste in gay literature leaned toward coming-out stories; I wanted to read about guys my own age seeing the world crack open for the first time, gaining their first shaky footing on promising new terrain. But I didn't want the books to go much further than that. I didn't want an instruction manual on how to proceed as a gay man. I was armed with the necessary arrogance of youth: I wanted to invent my own life, in some completely original way.

Not to mention, I was scared. The world of Ethan Mordden's "Buddies" novels is largely a world before AIDS. By the end of the third volume, *Everybody Loves You*, some shadow is beginning to fall, but for the most part, Mordden's milieu in these stories is, epidemiologically speaking, ancient history. When I was coming out in the mid-1980s, I felt a real impulse to run away from the first post-Stonewall generation. I'll now admit, with both embarrassment and contrition, that I somehow linked Mordden's characters, along with their symbols and styles, with a disease. And so I shut the books on them.

After graduation, Boy Perky and I went our separate ways. I soon learned that he had taken off to explore Europe with a man twenty years our senior. The very thought of it frightened me.

I stayed home and read.

From my earlier interest in coming-out stories, my taste in gay literature moved on to contemporary work that addressed AIDS head-on, books like John Weir's *The Irreversible Decline of Eddie Socket*, Allen Barnett's *The Body and Its Dangers*, and David B. Feinberg's lacerBarnett's *The Body and Its Dangers*, and David B. Feinberg's lacerat-ingly funny *Eighty-Sixed*. Next came an ongoing interest in domestic and social dramas in which contemporary gay men and lesbians do not exist in self-selected or demonized subcultures, but struggle to integrate themselves in the heterogeneous world at large, including the works of David Leavitt, Michael Cunningham, and Douglas Sadownick's dazzling *Sacred Lips of the Bronx*. For years, my reading was all about what's now, and what's next. I never looked back.

Here's the thing about acquired taste. You really do grow into it. A kid doesn't *acquire* a liking for asparagus by being force-fed a spear or two every day. With some trepidation, he decides to take another nibble years later and is taken aback to find that he enjoys the complex flavor.

When it comes to food, it turns out that the notion of acquired taste is backed by science. Kids' tastebuds have different sensitivities to chemicals than adults' do. It's about immaturity. Things really do change as we get older. And if we're brave enough to go back and try something again, years after we first spat it out, we are sometimes amazed at the new pleasure we find.

When my editor assigned me to write about *Some Men Are Lookers* in 1997, I finally sat back down with its three predecessors and, to my surprise, found them quite delicious. With ten years in the gay world under my belt, I found the sexy, bitchy surfaces of these stories much less threatening (and I recognized how expertly styled they are, with dialogue as pitch-perfect as you'll find anywhere).

Through my experiences both in reading and in living, I'd also developed an ability to see beyond these surfaces to recognize the heart of Mordden's work, a fiercely intelligent and unsentimentally poignant comprehension of gay psyches. He illuminates our need for deep friendships that might include, but must transcend, sex. He limns our desires both to form newfangled families, and to find points of reconciliation with our old-fashioned families.

Yes, the original trilogy's stories happen to be set amidst the celebratory, in-your-face gay scene of the late '70s and early '80s. But when I reacquainted myself with the tales' four central characters—writer Bud, schoolteacher Dennis and their younger companions, Little Kiwi and Cosgrove—in the more circumspect mid-'90s Manhattan of *Some Men Are Lookers*, it became clear to me that what Ethan Mordden has to tell us about timeless human yearnings transcends the relevance of the particular historical moment in which each tale happens to be set.

Reading these books, and exploring the continuity of these richly drawn characters, from the exuberance of the post-Stonewall moment to the ambiguity of the AZT era, can help provide a bracing literary antidote to one of the biggest ongoing problems within the gay community, the generational rift that spun out of AIDS.

Just out of college, I was terribly quick to assume that Boy Perky had no reason to be spending time with a man who was gay before there was AIDS. They were different species, weren't they?

If you came of age in the '80s or beyond, read the "Buddies" books with an open heart and an open mind. Don't think of it as nostalgia. When you recognize yourself (well, a wittier version of yourself) in Ethan Mordden's tenderly drawn characters, you'll feel reconnected to a body of literature and a generation of men that deserve our attention, and our affection. Perhaps, as I did, you'll learn that a work of fiction can be an acquired taste, and that, through the prism of reading, you can see your way to becoming a more mature person.

— Jim Gladstone

I'VE A FEELING WE'RE NOT IN KANSAS ANYMORE

TALES FROM GAY MANHATTAN

To Michael Denneny,
sine qua non

Contents

Acknowledgments

The author wishes to acknowledge the strategic collaboration of the house team, which, he is glad to note, still includes the masterful Ina Shapiro, one of the most precise of stylists. Paul Liepa keeps a yare ship, Deborah Daly is indispensable in jacket-art meetings, Izume Inoue presents a unique rendering of The Emerald City of Manhattan on the cover, Laura Hough designed what IBM would call a "reader-friendly" book, Carol Shookhoff assisted in the typing of a printer-friendly manuscript, and, for the home side, there remains the redoubtable Dorothy Pittman, the author's best friend and agent, in that order. As for Michael Denneny, the editor of this book, I have expressed my feelings a few pages to the fore.

In particular, I would like to thank Charles Ortleb, the founder and publisher of *Christopher Street,* where a substantial share of post-Stonewall gay lit has originated—not because writers have battered their way in, but because Chuck personally stimulated, encouraged, and in some cases helped subsidize their careers. Without his insistence that gays maintain at least one forum for new journalists, storytellers, and poets, gay publishing might have consisted of nothing but an occasional shuddering of the linotype's chromosomes.

Preface

I have sat with friends—and I mean very close friends—on those long nights at the Pines, listening to the ocean dancing about our mysterious island, and on those long days at the brunch table, trying to remember to be urbane, and on those odd, ironic afternoons of confessing feelings of such intimate enthusiasm or disappointment that one regrets having made them for the rest of one's life. We have traded tales, my buddies and I: of affairs, encounters, discoveries, weekends, parties, secrets, fears, self-promotions—of fantasies that we make real in the telling.

Well, it occurs to me that all of gay life is stories—that all these stories are about love somehow or other, and that many jests are made in them, though the overall feeling may be sad. One's life breaks into episodes, chapters of a picaresque adventure. As each episode ends, the material for the next shifts into place. Defunct characters cede to new ones, though a few figures—the best friends—hold their places throughout. A happy ending must be temporary, and a gloomy one may yield to surprising amusement without warning. It is a lively life I sing, with but two constants: humor and friendship. I am looking back now on what I have seen and heard, and on the men I have known, and on certain perceptions I am reluctantly compelled to share. And these are my tales . . .

fifty. Black cocktail dress, spike heels, cabaret mascara, and opera jewelry.

"When Miss Titania gave an order, you obeyed or that's it, you were out! You were glue. You were *grovel!* I mean. Miss Titania was the very certain queen of the Heat Rack—and was she big, I ask you? Bigger than a Zulu's dingus on Thursday night. Big in *spirit!* Miss Titania had her court, and everyone else was dogmeat when Miss Titania got through. Ask anyone. I don't know where they are now, but you ask them."

My pen flew. "Where's Miss Titania now?" I asked.

The drag queen shrugged. "It's all gone, so that is no question at all to me. Now every man in the city looks like trade in those muscle shirts, with those demure little bags like they're carrying their makeup kit or I don't know what. I don't think there's a man in New York who isn't available. Once even the gays were straight; now all the straights are gay. New York doesn't like queens anymore, regardless. We're the old revolutionaries. They say we dressed up because we were flops as men. Born to be freaks. They say we didn't care what other folks thought." She lit a cigarette like a woman, blowing the match out; and held it like a man, between thumb and forefinger. "Well, it's not true. We dressed up so they could see how lovely we are. We hope they see it."

"What if they don't?"

"Then we say something pungent."

"Tell me about Miss Titania."

"She was ruthless. The Heat Rack was her court, and *no one* upstaged her. The dire episodes! Once an upstart southern belle came in out of nowhere—I suspect Scranton—and there she was, taking up space and flouting Miss Titania. I will never forget—'Mr. Sandman' was playing on the juke, and Miss Titania liked to sing along, you know, such as 'Mr. Sandman, please make me cream.' A slightly altered version of the original, as I recall. Well, La Southern Comfort cries out, 'Deyah me, it would surely take the entiyah football teyum? at Ole Miss? to make you-all creayum, I'm shuah?' And there

2

Preface

I have sat with friends—and I mean very close friends—on those long nights at the Pines, listening to the ocean dancing about our mysterious island, and on those long days at the brunch table, trying to remember to be urbane, and on those odd, ironic afternoons of confessing feelings of such intimate enthusiasm or disappointment that one regrets having made them for the rest of one's life. We have traded tales, my buddies and I: of affairs, encounters, discoveries, weekends, parties, secrets, fears, self-promotions—of fantasies that we make real in the telling.

Well, it occurs to me that all of gay life is stories—that all these stories are about love somehow or other, and that many jests are made in them, though the overall feeling may be sad. One's life breaks into episodes, chapters of a picaresque adventure. As each episode ends, the material for the next shifts into place. Defunct characters cede to new ones, though a few figures—the best friends—hold their places throughout. A happy ending must be temporary, and a gloomy one may yield to surprising amusement without warning. It is a lively life I sing, with but two constants: humor and friendship. I am looking back now on what I have seen and heard, and on the men I have known, and on certain perceptions I am reluctantly compelled to share. And these are my tales . . .

Interview with the Drag Queen

At night, writing longhand in a spiral notebook at my desk, I can see my reflection in a window washed in lamplight, as if I were working before a mirror. I have a romance going that I am my characters, and can put on any of their faces at will. I can be all forearm and fist, or startled behind spectacles; I can wear my college sweatshirt, or hold my pen in an old-fashioned manner. When I view my reflection in the window, I am telling stories.

I say this because I recall that the drag queen recounted her saga into a great mirror that stood just over my left shoulder. She scarcely looked at me, or at her friend Paul, who had brought me to her.

"You must tell her story," Paul had urged. "This is gay history."

No, I was writing nonfiction then. I had no reflection. "I wouldn't know where to sell it," I told him. No stories.

"Try," he said. "Just take it down. *Someday.*"

I was intrigued. Paul arranged it, took me to a shabby walkup where Bleecker Street meets The Bowery, introduced us, and—breaking his word of honor not to leave me alone—walked out. "You'll see," he murmured. "See what?" I answered; he was already at the door, waving.

"'Who was that masked man?'" I quoted, to cover my embarrassment. And: "Why does everyone I know run out on me after five minutes?"

This was eleven years ago. The drag queen was perhaps

1

fifty. Black cocktail dress, spike heels, cabaret mascara, and opera jewelry.

"When Miss Titania gave an order, you obeyed or that's it, you were out! You were glue. You were *grovel!* I mean. Miss Titania was the very certain queen of the Heat Rack—and was she big, I ask you? Bigger than a Zulu's dingus on Thursday night. Big in *spirit!* Miss Titania had her court, and everyone else was dogmeat when Miss Titania got through. Ask anyone. I don't know where they are now, but you ask them."

My pen flew. "Where's Miss Titania now?" I asked.

The drag queen shrugged. "It's all gone, so that is no question at all to me. Now every man in the city looks like trade in those muscle shirts, with those demure little bags like they're carrying their makeup kit or I don't know what. I don't think there's a man in New York who isn't available. Once even the gays were straight; now all the straights are gay. New York doesn't like queens anymore, regardless. We're the old revolutionaries. They say we dressed up because we were flops as men. Born to be freaks. They say we didn't care what other folks thought." She lit a cigarette like a woman, blowing the match out; and held it like a man, between thumb and forefinger. "Well, it's not true. We dressed up so they could see how lovely we are. We hope they see it."

"What if they don't?"

"Then we say something pungent."

"Tell me about Miss Titania."

"She was ruthless. The Heat Rack was her court, and *no one* upstaged her. The dire episodes! Once an upstart southern belle came in out of nowhere—I suspect Scranton—and there she was, taking up space and flouting Miss Titania. I will never forget—'Mr. Sandman' was playing on the juke, and Miss Titania liked to sing along, you know, such as 'Mr. Sandman, please make me cream.' A slightly altered version of the original, as I recall. Well, La Southern Comfort cries out, 'Deyah me, it would surely take the entiyah football teyum? at Ole Miss? to make you-all creayum, I'm shuah?' And there

2

was such silence in the whole place. Except for 'Mr. Sand-man.' I *mean*. Even the toughest trade shut up. And Miss Titania. She looks at that no-good, lightweight daredevil, and smiles her famous smile and puts down her drink and fan. And suddenly, I don't know, it couldn't have been more than a few seconds, but Miss Titania flies across the room and rips the hair right off that southern girl's head—I mean her wig, truly; did you think I meant her skull hair? because, really, what an odd look you're wearing—and then Miss Titania rends the bodice of the southern girl's gown and pulls off her pathetic training bra or whatever she had on, and we are all roaring with laughter, so that southern girl runs into the ladies' and won't come out till the place is closed. We never saw her after that. Because you *don't* challenge the queen in her own court.

"And Miss Titania was the absolute queen. Even the Duchess of Diva, who presided over Carney's on Thirty-eighth Street—even she knew better than to tangle with Miss Titania. And the Duchess was a gigantic mother. She must have weighed three hundred pounds. Always wore black, for her husband. He died in the war. And did she have a savage streak. Everyone feared her. But Miss Titania had the pres-tige."

"Tell me more about the Heat Rack."

"Or the Pleasure Bar, or Folly's, or The Demitasse, or Club La Bohème, or sometimes no name at all. It changed by the week. To me it was always the Heat Rack, because that's what they called it when I made my choice."

"Your choice?"

"Between love and beauty. Surely you know that every queen must choose between living for the one or the other. You can't have both." She rose and presented herself to the mirror pensively. "I chose beauty, because I imagined that those who know about love can never have it. Do you think so, too?"

I was young then, and never thought about it. Now, in my window, I wonder. The woman across the way, in direct

3

line of my desk, becomes unnerved at my concentration, and lowers her blinds.

"The bars today are just saloons," the drag queen goes on. "The Heat Rack was our fortress and fraternity, the only place where *we* made the rules. We rated the beauty and arranged the love stories." She sweeps through the dismal room, touching things. "The whole world is just queens, johns, trade, and cops. The whole world. And Miss Titania kept them *all* in line. Yes. Yes. Yes. And she was kind and beautiful."

She is not speaking to me.

"The johns you respect. The trade you screw. The cops you ignore. Life is so simple in the Heat Rack. Now I'll tell you the difference between queens and trade."

She is looking hard at me for the first time.

"Queens are afraid that every horrible insult hurled at them is true. Trade is impervious to insult."

I take notes.

"That's why these Stonewall men all look like cowboys. They think if they play trade they won't have their feelings hurt. I would imagine that is why you've got dark glasses on right now."

"I always have dark glasses on."

"That's fascinating, no doubt. But how nice of you to wear a tie for me, all the same. The johns always wore ties."

In my window, it's always T-shirts. Once I came home from the opera so keen to write I sat down in my suit. Then I looked up and thought, "Who is that man?"

"The johns were so nice. All those years at the Heat Rack, never did I have to buy my own drink. Of course, they were living for love, so they were always getting wounded."

"What does trade live for?"

"To torment queens. That's why Miss Titania had to enforce the regulations so strictly, to keep trade from cheating the johns and breaking their hearts. Or making a ruckus, which they always did. Or showing off their stupid tattoos with a lady present. And some of them never washed and you

4

could smell their asses all the way across the room. Now, the Duchess of Diva, she let trade run *rampant* in her court. Mind you, I'm for a free market. But you give trade their liberty and what do you have?"

"Tell me."

"A world in which beauty passes the laws and all lovers go mad. I'm sure you know this, a writer. Do you write poems?"

"Never."

"I yearn for poetry. But no one rhymes anymore. No one lives for beauty. Everything is . . . *meaning*. There's always a message now. What's the good in a message when a pretty picture tells you everything you need to know?

"Now, I can tell you, on some nights the Heat Rack was the prettiest picture you ever hoped to see. In summer, let me say. The johns in the dark corners or sitting in the back booths, out of the way. And trade all around, some shirtless and so still, not looking to see who saw them. Three or four, perhaps, loafing at the pool table—not even playing, I expect, just filling out the tableau, making silly jokes and rubbing each other's necks and getting pensive. And the queens were near, doting. You would look for a moment at all this, all around, and it was like a painting. It was magic, regardless.

"But you can dote too much. And trade will take control if they can. That's why Miss Titania . . . once . . . I shouldn't tell you this, I suppose. You Stonewall boys don't understand the patterns of love discipline. What do you live for, you cowboys? What stirs you? Does the sight of a trade's crack, all trembling and open to assault . . . does it stir you? Do you want me to stop?"

"Go on."

"Well, once Miss Titania determined that a certain trade would have to be disciplined. A beautiful galoot, big and dark, the cruel kind. Like your father or some such. *Tales of the Woodshed?* Big, breezy galoots, so lazy and mean. This one was called Carl, and he was swindling the johns. He'd go with them but wouldn't let them do anything. Then he'd flex

his huge muscles and say they'd better give him a tip, and he'd empty their wallets. He even pulled this on the queens! I mean, in Miss Titania's court, you *never* smooth a queen! Well. So Miss Titania and the Duchess of Diva made a date at Miss Titania's place with this trade, Carl. Funny name for trade. They're usually Blue or Tex or so what. Miss Titania and the Duchess, they knock Carl out with a mickey . . . do they still call them mickeys?"

"Oddly enough, that's exactly the word a friend of mine used recently when some guy got into his apartment and—"

"Who's being interviewed, anyway?" she cried, all chin and cheekbones.

"Carry on."

"It was a *rhetorical* question. So Miss Titania and the Duchess strip Carl and tie him to the bed on his stomach, and they call the court over to watch, because you have to humiliate trade to reform them. And I thoroughly approve of this, because they can become almost sweet after they've had their asses whipped. The Duchess of Diva—whose sense of tact, I must tell you, runs way to the left of disreputable—wanted to tie Carl down face up, so she could whip his chest and cock and even his face. She would have, too. But Miss Titania knows what's right. Except as she was getting ready to whip that boy's ass, Miss Titania begins to realize what a beautiful thing it is to tenderize a man like that. Sweeten him up. Make him so sweet. It's a dreamy thing. Meanwhile, Carl is coming to and the Duchess is telling him off but good about how he'd better not try his tricks in *her* court, which is very funny because he's so groggy he doesn't know what *planet* he's on. And Miss Titania is just gazing upon him. How his shoulder skin ripples as he's struggling against the rope and how his ass quivers as she lays the whip so gently upon it. And then Carl is bellowing like a bull, how he'll kill us all. But Miss Titania knows that a beautiful stud was born to be whipped, and to see him stretched out nude and helpless is the most beautiful thing in the world. And his ass is so lovely as she parts it to inhale the stink of him . . ."

6

I would rehearse dialogue in my window, but how does one look saying this? Because truth is not beauty. Is *not*.

". . . and she knows that he must be whipped, and how good that would be, and of course the Duchess is shrieking, 'Let's rip him up!' all over the room. She has *no* sense of timing. But Miss Titania spreads Carl's legs wider and wider as she strokes his thighs. She must calm him down, it's true. And then he's quiet. He knows he must be sweetened, and that is the secret that queens and trade share. You couldn't hear a sound in the place as Miss Titania soothed Carl's hole with her tongue and slowly worked it open, and Carl's groaning like a wild beast who doesn't care what anyone knows about him. I truly believe that that is the most beautiful sound in the world. Don't you?"

"No."

She looks at me now, quite frankly. "To be sure. And what do you call the most beautiful sound?"

"*La Mer?*"

The drag queen looks away as if she would never look back again. "Who's she?"

"It's music."

"Miss Titania rimmed and rimmed," the drag queen insisted. "It was the most spectacular rim job since Scheherazade. Even the Duchess of Diva held her peace as she looked on, and there wasn't a soul in that room who wouldn't have given a year of life to be in Miss Titania's place. Carl's head was swaying on his neck like a broken toy, and he kept saying, 'No. No. No. No.' I wonder why he said that. He was crying. A big, dashing, empty fuck-monster like that, crying. Can you imagine? And when it was done and Carl had been rimmed inside and out, the Duchess of Diva untied him and all the court looked upon him. He had not been whipped, yet he was sweetened. As if he had been cleaned out in his *mind*. He would give no trouble from now on, because everyone had watched. They saw him, do you see? But Miss Titania saw nothing. She was swaying in mid-air as if in a trance. I believe she was in a state of grace, truly. And Carl went into the bathroom and he wouldn't come out."

"Just like that southern queen who offended Miss—"

She flared up like a lighter. "How dare you? It's not the same at all!"

"Well, in outline—"

"*Trade is not like queens!* Now, do you understand? And they *never* will be!"

"Which would you rather be, if you could choose and start all over?"

She is quiet. "I lived for beauty. That was my choice." I take notes.

"You don't think that is sufficient, you Stonewall cowboy. Do you? I suppose you live for music. How grand."

"Music is a form of beauty, isn't it?"

"No. Beauty is not music. Beauty is a pretty picture. I told you that. Oh, no—no, I'll give you something for your piece. Yes. Someone asked Miss Titania once, 'What is beauty?' You know what she said? And I quote: 'Beauty is the death of the drag queen.' *There!*"

She sighed as I wrote. Eleven years ago there was no place to print such tales as this. "Just take it down," Paul had said, and he added, "You'll see."

She lit another cigarette. "It's true. We had to die so you cowboys could live. Not that we wanted to. No one asked us, regardless. But people who believe every horrible insult are of no use to anyone now. That is not part of survival. No. This society believes in trade. Even if all the trade is imitation. Cops and johns, that's all that's left. That's all that's real. The need and the threat. Where's beauty now, penscratcher?"

I looked up from my notebook. I looked at her and she looked back. She smiled.

"You think we have no feelings," she said. "Is that it?"

I waited.

"Feelings, dressed like this? Feelings? In a place called the Heat Rack? The Demitasse? Feelings, that I am thrilled by the simple sight of a tie? I don't have feelings, right? Yes?

Yes?" She screamed in that dreary room; I hear it yet. "*Say yes!*"

And I said, "Yes." Because that is the impression they infix.

She calmed down quite suddenly. "Yes," she said. "Yes, thank you." She nodded. "How right you are. We don't have feelings. We learn to live without them."

That sounded like the end of the last stanza. I rose to go.

"Where will your piece be printed," she asked, "and when? I must order copies for all the gang."

"You still see them, then?"

"Alas." She raised her hand, palm to me. "Not for a terribly long time. But wouldn't it be dramatic to track them down for the occasion?"

"Do you think you could find Miss Titania?"

"No one will ever find Miss Titania. She was the first to die, you see. Now, tell me—*The New York Times? McCall's?* Would they want a picture, dare I hope?"

"Let's wing it," I said, while visualizing the editors of the *Times* coming upon that line about the Zulu's dingus. And *McCall's!*

"What did you think?" Paul asked me on the phone a bit later.

"I think Miss Titania is the one I should have interviewed. There the story lies."

"You jerk," he said. "That *is* Miss Titania."

That *was* Miss Titania, my window tells me, eleven years later; it took that long for me to believe my ears. My eyes I trust by the moment, but who is that masked man? Who tells me these terrible tales? I wish I could choose between beauty and love; I wish life were so trim; I, too, like a pretty picture. But I think the meaning matters more. Staring straight into my window to the disgust of my neighbor, I am bewildered, saddened, offended, and amazed. God make me as honest a storyteller as the drag queen was.

The Straight;
or, Field Expedients

When my windows are not reflecting the local countenance, they give out on a great hole from which an office tower has been rising, somewhat feyly (I think) referred to on the hoarding as "Third Avenue at Fifty-third Street."

So be it. But in the early 1970s, it was all brownstones— especially one, a great box of stories that I would gaze upon from my desk. There was the ancient couple, top left, who never washed their windows. There were the Spanish-speaking queens, middle right, with the yapping chihuahua and the live-in Puerto Rican who watered the hanging garden on the fire escape in the nude. There were the bohemians next to them—he played cello and she painted—and my friend Alex just above. Next to him was a plain straight couple; the woman was seldom seen, the man always around.

As I wrote, typed, and fretted at the dictionary, I would spot this man in his window, looking, sitting, guzzling beer, waiting. He had very long hair, which he sometimes wore in a ponytail, heavy arms and thighs, and (apparently) no clothing but boxer shorts. Gay, he would have gymmed himself inside of a year into a gleaming demon. But straights often like themselves as they are; it's an arcane grade of hot I've never understood.

My friend Alex would regale me with tales of this couple. One season, the woman was cute and the man a nerd. Next season, she was standoffish and he vaguely sweet. They fought, they cooed, they bought a stereo, she made perfect strudel, he got a job. . . .

10

"Why tell me these stories?" I finally asked. "All straight stories are the same. What's in it for us?"

Even when they broke up, the tale lacked interest. But my best friend Dennis Savage was thrilled. "Nowadays," he said, "when a straight couple busts up, the man always turns gay. Or the woman. You never know with straights."

"This woman isn't gay," said Alex. "Karen. She left him because he wasn't smart enough for her."

"He was smart enough to keep the apartment."

"She went to California. *That's* smart."

"Anyway, I've seen this guy but plenty," I told Dennis Savage. "Nothing."

"How can you tell this far off?" Alex countered. "Besides, you've never met him. He happens to be—" Noting that we were watching him like trolls observing a Billy Goat Gruff crossing our bridge, he stopped. "He's a nice man. Joe Dolan."

Dennis Savage went into a barfing pantomime as I held my nose.

"That," I said, "is the straightest name I ever heard."

"What's a gay name?" asked Alex.

"Dorinda Spreddem," I offered. "Nosy Porker."

"Maytag de Washer," Dennis Savage suggested. "Rosemary de Tramp."

"Humungous Layman."

"Will you stop?" Alex pleaded. "Will you, please?"

"Don't get serious about him," Dennis Savage advised. "Those crushes on the straight next door are destructive. Because straight is straight and they never cross that line, no matter how drunk they get, no matter how mad they get at women, no matter—"

"We've already had sex," Alex said. "All the way, everything. Several times."

The room was so quiet we could hear the appliances depreciating. Alex got up and looked out the window at his building for a long while. "He's there now, watching a baseball game or somesuch. And when it's over he'll knock on my door. He says I'm good to talk to."

"So he is gay after all," said Dennis Savage.

"He lived with Karen for two years. They were lovers."

"An act."

"I was there! I saw them together! You can fool your parents and your co-workers, but not your gay neighbor. It's no act."

"You're saying that this man came on to you several times and he's not gay?"

"I'm saying that everything about him is straight. Including the way he comes on."

Dennis Savage sighed. "Now I'm fascinated. Tell."

"I certainly will not!"

"Oh, let me guess. He came over one night and asked if you know how to give a backrub."

"No, it wasn't—"

"He was in red velvet, a stole, and a cloche hat, and you said—"

"How can you make fun of something so *intime* and dear, and so terribly secret?"

"Will you hark at him?" Dennis Savage exclaimed to me. "*Intime!*"

"All right!" Alex paced, stopped, and paced again. "All right, I'll tell. Just don't jeer any more. Don't mock things you don't understand."

"Listen, Alex," said Dennis Savage, "I was setting Stonewall style when you were running around in a propeller beanie, so don't tell me what I understand or don't." He turned to me. "Do I know gay or don't I?"

"I'll say," I agreed. "You've gone down on everything but the Lusitania."

"Look!" cried Alex. "Do you want the story or not?"

It was a familiar one: boy loses girl, boy turns to local ear for sympathy, and a friendship is born. "He'd visit every night, or I'd go to his place. Dropping in, you know? We just talked. For hours, sometimes. He'd be going on about 'ladies'

12

all the time. This lady in Dallas, this lady in Chicago, do I have a lady, how do I address a lady. And I just wanted him to scoop me up . . ." He gazed out my window. "Not once did he look at me ambiguously. He never laid a hand on me. I could have been his uncle.

"Then one night, while we were watching some football or basketball game on television, he started to tell me how ladies never really liked him. How they'd put up with him when they were between true loves. *Put up with him*—that was how he said it. Even Karen, after all that time . . . even she thought he was a goon. A goon, he said. Because he didn't . . . he wasn't . . . smooth enough or something. Well, one woman's goon is another . . . man's . . . if you see what I mean. And he was telling me about the different ways of turning ladies on. Some men have a tattoo in a fancy place. You know? And they show it. Or some have subtle speeches worked out. And one friend of his, he said, used to show his ladies photographs of himself kissing another man. And he . . . asked me what I thought of that. I was thinking that if all the women he liked thought he was a goon, maybe he should . . . maybe take some photographs himself. Because he isn't handsome, I know, but he's . . . strong. He's nice to me." Alex cleared his throat. "He only wants to be liked, you know? He'll do anything to be liked. And I saw that. And I . . . well . . ."

"You liked him," I put in. "That's what it is."

"Well, I told him maybe he should try making such photographs. And he laughed and said, 'Would you make them with me?' I guessed he was joking. But he kept talking about it. He told me Karen doesn't really know him. And how I'm so much nicer to him. And how . . . how we should make those pictures. And . . . out of nowhere . . . he said, 'I sure would like to ream you.' Just like that. I was so startled I couldn't speak. I thought I'd misheard him. But he went on. 'I won't hurt you,' he said. 'I just want to put my cock in you and see what you're like. We can be buddies, okay?'" He turned back to us. "Come and see. He's standing in the window."

We got there so fast we almost crashed through the glass. There he was, looking at us. Alex smiled and waved, and Joe wiggled his index finger at him in that "Come here" gesture that kids use.

"So you're buddies," Dennis Savage said as Alex got his coat on.

"One catch," Alex replied. "We can't call it by name. It's okay only if you don't admit you're doing it. The day I say 'gay' he'll drop me."

"Or kill you."

"He wouldn't hurt me. He only gets mad at strangers."

I don't know whether Alex thought of Dennis Savage and me as the natural strangers of Joe Dolan, but he kept the man to himself. Perhaps he thought exposure to outright gays might threaten their touchy diplomacy. A lover who won't bear the word *gay* obviously won't be comfortable around practitioners of the style.

So we all left it thus. From my desk, spotting Joe watching at his window, I gave him no more than a glance. And the days stole by me; and I wrote; and it was with some shock that I noticed one time that Joe the Straight had cut his hair and grown a clone moustache. Alex tried to shrug it away when I ran into him in Sloan's. "I don't know," he said. "He just . . . he decided . . ." He faked an elaborate pantomime with the tuna cans, apparently dismissing me.

"I'm not moving," I told him.

He wouldn't look up. "He joined a gym, too. He's really gotten into it. He's quite . . . different . . ."

"Are you disappointed? Or Columbus sighting America?"

He grew fierce. "I wish you'd stop."

"I'm too curious to stop. Is he gay or isn't he?"

"Is it always war or peace? Comic or tragic?"

"If you're fighting, it's war; if you're not, it's peace. If it's about courtship, it's comic; if it's about honor, it's tragic. And if it makes love to men, it's gay."

14

He stared at me for a spell, said, "I can remember when I thought you might be my best friend," and walked out.

What had got into me? It's none of my business whether Alex plays comedy or tragedy. Two days later he called, apologized, and invited me to dinner.

So I officially met Joe, who couldn't have looked gayer in his white T-shirt, Levi's, and Frye boots. He didn't *seem* gay, lacking both self-willing sensuality and self-spoofing satire. But he also lacked the self-righteous coarseness of proletarian straight culture. He was placeless, a man without a side in the war. He seemed unaware of Alex unless directly addressing him, yet I felt a marvelous tension in the averting of their eyes. While we were clearing the table, I caught him watching Alex, who was at the sink. Joe picked up a glass, took it to Alex, pressed it into his grasp, and gently rubbed his fingers. "Yeah," he said. Then he put his hand on Alex's neck and traced a finger along his eyebrows, shifting weight from foot to foot as if dancing. "Oh yeah," he went on, nabbing Alex's eyes with his own, and he purred a little, then concluded, "Oh, that's real nice." It was the most pornographic act I'd ever witnessed.

"Well?" Dennis Savage asked later. "Is he or isn't he? And if you don't tell me, I'll make you rim the Roach Motel."

"Let me point out that there is an incredibly vicious dish-queen in this room and it isn't me. Can I tell who it is?"

"Can we please stop with this and tell me if Joe Dolan is gay!"

"I don't know what he is. He doesn't seem straight and he doesn't seem gay."

"Is he still a big dull lump? Sexually?"

"Well . . . no."

"You mean he's hot?"

"It depends on . . . actually—"

Dennis Savage closed in. "You wake up and he's in your bed. Either you say, 'Get out of this bed' or you say 'Help me

15

make it through the night.' Which? Pick one only." I just looked at him. "He's hot, isn't he? He has the look, doesn't he? He knows how to do it, right? *Right?*"

"Maybe."

"I hope you never join the CIA. Because if we're West Berlin, and the KGB is East Berlin, where would you be? *Middle* Berlin, right?"

"This is where I paint a telephone on your face and dial you with ice-cube tongs."

"Does he have feelings?"

That halted me. "Who doesn't?"

"Most straights don't. Or no one knows for sure. Only a straight could tell us, and no straight is sensitive enough to know what feelings are."

"Are you saying that straights are androids?"

"No, I'm saying that straights are video games."

"You know," I said, "it's just possible that he is straight. That, in fact, he took Alex to bed because after a lifetime of failing to get women to regard him as anything but an ork, he decided to go with someone who admired him. Or . . . I don't know. Maybe he's just another nerd exploding out of his closet."

"Does he, I repeat, have feelings?"

"Did gays have feelings in the 1940s, when no one tolerated their feelings? Joe Dolan may simply be an uninformed homosexual."

"That's gay."

"Stop playing king of the Circuit and look at it from someone else's point of view, all right? He comes from some small town where everything is *Father Knows Best*. He has no access to all the media snitching. He never reads a book, much less hangs out at the opera or blunders into a gay bar. He could miss the whole thing. And he grows up thinking he'd better hide his sexuality, because he thinks he's the only one—or, who knows?, maybe everyone hides it. But it's hard to be selective in such matters, so he hides *everything*. Including his feelings. That, my friend, is what gay life was like in

16

the old days. One man befriends another, opportunity strikes, they become buddies. And only the other buddies know what they are. Do you like that story?"

"He's hot, isn't he?"

"Yes, he's hot."

"Not handsome or charming."

"No."

"Not even fun."

"Not yet."

"But strong and loyal. Am I correct?"

"You are smug, but correct."

"When will he reveal his feelings?"

"When Alex hurts him, and he weeps in despair."

Dennis Savage exhaled with contentment and went into the kitchen to refill the glasses. "I didn't care for this adventure before, but now I love it. Except you're wrong about one piece. Alex will not hurt Joe Dolan. He's been left out of too much to blow something this good."

"You don't know Alex."

Dennis Savage handed me wine. "Did he hurt you?"

I raised my glass. "To new friends," I said.

Our new friend was Joe, because Alex was now bringing him out. Joe still thought of movies as something you see rather than discuss, had no use for cabaret, and didn't know how to dance: there was nothing to bring. But his months at the gym had styled him smartly, and he could pass. He had lost his nondescript straight's fleshiness; he was cut and basted. His pants were tight, his hands heavy, his nipples offensive. At the Tenth Floor one night, Dennis Savage and I overheard two kids discussing some avatar when suddenly we realized that they were referring to Joe, dancing shirtless with Alex. We watched the crowd watching them, knew that Joe was crossing over, wondered how it felt to him, took in the music and the crowd and the hunger, and joined Joe and Alex on the floor.

It was a gala last night before the summer break, and the room was packed. How amazing to think back and realize that the scene that would eventually fill and jade The Saint had started out in that undecorated little den of innocence. It was hard to dance without jostling one's neighbors, yet someone behind Joe was taking up far too much room, throwing his arms around, clapping and posing. He was knocking into everyone around him, and finally Joe told him, in a neutral tone, "Look, would you mind keeping your hands to yourself?"

"Why don't you fuck your panties, you frump?" said the stranger, a high-voltage little queen with the voice of transvestite Brillo.

"Okay," said Joe, still evenly. "Now you can move out of our part of the floor, or you're going to wish you did."

"Says who, you bitch?" With that the stranger shoved Joe at the rest of us, a foolish act given their respective sizes. Joe hauled back and, with a hoarse cry, felled his foe.

"Oh shit!" the queen screamed, feeling blood at his nose, as his friends whimpered and giggled. "Oh, help me!"

"You asked for it," Joe told him.

Alex was furious. "Did you have to fight?" he whispered through his teeth. "What is this, a circus? A SWAT encounter?" He stormed off the floor. The rest of us followed, while Joe's opponent, his coterie, and thrilled bystanders played out The Theatre of the Punched-Out Queen.

Had we been smart, we would have called it a night. But no, we went on to Dennis Savage's place, with Alex seething and Joe bewildered. I knew there was more to come, and, yes, no sooner did our host pour out the wine than Joe gave Alex his opening by rehearsing the episode.

"He shoved me, didn't he?" he asked. "What was I supposed to do, thank him?"

"You don't fight," Alex spit at him, "at the Tenth Floor."

"It's not my fault where it happened."

"*Your* behavior is *your* fault!"

Joe turned away, struggling to control his anger.

"How about some music?" I asked. "Some Nino Rota?"

"*Otto e Mezzo!*" cried Dennis Savage.

"*Giulietta degli Spiriti!*"

Alex viewed us as if we were the Barry Sisters making a comeback singing "Que Sera, Sera" in his bathroom, and returned to Joe. "You're like something just off the bus from Akron. You're not ready for the social life. You're a pushy clod." "I never said I wasn't. And why do we have to go dancing? Or out to dinner with your ooh-la-la friends?" He turned to us. "I don't mean you two." We felt like the Barry Sisters, barred from presenting an Academy Award backstage at the last minute on account of deficient ooh-la-la. "But some of your friends treat me as if—"

"And they're *right!*"

"I don't want to go to these places. Why can't we just be together? That's all I want." He went to Alex, held him by the waist, and saw him so acutely all three of us were transfixed. Looked and *saw.* "Just to be with you. To pump you and cream you."

"You beggar!" Alex shouted. "You *filth!* You dare say this in front of them?"

We seemed to be the Barry Sisters, stumbling onstage during a performance of *Private Lives.*

"Why shouldn't I? They know we're buddies."

"We're *not* buddies! *We are not!*" Dennis Savage had never seen Alex like this; I had. "We're *lovers.* We're men who fuck together. Your cock in my ass. Lovers, Joe. Say the word 'gay.' Say 'lovers'!"

"That's *enough!*"

"Gay is the word, Joe. That lovers use, you know? Gay means you're a beautiful muscle dude who rides me out of my mind. Tell them how your body moves. We're filth. We'll tell them together. Then you can sock me, too."

Joe grabbed Alex, to hold or to hurt him, but he kept changing his grip and finally he put his hand over Alex's mouth. "I know what we are," he said. "I know about love and things. I'm not a beast. I'm *not* a beast. I just don't want

19

to be pushed around. That guy at the dancing was asking for it. He started it." He let go of Alex and faced us. "He says I'm filth and then he says I'm beautiful. What am I supposed to think?"

"You're supposed to think you're gay," Alex told him. "Say it: say 'Joe Dolan is gay.' Say 'Joe Dolan is a beast.'"

Joe hesitated, shook his head, then tried to grab Alex again.

"A beast," Alex pursued, pushing Joe away. "How can you love men when you fight them? You have no smarts. You have no patience. You have no ambition. You have no sensitivity. You're a stupid hunk with thighs of death, that's all. And when I tire of you or you tire of me, you'll be nothing but Karen's castoff memory. How do you like it, beast? So you punched a pantywaist in a dance hall. Wow! Nice job, Thighs. Inside of three minutes, you can alienate everyone in a room. You've got the touch, Thighs!"

And Joe was weeping. "I did the right thing," he said. He wiped his eyes, but the tears kept coming. "How can you say that to me, Alex?"

"How beautiful," said Alex, "to see you cry."

"Would someone like a toasted bagel?" Dennis Savage asked.

"I'm not a beast," Joe insisted. "I'm your buddy."

"You're human garbage," Alex replied.

"Leave him alone, Alex," I said.

"He's a bully."

"He's had a good teacher."

"I did the right thing!" Joe grabbed Alex, spun him around, pushed him, held him, stroked his hair. Dennis Savage and I might have been the Barry Sisters screening *Psycho,* or perhaps *She Married Her Boss.* "Okay?" Joe went on. "Please! Okay?"

"Only if you call it by its name," said Alex. We could see his cock stirring at Joe's touch.

"Take me how I am."

"How you are," Alex persisted, "is a lewd queen."

20

"I'm a *man.*"

"We're all lewd queens," Dennis Savage observed.

"Dennis Savage is a lewd queen," I explained. "I'm a man."

"Excuse me, but you're a princess."

"And you're the pea."

"Will you shut up?" Alex screamed. "How can we quarrel with you two playing fag vaudeville?"

"I love him," Joe told us. "I truly do. To hold him and talk with him and . . . the rest. Is that enough? I am saying that I love him."

"Make him say the word," said Alex.

"He cried before God and gays," Dennis Savage noted. "Justice is served." To me he added, "You were right—he wept."

"I don't know what anyone is talking about here," said Joe. He kept wiping his eyes and crying. "Do you think I'm a beast?" he asked me.

"That little queen started it and you finished it. As far as I go, you did the right thing."

We solemnly shook hands.

"Oh look!" Alex cried. "Look at the two *men!*"

"Now I think I *will* sock him!"

"No, Joe. Tell him to go fluff his puff."

"His . . . puff?"

"Just say it."

He gave me an odd look, but he said it: "Alex, go fluff your puff!"

Everyone was laughing. The fight was about courtship, not honor: a comedy.

"You call me horrible names and make fun of my morals," Joe told Alex. "You say you're glad that I cried. You call me a beast. And now we're all laughing. It's crazy! My face is wet with my own tears and I'm laughing!"

"Well, there you go, shweetheart," I said in my Humphrey Bogart voice. "Welcome to gay."

"That," said Dennis Savage, "is the *worst* Greta Garbo imitation I have ever heard."

The Mute Boy

Everyone has a smartest friend, a handsomest friend, a most famous friend, and a best friend. Mine are Lionel, Carlo, Eric, and Dennis Savage. Some of us have a sweetest friend, too; mine was Mac McNally. In a city where everyone you're supposed to want to meet turns out to be a ghoul, Mac was a hobbit: whimsical, sentimental, and tactfully frisky. He adored his friends; he was faultless and true. I wondered where he had got it from till the day one of his brothers showed up from the family seat near Racine. Over dinner, I saw Mac in an older, larger version—the same quick grin, the same eager nod of agreement, the same unselfish strength. I have seen (and had) my fill of brothers, but this one seemed to belong to some new genre in relationships, one of pledges made early, freely, and permanently. There were no delicacies of regret or disapproval in his affection for Mac, no fascism in his beautiful morals. He was that unheard-of thing in families, the relative who treats you as a perfect lover. Their intimacy was fearsome, like a ballet without music. I had heard it was a big tribe. "Are they all like that?" I asked later. Mac grinned and nodded.

By day Mac was a computer programmer—by night too, sometimes, depending on the project—but his great gift was writing, in the tightest, leanest style I've ever known. So, too, was Mac tight and lean, very light, very swift. But his eyes weighed a thousand pounds. Letters were his forte. I met him in the mail, in a note congratulating me on some book or other, forwarded by the publisher. I answer the nice ones, and so found myself in correspondence with an address just up the avenue, reading arresting disquisitions on a host of subjects, all of them love, in penciled block letters. One letter arrived with photographs, of Mac and four friends on summer holiday in Portugal, of Mac and an older couple camping in Maine, of Mac and his three brothers and their wives and children at the Thanksgiving bash.

"What is he, a tour guide?" asked Dennis Savage, when I showed him the pictures.

"You don't miss a chance to bring ants to the picnic, do you?"

"How come he's never alone? He's cute, anyway. When are you going to meet him?"

It comes down to that, doesn't it? The quest. It was Mac who broached the question, asking me to dinner—but it was a friend of his, Rolf something, who did the phoning.

"Mac's held up at work," he explained, "and we didn't know how late a day you keep." It sounded dotty to me, but I went along with it. On the afternoon of the date, Rolf called again. "Are we still on for tonight?" he asked.

"Of course."

"Fine. Just checking. We don't want Mac's feelings hurt in the slightest way, do we?"

"Did you hear I was going to hurt them?"

"No offense. But some New Yorkers are unreliable and I didn't want any misunderstanding."

"Have no fears. When it comes to appointments I'm sure as steel."

"That's what Mac's friends like to hear."

Maybe he is a tour guide, I thought as I hung up. I haven't had a call that strange since the last time I spoke to my mother.

Rolf opened the door. He was tall, handsome, and slightly gray, of the stalwart type that, I was to learn, marked Mac's cohort. My handshake is pretty solid, but his was a grip of grips: I felt like a glass of water meeting the North Sea. As

I came in, Rolf stood aside and there was Mac. He pointed at himself, pointed at me, touched his heart, and indicated the apartment with a sweep of his hand.

"I'm very pleased to meet you," said Rolf, "and my apartment is yours."

I looked at Rolf. Rolf looked dead on at Mac.

Mac and I shook hands and he picked up a glass, looking enquiringly at me. "What would you like to drink?" said Rolf.

I asked for wine.

Mac made a "fork in the road" with his index fingers, then upturned the palms in a questioning gesture.

"White or red?" said Rolf.

An incorrigible lush, I answered, "Whichever you have more of," making my lip movements as clear as possible. I must have looked like someone in an early Hollywood talkie, overtly proclaiming the new miracle of dialogue. Smiling, Mac slashed the air with a finger, put it to my lips, jabbed himself with his thumb, and, slowly drawing his open hands up to his ears, nodded once. "Speak normally," said Rolf, who was beginning to sound like a Conehead. "I can hear."

Mac poured wine for us. We sat. "I have to tell you," I began, "you write wonderful letters. I'm amazed at how many ideas you cram onto a single page."

Mac shook his head vigorously, pointed at me, deftly suggested writing as he pulled the finger back to stab his heart, made a circle with thumb and forefinger as his eyes appeared to read, raised the circle high in the air, and read more. "No," said Rolf, "your letters are the wonderful ones. They move me so I must reread them."

"I got it," I murmured, staring at Mac. Rolf was no longer the translation, but an echo. Mac's sign language was as eloquent as his letters were: his hands gave the message, their speed or angle lent nuance, and his face showed how the message and nuances felt. All you had to do was look. By the time the food appeared, I myself was performing Mac's "sounding"—his term, a correction of my faux pas, that delightful and exhausting night, in verbalizing the notion that I

24

was "speaking" for him. Fiercely shaking his head, he reached for one of the little pads lying all about the apartment, and with mischievous grace wrote me in those block letters I knew from the mail: "I do speak—without noise."

He was not deaf, only mute, apparently the reverse of the usual condition; even a fluke, for all I could guess, for I never asked. He was proud of his ability to cope with his impairment but, if not ashamed of it, reticent about it. His many friends protected him—crowded him in theatres, blocked and ran passes for him in bars, sat in on his dinners with new friends, sounded for him in banks and restaurants. His family constantly found reasons to come east and check up on him, bring him things, kiss him. I, who was to turn thirty before I dared embrace my father and have never done more than shake hands with my brothers, was dazzled. Still, I wondered how much protection one needs. Mac's friends insistently set him up with Good Husband Material; their dinner parties looked like the waiting room at Yenta the Matchmaker's. And Mac's family had their version, prodding him to Come Home and Settle Down—meaning, translated from the straight, "Give up the rebellious gay phase and do what is done."

But Mac loved the city. He loved crowds and dinners and doing eight things every evening. "Do you realize?" he had written in one of his earliest letters, "that there are probably a million gays in New York? Allowing for variables of looks, spirit, vocation, and bad habits, each of us may have a thousand ideal mates within immediate geography. We need but look."

What can you project without a voice in this town of the insinuating opener and the whipcrack reply? You might show optimism, hesitation, disappointment, pain—and all too clearly. Speakers grow up learning to develop or hide their emotions; Mac had learned only to display his. Thus did he speak, as he claimed. Better, he charmed. And I mean strangers. Belligerent strangers. Even belligerent, tough strangers on a mean bad day.

I went walking with him one afternoon when he had just received news about an aunt who had cancer; like a puppy, Mac perked up when you walked him. I'm champion at distracting wounded comrades—when all else fails, I start a fight—but Mac was half in a daze, and blundered into fresh-laid concrete on Forty-ninth Street, east of Park. One of the masons, foully irate, came over to berate him. Before I could intervene with my usual exacerbating ruckus, Mac stopped me, indicating the laborer with the philosopher's upheld index finger and himself with a down-turned thumb.

"He's right and I'm wrong," I sounded, dubiously, for Mac. He showed us the sidewalk, ran a hand over his eyes, and chided the hand with a look. "I should have been watching where I was going."

As the laborer blankly surveyed this latest charade of the Manhattan streets, Mac tore off a message for him.

"'I have had bad news,'" the man read out. "'I'm sorry.'" He looked at Mac. "Family news, huh?"

Mac nodded.

"Yeah, well . . . yeah, sure." He shifted his stance and patted Mac's shoulder. "It'll be all right. I'm sorry, too. For yelling."

Mac hit his chest with a fist and shook his head. "No," I sounded. "It was my fault."

"No—"

Mac hit himself again.

"*No.*" The man grabbed Mac by the shoulders. "No, you . . . look . . . I gotta get back to work." He touched Mac's nose and gave him a quarter. "Be a good boy, now."

Mac smiled and nodded.

"Right," I said, after we had walked on a bit. "I've been in New York for seven years and I've seen, I think, everything. But did that really happen?"

Mac shrugged benignly.

"He gave you a quarter!"

"People like me," Mac wrote. "I'm nice."

"What's the secret of nice?" I wondered aloud.

"Forgiving," he wrote.

He could have used somewhat more in height and weight, no doubt; it doesn't do to be quite so boyish after twenty-six. Yet he made it work, for his short and thin suited the grin and the nod. He was the kind of man who could grow a moustache and no one would notice—would see it, even. He was the eternal kid, tirelessly seeking his mate. Fastidious, he wanted true love or nothing. But love is scarce even when forgiveness makes you nice, and I wondered what Mac did to fill in meanwhile, till one afternoon when Dennis Savage and I were hacking around in Mac's apartment and Mac pulled out the world's largest collection of porn magazines.

He did it, typically, to stop a war. Dennis Savage was cranky (as usual) and began to growl at me about something or other. Who knows, now, what? My taste in men? My dislike of travel? The Charge of the Light Brigade? Anyway:

"I'm going to get a huge dog," says Dennis Savage. "And you know what I'll train him to do?"

Mac touched us urgently, him then me. "Please don't fight," I sounded; adding, for myself, "Okay."

"Bite up your ass," Dennis Savage concluded.

"You don't need a dog for that, from what I hear."

He rose, fuming like Hardy when Laurel puts a fish in his pants, and Mac got between us, scribbling a cease-fire: "Sit down to play Fantasy." Bemused, we held our peace as he hauled stacks of magazines out of a closet. "I usually play by myself," he mimed to my sound, "but it works in groups, too." He handed us each a number, prime porn. "Browse and choose," he wrote. "Each gets anyone he wants for one night."

"Get him," said Dennis Savage.

Mac wrote a note just for him: "Pretend!"

"Where did all this porn come from?" I asked. "It's like the Decadent Studies Room in the Library of Congress."

Mac went through an elaborate mime. "I threw up on the bureau of my aunt?" suggested Dennis Savage.

Mac made a wry face as he picked up the pad. "It keeps me off the streets," he wrote.

"Strange men give him quarters," I added. "They touch his nose."

"He forgives," Dennis Savage noted, "and his kisses are as sweet as the bottom inch of a Dannon cup." Innocence is Dennis Savage's party.

Mac reverently showed us a spread entitled "The Boys of Soho." Writing "This one's my fave," he pointed out a dark-haired chap of about twenty-five, standing nude, arms folded across his stomach. There was nothing splendid about his looks or proportions, but something arresting somewhere; his face, you thought; you searched it, found nothing, but kept looking. Amid a load of musclemen, hung boys, and surly toughs, here was a man of no special detail but an attitude of sleaze too personable to ignore. I imagine evil looks like this.

"'Nick,'" I read out. "'A typical Soho boy with an air of fun and a taste for the finer things.' What does that mean, I wonder?"

"Hepatitus B on the first date," Dennis Savage answered.

Mac mimed, and I sounded: "Do you think he would respond to a letter?"

"Mac, you wouldn't fall in love with that! What would your family say?"

"Just for a night," Mac mimed, then, by pad: "How would you contact such a person?"

"We wouldn't know," said Dennis Savage, "so forget it."

"You could write him a letter in care of the photographer," I put in. "Or even call the photographer and ask—"

"You bonehead!" Dennis Savage pointed out.

"Let the kid have some fun. Why should he go through life only imagining where such paths lead? Everyone alive who isn't a coward or a creep deserves one glorious night."

"Which are you? Coward or creep?"

"Glorious."

He waved this nonsense away and concentrated on Mac. "I'm going to set you up with some very excellent Italian accountants in the West Seventies. They make the best husbands, believe me. Always remember The Three Advantages of the Italian beau: hairy chest, volcanic thighs, and the commitment of a Pope."

"*Volcanic thighs?*" I howled. "And dare I ask where the lava comes out?"

Slowly he turned. He regarded me. He was stern. "You know, you should take care where you go. Fag-bashing incidents have been reported in this area."

"Such as where?"

"Such as in this apartment in about three seconds."

"I dream of Nick," Mac had written, and now showed us his little pad. "I think it's always Nick."

"Another good boy goes wrong," said Dennis Savage. "Is that why you left Racine? To meet Nicks?"

Mac gazed at the photograph. "He's such a beautiful dude," I sounded, watching Mac's face.

"Will you shut up?" Dennis Savage roared.

"It wasn't me."

Porn models are surprisingly easy to meet—as if their photos were meant as credentials for work. Despite Dennis Savage's reservations, I helped Mac make contact with Nick. This was 1976, when dubious encounters were quaint adventure rather than mortal peril; so let the harmless fantasy come true for a night. Very little trouble yielded Nick's telephone number, and I made the call for Mac and set up an appointment. Nick sounded as one might have expected, trashy and agreeable. No, you wouldn't kick him out of bed—but you wouldn't want your brother to marry him. He wasn't in the least thrown to hear that his date couldn't talk.

"You should see some of the things I get with," he said. "Once I went to a meet and this guy had no legs." He laughed. "So whattaya think of that?"

Instinct warned me to arrange Mac's date for as soon as

29

possible; I did not picture Nick keeping a terribly precise engagement book.

"How about now?" he asked.

It was a Saturday afternoon and Mac was game, so we cinched it—but it worried me that he didn't want me to stay and set things up with Nick, not to mention check him out for weapons. I never heard of Mac's taking an adventure alone. But he was adamant. "This fantasy I must not share," he wrote. The urgency was unnerving.

Worse yet, Mac refused to tell how the date had gone. That he had had a wonderful time was unmissable; the grin was showing about twenty-five more teeth and the nod came a hair more slowly now, as if Mac had grown younger and wiser at once. Bits of dish would slide out of him perchance: Nick had spent the weekend at Mac's that first time; Nick lived in a hole in darkest Brooklyn; Nick was seeing Mac regularly at bargain rates; Nick was very pleasant under the mean-streets facade.

Suddenly Nick moved in with Mac.

Dennis Savage, when he heard, was shocked silent for a good two minutes, an ideal condition for him. Our Mac—so he had become, for to befriend him was to own him—consorting with sex-show debris? When Dennis Savage regained his voice, he went into a ten-minute tirade reproaching me for encouraging Mac in this vile stunt, for having the sensitivity of Mickey Spillane, and for living. How was I to know that a date with a hustler would yield romance? Whoever heard of the fantasy coming true? I had always thought hustlers were the ultimate tricks, guaranteed for one time only, impersonal and beyond reach. Would not fantasy begin to dissolve at the touch of real life? Why else is "the morning after" as terrible a term in gay as "no exit" is in hell?

Yet Mac's fantasy held. I saw it in the way he spoke of Nick and to him—and Nick, fascinated by the gestures of hand and face that made words for the rest of us, would stare in smug wonder and cry, "Go for it, sport! Go for it!"

Mac did, all the way. It was dinners with Nick, cinema

and hamburgers with Nick, Monopoly with Nick—the first American I've known, by the way, who couldn't play the game. You don't realize how broad our range of kind is here in the magic city till you meet someone who doesn't know what Monopoly is. I've played it with Ph.Ds and little kids, with the birthright wealthy and users of food stamps, with actors and construction workers, with competitors and nerds. Some had mastered it—to the point that they virtually knew where they would land when they were shaking the dice—and some learned by playing, and some were frankly not apt. But everyone knew what it was. Nick had never heard of it— could not, moreover, pick it up no matter how carefully we explained it. My friend Carlo, who likes just about everyone and has a superb ability to forgive hot men their little misdemeanors, walked home with me after this Monopoly game and, in a lull, pensively regarded the traffic and said, "Tell me, who was that extremely terrible boy?"

Mac's coterie shook their prickles at me for bringing Nick into his life, and, believe me, I did not rejoice. But the man was happy. No, he had always been happy; now he was cocky, getting around more by himself, doing what he wanted to on spunk, not on the assistance of his chorus of Rolfs. I found myself sounding, again and again, "I am glad," for him. I hear tell of a chemistry bonding the socioeconomically energetic with the intellectually needy: yet what lies below Baltic Avenue?

I learned what at one of Mac's dinners. He was held up at the office again, and the other guests, respectably employed, could be reached at their places of business and told to come along later. But I had been out mooching around in the streets, viewing the town for adaptable incidents, and so arrived for the party before I should have: when Nick was alone.

"This fantasy I must not share" ran through my mind that evening, as the Theme of Alberich's Curse runs through *Der Ring des Nibelungen*. And there before me was a kind of Alberich, the dark lord, wearing nothing but navy blue corduroy pants held up by suspenders. Just as Nick was ignorant of this nation's essential board game, so was he a gracelessly unknowing host. He offered nothing, not even a chair. He said nothing, not even about Mac being held up. He seemed to regard me as if I were a movie: he paid complete attention without doing anything himself.

I went into the kitchen and poured myself some wine. When I came out, he was where he had been, spread out on the sofa, idly shifting a suspender arm from the curve of his left pectoral to the nipple and back again.

"So whattaya say?" he finally uttered.

What does one say to the kind of man who looks naked in pants? "How does it feel" was what I came up with, "to switch from free-lancing to a steady position?"

"Yeah."

"You don't miss the scene?" Living as I did along Hustler Alley on East Fifty-third Street, I had seen the dire fascination that brought certain of Nick's colleagues back to the neighborhood night after night, some restively pushing the agenda early of a Saturday or dully clinging to the illusion as the sun came up on Sunday. Passing by with my groceries or my playbill, I had the impression that they had nothing but this for life, that the success of a paying rendezvous was less important than the simple fact of membership in the club of hot.

"Miss the scene?" Nick repeated. "I miss it like my last case of crabs."

"Ah."

"Miss the scene?" He laughed. "I could tell you about that. I could *tell* about the *scene!*" He laughed again. "You know what they are?"

"Who?"

"They're garbage is what. They'd rob blind cripples."

"Don't you have to stay in touch with your clients?"

"My what?"

"Your regulars. The johns."

"Oh. *Wallets.*"

"That's what you call them?"

"That's what they are. Money. Talking money. Asshole money. Fat, drooling money, and hair all over it like stupid. What do I want with them now? I got a deal here. I can sleep late. No hassle. I can do like . . . anything. And then Mac comes home and makes me feel good. Little Mac. He makes those cute things with his hands. He cooks dinner. All I have to do is lay him nice and easy. Sometimes they like it when you hurt them, you know? But Little Mac likes it lullaby-style."

"He makes you feel good?"

"You bet. Like when he smiles if you put your arm around him. He feels nice. You know, he's pretty. A pretty little nice boy. You know that kind? I like to feel him up. Tickle him, you know? Watch him shake. That's real dandy. I make him dance. Did he ever dance for you? Real pretty, when they dance. So pretty. He's not like a wallet and he's not like dig. You know?"

"Dig?"

"Dig is what I am. A wallet pays a dig, right?" He toyed with his suspender again. "Oh, what's he like, now? He's like a brother I had once. Kid brother. I made him dance, too. But like who could tickle a wallet, you know?"

"Dig is what you are."

"He should go pro. Let me turn him out. We could make two hundred a night, easy. These East Side wallets, they've got these videos? Pay you anything to make tape for them. They like tell you this story and then you do it. Acting. Maybe I'll be an actor, right? But the best thing I do is dance video. That's my hottest." He sat up.

"Dance video?"

"Mac'd be good at that, too. I like to dance. I like to fuck and dance. You got video? You want to make some tape, now? Bargain rates, 'cause you're a friend. We'll make one together, you know? Anything you want. Anything."

I looked at him. It was quite a long moment.

"What's with those shades, anyway? You doing something bad?"

He took hold of my glasses at the bridge and pulled them off. "Uh-oh." He replaced them. "No video. Gotcha." He laughed. "The man doesn't dance. The man does *not* choose to dance."

"Not with the likes of you."

He stopped laughing. "You got the eyes of a cop."

I've witnessed various liaisons with hustlers over the years, the street kind as well as the call-boy elite, on a dating and live-in basis; each has ended differently. One hustler drifts out of reach like a balloon in the park, another dwindles into a sexless chum, one vanishes, another gets pushy about money or moves on into his host's coterie or turns lawless and ends in jail. I even know of one—I'll get to him some pages hence—who was thrown out by a man who couldn't live with perfection. Nick adds another trope to the catalogue: the fuck machine plugged into a good gig, he simply hung on. Mac's friends fretted and his visiting brothers scowled, but something like a year went by and everyone but Mac was still waiting for Nick to clear out. Dennis Savage thumbed his black book to tatters manifesting Italian accountants, and dinners were duly arranged. But it was the dark lord whom the accountants loved, not the mute boy. Like it or not, Nick was hot.

So it stayed Mac and Nick, though no one ever tied them verbally, out of fear of giving their duet legitimacy. I think most gays respect the mating of twins, not the sharing of fantasy. Mac had offended custom, and this sin above all bills its dues. And Mac paid, when somebody with money beckoned to Nick.

It hit suddenly, at another dinner—perhaps my thousandth in New York, and never have I been given enough to eat—and Dennis Savage and I arrived to find Nick throwing clothes into a backpack as Mac followed him around frantically signaling.

"I know when it's time," Nick philosophized for our benefit. "It's time for L.A. Because I hate this fucking snow, and bartenders, and niggers on bicycles—"

Mac grabbed my arms, pointed to Nick, then hugged himself, watching me with huge asking eyes.

"I don't know what you're saying," I told him.

"This guy saw me in Studio, right? He dropped his glasses on the dance floor and who picks them up?"

"A wallet," I said.

"No, he's okay. I'm going back with him. On a *plane!*"

Mac moved to Nick, indicating their faces, their hearts, trying to smile. Nick turned away, muttering, "Sure, sure," but Mac took his hand and touched it to Nick's forehead.

Nick jerked his hand away. "Make him stop that stuff."

"After what he's done for you, my friend," said Dennis Savage, "the least you should—"

"Hey," said Nick, his arms as wide as his smile, slurring the word out the way grown-ups do when talking to children, "I earned it, didn't I?" He patted Mac's head and headed for the door. "Stay loose, boys," he called out. "And remember our motto: 'Don't screw anything made of wood.'" He laughed and pulled open the door as Mac ran up, pencil dashing across the top leaf of a pad. He tore it off and handed it to Nick.

"Give it to the next guy," said Nick. He crumpled the note, let it fall, and closed the door behind him.

Mac stayed where he was, facing the door, shaking his head. Finally he turned, touched his eyes, indicated us, and militantly brushed his palm across the air.

"I don't want you to see me cry," I sounded.

"We've seen you smile so much," said Dennis Savage. "I don't think a little crying would hurt."

Mac shook his head, holding back the tears. We didn't move, and he shook his head again.

I took the pad and pencil from him, and wrote, "Would you like a quarter?"

He read it, reclaimed the kit, and wrote, "It hurts to be nice."

I furiously shook my head.

He nodded grimly.

Dennis Savage held him very, very gently from behind, as if afraid of being pushed away. "Come on and cry," he urged. He had picked up the crumpled note, and put it in Mac's hand and closed his fist around it.

Mac looked at me.

"What?" I said.

He handed me the note. I opened it. It read, "My aunt died today."

"Mac," I said, "why did you write this?"

That was when he began to cry.

Mac went home for the funeral, returned to New York, and, bare weeks after, went back to Wisconsin on a long vacation. Letters poured out, somewhat less ebullient than usual; or perhaps as ebullient, but about unusual things—the nightingales at his window or losing to his nephew at chess. He would sneak back to the city, not calling any of us—Mac, the most intent comrade of all. How dare the little bastard, I thought, spotting him in the D'Agostino midway between our apartments. He's supposed to be in Racine! At least he had the sense of style to be embarrassed, which made it worse. I followed him to the checkout line, and sounded for him to the clerk: he had forgotten to take his pad. This is like forgetting to wear your shoes in a blizzard.

The Racine trips grew longer, but Mac continued to write. However, the letters grew shorter.

"Is it Nick?" I asked Dennis Savage. "All this mourning because a love affair ended?"

"Where do you get off reducing it to 'all this mourning'? Who are you to point a finger—you who set it all up, as I recall?"

"I hate you for that."

"And you aren't joking."

"I was helping! How was I to know that Mac could stay intrigued by a Nick?"

"Who made you the social arbiter of gay romance?"

"It was supposed to be one glorious night. *One.* It does *not* follow that a . . . a player of Monopoly would want to coexist with someone who can't tell a house from a hotel!"

He looked pensive. "Who knows less about love than you? The Wicked Witch of the West?"

"All right, what happens now? Is Mac's life ruined because that slimy hustler busted his heart? No doubt you know much of one, true, life-long love—no one I know has been in and out of it more variously than you."

"Jeers from a left-out."

"So tell me: can it destroy as surely as it exhilarates?"

"We must watch developments," he replied. "We must see and know."

Developments proved invisible, for Mac gave up his apartment and resettled in Wisconsin. Odd letters trickled back, drab ones now. Mac's mail used to soar. He never mentioned Nick, though there were what I took as oblique references, in phrases like "the fantasies of Manhattan" or "the grip of wishes." I would respond with carefree dish and, perhaps two months later, back would come another feeble laudamus of rustic places. "More and more," he wrote, "I have come to appreciate the plain heart of the midwest." I felt as if he had spit on me.

I continued to write, as breezily as I could manage. There was pleasant news: Lionel was teaching at the New School, Carlo lucked into a job at a ritzy boutique and became solvent for the first time since grade school, Eric sold his first novel to a major house, Dennis Savage had met a dazzling young man in, of all places, the Forty-Sixth Street Theatre, and the boy was so pure it took our Circuit paragon four dates to bed him. Are Manhattan's fantasies so blameful, then? We were all pushing thirty, and great dreams were slipping within our reach. And so I said to Mac, straight out: "Some fantasies must be shared."

Mac never answered; his wife did, enclosing photographs of the wedding. Her name was Patricia; she had known Mac all their lives, and had married Mac's high-school buddy, one of the last American casualties in Vietnam. Shortly after his death, Patricia had given birth to their son, Ty. A very midwestern story. I saw them all in the pictures: Pat quite pretty, Ty a handsome and sombre little boy, and the Mac I had known in New York, glad and lively. And still believing in fantasy. A thousand McNallys surrounded them, held them, admired them. There was even a tiny Ty with the model couple atop the festive cake. "And Mac," Patricia ended, "is a natural-born father. We put on a record of 'The Parade of the Tin Soldiers' and Mac and Ty march around the room. You should see little Ty, how seriously he takes it. There is so much love in the world, I cannot know why I have been so lucky." And she closed with, "Your friend, Patricia McNally."

I never heard from Mac again.

I did see Nick, though, some years later, in some other spread in some other magazine. What, *Cockstorm? Bullstick?* And the spread—"Fantasy Boys"? It might as well have been. Nick was fondling a younger man, who gazed up at him in tender terror. No doubt Nick was making him dance. I was in a room full of men at party, and they passed the magazine from hand to hand to see.

"My God, that one's hot!" someone exclaimed.

"How . . . hot . . . is he?" said another, in the cue-up style of Ed McMahon.

"He's so hot," said the jester, "he could make a straight turn gay."

I let it pass.

The Homogay

These stories, reader, are meant as mine in particular, not as gay stories in general—not depictions per se. Each life bears its own tales. Still, I am concerned at how often people cry in these pages. Life is not that sad. I've made up my mind that there will be no crying in this one.

I come from a town so small that every mother's son is born at home in mother's bed. So small the school bus made but three stops. So small the bully had to double as the sissy.

His name was Harvey Jonas. He had a high-pitched voice, his frame carried a pudding of blubber, and he was a fiasco at sports: the classic adolescent queer. Yet he was intently aggressive, even sadistic, especially with those smaller than he: a classic adolescent tormentor. I frankly admit I was afraid of him. With a little warning, anyone could outrun him, but sometimes he would lie in wait, then come hurtling out to nab you, braying like a monstrous donkey. Once he caught me while I was pumping my bicycle tires and, without uttering a word, snatched the air pump and marched off with it.

Our meanest encounter happened up by the swings one summer evening. Harvey came upon me and my two little brothers while we were in the air and couldn't run off. Anyway, you can't run in front of little brothers. I stood my ground and had the first extrafamilial fight of my life, outclassed by Harvey's superior weight and a warrior's will I had yet to develop. My brothers came to my aid—Andrew socked his head and Tony bit his foot—but I was losing badly until my older brother Jim happened by.

Jim was one of those cooly murderous youths who, if not strangled at birth, grow up to comprise a sizable fraction of the straight male population as cooly murderous adults. I must admit, though, that it was rather grand knowing him on this occasion. Always decisive if sloppy on the amenities, Jim grabbed Harvey by the hair and swung him with a grunt into one of the metal posts that supported the swings. Harvey lay where he landed, and I feared he might be dead, but suddenly he reared up and ran off. At a safe distance, he turned around and brayed at us.

"That," Jim observed with disgust, "is one champion queer."

"Yeah," I said.

"He sure is," agreed Andrew.

"I bit his foot," said Tony.

"And you know what you are?" Jim asked me, getting around to one of his favorite subjects. "A stupid *jerk.*" He shoved me. "Because you can't even defend yourself from a *fag* with an *army* to help you!"

"I bit his foot," said Tony.

Jim shoved me again. "Because you were *born* a jerk and you'll *die* a jerk!" He stared at me as if he could see another Harvey Jonas on the rise. I was there; I know it; I can feel how it looks to this day. And Jim stalked off.

It's tricky being the middle child: half the known world looks up to you and the other half looks down. Andrew and Tony waited for the next move, but I was too crushed to initiate anything.

"Do you want us to grunch his room for you?" asked Andrew, to cheer me up. "Grunch" is to ruin, to trash.

"The Revolt of the Moon Mice!" cried Tony, planning the marquee. "Let's chew Jujubes and dribble them in his sneakers!"

Childhood is hard. I'll skip ahead now to my grownup years in New York—you'll see why directly—to a fey and raucous party of gays and their friends in the West Nineties. I knew no one; the other guests all seemed to be old comrades. There was a lot of liquor and smoke and by midnight the place was roaring. A few couples were openly smooching, a Puerto Rican teenager was wandering around wearing nothing but a Melitta coffee filter paper around his middle (it was large and he was small), and, in the main room, two queens were doing show-biz impersonations.

It appeared to be a set routine. After a handsome actor type smoothly intoned into an imaginary microphone, "And now, it's time for *Dish Maven*, with the first legend of stage and screen, Miss Katharine Hepburn," seven or eight people hummed "Fine and Dandy"—*Dish Maven*'s theme song, I guessed. And "Hepburn," on a couch, ran through the rituals of the talk show, with preposterous commercials, rampant plugola, and unwitting egotism.

"And now, Miss Hepburn," the actory announcer cut in, "it's time to bring on your special guest."

"Damn. I was just going to do *Coco* medley," said Kate.

"Too late now, for here comes your dearest friend and competitor, the scintillant Miss Bette Davis!"

To a reprise of "Fine and Dandy," a second queen joined Kate on the couch, eyeing her as Hamlet might eye King Lear.

"Deah, deah Kate!" rasped Bette.

"Miss Davis' clothes," Kate told the crowd, "designed exclusively by K-Mart fashions!"

"Who is older, Kate?" Bette asked. "You or the Gobi Desert?"

"Quick!" Kate cried to an imaginary orchestra. "*Coco* medley!"

"*Coco?*" asked Bette. "I pronounce it with cedillas: *Soso!*"

"Well, you never won an Oscar!"

"You slept with Howard Hughes!"

"You made *Beyond the Forest!*"

"Ladies, ladies!" urged the announcer. "Surely you great

survivors can stop feuding and tell us of Hollywood's golden age."

The two stars fell into each other's arms. "We'll reminisce!" Kate swore; and Bette was overwhelmed. "Yes," Kate went on, "yes, we knew them all: Gable, Hank Fonda, dear little Deanna Durbin, sweet as halvah. And, of course, Bette, I had my marvelous Spencer and you had no one, but they were great, great times!"

"I had William Wellman."

"I want to ask you a very important question, Bette. Now, it may seem academic—and I know our guests are waiting for golden-age dish—but, seriously, Bette . . . you knew them all. The directors, the writers—"

"Such as F. Scott Fitzpatrick, my favorite, who wrote *Tender Are the Damned!*"

". . . the actors . . . and you knew what greatness was, as I did, and you knew the beauty of the art. You knew it! You *knew* it!" It was like Hepburn in *The Lion in Winter,* running, mounting, soaring. "Griffith and Gish! *Gone With the Wind!* The comebacks and the glory! And what I want to ask you is . . ."

"Yes?"

"Who had the biggest boner in Hollywood?"

And of course everyone laughed and clapped, and someone cried in a Tallulah voice, *"I* did, dahling!," and people refilled their glasses, and I was bowled over. I had come to New York for fast-moving hip, freedom from straights, and a touch of dada; here they all were at once. While musing on this, I suppose, I was unconsciously staring at the man who had played Hepburn. He was tall, not good-looking, and strikingly weightlifted; another year or two of iron and he could have entered a contest. The contrast between his physique and his performance was like a standoff between homosexuality as a feeling and gay as a style, the clipped hunk look warring with the camp. Half of him was more homo than gay, the other half more gay than homo. He was *homogay;* and he was, I suddenly noticed, aware that I was looking at him. He came over, posed, and said in a sultry voice through Jane Russell lips, "They call me Lorinda."

"That was expert satire," I told him. "You got television, Hollywood, and show-biz megalomania all at once."

He was looking at me oddly; was I too stiff for this party? "Go on," he said, in his own voice. "Say something else."

"Why?"

"Because I know you."

"No, you don't," I told him, strangely fearful.

"It's Bud Mordden, isn't it?"

"Who are you?"

"So!" he screamed, Lorinda again. People were looking. "Have you forgotten that night in romantic Mahony City when you pledged to be true?"

It was Harvey Jonas. Most gays conquer an atrocious childhood by going either completely virile or completely fag. Harvey had done both. No wonder I hadn't recognized him: he was twice disguised. Nearly speechless, I said the first thing that hit me: "You stole my bicycle pump."

"But not your heart, I see." He squeezed my thigh and "whispered," "What are you doing after the game, fullback? Let me teach you some new positions." More people were looking, and I backed away from him.

"Slow down," I said.

"A hometown girl like me needs her sweetheart by her side!" He was screaming again; now half the party was watching, including, inches away, the Puerto Rican in the Melitta filter. Briskly switching over to Eve Arden, Harvey told the boy, "You have an emergency call—coffee for three in Room 308," turned him around and pushed him away. "They'll want plenty of hot cream from your spigot, too," he added, and turned back to me.

"Now, my old friend," he said, in quiet, even, masculine tones, grasping my shoulders. "Let's understand each other vividly. If you tell a single soul . . . and I mean *anyone*: a judge, a ribbon clerk, a bag lady . . . if you tell anyone about

43

my past, I swear I'll rip you apart, limb from limb." Grasping harder, he flexed his right biceps. "Feel that."

"No, I'll take your word for it." Twenty years after, the same bully was still harassing me.

"If you're nice to me," he added, softening, "I'll be nice to you. Silence?"

"All right."

"Will you shake hands on it, in our simple country way?"

"No. But I'll give you my word."

He regarded me for a bit, then nodded. "I'll trust you."

Suddenly a voice rang out: "Auditions for the chorus line! Auditions for the *Hello, Dolly!* number!" Harvey swept back into the throng; now he was Carol Channing. "And *I'm* Dolly!" he announced. "Hello, everybody!"

"Hello, Carol!" they replied. And that day at the swings, which I had almost succeeded in burying, came flooding back into me like poison.

I would have been glad to give Harvey a wide berth, but for some reason he adopted me. He was utterly uninterested in me physically and we were not compatible as friends; however, he often included me in a crowd. I went along because I liked his crowd; after all, I had come to New York to join it. And never once did he revert to the threat he had voiced that night we reconvened. He had learned to project his toughness at genuine enemies, from impedient bureaucrats to sullen doormen, casually and fiercely. He was shameless. A scene in a bank or restaurant energized him. One minute he would be regaling the dinner table with his Tallulah and Carol; the next, he'd have a flippant waiter by the hair threatening to wash his face in soup if he didn't snap to. And he meant it; and he was over two hundred pounds of total beef.

He could be very funny. Once, in his apartment, he performed a version of *A Little Night Music* with Bette Davis in the lead, bungling the lyrics, quoting lines from her films, haranguing the audience with homophobic paranoia. He did Hal Prince, shaping Concept Production. He did Sondheim, tearing his hair. He did Kate Hepburn, sneaking into the show during "A Weekend in the Country" and trying to usurp Bette's role. I was literally on the floor, holding my stomach and screaming for mercy.

He was popular but loveless: the face was wrong. He worked out at Sheridan Square but, on the street, never nodded to the others who did, as most of them do. He scarcely cruised at all. His queen act centered on romance and sex; in real life, he stepped around them. There were times, rare ones when we were alone together, when I thought he was about to say something intimately sad, *homo,* but then he would cut over to some slashing line, *gay,* like, "You want hot truth? Love is so stupid they should give it to straights" or "I'm loud and crass and that's my fun—love me or leave me!"

One spends the first years in New York collecting coterie, one's next years trimming it. I moved on to a crowd in a lower key, given to ties and quiet pricey restaurants. At L'Aiglon one night I told them about Harvey's routines and they just looked at each other blankly. (It was a dull group, but the clothes were fun.) I kept in touch with Harvey and told him of my doings, and he became fascinated by the company I kept. They had names like Crosby and Raymond and were smooth operators. In their gentle way they made good stories, and in his rowdy way Harvey took them into his act. "Bette Meets Crosby," he would announce, then show me how the diva fared among the townhouse gentry. The adventure varied with his mood. "Tea is served," he once narrated, enacting it, "and Bette deftly raises a pinkie. But the potent tea has unaccountably excited her, and she finds to her horror that she has erected a *tremendous boner* just as Lady Fashionbury leans over to enquire after her health!"

He stopped and looked at me. "We aren't close, are we?"

I said nothing. It always unnerved me when he went into his own voice.

"Still, I'm going to ask a favor of you. If you say no, we won't mention it again, all right?" He came over to me, smiling. "I want to come along with you to one of those dinners you have with your gentlemen friends. The Crosby gang. Harvey Meets Crosby. Yes or no?"

"Well . . . actually . . ."

He waited, towering above me. "Yes or no?" He grabbed my arm and pulled me to my feet. I saw the swings again, and my brothers fighting alongside me and Jim hating me. "Just say yes or no."

"Yes or no."

He let me go and moved away. Then he roared with laughter. "How's your love life?" he asked.

"Fine."

"You never speak of it."

"I keep secrets."

"Yes, I'm well aware. You keep a good secret. Do you ever think about . . . back then?"

"You know," I said, "I'd rather direct this scene than be in it, but I wouldn't know what to tell the actors. What is this scene about?"

"Why won't you take me to meet the Crosby gang?"

"Because you threatened me."

"Is that the only reason?"

I lied. "Yes."

"You want hot truth? I don't even want to meet them. I truly don't. I'd just make them angry, wouldn't I? I'd dip my spoon into the fingerbowl and say, 'What delicious consommé!' And, tasting my pheasant, I'd turn to Crosby and say, 'It's absolu de*lish!*' No, I wouldn't say it. I'd *scream* it, right there in Le Grand Can-Can or wherever it is you go to." And he did scream it, right there in his apartment. "Absolu de*lish!* It's *ab*solu de*lish!*" He paced and frumped like Davis in her Elizabeth movies. "Why, Layt-ty Crospy, how haugh-ty you seem tto-ttay!" He pushed me back down on the couch. The damned aren't always tender. He was furious—not, I think, at me. "They all have lovers, don't they, the Crosby gang?"

"No, not all. A few. Nothing long-lasting."

46

"That type doesn't need lovers, anyway. They have fuck chums." This too he screamed out. "*Fuck!Chums!* Once a month, with the lights turned down and a little Mozart in the background. Oh, it's delicate and soigné. I'll bet they don't even fuck. Fuck is too lewd for that coven. They *cuddle!*" He sat down across the room from me and kicked off his shoes, calming down. "That brother of yours, the handsome one . . . Jim. He's gay, isn't he?"

"No."

"You're wrong."

"No, I'm not."

Harvey pulled off his socks and threw them in a corner. I cleared my throat. "What *is* this scene about, by the way?"

"The scene is about how to hold a lover. Do you want a lover? Don't answer; almost everyone does. Almost everyone." He began to unbutton his shirt. "You're my oldest friend and you know my secrets. Not all of them. But some of the best ones. Now let me tell you how to hold your beautiful gay lover. By being terrific in bed? No. That will guarantee a good premiere, but beautiful lovers by nature have already had much taste of fabulous carnal technique. You won't hold him that way. Am I making you nervous?" He got up and slowly peeled off his shirt. "What else? By having pecs or thighs of death? No. Who doesn't, nowadays?" He unbuckled his belt, opened his pants, and took them off. Nude, he presented the most spectacular member I've ever seen. A bit longer or heavier and it would have been grotesque; like so, it was . . . well, champion queer. "Cock of death, too, has been called premium. But cock, I've discovered, is made for tricking, not love. Oh yes . . . yes, how often you've heard a man sigh that cock is everything. Once you've been fucked by a big one you can never go back to the minor leagues. Have you heard this?" He stroked himself fleetingly. "I've seen men weep as they lay before me, vulnerable and poetic, waiting for me to begin. They weep for joy. For a moment, one imagines that nothing else in the world is as important as cock. The wonder of it! But they don't stay. They don't take you in their arms and just hold on so quietly and happily. They don't look at you, at any time of day, with those wild eyes one hears tell of. They don't need you. Nor, I'm sorry to say, will wit or social grace avail you. No, there is only one way to hold a lover: by having a handsome face. You may have noticed that I do not. Not partly or nearly. Not *possibly*. And once one isn't handsome, one never will be. Everyone talks about power, but everyone wants beauty. It's sad, because you can acquire power but you can't acquire beauty. Do you know why everyone wants beauty? Because beauty is the only thing in the world that isn't a lie."

He extended his arms, palms outward. "I am not offering myself to you, incidentally. I simply wish to show you, as generously as possible, a choice irony of contemporary urban life. Would you ever so mind going now?"

I got up. At the door he said, his eyes on the floor, "Somewhat needless to say, if you tell anyone about this . . ."

"I'm not afraid of you anymore."

He looked up. "Were you ever?"

"All my life. Till about five minutes ago."

He opened the door, then gently pulled me back as he thought of something. "Tell me, where is your brother now?"

"Here. He lives a few blocks from me, in fact."

"What would happen if you said hello to him for me?"

"I haven't spoken to Jim in years."

He considered this. "You always had a very strange family. What was that littlest one's name?"

"Tony. He bit your foot."

Naked in the doorway, he watched me wait for the elevator. "That was all a long, long time ago," he said. "You can forgive me now."

"No, I can't. And I never will."

"Was I that awful to you?"

"It wasn't just you."

"Who else?"

I shook my head.

The Precarious Ontology of the Buddy System

Thinking back on the couples I have known, I note how many of them were unsuited for each other—Alex and Joe, for instance, or Mac and Nick. What is surprising about the gay fascination for the misalliance is how many odd couples actually seem rather made for each other, once they hook up. I marvel. When Dennis Savage, that very exponent of Stonewall-era sexual cosmopolitanism, picked up a youngster at standing room for *The Best Little Whorehouse in Texas,* I took it as usual news, at best a passing headline: ALLURING VETERAN NABS NEW BOY IN TOWN. But this was the boy it took four dates to land, and when their spotty rendezvous schedule grew constant, then insistent, I stood by, amused and supportive. When I met the boy and found him very young, very silly, and very uneducated, I held my peace. And when I saw this archon of the Circuit, the notable (if fiercely flawed) Dennis Savage, become so involved with this boy that he began to lecture me on the evils of the single-person family (especially mine), I smiled. One must. But then this kid moved in with Dennis Savage, and the kid was called Little Kiwi, and Dennis Savage acted as if he owned every place Little Kiwi was in, like a father, a creditor, and a king all at once. What was I to do? Especially as they would show up at my apartment whenever they chose. Actually, what I did was: I thought, There is a tale in this now. Another story begins to stir in this our gay life.

As Lord Mayor of the Circuit, Dennis Savage intends his visits as an honor, but somehow he always shows up when I'm

50

"It's ancient history," he urged. "An old story."

"This story isn't finished yet."

"If you're nice to me, I'll be nice to you."

I just looked at him and he shrugged and closed his door. So who did have the biggest boner in Hollywood? Harvey Jonas did, for all the good it did him; and it did him none; and that's fine with me. You want hot truth? That scene was about the ruin promoted by childhood calamaties. About how something goes wrong in infancy and nothing feels right thereafter. About being haunted by nameless worries.

I promised not to expose the secrets of Harvey Jonas. But he owes me satisfaction: for my bicycle pump, for what happened at the swings, and mainly for some other matter that I'd rather not mention just now.

There is no crying anywhere in this story.

pushing a deadline and, as he lives in my building, there's never a warning. If I bar my door to him, he goes into some grotesque routine in the hall, which makes for crabby neighbors. Worse yet, now that Little Kiwi has moved in with him, they go everywhere together, often in the company of Little Kiwi's disreputable dog, Bauhaus. But people tell me how lucky I am to have Dennis Savage's confidence—"and that fetching number who walks in his shadows! My, my, *my!*" Will you listen to the sound of them? As if we were still in the late 1940s, when all the bars were unmarked and only bombers wore bomber jackets.

I've told Dennis Savage to call first. I've lectured him on the rudeness of poking into my fridge uninvited. I've warned him that Little Kiwi's fabled charm is lost on me. And all he says is, "Have you noticed how lamplight picks up the tones in his hair?"

"How old is that kid, anyway?" I once asked him.

"Old enough to love."

"He has the interests of a child of eight."

"He voted in the last election."

"For whom? The Velveteen Rabbit?"

"Everyone adores him. They dress up for him and bake a pie. Look at you." I keep house in jeans and a sweatshirt. "And what do you give us to eat? BLTs!"

Actually, I give Dennis Savage BLTs. Little Kiwi subsists on grilled-cheese sandwiches and sliced tomato.

"Everyone wants Little Kiwi," says Dennis Savage. "You should know this. Except no one can have him but me."

"Oh, yeah?"

Dennis Savage chuckles. "I dare you."

How satisfying it would be to outfox Dennis Savage, though on the other hand his relationship with Little Kiwi is too fascinating to menace. I always listen for the sour notes in the gay duet, perhaps because the local Sloan's, at First Avenue and Fifty-third Street, seems at times to be populated exclusively by quarreling moustaches. But in these two I see the seamless fraternity of the worldly and the naïve, the hip and the unspoiled. Dennis Savage has been everywhere; Little Kiwi knows nothing.

Despite my complaints, I enjoy their visits, though they do tend to take over. One evening, as spring gave way to summer and my workday dwindled into daydreams and staring out the window, the two of them and Bauhaus paraded in. Dennis Savage went into the kitchen to see about a snack, Little Kiwi was poking into the two huge cardboard boxes my new stereo had come in, and Bauhaus grabbed a sneaker in his mouth, ran around in a craze, crashed into the piano, and lay there.

"Hey! This would make a great boat," said Little Kiwi, laying one of the boxes on the floor. "Would somebody push me around in my boat?"

"I'll push you, little darling," I said. Suddenly Dennis Savage came roaring out of the kitchen, steel in his eyes.

"Well, well, well," I remark. "Look at somebody nervous about something."

Dennis Savage takes a long breath and smiles. "This is a funny apartment and you are a funny man."

"It's a funny world."

"How would you like no head?"

"Now I'm playing store," Little Kiwi announces, hauling the box up on its side. "Who wants to buy a dog?"

"What else do you sell in your store?" I ask. "Kisses?"

Little Kiwi looked at me for quite some time, then shot the same look at Dennis Savage: confusion? distrust? fear? I must admit, lamplight does rather pick up the tones in his hair.

"You know," I said to Dennis Savage. "I think it's time you and I took Little Kiwi to the Island."

"What island?" Little Kiwi asked.

"Fire."

"Could Bauhaus come?"

"Surely," I replied. "What's Fire Island without Bauhaus?"

"I'm going to pack!" Little Kiwi cried, racing out with the dog.

"It so happens," says Dennis Savage, "that I had just such a trip in mind."

"Of course," I agreed. "Of course. Of course. Of course."

"But since you brought it up, you can make the arrangements."

"My pleasure."

"It'll be grand showing Little Kiwi all the places. Like revisiting our youth. There are three memories that every gay lives on—the first Gay Pride March, the first sight of the Saint, and the first trip to the Pines."

"Aren't you afraid of losing Little Kiwi out there?" I asked. "It's been known to happen."

He nodded, smiling vaguely, nodded again. "I've got Little Kiwi all wired down."

"You didn't seem to think so a minute ago. You came rocketing out of the kitchen like a husband."

"I just didn't want to miss anything," he said airily. "You put on such an amusing act. Yea, if I'm the husband, what are you—the iceman?"

"Maybe."

"Make sure you set us up in a real *bijou* of a house, now. We want to do the Island in top style."

"Shall we say the weekend after Memorial Day?"

"I can't wait to see Little Kiwi on the ferry—the wind in his hair and such. We could arrive just in time for tea and step right off the boat into the throng, Little Kiwi a sensation in lederhosen and I, Lord Mayor of the Circuit, greeting my fans." He regarded me with something like scorn. "Do you suppose you could, just for once, try to look famous? Nothing spoils an entrance like one of the party clomping in like somebody's uncle."

As he reached the door I said, "Please, don't worry about Little Kiwi and me."

"Was I planning to?"

"You know what they say about the iceman."

"What do they say, you bum sheik?"

"He cometh."

It went off like a dream. We claimed the hospitality of a wealthy friend of mine with a house on the surf, two decks, a pool, endless room, and the honest generosity of a golden-age host. We caught the Islanders' bus at Fifty-third and Second, Bauhaus and all, and Dennis Savage planted Little Kiwi across the aisle from us on his own. "He has to get out in the world," said Dennis Savage. There Little Kiwi entranced an elderly man with Wacko the Puppet, a character Little Kiwi creates by smushing his hand into a paper envelope to form a mouth. Wacko speaks in a crackly voice suggestive of Wheat Chex coughing and hasn't a shred of wit; his charm lies not in what he says but in the fact that Little Kiwi gets such a kick out of him. It's like Joan Crawford's acting: you don't admire the talent; you admire the commitment.

"I have a beautiful home on the bay," the old man was saying. "I'm looking for a houseboy. Would you like the job?"

"Don't do windows!" Wacko warned Little Kiwi.

"The duties are light," the man went on.

"That lets Little Kiwi out," Wacko observed. "He likes a lot of structure in his life."

"The salary is very negotiable."

"Now, Wacko," said Little Kiwi, "tell the folks that story about the Polish elephant."

"Please," the man pleaded. "Please."

"Why don't you trade seats with Little Kiwi?" I asked Dennis Savage. "He's shattering the social contract."

"He has to see life and learn. He's been very sheltered till now."

"He's about to give that old man a heart attack."

"That is the role that old men play in the gay world. If

you haven't accepted that by now, you'll never know anything."

As we disembarked at Sayville, Dennis Savage got teary. "Remember?" he kept saying. "Remember? The magic of the Island!" As the boat pulled out of the slip, he gripped Little Kiwi's shoulders and promised him the most spectacular experience of his life. Wacko immediately bit his nose and he calmed down; but, true enough, the spell of the Pines came upon us as we cut through the bay.

"There is a tale," I began. "In ancient days, when the Pines consisted of a few cottages and the ferries stopped once a week, a collection of very special people sped over the water to the Star Party. Everyone would come as a Hollywood personality, full kit. The food! The prizes! The guests! This was a festival to redeem an era!"

Mention elitism and all gays are transfixed. "When was this?" Dennis Savage asked. "Was Wacko there?" said Little Kiwi. "The puppet?"

"With so many stupendous guests, it was agreed that all would enter at the same moment. Consider them boarding the ferry, each thinking of his personal *grandezza,* retouching his *toilette,* planning his *mots.* Each had a secret dream of who he might be, could he but *become.*"

"The magic of the Island!" Dennis Savage breathed.

"What a tension there was as each came unto the ferry, the many dog-pets—impressed by the crush of celebrity— barking and whining." Little Kiwi patted Bauhaus' head; Bauhaus growled. "As the ferry neared the Island, the company tensed, wondered, thrilled. Consider their state." We too were nearing port, cutting by the ambiguous coast. All you see is greenery broken by roofs, but you sense the extraordinary. You have heard amazing stories; you look at the place where they happen.

"Just as the boat sighted dock," I went on, "disaster struck. The ferry lurched, struck bottom, and sank. Everyone drowned!"

"No," said Little Kiwi. "Wait—"

"Ridiculous," cried Dennis Savage. "The bay is four feet deep."

"It sank. Yes. Horrible and true. They held no party that night."

"No *party!*" Little Kiwi repeated, with a miserable groan, as if I had told him that the world's supply of grilled cheese had been exhausted.

"And, so they say, when the moon is full and the Island humming, that ferry rises, a ghost. As midnight strikes, if you approach the harbor, you can hear . . . *the ghastly yapping of a hundred poodles!*"

"*Satirist!*" Dennis Savage hissed, as we pulled in. It was just after lunch. We turned south on the boardwalk to check in with our host, Wacko commenting avidly on the passing scene, and the passing scene, in whispers, commenting avidly on Little Kiwi. About halfway there I looked back and saw that the old man from the bus was following us.

"Maybe he lives in this direction," Dennis Savage said.

"No, he looks guilty. He's *lurking.*" We had stopped, and so had he.

"I'll take care of this," Dennis Savage snapped, starting back.

I grabbed his arm. "Let me talk to him. You're not gentle enough."

"You? You'll throw a drink in his face!"

"That's telling him!" cried Wacko. "Put him in the blender and dial puree!"

Dennis Savage sent the man away, weeping; and Little Kiwi went on snagging hearts. Our host had been having drinks with a friend, who greeted Dennis Savage and me with vacant politesse. But when the friend's eyes lit on Little Kiwi, he turned vivacious. We dropped our luggage at the door and plopped down with dim smiles and nothing to say in the Pines manner. But the man went on and on, addressing himself to Little Kiwi, going for broke. He hung around so long he practically had to be asked to leave. Of course he insisted on kiss-

ing us all good-bye. Our host endured it, Dennis Savage made his usual lateral cheek-to-cheek bypass, and I simply picked up some luggage and carried it into a room. But Little Kiwi, the real object of this exercise, wailed, "It's the kiss of death!" and backed away.

I returned to a room made of embarrassment and horror. Apparently this was an Influential Man. Our host turned to me and whispered, "Get him out of here!" through his teeth. I grabbed the man by the collar and was about to swing him toward the door when our host restrained me. "Not him!" he cried. "The *kid!*"

"Come, Little Kiwi, we'll view the ocean."

"He has boils on his nose," Little Kiwi screamed as we left, Bauhaus staggering after us. "He has liver lips!"

"Hush."

"Meet us at tea," Dennis Savage called out at the door. "And do me a favor—lose the puppet."

That part was a cinch: Wacko fell in the water and drowned, and, Bauhaus barking at every wave, Little Kiwi and I walked west along the water's edge. I never know what to say to him, so we moved in silence all the way to the Grove, which Little Kiwi wanted to explore. "This one looks different," he noted—from the Pines, and indeed it is; cramped, campy, and heedless of fashion where the Pines is expansively tense with it. The Grove is like a stomach that has sagged atrociously for twenty years; the Pines is abdominals perfectly turned.

"Why are we here?" Little Kiwi suddenly asked.

"We walked here."

"On Fire Island, I mean. Us three."

"For fun."

"No."

"For adventure."

He shook his head.

"Okay, you tell me."

"No, it was your idea to come out here. What are you two planning?"

I said nothing. We were walking back along the beach, admiring the sunset. The sand was nearly deserted, though here and there solos and small groups were playing out the day's concerto of desire and regret. Ahead of us we saw a tall, dark-haired, very well-built, and extremely handsome man of about thirty-five stalk down the beach toward a young, fair man in the surf up to his thighs. As the older man neared him he turned and they stared at each other for a long moment. Everything else around us seemed to stop, too. The older man very gently stroked the youth's chest. The youth returned the gesture, but not willingly—uneasily, maybe, in a beautiful alarm, never taking his eyes from the man's own. They went on trading these compliments in a kind of reverie, hypnotized by the setting, by their utter disregard for the received inhibitions of Western civilization, and perhaps by their own grandeur as archetypes, like unto like. It was awesome: turbulent and still. So open, so secret. It was the magic of the Island. Oblivious of the rest of us, the two finally stopped touching and just looked. Then the man put his arm around the boy's shoulders and together they walked out of the water and across the sand to the boardwalk.

Little Kiwi looked at me. "Do they know each other?"

"I don't believe so."

"They just . . . met? Like that?"

"It happens."

"Is it going to happen to me?"

"Do you want it to?"

He was silent. Then: "What is it *for*?"

"What's an orange for? Or shoes?"

"I *ate* an orange," he replied. "I *wore* a shoe."

We reflected, looking out upon the sea. Bauhaus, whose existence is an endless chain of wrong choices, rushed sneezing out of the surf, wrestled frantically in the sand, gobbled seaweed, and threw up.

"That dog of yours," I said, "is going to make a big hit at tea."

We arrived late and put in the worst sort of entrance: moodily pensive. Dennis Savage's eyes narrowed as we joined him. Our host was high, however, and forgave me five or six times for our faux pas with the Influential Man. "Well, he really is a troll," our host admitted. "He has everything but the bridge. Dear me, that little boy has a nice frown. Where did Dennis Savage find him, do you suppose?"

We gazed dotingly upon Little Kiwi. A huge weightlifter in silk pajama bottoms also took note of him, moved near, and smiled down like a rainbow as Little Kiwi slowly looked up at him. "You're the sweetest little thing on the Island," said the weightlifter, "and that's a fact." He ran a finger down the front of Little Kiwi's shirt and hooked it on his belt, pulling him closer. "Think we could arrange something, babe?"

Little Kiwi dropped his eyes; his fingers rustled as if Wacko the Puppet were turning over in his grave. Then he looked at the man and said, "Little Kiwi is afraid of you."

The weightlifter laughed, patted Little Kiwi's head, and moved off as Dennis Savage glared daggers in my direction.

"Don't look at me," I told him. "I'm not in this scene."

Oh yes, I was. As our host and Little Kiwi collaborated on dinner in the kitchen, Dennis Savage laid me out to filth in the living room.

"What have you done to him? What did you say? Where did you take him? I've never seen him like this before. He's . . . *crestfallen.*"

"He saw the magic of the Island."

"I'll just bet he did! When he left this house today he was a Pan of the Circuit. He had presto, mistos, contempo."

"Sounds like a new series of designer bank checks."

"This always happens when I let him alone with you!" Dennis Savage raged. "That time I had flu and he had dinner at your place, he came back saying the world was going to end. He was afraid of the dark for weeks!"

"He asked about Spengler's theories because he saw—"

"Spengler! *Spengler?* Little Kiwi wouldn't know Spengler if he caught him rimming Hegel in Xenon!"

"The book happened to be lying open on the ottoman of my armchair and he asked me—"

"I suppose you and he discussed Kant this afternoon and that's why he showed up at tea in such a merry mood!"

"Oh, Christ! What should I have done, then—taken him to the meat rack? What do you think the magic of the Island is, pray?"

"It's ever such delicious quiche, of course!" cried our host, sweeping in with a hot one. "And salad! *Vino!*" Trivets and flatware erupted and settled. "Now, get set for, yes, the *pêche de résistance!* Okay, Little Kiwi!"

Out came Little Kiwi, solemnly bearing a bowl of fruit.

"Look," declaimed our host, "at what Little Kiwi made!"

"Grapes and a peach?" I asked.

"He made *fruit selection!*"

"By myself," Little Kiwi added.

We tried to make dinner festive, but Little Kiwi's funk seemed to have deepened. Every innocent gambit of conversation I played somehow kept coming around to Heavy Topic, Dennis Savage could utter nothing but insults (directed at me), and our host became so dizzy trying to enliven us that the table might have been flying through the air at a drag ball. Even Bauhaus picked up on our troubles; he was whining so, we had to tie him up out on the deck. Finally, in desperation, we tried eating in silence, whereupon poor Little Kiwi put his head down and wept.

We were too shocked to do anything. Or no: we did that stupid, helpless, wasteful thing—we sat and watched.

"I don't want to," Little Kiwi told us. "I don't like it."

Our host started to get up, but Dennis Savage signaled him not to. "What don't you want?" Dennis Savage asked evenly.

"I don't know what to call it." Little Kiwi wiped his eyes but they just got wet again.

"You know what it might be?" our host suggested. He lives quietly, has never had a lover, and isn't used to Scenes. (I could visualize him asking, like Little Kiwi, "What are they *for?*") "We raced home from tea-dancing and went right into the kitchen, so we never took that wonderful Fire Island time out on the deck to sip a cocktail and watch the sun go down."

"That isn't it," I told him.

"Don't be too sure," he replied. Little Kiwi was still crying, head down, grabbing the sides of his chair, a sweet doubting no with hurt feelings and soft black hair. "Almost all my guests tell me how much they love just sitting out there in that silence with their friends. I would read Walt Whitman aloud to them, but I don't dare, of course. Still, the atmosphere is so . . . well, so magical that—"

"Look," I said, "I'll tell you about the magic of the—"

"Little Kiwi," said Dennis Savage dangerously. "Stop crying."

"Oh dear," said our host, "you don't think it was the quiche, do you?"

"And this," Dennis Savage went on, eyeing us two like Monstro the Whale, "is not the time to discuss the magic of the Island. *Do you mind?*"

Clearly it was time to leave them alone, though I must say our host handled it more suavely than I. "I love to go walking on the beach at night," he began; I just grabbed a pear from the fruit selection and shouted "Amscray time!"

We took Bauhaus with us, and traipsed along the water's edge dishing the day's events. I told him about the two men we had seen making magic in the water and he laughed sadly. "Love in the fast lane, isn't it?" he said. "You know, when the three of you arrived, I thought that little boy was a hustler."

"Little Kiwi? Good grief, he's from Cleveland or something."

"Hustlers come from Cleveland."

"Hustlers come from Queens."

"Hustlers come *in* queens."

Another of those elegant nights in the Pines.

Dennis Savage caught up with us after a bit, his cool recovered. As to what had troubled Little Kiwi, he would say nothing other than that the storm was over and the boy had gone to bed. Now it was time for the Lord Mayor of the Circuit to touch base with his cohorts. Our host begged to go along and I proposed to take Bauhaus home and make my fortieth attempt at *Middlemarch*.

"Aye, ever improving himself," said Dennis Savage as we started back. "How inspiring the variety of life in the Pines. Some to their books . . . others to hold court."

"And still others to make a pilgrimage," I added, "slinking through the trees toward love."

"That," replied Dennis Savage, "is your gay materialism speaking. It will be the ruin of you yet."

If there's a lightbulb in all of the Pines bigger than ten watts I've yet to see it. One comes here to be in stories, not read them. Holding *Middlemarch* about three inches from my nose, I had the sensation I was back in the days of the Inquisition, reading forbidden text by secret light. I gave it up, fixed myself a triple Scotch, and went out on the deck to listen to the ocean. There Little Kiwi joined me in running shorts and Dennis Savage's old Hamilton College sweatshirt.

"I'm still embarrassed," he said after quite some wait.

"Dennis Savage went visiting with our host."

He sighed. "I guess I'll have to try to be older, won't I?"

"Now, that's a Fire Island first. Everyone else here is trying to renovate."

"I could have a secret dream and become. Like those party guests on the ferry that sank."

"What would you become, do you think?"

"Virgil Brown."

"Say what?"

He sat on the bench along the deck railing, facing the ocean. "Could I have a sip of your drink?" He tried it and shuddered. "I don't like liquor. I like the sound of the ocean, though."

"It's restful, isn't it?"

"That's my name: Virgil Brown. You can call me that, if you like. Virgil Brown. Mister Brown. That Brown man. You know."

"Okay."

"Do you think Dennis Savage will call me that?"

"He will if you ask him to."

We watched Bauhaus ooch along the deck planks on his stomach, growling.

"I like to listen to the waves," he went on. "I've been to beaches before but I've never heard them sound like this." Bauhaus whimpered and drooled. "Is our host sore at me?"

"On the contrary, I imagine he found it all very stimulating."

"He thought it was the quiche." Little Kiwi laughed very gently. "That was so . . . nice . . . of him. Wasn't it?" Bauhaus rolled over on his back and posed with his legs in the air, a big dead roach.

"Are you cold?" I asked him. "I brought an extra sweater. It's in my satchel."

"Could I sit on your lap and put my arms around you?"

"Of course."

"Grownups do this sometimes," he said, settling in. "It isn't only for kids."

We listened to the ocean pound out its rhythm in the great empty dark of the place where all men are forms of lover because they hunger so, the gayest place on earth, all ours.

"This is the magic of the Island," he said. He lay his head on my shoulder and closed his eyes, listening.

Three Infatuations

All gay is divided into three parts: looks, money, and wit, in that (descending) order, and my friend Carson had some of each—decent looks, tons of money, and competent wit. He'd get by. Perhaps he expected too much. He was always *casing* men—not cruising them as much as considering how they might figure in his plot. Let a waiter come to our table happy with menus, or a truck driver ask the time, or an actor cross a stage, and Carson would be wondering what he would be like to live with. Later, he would ask you where you thought the waiter went, or whom the trucker knew, or what the actor thought.

"I could buy all the men in the world, I expect," he told me. "I could rent the Colt stable, one after the other, night of my nights. But *then* what happens? What is life without mystery?"

Let the rest of us buddy up with persons very much like ourselves, clone for clone; not Carson. He craved the ad, the rendezvous by graffito, the remote, posed photo. Yet all his archetypes ordered out of the catalogue kept turning into real people. There was the weightlifter Carson met in his gym, an agreeable, speechless hunk who fascinated Carson till the night he returned early from a family trip to find the weightlifter dancing around the room in a picture hat to Carol Channing records. Or there was the swimming champ from Rutgers who used to wake up screaming from unspeakable dreams (but he spoke of them); or the vocal coach with the wonderful beard who suffered temporary impotence every time he heard

64

Leonie Rysanek mentioned. There was another weightlifter, a German who knew no English and was turning out great till Carson took him to Fire Island and he went crazy at the quality of the competition and wrecked the house they were staying in.

My favorite was Kurt, a trim dark kid Carson picked up on Christopher Street and took—and kept—home. Carson's term for Kurt's type, for reasons that I'm glad to say were kept obscure, was "sweet gypsy butt." Yet, overnight, Kurt turned into what is generally termed a wife. Carson said Kurt was incredible in the lay, but, underneath Kurt's "I will do anything and I'll do it better than anyone and what's more I'll scream while we're doing it" façade, this kid was against (1) good food, (2) whizz entertainment, (3) hot dancing, and, generally, (4) life. Carson had a tendency to stomach, so Kurt put him on a diet of what looked like hay, and went on to institute farm yard bedtimes and reveilles and refused to go anywhere that held more than eight people.

The night Kern Loften turned forty he threw a stupendous party, and Carson somehow sneaked away from Kurt, arrived early, and dug into his first real food in months. He ate like the Cowardly Lion, ravenously but with a fearful eye over his shoulder watching for Kurt. Remember, this was a kept boy, living with Carson rent-free, board taken care of, pocket money discreetly supplied. And listen to how he carried on with his master:

"What's that in your mouth?" he cried, suddenly upon us and eyes blazing.

"Carrots," said Carson, shooting cookie crumbs all over the place.

"What do you have behind your back?"

"The wall," I whispered.

"You've got pastries and tarts there, haven't you?"

"No," Carson replied. "Celery sticks!"

"Why are they hiding from me?"

"They're afraid you'll gobble them up," I told him. "They want to live."

Kurt regarded me balefully. "I know about you," he said—he always said this when one of Carson's friends picked on him. God, was he cute; but what a bore. "We're leaving *right* now!" he told Carson.

"*You're* leaving. In many ways." And he took his arm from behind him to reveal a bowl of M&Ms. We cheered as Kurt stormed out.

"Well," Carson remarked. "That's the end of him, isn't it?" He meant it, too. When Carson froze on you—he did so, at times, on a whim—he stayed frozen. "Here we go again with the locksmith."

"Poor Kurt," said someone.

"They always have somewhere to go," Carson noted. "With the usual check."

We made a night of it, repairing to Carson's apartment for dish therapy and silly acts. Carson celebrated his freedom in the kitchen, heaving out Kurt's pita bread and bran. "Thank God," he screamed, "I'll never have to eat another dish of tofu!"

In the living room, he surveyed us gloomily. "On the other hand, here I am again: rich, young, and reasonably pretty with no one to pet me. What's the use of money if it can't buy love?"

We wondered.

"I've tried all the kinds, haven't I?" he went on. "Man dudes, sweet gypsy butt, disco league"—here Kurt slammed in, eyed us with ire, and marched off to his last night in the local bed, as Carson wryly ignored the whole thing. "I even had a preppy once. The summer," he sighed, "of '74. So now what?"

It was time for Dennis Savage to theorize. "You've been buying the wrong kind of love," said he. "You haven't had hustlers; you've had gays who charged money. You need a real hustler, who knows his trade and works at it."

Sensation in the room.

"What *is* a real hustler?" someone asked.

"That's a good gay question," says Dennis Savage. "What does a hustler have, besides expert love technique?"

"A hustler doesn't have anything," I offered. "A hustler lacks."

"Yes!" Carson cried. "Yes!"

"All your protégés had things—hang-ups, rules, plans. A hustler is the essence of the thing, a poster made flesh."

"What *doesn't* a hustler have, exactly?" asked Dennis Savage.

"No background?" Carson suggested.

"No mind," someone put in.

"No ambition," said another.

"No interests!" said Dennis Savage, hoping to cap it. But I love to flunk him:

"A hustler," I announced climactically, "has no opinions."

There was silence; then Carson leaped up ecstatically. "Where do I find someone like that?"

As we know, I live on Fifty-third Street between Third and Second, Hustler Alley, and it was there, of course, that Carson would find one, if one could be found. I had doubts. The hustler, after all, is a platonic essence, and real-life humans are less concisely derived.

"I'm auditioning," Carson blithely told me when we bumped into each other one summer evening, I with a bag of groceries and he with about nineteen eyes, all going at once, up street and down, to right and left, quick shots, double takes, and pans, swiveling to follow. It's standard but it's rude.

"Aren't you afraid you'll catch something?" I asked him.

"I'm not actually doing them yet. We're still in the interview stage. To screen out the ones with opinions."

He winked and moved on; I'd never seen him so urbane. But then spending power tends to emphasize the suave in the wealthy.

I took to having the evening cocktail with Dennis Savage. His apartment, two floors above mine, fronts on Fifty-third, so we could sit at the window and watch Carson's auditions. Actually, he seldom materialized. I gather he spent most of his time in the neighborhood's several hustler bars. But we did see quite some parade: the most spectacular boys alongside the most atrocious, the latter as confident or druggy or disturbed as the former; hunks and skeletons; outfits and rags; slick buyers in vested suits and hopeless browsers with damp polyester underarms. You'd think the stage had but two character types, the beauty and the beast, and one topic, their encounter. But every viewing brought new themes, startling variations.

"Is it a microcosm?" I asked, playfully.

"No," says Dennis Savage. "No, it has no texture. Here you see gay reduced to one element: porn. It will be amusing to see what Carson comes up with. Will he find the male who is made of nothing but sex? Think of it: an unconflicted gay!"

We thought of it.

"However," he added, "I've never known Carson to finish anything he started *and* it takes him years not to do it. If he were the captain of the *Titanic* it would still be sinking."

But Carson came through on this one. Jimmy was about twenty-four, tall, and handsome, with straight sandy hair, a roguish smile, hot slit eyes, and a classic kid's frame opulently fleshed out. He had none of the gay things—no quickness, no points of reference, no curiosity. I doubted he had ever seen the inside of a gym or a cabaret. He was amiable and quiet. Carson had us all over for drinks, one by one, to show him off, to get him used to us, and to acclimatize him to gay society. And of course, like those characters in *The Wizard of Oz*, we all compared notes to learn if we had each met the same god. Oz, a figure entirely made of fantasy, appeared differently to each beholder; but Jimmy, no matter who saw him, was one thing: a lost boy.

At Carson's urging, Jimmy told us stories about his adventures, our coterie ranged around him, a Central Committee on gay style, as Carson wandered in and out with *table d'hôte*. It sounds stiff, but I remember being spellbound. Jimmy had actually grown up in an orphanage, run away, held a thousand jobs, and lost them for reasons he never understood. (I could have told him: a boy this beautiful has to keep moving—at liberty, he could blow a community apart.) I saw, as he spoke, that I had misconceived what a hustler is. He doesn't lack opinions—he lacks psychology. Jimmy knew nothing of human interaction. He couldn't read a face or gauge vocal tone, couldn't extrapolate vibe, could scarcely tell you what someone looked like.

And what ghastly tales he shared. From anyone else, these stories would have been ace dish. After hearing them from Jimmy, I wanted to run into a church and shiver. Once he told us about a bordello he worked in Dallas, where the boys were never allowed to leave. The place was run by a huge fat slob and discipline enforced by a nameless hunk covered with tattoos.

"He had no name?" Dennis Savage asked. "None at all? What did you call him?"

"I never said anything to him."

"No, how did you refer to him when he wasn't around?"

"We called him The Man."

"Tell them what you called the fat guy," Carson put in. "Sheila."

We laughed; Jimmy didn't. He was like a TV news reporter reading text, each story a meaningless announcement. He told us that when one of the bordello boys tried to escape, as deterrent punishment The Man would strip the culprit, paddle his butt, then roughfuck him.

We were scandalized; and somewhat aroused. "*Roughfuck* him?" cried one of us. "Fan me with a tulip, mother!" cried another. "What on earth," I asked, "is roughfucking?"

Jimmy looked at Carson, got a nod, and said, "That's when the top man lays you face down on your junk, and after he starts to punk you he turns you on your side and locks his arms around you so you can't pull away. Then he finishes you off by pumping as deep and hard as he can. It hurts a lot after your ass has been paddled."

Of course we wanted more details. We have read Mann, Joyce, Proust. We are the cream of the cultural capital and we want the *eyes* of the story. "Was he ruthless?" we asked. "The Man? Did he get off on hurting you? Would he comfort you afterward?"

Jimmy thought. "No. He just . . . he came in and did it and then he went away somewhere."

"Your junk," we were murmuring in a daze. "What's the other side called?" and when Jimmy answered, "Your candy," we weren't sure what move to make. Then he added, "The Man called it your honeycomb—because it's so sweet to rim, I guess," and we became quite riotous.

Walking home, Dennis Savage and I marveled at this noble primitive brought among us.

"I wonder," said Dennis Savage, "if I should try rough-fucking Little Kiwi."

"Oh, for heaven's sake!"

"On the other hand, I wouldn't know where to buy a paddle."

"Carson," I said once when we were alone, "can this story be true?"

Carson beamed. "He's the real thing, my boy. Just keep encouraging him the way you do, you and the old gang. I've got to get him into shape for the gay life, don't I?"

"Do you?"

"These are just the tryouts. When he's ready, I'll take him out for his debut." I must have had an odd look on my face, for he patted my shoulder and said, "No, don't worry, my old. He picks things up very easily. And he looks *marvelous* in a sweater."

Carson had us over for dinners and Jimmy was the conversation piece, fascinating as such. We had had our fill of collegiate dazzle, show biz dazzle, and porn star dazzle; proletarian dazzle was a novelty. It was like meeting Wild Bill

Hickok after a decade of Guy Madison. Paradoxically, Jimmy did look marvelous in a sweater. And he was picking things up, as Carson said. He had the ability to *listen* that makes genuine charm. He was learning the nouns and terms. He never read, but he took to fine music and was wild for film. By the time the opera season was in swing, barely three months after he had moved in with Carson, Jimmy had seen more Ingmar Bergman than I had logged in ten years. It was at the opera that I met them, in fact, the two superb in pinstriped vested suits with identical grins heading toward me on the Grand Tier promenade.

"Isn't he something?" Carson asked me of Jimmy. "He outclasses half the people I know." And Jimmy looked around us to see if it was true.

It was. Gays were spraying the Met with bitter *mots* and anguished looks, their input and output alike a distilled putdown, while Jimmy could shake your hand, hold your eye, and ask about the things he remembered you liked. Others went through motions; Jimmy, because he had to learn them and was warned that they mattered, legitimized them.

"Everyone's looking at you," I told them. "You couldn't attract more attention in this place if you were Leonard Bernstein and Franco Zeffirelli. I can feel the eyes on my back."

"Leonard Bernstein conducts my record of Beethoven's Fifth," said Jimmy, in a tone you might use for "Leonard Bernstein eats asparagus tips" or "Leonard Bernstein roughfucks Sylvia Sass when he's in Budapest."

No opinion, still. But he was smiling now, often. There cannot have been a nicer hustler in New York; Carson's friends would call up when Carson couldn't possibly have been in just to hear Jimmy's voice. I wondered if anyone of the gang fantasized slipping into Carson's shoes, or perhaps assuming Jimmy's contract when Carson finished with him. Of course, without Carson's amazing apartment and amazing bank account and amazing social calendar, a Jimmy might seem questionable. And was there not, in some minds, a sense of failure attached to the taking of a lover on salary—

71

though we know that half the romances in the Great World are predicated on the doing of a deal?

Everyone hungers, but who *loves?* I wondered, when Carson took me to lunch for my birthday and spent most of it picking the absent Jimmy to pieces. I was thinking of the subculture's great love stories. Did a single one of them involve a hustler? You can be destroyed, as Mac was; or amused, as Carson is. But loved?

"He asks too many questions," Carson was saying. "Why doesn't he quit while he's ahead?"

"Stop complaining, Carson. You've got the hottest partner in the seventeenth precinct."

"Oh, I admit his sense of devotion is touching. And he does have the most spectacular nipples on the east coast, big as half-dollars. Yes. True. Yes." He sighed. "I just wish he'd stop . . . what do I wish?"

"I wish you appreciated what a neat couple you make."

"I wish you knew what it's like working the Circuit with a god in tow. Everyone comes running up to ask *Who is that one?* in that breathless way." He imitated: "*Who, Carson, tell? It's sizeable, isn't it? What's his service? What's his code name? Does it talk?* How would you like to live with that?"

"His code name is The Man."

"You know what he calls the stereo? The 'record machine'!" He made a face. "I wonder if I suffer from sex nausea. Like Shakespeare in the late romances."

"Your trouble is, you can't accept good fortune."

"*It's sizeable, isn't it?*" He snorted.

It lasted through April, and ended sweetly, calmly, and sadly. This was Jimmy's doing, those his qualities—Carson always liked to go out fighting. He told it far and wide how he threw Jimmy out, and no one believed him. The likes of Carson seldom make it into a room with a Jimmy, let alone dismiss him. But I know it was Carson who pulled the cord, because Jimmy came over to my place when he left on his way to the rest of his life. Everything was wool and cotton; the

72

boy had been done over so completely you might have glimpsed him in *GQ*. Yet he retained his honest incomprehension of the patterns by which we enact ourselves—so well that if he were to appear on a soap opera his artlessness would shatter the great American television screen.

"I have to talk," he said as he set down his suitcases. "And I don't know what to say."

"We need a drink."

"Scotch, neat. A twist if you have one."

You churl, I told myself in the kitchen, because I was thinking I knew him when he couldn't have named a brand of beer. Not surprisingly, he had had no trouble securing a place to move to; he was already set, in fact. I couldn't identify the name he gave me, but I could visualize the scene: more money than Carson, less to do, and atrocious friends. Love seats, plane trips, and cast parties. East Seventies stuff. Was this the step up or down?

We talked. "There's only one thing I can do," he told me. "I tried to be so hot in bed that he would never let me go. And I know I'm good. I know I am. I spoke to him, you know, giving the choices. There's pimp style, little-boy style, party style . . ."

And roughfuck, I thought, trying and failing to see Carson getting paddled. Junk side down, I thought. Flip over on your candy, I thought. Should I offer him my money and my life?

". . . if someone would pick me out of the crowd like that and . . . well, keep me. I used to wonder about it. You know? Imagine it? How he would look and the things he'd say to me." He grinned, sadly. "He wasn't anything like Carson."

I told him that we all fantasize.

"I admire him," he said.

I told him that Carson was beyond admiration, or too far before it.

"He isn't easy to get along with. But I'm going to miss him. I'll miss all of you. This was a wonderful year. It was the first thing I've ever belonged to."

I didn't tell him that the only thing he had ever truly belonged to, because gay is the most class-conscious of cultures, was Sheila's bordello. Because opinions are what define us. Because, despite our best intentions, Jimmy was all candy and all junk. Hell, most of the people I know divide you in half if you didn't go to Yale, Chicago, Penn, or Swarthmore. *I tried to make myself so hot in bed.* Who doesn't? I told him, "You're a gay Galatea."

He waited for the explanation, as he always did, antennae quivering. "Pygmalion sculpted Galatea, *created* her. Then he fell in love with her."

Jimmy nodded. "Only this time he didn't."

"Next time," I said. "In fact, I was going to suggest—"

Suddenly he blurted out, "Why do I like him? Why? He was so cruel . . . last night he said . . . he said . . ."

"Because we get crushes on the men who teach us to be wonderful."

And in crashed Dennis Savage and Little Kiwi, at least without Little Kiwi's endlessly horrendous dog Bauhaus. The commotion eased the atmosphere, and Jimmy took his leave, clapping us all on the shoulder and swearing to stay in touch. Little Kiwi, who had had limited exposure to this son of sex—father, should I say?—stared at Jimmy and, at the last minute, impetuously rushed forward to throw his arms around him. Jimmy rubbed his back and kept saying "Okay, okay, okay." Little Kiwi backed away as red as some people's underwear, Dennis Savage and Jimmy shared a grave look, and off went the hustler with his suitcases.

That should be the end, Jimmy vanishing into the cashmere despair of the service routes. "He came in, he did it, then he went away somewhere." But, some years later, as I walked up the aisle after *Evita*, a strong hand gripped my arm and I turned and there he was, the pair of us too stunned to speak. He was with a grisly moneygay group, one very tall haughty queen in a fur shako especially regrettable.

"Jimmy," he sizzled, "if you would *detach* yourthelf. We have to get to Roddy and Roberto'th thoiree."

Gosh, I thought, somebody still lisps. Jimmy held on to me, whispering as if he were passing contraband.

"Do you see Carson?"

"Yes, of course. He—"

"Would you please tell him something for me? Something important?"

"Surely, but why don't you—"

"Get out of it, you Tribeca queen!" screamed the haughty shako. "Somebody puth him *away!*"

I reached up and dislodged his hat, and he would have charged and queened me to death but for the crowds pouring past us.

"Look," I said to Jimmy, "why don't you call him yourself? Or you could even drop in on him. Messengers aren't all that effective outside of Sophocles."

He shook his head. "You don't understand."

"Leave these dreadful people," I told him. "Come home with me, and we'll call Carson, or even—"

"Jimmy, please." It was another of the Roddy-Roberto set. "Hugh is having a fit. You'll blow the whole deal if you don't come now."

Jimmy clasped my hand, said, "I remember all of you," and left. And I stood there thinking, Why *Tribeca?* This sweater is from Bloomingdale's.

Naturally, Dennis Savage scoffed when I told him. "That old dish!" he cried. "Half the guys in town don't even know who Jimmy is! And look at you waving an *Evita* playbill at me, you *follower!*"

"Oh, Christ."

"How many times must I tell you? Gays *create* sell-outs; they don't attend them."

"I come to you with the last paragraph of a romantic tragedy and you lecture me on hip!"

"All right," he said. "You met a devastato at the theatre

and he asked you to take a message to friend Carson. Now for dessert: *What* did he want you to tell him?"

"Just for that, I'm not saying."

"I'll guess: 'Carson, please take me back for you are the love of my life.' Right?"

I said nothing. He remembers all of us.

"Or, rather," he went on, "that's what you *hope* the message is, don't you? The name is love. And that is so bizarre, and so inane, and so likable, that it could almost be true. I've always said gay needs more romanticism. You may hawk antique dish and attend old shows, but emotionally you're in the vanguard." He went over to the window and gazed down on Fifty-third Street, upon the parade of the bribed and deluded. "The name is love," he repeated. "The name of a thing is strategic. And there are three names in gay: your own, the name of your one true best friend, and the name of your imaginary lover, whom you never meet."

I joined him at the window. "I can cite one person who met him."

Dennis Savage smiled, utterly misconstruing the allusion. *Three* infatuations, I say. "Who but you," he asked, "would get sentimental over the story of a hustler who developed an opinion? I believe you wear those dark glasses so we can't see you weeping at the pathos of a loveless world."

"*Never!*"

"Look! Down there. Look at them all, the strangers! As if callous, impenetrable beauty were more attractive than feeling intimacy. As if no one dared face himself. I tell you, all gays are liars."

"I haven't wept since I was a child!"

"And that," he said, "is the most stupid lie of all."

The Case of
the Dangerous Man

I hate to give Dennis Savage credit for anything—he'd only get pompous—but his concept of the Imaginary Lover is all-basic to gay culture. It is everyone's direst secret. Few men will as much as breathe his imaginary name to their best friend, much less provide a physical description or character sketch. "This," as Mac McNally once said, "I must not share."

Yet one notes references to the Imaginary Lover everywhere. You are conversing to the dim accompaniment of some dreary television show, a nameless hunk appears, and your comrade discreetly stiffens: this is a clue. You are strolling along the street, something elegant strides by, and your companion murmurs, "I want to bear his child": this is annotation. The unique charm of the Imaginary Lover is that he can never lose his appeal as real humans do, invariably, eventually, for he is a fantasy—plausible but a dream. You may spot someone who looks like him, or cracks his jokes, or lives where he ought to live. You even seem to know what it's like to climb his stairs, and press his buzzer. But to run across the man who accommodates your precise measurements of the romantic utopia is unlikely.

This is just as well, I think, for keeping the fantasy fantastical allows everyone to play. In a culture run by the fascism of looks, the Imaginary Lover is a democratic exercise. A beauty knows he might well land something comparable to supreme, even be one. A nice-looking fellow has a shot at it. A homely-but-hot man is ever loveable. And certain *objets trouvés* may win out through force of personality; unthinkable but true, my favorite combination. Below a certain level of appearance, however, a gay man is in big trouble; yet everyone can dream. And, though no one likes to hear about this, I know that the ugliest man in town visualizes himself being fondled, or toughed up, or tucked in by some divo just as easily as the handsomest man can. But why does no one like to hear about this?

Carlo shook his finger at me when I spoke of the matter late one night. And when I went on undeterred, he held his hand over my mouth and said, "I want you to please stop. I don't want to know about morals, or politics, or death, or feelings, or any of the other things that ruin everybody's fun."

"What morals?" I asked.

"Trolls," he said. "Talking about trolls is talking morals. Or politics."

We were confessing our episodes to each other—My First Time in Bed, My Worst Time in Bed, My Sleaziest Pickup (Carlo had about twenty-five possibilities to choose from; I had none), My Most Daring Pickup (mine was my neighbor Alex: after watching him for a year, I held up a sign in my window asking to come over and watch the Oscars). Suddenly it struck me that all over New York gays were exchanging these stories, and the stories were all the same but the storytellers all different. I wondered how it felt to hear smoking-car braggadocio from a troll, and I verbalized it, and Carlo got upset. But why?

"You always want to make a case out of everything," he said.

This is highest offense to Carlo, the paragon of the carefree gay. There are no cases in Carlo's life. Everything just happens; nothing is questioned, challenged, repudiated. Naturally, he is one of those typeless beauties whom everyone craves, dark but smooth, bright but uneducated, solid but slim: nice and hot. Naturally—you've got to be super cute to enjoy a heedless life. Carlo has more best friends than anyone else I know, all former lovers, for if his erotic appeal is con-

78

siderable, his gift as sympathetic company is overwhelming. Some men don't truly love him until after their affair has ended.

He is perhaps the most "episodic" of my friends in that he would fall hopelessly in crush every year in late fall and fall out again by the following spring. He favored size, age, and the Latin school of charm, and his lovers were so good-natured that they never held it against Carlo when he abandoned them. Except he never did abandon anyone: he simply collected another best friend. And I note that none of them was spectacular, in the Imaginary Lover manner. They were teddy bears, a little coarse but terribly nice, probably fun in bed and even more fun the next morning. They were all alike, yet they had nothing in common; like Carlo, they had not defined themselves in any certain way. After I had known all of them for years, the thing that sprang to mind when they did was not something any one of them had said or done but how large they all felt when I was jammed onto a couch next to them.

And this is possibly because they did, after all, have one thing in common, something Carlo shared with them: they had jobs but no career. They were gym trainers, or hotel orderlies, or movers. Now and again they hustled. They were the kind of people who never receive junk mail or utter beliefs or yearn for something that happens later than next week. They could be amazingly loyal, even valiant. They just didn't subscribe to anything.

Does it matter? I suppose that depends on what set you run with. But I was raised by a couple who urged me to make something notable of myself, and they didn't mean a banker or a doctor. The world is full of these; artists are ever few. So they sat rapt before my puppet shows (though they were always Punch–and–Judy *guignol* in which all my brothers were murdered), and gave me piano lessons, and took me to Broadway. And when it was all over I was a little crazy and very smart, and I was bound to regard cool Carlo and his unsophisticated lovers with befuddlement. They lacked a theme. Or I would come back from the Eagle having approached someone because of his charm and deserted him because he was professionally unmotivated, and Dennis Savage would chide me, one of his most enthusiastic activities. "Stop making judgments," he once said, "and consult Chatty Cock."

Well, you know, we have these little talks, and, much as I would enjoy kicking his bum in, he is the dearest thing I own. So I say, "Who is Chatty Cock?"

"Chatty Cock," he replies, "is the spirit of the Circuit. He has perfect instincts. He knows what to wear, whom to go with, whether to prevaricate or denude himself—"

"I'll bet a piaster on that."

"—because he doesn't agonize over bourgeois ethics. He doesn't weigh the advantages, as you do. He doesn't try to comprehend the Circuit. Life is short. Consult Chatty Cock and let a thing happen. You need spontaneity."

"You need a muzzle."

"When things get tough, you might assume a restorative posture of comic resistance, reducing the Circuit to a vanity." Dennis Savage doesn't merely theorize; he dictates a proposal to Yale University Press. This is what comes of letting your children attend small, elite men's colleges with pungent English departments, like Hamilton, instead of Sensible Preppy Places like Duke. "When comedy is called for, you might turn to Satyricock." I swear I heard him pronounce the *y*. "Satyricock doesn't get much, I admit, but he's popular and famous."

"I visualize President Taft."

"He's not dear to look at, but he has balance. He'll never figure in disreputable dish, as someone I know so often does."

"What if I don't believe in comic resistance? What if I take everything seriously, including the question of a person's vocation? What if I want my associates to *stand* for something? What about ideas?"

"Then you're in the grip of Murder Cock, and no good can come of it."

"Murder Cock? *He* sounds like the boy to follow."

Dennis Savage shakes his head. "See, with Chatty Cock, everything is casual narcissism: do I want to or don't I? With Satyricock, everything is burlesque. Note the choices?"

"And with Murder Cock?"

"With Murder Cock, everything is resistance and counterattack, death and debris. Follow him and no one will like you anymore."

I must admit, he remarks something there—you can have love, war, or nothing. But the trouble with Circuit Theory is the Circuit doesn't observe it. The Circuit is inconsistent, volatile, pandemic.

"Why don't you be like Carlo?" Dennis Savage goes on. "Carlo is Chatty Cock personified."

"Men are what they do," I grumble.

"Not Carlo."

"My point exactly. Carlo doesn't do anything."

"Carlo is a lover," he replies. "That's his calling."

Surely it was; some calling. And what happens when the ace handler of teddy bears runs into a grizzly—better, when the eternal amateur hooks up with a man who does something? This episode is about the marriage of Chatty Cock and Murder Cock.

Carlo would launch his affairs by taking his latest beau around for coffee and commentary, and this year the event fell on My Usual Evening With Dennis Savage.

At my knock, Little Kiwi opened the door a crack, studied me through a magnifying glass, and said, "I detect a literary man."

"I detect a little crumbun," I replied, "who'd better—"

"Little Kiwi!" Dennis Savage cried from behind the door. "I told you to—"

"Inspector Wilberforce," Little Kiwi corrected, as I passed inside. "The Supreme Detective."

"They're not here yet," Dennis Savage told me. "But soon. Autumn doesn't really get going till Carlo pairs off in his annual rite."

"Plus the intrepid canine wonder," Little Kiwi went on, "who has a mystic alias never yet revealed." This, of course, would be Bauhaus, Little Kiwi's phenomenally D-list dog, just then cheezing up under the sofa.

"Oh no," said Little Kiwi. "He ate Oysterettes again."

"Well, who *gave* him Oysterettes?" When he gets tired of palling around with me, Dennis Savage can get a job as a young George Burns in some vaudeville act.

"He eats the box, too," said Little Kiwi, examining my belt buckle through his glass.

"If someone I know doesn't leave off detecting the guests," said Dennis Savage, "he's going to get the spanking of his life tonight."

"Oh, you always say that," said Little Kiwi. "And then nothing happens."

Something did happen: Carlo's new lover, Daniel Johnson, came in. I think the word for him would be "stalwart." He looked like the hero of a western, and moved like one, and sounded like one. Even Carlo seemed awed, and the rest of us were notably subdued, for us. Inspector Wilberforce quite neglected to introduce the canine wonder.

Daniel Johnson was not shy, and he appeared to be observing us keenly. No doubt Carlo had told him something of us, and now he was matching the tales to the subjects. What had he heard? Did Carlo mention the time Little Kiwi blundered through an arcane door, found himself locked in a strange hallway, and disrupted Bloomingdale's housewares department trying to get back into the store? Or the time Dennis Savage and I followed Kern Loften around at a party for hours waiting for him to sit down because we wanted to put an egg under him just before he landed? Mild tales, I know. But they're ours, all the same. Our secrets. Daniel had us at several disadvantages: one, he knew our dish while we didn't know his; two, as the honored guest he commanded our courtesies; and three, he was to die. And he knew it; but he seemed not to care, which is a new one in my catalogue of the Gay Mentalities. I've checked off archetypes who luxuriated in their distinction and archetypes who suffered it, but never one who behaved as though there were some eight or nine things that mattered more. And, to judge by the tone of his conversation, morals, politics, death, and feelings were clearly on the list.

Carlo was in bliss, as always at this time of his year, so he was missing a lot. But I noticed that Daniel responded to my mention of *Vile Bodies* not with some bawdy slogan but with a reference to Waugh, and that he nodded in affirmation when I suggested that if Cyrus Vance had been one of the hostages in Iran, the whole crowd would have been freed the first night, and, for that matter, that no one tried to call him Dan or Danny. This was a very self-possessed man.

"Is it permitted to ask how you two met?" Dennis Savage asked.

Carlo grinned.

"I picked him up on the street," said Daniel. "It's not something I normally do. But I saw him and I wanted him, and I figured maybe he ought to know about it."

"In those words?"

"Just about."

"I have never been so completely picked up in my life," said Carlo. "And I've been picked up by experts."

"Where did this happen," said Little Kiwi, recovered from his shyness and strutting around with his hands behind his back like someone in a tweedy salon thriller of the 1920s, "may I ask?"

"This happened at the corner of Bank Street and Seventh Avenue," Daniel replied, suppressing a smile.

"A likely story!" cried Little Kiwi, whirling around and pointing. "I suppose," he tried to snarl, "there were a hundred witnesses?"

"A nun smiled at us," said Carlo.

"Inspector," I put in, "why don't you show Carlo and Daniel your new sweater?"

"Okay!" Little Kiwi loves a new idea. Racing off, he

paused drastically at the bedroom door. "Don't anybody leave this room."

"Go! Sweater! Put on!"

He vanished.

"*This* takes him shopping," said Dennis Savage, meaning me, "and lets him buy a large."

"He insisted."

Carlo was fastened on Daniel, but Daniel was listening to us, and each time his eyes blinked I felt as if a camera had gone off in his head, freezing us in our sport. This was something new in Carlo's love life for certain; his other beaux never saw anything but Carlo.

"Look!" cried Little Kiwi, in his new sweater.

"It goes back tomorrow," said Dennis Savage.

"No!"

"It's too big for you!"

"It makes me look tough!"

It made him look, actually, like a lollipop wearing a teepee. Sensing sympathy for lost causes in Daniel, Little Kiwi turned to him and said, "What do you think?"

Daniel regarded him for a moment, took him by the waist, and said, "I think you're a very sexy boy."

"No, I didn't," said Little Kiwi, breaking loose. Erotic directness still panics him and even jumbles his syntax. He has a way to go yet. But he is picking up defenses here and there: grabbing his detecting glass, he held it up to Daniel's nose and faced him down till he laughed.

"A likely story," Little Kiwi repeated triumphantly.

"How does it feel having your own detective on the premises?" Carlo asked Dennis Savage.

"Not to mention the writer downstairs?" Dennis Savage replied.

"Or the schoolteacher up," I added. "Though he mentions it seldom."

"And me," said Little Kiwi, "Inspector Wilberforce. Plus the canine wonder with a mystic alias never yet revealed."

"The canine wonder?" said Daniel.

"He's hiding under the couch because he ate too many Oysterettes. Daniel, what do you do?"

Daniel smiled, friendly but firm. "That's a secret."

"It is?"

"Yes."

"From Carlo, too?"

Carlo looked baffled. Of course he hadn't yet thought to ask what Daniel did for toil. A job is an obstacle, something that precludes pleasure, like a dentist appointment or going home at Thanksgiving. You wouldn't ask about it. But who would bother to keep it a secret?

"Why can't you tell me?" Carlo asked Daniel.

"Because I can't."

Carlo said, "All right," but he looked as if he wasn't sure it was.

"What do you think of Daniel now?" was the question of the month, as more and more of him showed. I thought he was generous, because he took us all out to dinner; and appreciative, as long as no one attacked the United States or the flag; and hard-headed, when he ran into anything that unreasonably barred his path. Little Kiwi adored him; Dennis Savage regarded him wryly. "He's too wonderful," he said. "There's got to be a flaw, some terrible hidden thing. No one's that . . ."

"Yes?"

He shrugged.

"No, go on," I urged. "Finish the thought and reveal one of your own bitter doubts. Criticism of wonderful men usually does."

"That strong, I was going to say. Is that so revealing, you human bedpan? And while we're at it, what did you mean when you said I seldom mention teaching?"

"Have you been stewing about that all this time? In fact, you never mention teaching at all."

"No one wants to hear about it."

"Most people talk about their work."

"Fascinating. Shall we call Little Kiwi in to tell us about life in the mail room at BBDO?"

In the succeeding silence, I was thinking that I for one talk ceaselessly about writing, my own and others'; it had never occurred to me that anyone worth talking to wouldn't find it enticing. Writing is the world entire: morals, politics, death, and feelings.

Dennis Savage looked away. Was he thinking that a man of education ought to do better in a lover than a mail room assistant? I was. But then I have seen him, over the years, crying, sick, nude, drunk, and raging in despair, so he has long since given up worrying about what I think. I suppose I resent that; but someone who worries about how you feel can be forgiven a lot.

"You know," I said, as carelessly as I dared, "I wouldn't mind hearing about teaching every now and then."

He took a while to respond. "Everyone has flaws. So no one is perfectly suited to anyone else."

"Is that Chatty Cock's wisdom or yours?"

"My wisdom for today is: Not being able to tell your lover what you do in the daytime is *molto* strange."

Carlo thought so, too, which was even stranger. "What could be so terrible," he worried, "that he can't let me in on it?" As so often, Carlo was living on unemployment insurance and had plenty of time for visiting. Most days, by my six o'clock break, if Carlo wasn't at my place I could go upstairs and find him at Dennis Savage's playing Guess Daniel Johnson's Profession.

"Maybe he's rich," said Little Kiwi, taking out his wallet and admiring, as he continually did that month, his first bank plastic, with a credit limit of something like eight dollars. "He's rich, see, but he wants you to like him for himself. That's what his secret is."

"He can't be rich," said Carlo. "He lives in Brooklyn."

"Maybe he owns a house there."

"Rich people don't own houses in Brooklyn," said Dennis Savage. "Rich people own Brooklyn."

"Have you ever seen where he lives?" Little Kiwi asked Carlo.

"No . . ."

Little Kiwi beamed. "Inspector Wilberforce rides again."

"Maybe he's a hit man," I suggested.

"Never," said Little Kiwi. "He's too nice."

"Hit men can be nice."

"Not," said Carlo, pensively, "to the people they hit."

Dennis Savage looked at him.

I looked at him.

Little Kiwi saw something going on and he looked, too.

"Oh, it's nothing like that," said Carlo. He said it too fervently, so we all leaned in for more.

"It's . . . no. Believe me. I was just thinking aloud. I didn't mean anything."

"You never truly know a man till you know what he does in bed," said Dennis Savage. "You know, Carlo. So tell us and we'll decide."

"It's not what you think," Carlo insisted.

"What do we think?"

"This is too deep. I don't want to talk about it."

"What do we think?" said Little Kiwi, baffled. He turned to Carlo. "Does he hit you? In *bed?*"

"You know him, Carlo," I said. "For good or ill, you know him. And it's for good, right? What difference does it make what he does for a living?"

"I should have known you'd take the fascist's side," said Dennis Savage.

"I'm taking Chatty Cock's side, in fact."

"Does Daniel hit Carlo?" Little Kiwi repeated. "Because he was naughty, or what?"

Carlo, who spent his twenties in San Francisco exploring some of the culture's heaviest scenes, said, "Little Kiwi, someday I will sit you down and tell you about dangerous men."

"Daniel is dangerous?" Little Kiwi asked. "He gave me a piggyback ride on Hudson Street!"

"Inspector," I said, "I think this particular topic is over your head."

"The Case of the Dangerous Man," Little Kiwi murmured, amazed.

"I just want to know what he does," said Carlo. "I just want to know."

"'I must see the Things,'" I quoted. "'I must see the Men.'"

"Who said that?" asked Dennis Savage.

"The crazy part," Carlo went on, "is I left San Francisco to get away from it. Do you know what I like? After all this? Do you know? I like playful men. Playful and affectionate. The trouble with S and M is that it . . . it does something. It's more than sex. It's like an act you would be hired to do in an after-hours club."

"It makes a case out of love," I observed.

Carlo nodded.

"But Daniel *is* playful," said Little Kiwi.

"You know what?" said Carlo. "Daniel is a lot of things."

I feel like something of an inspector myself, as I unravel my tales, making cases of everyone I know. As I write, my neighbor across the way is standing in her window with a male friend, pointing at me. "See?" she says, I guess. "There he is again, watching." Yes, I watch; but not her.

Or yes, sometimes I do, fleetingly. She is very attractive, dresses for power, and constantly changes her clothes: for the office, for dinner, for rendezvous. The man is older than she. When he comes in at night, he wears a lawyer's suit, but peels down to Oz-green jockey shorts. Once I saw him push her onto the bed, and without anything else to go on—the lights immediately went out—I could not tell whether he was being playful or dangerous.

"We are not alone," my friend Eric told me once, as we walked up Third Avenue after dinner. "*Everyone* is mad." Only the truly bizarre is normal in New York, where spiffy men in Lord & Taylor trench coats and bearing haughty at-

88

taché cases walk past you carrying on irate conversations with invisible associates. Then I encounter Little Kiwi at the treats section in Sloan's, looking as wan as Tiny Tim because his favorite flavor of Pop-Tarts—brown sugar–cinnamon—is out of stock. And I think, thank heaven, *someone* is still sane.

We trudge home together past the little kids solemnly pushing their own strollers, and the people with the latest Bloomingdale's bag, and the dreary hustlers attempting industrial-strength come-hither smiles, and Little Kiwi asks me, "Does Daniel really hit Carlo?"

How do you explain S and M to someone who thinks belts grow on pants? "He doesn't hit him, exactly. He . . ."

What? "He romanticizes him. He takes him out of the world and engulfs him."

"With what?"

"Concentration."

The doorman hands me a messengered package as we turn into our lobby—page proofs of my latest book.

"What's this one about?" Little Kiwi asks.

"Same as the others. Morals, politics, death, and feelings."

"No wonder you're always grouchy."

Carlo met us at Dennis Savage's door, in the heat of debate. "Isn't it a lover's job," he asked, "to be honest and true?"

"Now what?" I asked Dennis Savage.

"Tell him, Carlo."

Carlo threw himself onto the couch as Little Kiwi and I sat with our brown paper grocery bags on our laps. We looked like steerage passengers awaiting our examination at Ellis Island.

"I found a gun in his room," said Carlo.

"You went to Brooklyn?"

"A gun in a leather holster."

"Instead of in what, a macramé potholder?"

"A gun in a holster in the top drawer of his bureau!"

"What must he have in his closet?"

"I didn't get a chance to check the closet. He went to the bathroom and I just had a—"

"*With gloves?*" cried Little Kiwi. "So you don't leave fingerprints? Carlo, can I come with you next time you snoop around in Brooklyn?"

"A man with a gun!" Carlo pleaded. "Don't you understand? Won't you please listen?"

Bauhaus, feebly barking, pattered in from the bedroom on the way to his water dish as we contemplated Carlo's predicament.

"Tell me what to do," said Carlo.

"Carlo," I explained, "you are one of the most experienced men in American gay. You helped break styles in in San Francisco, Los Angeles, and New York. Factions have formed around you. Bars have mooed in wonder upon your entrance. If James Joyce had known you, Molly Bloom would have been a man. How can anyone tell you what to do in romance?"

Carlo heaved a sigh of profound discontent. "If only I knew what that gun does."

"I'll find out!" cried Little Kiwi. "This is a job for Inspector Wilberforce! With his intrepid canine wonder, whose mystic name . . ."

The canine wonder slunk past us with the biggest dog yummy I've ever seen between his teeth.

"What are those?" I asked. "Elephant biscuits?"

"Little Kiwi," said Dennis Savage, "I don't want that dog eating in the bedroom."

Little Kiwi shrugged. "He likes to dine in utter silence. It's too noisy in here."

"I'm going to break it off with him," said Carlo suddenly. "I mean it."

"Carlo, if you love him—"

"Love is for twinkies."

"*What?*"

"I'm not like you." He looked at us, all of us, and this

90

time we leaned back and away. "We don't believe the same things."

Silence.

"Don't be sore at me," he went on. "I'm not saying I'm better than you. I just know about other deals. I don't make cases out of everything."

"Deals?" said Dennis Savage. "You think love is a deal?"

"You're making a case out of Daniel Johnson," I observed.

Carlo nodded. "Good for me. Because he's not doing what he's supposed to do. And I *will* drop him, watch."

More silence, penetrated by the sounds of distant teeth breaking up a biscuit.

"I have to go," said Carlo; and he went.

"It isn't the gun," said Dennis Savage, after a moment. "Or the mystery job. And Oscar Wilde knows it's not S and M."

"Then what?" I asked. "Is Daniel too dangerous for Carlo?"

Dennis Savage slowly shook his head. "There's a missing piece somewhere."

"Is it possible," I asked, "that, for the first time, our Chatty Cock has come face to face with Murder Cock?"

"It wouldn't be the first time. Carlo is smarter than he likes to think he is, and he learns by doing. What has he done for fifteen years? He has made love to men. Men is what he knows, all the kinds. Believe me, Murder Cock and Carlo are graduates of the same school. And so is Daniel Johnson."

"So what's the missing piece?"

"I think I know," said Little Kiwi.

Dennis Savage patted the sofa next to him and Little Kiwi dutifully arrived there.

"No," Dennis Savage told him. "You don't know. And if I have any contribution to make, you never will. Okay?"

"For the sake of heuristics, Inspector," I put in, "what do you think the missing piece is?"

"Love."

"How so?"

"I don't think Carlo has ever been in love. You know how I know?"

"How?" asked Dennis Savage, putting an arm around him.

"Because he isn't afraid of anything."

"That may well be," I said. "He has never thought about what it's like. Right? He just does it."

"What's 'it'?" asked Dennis Savage.

"Love . . . no, I mean, a lover—*No,* I mean, the Imaginary Lover. One's concept of what love is supposed to feel like. That's 'it.' And Carlo has no concept. He is his own Imaginary Lover. And you know what I think? I think Daniel wants to be Carlo's Imaginary Lover, and things are getting hot. Very, unbalanced, true-love hot. And Carlo is uncertain. For the first time in his life."

No one said anything for a bit. Then, "If I were Carlo," Little Kiwi observed, "I would be uncertain, too. I might even start being afraid."

After that, there was little for me to do but take my groceries home, sit down at my desk, open the notebook, and distress my neighbor.

Carlo did throw Daniel over, spang in the middle of winter, completely upsetting everybody's schedule. Our friend would be available when he should have been occupied, the droop when he ought to be the hedonist, and chaotically in doubt when he owed us the directness of a pilot. I had not realized before how much a guide Carlo had been, trading his lack of sophistication for our hunger for data on sensuality. We taught him how to bluff his way through brunch; he taught us how to play a bar. If the Circuit is ice, Carlo had slipped; now he was breaking through and would drown. "Tell me what to do," he had said—*Carlo* needed telling!

He certainly didn't need any tutorials in how to drop a lover. He believes catastrophic announcement works best, and drops mates the way gunfighters of the Old West dropped their challengers: he shoots them down in cold blood. As far as I can see, he doesn't give off warning signs of recalcitrance or hostility, or arrive late for dinner, eyes avid after some rebellious tryst, or become inexplicably unavailable. No. It is as if it has suddenly occurred to him that he doesn't want a lover anymore. And he will turn to his innamorato and say, "Would you mind if we didn't see each other for a while?" He's very nice about it, almost gentle, once he detonates his bomb. He just means to announce that he's had enough, thank you, enough.

But every so often we run across someone who doesn't suit our behavior patterns—indeed, one who plans to overwhelm them. For the French, it may be the German army. For writers, it may be your editor's replacement, who ushers you into a third-rate café, smiles engagingly, and says, "There's a problem." For gays, it may be the man who doesn't take no for an answer.

Carlo's no had never been challenged, because, frankly, the man is so good-looking that most other men accept his rejection as their due—the sole instance, I believe, in which gay is inferior to straight. The average heterosexual man, turned down for a dance, a date, or a fling, tends to think the woman had made a foolish mistake. Gays in a comparable position mope or frantically double the weights in their workout. Perhaps Carlo got his first no this time around because Daniel is even better-looking than Carlo; perhaps because Daniel really is dangerous; perhaps because it was high time. Anyway, Daniel did not take no for his answer.

"He's after me," said Carlo, walking into my apartment one afternoon, as you might say, "The grocery clerk overcharged me."

"After you?"

"He won't let me alone. Daniel. He says if I don't talk it out with him he's going to . . ." I was trying to look blasé, but I don't wear dark glasses in the apartment and my eyes gave me away. Carlo stopped; he has no more desire to become Dish of the Week than you or I, boys and girls.

I thought of all those sizeable sweethearts Carlo had acquired—Wayne Hibbard, the only man I've met who cries when his favorites don't win Oscars; or Scooter Smith, so kind-hearted he has had mercy sex with some of the most atrocious men in New York; or Big Steve Bosco, so ebullient that he hugs strangers on the street. Daniel was broader, cooler, and more judgmental than they, and I could easily see him refusing the role of the discard.

"He's tough, isn't he?" I asked, though it wasn't a question.

"Do you know what he did? The night of the Blue Party, we were going back to my place, and at the corner of my block this guy came up at us with a knife."

My face must have been too blank, for Carlo decided to backtrack. "The Blue Party, remember? When Frank Donner came in Arabian pajamas and Eddie Palladino grabbed his—"

"I wasn't there."

"How could you not be there?"

"Probably because my pen was flying and I didn't want to throw away an evening of A-list work just to go to another night of . . ." I trailed off. He doesn't approve and he never will, no matter how I explain it.

"I've been to so many parties," I tell him.

"I know, Bud. But each one—"

"Is not as interesting to me as what I can do at my desk." He shakes a finger at me.

"You and my neighbor should get together," I tell him. "She thinks I should get out more, too."

"Sometimes I don't think I can talk to you anymore."

"A guy with a knife," I prompt.

"Yeah." He nods. "Yeah. And he was whispering. Listen, it was like . . . like 'Some for me, now.' Like that: 'Some for me.'" Carlo paused, shifted position, brooded. I always take my desk chair and leave the big black armchair with the ottoman for the guests, giving me the chance to tower over

94

them in an academic manner, like a psychiatrist. I might lay in a supply of threatening little pads and take up saying, "Any dreams lately?"

"Well, so Daniel did this . . . maneuver, or something. I didn't see it, exactly. Something like karate. Turning and kicking. And the guy went down like . . . like he had never been there. Didn't even scream. And Daniel picked up the guy's knife and said, 'Let's go,' and he took my arm and he kind of . . . pulled me along. About seven doors down the street he threw the knife into a garbage can. And I was so hot for him, then. I was, okay. God, he's such a *man*. But I don't . . ."

This was key.

". . . I don't want him asking me for any more details."

"*What?*"

"Well, he does!"

"About what?"

"My family. And where I'm from. You know. Faggot questions. He won't tell me what he does but he wants to know what I was like in sports when I was a kid. That's really neat!"

"All right, all right."

"Yeah, I really want to talk about it, don't I?"

"All right!"

"Yeah." He went over to the piano and picked out the right hand of the *Moonlight Sonata*. "'Some for me,'" he repeated, shaking his head. "You know why everyone's in San Francisco? Because this town is a madhouse. It is a *madhouse!*"

"So I hear. Eric says—"

"Just listen, okay?"

I shut up.

"He kisses me . . ." Carlo regarded me, considering. Maybe he shouldn't tell me. But he goes on: "He holds me down when he kisses me. On top of me. Listen." He left the piano, gazing at his hands, trying to show me what Daniel's hands do. "He kisses like he's eating you up—or no, *drinking* me, gulping me down. Like . . . I'm a glass of punch and he's going to drink me and then go out for seconds somewhere." He turned his hands over. "No. No . . . Only me. He only drinks me. That's what makes it so . . . I can't even breathe. When I pull away to gasp for air he grabs my head and holds me there and goes on drinking me up. He won't let me breathe!"

No, I was wrong before. *This* was key.

"When I first met him, you know what I thought he was? Don't laugh."

I waited.

"A knight. You know, in shining armor? A *hero*."

"Isn't he, now?"

Carlo showed me his hands again, how they hold him down. "If he's a hero, why won't he tell me what he does?"

"Maybe he wants you to guess."

"'Some for me!' Do you believe that?"

"Meanwhile, if you don't see him again, what will he do?"

"Oh, he's just bugging me. He's making a case."

"Are you afraid?"

"Of what?"

"So you aren't." But your days of carefree love are over, I thought, and you will know fear in time—because Chatty Cock is no match for Murder Cock.

I knew a little fear myself when Daniel called me to ask if we could meet. I feared scanting the etiquette by talking to him—it was Carlo, after all, to whom I owed fealty.

"I think not," I said.

"In the open," he urged. "Wherever you want. What could happen?"

I agreed, finally, to connect with him downtown in Footlight Records, a treasure house of old collectibles and an ideal meeting haunt because the later my associate, the more time I have to parse my sections of devotion. Records are my vice. But Daniel was standing outside when I got there. I dragged him in, though he was obviously eager to talk, and—while I don't enjoy Collecting with someone breathing over my shoulder, whether of or against the sport—I tried to make a game of it.

"Look!" I said, holding up an album. "The June Bronhill *Bitter Sweet!*"

Daniel put a gloved hand on my shoulder and I turned around. He looked at me; only that, but that sufficed. So I took a deep breath and went outside with him to find some lunch. Just don't charm me, I silently warned him. I'm doing this for Carlo.

Well, you know these dangerous men can be very attractive across a table from someone they want something from. Daniel wanted me to give a dinner so he could get hold of Carlo again. "I just want to talk to him," he said.

"You'll have to tell him what you do."

"I intend to. I always meant to, right along. But he's delicate. He doesn't look it, but he is. The trouble with Carlo is, he . . . he lacks inexperience. He never learned the hard way, like most of us. He likes the same thing every time. The easy thing. And he could be so . . . so *wild.*" Daniel spills this out calmly as he sips coffee. Sure, let's all talk about our sex lives. "He's a very hot man. But he stabilizes. Now, I say the interesting thing about taking a lover is letting him expand your sensuality. *De*stabilize. Love isn't forever, anyway. Why not make an adventure of it?"

So that was the missing piece after all: Carlo didn't want to be on his back with someone who gets so much out of being on top. It's innocuous, even amusing, with a switch-hitting buddy. But with Murder Cock one may feel plundered.

"The odd thing," he went on, "is when I first picked him up, I took him for a man who would do anything. He looks like a sort of degenerate saint."

"You're too smart for him."

"There's no such thing."

"You're like a lot of people I know. You verbalize."

"Don't you?"

"Sure. And I worry Carlo, too. You see, he thinks it's bad luck to know about something. He thinks it's good luck to do it."

"I can't live that way."

"Morals, politics, death, and feelings."

He sipped coffee and looked at me, considering what occult antecedent might have inspired that declaration. "I'm a policeman," he said.

"I don't catch the metaphor."

"Literally. That's what I do."

I was startled silent for a good twenty seconds. Then all I could say was "Good grief."

"See?" he said. "That's why I keep it a secret. I'm the best friend of all the men I have no use for, and the natural enemy of all the ones I like. Don't get me wrong: I'm on the right side. I just don't care for my teammates."

"That's politics and morals."

"You can joke about it because you don't live it. You're not on a team. You work alone."

Except for my neighbor, I thought.

"But, I'll tell you, everyone who sees me in uniform thinks I'm a hundred things I'm not and refuses to imagine the things I am. Think about it. What if you had to go around as a . . ." He searched.

"A commissar?"

He eyed me sagely. "We understand each other, don't we?"

"Not entirely. Policeman are a universal gay fantasy. Half the culture dreams of being arrested and treated to the protocols of interrogation. You have it made."

"That's just it, right there," he said heavily. "I'm not a fantasy. I'm a man, like you, like Carlo, like your fathers and brothers. I don't want to have to arrest my lovers."

"You're a person."

"Exactly."

"That's feelings. Three down, one to go."

"Look, I'm proud of what I do, and I'm tired of trying to talk my fellow gays into being proud for me. Look . . ."

"Look."

"Are you going to help me or not?"

"If you hadn't told me this, I wouldn't have done. I have to respect what Carlo wants. But I believe he'll want to see you again, on one condition—you have to come in uniform."

"Why?"

"Trust me."

He thought it over. "What could I do in uniform that I can't do out of it?"

"For one thing, you could have arrested the man with the knife instead of just neutralizing him."

He folded his hands on the table and looked at me.

"Is that my neck between your fingers?" I asked.

"I just want to tell you one thing. I'm very fond of Carlo. He's a very, very beautiful man. A beautiful man. If this doesn't work, I may want to neutralize you."

"I wonder if a New York City police officer should speak to a citizen of New York in that manner."

"Policemen are like everyone else. We break our oaths to make an effect."

"Anyway, that's all four, isn't it?"

So, on a night that timed to Daniel's schedule of patrols and breaks, I gave a dinner, the only one I give: Tree Tavern frozen pizza, spruced up with extra cheese, ketchup, oil, and oregano, and martyred in a raging oven for dark crust. I think the recipe (my mother's) is older than I am. With the most banal possible green salad, a boisterous dessert, and a lot of liquor, it'll do; anyway the people I know like pizza.

If Carlo was uncommunicative before the meal and tac-iturn during it, he was dead silent when Daniel walked in. In fact, he was stunned. Indeed, Daniel was a policeman. In his blues and accoutrements he looked . . . well, yes, stunning—like a knight. A hero. Dennis Savage exhaled audibly and Little Kiwi whispered, "Oh, yikes!" Diplomatically, I rattled on and then ran down, and there was absolute quiet. The rest of us watched Carlo, who looked like the little boy who would pray, "Oh God, make me good, but not yet."

"Are those handcuffs real?" Little Kiwi finally asked Daniel.

"They sure are. Want to try them?"

"I'm not allowed to. I'm glad you're back, though. You're not dangerous, are you, Daniel?"

"Only to bad guys."

Bauhaus doesn't fit under my couch, so on his unfortunately frequent visits he sits in the bathroom and barks if anyone tries to get in, or if anyone doesn't. Now he barked.

"Do you want me to tell you the alias of Inspector Wilberforce's canine wonder," Little Kiwi asked, "never yet revealed?"

"I wish you would."

Little Kiwi gave a stage whisper into Daniel's ear that could be heard clear to Baker Street. "They call him Secret Mantis."

Daniel looked at Little Kiwi for a bit, then took him by the arms and said, "Inspector, if you weren't securely accommodated with Dennis Savage here, I'd really worry about what would happen to you."

Little Kiwi looked up at him. "Why?"

"Because there are men who would spot you and cart you home and treat you real tough."

"And hit me?"

Carlo laughed. It was the first noise he had made since Daniel had joined us. He laughed so long that he held himself, and dropped his dessert plate, and made a mess, until Daniel was standing over him, and pulled him up, and Carlo held Daniel back, but he stayed near him and felt his badge and read out the number on it. Then he said, "Okay. But this time you can be Carlo. You."

Daniel nodded. "Midnight again."

Carlo said, "Yes. Again."

Daniel shook hands with all of us one by one—with Little Kiwi he pretended to groan and hold his hand in pain—and left.

"Is that why he had a gun, after all?" asked Little Kiwi. "Just that?"

I nodded.

"And doesn't like the U.N.?"

I said, "Only Communazis and their dupes like the U.N.," a remark that has enlivened many a party. This was not a political group, however, and my words landed unchallenged.

"But how can he be Carlo?"

"How can you be Inspector Wilberforce?"

Carlo's eyes clouded as he thought of something.

"Look at him," I told them. "He's had his first taste of an Imaginary Lover."

"What?" said Carlo, but dimly.

"You've made a breakthrough," said Dennis Savage. "Apparently."

"No," Carlo replied. "I always knew about this."

"About what?" asked Little Kiwi.

"About," I answered, "what Carlo is. And what his lovers are. And why they ask faggot questions—though I've always thought sex itself is the highest form of inquiry."

Carlo looked at me, and shook his head.

"And," I went on, "he is getting to know about fantasy."

"I don't believe in fantasy," said Carlo.

"'I must see the Things, I must see the Men,'" I exulted.

"Who said that?" asked Little Kiwi.

"Edmund Burke."

"Who's Edmund Burke?"

"Well, who are you, for that matter?"

Secret Mantis, the canine wonder, thrust his head out of the bathroom, cagily watching.

"I'm Inspector Wilberforce, as is well known," Little Kiwi explained. "But we don't know who you are."

"Yes," said Dennis Savage, coming up behind Little Kiwi

and putting his arms around him. Carlo, still half-dazed by the revelation of the uncertain in the familiar—and is this not what the Imaginary Lover is?—slowly joined them, putting his arms around Dennis Savage. "Now tell us, my friend," Dennis Savage pursued. "Who are you?"

"Well," I said, "sometimes I think I'm Edmund Burke."

And Eric Said
He'd Come

Christopher, an opera director with a twin brother who is also an opera director, invites me to a cottage by the sea. His friend Helen has taken a place in the Grove for a week; they want scintillating company. I'll do my best.

I met Helen once, at the Met. Inside of twenty seconds she asked what my middle name is, where I got that tie, how I met Christopher, if I knew where the Wagnerian contralto Ottilie Metzger died, and if she could try on my dark glasses.

I never turn down an invitation to Fire Island. Christopher met me at the ferry, where I feigned the necessary suave. I had dressed precisely, as if for a sacred pageant set on the sand, which, in fact, is what the Island of Fire is. In gray corduroy shorts, striped T-shirt, Mickey Mouse watch, running shoes, and punk socks, I'm so *right* that if there were grapefruit sections in my hair, I'd start a fad. Think hot to be hot.

Helen greets me warmly, on the deck of a trim little thing of a house on the ocean, west of the Monster. There is another guest, one Larry.

"Welcome to the D-list," he tells me. "You realize we're the only people in the Grove under sixty-five!"

Christopher laughs. Helen glowers. I'm bemused.

"The *Grove!*" he cries. As if to say: "The Black Hole of Calcutta!"

"What's for lunch?" I ask, to cue in the next scene.

"Decay. Ugliness. Stupidity." Larry marches off to the

beach, I presume to head for the Pines. Dire on a dune, he adds, "If you can't get into hell, they send you here." Exit.

Silence.

"Good grief," I explain.

"I forgot to warn you about Larry," says Christopher.

"Whose friend *is* that?" I ask.

Helen and Christopher share accusing looks.

"Never mind," I tell them.

Helen can't let it rest. "The worst of it," she begins— then checks herself, looks away, goes out the front door and immediately surges in through the back—"The worst of it is: he's *such a* schmarotzer!"

"Helen," Christopher begins.

"But your friend must be thirsty from his trip. Quick, a tea, some cheese wedges, a boiled egg. Schmarotzer means 'parasite.' The Nazis used it against the Jews, as if they were cultural parasites battening on Goethe, Schiller, Brentano, without contributing anything of their own. *Battening!* I would mention Heine and Mendelssohn. I lived in Germany for two years. Munich."

"Why is Larry a schmarotzer?" I asked, feeling my way into a new word.

Helen became tragic. She looked off to a remote prospect—the colored frieze atop the facade of the Munich Staatsoper, I imagined.

"He comes and he takes, and he takes, and he takes," Helen observes.

"He brought fruit," Christopher puts in. "He made pasta primavera."

"With marinara sauce!"

Helen dramatically reveals a tub of cold rigatoni, stained red amid broccoli and cauliflower. "The last supper of a schmarotzer!" she screams.

"Egad," I say, to fill in a pause.

Now Helen is quiet, showing us what patience looks like. "Does he offer anything to the group? Tell me that, please!" She turns to me. "And he has the nerve—no, I can't! It's *too*

104

much!" She claps a hand to her mouth, but it flies right off again. "He had the nerve to ask for *Irish Coffee!*" She bustles to the fridge. "Now, there's five kinds of cheese . . ." Eventually, I note that planning a cheese tray is Helen's most constant activity. Christopher has taken to calling her the Cheese Gräfin, and I join him. She seems to like it, or any kind of attention. It's hard to give her as much as she wants, though, as she never stops attending herself—asking, remarking, planning, promising. At length, in a daze, she says, "I must do the dishes," though the sink is empty.

Ottilie Metzger died at Auschwitz.

After lunch I excused myself for a solo flight in the Island manner and headed for the Pines, my favorite place. Here I learned to admire or tell off, here comprehended the pride of the beauty and the passion of the troll, here conceived the classes of gay and learned the nuances that separate tough from stalwart. I was a kid here, and grew wise. There are a number of stories that are assigned to each gay man's collection whether or not he'll have them: "The Day I Told My Parents," for instance, or "What I Saw in the Bars." There are perhaps fifteen such titles, and I think it notable that while those with an urban, rural, business, or family setting can take place anywhere in America with acceptable resonance, every beach story must take place on Fire Island. For here we find gay stripped to its essentials. The beautiful are more fully exposed here, the trolls more cast out than anywhere else—thus their pride and passion. The beguiling but often irrelevant data of talent and intelligence that can seem enticing in the city are internal contradictions in a place without an opera house or a library. Only money and charm count. Professional advantages are worthless, for, in a bathing suit, all men have the same vocation. Yet there are distinctions of rank. Those who rent are the proletariat, those who own houses are the bourgeoisie, and houseboys form the aristocracy.

Of course you cannot tackle the place alone.

Here you learn to focus your view of the scene. You decide which options you will take—say, toward fashion or naturalism, favoring colleagues or competition, dealing in aggressiveness or self-protection. It is too extreme to say that one's first trips to the Island will govern the rest of one's life in gay; but if it isn't true, it should be. New Yorkers virtually come out in this place. Every other gay beach is a strip of sand, merely theatre. But the Pines is a culture, really life.

There are three rules: You must let a veteran squire you about on the first jaunts, you must take to it gradually, and you must find your gang and join it. You *cannot* tackle the place alone.

Helen's "Does he offer anything to the group?" resounds in my head; suddenly I run smack into Eric, ensconced with friends between Pines and Grove. Between: as if respecting fashion but resenting it. Fearful of the sun, Eric is swaddled like an Arab. All I can see are his eyes, nose, and mouth. He is thrilled that I materialize by chance, for anything that wants to occur by arrangement unnerves him. "And Eric said he'd come" is this famous, useless remark we make at parties, our voices trailing off as we survey a dismal gathering that needs an Eric.

Once, a wicked friend envisioned satirical Ph.D theses for all the famous gay writers. A lapidarian storyteller and essayist got "The Use of Style in Filling a Vacuum." A veteran of pre-Stonewall got "Beauty and Truth: The Positioning of Jeans in My Dust Jacket Photos." Unfair, I thought, but I laughed. Eric, by miles the best writer of the lot, got "The Swank and the Drab: Philosophy and Technique." Yet here he was, hiding from both the swank and the drab, hiding *between,* as if instituting a new sort of gay in which neither praise nor blame will be freely given. A quiet place, this, just around the corner from the turmoil of keeping up with Jones, with his Chelsea lats, Perry Ellis sleeves, and Greek tan.

I tell Eric of the schmarotzer and the Cheese Gräfin. He is mildly fascinated, but mainly he wants an ice-cream cone. I feel I should get back to my house. We decide to drop Eric's things off at his friends', head for downtown Grove for ice cream, and then . . . but he won't plan farther ahead. He may stay over in the Grove. He may return to the Pines, where he spent last night with a group of queens so ritualized that their place is known as "the house of good taste and bad manners." Then, again, he may simply vanish. He is always in flight, fearful of fame, and seldom seen.

On the way to ice cream we pass the baroque guest house called Belvedere, where a gorgeous blond houseboy stares balefully about him.

"A beauty in the Grove," we murmur. "How bitter he seems." Who wouldn't be, here? "What does he bring to the group?" I almost ask, thinking of Larry the schmarotzer. Larry had spoken of "Pines People" and "Grove People"; but only the losers divide the world into winners and losers. You cannot redeem yourself by joining the people who—you think—hate you.

Eric suffers a raptus of indecision when we hit the ice-cream stand—should he buy a sandwich in the grocery instead? He does, and there we meet the Gräfin, her basket filled with goodies. She's thrilled to meet Eric and insists he join us for drinks. "Blueberries," she cries, showing us. "I thought we'd have them with sweet cream." And "Cheeses!" she reveals. "Do you want biscuits or crackers with them?" Ensues a pause as Eric and I try to remember what the difference is. "I'll get both!" she vows.

I gather that Christopher also stole away; the Gräfin hopes to lure us back with tasties. Surprisingly, Eric wants to come. "It's the blueberries," he tells me. "Only food impells me now." He is worried, though, about meeting the schmarotzer. He doesn't want to confront the injured nagging of the disinherited gay, that terror born of taking one's reading at others' evaluations. It reminds me of a few unpublished writers I have met, who believe there is a conspiracy to keep them out of the top houses, the hot magazines.

Actually, no one thinks about them whatsoever.

"The schmarotzer is Pines bound," I tell Eric, "and now he is out of the saga." Eric smiles and looks away. He imagines that half the things I say are allusions to obscure lit that only I would be mad enough to read. He is intent on the blueberries, and refuses to speak of anything else. "How many will she let me have?" he wonders.

"She's so impressed with who you are that she'd give you the box."

References to his public radiance disenchant him; now he won't talk at all. But he's *thinking* of blueberries.

Christopher has returned, and we drink tequila with lemon while waiting for the Gräfin to accommodate us. Christopher works hard when he directs opera, but at socializing he turns himself way down, seldom talking and scarcely listening. We have been friends since college, some fourteen years now, and have long since accepted each other without qualification.

It is not a dangerous relationship, and I wonder if that is enviable or pitiable.

The Gräfin returns with her groceries and we cheer. Eric gets ready. But for once she does not produce a tray. She unpacks in the kitchen, as noisily as possible—do I actually hear her calling out the items as she unloads?—but joins us with nothing in hand.

Eric is worried.

The Gräfin asks if Eric will stay for dinner, asks again, urges—he is evasive throughout—and I suddenly realize that she is using the blueberries as incentive. Hopeless. Promising to come by tomorrow if he's still here, Eric beats his retreat. The Gräfin is startled. It is her habit, whenever someone is leaving, to call out hysterical attempts to detain him—dire requests, pathetic mandates, whimpers of pain, anything. It is a relatively minor maneuver in the practice of high kvetching. Eric will have none of it. He smiles, says something wonderful, and goes.

"Will he come to dinner?" Helen asks me.

"I think not."

"He offers," she sighs, "so much to the group."

"You promised him blueberries."

"For dessert!"

"You made it sound as if the blueberries were hors d'oeuvres."

"Blueberries for hors d'oeuvres!" Christopher cries in mock society-horror. "What would Lady Gumbo say?"

I went walking through the Grove to think. Every time I stay in the Pines I have epiphanies and adventures; in the Grove I just have a stay at the beach. It's like the Jersey shore gone gay. There's no group there to offer anything to.

But the Pines one must join. Is this why it has its outraged detractors? Were they not invited to belong? A friend of mine denigrated the Pines in favor of the Grove, till one day a friend of his bought a ritzy house in the Pines with a pool on the ocean: and very quickly and quietly the Pines-hater transferred his affections.

The Pines gives back what you offer, no more. You don't come out looking like Fatso McDump, knowing no one anyone wants to know, and expect to be crowned King of the Pines. Yes, there is more beauty gathered here than elsewhere, and the beach insistently reveals it; so is this elation or despair? Does the congregation of dream palazzi with their two-story love dens under skylights of stars reproach you for lack of swank?

I think the Pines is friendly. It is young, and was founded on elation; the Grove died years ago, in despair. It is never inclusive or convivial, as the Pines routinely is; of course a beauty is bitter in Belvedere—in the Grove, beauty is suspect. How often I would trade hellos with some dazzling stranger as we passed on the Pines boardwalk. Never once did this happen in the Grove.

Till now. I was wearing a Yale T-shirt, light blue with the letters in huge white blocks across my chest, and one of those swank workmen who are forever tooling along the planks in motor carts suddenly stopped and called out, "Is that Yale for real?"

"Surest thing you know," I answered.

"Harvard, '61," he said, smiling. He looked too young to be class of '61—maybe he meant he was born at Harvard in '61. "It's a small world."

"That it is." I smiled back, and off he went. Well, it's a loose confederation to make a coincidence of, but 'twill serve. I felt chipper when I got back, and, as Christopher was out, I took the Gräfin to tea in the Pines, proudly leading her through the Grove like L'Enfant touring friends about D.C. At Belvedere, she stopped and stared at the place, at the empty courtyard, the dizzy pile, the discreet nameplate. Eric and I had rushed past, panicked by the angry houseboy who knew he was in the wrong place. The Gräfin pauses to take this wonder in. "Belvedere," she reads out, looking through the gratings at the turrets and gingerbread. "Belvedere," she repeats, listening to the sound. "Not Jewish." She shrugs and moves on.

"Why do you make such a big deal about religion, Helen?" I ask. "Are you forming a club?"

"The club is already formed."

We were passing into the Judy Garland Memorial Park that lies between Grove and Pines. I'm never sure exactly where I'm going through all those paths and copses—Eric can do it in the dark—but we glided along without a step wasted, arriving at tea just after seven.

"Will you know many people?" The Gräfin asks as we snake around the cut of the harbor. She senses that Eric is a celeb, and it takes one to know one. "I may know some," I say doubtfully.

I know one, in the event: Michael, one of my publishers, who has the sexiest hair in lit. Michael knows everyone. The Gräfin is thrilled to meet him, too, but Michael is taken aback when the Gräfin tells him she never reads; reading is highest calling to Michael. As the talk proceeds, the Gräfin wanders off, and moments later I see her engaged in conversation with a stranger. You have to admit, she has nerve. Rejoining us, she says, "That is Bob the Accountant. Very nice. But I suddenly remembered that I have to take my mother's jewelry out of the bank and wear it every so often." She turns to Michael. "Do you prefer the necklace? Or the ring?"

Michael looks at us as if we were a mountebank and his zany, stirring up a medieval plaza for strolling theatricals. Still, he invites us to drinks at his house on Beachcomber, on the way back to the Grove. The Gräfin celebrates by picking up Bob the Accountant once again on our way along the boardwalk.

Michael looks back at them, as if to say, "What *is* this?" He's too polite to ask, but I answer anyway: "Helen is very into non sequitur, but she has a sweet heart." It sounds like the first line of the last hundred novels Michael rejected.

Michael has a palazzo. The entree takes one up to the kitchen, where we meet one of the most Nordic-looking people I've ever seen, shirtless, tending a huge pan of chicken breasts. Michael introduces him as Erhart. Helen disengages Bob the Accountant at the very doorstep, which I think is strangely cute. But after one look at Erhart, she parks herself outside the kitchen window and stares.

I think of her words outside Belvedere: "Not Jewish." Erhart stirs the chicken, noting Helen, as Michael pulls out glasses and vodka. Finally she speaks, and what she asks Erhart is:

"Is that your bar mitzvah watch?"

"Helen," I warn her, "no kvetching." I turn to Erhart. *"Wollen Sie Deutsch sprechen mit dieser Frau, Erhart? Sie hätte es gern."*

Erhart looks confused. "I am Swiss," he says. It sounds relevant, but it isn't.

The Gräfin has entered the house. "Is that tarragon chicken?" she asks. "You speak English very well for a Swiss."

"I am not Swiss," he says. Erhart, *please!* (It later turns out that he means that his parents are Swiss, but he is total American, and speaks no German.)

Michael shows us the house. Quel palazzo—and guess who owns it? Erhart. It has a pool, a superb viewing aerie on

111

the roof, separate decks for each bedroom, and a sunken conversation nook. How would Larry the schmarotzer feel if he were here? Better? Famous? Included? The nook is so comfortable that I decide that the combined cow-hurling teams of Zürich, Bern, and Luzern won't move me, but the Gräfin, as always, is restless. Away we go, then, racing down the beach through that virulent wind that patrols the space between Pines and Grove. "He's so warm!" the Gräfin screams of Michael as we run the sand. "He makes you feel as if you'd known him all your life!" No, Helen, I carefully fail to say. He is, like anyone with will and intelligence, heedless of those without it. Everything is forgivable but non sequiturs; the strong warm to the other strong. We stagger through the Grove, drunk on swank, and find Christopher inside on the couch, reading in the dark— indeed, holding his book up to the window to catch light that went dead an hour before.

He has eaten all the blueberries.

Still, we have a merry time, high on tequila sunrises, planning a cookout, and making up risible songs. The Gräfin sings "Surabaja Larry" and "Un bel dì, Schmarotzer," and Christopher and I use *Schmarotzendiva* and *Schmarotzenkunst* in every sentence. It's a little like a Boy Scout Jamboree, eating hamburgers under the stars and singing around the dying embers of the campfire. Except at a Jamboree you're not allowed to be silly. I wonder if I should be having quite so good a time on a sexless jaunt to a sexual paradise; when I'm forty, I bet, I'll regret having missed every single opportunity to score.

The Gräfin, at least, is having a ball, raving over the view from Michael's roof and instructing me to get into that house next summer so as to invite everyone out. Even Erhart, by the chemistry of the Gräfin's self-delusion, has become an icon, a collectible. The Gräfin is telling Christopher he could not hope to eat such chicken as Erhart cooked; but she never tasted it.

Did I not warn you that gay life is a chain of tales? Sometimes outsiders claim a tale or so, and we become merely characters in their adventures. In Helen's view, this story is called, "And Eric Actually Came." One of the island's attractions is the sudden cold of the night, invigorating amid the lurid Manhattan summer, when everything is made to feel the way a fun-house mirror looks. But even inside the house it's too cold for fun. The wind is fierce. As the Gräfin tries to close a window, it flips its seams and smashes on the deck, immediately followed by all the other windows; the big glass-topped dining table on the porch decides to go, too. This is so shocking that we bundle into our beds without another word.

The next morning we were standing around drinking coffee and giggling in a pile of broken glass when Eric walked up. "What is this," he cries, "the Amityville Horror?" The Gräfin is thrilled all over again and scampers off to the kitchen to enthrall us with an imperial breakfast.

Eric has come to go. He is positively considering possibly leaving the Island maybe this afternoon if but. I say, "Let's." Then he doesn't want to.

I will make him, for I have had enough of a good thing. I pack, we make farewells—Christopher is as ever bemused at my emphasis on handshaking; he thinks close friends don't have to. As the Gräfin calls out desperate envois, entreaties, passwords, and inconclusions, Eric and I depart to buy sandwiches at the Pines Pantry and watch the beach parade. Dressed, clutching bags, eating sandwiches on the steps commanding the beach, we seem to be waifs kicked out of their houses. "Well, I'm *not* walking past David's blanket!" a queen tells his companion as they approach the sand. Seeing us, he adds, "Do you *have* to be here?" as he brushes past.

Do we? I tell Eric about Michael, Erhart, and the palazzo. "You had Major Tea," he cries.

"What do you recall most when you leave? The beauties, the attitude, the sand sculpture?"

"What's in your sandwich?" he counters.

"Salami, cheddar, Swiss, lettuce, tomato, peppers, mayo . . ."

"On a roll!" He is scandalized. "And they charge extra for each item!"

We watch the beach parade. The Belvedere houseboy is there, now in his element, grinning.

I think of my Pines visits: first one, hottest one, most social one, most lavish one.

I think of my own "What I Saw in the Bars," that it would take me back to the summer of 1973, when I walked into a gay place for the first time. A high school friend, who was by then an old campaigner in the scene, from back rooms to status-skirmishing over cocktails, outlined the stylistic differences, from Harry's Back East way down to Keller's. I decided on the Eagle, and boldly strode in only to feel an arm swing out, grab me, and pull me over to the wall. It belonged to a man I'd never seen before; he was smiling; it was Eric. My high school friend, standing next to him, had said, "There he is now" when I walked in. Though they would not have stated it in precisely these words, they had come to welcome me. Eric and I immediately began to speak as if we had known each other all our lives, and though my high school friend was notorious for being able to charm anyone inside of two minutes, the speed of the intimacy he had helped fire unsettled him. "Now I'll lose both of you," he complained.

"Look at that one!" Eric gasps, as a ruddy gymnast strolls along the parade, rippling with attitude. "Right now, he's devastating, but in five years he will be unbelievable!"

"Unless he burns out on drugs of pleasure," I suggest, my mouth full of sandwich. "Or has been had by everyone who ought to have him. What'll he do then? Do you think he'll keep any friends?"

"Are you kidding? Look at those shoulder caps!"

"Ah," I reply. "But are they his own?" An old Broadway joke.

I think of how neatly this scene would transfer into cin-

114

ema, most likely French: two writers perched on a kind of bleachers, watching and commenting as birds of rare plumage stalk past.

"Do you by any chance remember . . ." I begin, then stop; he is already shaking his head and smiling. He never remembers what I remember. We entertain contrary nostalgias, even for Pines weekends we spent in each other's company. I was going to ask him if he recalled an afternoon when we sat way far back against the dune pickets. The beach was empty and the wind tart. Even in sweatshirts we were shuddering. I had just told Eric that *A la Recherche du Temps Perdu* was the only great book I had never read and he was testing this with other possibilities. He jumped from Frank Norris to Petronius to Flaubert; still, he couldn't trip me up. Then he was silent, determined to find a sure thing. At last he spoke, with the ring of triumph: "*The Man Without Qualities!*"

"Do you really think that's a great book?"

Just then a man we knew of from the Eagle's great old days walked into our line of vision. He, too, had been there on my first night, and like the rest of us was there on most other nights too, a golden-blond hero who, for some of us, was kind of a poster for gay: Join up and you'll look like this. Now his hair was almost gone and his famous stomach had given way to creeping metabolic slowdown, yet he moved as if he still had it. Somewhere off to the right, we heard a woman's voice calling, "Kokomo! Kokomo!" A cocker spaniel came running up to the man, who knelt to pet him as he frolicked. "Kokomo!" the woman insisted. The dog at last obeyed and ran off. The man saw us as he rose, recognized us from the old days, and, though we had never spoken to him in our lives, shot us a marvelous smile and waved as he turned to go.

"Harvard, '61," I murmur, thinking of this.

"What?" says Eric.

"Nothing."

I wonder how long it will be before the threatened beach erodes right up to the house line.

I consider what I offer to the group.

I eat my sandwich.

"'Do you *have* to be here?'" I echo. "That's a good question, isn't it?"

"What happened to the blueberries?" Eric asks.

At the ferry slip he gets into a confusion over the possibility of an ice-cream cone. I buy one; he doesn't.

And the ferry glides into the harbor, filled—as my little brother Tony used to say—to the grim. Except no: everyone's smiling, expectant, tolerant. It's exciting to be here. As the boat passes the tea crowd, a few people wave, some wave back, someone calls out a real name like Jim or Steve, more people wave and others cheer, the ferry toots a whistle, and now everybody is cheering from the island to the boat and back. Everyone is waving and smiling.

"Do we have to be here?" I asked Eric as we climbed to the ferry's upper deck. "We ought to, yes. But do we have to?"

"Isn't that the Cheese Gräfin?" he asked, pointing.

It was: sitting at the dock, watching, forlorn.

"Where's Christopher?" I asked.

Eric waved.

The Gräfin watched.

Now I waved. "Helen!" I called. "Helen!"

She watched.

"Why is she there?" Eric asked.

"To see us off in a kvetching manner."

At last she waved, a sad, fulfilled wave of the most thorough good-bye. There would be, she seemed to acknowledge, no Michael house next summer, no more Jamboree. *Her* story ends here. But there was Christopher, lapping a cone. You cannot tackle the place alone.

The tea crowd cheered us as we floated by.

"Whom are you waving at?" Eric mused.

"At the gay community."

We looked back at the dock. Helen and Christopher had vanished.

"The swank and the drab," I told Eric, "and all between."

"There is nothing," he said in mock queen, "between swank and drab except early-middle Nazi punk."

"You sound like one of your characters."

"Was that an insult or a compliment?"

"Everything I've ever said to you or about you, in your whole life, is a compliment."

"Yah." He nods vigorously, looks away, hates hearing that, more praise to suffer.

And what I'm thinking is, If I use him in a story, he'll probably never speak to me again.

The Shredding of Peter Hawkins

My fourth best friend fell in love for the first time in his life when he was thirty-four.

"Ridiculous," someone told me. "Peter's too shallow to love."

"Disaster," said another. "No one that layered should do an affair."

"Heaven," a third pronounced it. "When you ask him what he's been doing he smirks like the Mona Lisa. And *have you seen the boyfriend?*"

"He'll be lacerated!" Dennis Savage exulted. "That ersatz Clark Gable in Speedos! He'll writhe and shriek like a rat in a Skinner box! He'll be shredded, and I hope I'm there to see it!"

"Has love shredded you and Little Kiwi?"

"No, because we're flexible. You have to give in all the time. You have to be humiliated and abused and it hurts like wild. Peter Hawkins thinks he can do it scot-free. Love without tears! That's like dessert without fat! Oh, just wait." He was whispering now, almost cackling, like the Wicked Witch dunking the poisoned apple. Tasty. Delicious. "Just wait."

I wouldn't have long to wait, because Dennis Savage, Little Kiwi, and I were about to share a house in the Pines with Peter and a fifth individual (contracted on the phone by Little Kiwi) who for unknown reasons never turned up when we were there. We put it down to sound social planning, and asked no more about it, though our mystery housemate left a trace here and there, especially in the pantry. It was a handsome house, by Pines standards. Significant others included Little Kiwi's possibly extraterrestrial dog, Bauhaus, and Peter's boyfriend, The Incredible Jeff McDonald.

Jeff was then living out the last years of his legend; one more little epoch and he would fade into the background of an Edward Hopper. But even at forty-some-odd he retained everything that had made him notable: a handsomeness that inspired cries of "Eureka!" from Morton Street Pier to the Thalia; a lazy walk that not five in a thousand could imitate; and thighs of, literally, death: once you glimpsed them, if you could not have them for your own, you died. In the 1970s, during High Middle Eagle and Tenth Floor Culture, everyone knew his name, but few knew him, for he wasn't a flirt. He was a lover.

I thought he'd be good for Peter, experienced and patient and maybe a bit worn down. Beginners don't usually handle an affair well, but veteran Jeff could ease Peter over the Three Fatal Mistakes in Romance: being late, being bored, and being hurt. I wondered, though, who would help Jeff deal with Peter's First Principle of Rational Living: being private.

"Always hold something back," he would tell me, "or they'll keep taking and taking."

"Who's they?" I asked.

"Little secrets build up your personal space. And make your associates make sense. We must admire the clarity of reason."

Peter lived for reason and personal space. Once his phone rang while I was visiting, and, consulting his watch, he told me, "This will be my mother, asking if I got the invitation to Cousin Patty's wedding and am I going."

It was. He got it. And no, he wasn't going—*because she asked.* "I've told you over and over, if you harass me about family things I won't attend them. . . . It's no use whining. . . . Nor will I give in to emotional blackmail. Yes, you are pushing. It's irritating, boring, and stupid. So give up because you can't win."

He shook his head as he rang off. "Some people simply cannot admire the clarity of reason."

Speaking as one who also suffers from wedding-crazed parents, I could admire the clarity of Peter's reason. But I wondered how it felt to be his mother.

I wondered, too, how Jeff would take to Peter's mode of living. One forgives much at the start of an affair; we are tough only with perfect strangers and imperfect intimates. So Jeff tolerated going to dinner alone because Peter had to catch up on some "unsharable" friend, or getting no answer when he phoned at midnight, or learning that Peter would not join him at a Mets game, period. "Baseball is for jerks," is how Peter put it; and Jeff took it.

I agree, I confess. Football and tennis are for sports, and baseball calls for a nerd's sensibility. Still, I had to ask Peter if he hadn't been a little hard on Jeff.

"In fact, no," Peter replied. "I don't drag him along to the theatre, do I?"

"Maybe he'd enjoy being dragged."

"He'd be bored, and he wouldn't like me as much anymore because I'd be boring him. He's a wonderful man, and I truly love him. Truly. You see, I'm not afraid to say so. It's . . . it's a miraculous thing, love. But it must be understood, and kept within reasonable bounds. It does not make sense for me to suffer through baseball games or for Jeff to suddenly have to like Stephen Sondheim. He just isn't cultured, and I am, and we have to work around that."

"What if . . . ?" I didn't have the heart to go on. Poor blind boy, I thought; are you in for trouble.

"What if what?" He was smiling, content that he had learned love's call number and could phone up as it suited him.

"What if love doesn't see reason? What if Jeff says, 'Come to a Mets game or else'?"

Peter mulled that over for a bit. "That won't happen," he said finally, yet with perhaps somewhat less than his usual authority. "He likes me too much to do that."

120

I nodded as uncommittedly as possible, the way you'd be polite on Mars.

"Well, doesn't he?" Peter asked.

"I know that you two are very much involved with each other. And I wish you a flawless romance."

He decided to accept that as agreement, and The Summer of Peter and Jeff began.

I would date the absolute first moment of this particular story to a Pines afternoon in mid-June. Jeff and I were on the deck tasting my favorite childhood treat, potato-chip sandwiches, when Peter ambled up looking breezy. Jeff asked, "Where have you been?" and Peter replied, "Nowhere," and Jeff said, "Where is nowhere?" and Peter said, "What difference does it make?" and Jeff countered with "It makes a difference to me," and Peter asked, "Why?" and I wished that a giant eagle would swoop down and carry me away. Or no, a winged Italian mesomorph with vulnerable eyes; but I'd take an eagle.

"I don't want you walking off on me," said Jeff.

Peter sat down and began to eat the filling out of my sandwich. "What am I, your houseboy?"

"Where were you?"

"If you mean, was I cheating on you, you know I wasn't."

"You're damn straight I know you weren't."

"That's all you have to know."

"I'm late for my bolero lesson," I began.

"Don't go," said Peter. "This is not the first time this has happened. But it'll be the last." He turned to Jeff. "I went away. Now I'm back. It doesn't matter where I was. End of scene."

Howling and barking on the walk warned of the return of Dennis Savage and company. Jeff pulled his chair closer to Peter's. "If it doesn't matter, why keep it a secret?"

"If it doesn't matter, why do you have to know?"

"Where were you? And I mean it."

Peter folded his arms across his chest and sighed.

Little Kiwi ran up. "Bauhaus caught someone's Frisbee just like that dog in the commercial and raced off with it! Now they don't know where it is! I expect he buried it, but he won't tell." He examined Peter: sullen. He saw Jeff: mad. "Oh no," Little Kiwi whispered. "The first quarrel."

Dennis Savage plopped the grocery bags on the table with a groan. "How does beef stew grab you? With new potatoes."

No one spoke. Jeff gently rubbed Peter's neck, but Peter wouldn't look at him. Little Kiwi took the bags inside. Bauhaus fell off the deck into the poison ivy for about the twentieth time that weekend.

"That dog is such an asshole," said Dennis Savage. Then he noticed. "What's wrong?"

"Nothing's wrong," said Peter, trying to smile.

"One more time," said Jeff, slipping his arm around Peter's shoulder. "Where were you?"

"Please don't do this," Peter replied. "I'm loyal, clever, and cute. I'll never let you down. Never, I promise. Isn't that enough?"

"Nothing is enough," Jeff told him. "That's what love is. The more you have the more you need. You aren't halfway there yet."

Peter got up and started for the walk, calling out, "I'll be back for dinner." Brisk. Nonchalant. The Peter I know. At the turning he paused, came back, and looked Jeff in the eye. "Okay," he said. He took a deep breath. "Okay. I went to visit Tod Graham. His father has cancer. He needs visits. The house was full of people. Is that what you want? Is that enough now? Is that love?"

Bauhaus barked.

"Little Kiwi," Dennis Savage called out, "come get your idiotic dog out of the grunge."

"Yes, that's what I want," said Jeff.

Little Kiwi joined us, eyeing Peter and Jeff nervously. "Bauhaus, come!"

122

Bauhaus made a pass at the deck, missed, and whimpered.

Jeff went over to Peter. "It's silly to fight over something so small. Let's save the fights for the big issues."

"I don't want to fight at all."

"But we will."

"It hurts me when you fight." Peter was pleading: a strange Peter. "It *hurts* me, Jeff."

"It hurts me when you aren't honest."

Little Kiwi dragged the dog onto the deck. "Now he's full of cooties. I *told* you not to fall off, didn't I?"

"I *am* honest," said Peter. Tears were rolling down his cheeks.

Jeff took him in his arms.

I looked at Dennis Savage. He was somewhat less than thrilled to witness the shredding of Peter Hawkins, after all. "Little Kiwi, he said, "come help me zip up the salad."

Little Kiwi was watching Peter and Jeff like Emily Dickinson viewing the dismembering of a butterfly.

"Shoo," I told him.

He ran into the house.

For the next few days, Jeff and Peter played together like puppies. "It's always like that," Dennis Savage informed me, "after the first fight. But then comes the second, and the third. . . ."

"What a horror show," I cried. "We've seen Peter crying—Peter who mutes ghetto blasters with a look."

"Yes, that really scared you. Because if our strong, sensible Peter can cry, anyone can, right?"

"Who's anyone, as if I didn't know, you dreary plop who rims scrofulous sheep?"

"The day you fall in love, I will personally phone in the item to Liz Smith: BOY WRITER STRICKEN WITH CASE OF FEELINGS. CONDITION CRITICAL. WEEPING, MOPING, AND PICKING LISTLESSLY AT HIS ZWEIBACK AND MILK."

"I always knew you secretly hated me."

123

"First Peter, then you, and that'll be the end of you arrogant sons-of-bitches who think you can take it or leave it. You're going to die, boyo, just like the rest of us. I'm going to fix you up with death himself."

A pause ensued.

"You know," I said, "sometimes these jokes get a little out of control."

Yes. And he nodded. Yes.

Peter and Jeff did start quarreling again; by August it had become a routine of the house, something always going on, like MTV or construction noises. There was a lot of Why? and When? from Jeff, and rebuffs from Peter. Why won't you come to Dick's party? When did you get home last night? Why do we have to go to Europe for Thanksgiving? When a wall of silence failed to prove deterrent, Peter worked out a way to answer Jeff's queries without saying anything, and their bickering took on an absurdist note, like a play with every third line missing. "Why aren't you?" provoked responses like "But I am—or I shall have had to be, before long," or simply "Because I believe that you are Attila the Nun."

Jeff was exasperated and bewildered, unable to battle through these rebuses. But Peter reclaimed some of his old dash. He would not surrender to the fascism of romance again.

"I know what," said Little Kiwi one lunchtime. "Every day each of you has to tell one true thing that you never told anyone before."

"Is that how you and Dennis Savage survive?" asked Jeff.

"We don't have to," said Dennis Savage. "We're—"

"Flexible, we know," I put in, thinking that he's about as flexible as the Pope's hernia truss.

"Now, for example," Little Kiwi went on, "Jeff could say who Peter most reminds him of. And Peter could tell about the cutest thing Jeff ever did. Or something."

"The cutest thing Jeff ever did," said Peter, "was when

124

he forgot to clean out the medicine cabinet when his parents were visiting, and his mother came out of the bathroom and said—"

"Shut up!"

Peter, lean and mean, smiled. "You want me to be honest, don't you?" he said.

"And loyal, how about that?"

"Oh, no." Peter shook his head, snapped his fingers, pointed at Jeff. He had found the stop in reason's mind that would put love in its place. "Loyalty needs lying. Do you want me to be honest or loyal? It's one or the other."

"And what does Peter remind you of?" Little Kiwi asked Jeff, merrily, but with an edge.

Jeff grinned at Peter. "He reminds me of—"

"You remind me of the Elephant Man!"

"*You fucking zit!*"

"But we have to be nice to you because you've got a terminal case of brainturd, that dread disease in which your brain slowly turns into a great, big, brown—"

Jeff leaped out of his chair and went for Peter, who dodged around the table. "What other wonderful games can you suggest for us to play?" I asked Little Kiwi, as Peter and Jeff lunged about us.

"I know Animal Lotto," he answered.

Eventually Jeff heaved into his chair and told Peter to fuck off. Peter did so with a purposeful look in his eye, leaving a sober quartet to assess and attempt to make remedy.

"You have to stop fighting," Dennis Savage told Jeff. "You're the top-okay couple of the summer. They were fainting when you and Peter walked into tea yesterday. Fashion and ad people in the six figures are lining up for dinner invitations."

Jeff shrugged.

"Why did he call you the Elephant Man?" Little Kiwi asked.

"Why do you think?"

"Because you like peanuts?"

"Size."

Little Kiwi paused. "Size what?"

"Of his, uh, trunk," I said.

"Mere trivia," said Dennis Savage. "The issues are sharing and candor and that's exactly—Little Kiwi, stop gaping—where Peter can't compromise."

"Why does he have to?" I asked.

"Because I said so," said Jeff. You should have seen his face.

"I admit that Peter is a pretty unbending character," I went on, "but isn't that in itself good reason to run this affair by his rules? Keep company, but respect your differences. Share what is sharable."

"He's too mixed up even for that," said Jeff. "He's been covering his insecurity so long that he can't open up at all."

"Two men can't give up the same thing at the same time," I said.

Well, that stopped them.

"What happens in straight romance?" I continued. "The woman gives up her independence and the man gives up nothing. That's why they're man and wife, not husband and wife. She has to change, not he. She pays the compromises. But when two men couple, no one is giving up anything. That's bound to create tension, and some men can compensate for it better than others. Peter compensates less well."

"Bullshit."

"That's the retort of an ignorant lout. I expect something more sensitive from someone in love."

"Look!" Little Kiwi shouted, pointing at Ocean Walk. "An ox!"

"A deer. Specialty of the Pines."

Bauhaus strained at his rope, fuming and groaning.

"Hush, Bauhaus."

So Bauhaus promptly barks and the deer runs off.

"It's done all the time," Jeff repeats. "*I* do it. Why can't he?"

"Why don't you give him a chance to edge into it?" I asked.

"If it doesn't start right, it's already finished," Jeff retorted, flaring up. "He'll do what he has to, or I'll find out why but good!"

"You made him cry," Little Kiwi blurted out. "You're the Elephant Man!"

"Walk time," said Dennis Savage.

Little Kiwi eyed the boardwalk. "Do ox bite?"

"*Oxen* bite. Deer don't. Come." Away they went, Bauhaus dragging on his leash.

"That kid is very pretty," said Jeff, looking after them. "But real stupid."

"He's bright enough to know how to behave in love."

"And how is that?"

"With ease."

He took a deep breath, tilted his chair back, and watched me. "Let me tell you something," he finally said. "I've gone to and fro in love, and walked up and down in it. I know love. Peter doesn't. Nor do you. So he's going to take my advice, and you're going to keep yours to yourself."

"Think I'll catch up with the guys," I said, rising. "One thing, though: next time you use the Bible for your text, don't quote the devil. It hurts your credibility."

"What Bible?"

"'Going to and fro in the earth and walking up and down in it.' The Book of Job."

He chuckled. "I knew that was from somewhere."

Peter stayed away all that day and night and didn't return till just before dinner the next day. Little Kiwi insisted on making the drinks, which he called Kazootie Koolers: white wine drowning grapes, melon balls, and strawberries.

"I hope no one drops in and sees us drinking these," said Dennis Savage. "I mean, I like them, but they'd be hard to alibi to anyone on the A-list."

"Why don't you do what you want to do without reference to what others think?" I asked.

"Because no man is an island!"

"*I* am an island!"

"So am I," said Peter, strolling in. "I'm Fire Island." Nice. Assured. "I'm the embodied truth of the Pines. I'm the destiny of homoerotic passion." He marched into the house and came out munching a hunk of cheese. "Aren't you going to ask where I was?" he asked Jeff. "If it doesn't matter, why keep it a secret, right? So where was I?"

Jeff ignored him.

"Hey," Peter went on, "what would happen if I took Bauhaus for a run?"

"You best not," said Little Kiwi. "He's afraid of an ox."

Jeff got up.

"Do you want a Kazootie Kooler?" Little Kiwi asked Peter, his eyes on Jeff.

"Hell, yes."

Jeff confronted Peter.

"I was with Jim Guest," said Peter, quite casually. "All night. He's hotter than you are. Now you know and how do you like it?"

Jeff fetched Peter a walloping blow to the side of the head and knocked him flat on the deck.

To Bauhaus' crazed barking, Dennis Savage and I jumped between them. Jeff threw us one by one off the deck into the grunge. Bauhaus came, too; it's possible that he prefers it there.

Jeff pulled Peter to his feet and smacked him down again.

"I knew you'd be understanding about this," said Peter.

"How do I like it?" shouted Jeff. "How do I like it, huh?"

Now Little Kiwi got between them. "Go away!" he cried, harrying Jeff with his chair as one tames a tiger. "Go away *now!*"

"This is how I like it," said Jeff, pushing past Little Kiwi to get to Peter again. Dennis Savage and I had just gained the deck when we saw Jeff haul Peter up by the collar of his shirt and Little Kiwi punching Jeff in the back. Suddenly, someone said, "What the fruit is going on here?" and we turned to find the most nondescript man I've ever seen, standing on our deck holding an overnight bag and a briefcase. He was a pair of glasses with no eyes behind them.

"Which of you," he went on, "is Virgil Brown?"

"I am," said Little Kiwi.

"I'm Orville McKlung. Permit me to point out that you said nothing about violence when I inquired about the tenor of the house. Nor did you speak of a dog."

Bauhaus grumbled in the grunge.

The man walked past us into the house in the flat-footed but hip-rolling gait of the queen who believes that everyone thinks he's straight. We could hear him rummaging in the kitchen. Sniffing. Put out.

Outside, our riot collapsed. Little Kiwi picked up the fallen chair. Dennis Savage examined Peter's ear, which was bleeding. Jeff stood off a bit, not taking his eyes off Peter, not even to blink. A moment later, the stranger was back, flourishing a cookie wrapper.

"And who, may I ask, ate almost all my Lorna Doones?"

"I didn't know they were yours," said Peter.

"I saved them for tonight! It's my Wednesday night special!"

("That sounds like you," Dennis Savage murmured to me." "Your mother wears a dribble bib," I replied.)

"Would you like a Kazootie Kooler?"

"No, Mr. Brown, I would like my Lorna Doones replaced."

"*Mea culpa,*" said Peter. "I'll go."

"Let me," I said. His shirt was torn almost in two.

"Peter and I will go," said Jeff. "Together."

"I'm not going anywhere with you."

"Do you want more of the same?"

Peter held his ground. "I won't cry for you this time."

We all stood and waited, except Orville McKlung, who muttered, "Swindlers," and went inside.

"Come on," said Jeff, extending his hand.

"No!"

"If you don't take my hand," said Jeff, "I'm going to drag you to the store by the neck for all the Pines to see. And when the dish queens get through with you, you'll be the laugh of the week."

"I don't believe you," said Peter.

"Bud," said Jeff, his eyes still on Peter, "do you believe me?"

"I believe you would try," I answered.

"I hurt you," Jeff told Peter. "I'll hurt you again. And I'll be sorry then as I'm sorry now. But you hurt me, too. You've been hurting me since we met. That's what love is." Jeff seemed to circle around Peter, surround him. "Now, come with me and we'll buy this man his cookies, and then we'll take a walk on the beach and talk about it. I can make it up to you."

Peter laughed softly. "How could you possibly?"

"Tonight."

Peter paused, looked away, shook his head, let Jeff take his hand. "I don't love you anymore," he said dully.

"That's when you love me the most," Jeff told him. "When you feel it hurting."

"Somebody . . . please help me," said Peter.

Little Kiwi whispered, "I'll help you. What do you want?"

Peter looked at Jeff. "I want to go with him."

"You don't need any help for that," said Jeff.

And away the two of them went.

"You know what's funny about extroverts?" I said. "They're just as dogmatic as introverts."

"Did you hear the other guy call me 'Mr. Brown'?" said Little Kiwi.

"Speaking of that," said Dennis Savage, "whose idea was

130

it to let Little Kiwi arrange for the disposition of the shares in this house?"

"'Mr. Brown,'" Little Kiwi quoted, striking a solemn pose, "'I would like my Lorna Doones replaced.'"

"Little Kiwi, get that menace of a dog back among the living!"

Little Kiwi helped Bauhaus onto the deck and said, "Now everyone has cooties but me."

"That won't last long," replied Dennis Savage, as I pretended to fan myself like a deb at a more than usually intense prom.

And when anyone complains to me that he's getting old and has no romance, I think of Jeff and Peter, and remark that I know someone who didn't fall in love till he was thirty-four.

Think of all you have to look forward to.

A Christmas Carol

My family has been celebrating a highly traditional Christmas since before I was born. We trimmed no trees—Mother disdained them as fire hazards. But we did everything else Americans do, from rummaging through closets to see what presents were heading our way to gloating over them on Christmas Eve as my father took home movies and mother served champagne to those of age and caviar to all. I mean the real thing, too, on a multi-leveled tray bearing chopped, boiled egg, minced onion, sour cream, and toast. (When he thought no one was looking, my dad would slip a spoon into the fish and glop it down neat.) The caviar tray was as much a part of our Night Before as was staying up late with my brothers to reminisce, bicker, and watch the Alastair Sim *Christmas Carol* on television. The great moment was when all five of us spoke, along with Sim, the immortal line, "Are there no prisons? *No workhouses?*"

On Christmas Day we bundled into the car for the larger, dynastic festival at my Aunt Agnes' in Connecticut. Some four generations made a day of it, with drinks and little meatballs at noon as the various cars pulled in, followed by the dread ritual of the Kissing of the Grandparents, the kids trundled into the living room where the old folks stiffly held court in high-backed chairs, my grandfather passing out antique silver dollars to all the dutiful children. "Was he good?" Grandfather would ask as my cousin Ellis filed by. "Very good," said my aunt Laura; and Ellis got a coin. "Was she good?" asked Grandfather, as my cousin Ruth came up. "Basically," my aunt Jane answered; a coin for Ruth. Now it's my turn. "Was he good?" my grandfather inquires of mother, who replies, "He's a perfect little monster-child!" I got a coin anyway, as Mother fumed.

The men sat in on the televised football game in the den, the women traded eternal wisdoms here and there through the house, and the kids repaired outside for touch football with something like twenty on each side, ranging in age from five to thirty. Sacred acts were committed, too, as when my cousins would bring their fiancées to meet their engaged in-laws. I can remember Ellis introducing Sally, person by person, as they moved through the house. Years before, when we were still kids, that time was claimed by the annual Monopoly game, with Ellis, Donald, Jeff, and I behind locked doors as my little brothers and cousins plotted raids outside in the hall. (Ruth still claims she can never forgive us for leaving her out.) Some years, there was a free-for-all upstairs on the third floor, more modern than the rest of the house and amply supplied with huge closets and magical attics. It was the best kind of game: no rules. Everyone just ran around screaming and hiding.

At length came the holiday dinner, in three seatings because of the crush of people. First seating was desirable if you wanted primary choice of the turkey platter, but the second-seating people would come up and stand behind you, grumbling in hunger. Second seating was more convivial but a little thin on the soufflé potatoes; and third seating, reserved for the drunks, who didn't much care whether they ate or not, was a touch campy, with too many green peas. Then came buffet-style coffee and dessert, of an endless suspense punctuated by us kids, who would ask, "Is it time yet?" every three minutes.

By 7:30 or so it was time: for the presents, enough to fill F. A. O. Schwartz for a year. My Uncle Willy was in the toy business, so his were the best—forts, gas stations, and building sets—but there was a general emphasis on things to play with rather than things to wear. My Uncle Mike would read out the cards through a megaphone—"To Bud from Aunt Jane and Uncle Sonny"—as various grownups clapped and the recipient bellowed out a law-abiding "Thank you!" Everyone leaned over to see what came out of the wrapping, and reactions were not muted. Uncle Willy's toys received ovations from the kids, plus cries of "I want that, too!" while the occasional sweater won oohs from the mothers and boos from the kids.

With so many presentations, fathers had to supervise the packing of the gifts in the big cardboard boxes each car had arrived with; the mean fathers dispossessed you of each item almost immediately, while the neat ones (like mine) let you stockpile your haul in the manner of Fafner. Finally, we would be summoned to the kitchen for ice-cream cones, the youngest of us already changed into pajamas. Then, family by family, the clan would disperse. We Pennsylvanians spent much of the night on the road, from Norwalk down through the Bronx to the George Washington Bridge, all the way through New Jersey, and home to Heavensville, my brother Jim and I up front and the oldest and the two youngest in the back with Mother. We had assigned seats for long trips, so she would know whom she was hitting even in the dark. One of my earliest and most pointless memories is of waking up, dimly and momentarily, whenever we stopped for a toll.

I grew up thinking that everyone had the same Christmas; happy families are alike. Coming to New York after college, I learned to my horror that some families simply traded a minor gift or two after dinner. My Jewish friends confirmed the wondrous rumor that Chanukah is like Christmas but *lasts eight days!* Yet they seemed rather blasé about it, and couldn't match Christians for generational pageant. One companion, shockingly calm, told me his parents were Communists and didn't celebrate anything. Worst of all were those who could claim a true holiday but wouldn't join their families. To me, this was like practicing to be an orphan. The sole advantage in having relatives is to be able to go to a Christmas.

Not long ago, my parents moved to California, where my younger brothers live. Then Uncle Mike died, and Aunt Agnes decided to retire from party-giving. Suddenly I was an orphan like many of my set, placeless on Christmas. As they did, I shrugged when asked what I was doing for the holidays. Inwardly, I worried. What could I do? Sit in my armchair scheming and sulking, I suppose; but I do that all the time. The meanest bit of the deal was that I had agreed to mind the Pazuzu-like Bauhaus while Little Kiwi and Dennis Savage were away.

I dropped in as they were packing for their respective trips, Little Kiwi to his folks in Cleveland and Dennis Savage to his sister's in Buffalo.

"Don't forget to give Bauhaus something super for Christmas," Little Kiwi told me.

"He'll be lucky if I fill his water dish."

"If you really wanted to," said Dennis Savage, "you could get a nice party together. Carlo, Lionel, Alex. Don't jive at us just because we've got homes to go to."

"After the Christmases I've known, I'm not going to hunker down with a bunch of overgrown waifs pretending to feel loved."

"Christmas," he says, "is not about love. Christmas is about being with people who are so used to you they take everything you do for granted."

"*You* could have that at the Ramrod."

"Oh? And where could you have that, may I ask?"

Nowhere. My Christmas had vanished: moved away, passed on, grown old. Had it even been available, it could only play as a nostalgic forgery, for touch football and toys have lost their magic now that I am the only cousin of age without a spouse and children. Even my juniors have coupled and are staging their own Christmases, in Scarsdale, Chicago,

Des Moines. A bachelor doesn't quite fit into the Christmas I was raised on. Christmas is about families.

And so, as Dennis Savage and Little Kiwi bustled about, I began to tell them of my Christmas. As I spoke I realized that, yes, everyone does take everyone else for granted: as part of his heritage and destiny. Christmas is the one time of the year when you look about and *feel* your blood. Your race passes before you, epic in little—for instance when my tiniest cousins run up to dance when I play the piano as the grownups dote and clap, or in the spaces left by those departed, very much sensed and even mentioned, almost alive. And there is film on this. I have seen myself at the age of two-and-a-half, from the back, walking up Agnes' tiled pathway in my camel's hair coat, my cousin Donald throwing a welcoming football at my father, my mother sharing a fast confidence with Laura. The camera turns to our car as my father demonstrates the convertible top, hot stuff in those days. Suddenly I turn around for the first time and lo, I'm wearing a Flub-a-Dub mask. Who was holding that camera, Federico Fellini?

"You know," said Dennis Savage, as I subsided, "sometimes your family sounds like *The Forsyte Saga* and sometimes it sounds like *Tobacco Road*."

"Well, your family sounds like *Attack of the Killer Macadamia Nuts*."

"Will you two stop?" cried Little Kiwi, pulling closed the zipper of his valise. "I know you're only fighting because you're both cut off from your brothers."

"Oh yeah?" I countered. "And what do you fight with?"

"I don't fight at Christmas."

"Anyway," said Dennis Savage, "we're packed."

I saw them downstairs to Third Avenue to get a cab, holding Bauhaus on his leash with one hand and a bag of his foodstuffs with the other.

"How cute of you," I noted, "to book simultaneous reservations on different planes."

"It's not cute," said Dennis Savage. "It's expert planning—which, I might add, would have saved you from the terrible curse of Lonely Christmas."

"We're going to have lunch at the airport!" Little Kiwi crowed.

"Hey," I said, "it's snowing."

"A white Christmas!" Little Kiwi breathed.

"Go home," I suggested, between my teeth.

"Don't be sad," said Dennis Savage. "I'll be back in two days."

As they rolled away, Bauhaus looked after them, looked up at me, and began to growl.

"Don't you start in, Buster," I told him.

It was Christmas Eve. Living in midtown, I observe New York's rhapsody of population more than many do, and I saw the crowds, as Robinson Crusoe saw the sea, when I stepped outside for a walk at nightfall. Shoppers, walkers, workers, cranks—the drawbacks of a Christmas lived on the blade. In the Village, Christmas is a rumor, in Brooklyn something done in dark alleys, in the suburbs an arcane rite shut away behind closed doors. But at Fifty-third and Third it's Manhattan at its most dense and fierce. I saw a dumpy little man loaded with wrapped boxes take a cab from a smartly dressed woman who socked him; and when he got into the cab without responding, she spat at him through the open window. A few feet away, two construction workers were trying to help an old man who had fallen, but he was afraid to rise. Behind me, a man in a suit was chasing a hustler, and the boy dashed past us as the man called out, "You'll come back sometime!" He seemed jolly. As I turned away a photographer in leather pants and a knitted cap snapped my picture and ran off. Too bad I wasn't wearing my Flub-a-Dub mask.

It was very cold. I felt like turning back, but I wasn't going to let Christmas spoil *my* holiday. I tried to whirl through the streets, but the crowds held me back, and the noise of the town, too, was heavy, from street musicians to the carol of shattering glass. The last straw was the eruption of Guy Webster out of Brooks Brothers, a dead-on meet, no escape. He wrung my hand and said that, as I was the smartest man in the world, I could save his life by helping him out of a terrible scrape, and, as I was his best friend in the world, I had to. I was thinking that the only thing worse than meeting Guy Webster was meeting Guy Webster's inevitable comrade, Claudia Luxemburg, when Guy added, "And Claudia's here, too!"

Now Guy, I must tell you, is the richest man I know. It's family money, of course: the people I consort with make salaries, not fortunes. Guy and I were in the same class in Friends Academy, and, though we were not chums, we kept bumping into each other later in New York and struck up a sort of acquaintance. I think Guy was fascinated by my independence, for he was very much subject to parental guidance. I know I was fascinated by his *bon ton* set, for at the time I entertained thoughts of becoming a society satirist and hoped to collect material. I gave up early on, after divining that the rich have no emotions. They have manners, they don't litter, and they're apt pretenders at all kinds of skills from boating to sympathizing. A few of them even have style—irony, anyway. But they cannot truly be said to be people, because there just isn't anything they want. However, I could not shake Guy, even when his lofty imperturbility began to get on my nerves and I became crabby with him. In some strangely endearing way he looked up to me—for advice, it seemed, but more exactly for gay glamour, for Guy was semi-closeted and knew neither clones nor queens.

What Guy knew was Claudia. Now, Claudia was what we in the trade call a *fag hag*. This is an almost unusably diffuse term, like "salesman" or "Spaniard" denoting a wide range of characters. Straights seem to think that fag hags are lesbians. No, never. Lesbians are lesbians. Fag hags are straight women who pal around with gay men. No one knows why. Some of them may fear the sexual competition of other women, or the sexual aggression of straight men. Some of

138

them share the gay's whimsically bizarre sense of humor and love of savage elegance and have deserted the straight world as boring. Some of them fall into gay company professionally, through connections in show biz or fashion. Some of them aren't properly of the genre at all, only seem so momentarily—like Helen, my Fire Island hostess, who is something of a genre herself. No two hags are alike, but the bitter term itself suggests the gay's ambivalence—and let's admit that the classic pre-Stonewall hag tended to be a rather unappealing sort, as disgusted by gays as intrigued by them. They hugged the more unappealing men, who would say—after the hag had gotten drunk and offended everyone in the room—"Isn't she *heaven?*"

Guy never said this of Claudia. Guy never said anything that couldn't be uttered resonantly at high noon in the bar of the Piping Rock Club. Claudia never said anything that could; she spoke but one language, High-Middle Cabaret. She was pretty and vivacious, and, in spasms, great fun. But anyone who can spend three hours in a piano bar and meet a request to leave with the statement that "We've just gotten started!" is not my idea of a companion. To top it off, Claudia was unreliable. She had no awareness of time or responsibility, and that drives me wild. Some people show up three hours late for dinner; Claudia would show up a year and three hours late. I can forgive almost nothing, but recklessness especially infuriates me. Yet reckless people somehow gravitate toward me, as if seeking the reproaches their parents spared. Sometimes I feel like every spoiled kid's surrogate father. "Lower your voice," I order Christopher in a bookstore, when he loudly eructates publishing innuendo. "People are starving in China!" I snarl at Little Kiwi, when he throws out leftover food. (He just says, "Oh." When I was young, we told my mother, "So send it to China.")

Claudia's tactless sense of obligation never offended Guy, because the rich don't have much sense of it themselves. There's nowhere that they have to be, ever, nothing that can't be delayed. And Claudia was useful. She gave Guy a feeling for gay without his having to be there in person, and she could show up on his arm when he needed a date. Claudia was what is known as Guy's beard.

"The writer!" Claudia cried, as husbands and wives poured out of Brooks Brothers, their gift lists fulfilled and the hearth beckoning. "Will he help us?"

"Of course he will. He has nothing else to do. Right, Bud?"

"It just so happens," I intoned, "that—"

"Guy," Claudia said, "I'd *kill* for a wee drinkie."

"It just so happens," said Guy, "that anyone alone on the street at this hour is a homeless Christmas bachelor. Now be good and come along and we'll tell you about it."

"Come along where?"

"What's near?" He thought. "The Varsity House."

"They don't have menus," Claudia enthused, as we walked. "You ask for whatever you want and they bring it."

I want my family back, I was thinking; but at least I was in on an adventure. The Varsity House, two blocks northeast of Brooks Brothers—the rich walk, but not far—is one of those places you know, rather than read about. It is nondescript, low-key, virtually hidden behind an unmarked door, and gives the impression that, if your parents didn't come here when they were dating adolescents, your business isn't welcome. The staff greeted Guy by name, and I was relieved to see that I wasn't the only man in a sweater: which reminds us that the rich don't dress up as often as you'd think. Claudia asked for a Scotch with lots of ice and a shrimp cocktail, Guy for scrambled eggs and canteloupe, and I ordered French toast, one of the things a place like this does really well. The rich eat anything they feel like at any time of day, even Cream of Wheat for dinner, if they so choose. Then you ask for seconds on dessert and they look as if they had caught you cadging your dinner out of a garbage can.

Saving Guy's life, it turned out, was simple: I had only to accompany him and Claudia to his parents' traditional Christmas Eve bash.

"Why?"

"Old man," said Guy, "you know how parents are. They *will* ask such-and-such, you know, and I keep fending them off. But now that I'm past thirty . . . well, all this evasion begins to seem ever so slightly tutti-frutti, doesn't it?"

"Why don't you just tell them that such-and-such in men past thirty means that they're. . . ." Guy died in a look, though I was speaking very quietly. "Why don't you tell them that 'bachelor' is a euphemism?"

"My dear fellow alumnus, they'd raving *shoot* me."

"I remember your parents. They seemed rather sweet."

"Well, they are sweet. They just think these incredibly grave thoughts about renouncing and disinheriting. My boy, it's like an opera. Anyway, my back is against the wall at last, so I told them I'd bring my sweetheart along tonight. I *told* them. 'My sweetheart.' The exact words."

"Guess who got the part?" said Claudia, simulating a resumé photograph.

"Where do I fit in?"

He patted my hand. "Imagine."

"Can't." Rich people think it's dashing when you leave out the subject pronouns.

"Well . . . my sweetheart Claudia and I can't face it alone, is the thing."

"He can't face it," said Claudia. "I sense it's high time I made my debut. And had another wee drinkie."

"They've never met her, you know. My parents." In this place, you simply point to a glass and a waiter refills it. Guy pointed; a wee drinkie for Claudia. "And if there were a group of us, I was thinking . . . well, just saying to Claudia, in fact. If there were someone we could *call* . . . and you came along like the cavalry. I mean, look: fellow schoolchum, old boy network, author and man-about-town, aunts and uncles gather 'round to worship, parents impressed . . . You can take the pressure off Claudia and me."

"I don't want to spend Christmas being your ruse," I

141

said. "And I'm not a man-about-town and I *don't* approve of closet cover procedures."

"Jeepers, man, must I sing 'The Red and Black Fight Song'?" This was Friends Academy's football anthem, the stirring performance of which before each game seemed to guarantee our stupendous defeat, though we probably would have lost, anyway. At least we played. When the wrestling team stood challenge to a public school, we sometimes defaulted matches because one of our side refused to go to the mat with a black. "I'll give you my watch. I'll give you my shoes."

"Guy—"

"Anything you want, for heaven's sake!"

"What I want, you cannot give."

"Unlike me," Claudia observed. "I want to star in a revival of *Flora, the Red Menace.* Guy could produce it, like a sugar daddy of the 1920s."

"Don't sing," Guy told her, because she often does, anywhere, loud.

But the sad truth of it was: What else did I have to do?

One thing you must not dare is to enter a rich people's Christmas in less than the higher threading; we repaired to my place so I could change. While Claudia poured herself another wee drinkie, Guy glanced through my closet and silently chose a suit, tie, shirt, and handkerchief. "Black socks and shoes," he concluded.

"I could have done that myself," I said.

"I'm faster."

"This is my fanciest suit " I noted. "Just how heavy is this party, anyway?"

"Well, it's the whole clan, you know. The one time of the year when we're all together. Even Aunt Eliza—and she doesn't come to anything." He put his hand on my shoulder. "It's the command performance, old chap. It's major, is what. So you can see how terribly eager I am to breeze through it, if possible. You see it, don't you?"

142

I took the clothes into the bathroom. "Excuse me for saying so," I whispered, "but aren't your parents counting on your showing up with some debutante? Claudia isn't exactly a Colonial Dame right off the *Arbella*."

"That's her charm." He winked at me. "You aren't planning to wear those dark glasses, are you? Have you any horn-rims or something like that?"

"Whoa!"

"Anyway, I don't have to show up with a fiancée, just a date. They simply want to assure themselves that I'm not . . . you know."

"Tutti-frutti."

He giggled. "Actually, Claudia is perfect casting. She's so colorful they won't put me through this again for at least a decade."

I stopped dressing and looked at him.

"But lest she overwhelm the place," he went on, "you can lend our company an air of . . . well . . ."

"*Zoom!*" said Claudia, edging in with her wee drinkie. "I want to zoom all over, like Liza in 'Mein Herr.' Can I go in dark glasses, too?"

We compromised on the glasses: I wore none at all, which makes me dangerously liable to nearsighted acts such as trying to charm people who are glaring at me.

The streets were deserted all of a sudden: New York had all gone home. In the cab, Claudia went into a medley of what she called "show biz goldies"—mostly *Carousel* cut with *On Your Toes*—but broke off when she took in the depth of the gathering snowfall and breezed into "White Christmas."

"Come on," she urged. "Somebody on harmony."

"It would be funny," I said, "if after all this I did something embarrassing at the party."

Guy turned a bland smile on me, which read, Anyone who went to school with Guy Webster is a perfect gentleman.

Traffic was moving so slowly that Claudia had time not only to put us through "White Christmas" but to drill us in descants and festive effects, such as adding "and emerald" be-

143

tween the two words of the title and having the men impose a descending chromatic line over the melody on "May your days be merry and bright." It sounded ragged but sweet, and I caught the taxi driver furtively joining in. Through it all, I was distracted by the humming of the meter, but Guy was perfectly at ease, as are all rich people when they hear money being spent, including their own. I don't mean just anyone with money, mind you, but the *genetically* rich, those born to a culture of largesse—a culture as textured and developed as the gay system is. One Christmas in my youth, I was given a cocker spaniel puppy who was so excited to be out of the kennel that he couldn't settle down and go to sleep, so my mother put a clock in his basket and the ticking soothed him. So it is, I believe, with the rich and taxi meters.

"Next could we do 'Good Christian Men, Rejoice'?" said the taxi driver.

"We only do Broadway-type carols," said Claudia.

"On the right, driver," said Guy. "Fourth house along."

It was literally a house: the Websters lived in the whole thing. The front door alone warned you that the building was like a human bank: an immensely thick bar of glass protected fore and aft by elaborate iron webbing. The man who opened the door actually called our host Mr. Guy, which gave Claudia the idea of going as Miss Glama de Ponselle.

"Claudia," Guy said, "things are touchy enough as it is."

"Miss Glama," she insisted, "is ready for her wee drinkie. Miss Glama de Ponselle."

"Guy!" cried a handsome man in the most beautifully tailored dinner clothes I've ever seen, sailing down the stairs. "Well, egad, old son!" They shook hands, and Guy introduced him as Cousin Brian. Another thing about the rich is that the men are usually good-looking but not sexy.

"And I'm Miss Glama," said Claudia, before Guy could say she wasn't. "Believe me, one day when I'm a celeb, you'll wish you knew me."

"I wish I knew you now," Brian answered, amused.

"Did Aunt Eliza make it?"

144

"Everyone's here, and there's a heavy air of Santa in the air. Come along, lad. Now is the time for the good little boys to claim their reward."

I bet it's somewhat more than a dollar, too, I said to myself as we ascended. Aunt Agnes' was never like this Christmas. True, there were the seniors sedately postured, the aunts and uncles grouped, the little kids in cute little versions of grown-up clothes racing around deliriously. But there was none of the sit-back-and-dish atmosphere that my aunts observed, none of my uncles' hearty thunder. There were no decorations, no presents, no bowls of pretzels. Surely no Monopoly game was in session down the hall. There were waiters wafting about with trays of fancy food that no one named Webster had cooked, little groups of people nodding to each other, and even the pianist noodling show tunes was clearly a hired man, not some obliging nephew.

"Piano bar!" Claudia breathed.

"Miss Havisham," I murmured, viewing a tremendous crone in a stupendous chair bearing a fabulous cane. Other family types posed behind her like lawyers at a board meeting.

"That's Aunt Eliza," said Guy.

"Claudia and I will scatter to the bar," I offered.

"No," said Guy, clutching us. "This is central."

"Guy," Aunt Eliza wheezed, as we approached. "Guy," she added, as he kissed her cheek. "Guy," she concluded, pounding her cane. "Do you smoke?"

"No, ma'am."

"Do you drink?"

"Sometimes."

"That's a good boy. That's a man. I hate a smoker, or a pantywaist who doesn't know his whiskey." She eyed Claudia, who curtsied as to royal majesty. "Lovely, child." Aunt Eliza proposed the kissing of her sere cheek, and Claudia managed nicely. "Whose is she? Ellen's? Is it Ellen's girl?"

"No, Aunt Eliza, this is my friend—"

"Miss Glama de Ponselle."

Aunt Eliza listened to the name as one attends agitated noises in the hall outside one's apartment door. "I sense New Orleans or such."

"Boston."

The old bag brightened. "Ah."

Now I was dragged forward, introduced as a writer.

"I love Dickens," Aunt Eliza declared, not to my surprise. "Are you Dickensian?"

"Sometimes," I said, as Little Nell, Smike, and Sidney Carton shrieked in their graves. "With a modern edge."

"Rubbish!" Aunt Eliza remarked. "Guy, you will appear before me later. I've something to give you."

"Yes, ma'am."

Having earned our dollars, we slipped over to the bar as Guy greeted his family.

"I know the pianist," Claudia told me. "He plays at Carstair's."

"Do you people hire out?" said Brian, coming up. "Guy's not the only one who needs support at parties."

"The writer's all booked up with Dickensian novels," said Claudia. "But I'm possible."

Brian smiled. Great teeth, and surprisingly broad shoulders for a rich boy. At Guy's signal, I excused myself, crossed the floor, dodged two adorable little girls imitating robots and screaming "Wind me up! Wind me up!" and found myself facing Guy's parents.

There are two kinds of rich parents. The men are either Ichabod Crane or Franklin Roosevelt and the women are Eleanor Roosevelt or Queen Elizabeth II. Guy had FDR and the Queen. Stunning; and they had this way of speaking so profoundly about such trivia that after two minutes with them you'd be ready to best Henry James at parlor banter.

"Layered," was all I said to Guy as we moved on. "Heavily layered."

"He published seven of the ten most imposing novels of the early 1950s and she opened the first surrealist gallery in

New York. They should have had you for a son. Now it's Claudia's turn."

"Do you know Glama sings?" said Brian, joining us. "At this very moment she's—"

"Oh, my gosh," Guy whispered, turning to the piano.

"You," Claudia was singing, very freely, "do," with her hands folded together, "something to me." The pianist swung gracefully into rhythm, Claudia's hands opened, and the guests gathered round as Miss Glama launched her vaudeville.

Brian told Guy, "You have gifted friends."

The odd thing was, Claudia was good. Hags who take over at the piano usually try to jazz up "Mister Snow" or tack a cakewalk finale onto "My Heart Stood Still." Claudia did not overplay, or blow lyrics, or go flat. She sounded like a pro doing a gig. She and the pianist were so in tune that on the second chorus they jumped the key a whole step without signaling to each other; something in her voice warned him and he followed. There was applause and, after scarcely a second's whisper, the pianist struck up "The Physician," Cole Porter's number about the doctor whose interest in his patient is strictly physical. It's what used to be called "naughty": wittily suggestive if you're worldly but shockingly doubly-meant if you aren't. I wondered how Aunt Eliza might take it. She was oblivious, busy with her inquisition; and those of the guests who were listening seemed appreciative.

"'But he never said he loved me,'" Claudia sang.

"Is she in the theatre?" Brian asked me.

"I believe so, yes."

"She's a brick. You so often hear this song camped about, don't you? But she's ace with it. Fresh." I was surprised to hear this knowledgeable commentary, but then I reminded myself that rich people often know about Cole Porter, because he was One of Them: rich. On the other hand, he was also One of Us: gay. Just then, Guy's father asked if he could speak to me upstairs.

I toyed with asking, "Why?" One advantage in attending rich people's parties is you can get away with anything, though of course they may not ask you back, which is their idea of punishment. But I was here as Guy's diplomat, and felt bound to "suave it out," as Little Kiwi has taken to putting it.

"'But he never said he loved *me*,'" Claudia sang, as I affably accompanied Mr. Webster up another rolling stairway into a room of leather and wood, books and prints—and, astonishingly, an old wind-up Victrola, which instantly gave us something friendly to explore. As every aficionado does, Mr. Webster pulled out treasures to delight me, and, as the disks spun and the uniquely reverberant sounds poured out, I thought of my late grandmother, an unlovably eccentric but fiercely musical woman who introduced me to 78s. Her taste was much like Mr. Webster's: symphony, opera, show music, and dance-band pop. As he retrieved Victor Herbert's recording of his "March of the Toys" from the turntable, Mr. Webster said, "I feel it important to tell you that Mrs. Webster and myself are relieved."

"Relieved?"

"That Guy has finally been honest with us." He said this mildly, as he said everything. "He may have wanted to protect us by keeping his . . . well, his love life . . . secret. But I don't think it truly serves a family to be too discreet. There is such a thing as intimacy, isn't there?"

"Surely."

He put no more records on, so this was what he had wanted to speak of. But why to me?

"I expect it is premature to say so, but I think Guy has done well for himself. I confess, I really wasn't sure what . . . sort of person, if I may say so, we were to encounter."

"Ah."

"Guy tells me you went to Friends Academy together."

"Yes."

"I always think it best when two people share a background. It makes the routine things so much easier." He

148

smiled. "As opposed to the notorious *nostalgie de la boue,* if you'll pardon my boldness."

Suddenly I had the impression that I was missing something. Not as much as I would have been missing if he had been speaking, say, entirely in Lithuanian, but something at the core of the topic.

"How long," he then said, "have you and Guy been lovers?"

That's what I had been missing.

"I will respect your silence," he went on, "if you would rather not speak of this."

I tried to collect my thoughts.

"Do you, like me, speak Lithuanian?"

No, he didn't say that—yet he might as well have done, given the flow of conversation. As so often with closeted scions, the parents were better informed than had been supposed. Well, what do you do when the father of your friend says he likes your friend's taste in romance, as opposed to the hard-hat or trucker he might have chosen if *nostalgie de la boue* had won out? I was still speechless, momentarily bemused by the picture of the meticulous Guy seeking something hot from the underworld. Guy's idea of rough trade is a Raggedy Andy doll.

I had to say something. "Who," I said, "is that masked man?"

"I beg your pardon?"

"My family gives a party like this, though rather more informally. Or we used to give them. And like other Americans we took movies. You know those old home color reels, that you'd send to Rochester in those yellow boxes?"

He nodded, intrigued.

"Well, my parents moved to California not long ago, and before they left we hauled out the films and ran them one last time in the east. There's one of me, at the Christmas party, in a Flub-a-Dub mask. And the strange thing is, I didn't just wear that mask for the movie. I wore it all day, from meatballs to ice cream, no matter what anyone said."

149

"But what is a Flub-a-Dub?"

"The Flub-a-Dub was a character on the Howdy Doody Show. Grotesque, animalistic, and illiterate. His act consisted of mixing up words."

If Mr. Webster was a publisher, he would know a theme when he heard one outlined.

"A rather piquant choice of alter ego for a writer," he observed.

"Well, I'm not illiterate. But I do mix up words, in a way. And the mask is the essential image, not the character."

"The mask?"

I nodded. "I am the masked man."

He thought. "But you were not . . . forgive me—not hired, surely?"

"I was beseeched."

"I see."

"Guy's got a mask on, too. And he'll probably be glad to take his off. If you tell him you know, and that it's all right. . . ."

He considered this solemnly, then slowly unfolded a Mona Lisa smile. "I believe I thought I *had* told him."

"In those words?"

"I don't suppose one ever does anything in precisely the words. You make it sound ingeniously simple. Was it like that with your parents?"

"My parents," I said, "are too attached to their children to let the luck of the draw cause trouble among us."

He thought this over, slowly winding up the record player. "Then," he announced at length, "I will play you one last side, and no pun is intended." It was Fanny Brice's "Cooking Breakfast for the One I Love." Superb. And downstairs we then went.

Claudia was on break, a wee drinkie in her hand, Guy and Brian flanking her.

"How can you not be sozzled by this time?" I asked her. "All those drinkies."

150

"Oh, they're mostly ice," she said. "And I never finish them. Drinking is entirely a matter of style."

"We have to talk," said Guy—but his father, Mrs. Webster attending, was pointing to him the way Guy had pointed to Claudia's glass in The Varsity House. Whatever you want, the rich are taught from infancy, just point to it. Gazing about me, I thought, This is the ultimate completion of the Christmas bachelor: to sanction the festivities of strangers. I hate party small talk. I hate food cut into tiny strips on silver dollars of white bread. I hate being served. I hate Aunt Eliza. How is one to feel his blood at such a party? You believe in the Christmas you were raised on; you cannot cross over.

"What did you tell him?" Guy asked me, a bit later, when he returned from upstairs. "Egad, they're . . . *happy!*"

"I didn't tell him anything," I replied. "They already knew."

"Knew what?" asked Claudia.

"That the world is full of masked men," I replied.

Now we were all summoned to the elders' part of the party, where the presents were to be distributed. There were no forts or gas stations, no megaphone, no Uncle Mike. There weren't even packages. It was all envelopes, even for the littlest kids; and thank yous were not hurled out but solemnly nodded. One gift put a stutter into this ceremonial rhythm, when Aunt Eliza pulled out a battered jewelry box of the kind that Edwin Drood might have kept his collar studs in. She opened it, gazed upon its contents, slowly extracted an antique watch, and said, "Come here, Guy."

He came.

"This was Grandfather's," said Aunt Eliza, her voice cracking. "You must have it now."

Hums and murmurs.

"It has tradition on this Christmas day," she went on. "It has a meaning in the family. And that is the most important thing to have."

There should be film on this, I thought. Too bad there

151

were no cameras about. Cameras and masks and watches, a Christmas!

Aunt Eliza handed the watch to Guy and commemorated the presentation with a crash of her cane. Everyone clapped.

"There are four of those watches in the world," Brian whispered to Claudia and me. "One for each of my great-great-grand-uncles. Three have been passed on, so this is the last of the group."

The casing was silver, elaborately chased, the inner surface inscribed with a name and date, the piece itself extraordinary. That's one thing rich people are good for: amazing presents.

They are also good for inviting you out to the Brasserie for some real food on plates, which Brian did after Claudia had sung another set and Aunt Eliza had raged at a minor cousin who had had the temerity to challenge her politics. I could almost hear her roaring, "Are there no prisons? *No workhouses?*"

We were all somewhat carefree as we paraded downstairs to get our coats, and on the far side of merry by the time we had reached the restaurant and made the first toast, to Aunt Eliza's cane. Brian was a grand host; without imploring or condescending, he made you know that he would feel disappointed if you didn't go for it and order something really spiffy.

I was jovial. Guy was utterly on top of the town, for the only serious problem in his life had been solved: his folks now knew of and proposed to live with his sexuality. And Claudia was shining, with three straight men playing to her—Brian in the literal sense, Guy in the Pickwickian sense, and I in the vaudevillian sense. True enough, she didn't really imbibe, just held. The rest of us, however, drank champagne, and Brian kept it coming. We men had reached that level of sauced euphoria in which we are still physically presentable but our mouths are blurting out confidences.

"This is the one, true Christmas," I heard myself say.

"Really. Consider its parts: relatives, champagne, presents, the Kissing of the Grandparents—"

"You didn't get a present," said Guy.

I shrugged happily.

After Brian excused himself, Claudia announced that she was up for a present that night.

"What?"

"Your cousin."

"Take care, Claudia," said Guy. "Brian's something of a womanizer, you know."

"Oh, that's my favorite kind," she replied. "What's a womanizer?"

"A straight Lothario," I explained.

"I'm in the nude," Claudia sang, "for love . . ."

Guy suddenly said, "You know what they told me?"

"'We still love you,'" I guessed.

"How did you know?"

"They always say that. The nice ones."

"A writer," said Claudia, "knows all the stories."

"Did you ever hear about the gay bachelor on Christmas Eve?" I asked.

"Do tell," said Claudia.

"He learns that if you can't spend Christmas with your family, then you have an adventure."

"That's good to know," said Claudia, "but the important thing is, you look so much better without those dark glasses."

"That may well be," said Guy. "I lost mine tonight, too."

"How does it feel?"

"Sporty."

Claudia raised a glass. "Christmas, love, and peace, fellow gypsies." We clinked and drank. "Now each of us make a wish for the new year."

"Mumps to my enemies," I said.

"No cab strikes," said Guy. "Claudia?"

"No more world hunger and an especially zoomy revival of *Mack and Mabel* with me as Mabel."

"That's two wishes," said Brian, rejoining us. "And who's Claudia?"

"What would you ask for?" she said.

He flashed a Piping Rock smile at her. "I like everything as it is."

That's the rich for you.

Outside the restaurant, we broke into couples, Claudia and Brian waiting for the correct moment in which to hail a cab and Guy and I doing that bashful, recapitulatory ceremony typical of gays who have shared an intimate experience yet do not really know each other. Rather than talk about ourselves, we admired the geography, Manhattan's great stupas lighting the snowfall, the towers concealed in a brilliant mist, the vision a rhetoric of power and daring and elitism. These are the principles of Manhattan capitalism, and its setting that night was an electro-industrial Switzerland, virtually a natural wonder. And we belong to it, and own it.

From a few feet off, the sounds of "White Christmas" floated over to us, Brian gamely holding the descant on "May your days be merry and bright." When we turned to see, they were kissing, and Guy and I shook hands like foxy grandpas.

Off the lovers went, and I walked Guy to Third Avenue before we, too, parted. We talked a bit more, aimlessly, then he put his hand in the pocket of my overcoat.

"This is a present," he said. "Don't take it out till you get home. Okay?"

"But I have nothing for you."

I started to put my hand in my pocket, but he stopped me. "I demand," he said, trying to cow me with his generations. "You already gave me mine."

He pointed at a cab and it skidded over. I watched him pull away, and waved; but the rich seldom look back.

The first thing I did when I got home was to take Bauhaus out for his walk, the second to call my parents, the third to light up a pipe, and the fourth to pull Guy's present out of my coat. It was a silver pocket watch, the inside of the cover reading, "Ch.ˢ Tuyler Webster, 1878."

"He must have been drunk!" Dennis Savage cried when I showed him. "You got him drunk and palmed his watch! You probably get your bed partners that way, too!"

"You ought to know."

"Of course you'll return it!"

"Of course," I agreed, thinking that could take years.

"Besides robbing the rich and starving Bauhaus, not that he doesn't deserve it, what else have you been up to while I was gone?"

"I've been writing up my Christmas adventure!"

"Branching out into science-fiction?"

"It just so happens, Mister Smarty, that I spent Christmas holding a family together, and teaching a closeted gay to have confidence in himself, and setting up a very cute straight couple. What did you do, may I ask? Add to your sister's already legendary Tupperware collection and try to lure your brother-in-law into wrestling matches. What's more, I'm writing a Dickensian story about it, with, I must admit, a modern edge. What have you written lately? And I have learned what place an orphan may take in the Christmas pageant, and that a bachelor may luxuriate in Christmas spirit as surely as any family man. After all, I can't go to Aunt Agnes' for the rest of my life. I can love tradition in other ways. Yea, I can undergo the rites. You think not? You are a benighted queen. I can give and be given to. And, by the way, contrary to what you believe, it turns out that Christmas is about love, after all. The name is love. And I have learned all this, and you have learned—and in any case know—nothing. So what do you have to say to that, you soigné debutante?"

He sat down, crossed his legs, and smiled. He mimed lighting a cigarette, puffing, exhaling. He smiled again. "You know what you aren't?" he said. "New wave."

The Disappearance of
Roger Ryder

Gay life has not only its episodic naturalism—its true stories—but its mythology, too. On those nights out at the Pines when heavy rain prohibits a walk to the dance hall and a table cluttered with dinner things reproaches the slightest attempt to Do Something, one of us will recount a legend or two, perhaps that of the most intense man in New York, or the most handsome, or the most betrayed, or the most bizarre. I prefer the tale of the most disguised man, the one who got to . . . well, listen and judge for yourself what he got. I have told this tale on many a night on the beach, sometimes including my listeners in the action. They may resent this, or laugh nervously, but they attend: for we are in these fantasies as surely as we are in our biographies.

I start with the unemployed actor Roger Ryder, standing on sand in the late afternoon, alone. The straight sweep of the beach, countless miles in either direction, is empty, as the code of the Pines recommends. Everyone else is housed and waiting. There will be tea, dinner, startling recreations: the summer begins.

Roger paces, carrying a Scotch and dying a little faster than the rest of us, because hope is an oik jeering in the gallery. Most actors arrive on some level by the time they're twenty-eight, a minority come through in their early thirties, and a very few squeak by later through fluke or some unspeakable arrangement. All the others—most actors, in truth—wake up at the age of forty to realize that they have scarcely been actors at all. They are waiters or word processors and will never be anything else. Roger, thirty-three-and-a-half, worries more than he hopes.

Once in a while a runner flashes by along the edge of the surf, a pure image of sport, boldness, health. What is their motivation? How would one portray a runner? Have they a rapt childhood, a contentious vocation, a favorite pie? Roger is up for a part in a soap—not a great part, nor yet a great soap. Still, in Roger's profession they say "Everything is potential." Given the right space, the right text, and the right lighting, you can be anything. Roger has played a dragon, a Chinese conjuror, a crazed vegetarian—even Hamlet, in Louisville, where it doesn't count. The dragon, in the second-grade Christmas pageant, was his greatest role; through perverse, cocky ad libs, he made such a hit that he was elected class president for the next three years. Things have slowed up somewhat since, and now there's Roger waiting for a break. Sometimes he tries to will something to happen.

How foolish, the Pines, to abandon the beach when it is most enchanting. By day what a dire festival, as competitive as an Olympic stadium; now, open and accessible under its darkening sun, it is serenely epic. The runners pass through as if anywhere were more useful than here, yet they always come back, their faces as concentratedly thoughtless as before. Who are they? Accountants, physicists, spies? *Waiters?* A man in running shorts tells you nothing.

Another man is walking the beach, about fifteen houses to the west. Black Speedos. Another runner probably, set for the gainless race. Roger sips his drink and admires the sea. Wednesday he has his soap interview; a reading too, if they like him. They might. It's one of those protean best-friend parts they plop in during a lull, to test viewer response before energizing the character with romantic commotion. Trouble is, they never warn you how to present yourself: what to act. They don't tell you because they don't know. They look and they listen. Maybe you hit them right; maybe you don't.

The man in black Speedos isn't heading for the wet sand

where the runners live. He prowls the dunes, like Roger, but not aimlessly, like Roger. As he nears, he breaks into outline: black hair and moustache, broad shoulders, spacious torso, trim waist. Tall and strong, with a take-no-prisoners air. Perhaps on his way to cocktails at the east end of the Pines, where the big money is. One of those parties in which fat garment center honchos audition houseboy talent.

Another sip of Scotch and Roger ambles toward the ocean, pondering Wednesday's choices. What do you project when no one knows who you're supposed to be? The brisk man? The ebullient kid? Sloppy grin, wanton eyes? Keen patter? Or silence? The less you give the more they want.

Give me a hit, Roger thinks, and I'd own this beach. I know how to use power. Especially here—the most sophisticated village in the world acting like the most primitive. It could be a Greek city–state of two or three millennia ago, waiting out a cultural intermission till the next god comes. Thebes, maybe. Thebes awaiting the next god. Turning to the line of houses above the dunes to raise his glass in toast, Roger sees the stranger in black Speedos, forty feet away and heading right toward him. My God, what a stunning man— no, *shockingly* beautiful!

"What's your wish?" he asks Roger.

"I'll bet you've heard this before, but if your smile isn't outlawed, I can't be held responsible for any consequent collapse of civil order."

"Nay, the collapse of order is what I plan."

"Nay?" Roger smiles.

"You must help." The stranger grasps Roger by the shoulders.

"Anything, to put it mildly."

"I've formed a gang. We'd like to tap you."

"Tap me?"

"For the gang."

"I thought 'tap' might be new Castro argot."

"If you join, you get to take any form you like. Physically. *Any form.* You change at will, every detail to your order. The professional advantages alone would be decisive. And socially, the possibilities are infinite, are they not?"

"Could I have my shoulders back?"

The stranger strokes Roger's hair.

"I don't know what you're on," Roger says, "but where can I get some?"

"Join us," the stranger urges. "You might be the thousand most handsome men alive. That would be worth . . . what? A million within three years. And our revenge program guarantees atrocious deaths to all your enemies. Have you enemies?"

"Just my agent."

The shoulders again. "I would be so glad to collect you, young fellow."

"Your place or mine?"

The stranger turns Roger to face the houses, holding him from behind. "So much. Look. You can encircle it. Look. Every day there's more. In a thousand years you couldn't exhaust the supply. And you'll have that long. Imagine. Taste it. Look."

"I love this."

The stranger smooths Roger's cheek. "So many possibilities!"

"You're wonderful. Who are you?"

"*You can change your looks.* Is there a greater gift?"

Roger pulls away. "Listen, ace, are you taking me home or not?"

"I offer you the world and you fasten on one! Use the head, young fellow: if you join my gang, you'll never need anyone again. You'll have it all. If the world is full of splendid men, can one be unique?"

"Okay, okay." Roger's eyes rake the houses. "Okay, whose idea was this? My entire house is on somebody's deck, watching through binoculars, right? Let's send the most gorgeous man in the Pines out to Roger and watch him get stirred up. It'll pass the time till tea. Well, let me tell you, gorgeous is as gorgeous does."

"Hush." The stranger puts his fingers against Roger's lips. "Hush, now." He smiles, and Roger becomes as peaceful as a melted Humorette. "I don't usually have this much trouble."

"I'll just bet you don't."

"Want proof? Where's your drink?"

Roger looks around.

"You had a glass of Scotch when I met you. Where is it now?"

"I must have put it down somewhere."

"Nowhere. We've been standing here the whole time."

Roger laughs. "Poof, you made my drink vanish?"

"Join my gang?"

"Are you going to tell me who you are, or what?"

"I'm the gang leader."

"All right, I'll join. One condition: I want to be initiated by you."

The stranger lets out a low, dirty ratchet-whirl of a laugh, the sole unattractive piece in his kit. "My gang will initiate you."

Roger is silent.

"The deal runs thus. Three months of unconditional transformation privileges, no quota, all types, clothes included. Change as often as you like. When you tire of one look, move on to another, or drop back into your born form as you choose. I ask you only not to take the form of anyone else, living or dead. It gets touchy, and you bring heat down on the gang, and that would make me enormously displeased with you." He very gently rubs Roger's lips with his thumb. "We wouldn't want that, would we?"

Still Roger is silent.

"Would we?"

Roger shakes his head.

"Now, what do you give for three months' free passage in the labyrinth of love?"

"I've been trying to give you my heart for the last half hour."

"It's customary for new members to run errands for us after their three months. We find it a pleasant way to instill a sense of gang loyalty. Unconditional loyalty, I need add."

"'Then is doomsday near.'"

"It's very enjoyable work: introducing corporate executives to drugs of pleasure, luring reformed alcoholics back to dreams of drink, making theatre critics cranky just before a Sondheim premiere, tripping nuns . . . a droll life."

"I don't think I'd be good at it."

"You'd be surprised what you'll be good at after three months of feeling the invulnerability of absolute beauty."

"What if I change my mind somewhere up the road?"

"Can't."

"What if I *do?*"

"Then I'll send for Jocko."

"Listen, does your keeper know you're out?"

"Now it begins. They're massing up for tea, and you'll make your debut. Go. Intoxicate them."

"Don't I get a magic kabunga or something? To transform myself with? With dials for face, physique, and points beyond?"

"Young fellow." The stranger rests a heavy hand on Roger's neck. "Your jesting hurts my heart."

"Why don't you come along to tea, anyway? I love walking in with something terrific."

"This day you will." He gives Roger a push. "Go."

Roger takes a few steps, then turns. "Will I see you again?"

"I'll be checking in to follow your progress. And good luck on Wednesday."

Roger comes back. "All right. Whom do you know that I know, and what's this about, really?"

"This is about deception."

"Yes, I see that."

"You've sharp eyes and a good mind. That's why I chose you. Savvy is moribund; and there's no fun in corrupting the dull. My gang is keen as razors."

They face each other for a moment. Roger nods. The stranger nods.

"You know," says Roger. "I . . . I like . . . the way you call me 'young fellow.'"

"That's all right, then. Come." They proceed to the boardwalk. "Do as I say and we'll be close. We'll talk of things, and I'll befriend you. Now go there."

Roger moves on alone. At the stairs leading to the boardwalk, Roger turns. The stranger waves. His grin shines for a mile. Roger climbs to the walk and, at an idle pace, deep in thought, Dionysus enters Thebes.

Actors are vagabond, and Roger Ryder jumped from house to house over the summers, landing at last with old friends in the thorny forest on the bay west of the harbor. They were short one share, and had been entertaining possibilities, thus far without luck. It was a quiet house, preferring dish to radio and chance to rules. The first weekend, someone brought out a gym-and-disco queen who kept house in a cockring and infuriated everyone with his "party tapes," largely strenuous rock spliced into remarks made during torrid encounters. The next weekend, someone else produced an academic whose field was the use of the gerundive in early-middle Millais. It was his only topic of conversation. A quiet house: but this was too quiet. The third weekend brought a live wire, who had the idea that he must win his place through divertissement. Armed with sets of Scrabble and Mille Bornes ("That touch of camp!" he cried; none knew why), trivia quiz books, and barnyard impersonations, he held the house in rumpus till someone slipped a synthetic substance into his Yoo-Hoo, whereupon he organized a variety show and led off with an act of pastiche farting, in the styles of various show biz personalities. Then he passed out. Heading for the Botel, everyone was in a sour mood, because, really, was there no one of minimally acceptable appearance, character, intelligence? Is that asking much?

Tea was tea, changeless: a validation of the eternally renewable fantasy. No backstory compromises the breadth of shoulders, no giggle ridicules the stomach-waist declension, no keening mother or kvetching father humiliates the ambitions of a truly inspiring nipple radius. Mystery, here, is the one honesty, truth in a glance. There is, sure enough, the tactless intimacy of gathered data, when last summer's most spectacular houseboy turns up in something like a dress, or when a man celebrated for decades appears sagging at the belt line. But there is always something new to browse. There is fame; there is notoriety; there is absolute visibility. And the day that Roger Ryder's housemates came fretting out of their cottage, still smoking from the entertainer's fire, someone whirled up out of nowhere and, in an instant, the hundred men present glimpsed, feared, and loved him. "Man of death!" Roger's friend Paul breathed.

Everything was big, pointed, bold. A fairy must have spun his golden hair, a sculptor cut his lines, an alchemist dyed his green eyes, a watchmaker tightened his parts.

He smiled at Paul.

Paul whispered, "He burned my face!"

Fifty men fell silent; the other fifty began to hiss. The blond stood at the top of the entrance stairs and scanned the population. He saw plops wither, clones glumly marvel, contenders defensively flash their best feature, two adorable punks silently whimper, and a smashing muscleman—who had one flaw, a raucous nose—shudder and go slack.

The blond strode to the bar and smiled at the bartender. "Let me have a beer."

The bartender also smiled, and didn't move.

The blond put a hand on the bartender's, caressing the middle finger. "Hey. Hey. How about that beer?"

The bartender stared. "Coming right up." Yet he was still.

"Take your time."

The bartender rummaged in a trance behind the counter. "One . . ."

"Beer."

". . . right . . ."
"Any brand."
". . . and . . ."
"Bottled or canned."
". . . yes . . ."
"Preferably bottled."
The bartender gave him three glasses, seven twists of lime, and a box of napkins. "On the house," he murmured.
"Thank you."
Suddenly awake, the bartender found a can of something. "And the beer, of course." He essayed a laugh.
The blond took another survey of the space. His eye lit upon a dark-haired youth whose cynical, hot-angles face played a fetching contrast with his elegant, hot-curves physique. The youth felt the blond's eye, turned to meet it, looked away, looked back, and held it.
The crowd rustled in wonder.
The blond nodded thoughtfully.
The youth walked up to him.
The crowd tensed.
The youth looked at the blond; the blond leaned over and whispered in his ear. The youth looked down and carefully nudged the edge of the blond's foot with his own.
The crowd moaned.
Locked eye to eye, the blond and the youth left together.
And fifty men turned to the other fifty men and said, "I want to die."

At about nine that night, Paul was checking the lasagna as Albert set to designing the table settings. "Origami napkins!" he decided.
"Penguins," Paul suggested. "Or little dinosaurs."
"If only I knew origami," said Albert.
The entertainer was still passed out.
Franklin got off the phone. "Even Barry Thompson doesn't know who he was. No one has ever seen him before. He's literally unheard of."

164

"Maybe he's Alexander the Great come back."

"Alexander was short."

"But great!"

"Barry says half the Pines has been ringing Wayne Calder's house and no one answers."

"Wayne Calder?"

"The boy he took home."

"Just remember," said Paul. "I'm the one he smiled at."

Roger came in.

"You missed everything!"

"'The players cannot keep counsel,'" Roger replied. "'They'll tell all.'"

"The *most* incredible man—"

"To die!"

"Wearing nothing but—"

"And whispered as if—"

"Stop." Roger peered into the oven. "Oh good, lasagna." He grinned at them. "I happen to know the case."

"Who is he?" They crowded, sat near, posed, twirled. The fun of the Pines!

"Who he is is not clear." Roger poured himself a drink. "But it is told that Wayne Calder wept for happiness as he was being stripped."

"No!"

"Name your source!"

"And, in a dear moment, they tell, Wayne murmured, 'If an officer finds us, we'll be put in the brig for life.'"

"Scream!"

"No!"

"*More!*"

"The question is," said Franklin, "is Wayne Calder beautiful or just sexy?"

"He misses being handsome," said Albert, "but the body is truly historic."

"Here's what I want to know," Paul put in. "What did the mystery man whisper to Wayne before they left?"

Roger said, "He whispered, 'I want to lay you on your back and deep-pump you full of joy.'"

Silence.

"The tactless majesty of the beautiful," Roger called it. "They speak their own language."

The conversation eventually passed to other matters, less weighty, such as true love, taxes, and who else might be invited to take up the outstanding share in the summer rent. Roger excused himself for a walk. While the others were clearing the table, a chestnut-haired Viking in jeans and a leather vest appeared at the door.

"Hi. Is Roger Ryder around?"

"No," said Paul. "But I am."

"Roger went for a walk," said Albert. "He'll be back any minute. Would you like to wait for him?"

"No, thanks. Just tell him I was here, okay?"

Albert's mouth had opened and Paul was hugging himself. Franklin coughed.

"What . . . name . . . should we give?"

The Viking treated them to a lovely laugh. "Describe me."

"Did you see that?" said Albert in a stage whisper as the footsteps died down the walk.

"Do you suppose he's in the same house as the tea man?" asked Franklin.

Paul sank into the sofa in a daze. "I'd wear a leather vest, only I catch cold so easily."

"Does a laugh like that get born with you?" Franklin wondered. "Or do you have to practice it?"

"This," Albert swore, "is going to be an arresting summer."

The Viking thought so, too. He raced down to the beach and danced in the darkness, his arms beating salutes in the air. Throwing off his clothes, he dove into the ocean where the moon gloated and swam like a champion. It's so easy! So incredibly easy! No doubts, no mistakes, no waste! A no-fault existence! We speak our own language!

166

He raced the wet sand like those crazy runners; so easy. Tomorrow, he'd give them a beach parade to set legend, then tea again . . . maybe something in a rough punk this time, with stupid eyes, the kind who dance as if their stomach were a snake. Cresting the stairs, he paused, his upper back shivering in the cool night, and he spoke his own language. "All you have to be," Roger Ryder said aloud, gravely and slowly, as if promising to take good advice, "is terminally beautiful."

The soap interview was a breeze, but what wasn't, now? For an hour or two, Roger stood at a crossroads: should he show up in one of his new "modes," as he called them, or in the form that matched his professional track record, résumé photographs, and appearances in Madame Podyelka's acting class? The modes, he had noticed, effortlessly won; the old Roger had had to fight for everything. But perhaps a separation of parts was not a bad idea; perhaps looks belonged to romance and talent belonged to acting. Pretty-boy roles were boring, anyway; they seldom led to anything but your total replacement two years later by the next pretty boy. This soap was unreasonably loaded with beauties as it was; two had been written out in the last three weeks. Roger decided to go as a character: as Roger Ryder.

They liked him. They liked his walk, his hair, his bluntness, his watchband. They liked his self-confidence, one of his best acts, always. They asked him where he had been hiding, and he laughed because the night before he had been hiding in the mode of a simian wrestler who dazzled a jaded veteran of Sheridan Square with his dangerous thighs, his unexpectedly shy recollections of life in the ring, and his mastery of the spanking arts.

They asked him why he had laughed, and Roger said, "Well, I'd say it doesn't feel like hiding. On the contrary, it's a rare chance to validate your feelings."

What is? they asked him.

"Acting is," he said.

167

They brought in an official to meet him and had him read. They told him to try one longish speech as if he were wildly in love with the woman he was addressing, a second time as if he hated her, a third time as if she were his dying mother. Then they took the script from him and asked him to play it from memory, because television is tempo, tempo, and the halt are left behind.

He won; and again he was thinking, It's so easy—before he remembered that this one he had done by himself.

We'll call your agent, they told him, and, you know, it'll go through channels, and like, keep your weekdays free starting June 5, and no, there's no script yet, so come in early and you'll have the morning to get used to it.

No language has words for how an actor feels when he gets a hot job without half trying and work starts in a week and this part can take him *anywhere*. For starters, world history begins to seem trivial in comparison with your future, and your feet get bigger. No, they do!

"You look happy, young fellow."

"You!"

"I knew you'd have good fortune."

They had met near Columbus Circle, minutes after. "You didn't . . ." Roger began. "You can't arrange this, can you?"

"I like my boys well placed," said the gang leader. "Depression clouds the mind. Euphoria clears it. The Norse thought the essential quality in a hero was luck. I like the Norse. Good lines."

" 'My wit's diseas'd.' "

"Ah, but you don't lack advancement, that's the important thing. Where will you go tonight? What will you be?"

Roger wondered about that every evening, as he prepared before a full-length mirror behind the bathroom door. He was a Mr. Wizard of the vanity lab, learning by doing. He would experiment with shapes of nose, depths of navel, formats of chest hair. Marvellous how the flesh instantaneously responded to the will; the imagination is quicker than the eye. But when you're already in the topmost class, what sets you apart from the others such—what's 101 percent? A really slick haircut? Roger fleetingly played with innocuous yet arresting flaws—scars, a mole, wild eyes, a limp. Maybe a cane? What will you be? he wondered again two nights after the soap interview, in the apartment of an old Village avatar, a king of the leather scene in the early Stonewall years and nostalgically resonant even in semi-ruin. Roger, a busty buckaroo, had taken particular care with his face that night, molding till he had something truly shattering. The old leather king very nearly shook his head in disbelief as they traded stares in front of Clyde's.

"I can't decide," he told Roger, "if it's the eyes or the mouth."

"It's both."

Two blocks away, in the tiny studio that had played host to uncountable young princes, Roger saw how raptly one obeys the command of attraction, what concentration lies in the borrowing of beauty. "As you open my pants like a burglar," the leather man breathed, and "I have no choice, as you lead me by the ass to the bed, to get me all set, to ream my ass out for me whether I'm willing or not." Captions to pictures Roger had never seen. "I know what it is, man," the leather man said as Roger laid him down. "You like to see some big stud throwing his rod as you stretch him out, huh? Big, fuckable stud, big dude, to give you what he has. Is that it? Tell me about it. Tell me what you're going to do."

Why should I? Roger thought. You're doing fine all by yourself.

"You make me so hot," the man went on. "And you know it. You're gonna go ahead with it. Yeah, you don't care. Like some guy I met once, this trucker, this big hot dude. Jesus, he was tough." Roger tried to shut him up with some mouth-to-mouth, but he talked right on through. "Oh yeah, romance me. It's so nice. So nice it hurts. So this big dude tells me he knows this guy who makes porn movies and maybe he should audition me. Yeah. So I said I don't know about that stuff, man, and he says, Just come here so I can

169

loosen you up. . . ." Roger stroked the man's thighs as he eased in and at last the man was silent, except, just before he came, when he whispered, "Oh, you are so damn what," which is a somewhat notable thing to have said. And no sooner were they disencumbered than the man more or less threw Roger out.

"I couldn't live up to that, man," the old king told him when Roger asked him to lunch the next day. "I mean, I have my good days, but . . . hell . . ." He looked at the wall, at nothing, faded squares where once hung nude photographs of an achingly beautiful man, this man. He laughed ironically, to please himself. "It's both."

Amiably donning his Stetson, Roger said, "Are you saying you didn't enjoy that?"

"No. I'm saying you didn't."

What will you be? Lose the cowboy, Roger warned himself. It's too hot for that clothing, anyway. I'll be contemporary, loose. No more mercy fucks for old-timers. Let's try some California-style kids, sheer looks and no complications. Three nights later, in the mode of a preppy football hero, Roger picked up a boy hovering near the garage of an office tower. Roger had seen him there before, whistling at women with his co-workers in the garage and setting the pace for the lunchtime stroll. Straights yield to beauty just as gays do, working-class straights especially, because they don't know how to behave around women who aren't their mothers. Instead, they court men.

This boy told his pals that Roger was a cousin and ambled up to him as if a motor were humming in his mid-quarters. The cheek, Roger thought. The cocky lack of cover dodges. That's what they're like; confidence turns them reckless. And their pals will look away and change the subject. His pals did. Everybody spoils them.

It took a long time to land the boy; they like to be persuaded in code. On the way to Roger's, they paused at a sidewalk fruit stand and the boy coolly palmed an apple while the proprietor was helping a fastidious business wimp collect a ripe banana. What did he save, fifty cents?

Roger cursed himself for caring. He tried to think of the boy's callous devilry as showmanship. The boy chomped on his booty as they walked, mouthing out "Like, man" and "Yeah, like" as if they were basic punctuation. He undressed like a peep show come unsprung, giggling and posing. Roger fucked him savagely, to avenge the stolen apple. The boy got mad and shoved Roger off him, so Roger grabbed him by the hair and bounced him off the walls. He was mad, too, it appears.

The boy cursed Roger as he dressed. He kept saying "Fucking crazy, man," and finally Roger grabbed the boy and his clothes and threw them all into the hall. The boy had to snatch the bannister to keep from flying downstairs.

"'Don't know m'own strenth,'" said Roger, in Bullwinkle's voice. You never know what you'll be.

Some actors see life as fun and work as terror, but Roger viewed acting as relaxation. If you're well cast and you know your lines and your public is with you, what else should it be? For the first few days in soap, his part consisted of showing up in General City, embracing about thirty-five relations in law and flesh, befriending twenty men, coming on to twenty women, and, at fadeouts, looking enigmatically menacing. Anyone could play it. But the first mail was good, and being recognized in D'Agostino's by appallingly delighted housewives of both sexes amused Roger. He admired the speed with which the whole thing moved, from "story lag" (the time between script composition and public airing) to "set time" (the taping). Once, they told him, their second biggest male sweetheart was written, taped, and presented dying in a hit-and-run automobile accident, all in four days.

Everyone should live this fast, Roger exulted, stretched out on the couch as he answered his housemates' daydreaming questions about the sudden rash of devastating strangers in the Pines. Sometimes he claimed intimate connection to well-sourced dish; at other times he chuckled when they challenged him. All the questions were, What are they like? Yet everyone thinks he knows what they're like. They speak their own language, converse in the instructive pictorial of bodily parts. To note face, shoulders, hands, is to know what they're like—everyone *thinks*.

How amazing, Roger thought, to know.

One thing he could tell about them: they are never shy. By the time they're seventeen or so even the dullest of them has noticed the interest he excites in others, in the way women show their feelings a little for him, and the way men try to cover theirs. Nice-looking people can be shy, but spectacular people have had it too easy to hold back.

There was a nice-looking fellow at Roger's soap; no one, ever, was shyer. He had virtually grown up on the program, playing someone's child through from early adolescence into young manhood. Roger's character was intricately and repeatedly related to his, yet thus far they had met only in the green room during breaks. His name was Roger, too, yielding a dozen nervous-actor jokes and breaking the ice for them.

"Sometimes I think it's safer to play the sidekick parts," the boy told Roger. "I've seen hot shots here today and . . . you know? But look at me. Twelve years of steady work. And I don't have to do anything. What else could I do, anyway? I never had . . . an ambition. I do what I'm told and I collect my check."

"You don't get much to play with, though, do you?"

The boy shrugged. "I'm not an actor. My dad was in TV then, so they cast me. And I'm easy to use, so I'm still here." He put down his sandwich and shook his head happily. "Believe me, plenty were who aren't."

He had a nice way of shaking his head—a nice head to begin with. He saw Roger watching him and looked away. "Maybe I shouldn't tell you this."

"Why the hell not?"

"Well, you . . . you never know how people will react."

True. Investigate a brazen Puerto Rican in a black muscle shirt and he'd turn out to be soulfully in need of cuddling; a taciturn bruiser might sniffle at an ambiguous comment; a dizzy kid would sacramentally produce rope from under the bed, his eyes on ice. You never know what they'll be.

Now, in Madame Podyelka's acting class, you knew what your fellow actors wanted to be just by what they did with their hands when they began a scene. You knew how the others would react, too. The performer's friends would offer praise tempered by quibble; everyone else would rip the scene to shreds.

"Children, it is life," Madame Podyelka would cry. "It is truth. Outside, it is false. Mistakes. Undirected."

"Do you think acting class would help me?" Little Roger asked Roger Ryder the day he blew a line three times in a row.

"Want to sit in on one? Madame loves guests. She thinks once anyone comes to an acting class, he's bound to come back for more."

"Where is it?"

"In her living room."

Little Roger shrugged in amazement.

"Madame thinks stages inhibit actors. She emphasizes acting in the round."

"I've never acted before an audience," said Little Roger. "I've never even auditioned. I was almost born on TV. Why don't you take me dancing instead?"

"Want to go to the Royal Party?"

The boy tried, failing, to look comically sly. "Does Erika Kane need a tongue-lashing?"

"You know, she's very sweet offstage."

Madame says, "Darlings, there is no offstage. There is not thinking. There are empty performance. Now, let's all practice our anxiety cough. *Odin. Dva . . .*"

Roger had gone out in the mode of a Colt model, more or less, picked up a real one, and had a jazzy time till the next morning, when the model went into a harangue about the infiltration of the American porn industry by extraterrestrials.

173

He gave Roger the ticket to the Royal Party. "They want the best," he told Roger. "Bring your hottest friend."

Everyone was there, they say, but they always say that: to those who weren't. There had been confusion as to how the title related to costume, so some came dressed as royalty while others simply behaved as such. A few discovered intriguing new places in which to wear crowns, and there was an unusual emphasis on drag. But otherwise the Royal was like all Great Parties, a place where one came to worship beauty and to dance—sometimes, but not usually, the same thing. It depends on who is dancing.

The two Rogers did some, but for much of the time they lurked among the sleek clutter. Here and there they grinned at each other. Once, in the excitement, Little Roger put his hand on Roger Ryder's shoulder, almost in passing; sure homage from such a bashful fellow. Paul and Albert came up to rave for a bit. At one point Albert gazed upon Little Roger, then nodded slyly at Roger Ryder.

"Oh! 'I Need a Hero'!" cried Paul, as the music swept in. "I have to! I have to!" He grabbed Albert and they rushed onto the floor.

"Do they think we're lovers?" Little Roger asked. He had seen Albert's signal of approval.

"They think we're dating. They'd think Nixon and Mondale were dating if they walked into a room together. Albert and Paul are romantics."

The boy pocketed his hands, released them, pocketed them. "Are we dating?"

Franklin wandered by. "I hear we have a new housemate."

"Anyone I know?" Roger asked.

"Silly boy," said Franklin, wandering off. "Albert told me *everything*."

Roger hugged Little Roger. "Want to dance?"

Later, waiting for Little Roger to return from the men's room, Roger heard a familiar voice over his shoulder: "The whole gang is disappointed in you."

Roger turned.

"The party of the year, and you come as yourself with a bus-and-truck Heidi."

"He's a nice kid."

"He's dreary as three Kansas picnics."

"I've been all over town, right? in a hundred snappy disguises. Don't I get a night off?"

"Not this night. Here's Georgie. Georgie ought to dance with you."

Georgie, in T-shirt and jeans, looked like the man in whose honor clonestyle was developed. His name was tattooed on his right biceps.

"I don't like beards," said Roger.

Georgie's beard vanished.

"Georgie," the leader warned, "no showboating."

Georgie took Roger by the arm. "Let's find a quiet corner," he said, "and get you nice and ready."

"Wait a minute, I have to—"

"Make it tasty, boys," said the leader.

There was no evading Georgie, Roger sensed; he'd get it over with and find Little Roger in good time. Way off at the edge of the party they found an angle shrouded in darkness. Georgie stood point, his huge back and long arms covering Roger as he flashed into mode as a surfer, dressed to match Georgie.

"Yeah, give me lots of package," said Georgie, feeling Roger's crotch.

"Let's do this thing."

Roger was so used to shifting look that he seldom bothered to view his changes anymore; he saw enough in the eyes of his witnesses. They followed Georgie and Roger as they eased onto the dance floor, reoriented themselves to observe Georgie and Roger, were heard to sing when Georgie wheeled behind Roger to simulate a humping motion.

"Let's take our shirts off together," Georgie whispered, his cheek smoothing Roger's hair. "Do it real slow, where you pull up from the waist with your hands crossed."

175

Who made him the director? Roger thought; but he did it, because once he had stood at the edge of this scene, wondering what doing it felt like. Smirking at each other like Krakens at a wake, Roger and Georgie parked their shirts in their pants; Georgie moved close to Roger and unfastened the top of his pants. "Yeah," said Georgie. "Now you. Me."

"I don't do windows," Roger replied.

He was about to leave the floor when the clacking of castanets caught his ear and two spectacular men joined them, similarly undressed, one—on the lean but lavish side—playing the instruments and the other—titanic—carrying an assortment of metal equipment on his belt. Each of the newcomers also bore a tattoo on his arm, like Georgie's, "Tony" and "Keeper." Grinning at Roger, Keeper, the metal man, flipped the top of Georgie's jeans open and ever so slightly nodded his head. Georgie reached for Roger and bought his lips with his own. Roger began to struggle almost at once, but Georgie held him so fast he couldn't even shift position, much less get away. Keeper sidled around, pinned Roger's arms behind him, and handcuffed him. Roger sensed every eye in the room on him as the other three men began to stir, sensed that he had been plugged into the vertigo of a million hungry men. Doing it is an elite fantasy for the conqueror; being done to, however, might be all-encompassing. Those who most fiercely resist it pay its fiercest homage.

"New boy, come," Georgie urged. "The handcuff dance."

Tony played his castanets so sweetly that Roger was mesmerized, as by a caress. In another life, somewhere, he heard clapping, music, dishing, shouting, and Keeper telling Georgie, "Make him happen." Swallowing his panic, Roger forced up a smile and slowly shook his head. "Take the cutlery off," he said pleasantly, "or I'll change into a hippopotamus in front of a thousand curious bystanders."

"It doesn't make animals," said Georgie.

"Arnold Stang, then."

"You're no fun," said Georgie, shooting an angry wink at Keeper. Roger was freed. Marching into the crowd to find

Little Roger, he met a rota of stares, as searching as Diogenes. Why was it so easy to smile? Some of them were loving couples, cheating. Roger could not bear a cheat. He found Little Roger sitting on bleachers near the refreshment table, looking like E. M. Forster when he realized that he might have sailors but would never be a sailor. Better: when he realized that, hell, he wasn't even going to have sailors.

"Hey," Roger said, tapping him on the shoulder. "I have a message for you from Roger Ryder."

"How did . . . I mean, what message?"

"He told me to tell you that he's networking with some advertising people. Stay put and he'll be with you in a few minutes. Okay?"

Little Roger stretched his legs and smiled. "I'll be here."

"One more thing."

"Yes?"

"He says he likes you."

Roger ruffled Little Roger's hair and sped away to meet the gang leader; trouble is never hard to find in an elite gay festival.

"And what," Roger began, "was that punk vignette supposed to be about?"

The leader made the naughty boy sign at Roger, left index finger scraping right one. "You were rude to the gang. Surely I told you how much we count on loyalty."

"Call your hunks off me. I'll make their acquaintance in my time and in my way."

"What better way than at a great place of the culture, and thus, in the disorderly conduct that inspires a million dreams?" He looked almost reverant. "You belong with your kind. You mustn't squander the elegy on wallflowers. You are to be our great invention."

"If you think I'm going to spend time with brainless disco freaks . . . You said they were sharp. And what's all this with the tattoos, may I ask? May I?"

"You'll have one." The leader traced a line of sweat

down the center of Roger's chest. "When your three months are up. Yes, young fellow. You'll take a look of choice, and your new name, and a whole catalogue of chores. Beauty is never boring—and you will party."

Roger calmed down, even laughed. "I still don't believe any of this." He reached behind for his T-shirt. His back pocket was empty.

"You don't believe? In the borrowed eureka of a Galahad? Don't bother; I disposed of your shirt. I hate over-dressing."

"Why don't you use your magic to build up my career?"

"I intend to, when you take the pledge. I fancy we'll call you Gordian, because you make everything so complex. But there is a central cord of inspiring simplicity: you need to succeed."

"That's true of anyone."

"At what, hey? Georgie only wants to dance and sleep. Keeper's great truth lies in the singing of lullabies to runaway orphans."

Roger surveyed the men promenading past them, looking, not looking; bright, drugged; dateless, booked. "And Tony?"

"The band's musician. An offbeat fellow. I support almost any kind of debauchery, but Tony is so heavy that when you speak of a conservative scene he assumes you mean the guillotine is hand-worked instead of electrical. Picturesque. And not without contacts. He was with James Dean at the end. Messy; that was before Jocko joined us."

"Who is Jocko anyway?"

"Jocko is the most irresistible man in the world. Our safety. The exterminator."

Roger looked at the leader, long and hard.

"We have to enforce discipline, no? Be sensible. Don't make me angry. Be useful. Actors can be so influential."

"Look, it's not . . . I don't get what I want out of it."

"You get what there is."

"It was fun at first, but they started stealing fruit and—"

"All men are alike."

"—babbling about aliens—"

"All men are whores."

"—and—"

The leader took Roger by the shoulders and bore down on him. "Trivia," he growled. "Performance is the factor! *See?*" He dropped Roger onto a bench. "I can't bear to hurt a beautiful man." He sat next to Roger, held his head, stroked his stomach. "Look around. Isn't it heaven?"

"You're beginning to sound like a costume designer."

"Take a sizzling young cocker home and break his heart or something. Do it for the gang."

Roger got up.

"For me?"

Georgie, Keeper, and Tony barred Roger's path, Tony's castanets dourly cackling.

"Let him go."

Roger went.

"I know better ways."

Roger was so eager to get back to Little Roger that he scarcely bothered to hide his transformation. Three men saw him change out of mode, so debilitated by drugs they could scarcely be said to have eyes at all.

"Your friend," said Little Roger. "No, listen. How did he know who I was? In this crowd?"

Roger paused. "I told him what you were like, so he knew what to look for."

"Come on."

"My point exactly: come on."

Madame Podyelka says it is very easy to play five things at once, harder to play to three, hardest to play one. "Intensity, children," she advises, "is never boring."

At Roger Ryder's apartment, Roger played desire and Little Roger played nothing, hardest yet to play of all. At a point, you must face the other eyes, and then how can you give them nothing? You can look away. But the rest of the cast will touch you.

179

"Would it be hard to believe," said Little Roger, "that this is my first time?"

Madame says there is no debut. "We have been acting since we were born."

"Just tell me what you're going to do," said Little Roger.

Madame says, "We play the roles as we are cast."

"This is nice, so far," said Little Roger.

"We are cast," Madame adds, "as we need to be."

Roger Ryder has sometimes wondered why, throughout history, men have risked ghastly consequences just to get someone into bed. It can't be for love. Is it because spectacular figures promise a density of sexual release not otherwise to be had? Is it for power or to make a wily story?

Maybe it can be love.

When Roger awoke in the middle of the night, he pulled a corner of the blanket over Little Roger's shoulder, and Little Roger, sleeping, patted Roger Ryder's back and said, "Okay, okay"; and the next morning they chattered while Roger Ryder made coffee, then drank it in silence; and when they were dressed and about to go out, Roger said, "Look—" and Little Roger said, "I guess—" and Roger was amused to think that spectacular men can say anything but everybody else has to speak his mind or stutter. These two decided not to say anything, and walked to the studio in happy confusion. On the way, a soccer player with the shoulders of Beowulf and a name tattooed on his arm waved at Roger.

Madame Podyelka may have been a charlatan, but any class that gives the actor a chance to perform is useful, and Madame's living room was filled with a colorfully various crowd. There were the few gifted actors, a natural clique respectfully hated by the second-raters. There were the opportunists, who would not rest till they were banking movie money. There were the non-pros, using the class as therapy for social problems. Most various of all was Madame, her fingers covering her mouth or eyes as she heard a scene, her body at a tilt, as if to look straight upon the art were to see it too well.

"Now, children, who will give us an improv?" Madame would say in her tenderly inarticulate palette of accents, roughly, "Chu fill gef es in em*prof?*" And the chosen one would be directed to the center of the room and excruciated in free-associative skits. Other students were called upon to play adversary roles, always The Father, The Mother, The Lover; and it was notable that, for all her almost brilliantly irrelevant advices, Madame always cast these supporting roles from the ranks of the crack troops. In his first days in the class, Roger Ryder had been about to drop out when Madame called him up, assigned him his prototypal partners with a doleful wave of her hand, and gave him the most provocative experience of his career. "The Father is very wrathful," Madame moaned, "because the boy wants to be an actor and not go to doctor school."

The Father, a compact, somewhat collegiate chap who had taken part in the Marriage Contract Scene from *The Way of the World* the week before, bore down on Roger with the eyes of Moses and the hands of Grendel. It wasn't Roger's story—his parents were lifelong theatre buffs—but it was *someone's,* surely, and the two men fought as if there were agents in the house.

Roger was barely holding even with The Father when Madame wailed, "The Mother lives only to quarrel with The Father. The boy is her weapon!" Was he ever. Two minutes later, when Madame had Roger seek sympathy from The Lover, he found himself shaking in her arms.

Odd how profoundly someone else's story can affect us. Roger scarcely heard Madame's analysis of his performance, or the tense discussion that followed, though a few assaults on his "honesty" pricked his ears. "It *was* honest, darlings." She turned to Roger. "Was it true?"

"It was . . ." Roger hesitated. ". . . fictions."

Behind him somebody snorted.

"It is a story," said Madame, smoothing out her dress. "It is a role. Is it a true story? Or just a pretty story?"

"I thought it was true," said The Father. "I felt it."

"Of course," said Madame. "I know that you feel, even if you are not tall enough for father parts. Next time, you must portray a tubercular heiress' sympathetic physician, from a poor family, and everyone has no neck and tiny eyes. Now, children, let us discuss *commedia dell'arte a soggetto.*"

Roger viewed improvs with a loathing fascination; they shattered one's defenses instructively. On the Circuit, from the Eagle to the Botel, one mastered evasions; improvs taught plain speech. Cramming soap script in the green room before set time, Roger realized that Madame had made him too good for soap; it was her kind of story, all confrontations, but the lines spun circles of themselves, with little hooks on the ends to snap into the next episodes. Roger's character had become enmeshed in an adulterous triangle, the refurbishing of a luncheonette by idealistic kids, and a tangled international espionage scheme. But, as the writers had to keep everything elastic, he had yet to utter the simplest declaration. It was a job, and a good one—but not acting. "'Why this is hire and salary,'" Roger told his housemates at dinner, "'not revenge.'"

"Have you noticed how much sexier Roger is," said Albert, "now that he's made it to TV?"

"Fame is sexy," Little Roger explained.

"I'm not famous yet," Roger said.

He was something comparable: a batch of notorious men. The Viking, the wrestler, the Colt model, and Roger's other modes were seen and seen again, at tea, on the beach, on Christopher Street, in Bloomingdale's, always in the inviolable solitude of self-esteem. He was emphasizing a short-and-slim creation, a teenager with extraordinarily pale skin and black hair. Everything about the youth was tender and subdued except his cock, which was perversely big. The one time Roger wore this mode to the gym, three men followed him from the locker room to the showers, one to glower, one to dote innocently, one to look pleadingly at him. The Father, Roger thought. The Mother, The Lover. Strung out on the opposite wall and knowing no joy. As the other two watched, The Lover crossed to Roger's side of the room two nozzles away, then moved to the shower next to Roger, so close you could smell the snot hardening in his nose. Roger turned his back on him, but The Lover sucked in his breath and ran a finger up the crack of Roger's ass. Roger jumped as if bitten. "Please," The Lover said. "Just let me touch you . . . please." As he knelt, Roger grabbed his towel and fled.

"At last you're playing for the team," the gang leader told him, tying his sneakers one locker over. "The boys will be so thrilled. They still resent your failure to dance for them at the Royal Party. Keeper says we'll have to tattoo the name Trouble on you, because that's all you are. You know, I believe I like you best of all like this. There's something so dangerous in the mating of youth and power. I notice you took that nerd out to the Pines last weekend. Don't, again."

"I don't take orders from you."

"Nay, you will."

"All right. Now, all *right!*" Roger dug in with a look. "So I ups to him," Jimmy Durante used to put it.

The gang leader examined himself in a mirror.

"We have to talk," said Roger.

"Bench press," said the leader, flexing his pecs. "Go for the burn."

"Listen."

"You made a deal. You were told the rules. You will observe them."

"It was a con. You knew I didn't believe you."

"Monty Clift tried that on me. Look what happened to him."

"It hasn't done anything for me."

"You're not using it, young fellow. You're so bright. Keeper and Tony, now, they are totally unreproachable in bed, ruthless kismet. But they lack smarts. I know. You know. They know. We want brains. That was you, my boy.

You were to be our entrepreneur. And look what? An affair with something in underpants from some shopping mall in New Jersey!"

"How about letting me ride my own wishes?"

"On whose magic?"

"No fightin' in da locka room, peoples," said the attendant, not looking up from his magazine.

The leader pulled Roger into the Jacuzzi room. "I dispose of the gift as I see fit!" he cried. "Six weeks of dabbling remain; then you work for me. Need I recall to you that the more you please me today, the lighter will be your chores later?"

"Fuck him! Fuck him now!" The leader and Roger turned to find the three men from the shower watching them. "That's what he wants!" The Lover spoke.

"No, it isn't," said Roger.

The Lover pushed forward furiously; the leader grabbed him by the hair, swung him around, and threw him against the wall. "Make him know!" The Lover screamed from the floor, as the other two discreetly dispersed. "Doesn't he deserve to know?" The Lover leaped up at Roger, and the leader downed him again with a kick to the stomach.

"Know what?" Roger asked.

The Lover keeled over, holding his belly and dry-heaving.

"Come," the leader told Roger. "Get used to it."

"Know what?"

"Yes; show no pity. I love a heartless man."

"Why should I pity him? He attacked me."

"Come."

The improvs impressed Little Roger, when he came along to Madame's.

Make me know what?

The improvs free you to say what you wouldn't dare say as yourself.

And Little Roger was coming out to the Island, though he could not afford to become an official housemate. He

184

stood on the top deck of the Fire Island Empress and shrugged because some of the passengers were old, and some were unattractive, and some were grouchy. "It's time they knew," Little Roger told Roger Ryder.

"Knew what?"

Little Roger was willing, nay eager, to try an improv. "What makes you think I can't take it?"

"Okay."

"I *can*."

"Children, what could be meaner?" Madame would say. "But an actor's life is a chain of improvs. No?"

At the soap, they asked him, Could he do a romance with Tina?

"Sure," he replied, though he had a feeling that somewhere deep in the show's plotting he and Tina were blood cousins.

"You haven't gone anywhere in three days," said the leader. "I'm violently peeved."

"Say nothing!" said Madame. "Be *eyes!*"

Yet her improvs were not mimed.

"Darling," she said to Little Roger, "it is now. We will let the friend play The Father, yes? So fitting. So true. And no Mother or Lover. We keep it simple, da? The Father is mad at the boy because he can never do a thing right. The boy is sensitive. The Father is strict. Out of ferocious love, he must teach the boy discipline."

Madame set them in an amusement park. "The boy has an ice-cream cone," Madame intoned. "He must not drop it. *Ferocious love.*"

Fear in his face, Little Roger endeavored to eat his ice cream and earn approval.

"The father loves the boy no matter what he does," Madame groaned.

Roger Ryder played a terse, conflicted father.

"The boy drops the ice cream," Madame mourned.

Roger Ryder slapped Little Roger's face. "Don't cry," he warned, "or I'll slap you again. *Don't you dare cry.*"

Little Roger cried.

Roger Ryder held him. Ferocious love, he thought. The caption.

"No," said Madame. "Yes, but no. It looks so pretty but it is not correct."

"Why was the little boy sad?" asked a student. "Children have the world to play in."

"It was sentimental trash," said another student, an actor who had never had a job in his life except as a masseur. "I feel degraded by your performance here today."

Roger Ryder still held Little Roger.

The leader had trouble finding Roger Ryder alone after that. They met at length early one Friday afternoon as Roger came out of the Pines Pantry with the groceries. "What drivel about an ice-cream cone," the leader reproved. "Real men don't have fathers."

Roger Ryder smiled vaguely.

"Real men kill their fathers, perhaps metaphorically."

Roger walked on.

Keeper loomed up a few yards down the walk in what appeared to be cellophane jodhpurs.

"Hi, Keeper." Roger gave him a minute flash of the Handcuff Man as he passed. "Taking your Hallowe'en early?"

"Yo hey, good buddy." Keeper fell into step with an arm around Roger's shoulders. "Listen, you got to make good with the chief. He gets mad at you, boy, and you are in *bad* news."

"We'll work it out somehow, I guess."

Keeper shook his head. "You don't know him. He goes crazy when he's mad. He's got like . . ." —Keeper searched for the precise term— ". . . these magic powers."

They had stopped at the ferry landing. At the far end of the harbor, a boat was gliding in.

"You got somewhere we could talk, man?" Keeper asked. "For your own good." Roger Ryder dumped his grocery bag on one of the benches facing the water, and sat.

"Talk, Keeper. I'm ears."

186

"Yeah. Because I just want to help you, see?" Keeper sat. "If you play along, it's a breeze. If you don't play, you lose bad. Now that is the deal. You got no choice. Look, I know you're smart. But I've seen smart guys go up against him before, and they all go down. They *all*. What've you got against us, anyway? We have fun."

The boat disgorged its singles and groups of clones and queens, reveling and grumping, along with the usual persistent straights, largely Mr. and Mrs. Potato Head couples from New Jersey.

"We have fun," Keeper repeated.

Roger looked at him, weighing the risks in honesty. Oddly, Keeper had not chosen to be handsome. It was a rugged face, a good match for the implausibly supreme physique, but not likable. The eyes were nice.

"It's not fun, Keeper."

"You aren't doing it right. Why don't you change into a runaway orphan and come home with me? I'd sure be sweet to you. You wouldn't have to do a thing. I do all the stuff." Keeper was murmuring, drawing Roger close. "Wouldn't that be nice? I love it when a little orphan begs me not to hurt him."

Roger shot him a bad look.

"Now, I never do hurt them. They just think I will because orphans are the most helpless little cuties there ever could be. Don't you see that? Huh? They're so hot when I teach them how to coco."

"Stop. Stop."

"Yeah—"

"Keeper!" Keeper stopped. "It's just not my part, okay?"

Keeper started again. "Do you do the muscleboy who needs a trainer?" He took Roger's hand in his. "One-on-one."

"Keeper, *no*." Roger pulled his hand away, rested it on Keeper's arm.

Keeper shook his head in disapproval.

"Listen, is that arm real or magic?" Roger asked.

187

"My muscles are mostly real. But I had no chin." They watched the last tired travelers shuffle off the boat, a queen led by an avid dachshund and two plops. One of the mainland teenagers who work the ferry line was rehitching the tyings as they passed, the queen pouting in mock swoon and the plops staring as if eyes were wishes.

"It's funny," Keeper went on. "We don't really look different now from before. You go wild during the first three months and then you settle down into something like you were. Just improved. Except Jocko—he's always changing around somehow. You should stay away from him, man. That dude is radical."

"Keeper, has anyone gotten free?"

"To what?"

"Free of the gang."

"That's what I'm trying to tell you. *No way.*"

"He tricked me. I thought it was some kind of joke—"

"You *used* it, man! He gave you what he promised and you took it. Now you're on the slate, you got to chalk up. Want to sit in my lap and I'll rub your neck?"

"In the dead center of the Pines on a Friday afternoon?"

"So somewhere else."

Roger laughed. "Tell me, do you catch as well as pitch?"

"I pitch to guys who are smaller and I catch from guys who are bigger. Except so far no one is."

Roger looked out at the bay and bit a thumbnail. "Keeper, is this all on the level?"

"You know what side I'm on, man. But what I'm telling, I'm telling straight."

"You want to shake hands? Man-to-man, solemn and honorable?"

"Hey," said Keeper as they shook.

Roger rose. "I like the way your eyes crinkle, Keeper."

"Come here," growled Keeper, throwing his arms around Roger. They held each other for a long time; when they broke, two handsome men on the top deck of the ferry cheered. Roger blushed. Keeper looked on as if he'd never seen a blush before. He felt Roger's cheek and said, "You're a softie, man. You'll never make it. You'll have to give in. Let's go."

Roger retrieved the groceries. "'It would cost you a groaning,'" he replied, "'to take off mine edge.'"

"Ah yes, the Mousetrap Scene. Have you played Hamlet, then?"

Roger blinked at him.

"Besides having no chin," Keeper explained, "I taught English at CCNY. And, now that the jig's up, take a note of caution: 'The play's the thing.'"

"'I'll mark the play.'" More sobered than diverted, Roger left.

"And?" asked the leader, joining Keeper on the bench.

Keeper shook his head. "He will not give."

"The harder the conquest, the surer the surrender."

"He thinks," said Keeper, biting off the words, "that he has something better."

"Gently so."

"Under that bon vivant facade is a smug little snob."

The ferry slowly backed up, veered 120 degrees to starboard, and chugged northward toward the bay.

"When he's done," said Keeper, "I want him. No limits. Okay?"

"Yes, sweet Keeper."

Even if he hadn't seen the look of confusion on Little Roger's face, Roger would have known that something was wrong; one needs a second or two to adjust to the added weight, to the different balance, to being who you are. Yet not till he set the groceries down did he realize who he wasn't: the Viking had suddenly materialized, in running shorts and a cowboy hat. He put the hat on the counter next to the groceries.

Little Roger sat there.

"Roger asked me to drop by," said the Viking.

"He's . . . networking?"

"Not any more."

It is hardest to play one thing. *Odin. Dva.* . . .

Little Roger got up. "Where is he? Now."

The Viking shrugged.

"Are you staying here?" Little Roger asked. "Do you want something?"

The Viking smiled.

"The others will be here soon."

The Viking said, "You look nice."

"We haven't met, have we?"

"We are meeting."

The Viking moved first, but Little Roger stepped forward, too. He smoothed the Viking's arms and sides as they kissed. There is no offstage. The Viking pulled down the boy's swimsuit and heated him up party-style. Little Roger dug his hands into the Viking's shorts and edged them down to his knees. The Viking stepped out of them, murmuring, "Yeah," as he fondled the boy. "Yeah," he urged. "Yeah?"

"Yeah," said Little Roger.

We play the roles as we are cast.

The Viking lifted the boy in his arms and carried him into Roger Ryder's room. He knew where everything was, every prop and feeling; and the one thing that he played was treachery. His own, and others'. A great many others'. So it was not one thing. It was a rich act. Roger noticed, as he expected to, that the boy responded to the Viking with unaccustomed enthusiasm, all shyness put by. Whoever thought he was innocent? And whose improv was it? The leader's.

Roger lay with the boy for a bit after he had had him, stroking his flanks as he purred on his stomach, his legs spread and his toes twitching for more. "What do you want me to tell Roger?" the Viking asked him.

The boy froze for a moment, then went limp again. "Don't tell him anything."

"If he asks, what then?"

"Lie."

"Not for you."

The Viking showered, donned his shorts, and stood in the doorway. Little Roger flipped over onto his back and kicked his legs together in the air. He seemed utterly content. "Where is your house?" he asked.

The Viking said nothing.

"Will I see you again?"

"No."

The Viking left the cowboy hat on the counter.

Roger Ryder found the leader sitting on the bench where Keeper had been. "Now what?" Roger asked him, sitting down.

The leader patted Roger's knee. "It hasn't worked out, has it?"

"Are you going to let me off?"

"Keeper yearns to date you. Will it be tonight?"

"Listen."

"Bad news at your soap, though. I hear you'll be dropped from the saga presently. 'Indefinite leave,' they call it. How did your little friend like the Viking?"

"So you did that."

"I gave you the outfit, no more. What was done, you did. You look so sad. Will you weep?"

Roger shook his head.

"Lucky, with all the boats pulling in. We wouldn't want to be the subject of satirical remarks. Do you surrender? At last, young fellow? Your time's nearly up, anyway."

Roger shook his head.

The leader tenderly scratched Roger's hair. "What am I going to do with you?"

Roger looked at the leader for a long moment. "How can you do this?" he said at last.

"You mustn't be manfully pathetic. Anything but that—one look and I crumble." The leader laughed his nasty noise. "I've taken everything from you. You have no work and no love. What more must I do, tear down your apartment building and revoke your plastic?"

"You cheated me."

"You cheated me, young fellow."

"I won't work for you. I'd rather die."

"Your mind is locked on this point?"

"Yes."

"Nothing will sway you? No consideration of fame or beauty?"

"Worthless."

"Is it now?" The leader sighed profoundly. "Keeper will be so irritated. I expect I'll have to send Georgie to the bus station to find another runaway orphan for him. But so be it. You're too sensitive for our kind of fun. Go. Take another of your reflective walks along the beach. No doubt the whole thing will pass like a mad fancy."

Roger stared at the leader. "Are you . . . letting me off?"

"Let's say that I'm dismissing you. Now go."

Roger ran till he reached the edge of the sea, to wade into it, splashing like a dope and feeling himself emotionally for the sense of reprieve. No one had taken anything from him, in fact; he was back where he had started, a mere summer older with plenty to do. He walked west, watching the sun burn red and the clouds catch it till the sky streaked fire. He would continue to worry more than he hoped, but that was true of most of the people he knew. The ones with great apartments were bored; the ones with great jobs were lonely; the ones with great lovers were penniless. No one has everything. If you could take true satisfaction in any one thing of your choice, what should it be?

Curious shapes drew Roger up away from the water to an amazing monster of a sand castle, a city of tunnels and turrets. Roger looked in wonder. How was such a thing sculpted? With molds and dainty instruments, perhaps, from some antique seaside toy box? It was Eldorado, Xanadu. Who had put in so much time on such a doomed project?

Away up on a patio someone was waving. Roger looked

around; he was alone. He waved back, and the figure signaled him to come over.

I don't know anyone in this part of the beach, Roger thought. As he drew near, he saw a man in cut-off jeans, a hooded sweatshirt, and dark glasses.

"I saw you looking at the castle," the stranger told Roger. "It's like a dream. Come close. Yes. Look." The stranger aimed Roger at the sea. "The water overpowers the dream city, and it sinks down, and is obliterated."

"Who built it, do you know?"

"Your smile is trembling." The stranger pulled off his sweatshirt, and Roger caught a glimpse of the man's tattoo as he reached for him. Roger struggled as the first wave swept upon the castle.

"Not yet," Roger cried.

"You won't feel a thing," said Jocko.

BUDDIES

To
Chuck Ortleb

Contents

Acknowledgments

The author wishes to acknowledge the guidance and stimulation of his editor and friend, Michael Denneny, who has committed a substantial portion of his career to the nurturing of a literature for the age of Stonewall. Some years hence, when the chronicles are written, his entry in the indices will be rich.

Introduction

The French tend to write about manners, the Germans about knowledge, the English about sex. Americans write about families, gay Americans particularly. The gay writer's unique contribution to literature, the *Bildungsroman* of gathering self-awareness and coming out, is essentially a family novel; and our secondary invention, the New York camp-surreal romance, is notable for its desperate flight from the family, its attempt to reconstruct an existence without any relations but those we choose ourselves. Yet our family haunts us, like it or not, in allusions rapt and rueful. At times, all gay fiction, even (perhaps especially) porn, seems fascinated by father and brother figures, masked and idealized as passing strangers, companions, lovers.

The human need for romance, for erotic affection, is basic to storytelling. Most narrative art, from *Ulysses* to *Carousel*, from *The Sheik* to *Love's Labour's Lost*, celebrates it; and it is everywhere about us in our daily lives, in the touch of strolling couples, in scandals and wedding announcements in the newspapers, in acceptance speeches on awards nights. This is why the younger and less worldly gays are surprised when straights express irritation at the slightest public show of gay romance. Gays think there's room for everyone; most straights are willing to make room for gays on the condition that gays pretend they don't exist. Thanking one's wife for support is a convention; thanking one's male lover is a subversive act.

Yet, despite straights' lack of comprehension and outright intolerance, gays inevitably comprehend straights, because, whatever our sexuality, we all grow up within the straight culture as participators. You can be homosexual from birth, but you can't be gay unless you voluntarily enter the gay world, a culture all its own. Gays understand straights; but straights don't understand gays any more than whites understand blacks or Christians understand Jews, however good their intentions. Gay is a unique minority: strictly elective. If, called to the colors, you resist, no one may ever know who you really are.

This may be why *The New York Times* is so fanatic about terming gays "homosexuals." It's like calling blacks "niggers," calling Jews "kikes." It demotes them, questions their right to a culture. But black and Jewish separateness is inevitable; visual, aural, historical. Gays don't *have* to be gay. Denying their right to be is the act of a repressive father trying to herd errant sons back into the heritage, into the life's roles assigned them: back into the family.

So if the gay and straight worlds touch, it is only in the experiential sensibility of gays. Yet the two share one important element, a need for friendship, for nonerotic affection: for buddies. It is an American obsession, from *Moby-Dick* through *Of Mice and Men* to *The Sting*; and American gay life, in what I believe is its most compelling iconoclasm, has bettered the straight world in combining romance and friendship. One's lover is one's buddy—and who knows if the father- or brother-lover is not meant as much to eroticize one's only lifelong relationships as to soothe the less permanent relationships of one's love life: to accommodate the fierce and the tender, rivalry and alliance, at once?

This book is about these unique friendships, mostly gay ones but also some straight ones and even a few between gays and straights. Here, too, are fathers and brothers and recountings of family legends, of men in their youth, when rivalry often develops more naturally than alliance. In an earlier story collection, *I've a Feeling We're Not in Kansas Anymore,* I tried to show how gay life behaves; this time, I want to show how it feels, how it pursues its self-discovery. This book is different also on the technical level, structurally, for these are more pieces than stories, counting character studies, nostalgic recollections, and essayistic analyses as well as outright tales.

As before, my setting is New York, where gay has most thoroughly, most variously, come out. If the first will of Boston is work, the first will of San Francisco is sex, and the first will of Los Angeles is money, New York cannot choose. It needs all three at once, and so do my characters. But they need one other thing, perhaps above all: comradeship. I have known men whose need drove them to a multiplicity of sexual adventures with partners they knew as slightly as possible, and men who could communicate sexually only through a personal intensity. Men who would do anything but kiss, and men who did little else. Men who would Go With Anything and men who could only touch themselves. Yet all traveled the Circuit, treated the metropolis as their private lonely-hearts club. Sometimes I think they seek someone better than they are; sometimes I think no, they seek themselves. And sometimes the two searches are one. This is what makes our times interesting.

On the Care and Training of Parents and Siblings

An introduction to the whole, in which our boy propounds his rules for growing up and coming out.

My two younger brothers have driven up from Los Angeles to visit my folks in Sacramento; I call in from the metropolis, New York. Brother Andrew is on the phone, and in the background the dogs and Mother are barking. "No, you can't make pizza!" she cries. "Get out of the refrigerator! Where did you find that revolting shirt? Your socks don't match! Wash your hair! Who left these dishes in the sink? Don't you *dare* touch that cheese—I said you cannot make pizza! The kitchen is closed! And stop that belching; I'm not one of your contemporaries, you know!"

"Guess who hasn't mellowed?" says Andrew.

Actually, she has. My dad, as a character in my childhood, was as peaceful as a Rodin, ensconced in his chair, dreaming deep in a book (whereupon we kids would hit him for advances on our allowance— by my fourteenth birthday I was overdrawn through 1997). But Mother was a series of interrogations, moralistic harangues, and grouchings. She would even attempt making corporal correction upon us (we would simply head for the dining room and run around the table until she wore out or caught my littlest brother Tony). Two less alike parents there never were. Yet they agreed on the basics: love them, give them culture, and treat them for life as if they were permanently stuck at the age of eight.

1

Parents are tyrants, even the nice ones. I recommend taking the offensive as surely and early as possible, never letting up—and my system works, for I had a reasonably cute childhood, an amusing adolescence, and a profitable teenage career. My oldest brother Ned, a vaguely Fitzgeraldian figure, made a stab at defining a code for us kids, but it wasn't a *conquering* code. It reflected too much, stuttered, yearned. A code should confront. Ned was more afraid of taking power than of suffering engulfment. Through trial and error, I trimmed his romantically elaborated novel of wistful resistance into a terse handbook whose name was *Defiance*:

Rule One: Don't try to love Them; just get along with Them. Love in families only makes for ghastly scenes that will haunt you for life.

Rule Two: Obeying Their rules only encourages Them to create new ones. *Dis*obey as often as possible: for gain, for sport, for the art of it.

Corollary: Pursue the rebellion by being perversely nonconformist in all things—try, in fact, to act as if you're committing an enormity even when what you are doing is technically permissible. For instance, on the day report cards come out, you—having achieved straight A's—arrive home with your face alternating looks of shame and dread. They will pounce on your card, gloating and drooling as they dream up new and terrible punishments. Then They'll see the honorable grades, perhaps Teacher's enthusiastic commentary (". . . though he does insist on organizing chic brunches during blanket hour"), and They'll begin to blush, stutter, babble. Don't grin at Them, revealing the art of the stunt: look innocent and ever so slightly wounded. They'll avoid you in fear for days.

More quotidian possibilities include eating corn on the cob with a fork (the kernels come off in sedate little rows, which for some reason exasperates all the males at the table) and developing ersatz but noisy phobias about bridges, escalators, and religious activities of any kind.

Rule Three: Never lie. Childlike honesty throws Them completely off. Moreover, as parents are virtually made of lies (e.g., "Don't be afraid of bullies; stand up to Them and they'll run away," "If you stop

crying and wait till we get home, I'll make you an apple pancake,"
"We have no favorites; we love you all equally"), your speaking truth
undermines Their ethical position. Furthermore, lying is a sophisticated art generally beyond even the most gifted youngster. Almost any
effort is doomed. And, remember: your failure is Their success. It is
essential to avoid any error that will invigorate Their sense of power,
and Their joy in that power. The sight of a small boy pathetically
trying to worm his way out of a spanking enchants Them even more
than administering the spanking itself. If you must be spanked, de-
spoil it of all savor. Be cold and adult about it, like George Will at the
dentist. Or try to look embarrassed for Them, as if you had spotted
Them committing some atrocious peccadillo in a secret spot. Advanced students may want to Do the Manly Thing and insist on taking it bare-bottom. With all but the most diehard parents, this will
force Them to retreat, perhaps even apologize.

Rule Four: Abjure reason and justice; only strength counts. As the
tenant of a house owned by grown-ups, you are not the inhabitant of
a moral universe: you live in a world populated exclusively by winners
and losers. Show me a good loser, and I'll show you a loser.

Rule Five: Choose the major battles very carefully. Go to the mat
over bedtime, food, and presents, major issues that will color your
existence for nearly two decades. Don't overextend yourself fighting
over the small things—and of course it's useful every so often to give
in and let Them think They're in charge.

This was where Ned went wrong. He let Mother set policy on such
vital issues as whether or not he would stay up late on Saturday nights
to watch *The Gale Storm Show*, or precisely what comprised an acceptable vegetable plate, but would fall into a Gatsbyian gloom over
the shade of brown in his new shoes. Romanticism is impedient in
childhood; it turns one inward, toward poetry perhaps but away from
power.

One must be Nietzschean. One must exercise power to gain power;
and be prepared for violence. Isn't liberty worth it? True, I blush now
when we all get together for viewings of our ancient home movies,

when reel after reel reveals tantrums and riot: devastated birthday parties wherein I smash boxes of insulting gifts to the keening of wounded aunts; peaceful afternoons in the backyard worried by the sight of some crazed adult chasing me through the trees after a revolutionary act; festive recreation around some neighbor's pool suddenly humiliated as I push deck chairs, a chaise longue, and the local poodle into the water because the hosts were serving an inferior brand of candy bar. So: there is no glamour in power. Yet it is worth taking; one ought to win; the winner lives.

My classic seizure of power in the house was The War of the Antiques; but I hesitate to set it before my readers, for fear they might turn from me in disdain and contempt—as, indeed, many have done at our celebrated metropolitan brunches, or at predisco cocktail stations, even at one Thanksgiving I spent with my *Pooh* editor Jerrett and her friends, grown-up children of the sixties, of the Great American Generational Rebellion, and surely thus receptive to a saga of youthful insurgence. Shock of shocks, when I told my tale, the Thanksgiving guests sat silent in suppressed fury, the men brandishing their fists, knuckles white, and the women shaking their heads in dire sympathy for the enemy, Mother.

The antiques, yclept Mary Gregory, were vases, flagons, bowls, and utility pieces of every imaginable kind, made of colored glass and marked by silhouettes of children painted in white bas-relief. Mother conceived a fascination and began to collect, filling the house with Mary Gregory, floor to ceiling in every public room, or here or there, especially vulnerable, on little marble tables. After some years, Mother had cornered the market, for each piece was one of a kind, hand-crafted, the only version of itself there would ever be. Mother even became Known For Her Collection, an exciting suburban event. Impressively hefty magazines you couldn't purchase in Wilkes-Barre bore her name, our name, my name; one even sent a photographer to the house, where we all posed before a particularly bulging breakfront, never knowing that I was shortly to engage a very pungent history with Mary Gregory. A true enthusiast, Mother assembled subsidiary processions of Mary Gregory's imitators, easy to unmask, with their uncomely colors and uncouth silhouetting. It was about this time that I undertook application of Rule Five, and it seemed to me that threatening to smash whole rows of antiques might enable me to defy oppressive edicts.

Do you dare? you ask, boys and girls? I scarcely thought about it as a dare. I saw it as a dash to freedom. Remember, reader: it's winners and losers.

I don't recall the issue that sparked my first sortie, but it turned into a "No, I won't!" "Yes, you will!" contest, broken only when I moved to the nearest breakfront, placed my hand at the end of a long shelf, and proposed to shatter two bud vases, a pillbox, three cigarette holders, a stationery chestlet, a mail caddy, six barony cups, a mirror case, a matchbook trunk, and an animal bank (Mother said it was a napping cow, but it looked like a deranged yak taking a whizz) if I didn't have my way.

Mother refused to give in and made a grab at me; foolish Mother—she knew me better than that. The ensuing crashes brought the entire family in, and the thunder was fierce. Yet I was already at another shelf, threatening, threatening. There were a few such episodes, but at length Mother had to surrender, for if I needed to I would gamely have raged through the entire Collection, and she knew it. Oddly, one piece I had had my eye on for some time ultimately eluded me: Grandpa busted that one (by accident, but then everything grandparents do is by accident). This piece was a gigantis egg, silhouetted to death and revealing, when opened, a miniature decanter and eight tiny toasting glasses. It was so spectacular—Mother said that Mary Gregory aficionados considered it the climax of the line—that we had never used it. Yet, with a sweep of his hand, inveighing in some political context, her father dashed it to the floor. The egg was so complex an architecture that the breaking noises went on for some little time, and serially, like the minuet movement in a twelve-tone suite. First, the egg itself went *crash*. Then the decanter and a glass went *floink, dizzle, kinkle*. Then the bracings gave and the egg's outer surfaces diminished into crystal sneezes. At last the remaining glasses gave up, each with its own *kmlip*. Mother was holding me in despair: for only I, of all, knew what she was giving up.

I believe it's that last aperçu, of the two hostiles pledging sorrowful complicity, that sets everyone off. Oh, it's *too* much! Why was I not punished, beaten down, chained, imprisoned? We just didn't have that kind of family. And look on the bright side: by partitioning the collection I at least drove the price up on all Mary Gregory, thereby heavily reendowing the surviving pieces.

Naturally, such exploits are designed for large families like mine, wherein the sizable cast of characters crowds the days with incident. It helps especially if one's brothers get into trouble by themselves; this deflects attention from one's own eccentricities. Andrew, for instance, was always losing things—hats, lunchboxes, pencil cases, a galosh. Once he came home on a rainy day missing the hood of his slicker, and it wasn't even detachable. Mother raged. "*Why* did you lose your hood?" she kept asking. "I want to know *why!*"

Years later, he and I reviewed the event, and he pointed out how senseless these questions were. "It was an accident," he insisted. "There is no 'why.' It just happened."

"It doesn't just happen that you lose a raincoat hood that doesn't come off," I told him. "That's like losing a leg of your pants. You *did* something to it."

"Well, what about the other times? 'Why did you lose your hat? Why did you lose your gloves?' That's like asking 'Why did you get cancer?'"

The foolish boy; one must interpret. "She didn't mean 'Why did you lose your hat?'" I explain. "She meant, 'Stop losing things, you sordid fool.'"

Actually, Andrew sometimes got into scrapes that made my antique wars look like a scuffle over dominoes. A favorite example in the family is the Celebrated Pizza Incident, the most notable event of the year we spent in Venice. In the square dominated by La Fenice, the opera house, there was a trattoria with outdoor tables that served the most exquisite little pizzas to order, and, as Piazza la Fenice stood on our walk home from the Danieli boat that took us, that summer, from the Lido back to town, we became familiars of the place—Andrew in particular. He is, without question, an outstanding amateur of proletarian junk food. He would babble in his sleep, and—aside from an occasional romantic confession—the burden of his nocturnal text was "Pizza and hamburgers," repeated over and over, sometimes for an hour. Naturally, he became the most intent of us all on afternoon pizza breaks. Sometimes Mother would agree, sometimes not. One certain day, Andrew demanded, and Mother resisted. Tomorrow, she said.

But tomorrow she was too tired. The next day.

The next day she had a headache. Another time.

No. Andrew would not budge, and the rest of us stopped to wait. There were rules about such things, at any rate a custom. One remained neutral, no more than a witness. (This suggests a corollary to Rule Five: Don't take on your siblings' battles. You have enough to do winning your own.)

"You said *today*," Andrew insisted, his head bucking as if for attack.

"I have a *headache* today," said Mother, rather dangerously.

Ned shot me a look reading, "This is not suave"—his fiercest condemnation. But Jim shot me a look reading, "Let's see how it comes out"—for nothing failed to amuse him.

This is how it came out: Mother solemnly promised that we would have pizza tomorrow, no matter what. Not today, but—*absolutely*—tomorrow. Andrew accepted this and home we went, over the Accademia Bridge and around the corners to 127 Rio Terra dei Catecumeni. But on the way, I told Jim I was a touch worried about the grade of commitment in Mother's promise. He said, "So what? It's not about us, is it?" This is the converse of the corollary to Rule Five: Don't count siblings as allies.

Anyway, the next day, when the moment came, Mother decided it was too late, too hot, and too nervous for pizza; perhaps she resented being boxed in by a promise. Or who knows what was happening?—

but Andrew had her by the contract and would not yield. "You promised," he kept saying. "You *promised.*" As we others stood around, the
two of them debated it, Andrew (about ten years old then), staunch
and stony, shaking with righteousness. She had put him off for days.
She had left her promise. He *must* collect.

"All *right!*" Mother roared, leading us to a table. "I'll show you!
Yes! Yes! I'll show you promise! Yes, *promise!*"

We ordered in an atmosphere laden with airs of betrayal and coun-
terbetrayal. But the pizzas came, hot as hell, and Andrew, forking his
in a hell-for-leather escapism, accidentally flipped it up into the air
and down onto his lap.

"So!" Mother cried. "*Now* you see! *Now* you'll learn! When I say
no, it's *no*. But you insist, do you? *So!* God hears us. God *sees!* And
God will make punishment! *Yes!*"

The hot cheese was eating right through Andrew's shorts; in fact,
steam was rising in their color, and he looked as if he were in shock.
Ned was regarding the façade of La Fenice as if moved to poeticize,
and Tony had begun to eat his pizza. Jim simply got up, smacked the
food off of Andrew's lap with a napkin, pulled his pants off, and tossed
our cold drinks at his flesh.

Andrew lived. But he glowers, even rages, when this classic tale is
retold. Brothers were born to glower. You can make peace with parents eventually, but only somewhat with brothers. Actually, if possible
it's best to keep sibling combat to a minimum. Why spend energy on
your fellow oppressed when the true war impends with the authorities? Besides, one should maintain diplomatic relations with
one's brothers for later years, when they come in handy for lending
money, showing up at Christmas so you won't have to, and serving as
models for villains in one's fiction.

I must admit I slipped here. Fighting with my brothers was irresistible, as stimulating as a Crusade. Unfortunately, as the middle child,
I had the natural military advantage only over my two younger brothers; and one's more instructive battles tend upward, in audacity:
against older ones. Actually, Ned ignored me—he ignored the entire

family and finally ran off to Europe without saying "May I?" and became a reporter for the Paris *Herald-Tribune*. But Jim and I were born to battle. He was only a year older than I, counting in years, but had a good decade on me in smarts. Some of his wisdom he passed along to me in an alternative handbook, *On the Care and Training of the Entire World*, with such rules as "Never let anyone know what you're thinking, but make sure they hear what you say." He was a cool number, distantly polite when my folks were around, by turns contemptuous or confidential with his siblings, slow to move but fast as the devil when he pounced: an enigma that looked you in the eye. I suppose that, given our respective natures, Jim and I could not have avoided confrontation. He liked a peaceful house, running smoothly on the theory that you verbally gave in to your parents in anything they they wanted; then unobtrusively, off the record, did as you liked.

Under public scrutiny, he was a David Copperfield, perhaps a re-formed Huckleberry Finn; back on the third floor, where we kids lived, he was John Dillinger. My rebellion irritated him; smashing antiques and making provocative statements, he warned me, would "bring heat down on the whole compound." But I could not submit to his two-faced system. I liked the clarity of honest insurrection. My way to freedom had a Tolstoyan éclat; Jim's reptilian accommodations seemed very downtown, mean-streets, like the little white lies work-ing-class men tell their wives when they come home late. He was pragmatic, I symbolistic. So he stepped in, to pacify me and relieve the agitation, and I found myself fighting something of a two-front war.

At least all this violence prepared me for life in New York. Long before I heard about mugging, I experienced it, in The Attack of the Moon Mice, a ritual of seek-and-destroy that Andrew and Tony con-cocted under the influence of horror movies, psychodrama, and Sat-urday morning cartoon shows. Starting in the bedroom they shared, they would crawl through the house, gnawing the ankles of any hu-man who happened by and chanting their louche anthem, which ran, in its entirety, "*We* are the *moon* mice/We *grunch* all your *stuff!*"

Reaching my room, they would crash in, snapping their jaws and trashing everything they could get ahold of before I could repel them and institute Draconian retribution. Of course they would go right for the Oz books, the records, and everything else I most valued. Worse yet, the moon mice would attack even when I wasn't around to defend my treasures.

Once I came home late from soccer practice, exhausted and exasperated. (I know soccer is in nowadays, but in my day it was the fag sport. However, Friends Academy had no gym class. Everybody had to be on some team or other, and the only alternative, football, seemed lurid and bogus.) As I dropped my books on the kitchen table and sank into a chair I heard, in the remote distance, cries of "Grunch his puppet theatre! Grunch his theatre posters!", the unmistakable noises of a moon mice raid. Roaring "I'll murder you alive!", I hurtled through the house to my room. It was a shambles, but deserted. Had they fled? Were they hiding? I sensed a presence . . . the closet! Fools, you have trapped yourselves. Gloating at the thought of chopping them into messes, I grabbed for the closet door. It held fast. I pulled, I tugged, I turned. No! They had locked themselves in from the inside. Damn, these crazy old houses.

"Come out of there, you cretins, and take your deserts!" I shouted.

Silence.

"I know you're in there."

Nothing.

"I'm going to get you if I have to rip that door off with my bare hands."

Whispers.

"If you don't come out by the count of three—"

The closet exploded in a hail of coats, headgear, shoes, games, and books, and out poured the moon mice in full cry. "Grunch his room!" they caroled, as I struggled to catch them. "Grunch his desk! Pull out the drawers!" Andrew exulted. "Pee in his bed," advised Tony. The things they think of.

I don't remember how this episode finished; there were so many of them. Did I punish them for six days and six nights when I was twelve, or for twelve days and twelve nights when I was six? Was I harsh? Mother says I became a writer solely to sentimentalize a vicious past, to cast myself as an innocent trying to get along. Yet consider what I was up against. It was not only moon mice raids and the battles over bedtime, never finally won—for, like evil Sauron of Middle Earth, parents may at times retreat but will never give in. It was the totalitarian climate of the American family in general, the tenderness applied as blackmail, the mischievousness expressed as "concern." It was the simple day-to-day madness of intimate strangers experimenting on one another. By day Andrew might be Tony's ally; after dark he would join up with me in the kitchen, where Tony, the world's foremost aficionado of presweetened breakfast cereals, would in advance of the morning have laid out a bowl, filled it with Sugar Jets or such, and arranged the box at an angle conducive to breakfast reading. Andrew and I would look upon this egregious decadence holding our noses, then, with delicacy, would each drop a dollop of spit into the bowl.

Don't look away, reader; for a wise man, asked what were the three most powerful forces in the world, answered, "the revenge of fathers, the suffering of mothers, and the guilt of brothers." To which I would add a fourth, the memorable vehemence of a mother whose kitchen has been violated. Eager to free herself of having to make lunches for her little men, Mother taught us all how to make bacon and eggs. On the other hand, our pottering around in the kitchen—anywhere in the house, really—made her nervous. She was only content when we were asleep or away. One day, I was fixing myself lunch while the maid, Mildred, sat to a cup of coffee, muttering gospel to herself. Confidently juggling the toast, the pans, the bowl, and so on, I poured the boiling bacon fat into the great American coffee tin with one hand while I broke the eggs open with the other. Too confidently. Fastening the plastic lid on the tin, I lost my grip and plunged my hand into the fat, yanking it out to see layer after layer of skin calmly peeling away. The pain was so terrible I couldn't say anything, just

stood there hypnotized. You could die in a kitchen, I thought.
Mildred screamed and Mother came raging in. In silent horror, I
showed her my wound. The damn thing was actually smoking.
"He burned his hand in the bacon fat!" Mildred wailed.
Mother looked at it in cold fury. "And who," she asked, "told you
to make bacon?"

The suffering of mothers! To this day, when I hear the word
"bacon" I can smell my hand cooking—and, as with Andrew and the
Celebrated Pizza Incident, I fail to smile when someone reminisces in
this territory.

The pressure did not let up as the years went on. On the contrary,
as I neared the end of my high-school period, I was expected to take
up the duties of man's estate—to wit, a summer job. The only jobs
available in summers on Long Island, whither we had moved, were
bagging groceries and pumping gas. Of course I refused. I had just got
my driver's license and a motorcycle, and looked forward to idling
away the days with my school chums. What was the point of belonging to the upper middle class if you had to waste a vacation laboring
tediously for a minimum wage? Here we see Rule Five in its most
practical application: this was a major battle.

How to proceed? The devil in me longed for an all-out offensive,
but wisdom advised me to whittle them down, bargain, stall. We skir-
mished. "Next week," I assured them, then the week after that.
"Now," they said—or no allowance. Fine. My comrades had wheels,
so they picked me up and we passed the time at each other's houses.
Who needed money? Anyway, I had a huge collection of rare opera
scores, and could always sell off the duller ones, or those irreparably
grunched by the moon mice, to used music dealers. It was delicious
seeing my parents fume, frustrated by their own law; nothing incenses
them more than a cure that doesn't take.

Finally they pulled out their ace, never before played in our life-
long game: "Get a job or move out."

I moved out. No forwarding address, no farewell, nothing. My father went into a panic, my older brothers shrugged, Andrew and Tony danced a jig and, as the moon mice, held solemn festival in my room. But Mother stormed through the house inveighing against my mutinous wickedness. "No more breakfast in bed for *him*! It's a new regime!" This was her theme song whenever one of us was in trouble, though we had never had, or wanted, breakfast in bed. The very notion appalls me—toast crumbs everywhere and jam all over the sheets. That Mother would make a mantra out of a notion that didn't even apply to the local scene reveals another convention of the parent, the stock retort. (Others in the repertory: "We nurtured you!," "Because I said so, that's why!," and, my personal favorite, "Every day is children's day.")

Naturally I reestablished myself in the family in due course. But I exacted heavy peace terms, including an immediate cash settlement and the promise that this nonsense about a summer job would be decked for life. Mother, when she heard, went into turbulent despair, like the melodrama character who cries out "Foiled again!" And I never did tell them where I had gone, nor ever will. But something interesting happened to me while I was away, and this much I will tell.

I had gone to Manhattan on a lark, yet for a purpose. This was the mid-1960s, before gay had asserted its style, and there were intriguing mysteries in the air, enigmatic looks from strangers as they passed, the sensation of belonging to a club so secret it hadn't yet held its first meeting. I had the feeling that to explode this mystery would be a major rite of passage in my life, the next thing to do now that I was on the edge of leaving home for college and the great world. My day trip to Manhattan, then, was by way of sifting and watching. I sold off a few scores, strolled here and there, and paid a visit to one of my choice haunts, a huge store on the west side of Sixth Avenue in the low forties, now long vanished, that sold old magazines of every kind. It was a grand place, where one could browse for hours as if in a library, and where two dollars netted one a week's elite reading. That

these "back-date" parlors were in fact the early equivalent of the porno
shop never entered my mind. They were stocked mainly with *Theatre
Arts, Popular Mechanics, Life, The New Republic,* and the like; and I
thought these were their intended ware. Actually, the respectable titles
were simply a front for the skin magazines, which—in a time when
Playboy was still considered daring—I ignored.

But while paging through an old *Opera News,* I found hidden inside it another magazine, called *Physique Pictorial* and filled with the
opulent beefcake drawings that I later learned to be the work of that
arbiter of classic gay type, Tom of Finland: men in cowboy hats
lounging by the corral, men in (and promptly out of) leather, lumber-
jacks, lifeguards, hitchhikers, hustlers. I feasted my eyes. I had heard
of this, or imagined it, but had never been there.

"So you've found Griselda's secret file. She loves to look, but she's
afraid to be seen. Isn't she silly?"

I looked up, and there was this tall, thin, fortyish, effeminate man,
arms folded and fingers twitching. I think he worked in the store.

"We call him Griselda," he went on. "His real name's probably Joe,
and he thinks he's fooling the world, reading trash behind the cover of
Opera News." He peered over my shoulder at the drawings. "Oo, look
at that one. Do you know Griselda?"

I shook my head.

"He comes in all the time. Poor thing. She's quite talkative, too.
Tells me all about his wife and his little girl. I hope you're shocked. *I*
am. Poor Griselda's such a mess—everything happens to her. Her car
breaks down, her little girl wears braces, her transvestite balls keep
getting raided. She's all upset now because she has to have a co-
lostomy operation—and she's afraid she won't be able to find shoes to
match the bag!"

He bustled away, and I noticed a pleasant-looking fellow about my
age across the table from me, who had been looking through *The
Illustrated London News.* He seemed as bemused as I was by what
had just happened. Suddenly, we both smiled.

"What was in that magazine?" he asked.

I held up the secret.

He nodded. "Griselda," he said, savoring it.

"I hear his real name's probably Joe."

He laughed. "What's your real name?"

"Dorinda," said the effeminate man, dancing by us. "Am I right?"

Now I laughed.

"And you're Samantha," he told the *London News*. "You know you must have a name that your lover can whisper to you like music. You *know*."

"Frank," said the *London News* to me, with a smile.

"Bud," I said, as we shook hands.

"Frank! Bud!" the effeminate man cried. "Oh, my goodness gracious, it's the Garden City Little League!" Nevertheless, the first meeting of my chapter of the club had come to order. For till that moment I had thought of gay life as a choice of Griselda or *Physique Pictorial* cowboys. It was neither—these are the fantasies of gay. Gay naturalism was Little Leaguers with real names and good manners. Gay was . . . possible, legitimate, a reflection of oneself. Returning to the family nest, I sadly realized that the war would be winding down at home, its great issues dwindled into a nostalgia, into quaint farces flickering through the home-movie projector. Now I reckoned the final entry in the handbook, Rule Six: Self-knowledge is the final power. And I came home ready to leave it.

I have always figured that my family was more or less like others, but the looks of horror my associates give off when we trade childhood anecdotes suggests otherwise. "You did *what* into your little brother's cereal bowl?" they howl. Replying, "Of course, didn't you?" makes it worse. First they're repulsed, then they're insulted. But, mark me, all of them now maintain extremely conflicted relationships with their folks, while my parents and I get on famously. Even my two younger brothers and I, after all that scrapping, get along. (I haven't crossed paths with the two older ones in quite some time now; I believe that trying to accept one's older brothers after adolescence is psychologically unsound, perhaps masochistic, not unlike keeping one's cast-off lovers in spare bedrooms.)

Younger brothers are vastly easier to handle than older, though they do grow up and shed their vulnerability. Tony is now in computers and Andrew took up weight lifting, went into business, and became generally impossible to push around, even arrogant. I think I liked him better as a moon mouse. Nor does he approve of my cataloguing our past in these pages. After reading one, he said, "You should be locked up!"—I wonder if he knows why. Mother thinks these pieces would read better if I didn't keep trying to slip touching incidents into them. Ours was a crisp family, no sentiment, except for my dad. His idea of family is like a TV Christmas special, in which six or seven grown-up, married offspring congregate at the manse with recriminations, wonder, outcry, two dozen grandchildren, and, at the fade, embraces and joy.

But our real-live Christmases are like "The People's Court": strict, neat, plain, at times grimly rowdy, and always somebody not getting what he wants. Mother set the tone for the household, but Mother lost all the wars. She dreamed of children tucked into their beds by nightfall, but, came the wee hours, there I was before the TV, taking in Ann Sothern in *Lady in the Dark*, or Rosalind Russell in *Wonderful Town*, or some other unmissable proposition for which I was willing to die. The *Mommie Dearest* movie stirred Mother: *there* was a parent who knew how to express authority. Mother didn't like the business with the hangers—it was sloppy, uncrisp—but the scene in which little Christine refuses to eat a blood-red steak and is not released from the table till she does eat it thrilled Mother. She talked of it for days, and I could see her thinking how different her life might have been if she had instituted such procedures early enough.

I was ready for it long before it came. "I wish," she said at last, "that you had had Joan Crawford for your mother."

"I did," I answered.

She laughed. She's a good sport.

Hardhats

*In which we start with an impressionistic study
and end with a story.*

As the son of a builder I spent high-school spring vacations on various
construction sites in and around New York. It was my first experience
of absolutely impenetrable men, not only tough but emotionally invulnerable. Ironworkers—the men who lay a building's steel skel-
eton—are a class unto themselves. Passing someone while carrying a
load of material, they don't say, "Excuse me," but "Get the fuck out
of my way"—yet they say it in the tone Edmund White would use for
"Excuse me." Challenged by their own kind, they can be vivacious;
challenged by an alien, they are fast and lethal.

It's an intolerant class, racist, sexist, fascistic yet patriotic about a
democracy; almost the only place to see the flag these days, besides
outside federal agencies, is on the trucks serving construction sites.
(They also mount a flag atop each building as the last girder is placed,
as if they had climbed rather than built a mountain.) Ironworkers are
not merely proletarians; they are proletarians without the barest internal contradictions, without ambition, pull, or PR. They are the
cowboys of the city, skilled workers who are also vagabonds with nothing to lose. They have one of the toughest jobs in America: exhausting, permanently subject to layoff, and extremely dangerous. The
raising of office towers routinely claims a life or two. At least

17

bridgework is worse. The Whitestone Bridge was regarded as a life-sparing marvel because only thirty-five men were lost on it.

There is one major contradiction in the ironworker, his endless enthusiasm for street courtship. What other set of Don Juans ever went out so unromantically styled?—casually groomed, tactlessly dressed, unimaginatively verbal? "Got a cookie for me, honey?" they will utter as a woman strolls by. Of course she ignores them; it wouldn't get you far in the Ramrod, either. Sometimes a group of them will clap and whistle for a ten, and I've seen women with a sporty sense of humor wave in acknowledgment. But there the rapport ends.

So why do they keep at it? Has one of them ever—in the entire history of architecture from Stonehenge to the present—made a single woman on the street? There are the occasional groupies, true: a few days ago I saw a young woman with an intense air of the bimbo about her waiting outside the site next to my apartment building just before quitting time with a camera in her hands. But this is the kind of woman these men have access to anyway, not least in the neigh-borhood bars where they cruise for a "hit." The ladies of fashion who freeze out these lunch-break inquiries are a race of person these men will never contact. After all, women like being met, not picked up, especially not on the street.

One of the workers next door eats his lunch sitting on the sidewalk in front of my building. Men he discounts or glares at; women he violates in a grin. The pretty ones get a hello. I was heading home from the grocery when I saw a smashing Bloomingdale's type treat his greeting to a look of such dread scorn that, flashed in Ty's, it would have sent the entire bar into the hospital with rejection breakdowns. But the ironworker keeps grinning as she storms on; "Have a nice day!" he urges. Emotionally invulnerable, I tell you. Yet are they really trying to pick these women up—sitting on the ground in a kind of visual metaphor of the plebeian, chomping on a sandwich while ladling out ten or twelve obscenities per sentence? This ironworker at my building is young, handsome, and clean-cut; still, he's riffraff. Sex is class.

When I started working on my dad's sites, I saw these men not as a social entity but as ethnicities and professions. There were Italians, Poles, Portuguese, and the Irish, each with a signature accent. There were carpenters, electricians, cement people, and the ironworkers themselves, the center of the business, either setters (who guide the girders into their moorings) or bolters (who fasten them). They were quiet around my brothers and me, not respectful but not unpleasant, either. We were, as they term beginners, "punks." Still, we were the boss' punks.

My older brother Jim fit in easily with them and my younger brother Andrew somewhat admired them; I found them unnervingly unpredictable. They were forever dropping their pants or socking each other. They'd ignore you all day from a distance of two feet, then suddenly come over and bellow a chorus of "Tie a Yellow Ribbon Round the Old Oak Tree" about two inches from your nose. Surpassingly uncultured, they were nimble conversationalists, each with his unique idioms, jokes, passwords. One might almost call them sociable but for their ferocious sense of kind, of belonging to something that by its very nature had to—but also by its simple willfulness wanted to—exclude everyone who wasn't of the brotherhood. Their sense of loyalty was astonishing—loyalty to their work, their friends, their people. Offend that loyalty and you confronted Major War.

Most of them were huge, the mesomorph physiques expanding with the labor over the years so that even fat wrecks sported gigantic muscles under the flab. Strangely, ironworkers don't throw their weight around, don't try to characterize themselves the way gay Attitude Hunks so often do. Ironworkers don't care whether you're impressed with them or not: they are what they are. *They're* impressed. And just when you think you've figured them out, they'll pull a twist on you. My dad built the Louisiana pavilion at the 1962 World's Fair, an evocation of "Bourbon Street," and one of the setting crew, a tall,

silent Irish guy who drank literally from start to finish of every day,
impressed me as being the meanest bastard on the site. "Hey, you,"
he said to me, on my first hour on the job, "what the *fuck* are you
doing?" I had been sorting material so bizarre I don't think it has a
name, and I said as much. He stared at my mouth for a moment,
then said, "Fuck *you* and fuck your *college.*" I avoided him as much
as was possible. And it happened that one day, some weeks later, the
wind blew a speck of dirt into my eye while I was on the roof, and
before I could do anything about it, he had come over, pulled out the
bandanna they all carry, and was cleaning out my eye with the most
amazing tenderness. "Okay?" he asked. It was, now. "Thanks," I said.
He nodded, went back to what he was doing, and never spoke to me
again.

The younger ironworkers had a certain flash and drove dashing
cars, but my dad warned us not to take them as role models; they
spent their evenings getting drunk and came home to beat their wives
when they came home at all.

"Is that what you want to be?" he asked us grimly.

"Yeah," said Andrew.

The superintendents on these various jobs were supposed to keep an
eye on us lest we get into trouble, but they seemed to delight in
posing us atrocious tasks, such as climbing rickety, forty-foot ladders
on wild-goose chases. Sometimes they'd give us a lift home, whereupon we'd be treated to an analysis of the social contours of the business: "Doze Italians, now, all dey wanna do is make fires. De niggers
are lazy good-for-nothings." And so on. Once, on lunch break, Andrew told my dad about this. "That idiot," was my dad's comment.
"Look," said Andrew, pointing to a group of Italians who had just
made a pointless little fire so they could watch it go out.

Unlike the rest of us, Jim stayed with it. After a year of Rutgers he
abandoned college forever and joined the ironworkers' union, an unthinkable act for a building contractor's son, virtually a patricidal betrayal of class. Yet I doubt he could have gotten his union book

without my dad's assistance; the building trade is harder to get into than a child-proof aspirin bottle. By the time I reached New York he was living in Manhattan. We ended up a few blocks from each other in the east fifties, and tentatively reconvened the relationship. My dad's "Is that what you want to be?" ran through my head when I first visited Jim's apartment, nothing you'd expect from a birthright member of the middle class. It was somehow blank and gaudy at once, rather like a pussy wagon with walls. Mae West, reincarnated as a blind lesbian, might have lived there. No, I'm giving it too much texture. It was the house of a man whose image of sensuality was a nude photograph of himself, his torso turned to the side to display a tattoo of two crossed swords. The photograph hung on his wall, and when I saw it I said, "If that thing on your arm is real, you'd better not let Mother see it." He pulled off his shirt, smiling. It was real.

"Girls like a breezy man, sport," he told me. No one else in my family talks like him.

I don't understand this craze for tattoos among working-class men. Permanently disfiguring oneself falls in with that hopeless flirting with inaccessible women and other self-delusory acts of the reckless straight. At least Jim's tattoo was high up on the arm, easily hidden even in a T-shirt; his pal Gene Caputo had a tattoo on each biceps, forearm, and thigh. Colored ones, no less—snakes and eagles and murder and paranoia. Socially, Gene had one topic, "layfuck." For the first three beers and two joints, he would expound on the attracting of "my woman." Four beers and another joint along, he would outline the various methods of layfucking them. By the eighteenth beer, he'd get into how to dispose of them. Then he'd pass out wherever he happened to be.

Plenty of ironworkers are happily familied, jovial, and intelligent. I even knew one who was—on the quiet—a Dickens buff. But it is not a settled life: the work wanders, the schedule is erratic, the weather can freeze you, boil you. It's not for anyone who has the chance to do something better. So ironworkers tend to be roughnecks—and in this Gene was the essential ironworker. He was a fabulously uninhibited

slob. He was also one of the largest men I've known. The flow of beer
bloated him a bit, but he had something like six shoulders and a chest
that could cross the street. A good man to have on your side, if you've
got to be in the war.

He was hard company, the sort who expresses his *joie de vivre* by
putting headlocks on you. He also laced his endearments with threats
of sexual attack, a typical ironworker anarchism. When I asked him to
stop mauling me, or do it more gently, he said, "I could screw your
butt. Would that be gentle enough for you?" Of course, one doesn't
take any of this literally. They like to shake up the taboos. Jim would
say, "I don't know why I'm so exhausted," and Gene would reply,
"Because I was fucking you all night and now your fucking asshole's
all sore." Imperturbable Jim would observe, "Yeah, that might be it,"
and they'd proceed to other matters. After a number of these out-
bursts, I began to wonder if something genuine might be pouring out
of Gene.

He was often at Jim's when I was, elaborating his theory of layfucking, and, out of loyalty to Jim, would attempt to draw me into his
philosophy. Or perhaps it was just because I was there; perhaps he
would have polled Eleanor Roosevelt for the dos and don'ts of layfuck
had she had been in the room. He would be deep in depiction of a
pickup, acting out the parts, even filling in for passersby who, he once
said, were "huffy and out of date." Then, he told us, tensing, showing
us how it felt, "My woman spots this briefcase dude and she is traveling. She is traveling away." Now he showed us Rodin's *The Thinker.*
"But what she don't know is, see, those guys in suits don't spend
money on my woman like an ironworker does! Am I wrong or what?"

"You're right, my man Gene," says Jim; and I'm trying to figure out
where all this lingo comes from.

"What about you?" says Gene, to me.

"What about *what* me?" I respond, trying to look about six foot
eight.

"What do you think of my woman dodging me like so?"

I took up my beer can, swirled the liquor thoughtfully, and offered,

"I read that as an uncanny act on the part of my woman." Had I made it, passed? Jim was nodding, but Gene was just looking at me. I looked back.

His face a puzzle, Gene asked me, "So like tell us why you didn't join the union like Jimbo here."

"Jim already knows," I said, backpedaling.

"So me."

"The punk's a writer," Jim put in.

"What kind?" asked Gene, his brow clouding. "Novels, fiction, stories?"

"All of the above," I answered, for they already *were* all of the above.

Gene looked dire.

"Fuck me and fuck my college," I said. "Right?"

"How come you could have joined the union and instead you're being a writer?"

"Well," I said, "every family has its black sheep."

Gene looked over at Jim, digesting this comic flattery, and I believed I had scored the point. But there was one more test.

"So tell us," said Gene, "some of your unique procedures in the enticing of my woman."

Jim smiled. I hadn't told him I was gay, but brothers always know. Sometimes they care; not Jim. Gay neither irritated nor interested him. It was like water polo or raising sheep: someone else's fucking problem.

As it happens, I am bent toward the analytic. I love codes, theories, lists. So, despite our differences, I easily fell in with Gene's taxonomy, following—and sometimes leading—him into theoretical situations calling for the most finely honed expertise in layfucking. And I laid one concept in particular on him that struck vastly home: the wearing of shirts with a college insigne, I had noticed, encourages people to talk to you. "It's a mark of class," I concluded. "Especially if it's a snappy college."

Gene thought it over. "Girls like college, don't they?"

"They admire a college man."

"Yeah," said Gene, slowly. "I could be the fucking football hero."

Well, rougher men than Gene have attended school on jock scholarships. Jim remembered a Rutgers sweatshirt in some closet at my folks', and I retrieved it the next weekend. It was early spring, a nice wind up—excellent sweatshirt weather, and apparently Gene did score a social coup in his new accessory, though he had had to cut it up to fit into it. He didn't win any women over to a date, but a few actually replied to his addresses; according to Jim the most popular remark was, "Did you *really* go to Rutgers?"

From then on, I was Gene's main man, after Jim, and he took to dropping in on me for confidence and advice. He called me "little brother." I put up with him, at first because I was trying to straighten out my standing in the family at that time and I thought it politic to tolerate Gene as a favor to Jim. After a while, however, I began to like Gene himself, for under the perversely insensitive behavior he had a rather touching sweetness, a Dostoyefskyan idiocy, maybe. Too, there was that amazing ironworker loyalty, something I've never encountered in members of the leadership classes, gay or straight. There was this as well: though his days were filled up with labor and his evenings with pub talk, he was a very lonely man. Jim and I were his only friends; the women he took to bed, I gathered, were whores of small quality. He disposed of them not because he was heartless but because there was nothing between him and them but a hit. One summer night he turned up at my place in his Rutgers shirt, drunk and sorrowful and inarticulate, but clearly heading toward something. The subject was love.

"When you got a buddy, man," he said. "Then you can show him how you feel about him, right? It's *radical*. Because when you really like a guy, and he trusts you, you *know* him . . . you know him right down to his cock, know him like a man. You get a buddy like that, you can do anything with him. *Anything.* You could ask him to lie down on his stomach because you're going to lock him up and ream his cherry out for him, and he'll do it. That's what love is. Loving your buddy." He gazed at me as if measuring my ability to understand what he was saying. "You hear me, little brother?"

I nodded.

"Now, your brother is really solid. That is a fucking solid guy, and there aren't many. You better know that. Right?"

"Right."

"Sure. Because if you don't know it I'll kick your butt in. Shit, he's solid. But he doesn't like to let a guy show him how he fucking feels. Know what I mean?"

"You're hurting my arm."

"I'll be good, little brother," he said, releasing me. "Because listen. This fucking city is filled with buddies. And they trust each other. Sure they do. But there comes a moment when you got to show your fucking buddy how you feel about him. You got to. There's no words. A guy just looks at his buddy, and he loves him. He *loves* him. Not just as a friend but as a man. He's got to show him, don't he? Put his arms around him, show his buddy. Am I wrong or what?"

"You're right."

"Say my name, too."

"Gene."

"Okay. I like to hear it. So, like all this time there's buddies together, and there's this one fucking moment, and they both feel it. They know it's true. It's fucking true. So one guy just takes his buddy and shows him how he fucking feels, whatever it fucking takes. That's how they know they're buddies." Finally he slowed down, took a deep breath, and shook his head. "I can't do that with Jimbo, little brother. Do you know what he's like?"

"I grew up with him."

"A rubber band. You can stretch it *just so far*, and then . . ." He pantomimed an explosion that almost blew me off the couch. "I just wish there was a place you could go and find a buddy. You know?"

A thought hit me.

"There is one, Gene."

"A buddy club, like."

"Listen, there is one!"

I had been going to the Eagle, and it occurred to me that what Gene needed and couldn't quite name was a man to take home. Or was I making the mistake of taking him literally?

"What is it?" he asked. "A gin mill?" Their term for a pub.

"Sort of. Potential buddies stand around and try to meet."

"Then what happens?"

"They go somewhere and show how they feel about each other." That didn't sound right. "No, they . . . they try to like each other."

"How?"

"That's hard to say." Then I added, "It doesn't always work." The greatest understatement in Stonewall.

He took a last swig of his drink. "I don't fucking care anymore. Let's go."

Thirty seconds after we entered the bar, I decided I had made a mistake. The Eagle, then in its heyday, was the showcase for tough men, and I knew Gene would never have taken it for a gay bar. It looked, in fact, like what he had asked for: a buddy club. Still, Gene may have been too authentic a buddy for this gang. There was always a lot of leather and muscle, and bar discounts for shirtless men encouraged a trashy savor. But that impenetrable invulnerability set Gene off from the others, and the tattoos, when he pulled off the sweatshirt, were a shock. After all, this was the place where I once saw two incredibly ruthless-looking hombres intently conversing in low tones, and innocently sidled over to eavesdrop. One of them might say, "So we stripped the kid and secured him and then . . ." The other might say, "Belts are kid stuff, just makes them giggle. You have to whip those butts." Lo, this is not what I overheard, boys and girls. One was saying, "Barbara Cook could play Sally and Angela could play Phyllis," and the other replied, "What about Liza?"

In fact, I couldn't have blundered worse if I had set up Ozma of Oz on a blind date with Leo Tolstoy. This was a place of sculpted hunks; Gene was lewd. They were practiced; Gene was improvisational. And they had polish; Gene was basic. He'd find no buddy here. A partner for the night, maybe: but he would have been repelled by the idea. A man has one-night stands with women, not men. Anyway, Gene didn't want a sex partner. He wanted a buddy he could like so badly he would be bound, almost incidentally, to fuck him. That particular stylistic riddle he could only solve among his own people, where tattoos are not exotica but a convention, and where loyalties fiercely combine. Sex is class.

Dimly, through the liquor, Gene realized this. He said he liked the place, and energetically approached a few men, yet nothing panned out. "Let's blow," he said; once we got outside, he didn't want to go: "Let's just talk." We leaned against a car on the corner and watched the others saunter back and forth between the Eagle and the Spike. We didn't say much, and, after a long silence, Gene put his arm around me. I looked up to cheer him with a joke and saw that he was crying.

We stood frozen like that for a long while, till he put his arm down and said, "I don't think those guys liked me."

"Maybe I should have—"

"I couldn't fucking understand half the things they were saying. And one of them called me a fucking *Bulgarian*! I never even been there! I never been out of this country!"

Hell, I thought, if Gene is a vulgarian, whoever called him that, *you're* a Firbankian!

"I want to deck somebody. Anyone here you don't like? Point him out."

"Let me call Jim."

"Huh?"

"He's your best buddy, right?"

"Yeah, but . . . look, does he ever come here?"

"No. But let's see what we can arrange."

Jim, roused from sleep, was annoyed till I explained the delicacy of the case.

"Shit, the fucker's on a crying drunk, that's all," said Jim. "Everyone does that now and again. He can stay with me tonight."

"Jim's coming to get you," I told Gene.

He mauled me in relief.

The Eagle–Spike parade had picked up notably—but for all the lingering stares, no one actually dared to cruise Gene. Is it possible that there's a man too authentic to be hot?

Gene was still crying when Jim's cab pulled up—it is, as they say, a jag. I thought, Everyone likes my brother except his family, as Gene threw himself at the door. Suddenly he turned back.

"Gotta thank little brother," he said, and, staggering back to me, he planted a huge wet kiss right on my mouth.

"The fucking meter's running, man," said Jim.

After they left I noticed that Gene had left his Rutgers shirt on the car with me.

Later, when I told friends of this incident, they invariably turned against me, one of their favorite activities. How did I dare bring one of those violent homophobes to a gay bar? What if he had wrecked the place? Or me?

Rubbish. I was protected by ironworker loyalty: your buddy's brother is *your* brother. As for ironworker homophobia, Gene would never have taken the Eagle for a gay bar, because ironworkers don't believe in gay. Males are men or faggots; men are solid and faggots are weak. A husky leather dude who beds his own sex is even so a man. A little *New Republic* nerd who proudly bangs his wife and sneers at gays is still a faggot. This is why ironworkers casually throw around what we regard as gay references, and why they can climb into the sack with a buddy without regarding it as a sexual assertion.

No doubt all Gene got out of Jim was the chance to sprawl in his arms all night. There are buddies you fuck and there are buddies you only love; and I think Gene loved Jim. And I also think there are ironworkers and there is everyone else, because in looks, world view, and behavior they are unique. I have been wrong about one thing: they are not invulnerable. When I pass a file of them, I look for

Gene, but he is probably working some other part of the country now; they move around a lot.

However, they never change, whether in their habits, dress, loyalties, or patriotism, though their fix on love of country is at times comprehensively ignorant. Just a few days ago, as I walked by our local gang lounging out the lunch break, I heard one of them casually call out, "Hey, traita!" Accustomed as I am to New Yorkers' public speaking, I paid no notice. About a block later, I began to wonder what the heckler had seen to inspire the epithet. Jane Fonda? La Pasionaria? There were only a few shoppers and businesswomen walking with me.

Then I realized that he had been speaking to me. I was wearing my Yale sweatshirt, and ironworkers regard the big eastern schools as hotbeds of Stalin-loving treachery. Inadvertently, I had challenged an ironworker's loyalty to his kind, and probably baited his sense of class as well.

Anyway, it proves my contention that college-logo sportswear encourages people to talk to you.

Confessions of
a Theatregoer

*Or: how to be precocious, single-minded, and
"pseudo" whether the world likes it or not.*

A housewife in Sheboygan writes, "Why is it that gay men always
seem so much more interesting than straight men? Many of them are
cute as the dickens, I have noticed, and they are always fun to be
around. When my husband Ivan comes home from work he just
drinks beer and grouches till he falls asleep halfway through *Cagney
and Lacey*. Whereas my gay nephew Lester comes home from the K-
Mart and just locks himself right in his bedroom to primp with the
stereo going. And though I must say he goes out in some pixilated
getups, as far as he is concerned the night is young and he is ready to
party."

I don't agree that all gays are fun to be around, but our culture does
surely bring out one's vivacity just as straight culture tends to dim it—
as witness the fact that gays tend to look up to people like Oscar
Wilde, Gertrude Stein, and Madame while straights claim Theodore
Dreiser, Midge Decter, and George Will. Ask yourself which set of
people you'd rather brunch with.

Where does the gay spirit come from? I think, possibly, from the
theatre; and the spirit runs toward theatre, too: toward its romanticiz-
ing fantasy as well as its cathartic grotesquerie. The gay mind, too,
raised on impersonation (of the straight style), comes out by rebelling

30

against that fascism with impersonations of antistraight in the drag queen's camp, the hoofer's bizarrely debonair tap, the juvenile's passionate love song. Rebellion. Defiance. Offensive alchemical caricature mixed of too much knowledge of them and too much spoof of us—and it works the other way as well. Notice that it was drag queens who launched Stonewall, in true war. I expect the queen as archetype will last as long as homophobia, for he/she is our reply. Straights think the queen mocks them: no, they disgust her. She *loathes* them. All of show biz is useful in this rebellion, but the musical is especially, for it is most subversive: apparently straight to straights but, as young gays learn, secretly and profoundly gay.

The musical was my key to the culture, for Mother was messianic in the Finer Things. She got us to Europe at an age when the availability of Special K was a crucial issue, favored series titles in books in hopes that we'd plow through a library of them, made everyone play an instrument (respectively violin, trumpet, piano, drums, and utility reed—it sounds like the Brandenburgs in the Busch version), and hit us with recordings of Classics for Kiddies. I remember a Decca 78 of the *Nutcracker* with Fred Waring's Pennsylvanians singing descriptive fantasy travelogue—I could echo it verbatim before I knew what half the words meant. And there was an adaptation of the *Iliad* set to the music from Prokofyef's *The Love for Three Oranges*, with the famous March treating the scene in which the Trojans pull the Horse into the citadel. The music was threateningly satiric and so caught my ear more than Sousa might have, and I listened more closely, and imagined. There was something rich here, some telling music for the tales. I asked for more, and Mother made the leap. For my third birthday, in late January 1952, she took me to Broadway to see *The King and I*.

I remember little of it. One moment stands out, when the king, about to beat Tuptim, meets Mrs. Anna's imperialistic gaze and runs off in humiliation. The psychology was too dense for me and I asked Mother what had happened.

"No talking during the show," she whispered.

I was taken aback. "Are you still my mother?" I asked, and she went, "*Shh!*" Still, it was a momentous afternoon: that day my life took on its format.

I could not have said why at the time, of course. But I knew that I was suddenly mad wild for theatre. Sundays, fine or bitter, I would study Section Two of *The New York Times* for the theatre ads and articles. (We called it "Section Two." New Yorkers refer to it as "Arts and Leisure," and today when I mention "Section Two" everybody goes "What?") Annually, I had one birthday show and one in the summer to grow on, so I had to choose carefully. It was never difficult: something in a logo, the ring of the names involved, the charisma of adaptational source—these were my map. I picked *The Pajama Game*, for instance, because Peter Arno designed the logo, and Arno was a *New Yorker* artist. I figured the more exposure I had to *New Yorker* types, the faster I'd grow up. Then, too, I would devour the playbills my parents brought back, especially the song listings, where a title like "My Home's a Highway" or "I Feel Like I'm Going to Live Forever" would tease my imagination.

Most telling of all, of course, were the show recordings. My parents were record-oriented, and bought nearly everything, some several times over—there must have been six or seven *Carousels* floating around the house at one point. Here was a vocabulary, and a catalog of ideas. What did it mean when Julie Jordan liked "to watch the river meet the sea"? What were "vittles"? "Gullets"? Why, in "June Is Bustin' Out All Over," has April "cried" and why was May "pretty"? Here, also, was a lesson in stagecraft, in how composition is made vivid, pure, just. To see a musical after having memorized its score is a rare pleasure, for you get not only the device of the entertainment, but the aplomb of verification. To see the dream become fact is to stoke the imagination for more and bigger dreams.

With all this homework to do before selecting a subject for the matinee, I couldn't hope to catch a flop. Only hits stayed open long enough for me to consider, sample, and clear them with the authorities. I caught the major statistics of the day: *Can-Can*; *Fanny*, perhaps my introduction to opera in its expansive vocalism; *Damn Yankees*; *Plain and Fancy*, which touched on the Amish folk and underlined the notion of a culture within a culture; *My Fair Lady*, to which I was more assigned than devoted, because I sensed that popular things were less interesting than recondite things; *The Most Happy Fella*, more opera; *Li'l Abner*, with its enlightening novelty of musclemen *en cabriole*; *Happy Hunting*, confronting a legend in Ethel Merman; *New Girl in Town*, more legends in Eugene O'Neill and, yet in the making, Gwen Verdon; *Goldilocks*, more terrain covered in the silent-movie setting and, once the allusions were explained, D. W. Griffith and Mary Pickford. I didn't realize it then, but I was learning history, genre, personality, taste. Friends, I was being activated. Of them all, one stood out experientially, partly on sheer size, partly for its spectacular voices and orchestration, but mainly because it played to the utmost that intent, deluded fantasy about romance that all Americans, straight and gay, long to believe in and find best articulated in operetta: *Kismet*. It blew me away.

I was as up for that show as Columbus was for new world, but when Mother and I got to the Ziegfeld Theatre and I made my habitual investigation of the streetfront photographs, I was somewhat unnerved to see that Alfred Drake had suddenly grown a beard. In the *Oklahoma!* and *Kiss Me, Kate* pictures he was clean-shaven; that's how I liked him; and everyone else. I was just turning six and beards were strangely threatening to me. I suggested that I wait outside, but Mother, who, like some of my friends, sometimes sounds like Bette Davis, wasn't having any. "The nerf!" she cried, propelling me indoors. "We nurtured him, and now he's afrait of a beart!"

That *Kismet* afternoon stayed with me long after *Promises, Promises* and *Two by Two* faded into nothing. The overture, always a crucial element in my theatregoing as the unalterably novel first moment of contact, was bigger, broader, and grander than any I had yet heard, filled with Arabian cymbals and bells and gongs, and ecstatic in the "Stranger in Paradise" section, with *lots* of piano. (Much later I learned the show biz term for this, "concerto style.") *Kismet* didn't have a show curtain to flash during the overture. *The King and I* didn't, either. *Can-Can* had one, a dazzling aerial view of Paris, and I eventually realized that operettas and the more serious types of musical play did without show curtains almost as a rule. An embellished curtain was a promise of guiltless fun, and a sober show meant to enlighten. I learned to distinguish lampoon from myth.

I suppose the Ziegfeld Theatre's interior was a show curtain in itself, but I only have pictures to go by, as I don't recall looking up. I was too intent on the stage, even covered, even dark, even waiting. Though curtained, the stage appeared to glow once the overture began—and, to my delighted horror, the overture didn't end. It grew quiet. The curtain rose on a dark street scene in Bagdad. A tenor wandered through singing "Sands of Time." As he reached the last note—"All that there is to know, only lovers *know*"—the gong erupted, the scrim rose, and the stage awoke as grotesquely high voices way up in the balcony imitated the cries of the faithful in the minarets of Mohammed. I gasped and trembled; Mother, who had already seen *Kismet*, assured me in a whisper, "This is only the beginning." "No noises during the show," I countered; I try to seize the revolutionary moment.

She was right, however. By the time the show had ended I was so enthralled I didn't want to leave the theatre. I wasn't alone, either. All around us were kids with parents, all the kids begging to be allowed to stay to see it again. We were entranced by expert show-shop marketing, yes, by the American musical's typical jumble of fun—jokes about sex, picture-book tableaux, steamy choreography, and in general a surprising amount of hotcha for a show thought to be one of the last of the old-time operettas. But at the heart of all this, unmistakable even to my tender youth, was a profound commitment to the fantasy of romance. Most musicals take the love plot for granted: comedy is about courtship. But *Kismet* was about the *intoxication* of romance: "And This Is My Beloved," "Night of My Nights," "Stranger in Paradise." The tender are impressionable; and I left the theatre in a daze.

It was not long before I was gathering such afternoons, Section Two, *Theatre Arts* magazine, cast albums, and playbills into a cult. It is at this point, I believe, that many gay men begin to share a profile, a quest, a sequence of discoveries. When I meet someone who tells me he never saw shows in his youth, I am staggered. "Where are you from?" I want to ask. Tucson? Lodz? The Sargasso Sea? Going to the theatre is *getting to the city*: sighting the place of the independence to come—for gay culture is city culture. It thrives on the sophistication and vitally needs the tolerance that cities develop. So being taken to the theatre is not the passive act it may seem. One invites it, wills it, *chooses* the event—or would a show choose you, put its name on your through an enchanting poster design, a startling song title, a performer of note?

A show was elite and you had to go. *Candide* was like that for me, from my first view of the logo illustration in Section Two, a parade of urbane-looking people bearing the credits on kites; from the charisma in the name Voltaire; from reverberations that Leonard Bernstein, Dorothy Parker, and Tyrone Guthrie gave off in jazz-classical cross-over, in New York wit, in British stagecraft. Look, you want to be urbane? Go for it; it's never too soon.

This one, I knew, I must have. *Candide!* I remember reading Brooks Atkinson's review in *The New York Times*, which opened with some reference to the Flying Dutchman—so would the vaults of imagination swing open! My friends only knew Captain Video and Sky King. I had always sensed that I was destined to know more than anyone around me, and somehow I comprehended that the theatre was going to be my education. *The King and I* and *Kismet* had not quite connected me to anything; they were autotelic pleasures. But *Candide* was interdisciplinarily instructive.

This would be my eighth-birthday visit and luckily the faltering run lasted just long enough for me to get there, quiet as a postulant throughout the interminable ride to the Martin Beck Theatre. Divining that this was a momentous occasion, my dad had nabbed us front-row seats; and all the grown-ups around us thought it was so cute that this little boy was blissing out at sitting close. It's cute at age eight, perhaps; but it would seem less cute than suspicious later on when I counted the amenities of theatregoing more heavily than those of making the team. Real men don't care where they sit at a musical. Real men don't watch spellbound, taking in every move that Barbara Cook and Irra Petina make, memorizing the show like a camera. I wonder if I sensed, even then, that a lot of things real men don't do were the most stimulating things done.

By this time my parents had begun to realize that they had called up a monster in me. My older brothers played touch football and my little brothers played Candyland; I played show albums. Who were their heroes? Mickey Mantle and Rocky Jones, Space Ranger. Mine was Alistair Cooke. My mother took to calling me "The Changeling." Perhaps I was too sophisticated, or too self-important in my sophistication. When our maid Sarah Lee Patterson purloined my *Mr. Wonderful* souvenir book, I fired her. I was nine years old.

My brothers were flabbergasted; my mother, for once, speechless. But Sarah Lee had been generally screwy, using the carpet sweeper on the lawn, eating TV dinners frozen, right out of the box, and spending her days in her room writing a movie script decorated with colored stick-on stars and stolen from *Raintree County*, with Sarah Lee all set to replace Elizabeth Taylor. Sarah Lee knew I had the goods on her, and went quietly. And lo, when the smoke cleared, it turned out that she had been systematically looting the house of treasures great and small. "Bud fired the maid" became a catchphrase in the family, admiration and horror at once. Real men don't fire maids at the age of nine. Real men have no relationships with maids whatsoever.

Theatre governed my existence to the extent that I can chart my *Bildung* through the titles: *Peter Pan*, my first chance to see the magic worked upon someone younger than myself—my brother Andrew, who crowed at Mary Martin. *New Girl in Town*, my first *musical noir*. *Auntie Mame*, my first nonmusical. *Redhead*, my first inkling that not everyone loves musicals to death, when my dad abruptly got up after ten minutes of—I must admit—infantile nonsense, told me he'd meet me in the lobby at five o'clock, and left. *Salad Days* (in London), an experience in culture shock: the playbill cost money, Britishers tend to cluster in the middle of the house (leaving me alone in the first row, cowering under the souvenir program), and the level of production was far below what Broadway took for granted. *Flower Drum Song*, the first show I saw twice, first with Mother and then in one of those dynastic theatre parties in which every living relative takes part, serried along an entire row of seats. My littlest brother Tony, who was so excited by *The Music Man* that he couldn't sit down once the curtain went up, did not take to the solemnity of Rodgers and Hammerstein, and wandered in and out of the house in search of the men's room, the candy counter, and other arcana, to my digust. Worse yet, my dad happily sang along with the orchestra during the overture—and I mean aloud, improvising lyrics when memory failed. "No talking during the show!" I explained. He just tousled my hair and went right into "Grant Avenue." You can't get anywhere with someone like that.

Not many real men get into musicals. My dad and Oscar Hammerstein II are the only two I know of. The rest of us do almost as a matter of course. Why? One possibility is what I call the *Candide* theory: musicals make you smart. I got more out of that one show— in lit, music, and social history—than some people got out of four years of college. Its overture taught me what a rondo and a Rossini crescendo were before I knew the terms. The auto-da-fé scene introduced me to McCarthyism. (My father caught the parallel and explained it to me during the intermission.) From Voltaire I leaped to Diderot, Leibniz and the Enlightenment, from Tyrone Guthrie to Olivier, Gielgud, the Old Vic, and the Kembles, from Dorothy Parker to the New York wits, from the word "satire" to the notion of irony. If I followed *Candide*'s allusions and implications to their ends, I would know everything.

Of course, gays have to. At any rate, we have to know more than the straights know: have to understand what we are as well as what they are—have to find *our* unique place in *their* culture. For some of us, isolated in the straight system, the stage gave off one's first whiff of the gay tang. Certain clues led one to postulate the existence of another system, a secret one. One saw signs in the behavior of the male gypsies and gratuitous torso bearings, in questionably quaint rhymes and sly jokes, even in Daniel Blum's emphasis on male body shots in his *Theatre World* annuals. I remember looking up *Kismet* in one of these volumes and being surprised by a photograph of Steve Reeves, that icon of pre-Stonewall calculus. The photo caught an insignificant moment of the show and was clumsily cropped; it didn't belong in a book. Why was it there? Because Reeves in Arabian pajamas was too toothsome not to be included? Obviously Blum thought so; his *Theatre Worlds* were like certain New York parties: always room for the beautiful. This is an exclusively gay notion, and coming upon it through my cult told me I wasn't alone.

Overtly, I pretended membership in the straight club; this was the 1950s. Yet we cultists found our way around it: for taking up theatre as a hobby was not unlike coming out in code, reserving a place in a possible gay future without having to challenge the hypocrisy of the social contract. Kids always want to be like each other, have what they all have and fashion clubs of belonging; to have something different and join one's own club was to practice for later, when the system was no longer secret. Thus, liking musicals was like a legalized coming out. The connection made sense: what other profession is as gay-identified as theatre?

Indeed, an ancient queen who has been everywhere and known everyone once told me that gay was invented in a theatre, in 1956. Yes, there were the Greeks, but all their secrets were lost. Petronius? Fragments, dreams. Ronald Firbank was a fluke and Nöel Coward was an abundance of suave, not a sexuality. No, the queen tells, gay came about at the City Center revival of *A Streetcar Named Desire* in which Tallulah Bankhead played Blanche DuBois. Everyone who attended that production was instantly struck gay, the old queen says, including the usherettes, the candy sellers, the stage crew, and—on Tallulah's good nights—even those who were passing outside the theatre. This must be gospel. What else is common to this scattered, unwieldy, and inherently contradictory condition we term the "gay community" but a bent for the stage? We all go; we all look upon those who don't as unintellectual, uncultured, gross. True, we don't all want the same thing from it. Some want a poetry of life, some a keen comix, some a colorful immortality. But I notice that *A Streetcar Named Desire* has all of these, as well as the two basic gay characters, the stud and the queen.

If attending theatre educates, putting it on stimulates, which is why most of the men who write, produce, stage, perform, or even drum hype for the theatre are gay, with emphasis on musicals. Why musicals? Because gays love boas and sequins? Or because they have been attracted by a unique form of music theatre that sophisticates all arts so deftly and—on occasion—profoundly that it sweeps other pastimes and enlightenments to the side? Musicals aren't a fetish, then: they are the stimulation of the cultivated.

This is why many of us get into playwriting in youth, laying down versions of our favorite shows, adapting novels and plays, even attempting originals. When I was scarcely old enough to stand I was herding my parents into my living room for cameo pageants, written, scored, and acted by our boy. This may be why I never liked little off-Broadway musicals, with their simplistic composition and undecorated staging style—mine were no smaller and no more terrible. Off Broadway was tyke theatre. It was the racy wisdom of grown-up Broadway that I prized—not the glamour, but the self-knowledge.

Yet, years later, as we graduates of this eccentric college congregated and met in the metropolis, I learned that some of them did not have any perspective on themselves at all. The theatre had instructed them, but never let them go to learn about other things. Socially, professionally, even sexually, they were unversed and unmotivated. They were overgrown precocious kids, using their love of theatre to protect them from all the other loves they could not collect. Disreputably dressed, showing up everywhere bearing bags containing the day's haul of records, books, or memorabilia, sporting the breath of a dragon, and blaring idiotic trivia about record matrix numbers, they put something of a punk on the image of the buff. And, of course, they were always gay.

Why of course?

Yet I wonder what they would have had if they didn't have the theatre. Musical comedy doesn't ruin them: it saves them, gives them a topic and a confraternity, even if, at times, that brotherhood consists of a body of strangers enchanted in a darkened auditorium. Their first love became a lifetime obsession; but if it set them strictly apart, it did set them somewhere. How much worse to have nothing to believe in, to be, like many people I have met over the years, utterly devoid of interests. Work detains them. Companionship eludes them. Only the bodily appetites impel them: food, sleep, sex. Absurd as it is to see Gene Caputo the ironworker as an aficionado—once I mentioned Liza Minnelli and he said, "Who's that? Some bimbo?"—if Gene had had the ability to be enlightened, redeemed, perhaps merely diverted by entertainers, he might not have been so lonely, a homosexual straight who couldn't touch men and didn't appreciate women, a truly single man.

This fraternity aspect of the musical comedy life is significant: types tend to cluster. When my father's hurtling success, my brother's implacable rivalry, and my own ornate precocity suggested something (respectively) fancy, remote, and advanced in the way of my education, my folks sent me off to Friends Academy in Locust Valley, Long Island. Friends no longer accepted boarding students, so I stayed, through some occult arrangement, with a family that turned out to be shockingly informal; had I been Ralph Bellamy, it would have been a screwball comedy. Their huge house stood a short walk from the Glen Cove railroad station, and I found to my delight that Mrs. Pratt saw nothing objectionable in my spending Saturday afternoons in the metropolis, lunching at the big Automat (now vanished) on Broadway at Forty-sixth Street, catching a matinee of just about anything, and generally nosing around. Here was when my coming of age really began, when theatre trips evolved into trips into city life, into the notion that a people as chosen as gays are must erect a ghetto not so much for segregation as for concentration: to learn what gay is.

True, this side of me was not useful at Friends Academy, where most of the students were sheltered WASP kids of Brookville and Old Westbury who, for one reason or another, didn't go off to Choate or Deerfield. They were sheltered from notions of race and class and what might be called disopportunity; and from the notion of art as well. I felt like young Lord Greystoke, set down among not apes but talking macaroons. At the end of seventh grade, however, I somehow wangled the lead in the senior class show, *Seventeen*, and this gave me access to the group known as the "pseudos": short for pseudo-intellectual and meant as a put-down, but in fact describing all the creative people at Friends.

The pseudos were considered radical. In some ways they truly were—Michael Hadden spent his weekend evenings at the Apollo Theatre in Harlem, an unthinkably daring diversion for a birthright member of the white bourgeoisie, and one that perhaps corresponds to

my own metropolitan jaunts, for gosh knows the Apollo gave Michael
Hadden a feeling for the richness of American civilization he could
not have got in Locust Valley. I daresay he was one of the last whites
to feel comfortable in Harlem before its politicization (or before its
innate politicization became militant), and it certainly spunked
up the yearbook, amid the drearily facetious Likes and Dislikes everyone else listed, to see his references to Harlem and the Apollo. He
genuinely liked black music; that, for him, was an agent of what you
could call straight coming out, learning what there is and what else
you are.

But most pseudo-activity consisted of theatricals, assorted acts of
arrogance (Sylvia Dawkins marched into English class, told Miss
Blade she had set so much English homework Sylvia couldn't do her
geometry, and proceeded to do it, as Miss Blade cried out, "*Sylvia*
Dawkins! Sylvia *Dawkins!*), and turning up in bizarre outfits on slave
day. More typical of pseudo-style than Mike Hadden was Clodagh
Millham, perversely silent with whimsical eyes. On *her* yearbook
page, instead of the usual studio portrait and "personality candid" (a
jock staring at the field of war; a pre-deb modeling a prom frock in the
kitchen as the staff looks on in a bemused manner), Clodagh had
nothing—nothing bearing the legend, "Draw your own pictures of
Clodagh Millham here." Given Friends Academy's value system,
Clodagh's rejection of yearbook glamour was more shocking than
Mike Hadden's disdain for middle-class scruples. Mike Hadden wasn't
really a pseudo, anyway, for he was on the football team and led the
debating club, whereas the true pseudo didn't join things. Pseudos
were nonconformists as a rule, and by the time I reached my seniority
in this society and became a pseudo myself, I realized how much
Being Different had to do with being gay. Half of it is being marked,
being *made* different. The other half is acting marked, *accepting* the
difference. To be pseudo (straight for "phony") was to be creative (gay
for "vital"). That is: given a drab environment, you either rebel or
grow up drab.

Creative is often a euphemism for "neurotic." But, boys and girls, you can be neurotic without creating anything. And lots of creative people have *not* been neurotic. (Name three, you say? John Updike, Lilo, and Jack Pumpkinhead of Oz. You say some of those on my list are imaginary? Well, who isn't?) Anyway, I'd say that creativity is the route to travel, for all its awkward poignancy. It can be rough in childhood, but it gives one an intent sense of mission as an adult; and think of all the salons and brunches it makes available.

So, to the housewife in Sheboygan and others who ask why gay men have this vitality, I would say it's because we steal from and pay back to the intensity of show biz. We adopt its tart glitter, and then, experimenting, develop our opulence, whimsy, intelligibility.

My records, for instance. A pleasantly unsavory amusement arcade halfway on to Wilkes-Barre called Playland had a recording machine. For fifty cents you could make a 45, and I made plenty. If Bernstein and Hellman could dare Voltaire, should I not tackle *The Wizard of Oz, Treasure Island?* The sixty-second side duration limited my scope somewhat, but I was ace in short forms, including parodies of television variety shows. One time I took my younger brothers into the booth with me—Mother had forbidden them some promised trip as a result of the usual contretemps, so I cast them into my cult to cheer them up. They were to play announcer and delicious mystery guest in my show, though Andrew could not bring himself to announce anything but "Here comes Mr. Pickle!" (an arresting footnote in what turned out to be an insistently straight sex life) and mystery guest Tony, sullen with the humiliation of punishment, refused to say even a word. I liked to make multidisc sets, just like the 45 versions of show albums, and by the end of the third side Andrew and I were giggling and capering. Tony, however, remained obdurately silent, despite our prodding and hard looks. At length, he piped up, "I hate Mom." There the record ended.

But not the story. Years later, the three of us turned up for Christmas at the manse, and stayed up late to reminisce and get into trouble in the kitchen. My mother, who spent most of her parental life starting at the sound of an opening refrigerator door to scream, "Who's in the kitchen?" from the bedroom, screamed it now.

"Do you remember," Tony asked, "when that struck terror into our hearts?"

"We should wreck a dish or something," Andrew urged. "Let's make something vicious in the toaster-oven."

It was as if we had never grown up. They were still the moon mice, as capable of smashing up my room as of sharing a pizza; and I am still the theatre kid, throwing the word "satire" around and speaking of "Section Two." My folks were about to move to Sacramento, and in going through my old chest I found many a souvenir, including some of my old amateur 45s. I took them out now and played the Mr. Pickle show, running lampoon and myth together.

We were bemused, transported back to a time when losing a hat or catching cold was mortal sin. In the silence that followed, Mother came downstairs in her nightgown to expostulate and dither, and, suddenly wrenched by the horror of leaving friends and family for a strange culture, grew tearful. "There won't be a Fortunoff's," she explained. "They put tofu into the water supply." Tearful is bad enough, but now came nostalgic, not one of her characteristic modes. "I wish your father were here to see the three of you spending Christmas like brothers instead of fighting."

"He's just upstairs in bed," said Andrew. "Shall I get him?"

"Are you talking over old times?" she asked gently. I'd had enough of this. Consulting the phonograph, I replayed the last bit of the Mr. Pickle show:

"Well, Mr. Pickle, what's new on the Rialto?"

Silence.

("Say something, you spaz!")

Silence.

("Kick his knee.")

("No, let's give him noogies.")

"Mr. Pickle, won't you say hello at least?"

Long silence, then:

"I hate Mom."

Mother regarded us in fury. "You wretches! Who said that?"

I pointed at Tony, Tony pointed at Andrew, Andrew pointed at me.

"He did," we chorused. Lampoon and myth.

Where did we learn our timing, you ask? Broadway taught us. Life is educational, if you know how to choose your college.

The Ideal Couple

After fraternities of siblings and of construction workers, we consider a third brotherhood, neither genetic nor professional but cultural.

Stonewall the event happened very unexpectedly, and Stonewall the culture developed, in response, almost overnight. All those men who had been living alone and quietly suddenly had boyfriends, Oscar parties, leather pants. The gay world took on its themes, conventions, and terms with a ferocious imagination—for these elements of our civilization were not revealed, brought out of hiding: they were invented on the spot. We were leaderless, but then gay had long been, like it or not, a somewhat freelance situation, a field of loners making do. And we began to find each other, trade observations, build up the folklore. Some rather essential items turned out to have been there all along—Fire Island, for instance. Some equally essential items came along a few years later—dancing, for one, officially launched at the Tenth Floor in the early-middle 1970s. Other essential items, however, were simply routined into place then and there. *The Advocate* appeared. Bars opened in revolutionarily central locations. Even the sex changed. As if to renounce the passive stance of the old trade-worshiping oral encounters, men began to insist on the more aggressive attack of all-night screwing. Staying over—especially if you had coffee the next morning and hugged at the door—became a political act.

Most important, trade virtually vanished. Not long before I came to

New York, homosexuals had no partners but hustlers. There would still be hustlers; but now most gays only knew of them from books like these. Hired help had become as useful as Victrolas: occult leverage raised by the lunatic fringe. Just as most record-playing people now relied on stereos, so did gays rely on . . . friendship. In fact, one of the first things you absolutely had to have in New York, fall of 1969, was a best friend.

With best friends, I believe: the older, the better. Long-term relationships weather idiosyncrasies more easily than new ones; and old investments are dearer. Perhaps it's a matter of simple arithmetic: after ten or twelve years, you've already fought about everything potentially available, and can settle back and just get along.

What of preferences, you ask? Who needs what kind of best friend? Boys and girls, there's no point in having preferences—even non-smokers can just hold their horses—because it was one of Stonewall's first rules that you can't choose your best friend: he chooses you. I got mine at the Met. It was that same Stonewall fall, and the opera season had begun; at the first intermission of a *Tales of Hoffmann* I ran into a vaguely familiar face at the bar, one of those you know well enough to start joking around with but not well enough to name. Finally I placed him. He and I had, so to say, cochaired a sit-down strike on the playing fields of—no, not Eton—the annual Valley Forge Boy Scout Jamboree. Small potatoes, you say. But how many men of your acquaintance ever led a sit-down strike *during* an all-American Capture the Flag? And called a scoutmaster a Nazi? (His assistant, an Eagle scout, was even worse, but he was also somewhat breathtaking, so we didn't call him anything.) Now it was ten years later, and my fellow rebel and I were men of the world, drinking champagne between the acts of a Met *Hoffmann* and comparing neighborhoods. I was living on the west side in a brownstone, he in the east fifties, in a doorman building with a fancy solarium on the roof. It sounded altogether metropolitan to me, and when some creep pushed my air conditioner in and robbed my apartment, I moved into my old friend's building. We had a lot in common and lived only two floors apart and thus became rather confidential. Also, we were the only two people we knew who had called a scoutmaster a Nazi and harbored ecstatic feelings for an Eagle scout. This will tend to draw men together. So we became best friends. His name was Dennis Savage, and still is.

Shocking to report, in those days you could live pretty much anywhere you wanted to just by moving in. Buildings were uncrowded and rents low. In such profusion, roommates were actually suspicious—except to gays. Our love lives were forming. Dennis Savage and I marveled as man after man buddied up and the crowd assembled the lists. The Five Most Colorful Couples. The Ten Most Passionate Couples. The Three Most Wonderful But Almost Certainly Temporary Couples. (There were a lot of those.) The Couple of the Month. Then I would say, "Couple of the Day would be more realistic," and of course everyone would get mad at me.

Part of Stonewall, I eventually realized, was not letting the side down, not admitting errors. But if straights are allowed to mess up their love lives, why can't we? Besides, as a storyteller I am bound for life to play a kind of devil's advocate about everything. I may not carry a notebook around, but I don't miss a move.

All of which is by way of introduction to the story of Greg and Calvin, because they were most frequently mentioned at list sessions as the Ideal Couple. Television was hesitantly taking up the gay scene, but no one was satisfied with the men the networks chose to interview. "Greg and Cal should be on the air," I was told. "They should speak for us, not those bitter political queens!" Another told me, "They're so handsome. So correct." Greg and Cal were a commercial for gays.

So it seemed. Greg was in his mid-twenties then, dark, quiet, slow-moving, and impressively solid. Calvin was a little older, fair, slight, mercurial. They mixed a notable chemistry, for while neither was astonishing on his own, together they were a compound of infinitely sympathetic currents, flowing between each other and outward to all around them. They were very social, very popular. They were always giving dinners, and because the guests were all, like Emma Wood-house, handsome, clever, and rich, you were flattered to have been asked. But there was something else going on, something clammy in the compound. You had only to let slip a faux pas—as I tend to, as a matter of course if not policy—and Greg would turn upon you the blackest, most intense eyes ever flashed. And once, when I was one of the last guests to leave, Cal pleaded with me to stay as if he feared to be alone with Greg. Fascinated, I took another scotch. But then Greg came out of the kitchen, sat down next to me, asked a few irrelevant questions, and ever so politely threw me out as Calvin stood against the wall like Saint Sebastian waiting for the arrows.

Calvin and I dated back to an East Side gym, now vanished, where two bodybuilders had a titanic fight over him in the weight room while he scrambled into his clothes in a panic and begged someone, anyone, to hide him out for a few hours. I spoke up. This was what we call a "mixed" gym (i.e., about fifteen percent straight and one hundred thirty percent gay), and the two bodybuilders—I had thought—were of the straight percentile. If Calvin actually had charm enough to draw strangers into the parish, he had to be quizzed, had to lend Stonewall his data. I took him to my place for coffee and sat entranced; he *was* that charming. Or was he rather a deftly tactful flatterer, the kind who makes you feel that you have somehow notched yourself up a rating or two and are about to have a wonderful life? I felt so elated when Calvin left that I had to go right up to Dennis Savage's apartment and stand to ten minutes of nonstop in-sults and grouching before I felt like me again.

Everyone called him Calvin then, in response to his whimsical dig-nity. Such a tidy bon vivant would bear no nicknames. *Calvin.* He was like one of James M. Barrie's lost boys who had found himself in one of the less onerous Professions. He wore high style without study. He was learned but he was funny. Anytime you ran into him—and you often did—he was on his way somewhere and took you along, to cocktails, surprise parties, screenings. He must have known a thou-sand doting people. And while you never quite caught the names, everyone present was lively and unique. You would hear the names again, when the times were ready. "Calvin," they would say, "tell us about it." And "Calvin, what did you do, *then?*" He never spoke of sex. He was the eternal kid, though he was getting on. And he did drink too much—this was something we of early Stonewall avoided almost politically, as reminiscent of the old have-not queer, dejected by hustlers and decaying with isolation.

Calvin and I lost track of each other after a while, as happens. I'd hear his name every so often, but we'd never meet. Then one day I ran into him: and suddenly he was Cal, not Calvin, and when he saw you he wouldn't blurt out some amusing confidence but tell you about people coming into inheritances. He knew a wholly different crowd, too; and Greg had entered the picture.

I disliked Greg at first sight, though I could understand why so many men liked to be around him. He was a hot preppy, and that's hard to pull off. He was so damn poised, so *ready* for everything. After a while, you began to feel that, every time you met him, he was reading from a script. And there was a new feeling of a collection at his and Calvin's dinners, as at that famous Bloomsbury jape at which all the guests had names ending in -bottom. Higginbottom. Pillbottom, Clambottom. The Calvin I had known never gave a thought to the luster of his cohorts. So I blamed Greg. He was the type who rated his associates on a scale.

Now I'll let Calvin speak for himself. We were having drinks at the Mayfair, and I told Calvin that he and Greg were the Ideal Couple, and he asked, "Says who?"

"Everyone but me."

He nodded. He was drunk. "We arranged it, you know. I'm sure you know. You know, don't you?"

"Look, Calvin—"

"It's Cal."

"*Calvin.* Don't give me secret dish. Or by the time I get off the phone tonight you'll be ruined."

"I hope so."

"Enough."

"No, *listen*. It's a hoax."

"What isn't?"

"We figured out what the championship would be and we scored it. We did, didn't we? We arranged it. Don't you see that? We aren't even friends. We're *partners*."

Why was he telling me this? I wondered. Isn't this sort of thing supposed to be a secret? Of course, you have to get people to reveal all sorts of privileged information if you want to understand the world, tell stories, be a writer. Stonewall had thrown up something like a hundred different words for what you can do in bed, but we still had only one name for love—that one. If Calvin and Greg were our Ideal Couple, I decided, we needed more words.

I thought that notion worth talking over with Dennis Savage. He thought it second-rate dish, but, like everyone, rather liked the picture Calvin and Greg made together. "If you were really smart," he told me, "you'd become a photo journalist and do a visual essay on those two. Catch them at the beach, in the park, on their terrace, in the workplace . . . Greg looks so amazing in those dark suits of his, and then he comes out in a sweater and jeans and you just think . . . what are you looking at?"

"What do you believe a photo essay would reveal about those two?" I said.

He was fumbling with a do-it-yourself framing kit he had bought to mount the *Follies* poster I had given him. "Why do they make these screws so tiny? Who has fingers small enough to—"

"Use a screwdriver."

"There's no screwdriver in the kit."

"Don't you just have one?" I asked. "Men are supposed to."

"Of course I have one!" he cried.

"Let's see it."

Without a word he marched over to the couch and folded up like old cardboard. He disgruntles easily. So I went downstairs, came back with my tool chest, and took over the framing.

"Actually," I said, "a photo essay on those two might disclose arresting aperçus about friendship."

"Poor Cal."

"Oh, suddenly it's poor Cal, huh?"

"Well, he *is* in over his head. Anybody would be with Greg." Dennis Savage and Greg went to college together. "He majored in intimidation."

"You got this wired all wrong," I said, readjusting the fastenings.

"He had this roommate he used to beat up all the time."

"Oh—"

"I was next door, wasn't I? I heard them."

"It was wrestling practice."

"Wrestling practice does not yield screams of 'Please, Greg, no! I promise! I promise!' Does it?"

"You surely did not hear—"

"I was there, you."

I silently drove the headbars into their slots.

"I was there," he repeated, coming over to watch the operation.

"'I promise'?"

"He promised."

Can I believe this? Dennis Savage is known to season his dish.

"The best thing," he tells me, "is once the roommate ran away from campus. Literally ran away."

"Why?"

"I suppose life in a small room with Megalon the Fire Monster made him nervous."

"What happened?"

"Well, it's hard to run away from Hamilton. There's almost nothing to take."

"So?"

"So Greg found him and brought him back."

"And it was hushed up."

"Hushed up? The spring mixer was entitled Runaway Roommates in their honor! Everyone knew about it."

"Did Greg get in trouble, at least?"

"The Gregs of the world never get in trouble," Dennis Savage opines. "The family's too powerful. Everything about Greg is right. His background, his address, his business, his looks. Think about it."

"And the lover? How right is he?"

"Come on, they make a marvelous couple."

"Calvin told me they aren't lovers. They aren't even friends, he said."

"What an odd thing to say. The two of them are inseparable."

"He says they arranged it."

"Well, if they did, they couldn't have arranged it better. No one person that I know of could afford that apartment, or attract quite that array of party guests, or just get that kind of respect."

"Manhattan's Ideal Couple," I said. "They won the contest. They arranged it."

"*They* didn't arrange anything," Dennis Savage laughed. "Greg arranges."

"And Calvin . . ."

". . . makes the promise." He shrugged. "Because we have to show the world what we're worth in our spotless white sweaters at our faultless dinners. Just wait. Ten years from now, when Hollywood makes a progressive film with a gay couple in it, that's what we'll look like. Greg and Calvin."

"Are you being ironic or do you believe that?" I asked.

"People respect a handsome picture above all," he said, surveying my handiwork. "Nice job."

"You know," I said after some thought. "I find it hard to visualize you at Hamilton. Or at any college."

He nodded. "And you're a pig."

Whenever friends would burst into a salute to monogamy, I would cite Greg and Calvin in a cautionary lecture on the terrorism of suit-

ability in gay coupling. Of arranging and promising. True, plenty of
men were showing up with the most unsuitable characters in tow—
hot little tricks no better than hustlers, idiots whose very presence I
took as a dire insult. Then I realized that I was falling into the Greg-
and-Calvin camp, demanding that categories of education and bearing be satisfied before romance could commence, before admirable
witnesses would form an admiring circle. Is this liberation? "I promise" haunted me. What, precisely, is one required to promise?

I had the chance to find out when Dennis Savage called me and
said, "You'd better get up here pronto. It's Cal and is he in a state!"

It's Calvin, I muttered in the elevator. It was Calvin before he
promised, when he was himself.

Dennis Savage was right enough about Calvin's state. At first I
thought he might be zonked on some new substance, so little aware
was he. But after a while I got the impression that he was just scared.
Carlo was there, half watching and half thinking of some pickup—
Carlo, pure hunk, and our set's contact with Stonewall as absolute
sex.

"Did you see the picture I framed?" I asked Carlo, explaining how
Dennis Savage didn't have a screwdriver—or, for all we knew, a
church key or a driver's license.

"Do you want to stay here tonight, Cal?" Dennis Savage was asking. "Are you afraid to go home?"

Calvin's mouth worked, but little came out. "I . . . I'm sorry about
all this. I . . . if only . . . I wished . . ."

"Has a story been structured?" I asked, plopping down next to
Carlo.

"Not yet," said Dennis Savage, gently patting Calvin on the back.

"So what's the new thing?" I said to Carlo, who could always be
counted on to report on some arcane sexual practice introduced in
San Francisco, or some outrageously exclusive party he could get us
into.

"Sure," Carlo said. He's a dazzling man; it's interesting to see how
quiet new people get when they meet him. "Last night I fucked this

beautiful kid, and then he got me to call his parents and say I was his teacher and I was keeping him after school."

"Okay," I said. "That's pretty damn new."

"Come here and do something," Dennis Savage told me. "Cheer him."

"Talk, Calvin."

"Could I have some more tea?" Calvin asked. He seemed ready to open up.

"Do you want to tell us what happened?" I asked. He sadly shook his head. "Was it . . . wrestling practice?"

"Wrestlers," said Carlo, warming to the subject. "Can you imagine what they might do to you in bed? They have all those holds and body locks."

"Why did you come here, Calvin?" I asked. "Are you afraid Greg will find you? Are you afraid he won't?"

"Don't listen to that waster," Dennis Savage told Calvin.

"He doesn't have a screwdriver," I told Carlo. "He can't put a frame together. Can you imagine?"

"He gives me yogurt," said Carlo, looking on the good side. "Blueberry. And he puts that healthy crinkle stuff on it."

"Wheat germ," Dennis Savage put in.

"So what's the deal, Calvin?" I said. "Do you want to break free? Huh? Are you afraid he won't let you? Is it time to stop trying to live life in the Movement's picture window?"

"Wheat germ is good for you?" said Carlo, enchanted by the oxymoron. "Wheat *germ?*"

"I'll tell you how easy it is to break free," I went on. "Make the relationship disreputable and Greg'll drop you like that. Let's try it. Let's see."

"You can't destroy a relationship on the moment," said Dennis Savage. "You don't—"

"A good paddling," Carlo put in, "could make an affair fresh. Especially when the guy who's going to be paddled is a little afraid of it."

"Greg goes for appearances, right?" I said.

Silence.

"Doesn't he?"

Still silence.

"He makes the arrangements, doesn't he?"

"It's really the threat of being paddled," Carlo went on, "not getting paddled in itself. Though some very sweet kids—"

"Sabotage the appearance," I offered, "and you're free. Ruin the arrangement. Break your promise."

"How can he do that?" asked Dennis Savage.

"What are Greg's values? Let's chart." I was a teacher once. "Greg's values are virility, money, correct taste, career success, and no passions, in something like that order. Make yourself useless to that system and he'll have to find another partner. Stroll through Tiffany's in a merry widow. Hang out in video arcades. Leave a Harold Robbins novel on your beach blanket. Wear purple. Get fired. Drool."

"Well, that's hopeless," Calvin said.

"Then go home and face the music."

Calvin sighed. "Would . . . would someone like to come with me? I wouldn't mind it if someone else was there."

"Mind what?" I asked.

"Stop being a bully," said Dennis Savage, "and take him home. Stay with him till Greg's under control." He helped Calvin into his Perry Ellis windbreaker.

"Then come back," said Carlo, "and tell us everything."

"You know what I think?" I said at the door. "I think someone or other made up that story about Greg and his college roommate and Calvin heard it somewhere and decided to boost the legend. And that's our picture. That's the respectable beauty of Stonewall. Because I don't believe there's anything in that apartment but a pompous lacrosse captain who's afraid he'll fart at a key moment of the awards banquet."

"Let's go then," said Calvin. "And you'll see."

"My, didn't you calm down," I noted. "You were quivering like a flan when I got here."

"Take him home, you beast!" Dennis Savage roared.

We walked. At the time, everyone I liked lived on the west side but everyone I knew lived in the east fifties. Greg came out of the bedroom as we walked in, pulling a tennis sweater over his jeans. Dennis Savage was right: he comes out and you just think. He was tousled and sleepy. He stood there, running his hand through his hair. We parked by the front door. Nobody said a word. I couldn't read either of their faces.

At length Greg spoke. "You know how I first hooked up with this guy? I raped him. He touched my arm and asked me to wait for another time. He promised to bring me beauties in his place. No one had ever had him, he said. He wept, but I held his hand and whispered to him. While I was stripping him, he leaned his head against my chest and pleaded with me. I told him if he didn't cooperate I would tie him to the bed and hurt him. I made him take his choice."

And he grinned.

Calvin turned to me, speechless, avid, his eyes wild. He was so turned on the air around us was crackling and falling to the floor in bits.

"What choice, Calvin?" I asked. "What choice did you make?"

Greg came up behind Calvin and put his arms around him. "Stick around for the drinks," Greg told me. "Quentin and Edward are coming. We'll probably go on to dinner." Calvin was smirking like a cowboy about to hang a rustler.

"So," I said. "The Ideal Couple. Continuous performances. All live acts. Come see the Celebrity Cocktail in the Dazzling Penthouse, where Best Friends Invent the Traditions of Stonewall. Starring the Big Scary Preppie Bear and his Christopher Robin."

"I'm not such a scary bear, am I?" Greg purred in Calvin's ear.

"Who says you're the bear?" I said.

"*Everyone* but you," Calvin replied. "I told you how it was with us."

"You told me something else." Was this the aim of Stonewall—to fill lavish apartments with the right sweater, the right brunch flowers, the right lover? Were we perhaps going to raise up a midtown suburb, a gay bourgeoisie voting Republican and muttering about interest rates? *Liars!* I thought, watching them. *Arrangers!* The puppet makes the promise and the stringmaster collects it. Then they put on the show. "*You* didn't make any promise, man," I told Calvin. "*Greg* did. Greg is your puppet, you lurid Bloomingdale's pimp!"

"What ever are you speaking of?" he asked, with a smile.

"So long, Cal."

And whenever I heard people call them the Ideal Couple, I said, "Oh, you mean Citizen Pain and the Battered Bride?" And of course everyone would get mad at me.

A Weekend with Straights

A trip to the island of fire—but, for once, to neither Pines nor Grove, and among Strangers.

I didn't mind being the only unattached male in the house, but it felt odd to be the sole person of either sex without a tattoo. My brother Jim and his pal Danny D., typical ironworkers, sported standard regalia on their upper arms. And Brenda, Jim's date, was of the downtown bimbo class: they'll do anything for attention. Even Norma, girlfriend to Danny D. and a strictly reared Italian from Bay Ridge, shyly revealed a tiny heart inked into her right instep—"so I can hide it from my parents," she told me. Thus all four representatives of the straight-couple class were decorated. And, of the freelancers, Laurie the tough-guy lesbian weighed in as well, with a death's head on her left shoulder. That left me as the only *tabula rasa* in the house.

This was Water Island on a July Fourth weekend in the early 1970s. I had just discovered Fire Island, just begun to sense how neatly it essentialized gay, made its complexes intelligible; and I never turned down an invitation. Water Island, the first colony east of The Pines, was where Norma and Laurie shared a four-bedroom house with two women who had gone off on vacation, and Norma, who knew Jim through Danny D., offered Jim and Brenda the third room and me the fourth. Perhaps because of her sweetheart upbringing, Norma liked wild men, and may have been disappointed by my mild

manner. *This*, she must have been thinking, is Jim's brother? Don't
they have something in a dangerous? "I'll bet you've got a *terrific*
sense of humor," she told me as we shook hands, one of the most
tactless salutes I've ever suffered. Besides, my sense of humor isn't
terrific: it's occult.

Laurie, at least, seemed pleasantly jived at my appearance. Better a
gay, her smile betokened, than another of these hardhat supermen.
Her handshake was a vise, and I was amused to watch Jim take up the
challenge and squeeze it out with her. He won. He's slim but deadly.

Brenda, an elated blonde, was my kind of person: she likes everybody. Danny D., too, was easy to get along with, provided you were
not a Commie, a groveling cheat, or a faggot. He used the terms
indiscriminately—Billy Martin he dubbed a Commie, Walter
Cronkite a groveling cheat, and Norma a faggot the night she refused
to accompany him to a Jets game. He had an engaging quirk whereby
he would converse avidly with himself, usually to express what he
feared to articulate directly. "What's this for?" he said at Jim's place
once, handed a present. "It's because someone likes you," he answered himself, holding it. "Open it, you jerk." "No, I'm not ready
now." "Everybody's watching you." "Well, maybe." "If you don't, I'll
deck you busted." "Okay, okay." Jim grinned at me as Danny D.
ripped off the wrappings, as if to say, See what fun ironworkers are?

Water Island let me down. A drab batch of broken-down houses too
far from The Pines, it didn't even have a ferry stop, much less such
amenities as a grocery or liquor store. You landed at The Pines, laid
in supplies, took the last leg by water taxi, and waded into the bay to
gain the blasted boardwalk. Nor was there much beach life, any coming and going. For that you had to walk to The Pines, and it was no
mere hop and skip. Here I was hoping to jade myself on gay data,
stuck in a straight version of Fire Island.

We had unpacked. Jim and Brenda into their room and Danny D.
and Norma into theirs had retired for nookie; Laurie nodded toward
the sea with a look of Let's go and I went. We sat topless in the late-
afternoon sun and she said, "Tell me about it."

I told her about my family, about ironworkers, about writing, about New York, about those opposites nostalgia and ambition, about gay men, and about lesbians, though she was better informed than I. And I told her, who knows why, about the time we were all at the Jersey shore when I was ten and Jim eleven and I jumped him to give him a dunking and he threw me off and, his eyes on ice, told me that was the last time I'd sneak up on him. Then he held me under the water so long my lungs were about to burst when some stranger pulled us apart.

"One of those quaint family capers," I concluded, "that most people never mention."

"How did you two make that up?"

"We didn't. They sent me away to school, so we didn't see each other much after that. We're still trying to sort things out."

She nodded and we watched the water dance.

"Now you," I said.

"Guys like me have no past," she said. "What you see is the whole thing." She was right, in a way: real men don't go around lamenting their fearful kismet. But then, as Ernest Hemingway finally discovered, you can be a real man or a writer, not both.

"Does it hurt getting tattooed?" I asked.

"Tickles. Kind of funny having a brother out here. Mostly all we get is lovers and dates. Jim know about you?"

"I imagine so."

"Ironworkers are pretty homophobic. Doesn't that boil you?"

"Does it boil you?"

"They don't figure me for gay. They wouldn't even if I plowed Norma on the dining table. Women are beyond their typing rituals, see. We're exempt."

"Pardon me for busting into heartthrob city," said Norma over our shoulders. I had the feeling that she wasn't being ironic. "But cocktails are served."

"We'll get there," said Laurie.

"If you feel that way," said Norma, leaving.

"Doesn't she know," I asked, "that one doesn't launch dinner on Fire Island till nine o'clock at the earliest?"

"Jesus, you *are* gay."

I decided to try her patience. "If I got a tattoo, could I too pass as a man?"

She eyed me cannily for a bit, then chose to answer seriously. "Fact, they're a bargain. Cheap. Though all the artists want to stroke you up, doing it. Had to bust three guys before I got one would do his job and leave me be."

And she was not kidding, boys and girls.

"It's the loveboats!" Norma caroled when we joined the others on the deck. Brenda, in Jim's lap, held a goblet of wine. The men had bottles of Heinekens. Norma was doing revolting things to helpless slices of bread, salami, and cheese with a kit of molds and styli almost certainly Not Available in Stores. Laurie took a beer, and, though I wanted one, too, I asked for wine to avoid showing solidarity with a particular side.

"It takes a classy person," said Brenda, "to drink wine." She sipped hers, smirking at Jim. "Tongue me, big boy," she urged.

A curiosity of the house was a battered but working upright piano just inside the doors to the deck. I took my wine over and rattled into some Gershwin, though I find playing by memory difficult. Norma was thrilled to have live music to entrance her weekend commotion. Putting the thumbscrews to a hunk of munster, she carefully mimed Alert Sensitivity as I flailed through the release of "Nashville Nightingale," getting not a single note right.

"That sounded very tricky," she approved as I paused, defeated.

"That sounded like Arnold Schoenberg," I confessed.

"Hey, piano man," said Danny D. "Know any Scott Joplin?"

"Danny!" Norma cried. "Don't barge in with your B&T mentality! Maybe Jim's brother will favor us with Puccini."

Danny D. looked behind him. "She talking at you, Harry?" "Not me." "Who's she talking at?" "I don't know, but she better watch her step. She talks that way to *me* and pow! she'll be touring the far side of the moon."

"Well, naturally—" I began.

"Him, too," said Danny D., indicating me.

"The kid's okay," said Jim. "He's with me."

"Bud," said Norma sweetly, blinding an apple, "can you play Musetta's Valse Song?"

That one's a cinch. Partway through, Norma began to sing along, in one of those dowdy translations common around 1905:

> *And when I go out twirling on the boulevards*
> *The men all crane their necks to spy me . . .*

By the end she had opened up and was letting it rip right up to the climactic high B, for which she executed an antique coquette pose and accidentally upset some of her hors d'oeuvres.

"Hey Caruso," said Danny D., "you dropped your foodies."

Jim and Laurie exchanged a look, but Brenda clapped as Norma explained that she had trained as a singer and gave it up on parental suggestion.

"So who can blame them?" asked Danny D.

Actually, Norma was, like thousands who dally in that quarter, not good and not terrible: she fielded a sweet, tiny voice with neither authority nor musicianship. But now she felt encouraged, and the show was on. Norma produced a book of arias from the piano bench, and we ran through it till Danny D. came over and banged on the lower keys. "What is this?" he asked, "an opera house or the beach?"

Facing the bay as the sun sank away somewhere over Passaic, we dined uneventfully till one Sal, a neighbor, popped in. Now, The Pines is intent and Water Island zonked. So, if everything matters in The Pines, nothing matters in Water Island. Yet I got an intent feeling, in the laden comments passed and batted back, that Sal tended to drop in moochingly at mealtimes, that he and Norma had a small bit of a past she would gladly forget, and that Sal did not realize that forcing one's welcome on women was not the same thing as forcing it on men like Danny D.

Because Danny D. suddenly said, without the slightest provocation, "Look, can I tell you something? I don't want to see your fucking ugly face around here till I go, which is Monday night. So shove off, you Commie jerksucker."

Sal, a mite stunned, stared at him.

"And you got five," said Danny D.

"He means five seconds," said Laurie helpfully, "or else."

Sal waited out the five—more through confusion than defiance, I expect. But when Danny D. rose up, Sal sprang for the walk. At a safe distance, he turned to reply. Danny D. was still coming, and Sal vanished.

"That smart chick knows the code," said Danny D., of Laurie.

Now, what I wish to note here is that, in any other social group I have access to, such a scene would have considerably changed the complexion of the evening. Amongst trendy liberals, direly subtle commentary would have broken out, positions established. The literati would have prowled Danny D. for backstory and parts of him would filter into the *Paris Review* and *Grand Street*. A gay crowd might fashion it into dish, a condign scandal to do into tatters over tea. But this group went on as if nothing had happened. And, by their lights, nothing had: Danny D. didn't like an intruder and thus efficiently disposed of him.

There's a directness, an eagerness to confront, that sets certain kinds of people apart, at the beach or elsewhere, in trunks or a suit, out to boogie or looking for trouble. There's a look in the eye, a grab of the hands, and you're in over your head, drowning. If men tend to start fights and women tend to avoid them, it's interesting that gay men tend to avoid them, too. Spend an hour in an Irish bar with ten people present and you're sure to see men fight. Yet who has ever seen a fight in a gay bar, no matter how crowded? (Carlo dimly recalls one in the Eagle about twelve years ago.) Is this because gays are too busy confronting profound questions of male identity to spare energy for fighting? Or is it simply a cultural matter, another facet of the straight style?

Whatever its basis, it does put a certain quickness into the air. After dinner Norma asked me to institute some intellectual sport of a Manhattan savvy—no, not in those words—and in response I suggested we all try an old favorite in my family, the Question Game, in which the participants (five brothers can play) trade questions that must be answered truthfully.

"It's all the rage at those New York loft parties," Norma gushed; this was wishful thinking. "Now, Danny, do you love me for myself, or just for my physique?"—pronounced "*fi*-si-cyew."

Danny D. looked over at me and said, "What the hell kind of fucking stupid game is this?"

Imagine your ten closest friends in Danny D.'s position, thinking what he thinks, and consider what response they might make, as opposed to his: and you'll understand what I wish to note about confrontation.

The next day, after lunch, Norma cornered me with her aria book and expressed a life's dream to attempt "In questa reggia." I obliged. It sounded like Thumbelina singing the piccolo part of "The Stars and Stripes Forever," but, as we pulled into the finish, she clasped my shoulders and kissed my ear, her life's dream accomplished. And there, dripping wet from the shower, nude and irate, was Danny D.

"Look," he said, "I don't know what it is with this opera stuff, but Norma's my girl. Got it?"

Like Sal, I was too startled to react. Jim, out of nowhere, came up and said, "Hey, Danny D.!"

"Yo, Jimbo!" came the reply, familiar on many a building site.

"Take it easy," said Jim, touching Danny D.'s neck. "He's just playing piano for her. She's singing. End of bit, right?"

"What I see is she's a girl and he's a guy, huh?" He swung the flat of his hand through the air, meaning, "Cut!"

Danny D. went back inside to dress, Norma followed him, Brenda came up to Jim whispering, "Did I miss something, Honeycock?" and

Laurie again beckoned me to the beach, now with a jab of her thumb.

"Numbnuts," she began, as we settled on the sand just above the wetline. "Stop interfering with that romance. I thought gays were supposed to be sensitive."

"What did I do?"

"You assisted the world's champion cockbaiter in baiting her man's cock."

"Norma?"

"Don't you see how she makes Danny D. feel when she pulls out that opera jazz? It's supposed to be something *she* knows about, and *he* doesn't, so he's supposed to feel like a clod. Or didn't you know about these punk Italian *signorine?*"

"Who do you think I am, Errol Flynn?"

"Well, man, it turns out they're choice touch. But getting along with them is another thing. Because they bust ass and bite balls and torch cock." She imitated them: "'Buy me *that!* Where's my *ring?* It must be *catered* or my girlfriend Teresa won't be jealous!'"

I considered this.

"Your brother's a neat guy," she went on. "The way he covered for you with Danny D. You didn't know what the fuck was coming down. And he did. That's sensitive."

"Yeah, he was *so* sensitive on the beach some years ago, as I—"

"I'm talking now."

"Look how you defend a man like that. Haven't you heard the word chauvinist? Don't you know how he treats women? They're just packages of sexmeat to him."

"He was *there* for you, man!"

"Oh, come on! Any brother will defend you! That was to show you what a great guy he is."

She stared hard at the water, said, "I'm going to hit you because I want you to remember the next thing I'm going to say. Remember it for a long while." Then she grabbed me by the scruff of the neck and slapped my cheek harder than I've ever been slapped, harder than I thought I could be.

"Some brothers don't defend you," she said quietly, holding on to me. "Come *on*? Some brothers will stand by and watch their friends rape you. Listen, they'll do it themselves, brothers. You'll think maybe they'd look away at the time, lay a little shame on it, at least? Don't think that, mister. Don't think it. *Come on*? Listen. You got a brother to watch out for you, you be real glad of him." She released me and hugged herself, trying to calm the breathing. "Chauvinism. I hear it. That . . . logo word. How do you think *I* treat women, huh? Who am I, Tinker Bell? Jane Austen? I lay 'em and leave 'em! *I'm* Errol Flynn! And don't hand me that sisterhood shit! *Politics!* What the shit do I care who's king this year? They'll never be on my side, will they? Yours, either. Or your brother's. Know whose side the kings are on? Know who the kings *are*, for Christshit? Do you? *Rich! Straight! Males!*" She stood, walked into the bits of water at the end of the waves, and looked back at me. "Rich straight males," she repeated. "You're a subversive. And your brother's an exploitable prole. And I'm not on the chart."

After a few minutes, I said, "You know, you should have been an ironworker."

She laughed. Hell, she downright roared.

"I've got a nickname picked out for you," I added. "Stinger."

"Do they all have nicknames?"

"The hot ones do. What do you think 'Danny D.' is? His last name's O'Brien."

"Speaking of which," she said, glancing over my shoulder. Danny D. was heading over the dunes toward us, hopping daintily from one boiling footprint to the next in green nylon trunks that might have gone out of style in 1956.

"Yo hey," he said, plopping down next to me. "Going to apologize for blowing off steam like that there."

"Forget it."

"No. First it's that groveling cheat Sal, then that piano. You know, Norma, sometimes she leans on me with the music, sort of." He asked himself, "What do you mean leans on you?" "Leans on me, like suddenly she's too busy to play with me, or like it's this big put-down game. Like she's flirting with the songs, see?" "I see, man. So even though he's your pal's brother, you got to wonder what he's up to, right?" "Right."

"Danny D.," I said, "don't wonder. I'm gay."

"Gay who?"

"No, *gay*. As in Not Straight."

He turned questioningly to Laurie.

She said, "He means he's a faggot."

Danny D. gave me a searching look. "You shitting me?"

I shook my head.

"You mean gay like . . . boy meets *boy*? Boy gets *boy*?"

"Let's hope."

He thought this over, regarded me once more, leaped up with a whoop of joy, ran into the ocean, and ran right out again, shouting, "Cold water! Run for your lives!"

Her mind on other matters, Laurie asked me, "What's your brother's nickname?"

"Jimbo."

"You never call him that, do you?"

"I don't know Jimbo. I scarcely know Jim."

"You don't say it like a name," said Danny D. "You know that?"

"How does he say it?" Laurie asked.

"Like a . . . a secret."

I shrugged. "This has been being a holiday of secrets."

Danny D. was laughing again. "Wait'll I tell that bitchen Norma. Only thing is, how the fuck do I get back over that sand? Coming down, I almost burned my footsies off."

"Get your feet cold in the ocean," I suggested. "Then run like hell."

"Hey, you're a smart kid."

"Danny D., I'm older than you are."

"Yeah?" He got into the water to his knees. "You're still a kid." He faced the houses. "Okay," he began, "let's go," revving up. "It's *banzai time!*" And away he went.

Norma accepted my decision to curtail the operatic end of my repertory; she seemed to sense that the men had made one of their handshake pacts and, wise girl, bore it without reproach. I even managed to essay Joplin's "Peacherine Rag" (with the barest hint of Second Viennese School harmony) for Danny D., and he told Jim, "That's a swift kid, pal. You raised him right."

"He was hell at first," said Jim. "But he's cooling out nicely. Right, sport?"

"I'd rather die."

"Commie punk," said Danny D.

The usual nookie session followed dinner, and Laurie excused herself to, as she put it, "make a blonde." She probably did not mean by origami. Alone, then, alarmed and amused at spending a weekend at Fire Island without touching base at The Pines, I elected to put the time to use and got out notebook and pen and just started writing, as if by Ouija board, aim and tone wandering. What eventually came out was a story, an early version of this one, in fact. I had written plenty of stories, but till now they had been fantasies, or dialect romances, or urbane comedies about people I had never met. Now, suddenly, one was about someone's real life—rudely so, but a hard pen has no conscience. I wrote straight through, and, reaching a temporary lull in the tale, this lull, I stopped, stimulated and exhausted. It was well after midnight. I decided to walk down to the beach before turning in.

The Pines boardwalks can be tricky after dark, but Water Island's planks are fearsome, dilapidated and unmarked. It was worth any hazard, though, to reach that vast healing velvet of black sky trimmed by its knowing moon, a Pines moon. I searched westward for the lights of the gay citadel, just out of reach. Tomorrow, I resolved, I'll pay a call.

I heard whistling behind me and turned to find Jim in jeans and a ratty old yachting sweater.

"Thought you'd be out here," he said. "I saw your notebook on the table, sport. Fixing to write a story about something?"

"Did you read any of it?"

He swung a foot through the water. "Can't make out your handwriting. Thought I recognized some names, though."

"You want to play the Question Game?"

He laughed softly. "Uh-oh."

"One last time?"

"Okay, sport. One last time forever."

"You first."

He had it all ready. "What do they say about me now? Back home?"

"They . . . don't mention you at all."

He thought it over, nodded. He thinks that's fair. "Shoot."

"That time on the shore. Were you really trying to drown me?"

"Oh, that." He came up to me. "That time on the shore, right." He looked me in the eye; at close range, Fire Island moonlight permits excellent vision. "You blew it, sport. One last time forever. You know the answer to that question. The answer is yes. The question you should have asked is, *Why?*"

"I don't want to know that answer."

"Sure you do. You're going to be a writer, you've got to know everything." He took my arm. "Let's go back to the house. It's cold."

"I want to stay a bit more."

"That boardwalk's all busted up. It's dangerous alone."

"I got out here, didn't I?"

"Suit yourself." He started off, whistling.

"Jim." I guess it does sound like a secret. Telling, not keeping one. "Why . . . did you try to drown me?"

After a long while, he said, "Sport, some men just weren't meant to be brothers."

I watched him head back up the dunes in the moonlight, and I

thought, Whatever happens, I can use it. I can observe, abstract, enhance it, distance myself from or embrace it. It was a great moment;
years from now, white-haired, fêted and crabby, I may do a
madeleine on this memory. I showed my fist to the virgin moon, to
leave a picture for me to recall, and someone grabbed it and pulled
me around: Jim, the brother I most resemble and am least like, more
boyish than I would dare be and more man than I am permitted to
use in my world of the *comme il faut* intelligentsia.

"Come on along," he said, annoyed at having to tell me twice.

One day they nearly drown you; the next, they want you on hand
for social comedy. Oh, I'll come on along; the only things I don't
resist are hard liquor and brute force. I'll come on and take a bead on
all of you. I am eager to confront, now, and I'll get a story out of it,
no matter what is done to me. From here on, I know everything and
you got five.

Okay, sports?

I Am the Sleuth

A droll tale of sociosexual crossover, containing a treatise on sexuality thrown into the middle of the plot, for which the author makes no apology to his readers.

Well, there I am, as all too often, at my desk to scrimmage with the muse while everyone else in town is out on the streets having terse encounters. It's a Saturday afternoon in late fall, when the opinion-makers stroll Soho in awe of themselves, when fashionable people do the latest sweater along Madison or Second, when bagladies shop with such abandon that one finds overturned garbage cans all the way from Eighth Street to the Park. But I'm at my labor, painfully ooching through a piece I would knock off in two hours if only this were winter—if possible during a blizzard and with emergency rations of Johnnie Walker Red and Mars bars laid by in the pantry. Dragging along as the sunlight robustly streams down and the great world frolics only blocks away (am I missing a Major Brunch?), I seem to start this piece over again with each new sentence, making it something like a tiny encyclopedia. This proves, I ruefully reflect, that New York doesn't have more sex than other places, just more opinions.

So I was relieved when Dennis Savage came in, his eyes brightly furtive and his tread a fidgety sarabande.

"Well, well, well," I said. "Guess what you've been doing."

Smiling, he led me to the couch, sat me down, and prepared to launch his report.

"Anyone I know?" I asked.

"Shut up and listen and maybe you'll get a nice tale out of it."

"That's the story of my life."

"Last night I met this guy at the corner of Twenty-first and Eleventh. He was sitting on the curb because he had no place to go. He looked like he'd been on the streets for—"

"Whoa," I said, getting all set up. Basically we're best friends, but we have these verbal duels in which we try to pulverize each other. It keeps the relationship fresh. "What do you mean you *met* someone at Twenty-first and Eleventh, as if that were the lobby of the Algonquin or some prankish salon? Twenty-first and Eleventh is the Eagle. You don't just meet anyone there. You pick him up. You molest him. You pause to count the bugle beads on his art deco shorts and—"

"I knew you'd do this."

"What would you say if you handed a small child a lollipop and he unwrapped it and put it into his mouth to enjoy? 'I knew you'd do this'?"

"When calm sets in, I'll tell the interesting part."

I went to the piano and played "Getting to Know You," grinning at Dennis Savage. He let me get all the way through the chorus, then said, "The interesting part is, he's straight."

"Oh please, these banal gay daydreams. Mission ridiculous."

"I swear on your mother's life."

"I don't know," I temporized. "Didn't I read in the *Times* that there weren't any straights anymore, just electricians?"

"If you saw him—be good and you will—you'd change your tune."

"What does a straight do in bed?" I asked, bemused.

His eyes glowed again. "Everything," he breathed.

"But what would a straight be doing outside the Eagle?"

"He didn't know where he was. He was almost raving with hunger and fatigue."

"How come *you* got him?"

He shrugged happily. "I came out and there he was."

"Good career move."

"Oh, he's so nice," Dennis Savage told me. "To meet him is to . . .
to—"

"To yearn to drill him, eh?"

"Will you clam up? To meet him is to understand him."

"Old news. Any gay can understand a straight because we all start
out as insiders in straight culture. The headlines are due when a
straight understands a gay, which will be never. And, excuse me for
asking, but what's a straight doing in bed with the gayest man in New
York?"

"Well . . ."

"Stop looking rapt and answer!"

"Oh, he was a mite shy at first. But you know how affectionate lost
boys can be, when someone proposes to take care of them. Can I tell
you what a pleasure it was to spend time with a man who wasn't
scared by his mother when he was three?"

"Are you going to see this waif again?"

"I can't help but. He's sleeping upstairs right now."

"You left him alone in your apartment? Alone with your check-
book, your plastic, and your complete collection—the world's only, I
fear to say—of Alice Faye lobby cards?"

"*You're* the one who—"

"Did you at least hide your—"

"His name is Ray and he's as sweet as they make them. Do you
want to come up and meet him or not?"

I was reminded of that scene in Tennessee Williams' play *The Milk
Train Doesn't Stop Here Anymore*, wherein two beldames remark a
splendid youth asleep in a bed, for Dennis Savage took me up to his
place and there in the bedroom was his vagabond lover, one of those
unruly innocents that delight at twenty-five, confuse at thirty, and
irritate thereafter; but Ray was twenty-five. Curled up, clutching the
pillow as if it were a teddy bear with a Mastercard, he looked trashily
angelic, a little haunted and maybe a little intelligent. Maybe a lot
intelligent: that's unusual in waifs.

Dennis Savage was beaming like Fafner over his hoard. Noting
banter bubbling to my lips, he held up a ssh finger.

"Isn't he cute?" he whispered. "How jealous you must be."

"Not at all," I whispered back. "I'm happy for you."

"What are you, a saint?"

"I want all my friends content."

He regarded his treasure. "Please be jealous. I want you jealous."

"Why?"

"It's half the fun of being gay."

"I'll bet he squeaks when he's screwed."

"He doesn't do anything you'd expect. He even talks funny." He pulled me over to the window. "Last night, when we were dozing off, he farted and said, 'Guess a bedbug just bit me.'"

A guffaw yelped out of me and Ray was awake, eyes fluttering as he took us in. Interesting eyes. "I was oversleeping, fellas," he uttered.

"Ray," Dennis Savage blissed—no other usage quite captures the noise he made that moment.

Ray squirmed, lazily smiled, and kicked off the covers. Dennis Savage soared right on to introduce us, and Ray said, "A happy Saturdays to you."

"To someone, anyway," I replied. He pronounced it "Saterdies," which was charming enow. "Well," I added, edging out, "I'm off to farandole class."

"Wonder if I could get up eggs and buttered toast with fruit spread," Ray was saying, and I chuckled all the way home. Once again, another thrilling chapter in the gay chronicles—*True Love at Long Last*, for instance, or *Bad Hat Reformed by Influence of Nice New Friend*, or, as in this case, *Dennis Savage Makes Sexual Crossover*—boiled down to the usual participants making the usual pickup in the usual places. Not that true love, character reformation, and crossover were all that elusive; but they were secret, invisible, while cruising and tricking were all over the place and hard to miss. And Dennis Savage, in those plague-free days, before he hooked up permanently with Little Kiwi, did enjoy his pickups. I was a little startled to learn that he and Ray ran their morning after into the night of the following day (complete with periodic breathless reports from Dennis Savage on the wonders of bedding a straight). But then I've seen a lot of moving in and out on the part of the homeless—Carlo has spent half his life as a leaseless roommate, and a number of Brooklynites of my acquaintance routinely arrange their affairs around the securing of pieds-à-terre in more central locales. What was amusing was Dennis Savage's enthusiasm for the appeal of straight: the pure hot of A Real Man. "He's so elemental!" Dennis Savage raved. "So true to life! At last I see it! All that old friends-of-Dorothy lore about waterfront bars and truck stops and dangerous men. That wasn't just because they didn't have preppie bars then. It was because they wanted to experience sexuality at its most masculine." He looked awed. He prepared his lecture. "Frustrated by their own giddy going-nowhere wit," he intoned, "by the covering-up, the apologizing, the hunger for peace, they fled their own kind and sought . . . what?"

"You know, that's about the most homophobic thing I've ever heard."

"Oh, great. If you can't be jealous, be political."

"They weren't fleeing anything," I insisted, "except the vicious credo of self-hatred laid upon them by everyone they knew all their lives. Society outlawed them so thoroughly they had to conceive their culture after-hours in secret places with murderous lunatics who have nothing to lose, and then society cried out in horror at 'the night world of the homosexual'! And when a dangerous man took them to a dark corner, lifted their wallet, and kicked them to death, with their last breath the contemptible faggots would sigh, 'Thank you, that was just.'"

His enthusiasm somewhat watted out, Dennis Savage regarded me resentfully. "I hardly think that boy upstairs is going to kick me to death."

"Why does he have to be straight, anyway?" I asked. "Would you enjoy him less if he—"

"He doesn't have to be. He is. Nothing embarrasses him. His world isn't a . . . a stage of drag shows and epigrammatic ripostes and all those delirious, skulking hungers."

"Oh, good."

"Shut up. His world is the world, and he's the center of it. I'm telling you, it's pure straight. As far as he's concerned, the universe exists to pleasure him."

"Sounds like an est instructor."

"It's more than the sex. It's like slipping through to the other side of the mirror. It's the difference between needing love and fucking love. Gays need love. Straights only need to fuck."

"According to Freud, then, gays are healthier than straights. Health is defined by the ability to love and work."

"I'm not looking for healthy just now," he fumed. "Do you mind?"

"Aren't we confusing issues, anyway? It's not a question of who's dangerous and who's nice. It's a question of who's emotionally available and who isn't. I would consider a man who is thus available to a gay man as gay. A man who is thus unavailable is straight—no matter whom he lies down with for what reason."

"Dick Hallbeck," he said suddenly, supporting my thesis. Dick Hallbeck is one of our favorite people, a man from Dennis Savage's hometown who turned up in the early days of gay cinema under a *nom de porn* screwing every man who chanced to come within camera range. Some porn actors are slithery hot, some less hot than hired, just there, minding the wrong business. Dick Hallbeck was hot. He outclassed men far more stunning than he and overwhelmed practiced veterans. Dark and forceful, he seemed on screen to offer a *summum bonum* of dead-on, take-no-prisoners promiscuity. He was the very energy of what Stonewall promised besides politics and art, virtually the protagonist of gay sex.

But he was straight. I don't mean latent. I don't mean bi. I don't mean avant-garde. I mean he was a straight who made his living fucking men. He appeared to be managing it lucratively. Ads offering stills, cinema, and even the kiss-and-tell journal of Jim Packer—Dick Hallbeck's public name—were everywhere one turned in those days, and the utterly humorless eyes that gave that ordinary face its show did not look like those of an exploitable man. There was no doubt that Dick Hallbeck held the major percentage on the marketing of Jim Packer.

Today Jim Packer is long forgotten and porn stars are in any case less prominent than they once were; we look to other heroes now. But in the first days of Stonewall, porn promised to be the most immediate source of gay independence, symbolically the unique defiance. Not every gay would revel in the emergence of a gay literature or monitor the airwaves for signs of "normalization" in the stereotype. But every gay responds to porn. Hell, what man doesn't, except George Will? Willing or no, there was no *Christopher Street* then, no Edmund White, no Gerry Studds. What there was was Jim Packer. To sit in the ruins of one of old Broadway's great relics—Henry Miller's Theatre as was, renamed the Park-Miller for purposes of porn exhibition—surrounded by hordes of hungry men, cruising, gasping, lurking, wandering, watching Jim Packer initiating applicants of many types in more positions than the *Kama Sutra* knows . . . well, to be there and to comprehend it, yet to hear Dennis Savage whisper that he had gone to high school with this man, and that he was as straight as our fathers are, was to realize that there might indeed be more things in heaven and earth than are dreamt of in my philosophy.

Naturally, I didn't believe this at first, partly because it was unbelievable and partly because I find it good policy not to believe anything Dennis Savage says, especially when he's in earnest. You have to understand that he was speaking of a man we had seen, over the course of an hour, plowing into a sizable fraction of the male porn population. And while I must admit that this man never cried out, "Hey, some fun!" or even smiled, still no one was holding a gun to his head.

I told Dennis Savage he was crazy, that the man was as gay as George Cukor (if different). Dennis Savage said that after all Dennis Savage's older brother was Dick's best friend, so he ought to know. But at the time all I could see—or all I could understand, and therefore all I *would* see—was that straight was one world and gay another, and that the two worlds were irremediably separate. I could believe that many a straight had lain with a man for personal, financial, or professional advancement. But would a straight so thrust himself into the gay scene that he could become its potent symbol? The question fascinated both Dennis Savage and me, and his old friend's names became our buzz terms. "Dick Hallbeck" signified a straight of possibly expansive virtues. "Jim Packer" was gay, wildly appetitive, but somehow impersonal. These were fantasy figures, largely—but came the day, then, that we crossed paths with the two men ourselves. It was a spring afternoon; we were on a bench in one of the plazas the Sixth Avenue office towers use in order to frill up their bottoms, and a man left the passing crowd to examine Dennis Savage. His wrinkled shirt was open to the belt, his boots were busted, his scraggly beard looked like something a wrestler would wear to a cockfight, and he said, "How's Cliff doing?"

"He's in Seattle," said Dennis Savage. I think he was stunned.

"Who's this?" the man asked, about me, sitting next to us.

"Bud," said Dennis Savage, "this is . . ." Yes, who, or which, was he? "This is my brother's best friend from high school."

"Dick Hallbeck," he told me, as we shook hands.

That's one way of looking at it, I thought.

The meeting was short, merely a "What's new? encounter—Dennis Savage reporting on the family Cliff was raising in Seattle, Dick on the bar he was planning to open in New Jersey as soon as he had assembled his venture backing, along with a few idle aperçus. But we spoke long enough for me to realize that Dennis Savage had been right: Dick Hallbeck—even Jim Packer—was straight. Emotionally unavailable to gays, possibly to anyone. Some gays swear they can tell a fellow from an outsider within two minutes simply by his dress and eye movements and allusions; but these are blandishments. I can tell a comrade by a certain sensitivity, a sometimes determined and sometimes furtive awareness of place, of people, of the vibrations bashing through the ozone. Gays are never strangers, even when they're uncomfortable. Straights always hold something back. Dick Hallbeck did, too; and better, perhaps, than anyone I've met. He was focused

entirely on us, never as much as glanced at the people storming by.
Yet he gave nothing to us. There was no real transaction: because
what he might have wanted, we could not supply. There was a barely
perceptible gap between us, a hitch in delivery, as when one of the
speakers in a conversation is not altogether fluent in the language.
None of us was shy or brooding. We were lively, forthright, and we
all spoke English. Yet we could not impress him. He could not touch
us.

Dennis Savage, once he got over his surprise at seeing Jim Packer
turn into Dick Hallbeck, became ebullient and began to flow with
picturesque recollections of small-town life. Only in New York, I reminded myself—only in this absurd metropolis could you find yourself sitting between a schoolteacher and a porn star as they review a
past of socials and canoeing. But once in this old-home convention
did Dennis Savage tighten up, when Dick referred to "that time you
guys bagged the Winky-Dink out by the sled hills." One of Dick's
eyebrows jittered, as if he found this a questionable act, though his
tone was noncommittal, and I made note to inquire into this matter
as soon as was indecently possible.

It was Dick, anyway, who held my attention, for I always enjoy
meeting proof that the riddles haven't all been solved—that some stories, after all, have yet to be told. What fascinated was not what Dick
was, but what he *also* was, for Dick fielded the tough form of straight,
based on the kind of self-reliance so brash it hardly needs to show
itself. In fact, I began to understand—at that very moment, that
chance meeting—that the straight-gay disparity was not a sexual but a
cultural matter. Isn't it? I stopped listening to Dick and started watching him, and I got a picture of a man who cares only about withstand-
ing assaults on his space, making women, filling his wallet, and
satisfying a few secondary appetites. He cares about nothing else: he
has no art, no representations, no themes. And that is pure straight.
The exceptions are salesmen, unemployed actors, and hustlers, all of
whom will go out of their way to engage you emotionally no matter
how straight they may be. But then, of course, they want something
from you; that gives them a theme.

"Who's the Winky-Dink?" I asked after Dick went on his way. "And why did you bag him?"

"Do you like me?" Dennis Savage countered.

"Uh . . ."

"Do you want to stay friends with me?"

"At least through next week."

"Leave it alone, okay? Just leave it, because it's a sacred, sad thing that no one should hear of."

"Okay," I said. Two beats, then: "Tell me or I'll make up something horrible and put it in a story."

"If I tell you, you're bound to put it in a story."

"Never."

"It already is horrible."

"I sensed that."

"I'd hoped to take it to my grave."

"None must know it."

"Exactly."

"Any who did would hate you."

"There you go."

"So tell me. Or else." I mimed a headline: "DENNIS SAVAGE MOLESTS MAYOR'S EIGHT-YEAR-OLD SON. 'HE BLEW ME APART,' CHILD REVEALS."

"Cut it out!"

"'IT HURT BUT IT'S FUN,' THE VICTIM WENT ON, AS HIS PARENTS SLAPPED HIM ABOUT—"

"I helped some homophobic straights beat up a helpless gay kid for a Halloween prank. We were so mean to him that whenever he saw us he quietly stood where he was and wept. Now, are you glad? And who made *you* head of the gay secret police, *huh?*"

He was angry and I was silent.

"Comes the revolution," he went on, "and you report me to the Committee, try to remember that the pressures to conform are tremendous in a small town. Tremendous, okay? And remember that many of us, in that last desperate surge of fake solidarity before we face up to what we are . . . what we need to be . . . pull one or two truly vicious stunts that hurt us for the rest of our lives."

"Imagine how the Winky-Dink feels."

He took a deep breath and silently counted to ten.

"Go joke," he said, in what may have been genuine melancholy. "Go ahead." He gestured feebly, like a dying insect. "Have one on me."

We were almost home by then; our encounter with Dick Hallbeck had made us long to get indoors, safe from chance meetings.

"What's bagging, anyway?" I asked. "Each time I hear it, it means something else. Carlo says it's where you pull off someone's pants in public. Lionel says that's *de*bagging; plain bagging is dunking someone in water. The way you use it, it sounds like a mugging."

He just looked at me.

"You have to tell," I said. "I told you about Gary Lundquist making me play Strip Candyland in the attic."

"You never told me that."

"Didn't I?" I held the door for him; we had gone to my place. "Well, I will, one day. Right now, it's confess or else."

He nodded. "It was Halloween night," he began, speaking in a slow drag, as if showing me how repentant he was. "We were in tenth grade . . ."

"*Pace! Pace!*"

"All right," he said, and we began to sail. "His family called him Lance and their name was Winkler, but we called him the Winky-Dink, for the imaginable reasons. Total queer. He was eccentric, as you might expect, and he liked to go out trick-or-treating. Well, two jocks and I decided to jump him. You know, teach the faggot a lesson. I mean, here's a society in which tenth-grade males excel in sports and design racing cars and do ingenious things with cherry bombs. And here's this narrow-shouldered potzie named Lance who likes to dress up on Halloween and collect candy with the eight-year-olds. You have to admit that's pretty limp."

"I think it's pretty daring."

He shrugged. "Maybe it was the biggest night of his year—the one on which it was actually legal for him to go out in costume."

"So," I said, giving him unsweetened apple juice to steady his nerves. "What exactly happened?"

"We waited for him out by the sled hills, where there's this big empty space and no houses. And finally he came by, singing happily to himself, and we . . . well, okay, we bagged him."

"Such as what?"

"Oh, we harassed him and then we pulled him off the street into the shadows while he said, 'Please don't hurt me,' and 'I never did anything to you,' and all those unbelievably *stupid* things that have absolutely nothing to do with your relationship with implacable men. Is that what they say in a prison riot, as they're held down while someone trims their skull with an acetylene torch? 'I never did anything to you'?"

"More."

"More . . . We threw his candy all over the place and we punched him around a little, and then we stripped off his costume and ran off with it, laughing all the way. I know you love to humble me and rake me around, and here's your big chance. Let's get it over with."

"Did you really do that?"

He was still.

"No," I said. "I mean, *why* did you do that? How *could* you? I thought I knew you. 'I don't like his looks so let's bag him.'"

"On the contrary, he was very cute. Black hair and very dark skin. All the girls were crazy for him."

"I thought you hated violence."

He nodded. "Maybe this is why."

"And how," I pursued, "could you agree to go along with those two cretins? Why didn't you get sick or have to look after the house or something?"

"I didn't go along with them. I led them. It was my idea."

We drank our juice and contemplated the strange footnotes of the gay biography.

"The sled hills . . ." I said. "What's the derivation of that?"

"Oh, there was a series of interconnected slopes that were hell to walk on but great for sledding in the snow, which we always had a lot of. And there were no grown-ups around to . . . you know . . ."

"Bag you."

"We only went on them for sledding, so they were—"

"That's a great naturalistic detail. Authenticates the story."

"You mean I would have been safe if Dick hadn't mentioned that?" he asked. "You wouldn't have proposed to expose my shame?"

"No, I would have made something like that up. But it's more amusing when it's real." I noted down the term, and turned back to him, smiling.

"I'll never tell you anything again."

"I always thought teenage violence was a strictly straight phenomenon," I said. "Kind of like the physical interpretation of the state of being emotionally unavailable. You know, when I was a kid there was a Dairy Queen on the town road, and the parking lot was a meeting place for adolescents looking for a fight. I mean, literally. A violence market. The outlet closed at nine, and by ten there'd be kids hulking in the shadows, looking each other over, approaching, psyching up . . . What does it sound like?"

"A bar."

"Exactly. Jim used to hang out there and collect scalps. He'd invite me along now and then, but I got all the fighting I needed at home— with him, in fact—and besides, who in his sanity would lurk in a parking lot for the purpose of engaging in battle with another teenager for mere sport? Jim would come back and describe his adventures, and you know what I was thinking? Better he had this release for whatever's inside him, because if he didn't give it to them he'd probably give it to me."

"What did your parents say about this?"

"Are you kidding? They never knew."

"Interesting that your father never needed this outlet."

"Why should he? They had wars then. If you have the chance to

serve in the O.S.S. as liaison between Polish partisans and the Russian Army, who needs Dairy Queen parking lots?"

"Anyway, wasn't Jim the aberrant Mordden?"

"I always thought so. But then Andrew took it up in his time, too.
There's something in straight blood. Something in the mind."

"Maybe they intake a substance gays don't know about—Gatorade?
Sen-sen? Or effusions from polyester?"

"Incidentally, what costume did the Winkler boy go out in the
night you bagged him? I visualize a helter-skelter Liz Taylor, but
where would he have gotten the wig?"

"He went as a Mountie."

That took a moment to sink in. I said, "What?"

"You think every gay kid's idea of dressing up is drag?"

"You mean a Mountie like Sergeant Preston of the Yukon? Like
Dudley Do-Right?"

"I want more juice."

"Whatever happened to him? Winkler? I could really use a confrontation ten years on. He forgives you. Tearfully. Makes a nice
effect."

"You're really going to use this, aren't you?"

I refilled his glass. "If you don't want to be in a story, don't know a
writer."

"Anyway, I haven't heard of him in twenty years. I venture to guess
that he's in Rochester or Buffalo, has timidly joined some gay organi-
zation or other, and is alone and unhappy. He was cute, but he was
born to be pushed around and neglected."

"I wonder if that's a difference between gay and straight—that gays
are unhappy when they have no one to be emotionally available to."

"That sounds more like women."

"Anyway, what have we decided?" I asked. "Who hurts? Who
needs? Who gets? And what if the Lance Winklers come to New York
instead of the regional capital? Would that make a difference?"

"Do you know, every time I think of that Halloween I wish I were

Catholic so I could describe what I did to someone who doesn't hate
me."

"The interesting thing about being a Protestant is you get to pay for
your sins in this life."

"In that case, gays are the Protestants of the sexual revolution."

By all of which, boys and girls, I wish to put Dennis Savage's boyfriend Ray in context: as a willowy, charming fellow with hard skin
and soft talk. He was far from the certifiably brusque remoteness of
Dick Hallbeck, yet no Winky-Dink, either. He entered upon our
scene in the early 1970s, at the height of our questing communications on the subject of the gay and straight identities, and so may well
have seemed more attractive than he might have in some other season, as a kind of conversation piece.

He himself had little to say; and one was relieved, after hearing
what little there was. Ask him a question and he'd say, "Huh?
Lookit," before formulating a reply, and to the ponderous statements
that we of the great world are prone to make, he'd offer, "Hey, that's
for sure!" Then he'd smile at you as if patting you on the back after
making a great save in the ninth inning against the other team's ace
batter. He was the kind of fellow you introduced simply as "Ray"—
only important people have last names—but he seemed content however he was treated. The official story told it out that he was staying
with Dennis Savage till he could find work and a place of his own;
and that was true in theory. But in fact Ray was around because Ray
liked to take it easy and Dennis Savage liked company. So okay. And,
unlike a lot of young men in his position, Ray did not horn in on the
conversations of his betters with idiotic opinions. Nor did he scorn to
do the marketing, the laundry, and other minor favors. Best (and
rarest) of all, he did not quickly become less accommodating in bed.
Ray was ideal for his role: there when you needed him and out of the
way when you didn't. Moreover, he seemed completely honest, unlike most if not all hustlers, who feel they're missing something if they
don't somehow sneak a little extra out of you one way or another. I

still felt that there was something oddly intelligent about him, that he knew more than he let on. He would hear things, and be quiet, uninvolved; but you could tell he had heard. He reacted by not reacting.

When I caught him at this, I would smile wittingly, the cabaret detective; but his smile came back open and unknowing. Then I'd turn to Dennis Savage and he'd do one of his "What's going on here?" attitudes, like the cop in the movies who wants to be fair but gets a useful edge out of being tough first and fair later. Something *was* going on here, but I couldn't assimilate it yet.

"You think you're so smart," Dennis Savage would tell me.

"I just want to learn about straight from your friend," I reply. "I'm checking him for emotional unavailability."

"I can see you on the Ark. There's Noah and the family beaming at this amazing achievement. They've saved the world. And you come in and say, 'We forgot the unicorns.'"

"I'm looking out for him," I protested. "I'm afraid you'll find out he's gay after all and then you'll call him a funny name and take his candy and—"

"Of *all* the low tricks, *that's*—"

"Come to think of it, he already has a funny name."

"You should talk?"

"He pronounces it funny, too, doesn't he?"

Dennis Savage stopped grouching and looked at me, thinking about it. Listen: "Holgrave," he said, with the long *o* as in "hole" that most Americans would use.

"That's not how he says it," I told him. "He makes it sort of English. Hahl-grave. You know. The way they say 'hamaseksyual.'"

Dennis Savage shrugged.

"Ray Holgrave," I repeated. "It's a rather elaborate name for a rootless kid, isn't it? I mean, can you imagine a hustler named Holgrave?"

"You keep trying to turn him into some form of opportunist. Can't you believe that there are people with flexible taste? A straight who can enjoy something on the side?"

"This is simple market research. I'm trying to figure out what defines a straight in terms of personality. What variables command an individual's sexuality. Because it's undeniable that Ray isn't like us."

"Aha."

"Because he's *trying* not to be," I insisted.

"He isn't trying to be anything—that's his charm. He's a perfectly styleless man." Dennis Savage seemed so glad to have reckoned it out that I had to humor him with silence. But he went on, "Nothing has been added to him and nothing taken away," and now I must speak.

"No one," I said, "is perfectly styleless. Whatever you do, that's your style. Your diction and grammar, for instance. Are you telling me the odd things he says don't feed into a style?"

"What odd things?"

"'Huh, lookit,'" I replied, in Ray's vapidly blithe manner.

"Everyone else thinks it's cute!"

"Yeah," I said. "Especially Ray."

It was rude of me, no doubt, to keep prodding in matters that were none of my business, but The Case of the Questionable Straight gripped me with its thousand riddles. The most arresting part of it all was the defiance of the traditions of gay sexual crossover, which emphasize mystery and menace—those dangerous men, again, lying in wait for the fluttery stone-age queers who covered the waterfront. What were those men, really? Latent? Committed? Tolerant? Hostile? Were they lovers who dared not speak their name, or reformers of the underworld observing an informal purge technique? What would they do? Lie back and let you go to town? Would they come along with you? Take your money and follow you? Want you? Knife you? Here was menace. But what was Ray? Innocuous, clean-cut. A sweetheart. Dennis Savage had, it seemed, domesticated the crossover.

And yet. Time after time, at Dennis Savage's for dinner, or strolling with him and Ray through the Village of a Sunday, or in a cab setting out for a West Side brunch, the detective in me would come up for air and trouble. I would satirically test Ray with intellectual call-outs—the Odessa Steps montage, *Zuleika Dobson*, June 16,

1904, Rosebud, the Mapleson cylinders. Ray's eyes—too big, too fully lashed, so pretty—would grow avid as he smiled at me. Was he aware that I was goading him to break cover or simply grateful for the attention?

"It's not good when you get like this," Carlo warned me over steaks at Clyde's. "You make it feel as if knowing things is all that matters."

"Come on, knowledge is power."

Carlo got intent applying mayonnaise to his steak, which is apparently traditional, or at least ordinary, in South Dakota, Carlo's point of origin and, to me, the most remote of all American provinces. Some states don't have opera houses; South Dakota doesn't even have Korean fruit markets.

"Origins," I said, having been thinking of them, "are very telling. You can tell a lot about a person if you know his origins—region, parentage, class . . . Did you know Dennis Savage and the porn star Jim Packer were in high school together? Dennis Savage says, and you won't believe this—"

"Jim Packer is a gringo?" Carlo's term for straights. "I know that.

"How?"

"I tried to take him home and he said no."

"That's proof enough for me," I said, not joking. "But don't you think a straight man in gay porn is a little pushy? I mean, we're not talking of someone in a jack-off scene, or getting tongued here and there. I've seen him. He does every activity in the checklist, and he does it with the opulence of an initiate."

"You don't know what he's thinking of, though."

"Carlo, he was a CIA agent or something in this movie, and he had a spy tied down on a bed and he was trying to get information out of him, yes? Think of it. The spy looked like the swimming champ of Walt Whitman High School or something, but let's move right on. And there's our boy, straight Jim Packer"—only it's not Jim Packer who's straight, it's Dick Hallbeck—"stroking the spy's tummy and pubic hairs and murmuring sweet nothings about 'the information,' and am I supposed to . . . I mean, let's face it, the spy's cock was so rigid you could have plugged the hole in the dike and saved Amsterdam. And the look on Jim Packer's face. I can't believe—"

"*Do you suppose* you could talk about something more suitable to decent public gatherings?" cried someone at the table behind me.

I turned around to find four men glaring at me.

"This is a restaurant," another of the four explained, "not a toilet!"

Carlo, who has done this a hundred times, got up and stood before them and said, with engaging mildness, "One of you come outside with me and settle it like a man or shut your mouths and mind your business. Because one more word out of any of you and I'll pick *you*"—he chooses the most vulnerable queen of the lot; it's always queens, by the way: clones don't start these scenes—"and drag you outside and kick your junk in." Then, paradoxically, he touches the arm of the man he addressed. "So keep your friends in line," he urges. It never fails.

When he sat down again, we began to eat in silence, thinking over the themes. Clones and brothers and fighting and love. Emotional availability. And that really is New York right there: someone's always got some idea to sell.

"Bud," he finally said, "you surely have to stop measuring people."

"I can't stop. It's my job."

"A lot of porn actors switch back and so. It's just work to them."

"What about Ray, Carlo? His current assignment—would you call that work or fun? Would you call Ray an actor? Or a true story?"

He ate, considering. "I will sincerely tell you what is true," he said after a bit, putting down his fork and leaning on the table. "Access," he said. "So you'd best include that, while you're scoring everybody up as gays or gringos."

"Access."

"Some people would call it chance. It isn't, because this is something people get to do without consciously willing it. They . . . they *contrive* it. That means they don't know what they want, but they know what they're afraid of. So they allow themselves to get into the position of being near the thing that threatens them the least."

He stopped, reached for his fork. I grabbed his hand. "No," I said. "Go on."

"Well. So, like." He's thinking; the talk comes out too fast in New York. Midwestern Carlo pauses to be sure of what he knows. "Why is it," he asks, "that so many men who can't deal with emotional involvements get into prison, where they either have to go without sex—which no one can do—or fuck men? Because when they get out, they go *on* fucking men, and they tell themselves it's because they got wrecked in jail, or because men are easier to get ahold of than women."

"Access . . ."

"But maybe it's because it's what they wanted in the first place. Not because they're gay, but because they want sex without affection."

"Emotionally unavailable . . ."

"They can always find a bimbo, I know. You know. Some women are as easy to take home as men are. But even those women scare them. They're different. Hard. Funny. Something."

He started to eat again, watching me, glancing out the window onto Bleecker Street, nodding, chewing. He's no literato, but there are more stories in him than in all the writers I know put together. Maybe that's why I like him so much.

"Carlo, you aren't saying that you've run into men like that. Convicts? In our bars?"

"They don't go to gay bars, boy. They wouldn't know where to find them." He grinned. "They go to other places."

"Working-class bars?"

He nodded.

"They actually go there to pick up men?" I asked, scandalized and incredulous.

Our very scion of the Circuit regarded me with forgiveness for, as usual, my lack of scope. "You think you can't take a man home from a Clancy's or a Blue Ribbon Bar and Grill, like with a Schaefer logo in the window? You think everyone there is guys and bimbos?"

How does he know so much? I was thinking, for we were all young then.

"It's a question of lifestyle, Bud. It's not hetero and homo. It's gringo and gay. It's . . ."

"Culture."

"Yes. It's how you learn to behave. People tend to stay in their culture. They avoid other cultures."

"So a homophobic hardhat," I posed, "is what?"

"A gringo."

"But if he secretly beds men?"

"He's still a gringo. Straight is how you act, not how you feel. You truly should know that by now. Do you *feel* gay? Or do you wear the uniforms and attend the dances and keep in touch with the politics? And feel like a man? Men is all it is. Men. Boys. Kids. All this. And you and Dennis Savage. Eric, Lionel, Scooter, Kenny. And Big Steve. Remember him? And the people you didn't see and the dancers at the Tenth Floor. All of us . . ."

"Carlo."

"We're all here."

"What do you—"

"Eat up, Bud."

"*Access*. Listen—"

"You have to stop. You're going to get yourself weird. The more you make rules, the farther you get from the truth. People aren't rules, Bud. People are exceptions."

"Ray is a gringo, right? But is he a hetero gringo? Could he be a gay gringo? Is there such a thing?"

Carlo speared the last of my broccoli and smiled.

"He's naive, I know," I said. "But is he clever naive? Or just naive? His eyes are . . ." Now Carlo was grinning. "What's so funny?"

"Are you going to spend the whole summer doing this?"

"I won't have to. Because nothing brings out the gay in the gringo like The Pines. Right?"

* * *

I was righter than I knew, but only by a fluke. As the summer began, Ray was still living with Dennis Savage, had found neither job nor apartment, and was going to serve as unofficial houseboy for Dennis Savage's gang. Ray was also still the coolest cat in our set *or* the most accomplished mimic alive, to the satisfaction of everyone but me. At his first tea, I carefully watched him noticing the girls who come over from Sayville to dance. He stayed in character, did not overplay. He saw them as one who knew what he thought they were for and would request an audition again one day, but for now had to abstain out of respect for the man who was paying his bills.

"Beautifully judged," I told him.

"Say what, now?"

"That, too."

He smiled, as he often did when I teased him, and gave the tiny shrug that meant, "I don't know what you're referring to, but I'll play along."

So I decided to press him a little. Maybe I was in a mean mood. "I'm on to you, Jack," I told him. "I'm looking and listening and you're going to slip, aren't you? I'll be there when you do."

"You don't ought to be so tough around me," he said. "I don't do nothing to you."

"If this were a movie, you'd be up for an Oscar."

"Lookit?"

"I wish Olivier were here for this. He'd want to worship at your feet."

He leaned over a touch, as if putting his ear closer to the words would render them intelligible.

"Oh, I love that one," I said. "Harry Langdon as Hamlet, right?"

He looked at me: bewildered but trusting.

"Instead of looking for a punk handyboy job," I went on, "why don't you become an acting coach? I mean, Robert de Niro's good, but you're better."

And did I see then, for a split second, a flicker of acknowledgment in those lovable eyes, a sign of the quick wit that knew the names, the notions I was throwing at him? But it fled so fast that Ray had squeezed my arm, said, "Catch ya later on here," and moved away before I could assess it all.

Carlo wasn't with Dennis Savage this summer. Some uptown gays had offered him a room in an oceanside palazzo rent-free, in order to improve the physical tone of their house. There I went after tea, to confess and be absolved of my vicious needling of Ray, to beg for advice in breaking the writer's congenital habit of sticking one's nose in. It was seven o'clock in the evening of the second Friday of the season, High Pines: yet the fabulous house seemed deserted, not only dark and silent but gloomy, as if Important People had seen unfashionable things inside and ordered it Closed. Could they all be having sex? I wondered, walking around to the back entrance at the dunes— rich gays made out like bandits in those preplague days. No, there was Carlo, standing in the middle of the deck, looking at the water.

He turned, saw me, and gazed at me wordlessly. He is the handsomest man in New York and, once you get to know him, the nicest; but when he gets moody nobody can do anything with him. A fierce wind was up; his clothes and hair were whipping around. I thought, If they ever make a commercial for The Pines, this is all they need, provided Carlo is willing to smile.

"I always forget to bring the right sweater at the beginning of the summer," he said. "Then I get cold."

"Why don't you borrow something from your housemates? Where is everyone, anyway?"

He shook his head. Not important. When he's like this—so beauty, too, is human, boys and girls—he concentrates on essentials.

"When I was growing up," he said, "if I was worried about something and I went to my father with it, he would give me a switching. If I went to my mom, she would make me a plate of Cream of Wheat with maple syrup."

"You must not have gone to your dad very often."

"Sometimes you have to."

He put his arms around me and we shivered together in the wind. "Now this is a study," he said. "She prays for me. But I don't know if it's working. I sincerely don't know. Sometimes I believe I can hear her, halfway across the continent." He hummed a snatch of something. "Praying for me," he said.

"I was mean to Ray at tea."

He held me at arm's length. "You want Cream of Wheat or a switching?"

"Maybe he is genuine and maybe he isn't, and it's absolutely none of my business. I admit it. But I thought of something. Why would he pretend to be a homeless, dumb kid if he isn't one? Why would a gay play gringo *in* the gay world? A homosexual ditchdigger or carpenter would have to play gringo because his culture runs on the gringo code. But Ray's in the gay world. It makes no sense."

"You should tell him you're sorry. I do believe he's very sensitive."

"Straights have no feelings, Carlo."

"*Gringos* have no feelings. Straights are something else."

"Isn't Ray a gringo, after all?"

"No. Gringos are tough. Like John Wayne or . . ."

"Jim Packer?"

He nodded. "I never met a porn star who wasn't born tough."

"Then what is Ray?"

"Why don't you ask him?"

"Oh, come on."

"Do you want some Cream of Wheat with maple syrup?"

"Can you make that here? With real maple syrup?"

"Sure." He led me inside. "Their kitchen looks like the movie *Metropolis*." As he got the fixings out of the cupboard, he said, "She's probably praying for me right now. That's what drove me away from them, back a while ago. And she knows that, but she prays all the harder." He was almost murmuring. "I miss them," he added, a highly accessible man.

The fluke that exploded Ray Holgrave's act occurred a few Sundays after, on the beach at noon with the squad, gathered from our various houses, in full congress. A number of things were happening at once. Carlo and Kenny Reeves had just come up from the ocean and were getting everyone wet, Lionel was reading aloud from *Valmouth*, two visitors from the Grove were grousing at a strange nosy dog, and a straight couple had come up to ask Ray if he was the Mr. Hamill who was the graduate assistant of Dr. Copelman's Hawthorne and Melville course at Bucknell two years before.

Ray said nothing, literally nothing. I couldn't see his face.

Well, was he? they repeated. It was clear they thought he was.

Ray shook his head. Everyone else was watching and listening.

"Are you sure?" said the woman, laughing at the absurdity of the question. "Because you gave me an A on my *Marble Faun* paper and a B- on my *Confidence Man* paper. I wouldn't forget the man who grades with that kind of enthusiasm."

Ray looked at Dennis Savage. From behind, I saw his shoulders slide up into that tiny shrug of his.

"*Perry* Hamill?" the woman went on. "Really you look just like him."

My eyes were boring into the back of Ray's neck, but he didn't turn. Nor would he yet speak, and the silence sounded rather loud.

"His name," Dennis Savage finally said, "is Ray."

"Well," the woman told him, beginning to sense, and surprised by, the tension she had created. "You've got a twin brother named Perry walking around somewhere."

I looked at Carlo, but he raised a hand, warding me off.

I looked at Dennis Savage, but he was looking exclusively at Ray.

I looked at everyone else, but they couldn't have cared less. Kenny Reeves put a wet hand on Lionel's neck and made him jump; the two Grove people were calling the strange nosy dog bad names in French; and the collegiate couple moved on down the beach.

I cleared my throat.

"In *The House of the Seven Gables*," I began, "there's a character named Maule who takes a pseudonym. Has anyone present read Hawthorne's *The House of the Seven Gables*? Anyway, would someone like to guess what pseudonym this guy named Maule takes in Hawthorne's *The House of the Seven Gables?*"

Ray turned around to see me, and it was the same ungrudging, mildly questioning gaze he invariably—almost invariably—presented. I decided I must not go on, because I was being churlish and intrusive and boring; and what did it prove, anyway? Ray was Ray, as sure as Dick Hallbeck was Jim Packer—you see the problem? Ray was *not* Ray. Because gringo is *there* and gay is *here*, yet every other time I turn around, the two are trading slave bracelets. All right, it's not my business what Ray may have been in a former life. It's not, all right. Okay.

But, for the record, the pseudonym that Maule takes in Hawthorne's *The House of the Seven Gables* is Holgrave, and it's pronounced with an Anglo flip on the vowel: Hahlgrave, just the way Ray pronounced it.

Ray never did find an apartment, but he was offered a job by a straight couple who, legend told, had made an unholy fortune in cocaine dealing and owned one of the flashiest houses on the water. Ray moved out on Dennis Savage and into his new berth simply by ambling along the boardwalk.

"Just as well," said Dennis Savage. "I must admit, he did lack something in entertainment value."

As it was over, anyway, I told Dennis Savage about the Hawthorne correspondence. He was amused but unimpressed. "It's not conclusive," he said. "What it is is slightly arresting."

"You slept with him. You must know. Could he have been a teacher's assistant at Bucknell? Please. Just think about it. Just know what it is. Just tell me."

He considered. "Bucknell, maybe. But he couldn't have hacked it at Hamilton."

"Look, don't play rep audition with me. Is he or isn't he?"

"Is he what?"

"Jeepers," I said. "You *know* what."

"That's just it. I don't. And you don't. Only Ray knows."

"The story without end. We'll never find out."

"Why does it matter so much?"

"Because I believe culture is finite and taste is fixed. I've built life and art on those precepts. I have to know what is true in the world."

"Why?"

"Because I am the sleuth!"

He shook his head. "When you write it all down," he said, "I hope you make it clear to everyone just how irritating you've been about this."

"You only say that," I told him, "because you think this was Ray's story. 'The Tale of the Drifter,' or something like."

"Whose story was it, then, may I ask?"

"Mine."

He just shook his head again.

Will we ever know what is true in the world, especially about sexual crossover? I guess not. The data is secret, the informants are inarticulate, and they are probably too shaken by their experiences to report fairly on them. We have to take the word of writers; but writers are mad. We try to be gallant, however. When I ran into Ray in the Pines Pantry near the end of the summer, I waited for him to check out, and, outside, apologized for baiting him.

"Sure, huh," he said. "It's all the same."

"No," I insisted. "No. I was tough around you, as you said. It's unforgivable. So don't forgive me. Just register my apology."

"Hey, sure." He put his hand on my head and patted me. "Sure, pal." His hand slid down to my shoulders. "I know you were only doing that 'cause you liked me."

I looked at him smiling away. The touch of his hand was forgiving, which suggests that he knew what I was doing, which tells us that he *is* more aware than he acts—but that way more madness lies. Life in New York.

"How are you getting on with your new people?" I asked.

"They're okay. Kind of taking me twiceways. First she likes to screw me with a rubber thing, and then I go on and do him. It's fun but it really makes my hole ache."

I was still watching him, noting him down; I couldn't help myself.

"Carlo's really a great guy, isn't he?" Ray said.

"We all think so."

"I always liked that Carlo."

Carlo had said, "Why don't you ask him?" and so I did: "Ray, it couldn't possibly make any difference now. You're off to a new job with moneyed people, and Dennis Savage won't mind anyway at this point, and I don't know why, but I do, because I'm not sure I can live in a world in which Dick Hallbeck is interchangeable with Jim Packer. So look . . ."

Walking, we had reached the ferry plaza, where we would separate, he to the west and I to the east, and I glommed him one last time, and there were the utterly untroubled eyes of a man who doesn't need what you have. But I asked anyway.

"Are you Perry Hamill, a former teaching assistant in a Hawthorne-Melville course at Bucknell?"

He smiled and gave the tiny shrug, and nodded me goodbye. He started off. I didn't move. He sensed that, and, ten feet off, stopped and turned. Two men with their groceries standing at the harbor.

"Are you?" I said.

He smiled and looked me spang in the eye and whispered, as he turned to go, "Wouldn'st thou like to know?"

Uptown, Downtown

A tour through the gay metropolis.

My friend Lucky very recently made his first trip to New York. He saw it as a great theme park, an agglomeration not of neighborhoods where different cultures flower but of sectors where entertainments present themselves. The West Village was Gayland, Fourteenth Street Scuzz Avenue, the Lexington IRT Terror Train. Most impressive to Lucky was Midtown, which he termed Businessville.

"Wow," he opined, as dashing men in dress kit stalked past us, dotted here and there with important-looking women. "It's swank!" Lucky lives year round in a pair of jeans; for solemnities he may go as far as to don a T-shirt. "What do you call those things they're wearing?"

"Suits."

"No. The handkerchief in their high pockets."

"We call those 'quibbles,'" I replied, thinking fast.

"Do you ever wear a quibble?" he asked me, as we walked on. It's petty to kid an Angeleno; too easy. But Lucky is so receptive to colorful trivia that it's a form of sustenance, a way of making love to him. He dragged me out on long walks, from the two big museums bordering the Park down to Wall Street, from Sutton Place to Hell's Kitchen. Every now and then I'd stop in front of some dreary brownstone and invent a backstory involving Theodore Roosevelt,

Boss Tweed, Texas Guinan, and others such, as Lucky shivered at the closeness of history, the wonder of having a past compounded of closed systems fiercely abutting one another. Who was the hero, the villain, the dupe? Which was the risky, the wealthy, the happy district? Where were the theatres, the bordellos, the banks? Visitors always think New York is like their town, but bigger. New York is not like any other town. It is all dupes, all risky, and its own theatre. To be young, beautiful, and Angeleno is to know nothing of parish phenomena, of the advantages and penalties of helter-skelter sectorization, of the inevitability of epoch. When I first came to New York, the upper west side as a cultural place stopped dead at about Seventy-third Street; north of that, it was nothing but hardware stores straight to Poughkeepsie. Now it's one great pecan pie as far as the eye sees.

Somewhere, Lucky heard the word "gentrification"—meaning instead of being overrun with roaches you're overrun with Akitas—and he wants to see an example. I take him to Chelsea, but we find little evidence of Coming Up. "Where's all the gents?" asks Lucky. He laughs. He has made a joke. But the many men in tank tops and net shirts grow rigidly sober as they pass us, reading Lucky's stomach and thighs. There's no fun in New York; everyone's too busy cruising, the only activity common to all the sectors.

Lucky notices the general malaise. "I thought New York was like one big party." It is; but no one's invited. Some make an entire evening out of rejection, lining up outside discos to turn their facades into wailing walls; others scheme to learn the phone numbers of the great, and dial to thrill to a "Hello" they daren't answer.

"Take me to the fun part," Lucky urges.

"That's not what New York is for," I almost say. Then I think of the Madcap Heiress of Seventy-fourth Street, and decide it is time Lucky saw the east side.

The Madcap Heiress was born to clown looks as well as a fortune, and has played the one into a unique comix and the other into a credential of glamour. In the Village, guests are lavish presents to be unwrapped. On the west side, guests are the intelligentsia. At the Madcap Heiress', guests are an audience to be charmed and scandalized. All queens are funny: because the only other thing they can be is bitter. But this queen is insightfully ridiculous, like Dali's mustache. To be absurd in a sullen world is a surmise—as those Park Avenue tramps know, shouting lurid nonsense at the officers of the Corporation as they lope up the street in their ties each weekday evening.

The Madcap Heiress is thrilled to see us, but sighs profoundly as we step in. "Utterly worn out," he says. "Crazy Bunny came for lunch and brought that awful Dizzy Wizard. The two of them rendered me helpless and then played with the toilet flusher till the whole apartment was . . ." Now he takes in Lucky. "Little Lamb, who made thee?"

Lucky had offered to put on a shirt for the east side, but I figured the Madcap Heiress would prefer him *al fresco*.

"I like your quibble," Lucky told him.

"Completely baffled."

"He means your handkerchief," I put in.

"Oh, my . . . *quibble*, yes. My . . . Crazy Bunny gave it to me, had you heard? For when I came back from safari. He lifted it from Bergdorf's, there's no doubt. Did you know I was on safari? Hunting and tracking or so?" He purrs, admiring Lucky. "Actually, I went on Jewish safari. Just like the real thing, except all the animals are in cages. Darling, who *is* the boy?"

"He's my western friend Lucky."

"Could I have seen you in a movie?" the Madcap Heiress asks him.

"Yes."

I'm startled.

"*Cousins Who Rim During Shavuous*, or something?"

"*Brotherly Love*," Lucky corrects him amiably.

"A movie star in my apartment! Utterly floored!"

"You made porn?" I ask Lucky, before I can stop myself.

"Come see the famous view!" the Madcap Heiress cries. "You don't have anything like this in the West! The Contessa Pigoletto came all the way from Milan for my famous view! Well, and for a certain Greek-American electrician. But still."

It is a spectacular view, a right angle of glass scanning the center of town—to the extent that this episodic town has a center.

"The billion lights!" our host exclaims, taking Lucky's arm. "The heights of rage and ambition! Right before our eyes, four hundred nobodies are becoming overnight stars through acts of indescribable corruption, one hundred sixty-five statesmen are selling secrets, seventy-eight people are trying to cure their herpes with leftover Kwell, and twenty-three innocents are being murdered by strangers. And you're unnerved, you . . . explosively ripping object . . . because here you are in the city of passion and awe, and all you know is brotherly love. Is there much love in the west?"

"Depends on who you run into and what mood you're in," Lucky replies.

The Madcap Heiress turns to me. "So *distingué*! Will he move here?"

"I'm only here on business."

"Terrified to guess what kind."

Lucky is a hustler.

"Are you up for another movie perchance? *The Shoulder Caps That Devoured Biloxi? The Incredible Abdominals That Never Stopped Moving In and Out?* Or just *Young, Cute, and Lewd?*"

Later, Lucky asked me if the whole east side was like this. Of course *none* of the east side is like this, but after a while all of Manhattan is, because the rhythm of its humor takes the tempo of the queen and the gauge of its glamour observes the queen's imperatives. My friend Tim came to New York bearing the open cool of Seattle and the precision of Washington, D.C.; two months after he arrived, he was referring to himself as The Marquise.

If the Madcap Heiress is basic Manhattan, then so must be the east side, for there are no Madcap Heiresses anywhere else. The rich don't live where you live; they live where they live. A century ago, they had one of their meetings and decided that the rich sector was east of the Park. But New York's rich is strange, like everything else in New York. If Lady Bracknell moved here, where would she abide? Only the very East Fifties would look right to her, but they move too fast. Bank Street would be slow enough, but the wrong chic. Put her on West Eighty-second for a week and she'd be mugging Puerto Ricans. New York is too commingled. It's densely shared.

Lucky appreciated the Madcap Heiress. Effortfully polite, he asked about Crazy Bunny and the Dizzy Wizard, not realizing that these, like many of the people we know and count on, are fictional characters. If I had asked the Madcap Heiress about Crazy Bunny, he would have been peeved. You're to listen, not ask. But devastating aliens may derail the patter. "Why, dear heart, Crazy Bunny is very simply the natural enemy of Colonel Snapper von Turtel, and you must take care, when they call, not to ally yourself with one or the other. So gruesome." He moved closer to Lucky. "Keeps you busy." He drew his finger along the curve of Lucky's left pectoral. "I love it when they fight." He circled the nipple, bold and high on the muscle. "I'll give you five hundred dollars if you let me taste your quibble."

West siders routinely attack the east side, I imagine because the west side is a slum. It acts like one, too. Here, only the gays are men; the straights are shapeless wimps in joke-shop eyeglasses. In a Yankees cap they think they're preening, and when a weightlifter walks by they sneer. Lucky failed to notice them. He saw the Korean fruit stands, the boutiques, the old folks on the benches—and these are New York, but not New York enough for him. There's too much there here, too many sights that obscure the character of the place. "Where's the intellectuals?" he asked.

"They live in New Jersey."

I took him to a west side party, so he could sample Manhattan wit. But the guests were glued to the television—not even entertainment-center video, but network ooze. At least it was Public TV. I blushed for New York at the sparkless comebacks thrown at the screen, but

Lucky wouldn't know irony from babble; just hearing people talking fast intrigued him. Half the gang were straights, so they couldn't understand why he was shirtless, but they were too afraid of the answer to ask.

Guests came and went. The notable arrival was a tall but undergrown character who managed to be brutally bald and excessively hairy at once. He made numerous philosophical statements, each as valid as the advice you get on a cocktail napkin, and went on to put–down assessments of the hobbies, professions, and eating habits (remnants of Chinese takeout were strewn about) of the entire room. Then he settled down to some concentrated mugging of a program about a recent American assault on Everest. Lucky had tuned the rest of us out; mountains fascinate him. So, I expect, did the climbers, of that blond, bearded, lanky, affably laconic type that always turns up on documentaries of the outdoors. They were clearly as exhilarated as challenged, and I could see Lucky realizing that there is no one like this in New York. He was sad; he had hoped there would be mountains here. There is no one like this in L.A., either, but there are some in Oregon, whence Lucky derives.

"Why do you do it?" an interviewer asked a climber.

"Because you're a schmuck," said the hairy baldo.

"Say, excuse me," Lucky began, and I froze. The last time Lucky said, "Say, excuse me," he chopped three San Franciscan teenagers into messes on Sacramento Street for making homophobic allusions. Like all Oregonians, Lucky is easygoing except about one thing for which he will not only fight but die—everyone raised in the state gets to choose his thing at the age of fifteen, then must stick to it for life, even if he leaves home. Lucky's thing is mountains.

By hap, the fight was taken out of Lucky's hands, for the others had had enough of hairy baldo, too, and they more or less harried him out of the party. Or maybe they had suddenly realized why Lucky doesn't wear a shirt: he punches bad guys.

"You must take care not to ally yourself with either side," the Madcap Heiress had warned us, so we flee both west and east and proceed to Below Fourteenth Street, a city itself. Here, many of the principles of uptown are observed in reverse. Dressing for success is despicable; punk, prole, and various nonaligned grotesquerie are the norm. Moving fast and intently, as if one's day were full of Enviable Destinations, is suspect; downtown, you lurk, wander, or at most stroll, and going into a trance every block or so is good taste. Up north, everyone carries something—an attaché, a gym valise, a tiny shopping bag filled with leisure-class chotchkes; down here, everyone is openhanded. In the caverns of Businessville, street musicians, breakdancers, and monte sharps are intrusive; around Washington Square, they're the only things happening.

I hate it here; everyone looks as if he might glow in the dark. Lucky loves it. "Look at you!" a woman in a Mohawk enthuses at him, apropos of I'm not sure what, and a couple of uproarious kids covered with tattoos call out, "Hey, Jive!"

"I thought New York was unfriendly," Lucky says.

"That's not friendly. It's cultural harassment."

Stand anywhere in Manhattan, and no matter how busy you look or how involved in conversation, a crazy will come up to share the most idiotic secrets. Once in a movie theatre, the man in front of me turned around to say, "This is the night when I like to eat cabbage, but I'm afraid of how it smells."

"Hey, Jive!" Lucky echoes, pleased with it.

"Friendly?" I mutter. "It's a city of lonely maniacs."

"*Hey*, Jive!"

"Don't do that."

He tousles my hair. "You have to loosen up."

"If New Yorkers loosened up, this might as well be Cincinnati. And if my hair must be tousled, it ought to be by someone old enough to be my father, not by . . ."

"By what?"

Now I tousle his hair and he cries, "Hey, *Jive!*" and a black baglady across the street warns, "Children! You play nice, now!"

"This is New York," Lucky whispers, not for me to hear. "This is the jive."

We move on to Christopher Street, gay tourism's Bridge of Sighs, but Lucky is pensive and watches with but one eye. "What does 'lewd' mean?" he asks.

"Well . . . going around without a shirt and making porn movies could be thought lewd."

"Are you sore at me for that? The movie?"

We take in street ballet: a lot of skin, and anyone not in shorts is a goon. Two devastatos, approaching on the same side of the street as imperious as nabobs on howdahs, burn glances each into each, pass on, turn around to look again, both, and, at the same moment, turn and move on.

"What's the matter with this place?" Lucky asks. "Don't those hunks know how to cruise?"

"They weren't cruising. They were admiring themselves in the mirror."

"I take it back about New York being friendly. I'll bet I couldn't even give it away here."

It is a city of browsing eyes. The favorite question is "Should I have heard of you?"—but the words mean "What are you like in bed?" As a rule, trolls are the most impetuous (they will do anything to be liked), hunks the most inspiring (but hard to reach), romantics the most expert, and cynics the most intense. Which are you?

"Show me another sector," Lucky suggests. "I don't need this one so much."

"This is the gayest part, you know."

"Show me the most New York part. The most . . ."

"Typical?"

"Yes."

Is there one? Lucky's tour tells me that there scarcely are sectors at all, that all New York's parts are equal, because everyone goes everywhere. The architecture varies—glass and chrome stupas in Businessville, cast-iron frames in Soho, belts of brownstones. But the characters are often interchangeable. I note lawyers on St. Mark's Place, artists in the East Eighties, Poles in Yorkville, Italians in Chinatown. Mr. Peachum assigned his beggars their uniform and location in John Gay's London. Is someone assigning New Yorkers posts and routes? We need a sense of neighborhood, a disintegration of atmosphere. We need muzzles and handcuffs on all straight male teenagers, a ban on radios, and the death penalty for littering.

"There is no typical part," I tell Lucky. "It's consistent right the way through."

"Then show me the opposite of typical. The outstanding place."

"There is none."

"I know one. I'll take you there." It was my apartment.

"See," he showed me. "You have no famous view and no Crazy Bunny."

"I can see the whole of Fifty-fourth and Third."

"You won't when the new office building goes up. And you don't wear a quibble. Or have friends who come in and mock everything other people believe in."

"Like Chinese food."

"No one can come up and bother us," he goes on. "No one has strange hair or dervish clothes."

"Dervish?"

"Wacko."

"I thought you liked dervish behavior."

"Not in my friends."

"Lucky, don't you realize that New York is the city of the dervish? My apartment isn't atypical—it's asylum."

"That's why it's outstanding."

"Resistance is taboo! They don't like to let you take shelter here. That's why Bloomingdale's clerks are snotty and cab drivers play loud horrendous music on their radios. Privacy is offensive. The week I had my phone unlisted, people who hadn't bothered with me in years accosted me on the street, demanding the new number." I pace, I worry, I exult. "Death to spies! I am invisible!"

"I have to go to the airport," he says.

"Now?"

"Now."

With Lucky, everything happens without warning. He picks up his satchel, shakes my hand, smiles, drops the bag, hugs me, won't let go. "Do New Yorkers do this?" he asks.

"Only when you're here."

"Any city with friends," he observes, "is a nice city. The others aren't nice. That's the difference from one to another."

I consider offering to keep Lucky in New York—he'd be better off as a houseboy than hustling. But I doubt New York could stand Lucky on any terms. Thieves and crazies, yes. Queens and ruffians, surely. And vicious wimps especially—New York can't get enough of them. But brotherly love is an affront.

At that, could Lucky stand New York? After he goes, alone in my apartment, I practice saying "Hey, Jive!" in an affable manner. A dangerous silence ensues: and I hear the city screaming.

Kid Stuff

*A tale of taboo and regional style, from which
some readers may turn away in confusion or
distaste.*

There isn't all that much to do in The Pines on the best of days, but
there is *nothing* to do when it rains. I keep Monopoly and Risk on
hand just in case; but one must be prudent. Once, one of my best
friends landed that summer's Hottest Man on the Island and brought
him to my house thinking we were all at the beach. Instead, the two
of them found six of us huddled avidly around the Monopoly board.
Worse yet, quaint show albums were tooting away on the stereo—the
kind with Helen Gallagher or George S. Irving. Worst of all, someone
had just landed on Boardwalk, and Teddy Anders, who maintained a
hotel on the property, announced that this was the most exciting
thing that had happened to him all summer.

Well, the Hottest Man on the Island took a penetrating look at this
pathetically maidenly tableau, dropped a withering glance upon my
friend, and strode off. As the others gaped in bewilderment, my friend
slowly told me, "I will never . . . never . . . never . . . forgive you for
this." And he never did.

Mind you, I don't defend this point of view. One cannot be having
sex or hunting for it every minute, even in a place as rampantly erotic
as The Pines. Still, perhaps a day-long Monopoly game is too comradely an activity for the ruthless beach, too fraternal. Do you want to
be known for a hot house or for clubby chastity?

At any rate, you can't be hot when it rains, and I recall one afternoon eight years ago when sheets of water were ripping down as if the next Flood were upon us: Dennis Savage, his lover Little Kiwi, Little Kiwi's fiasco of a dog Bauhaus, Carlo, Ron, and I. All possibilities in reading, eating, and laundry had been exhausted. There was nothing left to do but lie around grumping, one activity Dennis Savage really excels at. Conversation lagged, till he suggested we trade Shameful Anecdotes. "We could start," he said, "with The Worst Thing I Ever Did to My Lover."

"How could you choose," I wondered, "from your many thousands such?"

He sat up, ready to strike. "Or you could tell us once again how you and your brothers committed incest night after glorious night right through your childhood and how it's just a typical American sport and *no one* would think you a gang of debauched cretins for a little thing like that."

"He committed what?" asked Little Kiwi, waking up.

"We didn't commit incest," I said. "We slept together, in total innocence. Haven't you seen puppies lying in a pet-store window? That's all we did. Doesn't everyone?"

"I never did," said Dennis Savage.

"I don't have a brother," said Carlo.

"I always locked my door," said Little Kiwi, "to keep out the scary clown monster."

Ron just blinked.

"What's more," said Dennis Savage, "I have never heard of any brothers sleeping in the same bed except yours. How does such a thing occur? What, do you wink at a brother and say, 'Who wants a backrub?'"

"I don't remember how it got started," I say. "I suppose someone was afraid of the dark, or had a nightmare, or was cold. We had a whole floor to ourselves, and one of us would just . . ." I trailed off. They were looking at me as if I'd told them we used to waylay strangers on the turnpike and chop them into sausage. "All I can say is it felt very normal to us. My older brothers used to carry me into their beds, and I did it with my younger brothers, or they'd pile in by themselves. Sometimes all five of us . . . I guess we just wanted company."

The rain beat even more heavily.

"They would carry you where?" said Little Kiwi.

"Nothing happened, I tell you."

"*Winesburg, Ohio*," said Dennis Savage.

"*Nothing* happened?" asked Ron. "Sexually? Are you sure?"

"We'd just snuggle up like bunnies."

"You know," said Dennis Savage, and I braced myself. "First it was dear little puppies; and now you say bunnies, suggesting visions of velveteen and cartoons and chocolate shapes with nougat eyes. But in real life bunnies are notorious fuckers. And I find it strenuously curious that you ladle out these tales of unapproachable *pornofamilia* and act as though you were merely playing hooky from Bible class. Are you telling us that five males—some of whom were heavily pubescent and others of whom were toothsome and easily overpowered—spent some ten years in bed and never touched each other?"

"He committed *what?*" said Little Kiwi, just grasping what we were discussing.

"A five-some!" said Carlo, impressed.

"All we did was sleep!"

"I know of . . . a couple of brothers," said Ron. "I mean, I know about two brothers who did have sex." He gulped, glancing at me. "I believe all five of you could have been together in bed and not . . . done anything. But it does happen."

We waited, listening to the rain.

"I wonder if Bauhaus is gay," said Little Kiwi. "Sometimes he walks funny."

"What brothers?" Carlo asked.

"In my town. Southern Indiana. You know, a little industry and a lot of farming. Three banks. One post office, two schools. See, the reason I know about this is it happened to my best friend. Tom Coley. I guess he had to tell someone, so he told me."

Ron is of that thin, pale-blond, long-necked type that doesn't get
noticed at first. At second, you think, "Who *is* this boy?"

"I'm not saying this is common. I always think a lot that happens
depends entirely on chance. Not on birth or education, you know.
Money. Things. But just who's near who at the right time. Anyway,
Tom had a brother named Elton, two years older. They could have
been twins, except Elton was bigger and broader because . . . well,
you know how much difference two years can make in your teens. I'm
not telling you that Tom or Elton were big wheels, now. In school, I
mean. Football captains or debating chairmen. But Elton was a slick
guy and Tom was . . . a good fellow. Did I say that he was my best
friend?"

Everyone was still, listening.

"Well, this happened when Tom was in ninth grade, Elton in eleventh. See, their father was dead and their mother had this snappy job
as a legal secretary. In a lawyer's office? And she always worked late.
So they had the house to themselves after school. She taught them
how to heat up canned spaghetti and TV dinners because she didn't
have the time to cook for them. She really worked hard. Everyone in
town thought she was the mother of the decade.

"Anyway, as Tom told it, one afternoon after school he was towel-
ing off from a shower and his brother came in from *his* shower and
they got to speaking about this and that." He grinned. "In our casual
midwestern way, you know. And somehow or other Tom ended up on
Elton's lap, just talking about . . . I don't know. School. Their father.
Maybe going to college. Except they're both completely bareass and
Elton has his arm around Tom's shoulder. And you know how close
brothers can be sometimes. And while they're talking, Elton is kissing
Tom. Just little pecks, like . . . like conversational punctuation. You
know, a sort of brother thing. To cheer him up. You kissed your
brothers, didn't you, Bud?"

"Never," I replied. "I scarcely shake their hands. I run when I see
them. They're worse than the scary clown monster."

"Oh. Well, maybe these two brothers were different because they had no father and their mother was away so much. They had to be kind of each other's parents sometimes, I guess."

"Pecks?" asked Dennis Savage. "On the cheek?"

"Well . . . actually . . . no, on the mouth. Kisses. Little demonstrative kisses between two brothers."

"Little between *what?*" said Little Kiwi.

"The thing is," said Ron, "that although neither of them would mention it, they both had hard-ons. And the kissing got . . . hotter. They were still talking, but in between they were virtually making out. They had their arms around each other and Elton was playing with Tom's genitals, and smoothing his skin, and stroking his hair. And I guess somewhere along the way they had stopped talking and were openly working on each other. And Elton got up and steered Tom over to the bed, and stretched him out on his stomach, and went into the bathroom for stuff, and when he came back he got right on top of Tom and screwed him. But you should understand that when Tom told me about this he underlined how careful his brother was with him, how gentle. Slow. And you know what was funny was they never seemed close in school or anywhere else like that. I mean, they *were* close, but they didn't make a big thing of it. It was like no one . . . knew about them. And then, after that first time, they started to take it up regular. Every day, same thing. They'd start talking and kissing in the chair, then move to the bed. And after each screwing, they'd talk again, waiting to get hot some more. And finally they'd roll over and collapse, and when their mother got home she'd find them lying in each other's arms."

"She knew about it, then?" said Carlo.

"Oh, no. She thought they were taking naps together. Two brothers who were so close they would talk themselves to sleep after school. She was worried about their not having a father figure, so it was nice that Elton was looking after Tom. Maybe it sounds more like the south than the midwest. They're very physical down south. Demonstrative. The midwest is almost as squeamish about personal contact as the northeast."

"Just a minute," said Dennis Savage, from upstate New York: snow-man country.

"Oh, come on," I said. "Would you call New York a relaxed, friendly, demonstrative city?"

"Not while you're in it."

"Gentlemen," said Carlo, raised in South Dakota. "The northeast *is* tense. I think that's why Bud's talk of sleeping with his brothers sounds weird. If you were from like Georgia, it would seem natural. And that's why Ron's tale is so interesting. It brings sort of a deca-dence to a place where we all thought men are men."

"And little brothers are nervous," said Dennis Savage.

"No, that's just it," said Ron. "Tom became very dependent on his afternoons with Elton. As far as I can gather, they never referred to it even in strictest privacy. They just did it. Every weekday, without fail. Over and over, the same methods every time. Elton sitting in the chair, and tilting his head at Tom, who would walk across the room to him. And if he got home first he took off his clothes and lay down to wait for Elton. There was nothing else in his life. He went through ninth and tenth grade in a daze because nothing was real to him except their . . . their . . ."

"Dates," said Carlo.

"Trysts," said Dennis Savage.

"Tango practice," I offered.

"Their love," said Ron.

"Of course, they already loved each other as brothers. They had a natural closeness. You know. But when they made it physical, it didn't just deepen. It became . . . I don't know how to explain it. It was not as if Tom had made a lover out of a brother. It was as if he'd made a *lover* into a *brother*, made him . . . I don't know, permanent, absolute. Close in a way no best friend can hope to be. And Tom made up this dream that he and Elton would stay like this for the rest of their lives. Keep on spending afternoons talking together and going to bed and falling asleep, and nothing else would matter. It's a strange story, isn't it? A strange dream to have for your whole life. I mean, the point of growing up is that you cut yourself off from the closeness of your family. You've already got everything they can give you in forming your personality. Your feelings, your emotions. They're all done with giving your character its shape. So you move on. You get married and start your own family and the whole thing repeats itself. Okay, you stay in touch with them and solidify the bond at special times. Christmas. A fiftieth birthday. But you don't stay a brother for the rest of your life, do you?"

"Not a younger one," I said.

"Imagine," he went on. "Imagine two men living somewhere, on a farm or something. And all they're doing is loving each other, and they're brothers! Can you imagine that? It's like being in the Boy Scouts for fifty years. It's . . . what is it?"

"It's a very sweet fantasy," said Dennis Savage, "in the wrong historical age."

"Anyway. Tom knew it couldn't last much longer. Because once Elton got out of high school and got a job . . . and some adult self-assurance . . . and learned how to talk to women, well . . . it was Elton's moving-on time. It was a terrible period for Tom, because they weren't breaking up over some curable incompatibility, or going through that crazy period some lovers hit after two years. They were breaking up because . . . well, because once upon a time Elton was horny as heck and women weren't available and Tom was. See, the bizarre part of this romance was that only one of the two men was gay. Think about that—and both of them knew it, too, I'm sure of it. It's like the birds and the bees without the birds. And then one day Elton was out of high school, and the next day he got a job, and some time after he got a little apartment over the record store. Drove him crazy Saturday nights when it was open late. And so of course Tom . . ." Thinking of it all, Ron paused, distracted.

". . . came out of his daze," Dennis Savage suggested.

Ron nodded.

Silence.

"I don't know," said Carlo. "Is this a sad story or a happy one?"

"It's a true story," said Ron. "That's what matters."

"Yes, but did they ever finalize it?" I asked. "Did they . . . well, did they ever say something to each other? About how they felt? What they had—"

"The midwest," said Ron, "doesn't work in that style."

"It's not what you say," Carlo suggested.

"You mean," I went on, "that never once in that two years those boys spent in bed did they say 'I love you' somewhere in there? Not once?"

"It's not what you say," Carlo insisted. "It's how you are made to feel."

"You have to remember that we aren't direct about our emotions. Not like New Yorkers, anyway. We're a country of poker players. Bluffers, you know?"

"Did they ever get into bed again?"

"How could they?" Ron replied. "Once Elton had his own place and was hitting the singles bars and smartening up his smile at the waitresses and such, what would he need Tom for, I wonder? You have to be fair."

The rain pounded on. Bauhaus shifted position. Carlo coughed.

"Anyway, it was as plain as it gets. There was that day they went out walking on a Saturday. Just walking. You're aware that two men might take a stroll with a lot on their minds and not say anything about it? This was like that. They weren't seeing each other much by then, just when Elton came home for dinner. And Tom didn't want to visit Elton in his apartment because . . . well, I'm not sure if he ever did know why. If you ask me, he was afraid to be alone with Elton and not go back to bed with him—afraid of having to face a formal parting of the ways. Because so far, no one had said anything about it. Yes, it looked as if it was over. But technically it was still an open question."

"Some affairs truly never do end," said Carlo. "It may turn out that you'll never fuck again, but you don't know that till years later."

"Tom knew then and there," said Ron. "Because they took this

walk. And you can imagine how Tom felt—I mean, this was one of
the very few chances he had to be alone with . . . his lover. And they
were just ambling around, seeing what was doing, and they ran into a
girl from Elton's class in high school. So it was like, 'What are you
doing now?' back and forth, which is what you tend to do in the
midwest for the rest of your life—unless you come to New York. And
Tom was just waiting till they could politely go off on their own
again, but it was dragging on and finally Elton invited her to join
them for coffee and she said yes. And there they all were, Tom just so
miserable and saying practically nothing and Elton and the girl flirting above and below the table. And of course finally they went off
together, and Tom went home alone, knowing that was how it was
going to be from now on. Tom was one thing and Elton was another,
and he had to face up to it. As we say in the midwest, 'That's how the
river gonna flow.' And this is where the story ends."

"Didn't they ever . . . say *anything* about this?" Dennis Savage
asked. "It seems a somewhat brusque way of dropping a lover."

Ron was quiet. So were we; we could hear his breathing.

"Well," he said finally. "It really isn't the way things work out
there."

"You keep saying that," I put in. "And there is something to it, I
understand. But is this a story about a place or about people? My
guess is every story is about people, even if the way they think and talk
and act and, I don't know, maybe even make love . . . even if all that
typifies the place they're in."

Ron nodded, but he said nothing.

"I mean," I went on, feeling crummy for pursuing Ron's feelings—
but hell, if I'm going to write this story I have to *know* it—"what next
passed between Tom and Elton?"

After a bit, Ron said, "Well, you're right. They did . . . refer to it
once. At Elton's. Tom had taken up visiting there every so often because it was so clear that it was over that he didn't feel any more left
out there than he would in the center of town. So he went over, and
Elton and he were talking about Tom's college plans. He was going to

be the first person in his family to do more than high school, so that was big news. And Elton was asking him about his major and so on, and after a while it ran down, and Tom knew it was time to leave but he just kept sitting there. You know how that feels. And Elton sensed that somehow, and he looked at his brother for a real long time, looked right at him. And Tom looked back. He was thinking about their two years together, and knowing what they were, and not asking for more, not even once more . . . just telling Elton how much . . . how important it was. How happy he had been. And Elton sensed that somehow, all that, and he . . . he nodded. Real solemn. As if to say he understood. And then they both got up at the same moment, and went to the door, but when they got there and Elton had the door open he suddenly closed it again. They were going to shake hands just then, you know. But Elton took Tom in his arms and he held him real tight. And he said, 'You're such a pretty kid.' He said that. And they stood there and held each other, and I swear it was as if . . . as if . . . I don't know. I don't know what it was at all now." A tear rolled down his cheek. "But he was so . . . damn . . . wonderful to me. So wonderful." Another tear. "We never fought. We never quarreled in our entire lives. About anything, never. And he came to all my track meets. Do brothers do that? All the time, I mean? I felt so safe with him. Jesus, I . . . I *don't care* who knows anymore. I *don't!* And let me tell you something—after him, all those gorgeous New York attitude hunks who think they're God's present are just pieces of ham to me! Pieces of fucking ham!"

"Canned ham!" said Dennis Savage, thinking to keep it light.

"Rotted canned ham," I put in.

Carlo, one of New York's most incurable gorgeous attitude hunks, made no-no fingers at us.

"He did *what?*" said Little Kiwi, finally.

"Oh hell," said Ron, wiping his eyes. "Isn't anyone hungry?"

He was shuffling lettuce and eggs when I came into the kitchen. "I thought omelettes and salad and this Italian bread," he told me.

"Terrific."

"You beat the eggs, okay?"

As I did, he said, "I was never going to tell anyone that. Not ever."

"Where'd you get the name Tom?"

"Oh, he *was* my best friend. Tom Coley. He died in Vietnam."
He set me to washing greens and cutting radishes.

"Are the others shocked?" he asked, quietly.

"Just Little Kiwi, and he's extremely unsophisticated, remember.
He didn't even know about lesbians till last week."

"Know what about them?"

"That there were any. Where is Elton now?"

He stopped, thought, patted my arm, said, "Stay here," and went to
his room to get a photograph of Elton taken at the last Thanksgiving
party. "Dayton, Ohio," Ron explained. "He's the superintendent of a
mattress factory. It's a good job in those parts. That's his wife Carrie,
that's Elton Jr.—they call him Tony—and that's Mary."

This Elton did not align with the one I had imagined pulling Ron
into his lap and leading him to bed. He was half bald, working on a
paunch, and sported an entirely dismal beard. Nice family, though.

Then Ron produced another photo, a dog-eared black-and-white of
two boys in swimsuits at the edge of a lake, and I gasped. Ron, I could
have guessed, would have been a spectacular teenager. But Elton,
perhaps fifteen then, his arm around Ron's shoulder, was about the
nicest-looking thing you ever hoped to be related to, or slip into bed
with: and, as Ron points out, sometimes you get both.

"Now that you've heard my story," said Ron, "are you ready to
admit that you and your brothers . . . you know?"

"Now that I've heard your story, I wish I could. But the truth is, all
we did was sleep."

He shrugged. "You may be better off that way. At least you came
out with no expectations. I had a tender, handsome man take me
through the hard parts of late adolescence, so I missed a lot of pointless anxiety. But where was I supposed to go next? I've been looking
for another brother ever since." He buttered the omelette pan. Typical

Pines: we have every kitchen apparatus known to man, including an artichoke guillotine, yet we're always out of clean towels. I think Bauhaus eats them.

I had one last question. "I can believe that an essentially straight man might pillow with an available male for two years out of adolescent horniness. But why would he then turn around—just as he's about to reform, so to say—and call you a pretty kid? Rather new-wave lingo for a midwestern straight. It seems sadistic, somehow."

Collecting the cutlery, Ron said, "Or generous. Maybe he was telling me what I needed to hear. As long as you're throwing someone over, why not let him think he means a great deal to you?"

"Surely you did. You don't sleep in someone's arms for two years without meaning something to him."

"Well, that's true." He was folding napkins. "A few years ago, at Christmas, Elton and I were joking around—shouting and punching each other, you know? Kid stuff. And Carrie asked us if we had always been this rowdy. And he said, 'No, when we were teenagers we were very serious around each other.' He said, 'Sometimes it was as if we were the only two people in the world.'"

"And you rent your garment and screamed that yours was a love that would never die."

He smiled, heaping dinner onto trays. "I kind of laughed and nodded and we went on to the next thing. Let's face it, gays have to do a lot of acting around the rest of the population."

They had the Monopoly stuff all set up when we brought the food in, and Carlo said, "There should be a Monopoly where you play for men instead of properties."

"There is," I reminded him. "It's called the gay world."

And, as the rain battered on, we got down to the really serious business of life: putting hotels on Boardwalk and Park Place and waiting for Dennis Savage to come around and land on them and go bankrupt.

The Preppie and the Clone

An east side romance.

Carlo decided that he wanted a preppie lawyer and no one could talk
him out of it.

"It's not for you," we told him.

"Their vested suits," he would reply.

"You'll be bored, Carlo."

"Their luncheon clubs and business talk," he would go on. "Their
fox trots, tennis rackets."

"What would you speak about?"

"They went to Harvard University! Look, I'm tired of hunks and
stars. I want something different this time. Maybe someone over
forty. I like them . . ." He grew blissful.

"Ripened," Dennis Savage offered.

"Practiced," Carlo corrected. "And they're nicer when they're
older."

"Grateful," Dennis Savage observed.

"No. They just have the time to be generous."

I grinned at Dennis Savage's lack of expertise. But then his taste
favors bashful youth, and we habitually take our reading of romance
from our own narrative, neglecting all other data.

It was the Friday after Christmas, a television afternoon at Dennis
Savage's: one of those amusingly wastrel days New Yorkers sometimes

schedule before plunging back into the grid of themes and ambitions and opinions that stretches across every social intersection of the town. Dennis Savage was free of his teaching duties, I was taking the afternoon off, Carlo was as usual living on unemployment, and Little Kiwi, on temporary enforced leave from the mailroom of BBDO because he had bitten a coworker for calling him "a derogatory epithet meaning an aficionado of oral gay sex" (as Little Kiwi put it, after working it out on a piece of paper), had been packed off to the grocery with his fey Godzilla of a dog, Bauhaus. We other three had settled down to cruise the soaps for skin. Strangely, instead of suburban bedrooms and health clubs, all we could find were political intrigues in exotic places, with heroines in tattered gowns crying, "No, Mark! Don't leave me here in the jungle, alone with the Ishtar Ruby!"

"Whatever happened to love?" I asked. "I thought soaps were about romance."

Dennis Savage scoffed. "Soap opera is about the illusion of romance. The characters fall out of love as fast as they fall in."

"Falling out of love is easy to do," said Carlo. "It can happen overnight."

We stared at him.

"You should go into it," he explained gently, "without expectations."

"You say this, after wishing for a lawyer?"

"I need a new adventure. I'm so truly bored with having a hot time and trading Circuit buzz terms. I want . . . I want someone I can *electrify*. That's what I want! Hot men are neat, but they already know everything, don't they?" His eyes lit with a wild surmise. "I surely believe I want a virgin!"

"Back to the sixties," Dennis Savage breathed. "Remember when no one knew how to do *anything*?"

"A lawyer with a terrace," Carlo went on, dreamily, "and a bulging briefcase."

"He'll be dull, Carlo," I warned.

"He won't, because we'll fall in love. Don't you know that everyone is good in bed when he's in love?"

A key clicked in the front door and Little Kiwi marched in with the groceries, the mail, and dire Bauhaus. "You're watching *soap operas?*"

"The best people watch soaps nowadays," I told him.

"The best people," he answered, "are otherwise engaged."

Carlo winked at him, and, suddenly shy, Little Kiwi turned away and threw his raincoat onto Bauhaus to watch it go. In the kitchen, sorting out his haul, he called out, "They didn't have Froot Loops, Snug, so I got Count Chocula."

"Snug?" Carlo echoed.

"*Froot Loops?*" I cried.

Dennis Savage blushed. "Little Kiwi, I believe it's time for your nap."

"Dennis Savage eats Froot Loops!" I exulted.

"Well, *you* eat zwieback and milk!"

"So I do . . . *Snug.*"

In the ensuing silence, we heard Little Kiwi slotting things into cupboards and watched his raincoat crawl evilly around the living room.

"What's new, *Snug?*" I asked.

"I could really enjoy tearing your head off."

"Little Kiwi should go first," Carlo told him. "He blew the secret."

Little Kiwi joined us, happy as a hatter. "He wouldn't hurt me," he announced. "He likes me a lot." He ruffled Dennis Savage's hair. "I guess I shouldn't have called you Snug, though," he added in a whisper.

"How long has it been now?" asked Carlo, looking at them thoughtfully.

"Four years," I said. "And they still sleep face to face, hot breath steaming their cheeks."

"Has anyone ever told you," Dennis Savage asked me, "that you are a vicious rotten oik who is completely fagola?"

Little Kiwi was taking in the television; a woman in a nun's habit was shouting, "Lars! Please, Lars! Don't rush off in search of The Golden Cone of Calcutta!"

"Soap opera is dumb," said Little Kiwi, picking up his raincoat. Bauhaus continued to slither around the floor, his eyes closed, growling.

"The conversations are funny," Carlo admitted.

"No class consciousness," I put in.

"It's not realistic," Little Kiwi insisted. "Out of nowhere, two people meet and kiss and shack up, and a few episodes later they're slapping each other. People aren't like that."

"Sometimes they are," said Carlo. "Like if they get to know each other too well."

"How could you know someone too well?" Little Kiwi asked.

"That's what love is for." He came over to Carlo. "Isn't it, Carlo?"

Carlo smiled at him. "Sure it is," he said.

Carlo was so serious about finding a lawyer that he harangued me about throwing a lawyer party so he could examine them and make a correct selection. Ridiculous. Everyone thinks I know suitgays because I live on the east side. On the contrary, you know whom you know and where you live has nothing to do with the case. Anyway, the only lawyer of my acquaintance is my cousin Ellis, who is straight, married, and the father of two splendid children. There didn't seem much point in setting him up with Carlo.

"Ellis?" Carlo said at a planning session in my apartment. "That sounds right. Where did he go to school?"

"Dartmouth."

"That's what I want! Fill a room with those and—"

"I know!" said Dennis Savage. "Hugh Whitkin!"

"Hugh!" Carlo sighed. "The names they have!"

"We were at Hamilton together, and he went on to Harvard Law. He knows a hundred preppie lawyers."

"Would he give Carlo a party?"

"Maybe I should skip the party and take Hugh Whitkin."

"Uh-oh!" Dennis Savage and I said in chorus.

"Is that a no?"

"Carlo, didn't you say you wanted a virgin?"

"Has Hugh been around?"

"Somewhat," Dennis Savage admitted. "When they discovered the Stone Age paintings in that cave in Spain, his phone number was on the wall."

"Is he cute?"

"Abnormally handsome," I said. "Nice shape. No muscles. Straight golden-blond hair . . ."

"I *love* Hugh Whitkin!"

"No Hugh Whitkin for you!" snapped Dennis Savage. "He's a jaded son-of-a-bitch who'll chew you, spit you out, and still have time for a lunchtime quickie with the mailroom boys."

"Look, I'm not exactly a novice—"

"No Hugh Whitkin or no party!" Dennis Savage walked to the phone, opened his address book, and laid his hand on the receiver. "I can set you up a party at Hugh Whitkin's or I can forget about the whole thing. It's your choice."

"Wait a minute," I said. "Carlo has been around the block, after all. I don't care how lurid Hugh Whitkin is, you can't throw a lion to the lions."

Dennis Savage slowly shook his head. "Choose, Carlo!"

Carlo chose. "No Hugh Whitkin."

"Attaboy."

But when Dennis Savage turned to dial, Carlo winked at me.

I should say something about Hugh Whitkin, though it grates me even to introduce much less develop him. He would make a dandy villain on the soaps: the smooth cad who will woo you till you grow to need him—at which time he tells you you're a dead issue. If Carlo is the gay brimming with romance, Hugh Whitkin holds as much romance as a colander. He is everything I despise in gay, closeted, selfish rich, politically resistant, and classy without culture. There was a time some years back when I moved with a nobby crowd. We were conservative in that old-fashioned, anglophile, James Burnham way, and dressed up when we socialized, and disdained a good many things. Eventually I realized that a conservative gay is about as valid as a Jewish Nazi, and Hugh Whitkin—the maximum leader of this crowd—was the main reason why.

I broke with my friends not so much for political reasons as for psychosexual ones. What did they think of themselves? What did they believe they knew of the world? What kind of men did they like? Little. Everything. Wimps, like themselves. You can't lead a successful life thinking you don't deserve one, or voicing preferences for the good old days of the men's rooms and the vice cops, or referring to the annual marching festival as Gay Shame Day. The first time I heard one of the crowd lament "the lost glamour of the tea-room rendezvous" my mouth fell open, and I disgraced myself passing heavy commentary at Harry Apgar when he brayed that line about "the love that dare not speak its name" becoming "the love that wouldn't shut up." Then, on a Gay Pride Day, when Hugh Whitkin smirked about "gay shame" I held very still—maybe I'd heard him wrong. But no: he smiled at me, daring me to challenge him; I think he knew I hated him before I knew it. I thought about it for a long while, as the others stirred about me and I refused to move out of the way of whatever was going on and everybody got the idea that I was going to do something horrible.

I didn't. I left and took a long walk home to think about it, and finally realized that I had been keeping company with men who embodied the straight's comprehension of gay: self-hating, devious, dreary pixies, as fearful of sensuality as hungry for it and terrified of women who aren't terrified of men. Solidarity of kind, to them, meant not comradely support but cold bodies to fit around the brunch table: a guest list for glum amusement between work and sleep.

The more I thought about the company I'd been keeping the angrier I got, till I was storming home promising myself never to see any of them again—and not to waste any words explaining myself, either.

I was resolute. But I feared I'd suffer a bad case of *pensées de l'esca-lier*—going over and over what I should have said when I had the chance—if I didn't confront one of them. And I knew which one. I called Hugh and told him I wanted to see him. The sooner the better. Maybe now. He laughed. "Everyone's worried about you, the way you hurried off. But I'm not worried, my friend." He laughed again. "I never worry because I have nothing to worry about."

Carlo is right in assuming that lawyers have terraces, and Hugh's is spectacular, a wraparound overlooking the East River. Chivas in hand, we went outside, Hugh sardonically smiling, as if he knew exactly what I was going to say and was ready to trip me up.

I began, "I'm going to tell you straight out—"

"What's that line from Oscar Wilde," he interjected, "about being absolutely candid when you have something unpleasant to say?"

I tried smiling sardonically back at him, but my sardonic lacks something in crust.

"Please go on," he said.

"I'm here to tell you what I think of you."

"My dear fellow, why on earth would I care what you think of me?"

That's a great comeback, boys and girls: no matter what the other says in reply, he comes off a fool. While I regrouped to renew my assault, Hugh moved closer to me, touched my arm, and said, "Have you ever made love to someone you loathed?"

Startled silent, I tried to overwhelm him with a bold cool, and stared into his eyes. But you can't stare down a man as handsome as Hugh Whitkin; you can only stare at him.

"You're on the wrong side," he told me. "You're going to be, the way you're headed. Leather jackets and mustaches and those circus-freak rags in the back pocket. Is that how you fancy yourself? Walking around like a human commercial for debauchery?"

I should have realized that you can't win an argument with a law-yer. I wasn't even able to start one.

"You're a smart fellow," he went on, his voice low. "Reason it out. You're not some pouf roughneck from Scranton. You're one of us."

Smiling, because he never worries. "You're going to be miserable if you join up with the wrong crowd." He touched me again. "Don't you realize that no one in America cares whether or not you're quietly homosexual? It's the gay stuff they hate, that's all. This public flogging of their feelings. You think the men upstairs are going to allow this filth to hector them indefinitely?"

He was stroking my hair, mesmerizing me. I was letting him. It came out a whisper when I said, "I hate you."

"No, you don't. You don't even wish you could."

"I'm not one of you."

He touched my tie, the handkerchief peeping out of my blazer pocket, the stripes in my Brooks Brothers shirt, as if taking inventory of my worth. "Linka Oelrichs remembers you from Friends Academy. She says you were in *The Boy Friend* together."

"She was thrown out in her senior year for rimming Phoebe Wadsworth in the common room without a permission slip."

"Linka Oelrichs heads the *Times'* Vienna bureau. Her brother Colbert is going to be the junior senator from Connecticut when the time comes. The family has been running their share of the Northeast for four generations."

"Cole Oelrichs is a bloody fucking crap-headed dildo and so are you," I said, but I had my hands on him then, pulling his jacket off his shoulders, remembering what I went through as a seventh-grader, five hundred miles from home and trying to fit in with the likes of Cole and Linka Oelrichs and various apprentice Hugh Whitkins, a pouf roughneck from, as it happens, not Scranton but Wilkes-Barre, one town over, and I suppose if I had given Hugh a beating I would have gone home feeling better but then I would never have known what it's like to screw the most elegant man on the east side.

Of course his theme, so to say, was that I *was* one of them, that I took him kind for kind, affirming that his patrician breeding and antique fortune were decorations as essential to the correct life as were the strains of orange and brown in his golden hair. But more: as he had never shown the slightest interest in me physically, alluring me and allowing me to be allured *and* to act on it was a lovely slur, a derogation fit for the blue book. At least I gave it to him gutter-style, standing in his bedroom, with our shoes on and pants down. And when I was about to leave I said, "To answer your question: Yes, I have made love to someone I loathed. Just now."

He was sitting on the bed, pulling off his shoes, and he laughed as I walked out. He laughed because he has nothing to worry about.

Even eight years later, I wasn't sure how glad Hugh would be to throw a party for a man he'd never met, a particularly gay man at that, and a distinctly unpatrician gay man, but for all Hugh's Us and Them he's probably as curious about what the other side is like sexually as the rest of us are.

I asked Dennis Savage if Hugh had remarked about my participation in all this.

"He said he's looking forward to seeing you again."

"Did he say . . .?" I caught myself just in time; Dennis Savage was watching me as Aschenbach watched Tadzio. No—as the hotel manager watched Aschenbach watching Tadzio.

"Is there something you haven't told me?" said Dennis Savage. "About you and Hugh Whitkin?"

"Of course," I replied.

It was the night of the party; we were dressing Carlo out of my closet. As someone who has lived his entire life on a wardrobe of T-shirts and corduroys (Carlo's trademark; supposedly he has never worn a pair of jeans since he came to New York), Carlo was naturally as dazzled by the accoutrements of the dress-up life as Poles, Greeks, and Norwegians were said to be by the stupas of Manhattan as their emigrant boats pulled into port.

"Look at these!" he cried, seizing my little clock cuff links, heirlooms I never wear. "Earrings that tell time!"

"Don't you ever buy new clothes?" Dennis Savage fussed, pawing through my shirts. "You must have gone through high school in these."

"I want a striped tie, okay?" said Carlo. "And perhaps I may have been wondering if I should change my name."

Dennis Savage carefully looked at him.

"Well, they're all going to be Ellis and Terence and Perry, right?" Carlo continued. "Maybe I should seem like one of them."

"Maybe they're as tired of their scene as you are of yours," I ventured. "So, like, opposites attract."

"Yes, okay. It's just . . . I do believe I thought of a name I might use. A party name, as you truly might say."

Dennis Savage, straightening Carlo's tie, said, "I don't like it already."

"Say, Coco," I advised Dennis Savage. "Why don't you concentrate on designing the outfit and—"

"*What . . . name . . .* did you think up?"

Carlo chuckled at him and patted his shoulder. "Whitkin McHugh?"

Dennis Savage slammed the closet door.

"I just thought—"

"We had a deal! No Hugh Whitkin! No thinking about or impersonating Hugh Whitkin!"

"Oh, gee."

"I *knew* he'd pull this!"

I took Carlo over to the mirror so he could see himself. He looked terrific as always, and a little different—wiser, maybe—and he saw it and grinned.

"Look," he said.

Then we collected Little Kiwi, bundled into a cab, and rolled up to East End Avenue to Hugh Whitkin's party, a soap-opera casting director's dream: two dozen men only a woman could love, cute but not sexy. Still, after a career of men called Slim and Blue, this was what Carlo wanted. It was quite some do, with catered food, a bartender, and a waiter. Little Kiwi had his first Perrier and sat upside down on the sofa, Dennis Savage performed fraternity nostalgia with Hugh, and I helped Carlo circulate.

Smooth, boys and girls. But Hugh always is smooth. He greeted me
at the door like a dear friend welcoming me back from having been
lost for two years in The Cloisters. Somehow he seemed backlit, as if
Greta Garbo had lent him William Daniels, and, of course, the debonair flurry beyond the entryway was impressive, with the most delicate
chamber music on the processed tape and the most admirable hors
d'oeuvres on the passing trays. "Guess I won't need this," Little Kiwi
whispered to me, showing me the box of Raisinets he had slipped into
his breast pocket.

Yes, smooth; still, I don't like these parties. I prefer the lit gatherings—tense, yes, but brilliant. This lawyer crowd could talk (1) mort-
gages, (2) Wall Street, and (3) shop. Someone with prep-school tact
led me to an alleged fellow opera buff who turned out to have seen
only three operas, all of them *La Bohème*. As my favorites are *Les
Troyens, Les Huguenots,* and *Francesca da Rimini,* we had little to
share.

Carlo was a wow. He was too intent on finding his fate to be shy
and too thrilled with the *richesse* of archetype to worry about how he
appealed to them. Yet as he charmed them they were unsure how to
charm back. "Where do you play squash?" one lawyer asked Carlo.

Imagine.

After squiring Carlo through the ranks, I went over to Little Kiwi
and dished the gang with him. He hasn't much to say but at least it's a
familiar mouth. Dennis Savage joined us and we watched the circles
form, close, and reform around Carlo. Whatever buildup Hugh had
given him to assemble his crew, Carlo was living up to it. Hugh
thought so, too. Slowly he turned, step by step, inch by inch. When
Dennis Savage and I got to them, Carlo was merrily enlarging on his
San Francisco past to an audience so enraptured they were dribbling
scampi onto their vests.

"Cockdudes?" Hugh was saying. "Cuddleboys?"

"Yeah, see, the cockdudes would spread out these mattresses,"
Carlo was telling them, "and they'd go out on the street to round up
some cuddleboys," as he shifted his focus to Hugh, "and then . . ."

because Hugh had taken Carlo's hand in his own, "you see . . ." and they locked eyes and somewhere great bells went clang.

Hugh took Carlo's other hand. "Yes?"

"They lay the cuddleboys on the mattresses."

"Ah."

"And they . . ."

"Tell me."

". . . they . . ."

"Yes."

Carlo grasped Hugh's shoulders. "This is a nice party."

"What do cockdudes do to cuddleboys?"

"I'm not allowed to talk to you."

"No one is."

"They loosen the cuddleboys up. Cream them up."

"Do they, now?"

"You're so handsome."

The other lawyers had drifted away; one thing a lawyer knows is timing. Carlo and Hugh kissed as Dennis Savage shook his head. "Get your coat," he told me.

Dennis Savage refused to discuss it; not a word. Of course Carlo had gone for Hugh. It was not blond hair after dark that he wanted, nor innocence after experience. He wanted mean after pleasant—or so I guess. Carlo had known hot without menace, fun without substance. Every other day he would tell me, "I've just fallen in love," but once, in one of those profound confessional sessions he abhors but gives so much to, he told me he had very seldom been in love in any real sense. "Very seldom," he had insisted. But was this love? In his several months with Hugh, Carlo's chest sprouted hair, his head whispered gray, and his stomach, so slightly, began to sag. He aged.

"It's astonishing," I said. "Dennis Savage and I tease each other about being jaded and decadent, but it's really because we happened to be there when Stonewall sexuality exploded. We were witnesses, more than anything else. But you, Carlo. You have done all this, everything. Yet every now and then you take some man to bed and suddenly the world cracks apart. You're like a kid wondering how far he'll get the night of the prom. Do the men with the most sex know the least about love?"

Carlo took out a bag of grass and butt papers and prepared to roll a joint. He can do it one-handed. "What was your first time like, Bud?" I didn't answer; it was not a question but an opening flourish. "Mine was in the back of a truck, when I was seventeen, on my way to New York. I hadn't even crossed the Mississippi then." He sorted the herb, flicked away a bit of twig. "This guy was driving a moving van filled with furniture. Someone probably got himself transferred from Denver to Toledo. Took his wife and kids and went on ahead. Anyway, the mover picked me up. Big fellow, bearded, rough hands, fancy green eyes. He flashed them every other second. Your typical gay kid's nighttime fantasy." He licked the paper, nodding at the recollection. "My first *real* time, I mean. All the way. I was scared, but I knew I wanted him, and I thought, There's probably a road in if I phrase it right. Because he kept looking at me, you know? Heavy looking. Two times, it's gringo rivalry. Three or four, you remind him of someone. Ten times with green eyes, he wants to fuck you." He folded the joint, lit it. "And that's what he said he wanted, right there in the cab of his truck." Took it in. He smokes too much, but other than breaking hearts it's his only vice. "He said he wanted to cornhole my cherry. Those words. Those words, Bud." He looked at me. "I'd never heard the term but I knew what it meant without thinking about it and I wasn't afraid. I was glad. We were passing a very empty stretch of road and he made it clear we could pull over and do it or he'd dump me right where we were. And I told him I'd be glad to let him cornhole me. He looked over again, the biggest look yet. What a fool I was. I was smiling, so relieved, after all that fumbling I had known in high school. And you know what he said? 'I don't want you voluntary.'"

He proffered the joint. I shook my head.

"Anyway, that's how I got to New York, hitching with truckers, and I swear every single one of them fucked me. One took me to a motel

in the afternoon, one got me out in the trees behind a Howard
Johnson's, and one gave me twenty dollars to do it with him in front
of his best friend—to settle a bet, he said. A bet. Okay. But there was
one you should know about, different from the others. This very man
took me to his mother's house in some small town in Ohio. It seemed
the same as the others at first—me face down and him on top, no
talking, just the gentle pounding in the darkness. See, they were all
men and I was a raw kid, so that was fair. But I wanted to find out
what it was like on top, making someone happy like that. Because
that's what it is, isn't it?

"Anyway, this guy with the mother. He wasn't much to look at, I
guess. Kind of clumsy. Said the wrong thing a lot, you know.
Laughed too much for nothing. But he was very nice, and I wasn't
used to nice men then, especially not big ones. Big men truly aren't
nice where I come from, you know. They're tough. Okay. That's how
we grow them. Anyway, this guy . . . I can't remember his name
now, but I can see him as clear as I see you. Brown hair, kind of
scraggly, the hair that never looks combed, like. Brown eyes, bushy
mustache. Gigantic shoulders, like he's been carrying stuff all his life.
Arms, too, big. Chest. Not cut up. Fleshy. With a light dust of hair
and nipples as big as a woman's. Stomach just starting to loosen up.
Squared-off ass, big junk. Oh, I truly see him. I see him, Bud." He
put the joint down. "He was the best of them all. He shouldn't have
been, but he was. Very basic, slow and certain. That means something, anyway. And like we were lying around talking and I asked him
if I could take a turn and fuck him and he said okay, and it was totally
different from then on. The moment he turned over and I got behind
him I felt . . . more involved, somehow. What could be more involved than being fucked, right? But this was. I sat on him and
stroked his sides as if I was giving him a massage, great long strokes all
the way down him, and each time he let out a deep breath, like he
was struggling not to moan. The lights were out, but the bed was by
the window and a ray of light from a street lamp was hitting him just
at the neck where the hair ends, and I thought that must be the sexiest

piece of flesh a man can have, just there. I ruffled the bottom ridge of his hair and he gave out this incredible sigh. We were using soap, you know, dipping it in a little bowl of warm water. It was like stepping back fifty years into the past. Like something *The Policeman's Gazette* might have known about but wouldn't care to mention." Stirred by the recollection, he paused. "Soap and a little bowl of warm water," he went on. He cocked his head, seeing it again. "We had dinner with his mother, and then we went upstairs, to a little room under the slope of the roof. Maybe he kept it especially for this. When we got up there, he said, 'What we need is some soap and a little bowl of warm water.' I guess I remember details like that more than I do what a guy looked like. But I remember this man. The way he looked all stretched out under me. The light on his neck. As I soaped him open, he began to spread his legs, bit by bit, wider and wider. And I thought . . . well . . . that I *knew* him somehow, like I was closer to him than . . . than anyone. He was my ally. My teammate. I was a real jerk about getting my cock into him. I guess I must have thought it would just slide in, but it took some practice. I had to pull him up on his hands to work it all in, and then we froze like that. I could scarcely breathe. I was filled with some wonderful feeling and I didn't know what it was. Never felt that before. Never." He paused again to relight the toke, nodding at some thought. "Well, so we hunkered down again and I began to fuck him and all I could think of was him, this man I was hitched up to, legs and arms and torso. All the way, right? All the way is how they put it. I kept saying his name over and over." He looked at me. "Jed. His name was Jed. Jesus, twenty years ago. Jed. And then I knew what the feeling was—I *loved* him. It was love! I did, I felt it. Him, that man, his skin and his muscles and his neck. Not just sex, not even just good sex, but love. I swear to God. I loved him. And I put my head down on his so our cheeks sort of touched, and I like nodded slightly, so my hair brushed his. It wasn't wild at all. It was serene. It was like . . . maybe like giving something to him and keeping it at the same time. That must be sharing. All the way. And when we broke apart, I grabbed him in this hug of death, and he laughed and said, 'You're a real live wire.' It may sound crazy, but I actually considered staying on with him, living in that house, in that room, maybe. With the street-lamp light and the little bowl of warm water. I didn't even care if we never fucked again, I just wanted to . . . I . . . what? *Touch* him. Say his name. And then he shifted over and put his arms around me and he nuzzled the back of my neck. And, do you know?, I was crying. My whole body was shaking. Lying with my head on those big chest muscles sobbing like an infant while he comforted me. I finally calmed down, and we lay there for a long time. Maybe an hour. We weren't dozing, either. Just lay there, nothing doing. All the way. Then he suddenly said, 'I'm forty-six years old.' That's all. I waited, and at last he said, 'How old are you?' And I told him. So then he put his hand on my head, stroking my hair. Playing with it. And then you know what he said? He said, 'You're going to be so happy.'"

"And are you?" I asked.

He stabbed out the joint, rose and aimlessly crossed the room, deep in thought. He came to a halt at the Victrola, lifted the lid, idly inspected the machine.

"Maybe I should have stayed with him forever. It was like that first night for a few days, and then I started to mind it when he'd roll me over for his turn to top me. I didn't want him to know me the way I could know him."

Here Carlo turned back to me. "And don't ask me why. Don't ask me anything. I just didn't. So I came here. And then San Francisco. Then back here, home. And I tried all the types and all the scenes. I had everybody. I did it and I did it, with the musclemen and the tender kids and the stars and the straights. But never again did I feel the way I felt that night in that little town with the ray of light on Jed's neck. I guess I wonder what would have happened if I'd stayed with him. What if that was love, that time? I want to go back to the way that . . . happened. That stranger. And maybe Hugh is the only stranger I have left."

"Even now?"

"Almost. Maybe. The way he lies on his stomach, waiting to be pleasured. There's something in him." He shrugged. "On the other hand, he's such a soft thin shell of a guy. God, does he need a gym." He turned to the window, watching the ironworkers bulling up the frame of the block's new office tower. "There's nothing as excellent as a big man. A really big, wonderful man. If I were a big man, I'd be happy."

"Carlo, you *are* a big man."

He turned back to me and grinned. "I only look big."

"You know, every other day I pass one of your ex-es. They always ask after you. Steve Bosco is moving back from Seattle. He wants to call you."

"Big Steve." He smiled. "He's a teddy bear. Every Sunday he made French toast in the waffle iron. He shouldn't call, though. I'm not free yet. But the bad things always end. Trust me. The good things hang on forever."

"So it is bad?"

"Not . . . not the way you think. See, I know Hugh is mean, so he can't hurt me any more than the nice men can help me. It's only your true friends who can hurt you, right? When they get mad at you."

I said nothing.

"It'll be over soon. I'm waiting for something."

"What?"

"You think I'm a sheltered sweetheart like Little Kiwi. Dennis Savage won't speak to me, did you know that? He gets off the phone so fast you'd think his building was afire."

"He wants to run you out of gay."

"You're all wrong about me. See, I'm truly not a cuddleboy. I'm a cockdude. I can risk anything."

"What are you waiting for?"

"I can't call it by name. But I'll know it when he does it."

He did it the night Carlo turned forty at a surprise party I threw in his apartment. The ruse was a peacemaking visit from Dennis Savage, piled on a dinner date Carlo had with who knew whom; and the guests were assembled an hour ahead, decorating, cooking, and drinking. What a comparison to Hugh Whitkin's lawyer party: half the group were in T-shirts, leather and lumberjack flannel lent an air, and Big Steve Bosco wore nothing but a netted pouch and running shoes.

Little Kiwi, in charge of the food, took offense. "His chest hair is infiltrating the lasagna!" he cried, carrying the platter back to the kitchen. "Make him wear something!"

"Be gentle," I warned him. "He's an affectionate elder who wants to stay in touch"—hanging on forever, I almost added, like a soap character.

"His hands are too big. He's always hugging people!"

"That's the mode of his circle. Don't be a monopolist, boy. Learn the modes. Welcome diversity."

He eyed me warily. "Will there be a quiz on this?"

"Lights!" someone cried, and out they went, but the footsteps traveled past the floor. "False alarm."

I took the lasagna back out, but had to drag it right back in again because in the darkness someone had slipped an ice cube into Big Steve's pouch and now he and several others were chasing around the living room in lighthearted melee.

"Is it true that Carlo is dating Hugh Whitkin?" Little Kiwi asked. "Snug won't tell me."

"Why do you call him Snug?"

He smirked. "I better not say."

"You can tell me."

"Like fish!"

"Lights!" This time was it, and we huddled grinning as the door opened. You know the festive moment, when the victim walks in and someone yanks the lights on and everyone screams "Surprise!" But this victim walked in with Hugh Whitkin and they were in the middle of a fight.

Hugh, of course, fights in undertone and Carlo never fights. Still, it had a nasty edge, the two of them framed in tight doorway light while the rest of us stood unseen at the far end of the living room waiting for no cue.

"You don't get to ask those questions," Hugh was saying. "I'll tell you what you can know. Everything else is none of your business."

"Enough for tonight, now."

"No. Oh, no." Hugh grabbed Carlo's elbow. "What do you mean by calling Randy Pinkerton a bohunk, you ghetto slime?"

"It's just a word, Hugh. I don't even know what it means."

"It means that you are a shabby slut and I doubt that we can continue this relationship on any level."

Carlo slowly pulled away from Hugh, spilling more light into the doorway. "You're truly a beautiful man, Hugh. No one else I've been with had anything like your style. They had the gym and The Look, that's all. You're perfect. Yet they were all terrific guys and you're a grungy prick. Why is that?"

"You little whore," Hugh rasped. He was actually angry. "You godless Christopher Street savage."

"I'm tired of fighting, Hugh. Let's be gentlemen and shake hands." He extended his. "Tomorrow, if you still—"

Hugh cracked the flat of his hand across Carlo's face, someone snapped on the lights, Little Kiwi yelled "Surprise!" and what a pair of faces the party then beheld. Carlo looked like a Munchkin the day the house fell on the Wicked Witch and Hugh like a truffle trapped in a gumball machine.

Big Steve hulked forward with dishonorable intentions toward Hugh's health, but Carlo intercepted him with a cry and an embrace. "You look great!" Carlo told him. "I must get the name of your tailor."

Hugh took a long look at Big Steve's jaw, a fleeting one at Big Steve's pouch, and fled.

"It's my birthday, right?" Carlo asked us all as we milled about, laughing nervously. "This is my party!"

Once we loosened up, it *was* a party. Carlo spent much of it in Big Steve's lap opening presents, Rick Conradi did a drag act in the discarded wrappings, and Kenny Reeves taught Little Kiwi the samba.

"You were waiting for something," I reminded Carlo. "Did it . . . occur?"

He grinned and patted his cheek. "You saw it occur, my friend."

"So was Hugh the stranger you wanted, after all? Did you electrify him?"

"Hugh is a stranger, I guess. But not my stranger." He looked around the room, at something like twenty men he had known for about four hundred years in the aggregate, nearly half a millennium of buddies. "Maybe there are no more strangers in gay life," he said. "Maybe you can only electrify yourself. Listen, that's what Stonewall gave us, right?"

"Do me a favor? Go home with Big Steve."

He laughed. Dennis Savage signaled me over to the salad bowl to pick out the last few cherry tomatoes.

"Thank God that wretched soap opera is over," he said.

"If it's over, it wasn't soap opera. Soaps never end, you know."

"I don't recall how this got started, but I'd swear it was your fault."

"I know why Little Kiwi calls you Snug."

"If you *dare* say so much as—"

"It's because you electrify him when you cuddle, you cockdude, you."

He said, "You would have made a good early Christian, you know that?" But I could tell he was pleased.

Rope

Notes on S&M, set forth by outsiders as well as by experts.

Strenuous, black-hearted Dick Tangent asks me where Bobby is.

I say I'm not aware.

He knows I'm lying, and takes the double-crostic away from me. I still won't look at him; fine, he'll wait.

I give in and turn to him. "Look—"

"Hey," he cuts in, mock-amiable, patting my knee. "Hey, now. Because the longer he stays away, the worse it'll be for him when he gets back. Tell him."

"He knows."

"I want that little chicken here, and I mean today. By the time I get back from tea. That gives him three hours." He leans against the deck railing, facing the ocean and me. "What does he think he's doing, anyway? He knows he'll come home. He's got a case on me, whether you like it or not."

"It has nothing to do with me."

He nods once, slowly. "Now you're talking." He looks at the puzzle, cut from the *Times* and set on a clipboard. "You do these in pen?"

"Pencil makes too light an impression."

"Belts make a good impression. You ought to try them sometime. Tell Bobby what I said." He hands me the clipboard and saunters off.

I have always had back luck in my Pines houses. My first year, I roomed with a temper-monster and an alcoholic realtor who, before my eyes, jacked off his poodle, Amahl the Night Visitor, with his foot. The dog cried out like a plucked mandrake when it climaxed. The second year I jumped from a house as structured as summer camp to one so open no one got around to making dinner. I lived on Lorna Doones; and by September I looked like one. I tried going freelance the next year, but I hated being a guest, so I bought out the share of a friend who was suddenly transferred to Los Angeles, and ended in a small rectangle surrounded by deckwork and perched high over the eastern end of the oceanside Pines: with one S, Dick Tangent; the S's two wonderful Labradors, Mortimer and Gridley; the S's M, Bobby Hackney; and a coil of rope with which Dick terrorized Bobby.

No gizmos for Dick—none of that *Drummer* kit of clamps, enemas, whoopie cushions, Cuisinarts, seltzer bottles, and other jazz. Dick was subtle, tactile, confidential. Tying up his partners was not the start of his scene, but its ultimate threat. What he would do to you then was, I suppose, your worst fantasy, Room 101; anyway, he had Bobby paralyzed. I had seen them in bed lying so skillfully intertwined they might have been a pretzel; and chasing each other along the beach splashing and shouting like little kids; and staring at each other on the deck as the sun was coming up, not daring to touch except at the eyes, and then Bobby would turn at my footsteps and I'd see tears running down his cheeks.

It was a good house logistically. Dick ran it, and ran it well. He and I got along because his dogs and I did. He let them walk me, which was not unlike driving a chariot without the chariot. He did all the cooking, saw to the landlord details, and even enjoyed cleaning up. All I had to do was play secret agent with Bobby, who was forever running off in fear of and returning in lamentation to Dick and the rope waiting in the bedroom.

Now, Bobby, I should tell you, was a very disadvantaged kid. Poor family, chance education, no ambition training. God gave him something: cuteness to die—but this too turned out to be a disadvantage, because as long as he could remember, men had been seducing and raping him. His cousins, his uncles, the minister, delivery boys. He called them "pirates." Too slight to defend himself from their advances, he took up karate training; but the instructor kidnapped him. Then Bobby joined a gym, but in the shower room everyone could view his gigantic cock—another disadvantage, the poor kid—and pirates would drag him home and commit disorderly conduct upon him. I suppose he concluded that as long as he was born to be possessed, he might as well select a permanent dreamboat.

That Dick Tangent was. He knew the Three Secrets, more valuable than the Three Cards of Pushkin's Queen of Spades, to wit: (1) have a lot of jaw, (2) smile seldom but dazzlingly, and (3) walk from the ass down. For my money, his dogs were more fun. Mornings, I'd come out on the deck and they'd frolic about, then I'd lie down and they'd take turns leaping over me. Yet everyone I knew was suing for dinner invitations, and not to meet the dogs. Dick ruled these out. "Take your guests to the Monster," he'd say. "Read your lease. I cook for the house."

Besides, he was busy with Bobby. There were other folk on the premises, but we were all in our late twenties and early thirties, and things were beginning to break for us professionally. They were often away: filming on location, setting up a Denver office, whatever. So basically it was a three-character play, a *No Exit*; or no, a duet with an audience, so Dick and Bobby could shock me, worry me, delight me when they lived happily ever after for a day or two, then challenge me when their contentious bond snagged taut and threatened to snap.

"How's World War III going?" Dennis Savage asked, when I repaired to his house for relief.

"You know this is the skid row of The Pines?" I replied. He was far west, deep in the woods on the bay side, where the mosquitoes are so big they wear cock rings. "If Elmer Fudd came out, this is where he'd stay."

"We had shrimp scampi for lunch," said Carlo, tidying up in the kitchen.

"Watch out, Carlo," said Dennis Savage. "Dick Tangent's been giving him macho lessons. He got an A in Tying Castanets to Your Balls So People Can Hear Them Clacking, and now they're working on—"

"Congratulations," I told Dennis Savage, "on getting over your accident."

"What accident?" asked Carlo, a dependable straight man.

"The night of the Green Party. He was putting toilet water behind his ears and the seat fell on his head."

"Does Dick still have that rope?" Carlo asked.

Sensing dish, Dennis Savage grew rigid. "Carlo! Did you—"

"No. I was out of S&M by the time I came back east. Does he?"

"Yes," I said.

Carlo smiled, nodded, shrugged; what a life.

"He never uses it," I added.

"Till it's time to," said Carlo. "He's quite a character. You remember what happened to Bert Wisner after Dick put the rope on him."

"He vanished," said Dennis Savage.

"He moved to Brooklyn," I corrected.

"Same thing."

"No," said Carlo, putting the dishes away. "No," closing the cabinet. "He left the scene, and he got into porn and hustling, and then you'd see him panhandling around St. Marks Place, and he looked so pathetic men took him home just to cash in on that sense of . . . of little lost boy. He wasn't attractive anymore. He was helpless. Some men go for that, you know? Like they collect pictures of amputees? And Bert had been a very, very cute man. He could've gone anywhere. He blew it all."

"Because of Dick Tangent?"

Carlo shook his head. "Because heavy sex is fire, and some people are made of stone and some of paper. The stone people are good for S&M, but the paper people go up like tinder. They fuck their brains away. They trade life in for fantasies. They become obsessed by stone idols." He packed away the flatware. "No, not because of Dick Tangent. But because some people shouldn't do anything more than cruise and screw and do an affair now and then. Haven't I always told you that certain kinds of love are dangerous before the age of thirty?"

Dennis Savage and I carefully attend. Carlo is not a great reader of Proudhon or Dickens or Nietzsche. But when it comes to romance, thus spake Zarathustra.

"Dick is a very deep guy, very loving," Carlo went on. "A strong man can survive him, learn from him, even. But a kid . . ." He shook his head. "It's like locking an altar boy in with twenty Popes."

"That's Bobby, all right," I said.

"Have you ever been tied up?" Dennis Savage asked me.

"Not for sex."

"Maybe," Carlo began, "someone should—"

"Whoa!" says Dennis Savage. "Not for *sex*? Then for what, an international incident?"

"My brother used to—"

"I knew it!" he exulted. "Another chapter of *Pennsylvania Gothic*." He turned to Carlo. "You know how parents send clan photographs at Christmas? The Morddens send their portrait by Charles Addams."

"Your brother?" asked Carlo, amused.

"Well, you know. Brothers will fight. And ours were pretty severe. So, finally, rather than chance killing me, he took to tying me up. Formalizing the punishment, so to say. I'm not defending it, but it was rather sensible, wasn't it? After a while, I didn't even bother to struggle."

"Listen to him," Dennis Savage whispered. "Listen to corruption."

"No, wait," said Carlo. "I happen to know about this. He tied you to your bed, didn't he?"

"Yes."

"Wrists and ankles?"

"No. Hands to the bedposts."

He smiled. "You had an old-fashioned house. And then what? He'd talk to you, right? Sit on a chair next to the bed?"

"On the bed."

He shook his head. "It's a tiny little thing of a world, gentlemen. So many men—so few stories."

"Did someone do that to you, Carlo?"

"My father."

"My God," said Dennis Savage, "I'm surrounded by perverts."

"No," said Carlo. "It's just punishment. An act of the middle class, like cruising shopping malls and turning on a television. It's discipline. But it's also a kind of flattery, I think."

"What do you say to a man you've just tied up?" asked Dennis Savage.

"You don't tie up a man," said Carlo. "You tie up a boy. Your kid brother. Your son. Men do the tying."

Dennis Savage said, "The two of you. Sometimes."

"It can be a very honest moment," Carlo told him. "I never felt so close to my father. Other days, you know, he was like steel. So sharp, so full of himself. But when he tied me up, he was gentle. So open. Intimate. Even soft. I was never so conscious of him—of the hair behind the top buttons of his shirt. Or the veins in his hands. We had this game we called, 'I'm Going to Touch Your Eyes.' When I was a kid. It was just another name for tag, really. But later, it turned into this like . . . this touching game. Where he'd sneak up on me and pin my arms and touch my eyes while I struggled. And I did it to him. It probably sounds strange, but, you know, it's like kissing him. It is. And so that's what my father said when he was satisfied that I had learned to be good and he was going to untie me: 'I'm going to touch your eyes.'"

"And would he?" asked Dennis Savage.

"Oh, yes. My God, how I miss that!"

"I can do without the rave review."

"Men have grievances one to another," Carlo told him, "and they are bound to express these."

"What is this," Dennis Savage cried, "Bible study group?" He raised an index finger. "And they made to divide the people, that those who knew reason would not know love, and that those who knew love, yea, would not know reason."

We laughed, and Carlo said, "That's what S&M needs, a sense of humor. The trouble is so many men got into it too early—tied up like that . . . consoled by it, too . . ."

"Patterned," I suggested.

"Yes, that's right. That kind of upbringing can make you very solemn about it. It's funny you never got into the scene, Bud."

"I loathe it."

"Oh, it was so wonderful a few years ago. What we called 'San Francisco Style.' It was like getting tied up by your father. Nothing to fear. No weapons or anything. Some quiet talk, then the buddy stuff. It was lovely. *Fun*. It wasn't touchy, the way it is now. Philosophic and so on." He grew informally nostalgic. "Oh, one night . . . you know . . . Big Steve decided he wanted to fist me, and I said no, and he got nosy about it, so I ran out of the house and he chased me up and down the boardwalk. It was one of those sweater nights, everyone all bundled up inside, and here were these two naked men chasing through the place. Finally I just ducked into a house and there were four queens sitting on a couch doing cocktails, and I flattened myself against a wall and winked at them. Wouldn't you think they'd be glad to have me around, a surprise happening to them? But they looked at me as if I had thrown up on their . . . antimacassar or something. So when Big Steve poked his head in and said, 'Hey, you guys see my victim around here?' one of them stood up and pointed to me and said, '*And there he is!*' So Big Steve looked at them and looked at me, and he broke into this . . . this great laughing roar, and he took me out of there with his arm around my shoulder, laughing all the way home. And I just liked him so much for that. I mean, he was no S. He was just doing what everyone else was doing then. You know? But

of course he had never been tied up or anything . . . patterned . . . so
he didn't realize . . ." His reverie dwindling, he blinked at us.

"Realize what?" Dennis Savage asked.

"Oh." He smiled. "Jesus. Remember when we were the new boys
in town? Trying everything for the first time? Wasn't there one encounter in there somewhere when you felt you weren't just sharing
something with someone but . . . well, opening yourself dangerously
to him? Totally, sort of? I mean, like feeling him pressing against you
through your emotions? And imagine now . . . imagine if you saw
that coming and tried to close yourself away from it, because you
don't want someone knowing you so well. But the other guy won't let
go. He presses. He presses, gentlemen. Closer and closer. He invades
you. A stranger. And, like if you pleaded with him to let you be he'd
hold you and he'd soothe you. You know. But he'd keep coming and
you'd never be safe. Never. Never. Never." He took up a sponge to
polish off the counter, but just stood there. "You guys tell me, what
kid could stand up to that?"

"What's going to happen to Bobby?" I asked. "Is he going to get
hurt?"

"Dick Tangent doesn't hurt them. The way he does it, there are no
visible scars."

"What exactly does he do?" asked Dennis Savage. "Is it like with
your father?"

Carlo shrugged and sponged off the counter.

"What did your brother say to you?" Dennis Savage asked me.

"Not another word," I announced, "shall pass my lips."

"Those talks aren't meant to be shared," murmured Carlo.

"Just tell me one thing. Are you comparing this family discipline
routine to S&M?"

"Not sexually," Carlo replied. "Family discipline isn't sexual. But
S&M is more than sex."

The dogs pranced about me when I returned. The house was still,
and Bobby sat despairing on the deck as the sun went down.

"What am I going to do?" he asked me.

I didn't know.

"I can't stay here anymore."

I nodded, looked sage.

"Wherever I go, he'll find me. They always do."

If this boy lives to be thirty, I thought, he's going to have an *amazing* backstory.

"Tell me something," I said, sitting next to him. "Do you love Dick—I mean, *really* do you? Or is he just an available sweetheart?"

"Oh, what difference does that make?"

"To a lot of Pines beauties like yourself, no difference. My point is: are you in this house because this is the summer of love or die, or are you truly hooked on him? If the former, you can get away from him. He's not the KGB, you know. If the latter, maybe you should work something out with him, with less S and more M. Or maybe he actually has a deep and abiding crush on you and together you can—"

"You fucking asshole," he said sorrowfully.

I rose. "Go to hell."

"I'm sorry." He grabbed my arm. "Please don't leave me alone. It's just . . . you don't know what you're talking about. You don't work anything out with pirates. They come in where you are and they say they're going to be nice to you but they aren't, whatever you do. It just eggs them on. I've tried joking with them, and getting tough, and running like hell, and screaming for help, and crying. You name it. They just keep coming in."

"Coming in where?"

"They're pirates, don't you see what they are? They're *pirates*! All they care about is . . . is . . ."

"Plunder."

"What's that?"

"You."

"So what do I do now?"

The dogs came up, leashes clamped in their jaws: time for my walk. "Come on. We'll spin along the beach and talk about it." The dogs romped frantically ahead down the walk while Bobby paced what looked like a last mile somewhat behind us. Every so often the dogs would look back and bark at him. Cute doesn't score any points with them; they think he's boring. Mortimer growled.

"Even his dogs are pirates," Bobby muttered.

"Well," I said, as we reached the water. "The way I see it, you have only to decide whether to go on with Dick and take what he dishes out or drop him for someone who isn't a pirate."

He splashed around in the water to his ankles, head down, shivering in the gathering wind. He sighed.

"What does he do to you?" I asked, trying to connect Carlo's lesson with Bobby's theory of the pirate.

"You know what he does. He cockfucks me to death."

"Besides that."

"He tells me things."

"What things?"

"Adventures we could have, like."

"Such as?"

He looked at me a long while. "No," he said finally. "You'll get mad."

"Not at you."

He made a face, designed to look wacko but very winning, a face to energize a pirate. "Fantastic adventures, that's all."

I waited.

"Like . . . there's a war somewhere. And the soldiers wreck this town and take hostages. And they're in this barn and all the soldiers get drunk and they decide to snuff the hostages. So each soldier picks out a prisoner he likes . . . you know. It goes on from there."

"I'll just bet it does."

He shrugged. "I don't mind those stories. Dick's not the first man who told me them, anyway. It's just that sometimes he makes me tell them, too."

"What?"

"It's funny what you'll say once you get going. Horrible things. Horrible, terrible sexy things. All made up. Things that could never happen. It's like I'm drugged, like he's pulling something out of me that shouldn't be there. The more we do it, the more comes out." He shivered again. "It doesn't sound so bad, I guess, talking about it like this. But after it happens, I feel so rotten and crazy. I feel like he's going to turn me into someone else, almost. Into . . ."

A pirate, I thought.

"Did this ever happen to you?"

"No." Yes. "Not really."

"And then he gets so tense with me sometimes. They always do, pirates. They get sore so easily. Oh, please don't be sore at me!"

He sent this over my shoulder: Dick had come down to the water, taking all four of us by surprise.

"Please," said Bobby, approaching him. "Please, Dick," stroking his arm. "I'll be a good boy and I'll do what you say," putting his arms around him and resting his head against Dick's shoulder as Dick moodily rubbed his back.

"We're going all the way tonight, Bobby boy," said Dick.

Bobby shifted position and held Dick more tightly, his feet almost on Dick's as if he were trying to climb into him. "Dick," he whispered.

"All the way to rope," said Dick.

Bobby was quiet.

Dick looked at me without changing expression. "I'll cook steak and mickies on the grill. You can make the salad. There's peppers and scallions and carrots. Use olive oil this time, and drop the chives *over* the bowl at the last minute. Don't mix them in with the dressing."

"Dick," said Bobby, looking up at him. "Listen. Not the rope yet. Okay? Dick?"

Dick took Bobby by the hand and led him up the sand to the dunes. The dogs and I watched.

"Dick is about to start losing his hair, I think," I told Mortimer, who was pulling on a leg of my jeans, trying to get me to follow his master. "And Bobby is about to be patterned," I told Gridley, pulling the other leg toward the ocean. "Dick will touch his eyes, I bet."

At the base of the stairs, Dick and Bobby paused and spoke a bit, and Dick ruffled Bobby's hair. They kissed, a good long one. As they mounted the steps, Bobby turned to us and waved happily. Gridley barked.

"I think someone just got a reprieve," I said.

Mortimer grumped.

"Of course, we should consider the possibility that Bobby is made of stone in the first place."

Mortimer sat.

"In the middle of this riot, you notice, I get gourmet reproaches about the chives in the dressing."

Gridley sat. Mortimer dug a little hole.

"All of which teaches us that, sooner or later, every gay gets roped. Sooner or later."

Gridley snapped at a beetle.

"Boys, I ask you; which is better: to take your roping early and grow up sophisticated, or come out innocent and work up to it?"

They hadn't a clue. I would have raced them to the stairs, but it occurred to me that at that distance Dick and Bobby looked like father and son, or perhaps two brothers, and I didn't want to shake up the picture.

Raw Recruits

*Ranging wildly through the years of Stonewall,
and perhaps more a discussion than a story,
although the most drastic narrative event in all this
book darkens the final pages.*

I was graduated from the University of Pennsylvania in the class of
1969 with a degree in Medieval Studies, for all the good that did me:
none. Mother greeted my return with, "Help, the monster-child is
back!" My dad, more whimsically, told me how much my education
had cost him—"door to door," as he put it, meaning *tout compris*,
from the tuition bills to my train fares to and fro and even the dinners
at Bookbinder's when they jaunted down for a visit.

All told, he quoted a whopping sum. I felt guilty. I decided to
devote the summer to Good Works, such as tending bar at weekend
cocktail hours. (With recreational amenities and a convenient suburban location, my parents did a lot of entertaining.) My specialty was
Tequila Sunrises poured into huge goblets over cracked ice and
topped with lemon juice, the fruit so overpowering the taste of the
liquor that the uninitiated took them for a kind of art deco orangeade.
In fact, it's potent stuff. One Sunday morning we came outside to find
Aunt Agnes, Uncle Mike, cousins Jeffrey and Rita, their children,
three locals, and an unfamiliar dog all passed out on the patio, and I
was in trouble again. Worse yet, I intercepted the invitations to my
graduation exercises and hid them so I wouldn't have to go back to
Philadelphia. By day I tooled around the north shore of Long Island
with my high-school chums; at night I worked on a novel of dubious
virtue. By the summer's end, Mother had had it. Coming into my

room one night, she said, "Monster-child, we all love you very much
. . . but why are you still here?"

She had a point. First I negotiated a settlement—years later, when
I told my agent Dorothy the terms of the deal, she was impressed by
their generosity. "It's like a contract with Knopf!" she said, deep
praise. Thus endowed, I phoned an older friend who had once offered
the hospitality of East End Avenue, packed a valise, sat in with two
grad students of old acquaintance on their drive into town for the start
of the semester, and, in September of 1969, at the dawn of Stonewall,
I moved into New York.

Like everyone else of my ilk, I was unlearned in metropolitan style.
But one meets people. There's a name or two to call. One event leads
to another—the opera, say, to cocktails on a terrace. You'd be surprised what doors the right tie will open. Hugh Whitkin's, of course,
was one of them, but at the time I had no inkling of what I would
become, and value, and despise. I had skipped two grades of grammar
school and ended up somehow always younger than my attainments
warranted. I was unformed, the raw recruit. But I did notice that my
old society of mixed couples going steady and gearing up for careers
was ceding to a more complex fellowship, all-male, of brunching,
cruising, and tricking. When my old friends got themselves placed,
aligned, married, they would ask of a stranger, "What do you do?"
When my new friends asked that question, it came out, "What do you
like to do?" and it meant: in bed.

There was, in fact, a veritable old-boy network still in operation
then—possibly because counseling the new boy in town on the nature
of life was not unlike learning from youth about the nature of love.
So, anyway, I took the transaction to be. At length someone brought
me to a spacious co-op in the east eighties for advising by a wise old
queen.

"First of all," that worthy warned me, "you must have a best friend.
First of all. So?"

What was I supposed to say? I tried to look concise and untouch-
able, yet warm. Enigmatic. Big-city.

"Second of all, so? You must have a dream of success, a work ambition. Do not be a waiter, a bar pianist, a masseur. Be avant-garde, but be respected."

"So," I murmured.

"Quite," he rejoined. "Friendship, ambition . . . yes: then comes love, thirdly. Do not expect it. Do not look for it. Do not believe in it. Are you willing?"

"I beg your pardon."

"Will you renounce love?"

"Of course not."

"So." He smiled. "I just wanted to see. Of course you believe in love. Of course. I believe in love, in my many years. Yet I've never known love. Do you think that strange?"

"Not in the least."

"Sweet chicken."

"I'm not a chicken," I flared up.

He considered me.

"Nor am I. Do you suppose that's interesting?"

Would I ever be doing this myself? I wondered. Do all gays become queens in due course? So I looked around and marked what I saw, noted whither the culture tended. The wise old queen put forth his three rules and I had mine. First of all, queens and clones stay the same, but kids become men, or nothing. Second, all gays have, somewhere, a touch of queen in them—or let's say an instinct for rebellion. Last, once a gringo crosses over into gay he can never get back. To attempt to retreat would be like giving up all your friends, your sense of brotherhood, of affirmed self. Or so I guessed.

It was, in any case, the age of the clone. The wise old queens were passing on, or keeping to themselves in their gala co-ops, and I thought how different a wise old clone's advice to some newcomer might be, how very potent the urge to friendship, how disinterested the line on ambition . . . and what does a clone think of love?

To Big Steve Bosco, a king clone, I said, "Some are born clones and some attain it. Does anyone have it thrust upon him?"

"You're a funny guy," he said. That means that Big Steve missed a few words in the sentence. But then, I had noticed, large, humorous, loving men were attractive even without great savvy. Ah, what would you talk about, you ask? But the odd thing is that clones never run out of things to say to each other. Nor do queens—though they prefer to speak to clones, as a rule. It's kids who lack tongue, who really don't know what is being said from one sentence to the next, or who, lacking attention, develop irritating allergies: to cats, soap, porcelain, whatever will disrupt a lover's life.

Big Steve thought anything a kid did was forgivable, as kids were on the scene for one purpose: to be bunked.

It was great to hang around Big Steve, soaking up lore, for I was gleaning copy and every third word out of him was a term.

"Bunked?" our boy asks.

"Sure." Big Steve was cutting up vegetables for some huge elaborate salad to be delivered to some party along with cold-cut platters and a cake. Like many gay men in New York—fantasy masseurs, or "actor-models," or makers of tape collages for parties—Steve chose a calling that had scarcely existed before Stonewall. True, he did not invent the profession of caterer. But surely he was the first caterer to guarantee caped and cockstrapped waiters among his help—and the only caterer I ever heard of who made a point of closing the evening by passing among the guests entirely nude (a truly awesome sight) to treat the host to a fabulous smooch. "It tends," he explained, "to make them sporty with the tip." But I think he did it for the hell of it.

"What's bunking?" I asked.

"You know what screwing is, right?"

"Yo."

"You know about sleeping over after, where you kind of nest the kid you screwed in your arms so you wake up all nice and warm together?"

"Sì."

He handed me a slice of green pepper, fresh, wet, gleaming. "And there's having a special breakfast, right? Like with honey toast or a farmer's omelette."

"Do."

"What's that?"

"Yes in Welsh."

"So," he went on, "you put all that together in one night for a nice kid who deserves it, and that's bunking."

Who deserves it? I wondered, examining the cake, a humungous rectangle sitting demurely under wax paper and bearing a motif of music notes and G clefs on its frosting, with the legend, "To my sleeping beauty: best wishes on the birthday from Cleve."

"What's this for?" I asked. "Some uptown faggot?"

"Don't use that word," he replied, evenly but with a fierce command. Something else worth learning: some gays don't think we can use straights' expletives, even for our purposes. Faggot is not our concept, therefore not our word.

"Besides," Big Steve went on. "Besides. What for do you want to put down someone you never met? That doesn't hardly make sense." He handed me a radish. "Everyone's got something to offer, if you look in the right place."

His ability to get along with practically everyone was legendary; but everyone, in Big Steve's world, was gay. He not only lived entirely in the ghetto, leaving the West Village only to deliver and serve his collation, but literally did not know a single straight, did not watch television because it was all "straight stuff," and would not open a bank account because banks were ungay.

"Have you ever bunked a man instead of a kid?" I asked him.

He paused. "You mean did I bunk a big old clone, like me?"

"I wouldn't put it like that."

"That's what I am, anyway."

"It's just that bunking sounds like sort of a fatherly act," I said. "Where you make the rules, you take the initiative, you have the power. Right?"

"It works best with kids because they like to be taken over."

"As a rule?"

"Never met a kid who didn't. See the idea is, when they're young they don't have the experience, see? They don't know what to do. You have to teach them. You might almost call it a clone's duty, teaching

kids. They've been raised by straights, so they're a little afraid of
what's going to happen even though they want it. So you have to . . .
what's the word?"

"Seduce them?"

He thought it over. "Seduce them. Yeah."

"Egad."

"See, you can't just take a kid home and say, 'I'm going to fuck
you.' They'd run. Instead, you say you know this photographer who
likes to shoot buddy pictures. Always looking for new talent. Kids like
that—you can't give them enough attention, for some reason, even
the really cute ones who've been getting attention since they were old
enough to love. So you get them to take their shirt off, like you're just
looking them over for the photographer."

He stops chopping up the salad to enlarge at ease. Big Steve is like a
gay Gene Caputo, the ironworker: sex is the topic that covers everything.

"So you move them around a little. Let's see this angle, or like, fold
your arms and turn this way. You get your hands on them, but it's
very professional. You keep it clean. It's best to take your time. Then
you say, 'This is very promising,' or something like that, and put in
about what the photographer pays his models, because kids never have
enough money. And you say, 'Let's try a certain pose like this.' You
get them out of their shoes, sit them on your lap. You say, 'Look at
the camera. Let's see you smile. That's a pretty smile.' Then you get
them to drop their pants, and that's when you can start working on
them. A little stroking here and there, and you're keeping it smooth.
No kissing or like that, just slowly bringing them along till their body
starts to tingle all the way to their toes. When you think they're ready
to go, you can start kissing them, and when they put their hands up to
hold on to you like little lost boys is the time to touch their behind.
Not before. Because by then they know what's going to happen and
they want it."

"After that treatment," I said, "Bob Haldeman would want it. What
if a kid believes you about the photographer and just wants to pose for

some money? What if he goes along with you because he's afraid you'll beat him up if he doesn't?"

He considered that for a bit, then smiled. "So what? I give them a real neat time."

I complained about this to Carlo, who was then, as Michael likes to put it, Big Steve's "current ex-lover." It seemed to me that Big Steve's technique was immoral, might well be taking in a number of innocents against their judgment. But Carlo, who has lived on the concept that good sex is its own morality, was not much bothered.

"That's his way of making friends," Carlo said.

"Oh, good grief."

"Come on. You and Dennis Savage and the other collegiates don't realize how difficult it can be for those of us who truly aren't born talkers. When we are trying to set up a social thing, I mean. Anyone knows how to talk sex. But getting to know someone, trying to make a friend . . . well, *you* always have something to say, sure. Big Steve doesn't. All he can do is cook and smile at you and . . . and touch you. That's all that man can do. And you have to make friends, don't you?"

"Hmm."

"Friends is how you survive. Besides, do you really think he's seducing anyone who doesn't want to be? Really?"

"You must admit, he's kind of overwhelming."

"Which would probably discourage anyone from coming home with him unless they were ready to go for it. For some of them, maybe the only way to come out is to have it done to them."

I thought of his tale of hitching across the country when he first came to New York.

"Admit it, Bud. Isn't that how you came out? Someone shows you what to do."

"Did he show you? Big Steve?"

"He truly showed me how to behave the next morning. I wasn't always so sure of myself, then."

"You're not exactly the kid type," I said. "A cuddleboy. It's odd seeing you in that position."

"There's a kid hidden away inside every clone, I sometimes think. Even Big Steve."

I wondered who might be more helpful to the raw recruit: a precise queen, dryly citing stylistic code, or an embracing clone, limited in what he knows but strong in certain manly virtues. Queens, clones, kids. As the years went by, I noted the new arrivals and heard dish on their metropolitan debuts, heard that this one had a smash gallery show in Soho, that that one burned out on drugs and whoring, that another was going uptown, trying yoga, or never seen by day, and that two others met one day, fell hopelessly in love, moved deep into New Jersey, and now would not come out even for brunch. Friends is survival, Carlo says, yet the recruits do not come to this city of utter trash and absolute power to make anything as mere as a friend.

I sometimes think.

But then comes an arresting exception and you have to reorganize your theories: as when Dennis Savage got bored one evening and hied himself to the theatre and there found himself next to a kid fresh from the midwest who agreed to go out for coffee and exchanged phone numbers and said, "I think you're a nice handsome man" when they parted—but that's just it, they parted: the kid would not go home with him.

They met for dinner and it went, I was told, really well. Yet still the kid would not budge in the indicated direction. A number of dates followed, after each of which Dennis Savage came running into my apartment like a fish whose scales have been stripped.

"He says he likes me!" Dennis Savage feverishly reported. "Now, why won't he let me—"

"Maybe you should send him to Big Steve for breaking in."

Dennis Savage paused, crushed by a thought. "Maybe he isn't gay?"

"Bring him over here for socializing," I said, "and we'll figure it out," realizing as I mouthed the words that I was showing signs of turning into a wise old queen. "On second thought," I added, "what do I know?"

"No, yes," Dennis Savage insisted. "Tonight at seven."

"Not good. I'll be doing my cartwheels then."

"Seven-thirty."

"That's seance hour," I said, panicking. I don't want to give advice. I want to take it. I want to be broken in, thrown around, snubbed, flattered, not paid for first-rate work . . . anything but regarded as a wise old queen. "Fuckin' A," I growled, to throw him off the track. "Fuckin' A. Let's pick up some bimbos and—"

"Eight o'clock."

"Gotta watch the Jets game."

"That's football. This is summer. They don't play football in—"

"Take him to Carlo!" I think I was beginning to scream. "Or—"

"Are you going to help me or not?"

Shattered, I collected the pieces of myself and shrugged. "Anytime."

"Eight."

At eight, Dennis Savage introduced me to a slender kid with floppy black hair, a blond's skin, and the most helpless cute appeal I've clocked yet. "Pay dirt," I—almost—said, as we shook hands.

"This is Little Kiwi," said Dennis Savage.

"No, Virgil Brown," said the kid.

I thought it over, surveying him. "No," I said. "Little Kiwi."

I served coffee—Little Kiwi wanted ice cream in his—and we talked of this and that. It was my job to get a bead on him, but he said little. He looked around a lot. He admired the antique model car that sits on my desk. He appeared to be perhaps fifteen, and was dressed in clothes designed to look like posters and menus. There was writing of some kind on every corner of him—we suppressed *that* damn fast—and, in all, the little he gave out revealed a young man unknowing, shy, and fearful. Later on, it turned out he was twenty and had done two years of junior college before coming east. But the oddest damn things spurred his fancy. A friend had given me an out-of-season pumpkinhead carving, and Little Kiwi asked me why it was smiling.

"I have no idea," I said.

"But I think I know."

He looked at me the way some waif might have looked at Horatio Alger the evening he launched his series of waif-makes-good novels. "Why?" I asked.

"He's smiling because he likes me."

I fought down the urge to pat Little Kiwi's head and went on playing the cocktail dandy with the two of them, but my mind was traveling. Are youths supposed to remind us of our own dear emergence? Or: was *I* that raw? This is the city of the debonair, is it not? Apparently unaware that one of our cardinal givens is that one does not eat four consecutive frozen Milky Ways out of the fridge of a man you just met that night (me), Little Kiwi ran on like a movement of one of those toy symphonies of Reinecke's day, with a plunk here and tinkle there. And finally everyone stopped talking. And Dennis Savage looked at Little Kiwi. And Little Kiwi looked at Dennis Savage, and how he looked was apprehensive. I felt *de trop* in my own apartment.

So I threw them out, and, at the door, as he shook my hand, Little Kiwi suddenly said, rather quietly, "I just wanted to be sure we were friends first," and he was looking at me but somehow he sent the message to Dennis Savage. Then they went upstairs to Dennis Savage's place and I didn't see him for three days. So it appeared that they had indeed become . . . friends.

And friends they stayed, which made it all admirably domestic, though it was some doing getting Little Kiwi out of his midwestern clownsuits and into something fit for life in the cultural capital. He took our advice in good faith, but there was a very great deal he didn't know, and sometimes, when things were explained to him, he became upset. You never knew how anything would hit him. A host of subjects, most of them sex but also talk of nuclear war and almost any social theory, would send him running to Dennis Savage like a lost babe found. And of course I would then get hell for the dread crime of Being Sophisticated With Little Kiwi.

Our circle in general found him amusing. All right, he was of age, but he *looked* so young; and he could find a turbulent whimsy in almost anything, as a child does. The rest of us brunched and dished, interpreted, analyzed. Little Kiwi romped and frolicked. In his life, the most risible acts were made conversant with the most sensible—as when he took pity on a stray dog and took him back to Dennis Savage's. Little Kiwi had had enough presence of mind to stop off on the way to secure food and plateware and even rubber toys, and he gave the dog a rather chic name, all considered: Bauhaus. (A bunch of us had been talking over Weimar at dinner the week before.) But the dog turned out to be eerie and pointless and klutzy, sort of a Carmen Miranda in Polish. Not long after Bauhaus moved in, I dropped in to find him parading around in one of those cardboard neck ruffs that vets put on animals to control their scratching a sore.

"What's going on here?" I asked.

Dennis Savage made a defeated gesture.

"Bauhaus saw an Airedale wearing that," Little Kiwi explained, "and he wanted one, too."

"Yes, o queen," I said, bowing to Bauhaus, "it shall be done as you command!"

"Oh, for heaven's sake," Dennis Savage roared. "Little Kiwi, take that foolish thing off that animal!"

"But he loves it so!" Little Kiwi protested.

My laughter made Dennis Savage yet more irate. "It comes off him, and I mean now—or he goes and you follow."

"We *will* go!" cried Little Kiwi. "*Come,* Bauhaus!"

But Bauhaus was very intent just then on doing a corn dance on his behind with his toy *Doggie News* in his mouth. Little Kiwi, perforce fending for himself, marched to the front door. When he got there he stopped, thought it over, lurched into the bathroom, slammed the door closed, and clicked the lock.

"And I'm never coming out!" he cried.

"As J. Edgar Hoover once said," I offered. "Okay, Mr. Smarty, you wanted a live-in boyfriend. Now what?"

"You might well look down on him," Dennis Savage whispered. "Yes." He nodded. His hands went out, palms up, like a rabbi's when a Methodist asks why Jews go to church on the wrong day. "Yes.

Because he's not educated. He's not particularly bright. His idea of gourmet food is you get fried chicken from a deli instead of in a TV dinner. But would you like to hear something personal from me? Would you?"

"Shoot."

"He's the sweetest damn thing I ever got close to. And the sooner you understand that, and share some of my joy, the more you'll know about the world."

"Love," I replied, "sure makes folks talk funny."

"You should hear me at night." He was knocking softly on the door as I departed—wondering why I had never noticed that the bathroom doors in our building have locks on them.

Alone of our squad, Carlo seemed to accept Little Kiwi without surprise—but then the rest of us kept viewing Little Kiwi's overgrown innocence in the context of our own watchful urbanity, whereas Carlo simply took him for a sexy child. He referred to him as "the kid himself." It shows how broad some men's views on sex can grow—beyond puberty, no age is inapposite, no place incorrect, no technique too radical. Everything is permissible because everyone consents.

Into this heady environment came one kid of my acquaintance not so much against his judgment as against mine: my houseboy Barry. Actually, he was more of an errand boy, as I wanted someone to run the street chores for me rather than disarrange the fastidiously coordinated office in which I not only work but live. A neighborhood kid not yet out of high school, and in a permanent state of quarrel with his parents, Barry had somehow or other taken up odd-jobbing along the Circuit at five bucks an hour. He was good at it, too, reliable and even imaginative at figuring out a substitute for a grocery item that wasn't in stock anywhere. His personal life, however, lay in disorder. One never knew for certain where he was staying, whether he was still legally a student, or even what his last name was. (He seemed to have several.) It occurred to me, too, to wonder how he had first launched his career as kid servant to gay men, and I imagined a wise old queen

version of Big Steve suavely alluring him with money and praise—
who knows?—even love.

I heard of Barry from a friend who was using him as a maid two
afternoons a week. His apartment had always looked like Calcutta.
Suddenly it was orderly; it gleamed, a showplace. Pieces of furniture
hitherto hidden under dirty clothes were revealed, to charm, and his
windows, once as dark as stained glass, lapped up light.

"Did you move?" I asked.

Barry came out of the bedroom just then, brisk and ready.

"All clear," he said.

We met—he had a soft handshake but a nice, slightly distracted
smile—and my friend his employer recommended him to me. He
was right, I realized: a cocktail dandy really ought to have someone
running tackle for him at the grocery, bank, laundry, and so on
(though, I must say, there's nothing like a walk home from The Food
Emporium at four o'clock in the morning with a cache of gourmet-
counter apricot-strudel cookies in your bag to remind you that you are
a New Yorker). I wondered if hiring Barry would spare me a New
Yorker's most onerous perquisite, shopping at Bloomingdale's; but this
was idle exercise. Barry and I struck a bargain right there on the site,
and, after he left, my friend said, "Believe me, you won't be sorry,"
his voice grinding like a burlesque attraction.

In fact, Barry tended to bring out the campy-seducer tones in older
men, which annoyed me. He seemed clearly to be a naturally unat-
tainable straight kid who had berthed his way into a field that calls for
tact and resourcefulness but no great intelligence or initiative. Yet,
every so often, when he would trundle in as I labored at my desk, I
caught allusions to passes made and, it sounded as if, not waved away.
I began to ask myself if I was being encouraged to make a move on
him. I thought back twelve years to Big Steve and his seductions; he
would have loved Barry, who had the scrubbed prettiness and pregym
slimness to coordinate with Big Steve's protective tenderness.

Like anyone else, I enjoy taking advantage of those encounters that
present themselves like ripe fruit, waiting to fall into hand should you
but reach up to pluck. But this was 1985, and like almost anyone else

I had become apprehensive of people who, like Barry, may for all I knew have been tanking up on bodily fluids. In fact, much as I liked Barry, I resented being tempted, and took to being elsewhere when he was expected. Finally one day he left a note for me: "Can I please talk to you about something?"

I stayed in for his next visit, and we talked. Rather, he rambled and I edited. He circled around a number of subjects at once, as if unwilling to confront his truths; I stopped listening to his words and tried catching the overtones. Suddenly he was saying, ". . . and Joe's mother said I couldn't stay over with him anymore, and she, like, told Alan's mother and *she* said okay, the same goes for her. Now, it's go back to my so-called parents or . . . or what? That's what I was asking, maybe."

"Maybe. Barry, exactly how old are you?"

"I forget."

"You know the term, 'jailbait'?"

"Look, that's not the problem. Mr. Lavery says I can live with him and be his houseboy, like. I just wanted to ask you what that means. You know, all together."

"It means you put out."

"To him?"

"No, to Princess Di. Who else, but to him? And his friends. Not to mention the hustlers he'll call in from time to time to enliven the action. Arnold Lavery is one of the shadiest characters in the east fifties—and that's saying something."

"His whole apartment is black."

"Do you like him?"

"Sure."

"You do?"

"He's my best customer. He says he's going to take me out to Fire Island when it's summer. He's even going to buy me . . ." He stopped. "Sure," he said.

"Buy you what"

"Just some clothes, he said."

I realized why Carlo could not share my disapproval of Big Steve's aggressive tactics. There *are* kids who are going to find their way onto the scene one way or another; and Carlo, wiser than I, knew that those who don't go Big Steve's way fall into the hands of an Arnold Lavery. For all our collegiate professionals and dashing brunches, this is still the city where those two opposites, beauty and money, dangerously attract. I wondered if I ought to send Barry to Big Steve for salvation, but Big Steve couldn't afford Barry. A kid without love or ambition doesn't want either. He wants luxury, and to be wanted, and not to care about anything.

"Barry," I said, "what is this talk about? Do you want me to speak against your moving in with Lavery, or to approve of it?"

"I don't know. I like thought . . ." He rose and looked down at the floor. "What exactly does it mean to put out?"

"You know what it means—the works."

He looked at me for a bit, then crossed the room and, without a word, left.

I tried to bring Carlo into the case, but he was too moody to help, and the little he had to say unnerved me. Like Barry, he was incoherent, but, unlike Barry, Carlo had a theme. "It's over," he kept saying. Then there'd be silence.

"What's over?" I asked.

He patted my arm; he wanted to be nice. But he couldn't phrase it properly and I wouldn't understand if he did.

"Tell me what it is," I urged.   .

He looked tired, as if he had lived through six or seven Hugh Whitkins inside of a month. In shorts and a T-shirt he seemed not sexy but sloppy, his hair going every which way, his face dark with stubble, his feet too big. We were in Big Steve's tiny apartment, where Carlo was, as he has been on and off over the years, something between a lover and a guest.

"*What's* over?" I demanded.

He said he was thinking of going back to South Dakota, and this was so absurd I could not address it. Carlo is the most metropolitan of gays, not in sophistication or wit but in strutting independence. I bet if an extraterrestrial, from a planet where the beings grow rather than carnally conceive their offspring, happened down to earth, and saw Carlo ambling along a summer street in his cords and striped polo shirt, grinning as he gave the world a once-over, the visitor would say, "Now I know what sex is, and sex is gay."

I made some joke about Carlo blowing the state of South Dakota wide open.

"It's the dishonor, I guess," he said. "More than anything else." He was looking out the window, and when he turned back to me he missed his footing and had to steady himself. He shivered as he tried to smile, and I realized he had been drinking, though he seldom does, and never in the daytime. "I haven't been able to figure it out exactly," he went on, "but that's how it seems to feel. The dishonor."

At least now he was talking.

"Because," he said, "the ones who go on having sex will die. And the ones who don't aren't men anymore. They might as well be . . ." He sat back on the couch. "Oh, what might they be, after all this?"

"Queens."

"Or dead," he whispered. "They might as well be dead."

All over town, men were having these talks. Some had actually quit the metropolis for small towns in Maine, Florida, Wisconsin. Some had gone to stay with their parents, who were startled but glad of the company. Others simply lit out and fled the stricken city, like Boccaccio's *Decameron* crowd. But those Florentines at least took something of great value along: their company. I couldn't imagine a gay man who had known Stonewall City living alone in the straight world.

"What's South Dakota like for a gay?" I asked.

"It isn't. There is no gay in South Dakota."

"Then why go there?"

"It's the only place I know, besides . . . these places. I want to think of getting along somehow. Your parents' is where you go when you can't go anywhere else. Isn't it?"

"When you're tired of gay life," I offered, revising Dr. Johnson, "you're tired of life."

"That's the nail on the ace, Bud. I *am* tired of life. This life, here.

I'm a man. I can't get along on bull sessions and . . . remembering.
It's like your hands are tied. I have to do what men do."

"You told me once, 'Friends is how you survive.' Now you're telling me you're planning to live without them?"

He crossed to the refrigerator and took out a bottle of vodka, three-
quarters empty. "I don't even know where you're supposed to keep
these." He took a short swig and came back to me. "Do you want a
glass?"

"I don't drink before dark," I said.

"When your hands are tied it's always dark." He went on drinking.
"Don't tell the others. Especially the kid himself. He looks up to me,
doesn't he?"

"He looks up to all of us, one way or another. He's like the local
kid brother."

A long swig this time. I thought back to the days when my brother
Jim lived in New York and his friends would sit around assessing the
mysteries of life and love, each with his own bottle.

"I know I'm hurting your feelings, Bud. But this brotherhood is
going to be a dead dream soon, and I don't want to see it die. I think
he looks up to me most of all, anyway."

His voice caught and he turned to me, crying. I started toward
him. "No, get back," he shouted, waving me off. "Not to soothe me.
I've done this show already, I know how it works." He went on, not
wiping his eyes. "I can know what it's like in South Dakota and I can't
know what it's like here anymore. That's the ticket, I truly believe.
Big Steve was so mad at me last night, he made me sleep on the
couch. He said I was a traitor and he wouldn't let me in his bed. In
South Dakota there are these truck stops. Then he came in here and
he turned on that lamp over there and he stood over me for a while. I
was awake. I could hear him there. I didn't pretend I was asleep but it
was dark so maybe he didn't know I was awake. You nod at the truckers real gruff, and if they nod back you go outside to their rig there.
See, and he knew and he said, 'Get up, Carlo.' He sounded angry
and I thought he might lick me for a minute. Because, you know . . .
but he didn't touch me. They have everything in the back of their

wheels. Towels, jelly, toke, cold beer. That's the whole life for them. They can be real men to you or they can be nice. There is no way to tell aforehand."

I'd never seen anyone cry like that, the tears roaring out of his eyes like those plastic-enclosed twenty-five cent globes of children's chotchkes spilling out of a broken machine.

"Carlo," I said.

"Shut up and please listen. This isn't joking. So Big Steve . . . he told me he didn't think it right that us two should be in separate rooms when we could be fucking. Because buddies like us were put on earth to take turns making each other happy. There are some things we tell each other, I recall. Some of the truckers have real long hair in the back because they're hoping someone will shoot a remark and they can slam the shit out of them, and they don't care where they are when they do it. They shouldn't have it that long. He said, 'Get up,' like that. And I said we should use a rubber and after all these years he is not going to do that with me, he said. That isn't buddies."

He was gesturing about the apartment, showing me where all this happened, and still crying.

"Well, I said it's taking precautions or nothing and that's how it is going to be, and he said it'll be how he wants it, and that's all the way and a rubber is like washing your hands with mittens on and he doesn't even have any and since he's trying to be nice to someone who doesn't deserve it and don't let him lose his temper, and Jim Fetters, who you wouldn't know because that was in tenth grade back there, he had gone out to a truck stop and he had this black eye all the next week and everyone said What happened? and he was just *white*. And don't tie my hands, that's all, because . . . because Big Steve and I had our troubles sometimes but he never hit me before. He just hauled off and hit me. But I don't have a black eye. And he kept going back there, shut up, and he kept getting these black eyes. Because Big Steve hit my jaw. He's my best friend, Bud. Even more than you. My best buddy. There are things we tell each other, and they started calling him Black Eye. He was proud of that. He even tied me up, he was so mad, and you can pray all you want to but that won't change anything, long or short. And I couldn't fight him back. I can, but I couldn't. They get the preachers out to talk to you. I don't see how they can tell, but they can. Preacher tells you, if you're that hard up, he'll do you right there, why not? They call you son. All of them. He tied me up. And I told him, Jesus, don't tie my hands. Don't tie me up. Maybe someone at the truck stop or a preacher but not you. Get back, this is not joking. Don't tie me up, I said. And he could see I wasn't joking. But he always had a weakness for that stuff . . ."

He was weeping now, but he had leaned back and thrown his arms out along the top of the couch as if discussing a quirk in the plot of the latest movie.

"Jim says it's been going on since the whole state was just forts and I expect it'll keep going on till all the gays are dead and it's just gringos and truck stops. I told Big Steve because he ought to know. And he was listening then. He untied me and put a blanket on me, and he went out. He hurt me very bad, Bud. Not just hitting me, though. Because I saw his eyes. And he was still mad when he came back, but he was lying next to me and holding me and that's all. I heard his eyes. The preachers tell your parents if you don't let them do you. He's still mad now. They say you were a wanton with Jim and you'd best be separated. We hardly did anything at all. They say the devil's in him. The devil's in his cock. His cock is talking to him, leading him astray, man shouldn't have a cock that size, that's a nigger cock or something, you got nigger blood? And your folks start praying, and the preachers are telling this to the town, the shame all over the town. They even hear it at the truck stop, nigger cock. They're waiting there now. I never hurt anyone, that's what I told them. Let me do you, they go, I won't say nothing. Never hurt anyone as long as I lived. Don't tie my hands. It isn't healthy. Some of those guys at the truck stop would do anything, but I wouldn't. Jim did more than I did. I tried to tell Big Steve, it wasn't hitting me, it was tying me up. He didn't have to do that. He knew he didn't. I thought Jim was giving himself black eyes for the attention. He didn't have to. He said it was a blunder. See, he can't say I'm sorry so he says he blundered. I told him I wasn't going to be fucked anymore, I was going to be top from now on. And he said he wanted me to be happy but I'm a rat. There aren't happy rats, are there? Because they know they're rats. That's why you always see them running around and hiding. Because they know people hate them. But people only hate them because they act like rats. Preachers are happy. Parents are happy. Jim was happy. He had his own devil. So we talked for a while, and then it was morning. This morning. I didn't sleep last night. I said, 'How could you tie me up like that?' He said he'll do worse to me if I don't stop being a rat. He says everyone's going to hate me because I'm a rat. And he looked at me the way those other guys did because I . . . they saw how easy I was going to be because I . . . wasn't ever really tough like them, I only . . ." Suddenly he began to sob again. "I'm not a rat after all this," he said, lurching to his feet, swaying, dropping the bottle; and I leapt up and grabbed him and told him to stop and took him into the back room and put him to bed while he whispered, "Get back, it's over" every twenty seconds. And "Don't tell Big Steve." And "Did I stop crying?"

It took me quite some while to find the aspirin, because it turns out that Big Steve keeps it in the refrigerator. I brought two tablets and some water to Carlo, who was asleep; but I woke him up, explaining that he had to take aspirin to stave off a hangover.

"Later," he said, turning over.

I almost threw the water in his face. "*Now.*"

He swallowed them dry, and said, "You won't be mad at me, will you? I can only do one mad at a time."

"I won't be mad."

He nodded. "The devil's in everyone. Even Diana Vreeland. But why did he tie me up, anyway?"

"He tied you up because he likes you."

He looked so sad then. "Everyone always liked me. My whole life. Because they wanted to pull my pants down. That's why I got so big, Bud. At the gym. Why should Big Steve be any different?"

"He is different," I said. "He tied you up because he loves you. You remember that guy you told me about on your way to New York way back there? The one with the little bowl of warm water and the soap? The one you said you loved? That's what you are to Big Steve—only you've stayed that all his life. That's why he tied you up. He wants to keep you in New York."

"He went to Seattle for two years."

"To try to forget you."

Carlo looked at me. "Oh, Jesus hell. Did he tell you that?"

I shook my head.

"Then how . . ." He wiped away new tears. "How do you know?"

"Because I was in that movie. We all were."

"I'm not a rat."

"Go to sleep, now."

"Don't go somewhere."

"Huh?"

"I mean, don't go away yet."

There was a bit of silence then.

"Did I say terrible things?" Carlo asked.

"You said . . . interesting things."

"About Jim Fetters?"

"Somewhat."

"Don't go. Okay?"

"I'm just getting something to read. As long as I have to play watch and ward."

In the front room, I nosed into Big Steve's five-inch shelf, settling on *The Silmarillion*—Tolkien is one thing Big Steve and I come to terms on.

"Read me from some of that," Carlo said.

"Carlo—"

"Just till I sleep. Please, Bud."

"'There was Eru, the One, who in Arda is called Ilúvatar,'" I began, thinking that, if I hadn't left Pennsylvania, I would never have found myself sitting on a bed in which Beau Geste lay listening to me read fairy tales as he slept off the direst drunk of his life. A uniquely metropolitan pastime. When I was sure he was asleep, I put the book down, and listened to him breathe for a bit, then left.

I never did get to talk to Carlo about Barry, to put it mildly; but Barry left my employ to live in as Arnold Lavery's houseboy. Just as well, that, for Carlo was in no tone to consider protecting reckless kids in an age that dishonors respectable clones. Our set tried to rally Carlo, but he resisted, out of fear, I imagine, that we would talk him down. Get back: he did not want to be soothed. He may well have moved in with Big Steve precisely to hop himself up, to force his own issue upon himself.

I was saddened. Yet he was right in a way. For it is the newcomers who recall to us the explosive truth that veterans live very near to the idea of fate: the Barrys and Little Kiwis who put the Carlos in perspective. What unites us, all of us, surely, is brotherhood, a sense that our friendships are historic, designed to hold Stonewall together. It is not rebellious sex habits that define us as much as the rebel coterie itself, the act of not bothering to adjust to gringo procedures. It is friendship that sustained us, supported our survival, and friendship that kids need more than seductions by Big Steve Bosco. For—not to put too fine a point on it—the difference between Barry and Little Kiwi is the latter's friendship with Dennis Savage, and Little Kiwi instinctively knew that, and so he held back on the touching till he was sure he had a friend. Barry, however, doesn't share that concept, that feeling of particular need—and where Barry is going, he'll not have many friends.

Carlo, who had more friends than anyone I know, left for South Dakota quite suddenly, just as the summer was getting under way. He did not call, and heaven knows Carlo doesn't write: my doorbell rang, without a summons from the doorman, because Carlo had just been to Dennis Savage's, and now it was my turn, and then South Dakota's.

As if making up for his demonstrative plaint at Big Steve's, he was taciturn, yet almost like his old, easily carried self. He smiled a few times, if adamantly, and when I offered him coffee he said he had to keep moving.

"Could I have your address?" he asked.

"Carlo, you've been coming here for over a decade."

"I don't know the number. I just know where it is. I thought . . ."

He was looking out the window at the site next door; one crew was attaching the curtain wall, another setting down the wooden forms for the concrete on the second-floor roof. "Another shirts-off day in New York." He turned to me. "I thought I might send you a letter."

I went to my desk to write down the data; when I was at *Opera News* ten years ago, we all got business cards, which I never used. Over the years, they've made ideal note stubs. I pulled one out, and, as I marked it up, Carlo said, "Look."

"Oh, her," I replied.

He was gazing at one of the workers, who, for several months, had been coming around at various times of the day to stare into my apartment. Perhaps he was fascinated by the thousands of books and records in view, or trying to figure out what the hell I was doing in by day when I should be out working like him. Who knows? Maybe he was entranced by my Bemelmans.

"He's kind of cute," said Carlo.

"Under the hardhat he's bald."

"That's not his fault. Sweet bod."

"Lugging things around all day will do that to you. Here." I gave him the card. I had included my phone number in case of emergency.

"Have you ever spoken to him? On the street."

"Never saw him on the street. Maybe he never *goes* on the street. Every time I look up, almost, he's standing there looking."

"He's sort of like a smaller version of Big Steve, isn't he?"

"My God, Carlo, you look . . . the way you used to look. Just now, like this. Carefree."

"Wave at him, Bud." Carlo pulled me to him, turned me to face the site, and the two of us looked out at the man. "He's lonely. How old is he? Thirty? Thirty-five? Italian. Lives with his folks. Never married. Dates when he has to. There are always those poor neglected girls who are glad to get any date at all. In between, he wonders what he wants. What he has a right to. Catholic, so everything he dreams of is forbidden anyway. But he looks in here and he senses somehow that you know what he wants. You can tell him. He doesn't know why, but he *knows* that you're clued in. That's why he stares at you. Help him."

Carlo waved.

"Now you," he said. "Give him a chance."

I waved, too, but the man stood there frozen, just watching, as he always did.

"He's shy," said Carlo.

"He doesn't know what we're doing," I said. "We might be making fun of him."

"He's a nice guy."

"How would you know a thing like that?"

"I can always tell." His grip tightened on my shoulders. "Bud. Don't see me out. I want you to go upstairs after I leave. The kid himself was crying before. Wave once more to him, Bud, with me, together."

We waved.

"Okay," he said. "I'll report to you on what it's like. We'll think about some things. You won't tell anybody what I said to you downtown, will you? Big Steve is really so truly sorry."

"Carlo—"

"No, Bud." He was holding me so I couldn't turn around. "Look, he's watching us as if we held his secret of life. There's always something somewhere else. I'm going to let you go, and I'm going to leave, and you're going to stay here, just like this. Okay?"

I nodded; the worker in the hardhat, fascinated by our melodrama, was still watching us.

Carlo let go of me, moved, crossed the room; I heard the door click open, but just then the worker waved at me, and by the time I turned Carlo was gone.

*   *   *

No one's irreplaceable, I told myself, as we went on with our dreams and dreads and brunches, which, on a really vital Sunday, may be formidably combined. But in summer the urban brunches dissolve in deference to the Island dinners—which can last even longer than a brunch.

I decided not to take a share this year, but Dennis Savage had finally gotten into a neat house on the ocean, in a reputable section of The Pines, so I guested. Each summer, old friends cross paths at the ferry, or the Pantry, or walking on the beach, and comparing the tones of the various years is an available topic. This year was generally thought unsuccessful, the weather boring, the ocean pugnacious, "and," as everybody pointed out, "no one's getting anything except older."

True enough. Pacing through the no-man's land between Pines and Grove, one would still run into the odd devotee here and there, never saying die in their come-hither poses, or even a nude or two. But where once one might have thought, "I should pause and collect that," now one wondered, moving right along, if the stranger had come out of a time machine from the 1970s. Anyway, there was less roaming now, especially in those old haunts; folks stayed buttoned up in their houses, and at night sometimes one had to strain to hear that former symbol of Pines in plenary session, a blaring stereo. Many people even avoided the beach on the sunniest days. They would lie around on their decks looking relaxed and content, but as you walked by you heard them tensely badgering each other.

When a grouchy wind assaults The Pines, Dennis Savage, of course, flies in the vanguard, and he was at me from the moment I set down my valise. Little Kiwi, however, was in a merry mood, though he would grow silent for a few minutes whenever Carlo's name came up; and though, more generally, The Pines as a culture tended to daunt him. Sending him to the Pantry for an item or two was like urging the Wicked Witch of the West to take a bath. He feared he'd be kidnapped if he dared the harbor alone. What he really wanted to do was stage little extravaganzas on the walkway that joined the two sections of the house's upper story. For anyone else, the walkway was a means to get from a bedroom to the bathroom. For Little Kiwi, the walkway was a stage.

I had scarcely arrived before he called down to me to sing "I Love To Walk in the Rain," an old Shirley Temple number that I had put on a cassette for him and which he played repeatedly till the neighbors threatened to mace Dennis Savage's apartment.

"I'm not in the mood," I told him.

"Sing it for him, you beast," said Dennis Savage. "He's been waiting all morning for this."

I started singing, in several of my favorite keys, and Little Kiwi dashed into the bathroom and promptly came back in a hooded yellow slicker and a Japanese parasol that belonged to one of the other men in the house. As I sang, he capered.

"Very nice," I said, heading for the fridge. Dennis Savage barred my way.

"He's not done yet," Dennis Savage said, through his teeth.

I sang some more, as Little Kiwi passed along the walkway, twirling the parasol. "Keep going!" he cried, darting into the bedroom to tow his dog out by the leash.

"It's Astaire and Bauhaus, the lovable Hollywood team!" he explained as he danced. Bauhaus had apparently been snoozing and was not happy to enter a musical revue. He whined and grumbled.

"Now this amazing effect," said Little Kiwi, taking a bag out of his pocket. The bag disgorged a few mushrooms, which Little Kiwi set up on the walkway. Bauhaus ate one as Little Kiwi hid behind the rotating umbrella and I reached the end of the song. Dennis Savage and I clapped.

"I've got plenty more of those."

"What a treat for later," I replied. "Much later."

Once things quieted down, it was again—for me, at least—The Pines as it has always been: our boy, his notebook, and a few intimate subjects. Your first years in The Pines you can't get enough of the beach parade, tea, the meat racks. After a while, the parade loses its glitter, tea is a chore, and—by 1982—the meat racks were pretty poison. The main purpose of The Pines, by then, is to provide a sanctuary from the outer world, a gay place. You no longer worry whether you're going out enough, dancing enough, getting enough. Just being there is being gay.

I prefer to lie around talking and writing. Dennis Savage, who as a schoolteacher has nothing to do in the summer, sat on the deck with me to watch Little Kiwi walking Bauhaus along the water's edge. Every now and then Bauhaus would break away and chase someone, and Little Kiwi would run off in the other direction. He says if he stays there, people yell at him.

"You know," I said, "this looks like a Paul Terry cartoon directed by Robert Wilson."

"I hate my work," Dennis Savage said.

I looked at him.

"Well, I do!" he said.

"I didn't make the world."

"You sleep as long as you want to, and I have to get up at five forty-five! And what's the point of pushing on those dumbbells to get them motivated? You speak to the cultured, and I speak to idiots."

"But you have free health insurance. And holidays. Seems to me every time somebody turns around in one of the boroughs, the schools declare a national holiday. I work day and night seven days a week, fifty-two—"

"Come on, you're always out playing!"

Someone was waving at us on the beach: someone in a crowd.

"Who's the kid?" asked Dennis Savage.

"My current ex-errand boy. Barry."

He was wearing a bathing suit so slight he would have been arrested at Cannes; but his friends were dressed—two of them, incredibly, in tropical suits.

"Look at the bizarre," said Dennis Savage. "Well, I'm going to see about dinner. Some of us run our own errands." He went inside.

"Who was that waving?" asked Little Kiwi, coming up from the sand with the dog.

"That's you without Dennis Savage," I said.

He looked after Barry's gang, remotely trudging, I would guess, to some furiously dreary cocktail shop. I was watching Little Kiwi, trying

to see him in a bathing suit like Barry's—made of the material super-
markets bag onions in—and attending those parties at which moneyed jitterbugs cop a feel while making small talk. I couldn't see it.

"What do you mean," Little Kiwi asked, "that he's me?"

"He's not you. That why he's in trouble."

Little Kiwi stared after Barry's group. He turned back to me. "He
looked happy."

"He is, today. But he'll get messed up and that'll be that."

"Why would he get messed up?"

"Because no one cares about him. He's alone."

"No, all those people with him . . . won't they—"

"They're his leeches. They'll milk him for fun and toss him away."

Little Kiwi looked at me. In the dying light, I could see him watching me carefully, knowing that I'm the one who says the hard things
to him. Our other friends treat him like a kid. I treat him like a clone.

"Why are they going to milk him?" he asked me. "He was nice."

"Yes, he's nice. He's helpless. Trusting. Likable. That's the type
they love to milk. If this were Paraguay, leftover Nazis would have
him brought to a party to be whipped for the fun of it."

Dennis Savage came out. "It'll be barbecued chicken, some pasta,
shiitake mushrooms for everyone's good health, and maybe something
green how about?"

"I don't want to get messed up!" Little Kiwi cried, running to him.
"The whippers are coming!"

"What have you been doing to him again?" Dennis Savage roared,
holding him.

And Bauhaus barked at me.

"We just saw a chicken on the way to his barbecue," I noted.

"Is Carlo coming back?" Little Kiwi asked, his voice muffled in
Dennis Savage's chest.

Dennis Savage looked at me. "Is he? He's your friend, mostly."

"Yes," I said. "Yes, he was."

Three Letters from South Dakota

I have corrected the mispellings, puncuation, and most severe infelicities, but here they are as he wrote them.

July 24

Dear Bud:

I told you I would be writing. You didn't believe me, I know. But this could be like those times when you and me would sit around and bullshit about the world. Only I'm not right next to you now. I always used to think you would get too heavy and I admit that once or twice when you were not around I thought about the things you said and I wanted to knock your block off. I even like argued with you, because I knew what you'd say, and I finally thought of the right answers. I'm glad you weren't there then, when I thought of the answers. I would really have pounded you.

My mom just came in and said, "Oh, are you writing to the Lord?" They do that here. They write letters to God. They don't mail them, of course. It's just to concentrate the prayer. (How they say it.) When I came back, they gave me a party, and it was like this. First, they all got here, aunts and cousins and things that I haven't seen in twenty years. So they all mass up, staring like I'm the figure of Jack the Ripper in the wax museum. Then comes the time when some of them go into one room to pray and the others stand around joking. It reminded me of some New York parties, where some guys went into the bedroom to fuck while some others stayed in the living room discussing opera. Because after that everyone had supper as if nothing had happened. And you know how there's always, always somebody who can't take their eyes off you but is afraid to say anything, but you can feel how hungry they are right across the room? Well, here it is my third kin Irene (which is pronounced Areenee around here). You can bet her folks and mine will be trying to set us up soon enough.

It sure was a crossword-puzzle thing, scooting around the old places. Everything's still there, I guess, but what about the people? And everybody calling me Rip, or old Ripper, or even Ripley (like my folks), mostly, because they don't go for New York nicknames around here. And my mom calling to me in the morning, and there's the Cream of Wheat just like before, which I liked to eat year round, even in the summer. And my dad grinning at me like I just broke the record at the Olympics for the four-minute mile or something. I guess they really are glad I'm back. They cry a lot, because they love me so much. This is the thing about parents that I will never get used to. They are a little different to each other, too, than I remember. Like they will pass each other on the way to different rooms and just stop and hug each other. It sure is a sight. I had to ask them not to treat me like that, and they said okay. I know what they were thinking— prayer is more certain, anyway. They are just trying to make me break down and cry. They call out crying for the Lord. You just have no idea what it's like.

I guess I cried plenty that morning you were at Big Steve's, and I wonder what you're going to do about that. Forgive me? (I hope.) You should have seen Big Steve later on, how sorry he was. But he started right in again. He made me tell him the names of all the people I love on earth, so he could count them. You know how I hate that stuff. I know I looked terrible that day, too, because I was drunk and it was not even afternoon. Did you think I was going crazy? But I never took drugs all those years, just toke. No poppers or anything. At least I have that. You might as well tell me what you thought of all what I said at Big Steve's. I hope you would tell me. Some of it was about

Jim Fetters, who still lives around here. But I am putting it off, meeting him again.

You know what's funny? The truck stop that some of us would go to for like a glory hole is now a Jesus Center. There are people with signs there—"Why Don't You Love Him? Because He Loves You!" and "If You Died Tomorrow, Could You Meet Him Fair?" It's like they were holding up cue cards for a big hymn sing. The one I like is "What Will You Do When He Comes?" I was staring at the sign and maybe smiling, and the woman who held it looked me right in the face and said, "You best think about it, because He'll be coming soon, all over the universe." And so many replies came to me. You know, like joking in the bars. Our kind of thing. But I just told her okay. They give you a booklet which tells you how to behave from now on.

The main reason I am writing is, I want to tell you what Big Steve said to me. But first I have to tell you something about him that you didn't know. I know how you get about a guy's profession, and how people are supposed to live in certain areas of town (like not Brooklyn, right?), and clothes and all. Like a tie. I did everything wrong, probably, except I don't think I ever lived in Brooklyn, even for the weekend. Anyway, way back there when you were still friendly with your brother, he mentioned something of great use, I think. To know about. It was about parents, that you can hate them, or call them every tough name there is, or hide from them, or not visit the house, or even like get married or something without telling them. And they'll always forgive you, he said. But where they draw the line is if you just lose interest in them. If you get neutral. That's where they draw that line. They can do love and they can do war but they can't do test patterns. And what I want to tell you about Big Steve is that he is like a parent. Like he's as good when an affair is falling apart and everyone's getting mad as he is when it's new and you're both so hot for each other all the time you don't get any chances to fight. But he can't deal with it when an old lover walks past him on the street as if he wasn't there. There's always got to be something. Anyway, what he told me was, he would give his life for me. Just like that. And I said, "Who wants you to?"

So he just went on about giving his life. And how many people were there that he would do that for. And how many would I?

Hell, have you ever thought about that? How many of those *you* have?

Well, I don't know what got into me, because I know he wanted me to say I would give my life for him. Because that was how he always was, that you shared what you were all the way. So like even on one of those nights when I topped him for a considerable full time, just as deep and slow as it goes, and we would doze off together just holding on, and what more could you ask? Except no, sometime later he'd be waking me up to say now it's his turn, because we have to pleasure each other. And I'd say I already am pleasured. He'd just be rolling me over. You know how he gets when he's after you.

Anyway, I said I wouldn't give my life for anyone, including him. And what I'm asking you is, Was that the fair thing to say to him?

So okay. Tell me what's doing with everyone, and say hello to the kid himself especially. Don't tell him this, but I truly believe I will have to remember the way he started to cry when I came over to say goodbye. I will have to. Because I kind of went for him to push him around for a joke, but he backed away from me, shaking his head. So now I started to make a list of all the nice things I did for you and the others all along, but then I thought that's too dumb. And you would know them anyway.

Remember to answer my question about what I should have said to Big Steve.

This is your old pal Carlo.

August 6

Dear Bud:

Well, you can see there's plenty of time for writing out here. Jim Fetters came over during dinner, which you will find shocking, but that's how we do things, at like six or seven o'clock. Because otherwise you can't find anyone home. Before, they're at work. After, they're in bed. That's our hours. I always love your rules about when to call, when to visit, and those things, like. You know what a New York attitude that is. But we have this midwestern language, where if we like a visitor we slap another plate down and if we don't we hold the whole thing at the door.

But Jim is an old friend. So my folks fussed over him, and said how's Marge and tell about the kids, and he did.

Now, you know, it has been about twenty years all the way, and Jim has hardly aged at all. It was my mom who opened the door, and when she said, "Why, Jim!" I felt guilty for not having gone around to him myself, us being best friends for so long all before. But the next thing I felt was just curious, and I got up and when I was at the door old Jim jumped me like a long-lost puppy dog, crying, "Hey, you big old Rip!" and stuff. Boy, he looked good. He truly did. He couldn't get over how I had grown. Of course they don't have gyms and all that here, not much. In Dakota we have a saying, "You don't make yourself into a clone, boy, you just better be born one." (That's a joke. We don't have such a saying here.)

So there was my old Jim. And my dad has already made a place at the table and we all sit around to hear Jim tell about his family, my folks just beaming away at us as if we were sixteen and talking out how the track season was shaping up. Then Jim asked what I had been up to all those years in the big New York City and my folks kept on smiling but their eyes sort of turned, you know. I almost imagined my dad saying then, "He was doing gay things in New York, which is a gay city, and now I'm going to switch him for it!"

You know what you do out here when someone comes back? You go visit all your old friends. It's sort of like if a New Yorker went around the Village looking up his old lovers. Imagine what you'd see. Some of them would be shacked up with new lovers and would they want you around? Some of them would be all alone and the sight of you would not cheer them up, would it? And some would be straight angry at you.

That's kind of how it was here that night when Jim and me went visiting, riding up the driveways to all these depressing houses. I guess the old gang didn't get to prove themselves. Everyone was married or living with someone, and even the guys I used to like didn't seem glad to see me. Jim was in rare form, like showing me off. He called me "Our New York boy from Dakota." Or maybe Our Dakota boy from New York is more like it.

You should have come along with us to get notes for your stories on dramatic pauses, because there sure were plenty. Jim was about the only one talking, most of the time. Meanwhile, all these little kids were wandering in and out, and one house was a real tornado, like there had been a married fight. After we left one place, Jim got real quiet, and after he started the car he said, "Hey, Rip, you think they still remember the trouble we got into?" About the truck stop and all. And his folks finding us together. The news around town, as I told you.

I said I guessed they did remember. And Jim didn't mean just *remember*—he means they don't forgive us. We drove back to my folks' and parked and took a walk around the yard. We have a lot of ground and things. Sheds and high grass and my old tree house, where Jim and I had a club when we were kids. No one else could join. And finally Jim said, "Oh hell." Like that. Just "Oh hell."

I said, "It's real neat to see you, good buddy." We weren't looking at each other. "I don't care about all them," I told him.

He said, "Me neither."

We walked around for a while, and then he stopped, and it was like an idea hit him out of the blue. He said, "I know! Let's get smashed. Got a bottle in my car."

I said great, but how about his family? He said it was all right, this was his night out, because it was like a holiday that I was back.

That's another thing we do around here that doesn't happen in

New York. Guys sitting around all night drinking. Maybe you could call this a Dakota brunch. My folks went up to bed not long after we started in, and my room is downstairs in the back, so we could make ourselves at home. And what do you know but Jim starts in asking me about New York and who are my friends and what we do. And hell, I told him. I told him, Bud. And he didn't play tourist on me, either. He took it. Sometimes he nodded, as if he thought that's how it was, all along. Nothing shocked him. And you know I have wild tales to tell if I loosen up.

I was stretched out on my bed and he was in the rocking chair, with the bottle between us. We drank it straight out, the way you do it here. One thing he said, was all the names were funny. Big Steve. Dennis Savage. He said they sounded like wrestlers on television. The only name he could relate to was yours, because we've got loads of Buds around. Then I said your name was really Ethan and he damn near choked his booze up.

Then I told him *my* name was Carlo. I explained about getting approached in the Eagle that time, and just in case you don't know about this, how this guy was looking for an escort for a friend of his. Or do you remember? That guy who owned his whole house by the river, and had his friend take pictures of me pretending I was going to hang him? He had a real noose there too, but it was tied all wrong. I fixed it for him, and he had this funny look on his face. Anyway, he took me to Key West, and after the whole thing was over he gave me five thousand bucks. *Do* you remember? (I guess that's a joke because Dennis Savage once said everything you hear goes right into the typewriter.) Well, Jim couldn't get over that. He kept calling me Carlo and shaking his head. And after I told him all I could about all of us, he said, "Rip, what does it *feel* like?"

He kind of stumped me there, so I said, "What does it feel like here for you?"

So then he got going about his life, and he said it plain away that he surely missed our adventures in high school because things slowed up after that. I could have said that seemed generally true from our drive around town. Jim said the only thing keeping him whole was his family, because his wife Marge is really great and they have a little boy just like Jim and a little girl just like Marge and they all play together and he reads to the kids and they all fall asleep in his lap. It sounded real cute, especially since I mostly remember Jim cutting these really Old Testament sort of farts in the library and riding his bicycle into a tree when the brakes busted, and other crazy stunts which do not exactly connect with him being a father.

He asked me how I could live without a family and I said my family is all the guys I was telling him about. Isn't it? But he didn't get that. He said no—a family like playing with them and learning from each other and living with them inseparable, and I said that's what we do. And finally he sort of got it, that my family is my buddies.

And I know what you're thinking, smart aleck, which is how come I'm *away* from my family, and that's just the kind of thing you always say that I have no reply to until I get home and think about it and wish you were handy so I could paste you a good one. Because you think you know everything.

Anyway, we were just into the second bottle when Jim started in again about, "God, you got so big, Rip," and "Why'd you get like that?" and "I'd be afraid to wrestle you now."

Which is how we got into trouble in the first place, because we used to wrestle naked, and the guy who won could make the loser do anything he asked. Like drink a bottle of ketchup. But one time we got into it in a different way. I know it was different because the other times we were just fooling around with it, but this time we went straight down the track, and all you could hear was us breathing.

You don't think I would remember something like that, at that age, no matter what the others do?

But the thing is, Jim asks me, What exactly did we do that time? I couldn't believe he forgot, after all the trouble we got into. I made him swear he didn't know. So he swore. Okay. And I told him, which was that I pinned him and I made him suck me off. And I like had to pin him again with his arm bent back, because he still wouldn't. But I knew he wanted to, anyway. And after he did it I started swinging on him, and I had him on his back holding his legs in the air gobbling him up when they found us, the preacher and his folks staring there right behind him. They must have known all along and called the preacher, because they were afraid to find us themselves. The preacher was so calm about it, he probably disappointed them. But then he had sucked us off himself often enough.

Old Jim was fit to be iced and put away for the summer when he heard about all this. I guess he really had forgotten. We were so pissed by then we started laughing, which is weird when you think of the terrible things they did to us. I guess the way we survived high school is I said anyone who said a word to us, I would put him in the hospital. And we already had a tough reputation because of hanging out at the truck stop. After all the laughing, we started getting teary, thinking about everything. So we took aspirin, a trick I learned from you, not to get a hangover, and I got up a jug of water so we wouldn't have to crash through the house when we got thirsty later. And I found a blanket. We sacked out in our clothes to sleep it off, just bundled up there. And Jim asked me if he should have come along to New York way back. Because I had asked him. He said, "Would I have had a family with New York names, like you? Would they have taken pictures of me too, and given me five thousand bucks?"

I told him, "You would have been a humdinger there, Jim."

We started to drift off, and I heard him say, "I missed you the whole time, Rip, because you're my best pal." So we went to sleep like that, and the next morning he was gone.

This is your friend, Carlo the Smith.

                                                    August 30
Dear Bud:

About time you wrote back, I don't care how busy you are. Or are you still mad at me? Because I know you are even if you won't say so.

You didn't answer my question right about Big Steve. I asked you if I said the fair thing. If I gave the right answer. I didn't want you to interpret Big Steve's question and turn it into something else. If he was really asking me if I loved him more than anyone else, why didn't he ask that? You and he really ought to get together now, and talk about love all the time, because that's all you guys want to do. You can't just accept something for the way it feels. You always want to know what to call it.

Anyway, I finally got off my butt and found a job, because that's another thing they do around here. None of that New York unemployment stuff in Dakota. My dad had a talk with me to see what kind of experience I had that we could put to use, and I burst out laughing, because what I have been is a hustler and a waiter for Big Steve's Kingdom Kum Katerers and a porn actor and a boutique clerk. But I was also a mover, and that's what I am again. I have to commute into Aberdeen in Dad's truck. It's mostly short-haul stuff in town, I can do it single-handed. You wonder why people want to move so much. They just go right into someplace as terrible as where they were before.

What did I tell you, that my kin would try to set me up with Cousin Irene? I guess they think I came back to change. Maybe instead I came back to be the same. I put them off, but they kept at me, and Irene's father called and said they're expecting me for dinner, so I just said okay and tooled off to town in the truck. If they won't take no for an answer, let them take yes. But I'm still not coming.

You're probably wondering after all this what I'm doing for fun. Well, it took me a while to find the right place, and unfortunately it's one of those real mean gringo taverns where every time the door opens every guy looks up to see if someone's brought a woman in so they can start a vicious incident. But I can't find a truck stop sort of place and of course we don't have any Ty's. The place is called Kicker's Bar and Grill, but I have this joke that it is really called Mars, because the men are all like Martians, you know. They can't talk, they can't smile, they can't do anything I'm used to from New York. You probably think they talk about sports or politics or women, but not even that. They don't talk, period.

The night I skipped dinner with Irene's family I was there. I spotted a guy who looked right, because he kept watching me. He was a big, bearded guy. I came over to his table and bought him a beer, and he turned out to be the most Martian of all, but I had guessed right, anyway, because he made me feel he was running his hand up and down my back just by the way he looked at me. That's a trick only gringos know how to do, because gays will do it by touching your arm, or smiling, or even by saying something pretty direct. Well, look, I know how the game is played, though after New York it's boring to pretend. Also, I have to tell you that even though this guy was no chicken, he was still younger than me, which just shows how things turn over, because I always used to be the kid. Probably for longer than I should have been.

We went through three or four beers each, and when you're drinking with a Martian it seems more like thirty beers. But finally we were near it, because he was staring real hard at me with a mean smile. He's missing one of his teeth. And when he was looking he leaned forward so our knees touched, and I could hear him sucking on his breath. His eyes were like fists. He said, "You want to try a little something new tonight?"

I said, "Like what?" real tough.

"Give me your right hand," he says, and he's reading my palm. "Look at what I see," he goes. "A tall dark stranger's coming into your life. With a beard on him. Tonight, looks like." Then he looks at me. "Right?"

"If you got a place," I said.

He laughs and says, "I got lots of places."

What he had was another dump over a store, like all the people I've been moving around town. He kept the lights out, and when we stripped he didn't take his shorts off, so I said, kind of joking, because it obviously wasn't, "Is this your first time?"

So he said, "What's your name again?" and I told him. And even though he already heard it, he starts using it a lot, like it's a new game he thought of. Then he says, "It's like this, Rip. You move around enough and keep your eyes open, you begin to realize that it ain't never *anybody's* first time."

I can tell you, it sure wasn't his. He said anytime I'm stuck for a place I can stay over some more, and I did a few times, and finally, without anyone saying this is what's happening, I just plain moved in with him. I guess that sounds familiar, huh? But you'd best not write to me anymore, since I'm not at my folks very often. This guy I'm with, whose name is Warren, is a typical supergringo. Anything he doesn't understand he puts down. Anyone he doesn't know he doesn't like. And he's a mean drunk. I tried telling him about me and like Fire Island and the things we do, and he got so nasty making fun of it that I just gave up. But at least he doesn't want anything from me except sex.

He did one strange thing, though. Just two nights ago, which I guess is why I had to write this letter, I got up real late to take a piss, and I was still at the pot when Warren suddenly loomed up behind me and tried to pull me around, and he said, "Where the fuck do you think you're going?" I said, "Let me finish this, will you?" and he was going on about he doesn't want me ducking out on him. It didn't take much to calm him down, because he was half asleep, and he even apologized, which is probably a first for him. But listen. When we got into bed he got all locked up around me, his feet and arms, like I'm his prisoner. I said, "Come on, quit it," and got him off me, but a few minutes later he came right back again. And then he started saying my name, and he said it over and over again.

Is there life on Mars? This is Ripley Smith, over and out. Please don't be mad at me anymore. Give Dennis Savage and the kid himself a hug for me after all this. And listen, whatever happens now, don't you forget me, boy! Because once you're buddies, it doesn't matter if you're there, just how you feel, and who you remember.

And what you can forgive. Okay, my friend?

The Hottest Man Alive

*A symbolic tale, projecting the first years of
Stonewall against the fall of a great man.*

Of course Carlo wrote no more letters. He was settled in—as he probably would be if you dropped him in Tibet, the Gobi desert, or
Middle-Earth—with a hot man who could busy, then puzzle, then
trouble him. With our resident hunk departed, my circle closed ranks
and went on with love and work. But we all felt the lack—not just of
Carlo the person but of Carlo the type, for the ideal confraternity
blends all kinds. Ironically, I was thinking of this when I ran into a
hunk even more essential than Carlo, or perhaps just more public.

It was late one night in the winter after Carlo left us, one of those
bad, bitterly cold nights New York can throw on without warning. I
was trudging along Third Avenue watching for a cab when I saw a
tall, broad, and familiar-looking man heading my way. He seemed to
recognize me, and came toward me—where had we met? My mind
jumped to pluck a name, a place, from cabinets marked College
Chums, Pines Housemates, People I Enraged at Parties (a dense file),
and People I Charmed at Parties (surprisingly thin). As he neared, I
started to smile, but he came too close, backed me against a car, and
said, "I'm hungry. Give me money or I'll hurt you."

Shoot, this *would* happen just when I'm starting to get famous.
Because, damn it!, I am not giving these creeps my wallet on demand. Anyway, it's too tempting to bluff them down. I disconnected

194

one footpad in the Village by grinning and nodding and speaking Russian; and when a kid fell into step with me on Fifty-seventh Street and said this was a holdup and he was armed, I told him nothing doing unless I saw the gun, and he ran away.

"Hand it over," my present assailant growled, bending my arm behind me, "or I swear to God I'll break it off."

He glared, to persuade me with bitter fire; but then recognition struck me, and I looked down at his left forearm to find the tattoo of a shield inscribed, "No. 1."

"Clark Ellis," I said, and he relaxed his hold on my arm in surprise. I had remembered where we had met before.

We had met, actually, twice, the first time in one of those "backdate" magazine stores where *Popular Mechanics* and *Boy's Life* had their sections, *Demi-Gods*, *Tomorrow's Man*, and *Rustic* theirs. *Rustic* bemused me as the name for a physique magazine. Here was not just the suggestion of the fact of beauty, but the sighting of it in a rural setting—putting real men into imaginary gardens. I was alarmed, alerted. Demi-gods did not exist; but hot farmers might.

One *Rustic* model in particular caught my eye. He was utterly unlike the dowdy hunks that prevailed in those days. They seemed to aim at an impersonalized ideal of flexing, a mere prowess. This one model, on the contrary, threw himself into his photo, aimed to reveal his personability, an expertise. At a time when a 1950s cover still hung over the emerging gay opulence, his parts suggested a sexy cartoon, each feature bigger than you could remember seeing on real flesh. The smile, above all, held me. It was more than dazzling: penetrating. It said, Forget the come-on—we're already there. The culture is here and I am among you. I had seen bedroom eyes before; this guy had room-at-the-baths eyes.

"Clem represents the new breed of poser," his caption ran, "with his conqueror's physique and sensual mentality that knows there is more to life than pitching hay and spreading the seed. We were glad to schedule his second photo session, but for some reason he never called." The oafs, I thought. Teasing me with availability and un-availability at once. Wise oafs: for it worked. That day, my teenage eyes wavering before the cashier's in fact dully tolerant gaze, I bought my first porn rag. I thought of these magazines as my textbooks in gay, though they taught me as much of fantasy as of truth: about what to hope for as well as what to expect. Over the years, some extraordinarily popular mechanics thus changed my suburban boy's life, but Clem's image stayed with me. Sometimes I wondered what his real name might be, as if a key turned into truth might make the fantasy all the more real.

I learned his name at Kern Loften's end-of-summer bash at The Pines the weekend before Labor Day in 1974. Kern's good qualities included a genuine palazzo, the hope of making his parties the greatest ever, and the ability to fill his rooms with his friends, their friends, and no one else. Private parties, without the bar-tension that the big public dos observe. The imposing bodies tended to belong to the bourgeoisie of the gyms, capable of love—not to the pornothespians who drifted in and out of the scene and were capable of anything. But Kern was rich, and some of his friends were rich; and the rich tend to hire help. Maids. Waiters. Lovers. You could always tell the hired lovers by the way they grinned: they already had what they wanted.

Entrance Kern's parties and he treasured you for life; to that end, an amazing soprano and I had put together a cabaret of show tunes, wacko Victor Herbert side by each with Harold Arlen art torch, the truth of sound musicianship fetching art back from mere diversion. We went on well after two A.M., made a hit, and spent the rest of the night basking in prominence. Sometime before dawn I started awake from a doze in one of the bedrooms facing the ocean. The house was dimly buzzing; someone had covered me with a blanket. A large figure stood gazing out at the sea. He turned as I stirred and said, from the shadows, "Nothing works, right?"

I wasted a smile in the darkness and said, "That depends on what you believe in."

He came toward me. "What do you believe in?"

"Will," I said. "Intelligence. Charm."

"What if you can have only one?" He sat on the edge of the bed. "Which would you take?"

It was Clem. I was so startled I blurted out something I had stuck into a story a few days before, one of those gnomic utterances that keep your mouth moving when you daren't speak your mind. "The wise," I said, "are troubled, for they trust only themselves and wisdom. The talented are twice troubled, for they trust only themselves. But the beautiful are most troubled, for they trust no one."

He thought it over, looking at the ocean. "You got that right."

His left arm rested close enough for me to spot the marking, "No. 1." He caught me, and said, "Got that in Denver. This incredible guy. The *most*. I think I thought he was straight. We ended up in this fleabag joint drinking, and he just went after me and did things like . . . like he'd invented sex that night. Hours and hours of it. We finished off the bottle as the sun was coming up, and I suddenly felt drowsy, and he said, 'I slid some stuff in your glass.' Strokes my arm and says, 'Right here, okay?' I didn't know what the hell . . . and when I woke up, he was gone and I—"

"Clark." Another stupendous man stood in the doorway.

"Coming." He rose and joined his partner, two carved idols breathing life into each other. Then he turned back to me. "Will," he said. "If you get your choice. *Will*."

"That's swift, because I've got plenty of will."

"What was that again about the wise are troubled?"

I repeated it, and he listened as if memorizing. His friend, chuckling, said, "The beautiful trust *no one*?"

"Neat piano playing, by the way," Clark Ellis told me, clapping his friend around the shoulders as they left.

"Thanks," I said to the empty room. The sun had nosed up; it was day, and the gang poured in.

"Clark Ellis!"

"What did he *say*?"

"I kiss this room!"

I told them, "He said the most important thing in life is will."

"Will who?"

"No, the most important thing is—"

"Politeness!"

"Sensible hats!"

"It's Sunday, it's The Pines, it's Kern Loften's," I announced. "I'm delirious. Everybody shut up and get out."

"What did he say?" Dennis Savage insisted.

"He told me how he got his tattoo."

"Number One!" they all echoed.

"The hottest man in The Pines!"

"The hottest man *alive!*"

"He'll never grow old."

"His ass will never fall!"

"Such hair—"

"That jaw—"

"He'll always—"

"I don't remember you," he said.

"How about not mugging me and I'll take you to dinner?"

Sarge's, the all-night deli, was a block away. He wouldn't look at the menu, kept searching me with his eyes, and said nothing to the waitress. From absolute aggression to complete passivitiy; strange. I ordered him a hot turkey sandwich, mashed potatoes, salad, apple pie, and coffee. I ordered myself a cheeseburger deluxe and coffee. So it worked out well, for if I'd gone home unmolested I'd have been stuck with cottage cheese and a hard pear.

"Cheer up," I told him. He had not aged badly, and, being naturally big, he had not lost his heft. But his expression was that of a man who never smiled, not even tentatively and certainly not dazzlingly. That did not jibe with the Clark Ellis I knew of.

"I don't remember you," he said again.

"How does a man as gala as you are end up mugging people? You were the King of Gay. You could have had anyone you wanted, and I know there's money in that. Why aren't you a millionaire model? Why didn't you let rich slobbos ply you with watches and yachts?"

He just looked at me.

"Spectacular men don't end up poor," I went on. "They *don't.*"

The food came quickly, everything at once, and he fiercely dug in. He must really have been hungry. He had cleaned up when I was halfway through.

"I want more," he said.

I called the waitress over. "The same again," he told her.

"How about a different pie this time? We got cherry."

"The same, the exact same," he said, grabbing a fistful of my french fries. "Turkey, apple, gravy, coffee, everything the same."

"One exact same coming up," she echoed, walking off.

He polished off my hamburger.

"Clark Ellis," I said. "Clark Ellis."

"Hot shit," he replied. "Tell all your friends another beauty wasted out. They're bored and lonely but their rent's paid, right? They're ahead of me."

"I think they'd be sad."

"Everybody's sad. Nothing works."

"How did you end up mugging people?"

"I broke a rich guy's crystal ball."

"That'll do it every time."

"I fell in love with Bill Post so I didn't buy the briquettes and I smashed the crystal ball into a thousand million pieces. And I wrecked the house and robbed them. So they threw me out of the whole world."

"Where do you live?"

"I don't."

Silence.

"Who's Bill Post?" I finally asked.

"What are you, a reporter?"

"Not unlike."

"You remember the pink boy with reddish-brown hair and hazel eyes who played Frisbee all over the beach in navy blue speedos? Your summer of 1980."

Who didn't remember him? I had seen this kid and his Frisbee, as had all others that odd summer, when, for once, the night weather lost its clever bite and took on the seamy intrusiveness of summer nights anywhere. Men I had known as professional smirkers would pace the boardwalk morose and sullen.

Like this man, now.

"I always thought of you riding high," I said.

"I didn't . . . I couldn't control it."

"The way you smiled . . ."

"I had those jobs, those messenger gigs. You know? The East Side co-op run. They're always sending these packages to each other, you can guess of what."

". . . as if you owned the world."

"They all expected me to fuck them. Like no job's legit. Everyone's a hustler or a buyer. So who needs a whore who won't screw?"

"This is one exact same," said the waitress, bringing the food.

He paused, holding his fork, stared at me, and nodded. "Appreciate it," he said, and ate.

"Clark Ellis fell in love with Bill Post," I murmured, trying out a first line. "It was late one night in the winter after Carlo left us . . ."

"Sure thing and so what?"

"Nice pairing. Man and boy. Dark and fair. Knowledgeable and pure."

"He *was* pure. The sweetest chicken there ever was. I am telling you this. But he didn't know shit. He was like me: wake up, listen to the time pass, take a spin in the gym, answer the phone, and go party. Letting it happen."

"Didn't you ever try to . . . well, do something?"

"Make the contacts? Talk them up? Every day. Planning. Everyone was so helpful, too. You know why?"

Silence.

"You *know* why. So finally one day you really are a whore. Not even an errand boy. Just a piece of ass."

"So," I recommended, some years late, "you pull yourself away."

He nodded.

"And?"

He shook his head. "Not so easy. I had Bill to watch over. He was taking what they gave, always said yes. Turn my back for an hour, he'd be doing some new drug, or picking up street cock. Always yes. But I was the man he loved. Know how I know? Because he wept when I flipped him. Only love makes them cry. The others smile. Hustlers. So many are hustlers, and that's why nothing works. Good sex is easy. Man, it's easy. You know what's hard? Love is hard."

"Smile for me."

"What?"

"Nothing."

"Smile for me," he repeated. He had heard. Be a symbol, Clark Ellis. Dazzle us, remember? The culture is here and you are among us. Or no, that was years ago, and the culture has since expanded, broken into factions—political, professional, sexual, intellectual, racial. It is no longer a question, sheerly, of identity, as it was when I was young: of learning that you were among us, that we had an *us* to be among. As he ate, I ran through my file of Hottest Men Alive. Did they all end up alone on the streets? Odd: many didn't appear to end up at all. Yes, there was the black-haired sex model with the unbelievable jaw who was made heir to a millionaire's estate and became a hit-and-run realtor, leaving slivers from the Brooklyn Bridge to Yorkville; or the Australian dancer who collected gasping crowds on the beach at the skater's house and who went on to a not unprominent TV series. Yes but. It seemed as if almost everyone else came to a dubious end, could come but not *dwell* among us. One rather expects it of fast boys, born to burn out; but a sizable man somehow suggests aggressive survival. *Will.* What is will but a sense of self-importance;

and is this not what size demands, looks like, is about? Is this not why Bill Post wept when Clark Ellis flipped him?

"What does 'flipping' mean?" I asked.

He held his coffee, recalling something, and, I hope, very nearly smiled.

"That's when they're done on one side, so you turn them over." He put down the cup, dark again, murky, as if fog masked our table. "He had the smoothest skin. If you knew where to touch him, he'd do anything. Anything. He howled when I laid him. Howled like a dog. God, he was beautiful."

"Now that you've had the appetizer," said the waitress, ambling up with a coffeepot, "how about some real food?"

I took the check.

"Bill let them use him up," he went on. "He fell in with a fashion crowd. Those parties where straight couples are selling drugs in the bathroom? He was going to be this one's houseboy, and then that one's. You know that street? They kept passing him from hand to hand, just another hot kid. And he'd let them, that was the stupid part. Some nights he was so drugged he didn't know where he'd been, come staggering home to me. Got so I had to beat him up. It was the only way to straighten him out, scare him. It would work, too. After, he'd crawl into my lap and say he'd be good and I'd tenderize him. I bet he loved that most of all, even more than laying. We'd just sit there, listening to each other breathe. And I thought, If only there was some *job* I could find, something to do that didn't connect with all those parties and the money, the phone ringing . . . and someone asks for you by your code name, and you're broke . . . so what else are you supposed to do?"

"What happened to Bill?" A Barry, I thought. A kid and a clone.

"Those fashion guys ripped him up. Filled him with junk. Said to him, 'You're a star.' See, they were trying to break us up because I was telling him what to do. I was with Lorenzo Fell then. You know him?"

"Of him."

"The ugliest mcgoon between Ocean Beach and Albania, I used to call him. Treated me like a servant, him and his pals. 'Clark'll do the honors, of course,' he'd say to some horror, and I'd have to take it to bed. Why do ugly men always have ugly friends?"

"They don't."

"You don't know shit. Who do you know?"

"I have to give you references?"

"Rich, I mean."

"Kern Loften."

"Yeah, I remember him."

"Nice fellow."

"Listen, anyone starts nice," he tells me. "Then comes life, and watch. Money changes them. Careers. Power."

"Looks?"

"How can looks change you? Looks are what you are. Looks are what change."

"You can't change your looks, surely."

"What's a gym for, then? Mustaches and beards? Clothes?" Don't you know *anything*? his tone said. Aren't you gay?

"Anyway, they were pulling Bill away from me. Lorenzo was in on it, the whole gang of them . . ."

The waitress and her coffeepot. "It's a little late to start a new elephant," she tells Clark as she pours, "but the chef might save you some of the moose if you feel like dessert."

Clark looks at her.

"That's a joke, honey," she says, taking off.

"Don't you ever laugh anymore?" I asked him. Smile for me.

"They made it so we could never be together. They were telling him the Coast, movies. Not porn, real ones."

Movies with *will*.

"We had to meet in secret. And all I could say was, 'Who were you with?' I didn't mind it for myself, because I know how to lay a mcgoon without getting dirty. But he was just a kid. Didn't know how to protect himself."

"How does one protect oneself with a mcgoon?"

"You pretend they're going to fall into an acid bath the day after. Maybe you're going to push them."

I forked off a bit of his pie and he pushed it to me.

"Finish it. I had some money saved, and I told Bill, 'Let's ditch these guys and set up shop. You know, porn, catering, hustling. I don't know, maybe all at once. Cook the food, serve it, then lay the host. It happens, doesn't it?"

Yes.

"But they got to him. Made him afraid. He had it going and he thought he'd lose it if they dropped him. They were going to take him to Europe after September. So like when I heard that, I just freaked. It was so heavy in my mind, I couldn't . . . I didn't hack it out right. He told me he'd never go away. When I was tenderizing him, sure. And I saw him cry so I thought it was all right. But then they'd get ahold of him, and he'd change his mind. Every minute at Lorenzo's, I'd worry what Bill was up to, what they were doing to him. And this one evening, we were hanging around the deck, and one of Lorenzo's toads sort of squirmed into position and said, 'Won't someone rub my back?' and Lorenzo pointed at me, like I had to. This fucking *toad*! And then one of those junky kids that always hung around Lorenzo came out and said, 'We're out of briquettes,' looking at me as if it was my fault. It's my job to get them, okay, but not to count them or something! They were all looking at me like I was . . . I don't know . . ."

"Someone they couldn't forgive for being beautiful."

A deep breath. "I left, and went to find Bill. I thought, You know, that's it. Fuck their briquettes. Listen. *Listen*, Jesus, he was gone! They'd just picked him up and took him away!"

"Where?"

"Where? Someplace Europe, where. Who *cares* where? They got him, slid him out from under me, just about. Figure it, how I felt. But, listen, Lorenzo had this crystal ball in his house. Something special, like there's no others but that one? Handmade, or something.

Had it in the center of the living room, and you had to be all this careful when you got near it. They held seances, telling the future. Lorenzo would dress up and do this cackly voice and say what would happen to you. You could always tell who was in favor with him from the fortune he told. He thought that glass ball was the hottest thing on the walk."

"Hotter than you?"

"Man, Lorenzo didn't know what hot was. He was even afraid to be laid. Wasn't even a *man!* All he did was suck and tips."

"Tips?"

"Nipple stuff. Ugly guys are so—"

"And you broke the crystal?"

He looked back on it. "Yes." Nodded. A story. Something happens, changes your life. "Into a thousand million pieces. Right in front of them. Shithead dufos. I picked it up, and I aimed it at Lorenzo's head, and I . . . *threw* . . . *that* . . . *mother.* And, man, they screeched like butchered cats. So I took them and smashed their fucking skulls together and I wrecked the whole place—furniture, clothes, even the walls, man, the whole *place!* The place, The *Pines!* And, the whole time—figure it—they were lying around sobbing in these . . . *positions,* like it was a *movie!* And I took the cash and split. They couldn't call the police, because I controlled some very heavy input on Lorenzo's Colombian connections, you taste? But they did something I couldn't fight back on—I didn't even know about it at first. This Dr. Conover, who runs the VD mill on Lexington? He's one of the gang. They got him to spread the rumor that I had AIDS. You should have seen how suddenly it all went away. It *all!* Friends were like strangers, and strangers . . . weren't there. Guys that used to stand around talking to me on the street, hoping I would say, 'So let's score'? Nothing. Didn't see me. Didn't hear me when I shouted their names. Your word is out, see? Suddenly everyone was a phone tape with no tape in it. And that's like suddenly you are unemployed. No prospects. No contacts. And that is the end of your career."

"Why didn't you try another town? San Francisco?"

"They give it away there, man. I'm an employee, so what do you want? A whore. Do you know what a whore is? A man without will, I swear."

He was about forty-two now, and still amazing. No doubt every-thing would catch up with him; already his eyes were as troubled as a prophet's. There was but one Clark Ellis, but many stories like his, of men dwindled from dish mythology into unemployment checks and evictions and fizzled jobs and injudicious hustling and death by drugs of pleasure. Smile for me, No. 1.

"Everyone can't have heard a rumor started by a single clique," I said. "It's such a big city. Couldn't you—"

"No. Stop." He held up his hand. "Just listen to me, okay?" His hand was shaking. "Because it's . . . it's more than that." He set his hand flat on the table, laid the other atop it. "The AIDS thing was just . . . it was to scare off the fancy-pants crowd. The mcgoons and the money. That's the part you see—on the ferry or in the Saint or at a big theme party. That's the part you know. That's your gay life. But there's more than that part. Stuff that doesn't come out all the time. It's there just the same, and it's connected to the fancy part. You don't know about it, maybe, and your friends don't. But it's powerful. It knows about you."

Whatever it was, it sounded like Santa Claus; and he saw me fight-ing a smile and glumly nodded.

"Listen to something else. The same thing, but it's different. Lis-ten. The world. You got your high-school football team and your college, and then some job and GQ clothes and your plastic, and you think that's the whole world. Everybody's world, okay, right? So someone didn't make the football team. Some got better jobs or more plastic or a dishwasher in the kitchen. So it's still the same world, isn't it? Don't look serious, just answer!"

"You haven't asked a question."

"Is that what you think the whole world is?" he almost shouted.

We both looked up guiltily at some movement in the room: the waitress again, with the coffee. "Now, now," she lightly warned, pouring. "He's probably upset," she murmured to me, "because he didn't get enough to eat."

She had cut into our momentum, and there was silence for a bit. "I played football in high school," he finally said. "Quarterback. Really the hero. There wasn't a girl in the whole school I couldn't have, including the teachers. And there was this guy on the team. Your strong silent guy sort. Never said a word to anyone. Good athlete, though. Good man. Good grades, even. He was . . . you'd say anything to him, he'd just nod. Last game of the season, there was a rumor that the cheerleaders were going to lie down for us, win or lose. Maybe it wasn't that big a deal, because they weren't exactly the singing nuns before that, but it had a quality. Like a pact, I guess. Something special for the team. It was like a party within a party, like it starts in one house and then a few of us get the signal and go somewhere else, with no parents or horny sophomores around. So we make our exit, and drive over to the duck pond. Real spread out there, dark, and it's got all these little hills and trees. Good place for the kind of thing. You can't tell who's doing what. And the guy I told you about, I saw him go off by himself and I followed him. We talked for a while. I mean, I talked and he nodded. He was really nervous. So I said, 'Come on, let's take a drive,' and we did that, and we parked somewhere, and nobody's saying nothing. Sitting there, fine. He's looking straight ahead, as if there was something to find in front of us, which there wasn't, and I'm kind of aimed at him. And suddenly he puts his hand on my thigh. He's straight back against the car seat like he's trying to smooth his way right through it. And then he looks at me, and I told him to go ahead. I should have known all along. He was so tense, I whispered to him to take it easy. So then I started to open up his pants, but he bolted out of the car and ran into the trees and yakked his guts out. Never saw anyone barf like that. Now he's probably a doctor with a big house and four kids somewhere in the Sunbelt and he never thinks about anything." He shook his head. "Now, why did I tell you about that?"

He looked sad and confused. I wondered if Bill Post had ever seen him so.

"Was it like that for you?" he asked. "Back then? First time?"

"Well . . . nobody threw up."

"Why the hell not? It's always like that. It's supposed to be."

I thought of Carlo and the man with the little bowl of warm water, and the excitement Carlo knew then that he could never retrieve.

"Why did you tell me that?" I asked.

"It was . . . about something. About the whole world. Things you don't see that are in the world."

Stuff that doesn't come out all the time.

"I wanted to tell you what happened to me," he pleaded. "To show you that there's more going on than you know about. That's why it happens. It wasn't just Bill or Lorenzo or telling everybody I had AIDS. Sure, you start on the squad and you go to the parties, and I guess in a way Fire Island and all that is more of the same. Making a different squad and going to other parties, but the same deal about who's allowed and who isn't. Who gets in. But look. When you start to slip, you fall into some really gruesome deals. I mean, some guys I know started dealing and they got so into the honey they took it and took it till they exploded. Or some guys got into shady porn. Or those waiter gigs where like all the guests are so friendly and they're all giving you stuff and you don't know what the hell it all is till you wake up three weeks from last Tuesday with half your head watted out, wondering how many people touched you and where." He took a deep breath. "Or you can report for a video date and take your chances." He gazed at me, the broken impresario of hot. The whole opera's gone bust and Rigoletto ran off with the scenery. "You know about those?"

"They tape you . . . in sport."

"You can even join a service for it. Unlisted numbers and so on. I mean, you could pick someone off the street if you wanted, but some of these people are into such kinky scenes that they need guys who, you know, perform the specialities. And that's how you go down, brother, let me whisper it to you. Because once you turn pro at this kind of thing, it isn't just Lorenzo Fell and his pansy sidekicks. It's the bottom rung of all the money you don't see. All the people who've done everything before they get to you, so, like, what's left to jolly them? But they'll figure something out, won't they? And that's what you'll do. Because you need the bread. Because it's there, you, in the dark rooms and all those eyes watching you. Maybe you can't even see them, but they see you all right. You hear them. Jesus, you can hear them *looking* at you, that's how heavy. Or a guy alone with a hundred whips and then this monster comes out of a door smiling at you like you're a piece of Danish and he's hungry. Or wives holding the camera, want to catch you porking their husbands. Video dates. Dark rooms and faces in a circle, that's what it is. And maybe anyone might do a spell in that world—but what if you're stuck there forever? Why didn't you get something better for yourself, huh? Why are you here? Why is this you?"

He stopped. "Say something," he told me.

"No, go on. Whatever it is."

"Why? What's the point now?"

"So I can understand about the other world."

"It's the same world," he said, slowly. "The same world." He leaned forward. "Okay," he said. "Now listen. This one time, I go up there. Huge place. Servant at the door, this way please, and I go in."

And I'm thinking that if Carlo didn't have Dennis Savage and Lionel and Big Steve and me and a few other friends to keep him busy and talk him out of things, he might have come to one of those dark rooms.

"They've got this kid tied to a chair. Sixteen, seventeen. Really sweet boy, scared as hell."

Or that it's not U and non-U but luck. The luck of finding the right apartment before the crunch hit, of not going down the street when the bad guys are waiting, of running into someone you half-know on a day when you feel the way George Will looks and the half-friend says, "Let's get ice-cream cones," and the next thing is the two of you are singing the entire score to *Follies* and you've made a friend for life. Or the luck, simply, of being one of the ones who doesn't take ill.

"All these people in suits. Sometimes they're in costumes and sometimes they're wearing like a plastic garbage bag, but these people were all dressed up. And the head man says, 'This boy is no fun at all,' meaning the kid, 'so you're going to liven him up for us.'"

I was thinking that this boy would look like Bill Post, for thematic symmetry, but Clark Ellis—as if reading my map—shook his head and said, "This chicken was pale white, like ivory, and very thin, with brown hair. He was no winner, just a stray kid. You know how many of those there are in this city? People were petting him, and they'd watch me, and pet him some more, and the man says, 'Let's see you, ace.' While I'm stripping they're getting the camera set up on this tripod. And the people were coaxing the kid toward this bed, and he's fighting them and he keeps looking at me. Just think of that, because the two of us are naked and everybody else looks like a party at the UN or something. I mean handkerchiefs and flowers and like feathers and lace. Fans and capes. And this kid was scared."

Like the football player in the car.

"The man gave me a gizmo like a combination carburetor and carrot grater and says, 'Slide this on your cock and fuck him.' Over on the bed the suit people were holding the kid down, and what do you think they look like? Grinning, like oh boy, some fun? There was nothing on their faces at all. See, they're holding this little boy down to watch his ass get all tore up, and nobody's home. Anyways, I told the man I didn't like the look of that piece of his, and he says he's got three big ones to lay on me if, but otherwise nothing, and what's my service going to say when he tells them I don't put out."

"This isn't the world," I told him. "This is land's end."

"That's why I'm telling you this story. Because you think that. Because you think everyone's got a place to live and enough friends and something funny to do on Sunday afternoon, don't you? You think Lorenzo Fell's as bad as it gets. Christ, all that fucking money! If only you knew about it, man. You would sure feel different in one of the dark rooms they got." He shook his head. "That rich friend of yours. King . . ."

"Kern Loften."

"He doesn't give dark-room parties, does he?"

"No, he gives very nice parties. Very official gay parties." The kind, I almost added, that you attended in your time of glory.

"He doesn't tie kids up and have them fucked with something you could cut your way through a jungle with, does he? He doesn't tape it? He doesn't have this woman in a mantilla or something who's looking at the kid and saying, 'Maybe get a towel for the blood, somebody.' Does he?"

Not exactly. Once Kern cut me off for weeks because I told him William Burroughs, despite a deplorable world view, was one of the greatest writers of the day. "How can you praise that kind of thing?" Kern asked while forgiving me. "Are you a New Yorker or aren't you?" And I replied, "What's a New Yorker?"

"He doesn't lay three bills on you because to him that's pennies and he wants to see what happens when you torture a boy who doesn't know how to make the exit? That's a neat sight to see, isn't it? Brings a lump to your throat."

There was silence then. Finally he said, "And so." He nodded. Gestured mildly. "And so. Good story, huh?"

I'll see what I can do.

"So they got this rope from somewhere and I said I don't need it. Look, I outweighed the kid by a hundred-ten pounds. He's just lying there, not even struggling anymore. I pulled a guy out of the crowd and gave him the camera and told him to be creative. And I scattered the people at the bed and pulled the kid up and stood behind him, like I was demonstrating him, you know. Showing him off. I felt him up but he was so scared he wasn't getting on. The camera was right on him and he kept trying to turn away from it. So I took him around through the guests so each one could touch him and kiss him, and they all got into that, stroking him with the camera on him. And soon he was hot. And they were getting pretty wild so I had to control them. That woman who asked for the towel? She was dancing in and out like the native princess in a jungle film. I looked over at the head man, and he was pleased. It was good for them, so I could make the bread without hurting the kid. I turned the scene around on them, see? I sat the kid on the bed, and I waved the camera guy in close, and I made the kid look right in there, at whatever it is. Then I asked the kid, 'Who are you afraid of?' He swiveled around to look at the head man, but I caught him back and I asked him again, with my hands on his neck, thumbs right on his throat. He was so damn sweet, he didn't understand what I was trying to do for him. But he saw my eyes, and I pressed his throat a little, and he got it. So then I said, 'Who are you afraid of?' a second time, and he said, 'You.' And then he was begging me not to hurt him, and crying, and that was it. That was all they wanted. Some of the others ran up and held him down again and now they were laughing and cheering us on and I could fuck him so gently and it didn't matter because I'd given them what they wanted. The man gave me five hundred dollars and I got dressed and I left the dark room and now, you tell me, Is that the world or is this the world?"

"What?"

"That dark room there—or sitting at this table now?"

"What happened to that boy at the party?"

"Drinking coffee like this, talking about it. Maybe they're showing that film somewhere this minute. Some guy's showing his wife so they can hot up enough to fuck. Maybe that's the world. That's what works. Money making adjustments for mcgoons. Ask a mcgoon how he's doing. He's doing great."

"It's not too late, you know," I said. "You're still a beautiful man—"

"Sure," he said. "Sure," holding his head, lowering it to shake and be sad and bewildered. And he said, "The beautiful are most troubled, for they trust no one."

"Where," I asked him, as quiet as a nail in a coffin, "did you learn that?"

He was still, didn't look up. "You told me. Didn't you?"

"Yes."

"Where?"

"At a party. In The Pines. It was—"

"Help me." He raised his head, stiffened, and looked sharp, as if apologizing for the outburst, for needing anything. "Please. Something."

"Kern Loften," I began, "always thought you were the hottest man alive. He'd probably send you to a doctor first and so on, but—"

"He gave that party."

I smiled. "It all comes back. Who was that man you were with? He was almost as—"

"He's dead. A lot of hot men are dead because they were hot. You should know that."

"Well, Kern might take you on. I could call him." A thought hit me. "What about Bill Post?"

He shook his head slowly. Dead also? Gone? Sometimes they simply vanish.

"I could call Kern tomorrow."

He nodded, and so we left it, but he seemed in no way relieved, and when he got outside he told me not to call anyone for him. Not Kern and not anyone. The wind had puffed up, the kind that burns your ears. We clearly could not chat it out. I said, "Do you want to come home with me?"

"Yes. And I'll smash you up and wreck your apartment and take everything you have."

There was a moment, just a flash of a bit of time, when I could see him trying to believe he meant it. I kept it light: "Better not, the doorman'll fuss at you. I think it's Ramon tonight, and he's—"

"You played the piano. With the opera lady."

"Yes."

"What do you do now?"

Well, for starters, I'm going to write this story. "Do you want me to call Kern for you?"

"No."

"You said, 'Help me.'"

"No."

"Why?"

"Because nothing works and everybody dies. Because it hurts."

He was about to turn, and I grabbed his arm and said, "Smile for me."

"No," he said. "Why?"

"To show me you're all right."

He looked at me for quite some time, then, and finally shook his head. I watched him walk off. After fifty yards he turned and stopped. We got into a kind of standing contest, then he came back and said, "What does it take?"

"Will," I said.

"No. To make you get lost?" But he grabbed for my hand and squeezed it, against the words, and patted my shoulder. "Go home," he said. "Okay?"

I grasped his left arm to see that caption of his again, No. 1, and I looked up at him, thinking maybe I would see the rest of him as he was, there among us once, really the hero, but his smile had busted into a thousand million pieces because nothing works. Because what you hope for isn't necessarily what to expect. And I am not a demonstrative fellow with people I don't know and Clark Ellis is very reserved, as many great beauties are expected to be, and the weather said move!, and I was so crowded with recollections of how matters have proceeded in those Stonewall days—which exactly coincide with my years in New York—that I scarcely knew how we ended up holding each other; but I would not make much of it, boys and girls, because I expect we were simply celebrating a pungent nostalgia, or marking our shared belief in certain things many others do not believe—or perhaps because it seemed correct punctuation, and easier than smiling. It was cold, and Clark Ellis went away.

When I reached my building and Ramon unlocked the door, I told him, "The beautiful are most troubled, for they trust no one."

And Ramon, who never smiles, said, "Good evening, sir."

Sliding into Home

In which unities of time, place, and action are observed—but not that of character, for even The Pines, Stonewall's most compact ghetto, may contain an intruder here and there. And herewith the author takes his leave.

I heard a strange voice ask, "What flavor of ice cream would you like, Virgil?" as I came up the walk. I opened the door to the patio, and stood facing a handsome, fortyish man in an outfit one rarely sees at The Pines, slacks and the kind of striped shirt you wear with a tie.

"Who's Virgil?" I asked him, though I knew very well.

"Don't listen to him!" Little Kiwi shouted, rushing up.

The man, completely at a loss, looked from him to me.

"If you're the garbageman, we don't want any today," cried Little Kiwi, trying to push me out.

"Don't call him Virgil," I told the man, using my valise to drive Little Kiwi back onto the porch.

"It's my name!"

"Yes, but it throws everything off."

"Then you're so mean," he said, "that I won't introduce you."

We introduced ourselves. The man in the outfit was Dave Bast, who had just moved to New York from Cleveland.

"How on earth," I asked, "does one move to New York in 1985? There's no place to move into."

"Unless you buy," he said.

"Ah. A professional."

Like me, he had come out for a stay at Dennis Savage's house in

215

midweek, when the other renters were job-bound in town. Dave Bast had been about to secure the lunch matter at the Pantry when I walked in.

"Little Kiwi's flavor, by the way, is Frusen Glädjé vanilla almond."

"Whose . . . what?"

Little Kiwi sulked.

"You'll have to go slower on this for me," said Dave. "I've only just got here and everyone is . . . well, kind of a stranger."

"Whose friend are you, anyway?"

"No one's really. See, I was Seth Brown's paddle brother in college, and—"

"*Paddle brother?*"

"Our fraternity. St. A's. It's just a . . . term. Read 'big brother.' Or 'sponsor.' Or something such."

I was impressed. For those of who you don't follow collegiate Greek culture, St. Anthony's is invariably the top house on campus, sporting not only the wealthiest and nicest guys but also the best looking. (Another interior contradiction in straight: if they're so stuck on women, why would they fill a frat house with gorgeous men?) When I left for Penn, my dad advised me to avoid St. A's—"it's kind of la-di-da," he warned me. I'll say. His idea of a sound frat was ATO, his old house, which turned out, not surprisingly, to be the third-toughest jock house on a campus noted for tough jock houses. In my first year at Penn, the first- and second-toughest jock houses were dissolved by university decree for hazing enormities. ATO was thrilled: number one at last! An ATO friend of mine, Bob Morgan, urged me to pledge the house, but I figured I'd already had everything ATO could offer just growing up with Jim. I went to St. Elmo's, a sort of vapidly sweet frat that had lost its building in a fire a bit before and had rebuilt in red brick and glass. It stood on Locust Walk, the main drag of the frat system, right in the heart of the campus, but it looked too neat and mod next to the Gothic mansions that characterized Penn's Greek community. (Funny how that word keeps slipping in.) Once, I left a group of friends in front of the house; it was the pledges' weekly night for dinner with the brothers. As I left, one of them said, "That's his fraternity? I thought that was the science building."

"St. Anthony Hall, huh?" I said, taking in Dave Bast. "No wonder you're so well dressed."

"It's supposed to be my junking-around duds."

"By Pines standards, that's black tie."

He smiled. "I guess I'm doing everything wrong. It's bound to happen when you fall in among strangers. I came to say goodbye to Seth before I left, and he . . . see, we've stayed in touch all these years, and I've known Virgil since he was a sprout. Seth asked me to look in on him when I got to New York."

I turned to Little Kiwi, sitting quietly with his back to us as if he were a figure in one of Samuel Beckett's plays. "You mean you're related to something human?" I asked him. "You actually have a father?"

"Now I will never talk to you again *forever!*" said Little Kiwi, leaping up. "*Come,* Bauhaus!"

Bauhaus didn't; Bauhaus seldom does.

"I better walk you down to the Pantry," I told Dave, as I ruffled Little Kiwi's hair. "First time out here can be tricky." Little Kiwi turned and put his arms around me; he's vulnerable to affectionate demonstration.

Dave regarded us quizzically. "I thought," he said. "I mean, it isn't the customary thing to . . . is it?"

"How do I know till you ask?"

"I understood there was someone else . . . in the picture." He looked like someone who catches children with their hands in the cookie jar, then gets flustered when they fail to act guilty.

"There is someone else," I said, stroking Little Kiwi's neck. "Dennis Savage. He'll be along presently. In fact, he's not someone else, he's some*one,* the whole thing. Right?"

Little Kiwi nodded. He's the only gay I know who reached his mid-twenties having had carnal intersection with one man and no others.

It's an accomplishment of some kind, certainly, but Dave looked as if
he were seeing something he shouldn't.

"Why doesn't Bauhaus come when I say?" Little Kiwi asked.

"Why don't you train him to?" I replied.

"I don't think he'd respond. He has such an artistic kind of tem-
perament." Little Kiwi turned to Dave. "We may be putting on some
shows later, so you should get set."

"Why do I have the impression," I asked, "that if this were the
1970s and we could still have sex with all the trimmings and not
spend the following week waking up screaming, I would nevertheless
be spending my trip watching you put on shows?"

Little Kiwi thought about it. "Because," he offered, "my shows are
a legend of the Island."

I was about to respond, but I caught sight of Dave, and he was a
sight. If he had known the kid himself since he'd been a, yes, sprout,
then he couldn't have been surprised at what passes, in our set, for
quaint charm. Yet he was staring at Little Kiwi as if . . . I don't know,
as if the kid were exposing essential secrets.

It occurred to me then that I really had no handle on Dave—had
no idea why someone so oddly out of tune was there at all. Who was
he, besides a friend of Little Kiwi's family? As we walked along Ocean
Boulevard—about a mile of wooden slats four feet wide—he said, "If
my wife and I had had kids . . . a little boy like Virgil, say . . . I guess
I wouldn't be here right now."

His wife?

"I guess raising children can wed a couple in a way that ordinary
mating can't. Sharing that flesh-and-blood thing, really, that
creativity. Putting those little people to bed, and holding them when
they're sick. Then they ask those funny questions, like—"

"Why are you here right now, on a gay beach?"

"I discovered I was gay after being married for twenty years."

I think he expected me to congratulate him or mount some club
demonstration, but I looked at him in disbelief. *Nobody* discovers his
sexuality after being anything for twenty years; you discover it in

youth, when it forms. And anyone who says otherwise is a bloody fucking liar.

"Anyway, if Amy and I *had* a whole family, I guess I would have let that carry me along."

We walked in silence.

"She was very nice about it when I told her," he finally said. "She didn't believe me, of course. Maybe I didn't even think she would. But I guess after twenty years of sex, they can't be expected to believe you're a faggot. She told me she figured there was another woman and that I was trying to spare her feelings."

More silence.

"Maybe we got too used to each other, after all."

He was carrying on a one-man conversation, answering questions I hadn't asked.

"I sort of knew about Virgil all along, so his dad was the first person I told. With his son and all, he'd have to understand."

You're really good-looking, I thought, but I don't like you. I'm not sure why.

"I caught Virgil here just before he left town, and he said if I was coming out I ought to do it here, because Fire Island is like . . . well now, I'm not sure I remember all that he said. I gather this is something of a homosexual amusement park, and as far as—"

"Just follow the walkway there past the ice-cream stand," I said, pointing. We had reached the harbor. "You'll see it."

I felt him gazing puzzled at my back as I marched away, leaving the impression that he had committed heavy faux pas. But so he had.

"What's the idea of inviting that gringo clown out here during my stay?" I called up to Little Kiwi when I got back.

He was on the balcony again, playing with the fancy umbrella Dennis Savage had given him for his birthday, the folding kind with a wooden handle colorfully painted and shaped to resemble a puffin.

"What clown?" he said. "Uncle Dave?" Suddenly he switched to a raspy voice as he animated the umbrella, handle side up. "Dave is no clown, *gskwark*! This is Randolph the Puffin speaking."

"Oh, not this again," I moaned.

"He's the nicest man in Ohio," the puffin said.

"Randolph," said Little Kiwi, "let's—"

"Just a minute, kiddo, he is *not* nice. He swindles a woman for twenty years—no doubt with lots of shadow-fucking along the way, whereupon he comes home and says, 'Not tonight, honey, I'm beat'—and then he grandly presents himself here in his . . . his Sears Roebuck party socks and expects the gay world to dance a jig, right?"

"Who's this nasty man?" Randolph asked Little Kiwi.

"I'm warning you, boy," I said. "I'm burning a short fuse today, thanks to your father's paddle buddy."

"If you don't start being cute," Little Kiwi warned me, "no one will like you."

"Or read your greasy books," Randolph piped in.

"Randolph," I said, mounting the stairs, "today a puffin dies."

With a yelp, Little Kiwi dashed into the bathroom, but I got my foot in the doorway before he could lock himself in, so he ran to the window, stuck the puffin out, and rasped, "Listen, gay America! A crazed fiend is after me, Randolph the Puffin!"

"O puffin," I told him in a Shakespearean manner, "thou hast bought the farm."

"Help! Danger! Fire!"

"*What the Judas heck is going on here?*" shouted Dennis Savage from below as he stamped into the house.

Little Kiwi and I froze. "Now we're going to get it," he whispered.

"I go to support a friend who, despite being celibate for the last three and a half years, is about to die," Dennis Savage went on, as Little Kiwi and I came out onto the walkway. "Have you *any idea* what that's *like?* Do you realize that right now I'm shaking with rage and fear because who knows which of us will be next? And *look* what I *find* when I get here! *Look what I find!*"

He heaved up one of the dining table chairs and threw it across the room.

"I find the two of you cavorting and yelling and making this house the scandal of the walk! What were you doing in the *bathroom*, for heaven's sake? You can't make a ruckus in the regular places?"

He crossed the room and picked up the chair. Suddenly calm, he sat in it, looking suavely up at us as if he had just devised some picturesque new Pines stunt that would soon be all the fashion.

"And," he went on quietly, "I see that umbrella's still with us. Little Kiwi, I told you, that joke staled after a week."

"It staled for me," I said, "after fifteen seconds."

"And the icing on the cake," said Dennis Savage, "is he won't take it out in the rain."

"I don't like getting wet," said Randolph.

I laughed.

"Don't be his audience," said Dennis Savage. He really was upset—not at us, but at the state of health in general. "Don't. Okay? Because he'll just go on doing it."

"I'd go on, anyway," said Little Kiwi, in his own voice.

Dennis Savage shook his head. "I'm just not in a mood for these games. Do you want to see me break down in front of you?"

"No," said Little Kiwi immediately, but then Randolph and I both said, "Yes."

"Very funny," said Dennis Savage. "Did your friend get here?"

"He went to the store for various assundries," said Little Kiwi.

"That's various *and*—"

"Did you meet," Dennis Savage asked me, "the new boy on the block?"

"Little Kiwi's paddle uncle?" I said, coming downstairs. "We met."

"Nice guy, I hear. But he picked a rather unterrific moment to come out in. Great timing they have in Cleveland."

"The whole state's like that," growled Randolph.

"Who told you he's a nice guy?" I asked.

"That time Little Kiwi's parents came to New York," said Dennis Savage, "his father went on and on about Uncle Dave. Especially about their college days. You may think you're joking about that paddle-brother stuff, but from the way he was talking, you'd have the idea that they were—"

Footsteps.

"Later."

"Had a hell of a time getting back here," said Uncle Dave, pulling in with the groceries. "Every street looks the same. The guys sure don't."

"What is that supposed to mean?" I asked.

Dennis Savage quickly introduced himself and busied Uncle Dave in unloading the haul. I stood aside, silently grumbling. Dave Bast was a resentable intruder, I felt. But I do believe that a book of coming-out photographs ought to include a view of Uncle Dave's face when Randolph the Puffin leaned over the edge of the walkway and asked, "What flavor of ice cream did you get?" Little Kiwi was crouching so he couldn't be seen on the main floor and Uncle Dave was a veritable study.

"What's . . . that?" he asked.

"That's Randolph the Puffin," said Dennis Savage, waving it away as if it were just another element of an ordinary day, soggy corn flakes or a burned-out light bulb. "Were you planning to cook this as well as buy it?"

"What flavor?" Randolph repeated.

"Do I talk to that?" Uncle Dave asked Dennis Savage.

"You do if you're gay," I put in. "Because if you're gay you'll have some taste, however slim or broad, for the camp theatrical. But if you're straight, you can talk all you want and it'll never hear you."

I spoke mildly, but I guess he saw what was in my eyes, because he said, also mildly, "Would you like to settle this outside?"

"I'd be glad to," I replied, "you gringo son of a bitch."

Dennis Savage exploded like a fresh mine. "*This*," he almost screamed at me, "is my guest, okay?" And he told Uncle Dave, "This is my best friend! So the two of you just cool off! *Now!*"

Little Kiwi, hanging over the walkway railing, looked—as he always did when these things happen—like the first person eliminated in an all-night Monopoly session. Uncle Dave held his ground but said nothing more. I retired to the deck with *Martin Chuzzlewit*, thinking that if Dickens had seen a gay America instead of the intolerant jackoff straight kind he did see, he might have had a better time here. But then there was no gay then. And, in the first place, Dickens was probably an intolerant jackoff himself . . . and there was Uncle Dave asking if I'd like to Talk It Out.

"Tell you what," I answered. "I'll stay out of your way and you'll stay out of mine. We'll get along."

"That's not good for me," he said.

"Who gives a flying fuck what's good for the likes of you?"

He stared at me as if I had the wrong man.

"You spend twenty years in the closet," I went on, "and you come out here with cruising tips? 'The guys sure don't'?" I stood up, because if you are going to fight, you don't give the enemy an advantage. "I don't know you," I said, "and I don't like you," I added, "and I don't believe in you," I concluded. "So huh?"

That usually does it. But he stood where he was and said, "I know there's a misunderstanding here, and I think we can compensate it."

"Compensate as an intransitive verb without the preposition. Now I've heard everything. What are you, an accountant or something?"

"Yes, as a matter of—"

"You compensate *for* quelque chose. You don't compensate *chose*. Got me, buddy?"

"I can't get why you're so down on me. We hardly met and you're . . . I could tell . . . you were mad about something."

What would Jimbo do at this point? I wondered. Jim would settle down and be amused.

"Was it something I said? Because I apologize. I'm new here, I told you. I'm bound to say the wrong thing, I guess."

I sat down, put *Martin Chuzzlewit* to the side, and regarded him.

"Virgil said you might point me in some directions. You know. Hints on how to . . . I . . . ."

"Start with the library. Stonewall classics. William Burroughs, Edmund White, *City of Night, The Movie Lover, The Boys on the Rock, Danny Slocum*. The life. The spirit. The themes."

Typical! I thought, watching him. He doesn't know what the hell I'm talking about.

"I thought I ought to start by visiting . . . the places. The right places. You know."

"No. Do I?"

"I mean, Where do you go to be . . . gay?"

I nodded. "Acceptable question. You could go to a Pasolini movie. You could go to a west side *conversazione*. You could go to the hospital . . ."

"Oh boy, you don't ever give in, do you?"

"Well, who gave you the right to be gay, anyway?" I said. "We don't run this club on open admissions."

"Okay, who does get in?"

"Everybody but straights."

He nodded. "I'm not straight."

It's a cultural thing, Carlo says. It's not whom you bed, it's whom you're kind to, whom you respect, whom you like in some important way. It's who your buddies are.

"I'm not straight," he repeated. "At least, not anymore."

"There's no crossing over," I told him. "What you've been is what you deserve to be. For life."

He looked at me for a moment. "Who let you make the rules, may I ask?"

"I don't make them. I discover them."

"Dave," said Little Kiwi, joining us with the unsavory Bauhaus, tethered and gamboling, "would you come help me walk a dog?"

"Go," I said, figuring that Dennis Savage had cooked this up so he and I could talk.

They headed over the dunes and I went inside.

"Mission accomplished," I said, finding Dennis Savage among the kitchen things, where he was halfheartedly setting up for lunch.

"I want to thank you," he said, "for making a difficult day so much easier."

"Oh yeah? How about thank you for brightening my stay by dragging in that gay Babbitt?"

"Actually, he's a rather eligible dude, all told. He's got money, he's intelligent, he's medically attractive, and, you must admit, he's awfully nice looking." He fussed at a stubborn jar top. "A nice, big fellow."

I shrugged.

"Yes," he said, "I thought you'd noticed."

I took the jar from him. "I'll tell you what I noticed." I opened it. "When that kind gets off the ferry, there goes the neighborhood."

"My hero," he observed, reclaiming the jar. "According to Little Kiwi, this guy really did just get off the boat a week or so ago, so it's too early to tell what he'll be like once he gets his bearings. I remember how rough-hewn you were when you first came out."

"Well, I don't remember you before three or four weeks ago. It's the charitable thing to do."

He spread peanut butter on right triangles of whole wheat toast.

"I hope that's crunchy," I said. "Smooth is for straights."

"Funny his waiting this long to take the step, isn't it?" Dennis Savage mused. "What must have been going through his mind all these years?"

"You surely don't buy this jazz about his not knowing he was gay till he was in his forties, do you? How can you not know what you're attracted to? It's like not knowing that you're wearing pants."

"How soon did you know?" he asked.

"I *never didn't*."

Silence and peanut butter.

"Have you never heard someone say," he asked finally, "that he wasn't sure what he liked?"

"A euphemistic cop-out for gays who can't confront their fate. Gays who keep looking over their shoulder to see what the straights are thinking of them. You remember Britt Kelso? One of the most effeminate characters going, right?"

"You and he were good friends, as I recall."

"Okay, we were. Till I got sick of his constantly putting down all his friends behind their backs. God knows what he was saying about me."

"I'll tell you sometime, when you're in the mood."

"The day I forgive you for that, they'll make me Pope. Anyway, we kept running into each other, and finally we had dinner. And while telling me about the superb hunk he is currently dating, he blithely lays upon me the scoop that he is also seeing a woman. We're talking about a male who was almost certainly known in high school, to his despair, as Britt the Flit. And after a lifetime of being the absolute bottom, he has become A Real Man. And did he enlarge upon the moral beauty of bisexuality, let me tell you!"

"If that's what he wants."

"He does it to impress himself! When Michael and I gave our joint birthday party, I told Chuck about this and he hit the ceiling. He called it 'gay fascism.' He said Britt was disputing my right of sexual choice."

"Aren't you disputing his?"

Bauhaus crashed into our midst like dirty work at the crossroads and began barking at Dennis Savage. Then Little Kiwi and Uncle Dave trooped in, and Bauhaus jumped up on Little Kiwi.

"What is it, boy? Speak!"

Bauhaus barked twice.

"You do?"

Bauhaus barked once.

"He says he wants to dance on a grape."

"Little Kiwi," said Dennis Savage, "enough is enough, okay?"

"He wants to dance on a grape?" Uncle Dave asked.

"It's his great new vaudeville act," said Little Kiwi, eyeing the walkway. "Later we—"

"Should we eat outside?" said Dennis Savage quickly. "Or is it too hot?"

"Oh, there were such breathtaking men on the beach as we walked there," Uncle Dave said. This sounded so odd, however true, that we all stopped and looked at him. "I mean," he added, "it's quite a place you've got here."

"He's getting the hang of it," said Dennis Savage, setting lunch out. No. It would be some while yet; he had much to learn. As we ate, he asked the questions one usually hears from the raw recruit—where are the places, who are the people, what are the terms, how do you *know*? Never in my life was it more clear how fully developed gay life had become in Stonewall's mere fifteen years, how much more there was to being gay than to being homosexual. Sexual taste you can be born with; but gay is a host of techniques to be acquired.

It's interesting, too, how differently the system tends in other gay places. San Francisco's gay, for instance, is less elegant and knowing and demanding than New York's, more fraternal and expedient and amiable. In New York, gays tell the recruits you must *become*—if you can. In San Francisco, they say You have *arrived*.

Perhaps Uncle Dave ought to have gone west instead of east, for with his big lumbering physique and shaggy blond mustache he'd already be in, whereas in New York he'd have a lot of nouns to memorize and concepts to assimilate. I'll give him some credit: he was moving fast.

"I don't know," he said as we brought the plates in. "Somehow I was expecting quiche."

"Real men don't cook quiche," Dennis Savage told him. "Real men *order* quiche."

"Real men," said Little Kiwi, "long to watch Bauhaus dance on a grape."

I was about to say something pointed, but Dennis Savage pulled Little Kiwi over to the sink to do the dishes—which unfortunately left me with Uncle Dave. I grabbed *Martin Chuzzlewit* and hotfooted it outside, but he followed me and, before I could sit down, said, "I hold the opinion that one of us owes the other an apology and I don't know who that is, but if you won't say you're sorry, I will. Now, how about that?"

Tell me, boys and girls, who can resist such an overture? I apologized for being short with him and we shook hands. Again *Martin Chuzzlewit* bit the dust, as we talked over breaking into the Circuit, and I then let him in on the Secret Sex practices of Dennis Savages, but the subject overheard us and came roaring out to chide me in what I can only term a viciously inflamed manner, and while he was out of the house Little Kiwi gave Bauhaus a grape to dance on (actually he just rolls over them on his back, whimpering), and then Little Kiwi came out and said, "Hey, everybody look at Bauhaus," and I gave Dennis Savage a few smacks to keep him in shape, and Little Kiwi put *Cats* on the stereo so Bauhaus could dance to something, and Little Kiwi told Dave, "They get fifty bucks for this on Broadway."

And Dave told Little Kiwi that it was amazing how much he looked like Seth when he was in his twenties, and that in fact the boy still looked the way he did when he was a little kid.

"He behaves the same, too," I put in.

And Bauhaus calmed down, and there was one of those pauses, and then Dave asked Dennis Savage if gay life was always like this.

I could see Dennis Savage thinking, Maybe, except when somebody dies—so I quickly suggested we take Dave on a tour of The Pines and the Grove, so he could see all of gay from clones to queens; and we could end up at tea, where the houseboys must be obeyed.

Away we went, Dennis Savage and I recounting events long past, some sage and some silly; and the names of those we knew and only knew of came rolling out. Here was where the last of the great drug fires occurred, there the house where the most spectacular party was given, here the site of the first and only annual Looks Contest, there the house so desirable that the wife gave up the kids in the divorce settlement in order to keep it.

"It must really give you a break to be so close to your history," said Dave. "To be a walk away from all the things you've done." He looked ahead at Dennis Savage and Little Kiwi, walking with their arms around each other. "Is that common, to walk like that?"

"It's more Grove style. The Pines generally tells its tales through eye contact."

He and I had slowed to a stop, and he said, "You know, I'm just beginning to realize how much there is in all this. Yet anyone can do it. I still remember, when Virgil left for the east . . . and he was so open about it. I thought, You just go and do it."

The other two had stopped and turned.

"Is he," Dave went on, "what you'd call . . . well, typical of life in the gay community?"

"Little Kiwi? I wouldn't call him typical of life on earth. How'd he get that name, anyway?"

Dennis Savage and Little Kiwi started back to get us.

"Oh, his sister Anne had a doll named Kiwi. A little man doll. And when Virgil was an infant she started calling him Little Kiwi, and the family took it up. I was the only one who called him by his Lord-given name."

"Why?"

"Because he asked me to. A man's going to grow up sometime, and his name's a part of that, I guess."

"So is his sexuality," I said.

He nodded. "So the little birds leave the nest."

"The big ones, too," I noted.

"Well, but he was the favorite in the family." Little Kiwi had reached us and was staring at Dave. "And it surely tore them up when he lit out of the state."

Little Kiwi put his arms around Dave and Dave riffled his hair.

"It surely tore them up, that's true."

"Well, *really!*" said a disgruntled wimpy older man, edging past us with, I expect, his wife.

"Yes, really," said Dave, in a contemplative manner.

"Oh dear," said the wife. Some people have to have the last word.

Well, we did the Grove, and we did tea, and we did the Pantry, and we did cocktails on the deck, and we did dinner, and during dinner Dave and I went back to a theme we had, shall we say, touched on earlier: that of the timing of self-awareness. How could Dave not have known he was a homosexual all those years? And Dave admitted that he'd had the knowledge all along, but could not accept it till the night he got into bed with a man he wanted sexually.

"What man was that?" asked Little Kiwi.

"Your father," said Dave.

And we were quite, quite still.

"Just remember how confusing puberty can be," he said. "Stimuli of so many kinds working on your senses. Heavy pressures from your gang to do what everyone else does. Your self-confidence trying to get organized. And all through this you're randy as hell. Of course you'd be confused—confused about a lot of things. You take a chance on a girl at a party, kiss her, and instead of getting mad she goes along with it and does nice things to your ego. So of course you think you're in love. That lasts for three days. Then it's some other girl—same thing. Another girl. Then your first crush. It's like flying to another planet— and that lasts three weeks. And you've got a best friend, too, and you know how teenagers get sometimes, swimming together, or rough-housing, and all. So, okay, you think he's got a great body, what's wrong with that? You're conscious of your own body, so why shouldn't you notice his? You get hard thinking about him, but teen-agers are always getting boners. You wake up from a very unusual dream, and he was in it . . . can you be blamed for what you dream? Maybe you killed someone in a dream once—that doesn't make you a murderer, does it?"

"Confusion," I said. "I guess I can see it."

"Besides, you don't want to think you're queer, so you're busy twisting everything around for yourself, rationalizing. And since you can't figure out what two men would do in bed, anyway, your dreams aren't all that risky. Meanwhile you're proving you're a man with the available girls. It gets so you can hold mutual bone-off sessions with your best friend and think of it as he-men keeping in shape for the ladies. And finally there comes one time, one event or something, with another guy . . . and I guess that's when you either face up to the truth and stop double-talking yourself, or you decide to live according to the confusion and turn away from the truth." He put his hand on Little Kiwi's head and stroked his hair. "Like father, like son," he mused, as Little Kiwi blushed.

"I'm dying to hear how this comes out," I said, "but since we're also responsible for introducing you to gay, why don't we walk along the beach before it gets too windy to bear and you can finish the story in the famous magic moonlight we have here?"

So we all got into sweaters and hooded sweatshirts—Dennis Savage had to outfit Dave somewhat; we wouldn't let him on the beach out of uniform—and we put Bauhaus on his leash, and off we went to the water's edge where the hard sand is, and there we made Dave turn back to gaze upon the strip of lights that comprises what may be the only gay colony in the history of the world. You say, "What of the Grove?", but the Grove was founded back in the days of the haunted homosexual, of the loving war of queen and hustler, when to be homosexual was to be faggot, queer, bent—Franklin Pangborn or Lucius Beebe, instead of . . . well, for instance, reader: you. The Grove is not gay. The Pines, for all its attitude and casually frantic code of behavior, is gay. And as we regarded it, now in its blasted morale of chaste amusements, of the no-fault cruising of look-but-don't-touch and the survivor mentality that hits those who have simply lived to be thirty-five, we began to tell Dave of its days of glory. Of riding the ferry in a bracing air of anticipation, being able to throw off our covers and be; or of heading for tea, a whole house in force, just to see who our people were, who we are; or of meeting, some weekend, someone's older friend, who would unveil forgotten mysteries of the pre-Stonewall days. Liberty, self-knowledge, anthropology: culture. Our place, in our time. Manhattan is ours, too, in a way—in several ways—but Manhattan we must share. In The Pines, we are the majority.

We all sounded off so thoroughly that we thrilled ourselves, and fell into silence, abashed at our exploits. Even Bauhaus was awed—quiet, anyway. We began to walk, though it was too cold and we should have gone back. And then Dave set in.

"During rush period, when the houses single out certain freshmen and make a play for them, we held weekly meetings, where we would discuss the possibilities. And Seth . . . Virgil's daddy . . . was on top of everyone's list. He was a very . . . attractive young man then. Attractive young man? Do you say that?"

"We say, a beautiful boy," I told him.

"A beautiful boy. Just like Virgil now."

Little Kiwi, still learning to endure these effusions, tightened his grip on Dennis Savage's hand.

"He was an outstanding character, too, on campus, because he went around in tweed suits all the time, and solid ties, and we all thought he was from the east. Like the Great Gatsby."

"Gatsby was from the midwest," I said. "He dazzled the east."

"He dazzled us, anyway. The girls were crazy for him. He really had to fight them off. That was part of his importance to the house, because most of the brothers were in the business school, and they didn't get to know many girls that way. I think they thought Seth might be able to set them up. Just walking around the campus with him you'd meet girls. But there was something else, too. Some of the brothers . . . no. No. It's just that he was very attractive. Beautiful. And everyone responds to that. So he was the first man keyed. And he accepted it, and he fell right in with everything—the brothers, the politics, the code. All the things you take for granted in a fraternity. That was what we called a 'solid man.' At the meetings, the question was always, 'Is he solid?' And Seth was. He was a little reserved, but underneath it he was very sure about things. Sure of himself. And that can be galling to men who aren't all that solid. They're going to go after it, test it, shove it up against a wall and see how solid it really is. The trouble with pledging is the hazing. That's when all the worst guys in the house come out of the woodwork. We tried to make sure we didn't have any worst guys, but somehow they get in. You know— impressive during rushing when they turn on their fireworks, then they get gloomy and solitary."

"Sounds like Dennis Savage's lovers," I would have joked at any other time; but this was a serious night in our lives. We walked along, listening. The wind was bitter, but the house lights cheered us.

"The worst of it is, those guys always take positions of command during hazing. They dream up the programs, administer the disciplines, run the sweat sessions. You can imagine what goes on. And they really went after Seth. It happened in other houses, too. Not to the big handsome guys, but the slight handsome guys. They get victimized. Even tormented. Well, I was Seth's paddle brother, so I could talk to them about it, throw some weight in his corner. They'd ease up on him for two or three days. It'd start in again. And I'd . . . I'd look up from my desk, you know, with your marketing data and your actuarial tables, and the books piled up, and your notes, and the papers of something like a hundred brothers before me. In a T-shirt and shorts, with the fire in the grate. The day was dying down. I'd look up at this . . . beautiful boy in one of his suits, looking so bright and so . . . dismal all at once. And he would ask for my help. And I just wanted to sweep him up and . . . and what? What would I have done after that?"

"My pop was like that?" asked Little Kiwi.

"Didn't he seem like that to you, ever?"

"I always loved him," said Little Kiwi. "I didn't know he was tormented."

"Well, I took care of that, finally. It really created a problem in the house, to interfere with the hazing command. That's not how it works. You're supposed to let them . . ."

"Give attitude," said Dennis Savage.

"Give what?"

"You'll find out."

"Anyway, I got the pledge masters to write what we in my business call letters of assurance to just about everyone in the house. It really put a damper on hell night—not that we had all that terrible a hell night in the first place. Some houses . . . well, you were lucky to get out in one piece."

"The olive race," I murmured.

Dave asked me, "What house did you pledge?"

I shook my head. "We didn't have anything like that. But the Betas and the Dekes . . ."

Dave nodded.

"What olives?" asked Little Kiwi.

"The race ran up the back stairs," I explained. "Five flights. Every pledge in the nude, with an olive in his behind. The loser had to eat the olives."

Even Bauhaus shuddered.

"Each club has its style," I said. "You find the club that suits your style."

"That's what I don't have, right?" said Dave. "The gay club style?"

"Stick with us, kid," I said, "and you'll be wearing leather."

"When my pop came into your room," said Little Kiwi, "was he sad? To ask for your help? Was he afraid?"

"He wasn't sad, but he was afraid. And that's the corn on the cob. Because he came to my room on a night in February, very late. I closed my books and we talked for a while. It had been snowing that day, a real blizzard on. I said he'd better stay over at the house. No point in getting wrecked in the snow."

"How far did he live from the house?" Little Kiwi asked.

"Three blocks. Four. But distance wasn't . . . what was happening then. I wanted to put him in my bed, because he was so vulnerable that minute, and that's why he was afraid—he knew what I was doing. I wanted to get him out of those suits. The ties. He even wore hats. He had a little line of hair that ran down his belly from his navel, and it was as if I could see it right through his clothes. I wanted

to trace my finger along it. I wanted to hold his body. I knew that. No
rationalizing. I wanted to touch him."

"My pop was afraid?" asked Little Kiwi.

"I believe so. But he didn't seem afraid, really. I turned out the
lights and we got undressed . . . talking the whole time, you know. I
was cool. I just smiled. And Seth smiled, too. But once I put him in
that bed I got my hands on him, and I wasn't confused anymore. I
was hard, and he knew it, because we were edged up together, spoon-
style. I wanted to squeeze him to death, to have him. But I didn't
know how to have him. I wanted to love him. And I told him that.
Just those words. Because if I didn't say it, no one would ever know I
felt that way, including me. And he turned around to face me, and he
had his arms around me. But he wouldn't say anything. I knew what I
wanted to hear, but I didn't know how to make him say it. So I felt
down for that line of hair, and I stroked it. I said, 'How does that
feel?' and I heard him gasp, but he didn't say anything. And, well, we
kept on like that. And we started to kiss each other. All over. And we
were juicing like crazy. But I might have been dreaming. I might well
have been dreaming, I can guess. I've thought about it so often, I
honestly don't know what happened by now. Virgil."

He reached for Little Kiwi, and we all stopped walking.

"Seeing you grow up. You're so much like him. Even Anne is like
him. Your whole family is like your father. Whenever I look at you, I
see him in my room, asking for help."

"I see him decking my allowance and such," said Little Kiwi.

"You should have been there when you were born, Virgil," said
Dave. "That boy loved you as he loved nothing else on earth."

We walked in silence for a time.

"Let's start back," Dennis Savage said.

"Is that all the story?" asked Little Kiwi.

"I guess it is," said Dave. "I never got him into bed again. We were
still friends, and when he moved into the house the next year we were
almost inseparable. We even had the same major, accounting. I guess

that doesn't matter. But sometimes we would talk real straight to each other, and once I referred to that night in the blizzard, and Seth denied it ever happened."

"How could he?" asked Dennis Savage.

"Press him," I urged, two decades late.

"He denied it," said Dave. "He looked me in the eye and said no. He seemed a little surprised that I would suggest that we could even . . . and he didn't get stiff on me or back away. He was very calm about it. So we stayed friends. But it had never happened. There was nothing between us except . . . except . . ."

I thought that if that *except* could be explained to the world, George Will would be out of business.

"My pop," said Little Kiwi, moving up to Dave with something on his mind. Dennis Savage and I hung back, allowing Bauhaus to lead us into the driftwood to reflect and comment.

"Aren't you going to rush up and eavesdrop?" Dennis Savage asked me. "Invade our privacy for some putrid story?"

"Putrid is right," I replied. "There is no story. Nothing has happened."

"We learned something, didn't we?"

"We learned that entering into any group will afford one assistants and imposters. Who doesn't know that already? Every club has someone at the door with a list."

A shadow moved at our house as we approached.

"What the hell was that?" asked Dennis Savage.

It moved again. We had left the lights on, and saw with reasonable clarity. Someone was on our porch. Someone waved something in the air.

As we moved up from the water, Dennis Savage tensed, Bauhaus began to bark, Dave looked from one of us to another, and Little Kiwi tore away to run up to the house. I heard him screaming but the wind was wrong and I couldn't hear the words. No matter. I got there soon enough. Bauhaus was leaping about and Little Kiwi had his arms around Carlo, who had been waving at us with a cowboy hat. Carlo threw his arms around us all, and when he got to Dave, he said, "Where'd you come from?" holding him by the shoulders. Dave looked like a character in a Robert Ludlam novel who gets the chance to slip into something by Richard Price.

"Can I get some of that?" said Dave, and Carlo embraced him, too. "Some more," Dave added, taking hold of Carlo as if to kiss his mouth, and Carlo pulled back; but I said, "He's been living in Cleveland," and Carlo grabbed Dave and took him so fervently Little Kiwi asked Dennis Savage if he ought to take Bauhaus for a walk.

"He just *got* walked."

"Who are you?" Carlo asked Dave.

"Carlo's back!" cried Little Kiwi.

"Is this permanent?" asked Dennis Savage, somewhat dangerously.

"We should drink on this," I said. "One gringo custom I've always been comfortable with."

"Who are you?" Carlo asked Dave again. "Why were you in Cleveland?"

"Why were you in South Dakota?" I muttered, heading inside with Dennis Savage to get liquor. We were too full up from dinner to contemplate any serious intake, and decided to ransack the liquor closet for brandy: a toast and a swallow. Carlo's "Who are you?" danced in my head, and as Dennis Savage rummaged I tried to imagine defining who Dave is to Carlo, and who Carlo is to Dave: explaining, in other words—to a man so imbued with the liberty of the sexy brotherhood that he offered to give it up rather than see it dully survive—how another man might be born to it yet try not to need it. Or explaining—to the man who went gringo simply because the world plays by gringo rules—that another man would make the informal challenging of those rules his life's work.

Heck, come to that, could I even explain Carlo to Carlo? I have tried to set him forth in these pages so others may comprehend, but Carlo believes a poem should not mean but be.

"Look at that," said Dennis Savage, coming up for air with a bottle of Grand Marnier, the label so faded it might have been older than we are. "It's funny about New York," he said. "You never see anybody buy this stuff. No one I know drinks it. Yet when you need a bottle there's always one there, way at the back."

"Pour," I said.

Little Kiwi came in wearing Carlo's cowboy hat. "There are two men making out on our deck," he said.

"Could it be love at last?" Dennis Savage asked, setting the glasses on a tray.

"Too early to say," Carlo replied as he brought Dave in by the arm.

"So," said Dennis Savage, passing the tray.

We all looked at Dave; it seemed his toast to offer. "Confusion to our enemies," he proposed.

"My mother would like you," I told him. "That's her favorite toast."

Then we all sat and talked—about Dave's new apartment (on Second and Fifty-sixth), about how best to enjoy one's first New York autumn, about whether or not it's fair to continue calling Virgil by a childhood nickname (it isn't, but we will), and about how long Carlo had returned for. He was evasive, but it was clear this was no mere trip. He was even planning to resecure his old place on East Third Street, a ghastly third-floor walkup he only uses when he's between engagements. It has been sublet so often over the years that the door has given up on keys; when it hears footsteps, it opens.

Some music was played, a late-night pizza snack was served (my famous Tree Tavern recipe), and at length the parties dispersed. Dennis Savage and Little Kiwi went to bed, Carlo, stretched out in Dave's arms for the previous half-hour, fell asleep, and I went up to my room to start this story—because, in the end, something had happened.

I put the lamp on the bed, lay on my stomach, and began to write; and I've taken it down pretty much as it happened. I've registered doubt, earlier in this book, about writing about everyone but myself; but when I put myself into a lead role I feel co-opted, disarmed, uncouth. Writing autobiographically should enhance one's image with dear lies; but a voice inside me warns that clones are invalid, kids are their own tragedy, that a drag queen should not tell but show.

Ontology, huh? That means I need a drink. I slipped downstairs to mix a double vodka—scotch doesn't suit The Pines somehow; it's a metropolitan liquor—and there I found Carlo and Dave still on the couch, asleep. I went into a vacant bedroom, copped a blanket, and covered them. Dave stirred awake.

He yawned. "Is it always so easy as this? To get a man?"

"Oh no. Some never get a man at all. And to come out, move to Manhattan, and get Carlo on a couch . . . that's a feat."

A Delilah is vodka on ice with crushed pepper, a Samson takes lemon peel, and a Samson and Delilah gets both. As I collected the makings of a both, Dave asked, "Why is he called Carlo? He doesn't look Spanish, except his hair and cheekbones."

"A wise old queen named him that in his first year in New York. He said Carlo needed a glamorous name because he was glamorous. Just one name, like all the greats—Charlemagne, Napoleon, Lilo. Something simple. Precise. Charismatic."

"Like your lad himself," said Dave, stroking Carlo's hair. "What *is* his name?"

"Ripley Smith."

Dave smiled. "Couldn't he have been Rip? Wouldn't that be a glamorous name? He looks like a Rip."

I sliced the lemon. Make it a hunk of a slice, for a double. Lot of work tonight, yes? "Be very careful with him," I said, grinding the pepper. "He looks tough, but he ain't."

I lit a candle. As I turned, drink in the right hand and candle in the left, Carlo wheezed and squirmed and hugged Dave in a hunger of death.

"He's exhausted," Dave told me. "He kept falling asleep as we talked."

"He probably traveled directly from Aberdeen, South Dakota to here. He's very impulsive."

"Why the candle?"

"I've a yen to write by candlelight."

"What are you writing?"

"Oh . . . a story about . . . you want anything before I go?"

"I want to hold this man in my arms for the rest of my life."

I nodded. "Romantic, nice. But wait till you get him into bed."

"Is he good?"

"We don't say good. We say hot. And he's not hot—he's sacramental."

I looked in on Dennis Savage and Little Kiwi. The latter, as usual, had thrashed himself into a position half on and off the bed. I righted him, and his eyes shot open. He breathed out, "Come back with Anne." Then he was still.

The house was now dark and abed, and I pulled my window open a bit to inhale the enchanted air and take in the slap of the water. Something had happened after all; yes. I thought thanks were in order: but whom to thank? I've been atheist as long as I've been gay— but I thought that if there was/were/might be a God, it could not be that paranoid Old Testament sheik with the plagues and the tantrums. I looked farther back, to the all-mother, probably less cruel and more forgiving than her male successor. As Carlo says, when you take a problem to your father, he switches you; your mother gives you Cream of Wheat.

So I thought, Hello, let's have some proof. If You exist, show us a lightning flash. You got five.

Nothing.

Maybe that was the wrong test. So I thought, Hello, if You exist, turn on the stereo. You got five.

Nothing.

So I thought, Okay, You don't exist; and the wind swept into my room and blew the fucking candle out.

EVERYBODY LOVES YOU

FURTHER ADVENTURES
IN GAY MANHATTAN

To Robert Trent

CONTENTS

ACKNOWLEDGMENTS

The author wishes to acknowledge the enthusiasm, audacity, and sage counsel of his editor, Michael Denneny, though after six books this is becoming monotonous: or let us say a fond cliché.

The Complete Death
of the Clown Dog

▰▰▰▰▰▰▰

THE RESTAURANT GOT A
rave in the *Times*, and it was *hot*. If
they didn't recognize your name, I was
told, they wouldn't take your reservation. It was not
that hot, it turned out, for they gave me no trouble.
Still, it was horribly crowded, as if they had decided
to run with the fame as long as it held out, and so
had filled the room with tables, to serve the vested
gentry at their lunches, then the chic cabaret watch-
ers who would learn of the place from their friends
because they never read, then the avid bridge-and-
tunnel tourists, who would hear about it in *Cue*.
Then the prices would go up, and the menu would
lose its energy, and the waiters would mess up your
drink order. And the place would falter and close.

I was taking an old friend to lunch to celebrate his
promotion to managing editor of a prominent fashion magazine. He had been given little more than a
few days in which to change the magazine's entire
"book"—the major columns and features—and thus

was invariably behind in everything that followed. Normally thoughtful and punctual, he became one of those nearly inaccessible heavy hitters who seldom return your phone messages or show up on time, the kind of Significant Other you are proud to know but can never see. At last I nabbed him for lunch, oddly timed to two o'clock, to fit into his schedule. Of course he was late, and as there is nothing else to do while awaiting the rest of your table but eavesdrop on your neighbors, I ordered a Kir and began to listen. To my right were three rowdy Communications people dishing a great load of apparently famous names; but I couldn't place those they cited. To my left were two men in their mid-thirties, whose quiet tone and conservatively sporty tweeds suggested the book trade.

They had reached the coffee stage. I supposed one was a writer and the other his editor, perhaps his agent, but I couldn't be sure because they weren't talking business. Many a telling silence passed between them. The one facing me—the authority figure, I guessed, whoever he was—sometimes smiled and sometimes nodded wisely. The one next to me, who was doing all the talking, had the heaviest regional accent I've ever heard, yet he spoke quickly, and filled his back country lingo with the articulate penetration of the literary man: as if he had picked up New York habits without losing his own.

What a backstory he must have, I thought—and suddenly, without preamble or explanation, he was spilling out his tale. I imagined that these two had met professionally and had just reached the moment—just now, here, at this lunch—when the

◆ 2 ◆

business relationship turned into friendship. I imagined that the one speaking was a writer, and that he was sharing some profound and painful secret with the man who published his work. I imagined that he had come a long way to arrive at this lunch, at this career, at this friendship. I began to hope that my friend the heavy-hitting magazine editor would be unforgivably late, so I could hear the stranger's story.

This is the story he told:

In Hanley, West Virginia, close on to Wheeling, where I was when I was little, there was a pokey little circus run by Hopey Paris. Most places don't have their own circus on the premises, not even a little one like Hopey's with almost no animals and a busted trapeze and these admission tickets that must have been printed up before the Civil War that you couldn't even read what they said on them anymore. In Hanley we figured it was okay to have this circus, though most of us didn't much care about it one way or the other. Anyway, you never knew when Hopey was going to put his circus on, because he ran it by whim. Also he owned the dime store. I expect what he got out of the dime store he plowed back into keeping the circus going, since he didn't own anything else.

It was like this about having the circus. Some night in light weather, mostly at the tip end of summer when everyone would just sit around and wait for something cool to happen, Hopey would come up from his end of town and find a crowd on the steps of wherever it was they were . . . someone's porch, whoever had beer. He'd wait about three lulls, nodding and shaking along with the gist of things as they got said. Then he'd go, "Guess I'll have to have the circus tonight." And everyone would get everyone else and go on over because, look, what else is there to do? You go to the circus.

What a funny circus—but how much do you want for free? Hopey handed out the admission tickets in a little booth at the entrance and you would take your seat inside the tent, which stood in Hopey's backyard, hanging on by a thread to these old poles. It wasn't a big tent, of course, but, as it is written, size isn't substance. And then Hopey would come in with a whip and this hat he got somewhere to be a ringmaster in. You'd want to think he would look pathetic, wouldn't you? Hopey Paris trying to hold down a circus all by himself in Hanley? He didn't, though. He didn't look much like anything. But he did have a star attraction, the clown dog.

It's crazy about dogs, how some can do things and some can't. I knew a dog once that caught softballs in the air if you threw them underhand. Then he'd go racing off with the ball in his teeth and you'd have to trap him and pry the ball out with a stick. That was his trick, I guess, is how he looked at it. And my father had a dog named Bill who was quite a hero in his day. Bill ran away finally and never came back.

But the clown dog sure was prime. He had this costume, a yellow coat-sort-of-thing with polka dots that he wore fastened around his middle and a red cone hat with a little pom-pom at the top. Whether the circus was on or off, and in all weathers, never, never did you see the clown dog out of costume. And his trick was he could talk. That dog could really talk.

This was why we would always come back to see the same old one-man circus, with no animals or clowns except one animal-clown, like that was all you needed to call it a circus. The tent was hardly alive at all, the big-top tent itself. But you always had to go back because you wanted to see how the trick was done. Because no dog, not even a circus trick dog, can talk. But the thing about tricks is whether or not you can figure them out. That's the art of tricks, right there. And the clown dog, though he often roamed around his end of town like any dog, free in the sun, except he was dressed . . . the clown dog would never do his talking except in the circus. This was probably the deal he made with Hopey, who was, after all, his master. You'd suppose that they must have come to terms on something that important.

That's what's so funny. Because, speaking of dogs, my father never did come to terms with his dog Bill, though he would try, hard as stone, to make that dog his. He trained it and trained it. It must have run near on to two years of sessions in Sunshine's field, and Bill just didn't ever submit and be trained. My father was a ferocious trainer by the standards of any region, but he couldn't get Bill to obey even the most essential commands. And he never could teach him not to chase around the davenport, especially late at night, when Bill most felt like a run. "I will have that dog behave," my father said, and I recall how he looked, like behavior was just around the corner. But Bill would not be suppressed. Sometimes he would come when you called, sometimes not. But when he did come, he had this funny look on him, as if he was coming over just to find out why you persisted in calling his name when it had already been established that he wasn't about to respond.

Bill was a mutt, not like the clown dog, who was a poodle, a very distinct breed. You can't miss a poodle, especially in a polka-dot coat and a cone hat with a pom-pom. But Bill was just another dog you might know, kind of slow for his race and disobedient but generally normal, except once when he was The Hero of '62. They called him that because he accidentally bit this management scud who was getting on everybody's nerves at the factory the summer before the strike.

McCosker, I think this guy's name was . . . one of those mouthy hirelings absolutely corrupted by a little power. He had been tacking up this notice by the front gate, some mouthy, powerful thing about something else you're not supposed to do, just busy as anything tacking away and being hated up by the people who were standing around watching. Suddenly Bill bounded over to where this guy McCosker was. I guess maybe Bill thought he saw something to eat near this McCosker's foot, but McCosker took it for some stunt and he made a sudden move and Bill got thrilled and bit him.

It was a tiny little bite on the ankle, kind of in passing, but McCosker screamed like he was being murdered and all the men cheered and patted Bill, and they all shook my father's hand, and mine, too. So Bill was The Hero of '62.

This is a funny thing. Because all Bill had done was what a dog will do every so often, whereas the clown dog was truly some kind of dog. Everybody said so. You just could not tell anyhow that he wasn't talking when Hopey Paris brought him on for his circus turn. Now, that was a trained dog if ever there was one. Yet nobody ever called the clown dog a hero. And the clown dog never ran away, either, which Bill did once. Once is all it takes.

I guess you have to figure that a dog that goes around in circus clothes isn't going to earn the respect of the community, besides him being a poodle, which is not one of your heroic breeds of dog. But I liked him, because he was the first thing I can remember in all my life. Hunkering back down in my mind as far as I can sail, the picture I reach is the clown dog talking in the circus, and the polka dots, and the hat. I wonder if he ever had a name, because he was always known as the clown dog that I ever heard, and I don't recall Hopey ever calling to him. Sometimes Hopey would act like that dog was this big secret, cocking an eyebrow and looking cagey if you asked after him, as if everyone in town hadn't seen the circus a hundred times.

I expect the clown dog must have liked me, because he used to follow me around some days that I know of with his coat and his dumb little hat. He looked so sad. I guess he sensed that he was supposed to be a secret, because he tended to hang back a little, like someone who has already been tagged out of a game and is waiting for the next thing to start. I don't recall that he even barked. And he never went along with us when we tried to get him to talk out of the circus.

Of course we had listened, with all the concentration of adolescents, to the exact words Hopey used in the act when the clown dog would speak, and we would try these words on the clown dog ourselves—imitating Hopey's voice, even, and standing the way he stood to be an imperial ringmaster. But we couldn't make it happen; never did the clown dog utter a word out of his context, the circus. It was the strangest thing. I was just thinking that I would have hated to be around Bill someday if someone tried to get him into a hat with pom-poms.

I was at college when Bill ran away, so I only know about it secondhand, from stories. I couldn't help thinking it was presumable in the end that Bill would take a walk one day and not come back. It was presumable. But still I was surprised to hear of it. It was Christmas, when I was a freshman, and the first sight I got of home when I got off the bus was my father cutting the grass with the Johnsons' lawn mower, and Bill nowhere to be seen. I knew something was wrong then, because Bill never missed a chance to play dogfight with the Johnsons' lawn mower, which always enraged my father. Bill would growl at it for starters, lying way off somewhere, and slowly creep towards it . . . you know, paw by paw. Then he'd run around it, fussing and barking, and at last he'd get in to rushing it like he was going in for the kill, only to back up snarling at the last second.

So when I saw the lawn mower and no Bill I

thought he must be sick, but my father said he had run off like as far back as October sometime. I listened carefully to this, though he didn't talk careful, not ever in all his life that I knew him. Whatever he was thinking when he spoke, that's what he'd say, as tough as you can take it. He didn't expect Bill back, he said, and he didn't miss him. He said it and I believe him. I can just see that now, what he said, and saying it, so plain it was like a picture somebody drew to prove something. I could see that way he didn't care right up front on him.

"No," he said lazily, because he is lazy. "I don't miss him. You run away from home and don't come back, nobody misses you at all. That's the rule."

I don't know of any rule saying you don't miss a runaway dog, even if he never comes back. If he's of a mind to run, there's usually a good reason. My father used to say, "There's always a reason for something, and sometimes two."

That was one of his wisdoms. He had wisdoms for most things that came up in life—lawyers, school, elections, working. He had his wisdoms for Bill, too, even when it was really clear that dog was born to go his own way in a nice wisdom of the animal kingdom.

I can see why that dog took off, anyway, because my father wasn't any too easy to get along with, especially when proclaiming one of his wisdoms. But despite what he said and how he looked saying it, I suppose he really did love that dog . . . or he *wanted* to love it, which would be the way people like my father express affection. It must have threatened to tear him up some when Bill deserted him.

◆ 9 ◆

That was a bad time, too, with the strike coming up sooner or later but sure as doom. I wasn't around for the strike. I was sixteen when I finished high school, and I could still have been young some more and not done much of anything with myself, but I had more ambition than to work in the factory or pump gas on Route 16. So I went to college on what you might call a soccer scholarship. My father always poked fun at me for playing soccer. "What kind of sport is that for a man, chasing a ball around with your feet? You look like a bunch of giant bugs," was his view of it. But soccer took me to college, on a full scholarship. It's true, I guess; soccer isn't much of a sport, and this wasn't much of a college. But one wisdom might be that college is college. Anyway, I went.

I came home for Christmas, because I was only two states away, one long bus ride. Besides, they closed the dorms on me and I had to go somewhere. That first night, Thursday, when I came home and saw the lawn mower and learned that Bill had run away, standing in the yard with my bag like a salesman, I decided to walk around town instead of just being home. Because I already knew about home, but I felt mysterious about Hanley, that it was a place filled with riddles that ought to be solved, even by someone who had lived his whole life of sixteen years so far in it.

I thought maybe I would take a look over to Hopey Paris's circus, in case that should be going on . . . or maybe I would talk Hopey into doing his show just for me, because it was extremely rare that the circus would happen in December. I had an idea that Hopey favored me over some others of my generation there in Hanley because I had always been keen to see the clown dog and figure out how he talked, and Hopey was pleased to be appreciated, even by kids.

He liked to think—I'm guessing at this—that his circus, starring the clown dog, which he celebrated as The Talking Dog of the World . . . his circus was what kept the town from feeling too complete. You might suppose that a town with a circus is more complete than most, but instead I sense that it is less complete, and therefore more open and more free. Because a circus is magic. And having its own private circus reminds the town of all the other magic things it doesn't have. It is like . . . it puts the town a little in touch with another town, a secret town that is the ghostly image of itself, a kind of myth in a mirror. Now, so long as the town is aware of its ideal twin, it will wonder about itself, and never think it knows everything there is to know, and not pretend that it is complete. Which I think is all to the good. So no wonder I liked to watch the clown dog's act. And that's why I went over to Hopey Paris's circus on my first night back from college—to watch the ghost dance by me again. Even after all those years, I still didn't understand how the clown dog did his trick.

This was the act. Hopey comes in with his whip and his hat and he stands in the ring. "And now we take great pride and the most highly principled pleasure"—this is exactly what he said every time—"in presenting for your delectation and enlightenment the one and only clown dog . . . The Talking Dog of the World!"

And out from behind a flap of the tent, in his coat and pom-pom hat, the clown dog would trot in. And he would sit on his hind legs looking expectantly at Hopey. That same old coat and hat. That poor little clown dog. Or I guess maybe he was well off, even if no one called him a hero.

In any case, Hopey would say, "Tell these folks here assembled who you *are*"—like that, with everything on the *are*. And . . . I swear to God, the clown dog would answer, as if he was going to growl first. But no, it was this funny talking—"Clown . . . dog." Like that, broken up into words. It was a high voice, tensely placed, like the sounds puppets make on television. And of course we were looking madly from the clown dog to Hopey and back to see the trick.

Then Hopey would say, "Who is the *clown dog*?" And the clown dog would answer, "Me." Something screwy would happen in his mouth, as if he was biting a fly or had bubble gum. And his head would tilt. But he talked, all right, and that was some trick. Just these two questions was all the talking, though. Because then Hopey would shout, "Leap, clown dog!" and that poodle just leaped right into Hopey's arms and licked his face. That was the whole act, and that was also the whole circus.

I miss that circus, for it is miles away from me now. But when I came home that Christmas, I didn't have it in mind as something you ever lose hold of, because I didn't realize about growing old. Now, that is a term for you, *growing old*. And it, too, has a trick: it contains the thought that things vanish. You don't grow old yourself as fast as old things grow old because even as you age you're still there but the other things are gone . . . what you might call completed. They function, and they pass, and you also pass along, and perhaps you come to the big city here, and you learn a new function, and think about who you are . . . and somewhere in there you remember the old things, and the other place, and suddenly you realize how much you miss them. And this tells you how you have your own completion to accomplish.

I didn't reckon on any of this at the time, passing through Hanley on my Christmas vacation. I was just out for a stroll. I should have stopped and seen everything the way a camera sees, marking it down so when I grew old everything that was there wouldn't have vanished even in completion. I just wanted a little peace.

The thing was, that if I was sixteen, the clown dog must have been well on to thirteen or fourteen. He just never acted old, so it was not something to realize. Fourteen is old for a dog, and that's as near as far as a dog can last without vanishing, even if he still acts spry and bouncy and leaps into your arms when you tell him. So I just went up to Hopey's door and knocked, thinking he'd be there like always and maybe he'd rustle up the circus just for me in honor of my coming back from college on my first holiday.

The house was lit inside but no one answered, so I went around to the back where the tent was. Except there was no tent there now. You could see the tracks in the dirt where it was, all the time before, and some of the bleacher seats were still there, a little wrecked, like someone was trying to take them apart and then suddenly changed his mind. And as I stood there wondering, I heard Hopey's back door open. I turned and saw him in the doorway, so I asked him where the circus had gone to.

"My little clown dog passed away," Hopey said, "so I cut down the tent and dissolved the circus."

It happened in October, he said, which would be only a few weeks after I left town for school. I didn't know what to tell him without making it seem like I was holding another funeral, and I was worried about words because I got distracted thinking about the clown dog's little hat and how sad he looked in it sometimes. You know how touchy it can be, lurking about a place and looking like a stranger. And what if I asked how did it happen and only made Hopey feel worse? I didn't ask. I must have stood there for a whole minute trying to get my mouth around a sentence.

"He liked you, you know," Hopey said suddenly. "Perhaps you suppose that I was busy in the store, but I knew who his friends were. He was a pickety chooser, but he had exquisite taste in people. Didn't you think so?"

"I think he was a shy little fellow," I said.

"Yes, that he was."

"I'm sorry, Hopey. I came over especially to see him again." Now that I'd found my tongue, I expected he would break down or get very quiet, but he was just so calm. The clown dog used to follow me around, I wanted to say. We tried to make him talk. But we never hurt him.

◆ 14 ◆

"Since he liked you," said Hopey, "do you want to plumb the mystery of how he talked?"

I had to smile now. "It was a trick, wasn't it?"

"It was a tip-top trick," Hopey replied, "because nobody knew how it was done. Bet I shouldn't spoil it for you after all this. Should I? Do you want to know?"

"I think I ought to plumb the mystery, if he liked me, after all."

"He didn't like everyone," said Hopey. "But I believe he was exceptionally popular in the town."

"I guess he had to be," I said. "No other circus dog that I heard tell of has ever been the headline attraction."

"Well, he certainly was that. And he led a rich life. He was The Talking Dog of the World."

Hopey asked me about college then, and I told him, and after a while there was this natural space to say good-bye, so I left. Hopey forgot to tell me the trick and I forgot to remind him that I should know it, but I didn't think it was fitting to go back there just then, and before I was halfway home I was glad I didn't find it out.

You'd think I would be unhappy to learn that the clown dog had died, but in a way that conversation with Hopey was the only nice thing that happened all Christmas. My father was in a terrible mood the whole time, spitting out wisdoms like he was on a quota system and falling behind. He kept talking about the strike that everyone knew was going to happen, and finally, a few days before I was due to go back to school, he asked me didn't I think my place was here with the people I'd known all my life instead of at some college?

It seemed to me that the place to be during a strike was as far from it as possible, and college would do as well as any. And that's what I told him. So he said if I felt that way about it, I might as well get going right now.

"Just like Bill," he said.

I was waiting for that. I didn't have anything prepared to say back to it, but I knew it was coming. I don't care. It was meant to hurt me, but it didn't, though I must admit it began to gnaw on me after a while . . . because I hoped it was true.

I really did. "Just like Bill," he said, but he meant more like: "Go vanish."

"Just like Bill"—because I was leaving him, too. Well, there's always a reason for something, and sometimes two. I never went back to Hanley, either; maybe Bill did, after I left, but I won't. I have heard those words often since in my mind, *Just like Bill*, in just the way he said it, looking so smug that he had doped it out at last, made the simple sum and added another wisdom to his collection. I could accept it if I had to, but the truth is I am no way like Bill, all told. I am not like anyone. Whenever someone asks who I am, I say, "Me," just like the clown dog did, because it cheers me to remember him, and to think back on how I could have heard the trick if I had wanted to, which is as close as anybody ought to get. That was a strange, but fine, animal.

▰

The speaker stopped there; he had finished. After a moment, the man who had been listening to him quietly took out some plastic and laid it on the check, and as the waiter bustled over to them, my magazine friend burst upon me, loaded down with apologies. I had to hear them, of course, and soothe them, and assure him that I wasn't in the least put off, and by the time we had settled down the two men to my left had gone.

"The worst of it," said my friend, "is that our star writer has gone on an autobiographical binge—*this* after ten years of that wonderful 'Letter from Paris' column, and 'Down and Out at the Venice Film Festival,' and 'Backstage at the Oscars,' all that kind of thing *no one else living* does as well. Suddenly, he can't so much as turn on his word processor unless he's all set to write about his childhood, and his family, and all these *grisly events that shaped him*, for God's sake. I mean, please, thank you, but *who cares*, right? We all have families, who doesn't? But do *I* go around telling about it? Do *you*?"

"Shall we order?" I said.

"That's the marvelous thing about New York, isn't it? No one really *has* families, because we all leave them somewhere when we . . . yes, we've *got* to order because I'm utterly . . . how's the veal, though? Do they do it Swiss style?"

So we lunched and spoke of metropolitan things, such as what well-known actor was beating on, absolutely *beating on* his wife; that the apartment crunch is starting to ease up a bit, unless you want a terrace or a really *dependable* no-frost fridge; and where you can get ceramic refrigerator magnets bearing the logos of classic Hollywood movies.

We parted on the street like boulevardiers, urbanely waving, and quick to move along, and quite, quite sure of ourselves, and without any family to speak of.

The Handshake Deal

I DIDN'T COME TO NEW York to write; I came to get published. But what I ended up doing was play piano in bars, make party tapes, put out romance comic books for the firm that published *Superman* and *Wonder Woman*, and update *TV Guide*'s squibs on old shows in syndication. (When you read about what's doing on *I Love Lucy*, *Surfside Six*, or *The Saint*—even today—it's mine.) In the spring of 1974, I got my first respectable job, on the staff of *Opera News*, and in late summer of that year I talked my way into my first book contract. I called my parents, a few friends. They were shocked and thrilled. Then I thought I'd tell my brother Jim. He wouldn't be thrilled, but he wouldn't be shocked either.

In fact, he was silent, distracted, holding a shoe in his hand. I was about to ask him to try to remake contact with the planet earth when I heard a pathetic mewing from somewhere in his apartment.

"What's going on?" I asked.

"Mice," he said. "Mice are going on."

"Mice squeak. I hear—"

"Laid in a cat," he explained, "to catch some mice here."

"Laid in?"

"Borrowed it."

I decided not to pursue that one. Somewhere outside, probably, some poor slob was pacing the street calling out, "Felix! Felix!"

"Something wrong with it," he went on. "The mice come out to play and that fucker doesn't even notice."

"You don't seem very impressed with my news."

"Must be a cheese factory next door or something. Why should I be impressed? You always wanted to be a writer and you knew you were going to get there, so what the fuck? Tell me some news and maybe . . ."

A mouse zipped out of the kitchen and disappeared behind the sofa as Jim heaved the shoe at it.

"It's like an army of them," he went on.

"Where's the cat through all this? Hiding?"

"I locked it in the bathroom yesterday to hunger it up so maybe then it'll straighten out and eat mice."

"Jesus!"

"Fucking coward cat. I'm not giving it any Puss 'n Boots Number Four or so when it isn't pulling its weight here."

Someone hit the buzzer downstairs.

"That's my man Dave coming around," said Jim, buttoning him in. "Now that Johnny Boy's tomcatting out on him, you know."

Whose story is it, who tells it, and what is the

story about? Walking the three blocks to Jim's, I had thought it would be my story, about my ambition. It wasn't. But listen.

Dave and Johnny Boy. Okay, they're hard to do. Because it wasn't what they said to each other or whatever was in their eyes—easy to record—as it was the threatening clarity of their pauses. Their hesitations around each other. The way they would start to move toward each other, freeze, back off; and they would be smiling right then. It was all rather highly charged, needs the visuals. And there were those things you would hear about them, too—like "Johnny Boy's tomcatting out on him."

So just listen.

Dave came in and got the cat out of Jim's bathroom, first thing, and told Jim, "You got to aim your boy at a project." He was in the kitchen opening a can of cat food. He petted the cat as it ate. "Don't you need to train this baby?"

"The fucking cat and the fucking mice," Jim muttered.

"You wait, my friend, and I'll show you what it is."

"Mice in my fucking house, you know."

Dave was about thirty-five then, a rangy, ham-handed, jocular, greying blond southerner who went through life in a blue T-shirt on top of a white T-shirt. Johnny Boy, his inseparable companion, was a trim, muscly guy in his early twenties. Like Jim, they were ironworkers, freelancing on construction sites in and around New York. Dave drove a motorcycle and Johnny Boy had a mustache. Dave took it cool and easy and Johnny Boy ran to the moody. Dave was the chief and Johnny Boy, grinning, did as he was told. It was Dave who had named him Johnny Boy, and this story, I learned on the day of the mice, is theirs.

"Now watch," said Dave, after the cat had fed, taking it over to where the mice were disappearing. He set it on the floor, knelt above it, and petted it some more as it arched its back and purred. He whispered to it. When it tried to move, he held it fast.

"Listen," he said. "Listen to the mice, cat." The cat vaguely listened. "Its name," Dave told us, "is Waterloo. Waterloo the cat is listening to mice."

Soon enough, the cat grew still, focused on something. I saw its eyes widen, and I knew some mice who were in a lot of trouble.

"When you have something in mind for your little pal, you got to aim him at it, see?"

"Dave," said Jim admiringly, "you are a gentleman and a fuckmaster."

"Yep. Look at Waterloo. Look at this swift mouse-killer. Waterloo the cat is going for it."

Sitting on Jim's couch at the nightly bull sessions, Johnny Boy would fall asleep in Dave's arms and no one as much as glanced at them, except me. "He ran all over the site today," Dave would explain, hefting the boy into his lap, "and now he's all tuckered out." And when the party broke up, Dave would stroke Johnny Boy's hair and say to him, "Come along, lad."

They lived together.

Dave petted the cat, enjoying its concentration. He looked at Jim and Jim nodded.

"You got to aim him, Jimbo."

"I see that, my amazing Dave."

Dave turned to me, smiling. "Or what?"

"You aim him," I replied, "because that is a righteous thing." You had to talk wild to stay abreast of Jim's buddies. They were wild men. I liked a few of them a very great deal.

"Hey, Dave, guess what?" I said. "I just sold a book to the Viking Press."

"Don't they got enough books of their own?"

"No, to write one. I sold a *deal*."

"Oh, so that," he said, coming over. "Now, that's a headline." He shook my hand.

Dave and Johnny Boy had this game. Dave would break into popular song, using a familiar tune but making up silly words. Such as:

> I'll bake a tart
> In Capistrano.

He'd sing this sweetly right into Johnny Boy's ear, and Johnny Boy would patiently say, "It doesn't go like that, Dave."

"How does it rightly go, Johnny Boy?"

"'I left my *heart*,'" Johnny Boy would tell him, "'in San Francisco.'"

"No kidding."

"Yeah."
Or:

> They tried to sell us
> Egg Foo Yong.

Johnny Boy would say, "'They tried to tell us we're too young.'"

Dave would reply, "You're too young, puppy. I'm old enough."

"Old enough for what?"

"Old enough to take you," Dave would pensively drawl, and they'd back off and pace around each other as if they were going to fight. Then Dave would feint and grab Johnny Boy by the waist and swing him around right there on the street, Johnny Boy yelling like a kid on a roller coaster.

I told Jim, "I think those two are lovers."

"You got to be wrong there, sport. Johnny Boy's a cinch with the ladies. They line right up for Johnny Boy, you know."

"What about Dave? Does he have a steady girl?"

Jim thought. "I expect he's married somewhere down south if you got the right state. Probably more than once if I know Dave. So what, though? Dave is not a guy to lay out his credentials for you. Dave is not afraid of what someone knows about him."

"Don't you think they're radically affectionate for . . . for . . ."

"Two straight guys?"

". . . right."

I hadn't come out to Jim, so I wasn't sure what terminology we were to use in this context. But he was.

"Those two boys are very close, I'll say that," he said. "They are very close. They love each other. But not fucking love. Friendship love. I've seen other guys like that. Something clicks off inside them, see. And like this one has this crazy sense of humor . . . and that one can get everything organized, which the other can't. And they just go right for each other, so they have someone to talk to, you know. To talk about things together and set aside the cares of the day. They think about each other all the time, too. But that doesn't mean they have to fuck together."

"We come from the same part of the world in the same era," I said. "The same *house,* not to put too fine a point on it. Yet I sound like a metropolitan *flâneur* and you sound like Zane Grey. How did that happen?"

He laughed. I don't know the answer myself and anyway this is not our story. But I am telling it. So let me put my oar in here: I had seen plenty of gay couples very much like Dave and Johnny Boy, usually hanging out on Sunday afternoons outside the Ramrod, their eyes dim after a long post-dancing love scene; or strolling the sand at the Grove to greet a lesbian couple and sit down on their blanket, the two women smiling at each other in memory of their own first years together. The cool man and the keen kid, that bracing union of grace and energy that means money in the straight world and love among gays. I tell you, I have seen gay couples exactly like

Dave and Johnny Boy—except if you had plunked those two down in our setting, outside the Ramrod or on the beach at Fire Island, they would have stood out like a cancan ensemble in Middle-earth. Of course, this is a difference of culture, not of sexuality. All those tales of tensely available truckers and butchers that I hear (a little too often) from my midwestern friends similarly takes in what you might call enemies of the parish. Still, were Dave and Johnny Boy uninhibited cutups or was something going on there?

So what is the story about?

I mean, was something going on that I should know of for future reference? (Like now.)

Let me tell you.

After Dave aimed the cat and petted it and told it to listen for mice, any time someone came through Jim's door that cat would run up and lay a dead mouse at his feet.

"Don't you ever run out of these?" I asked, stepping around the mouse to hand Jim the sweater he had asked me to bring back from our folks'. "What is this, Walt Disney's *Cinderella*?"

"This is cat heaven," said Jim, throwing the sweater at the couch.

Dave, holding a quart of Dewar's, caught it in the air. "I'll drink to that," he said. After taking a swig the size of the wave that obliterated Atlantis, he told me, "Tell Waterloo the cat how your book is coming."

"Fine."

"Hear that, Waterloo?"

"Fucking mice bodies," said Jim, kicking the latest one out into the hall.

Johnny Boy was still out—as Jim put it—tomcatting on Dave. That means that one of the girls who lined up for him had lucked in and Johnny Boy was bunking with her and only saw Dave by day on the site.

"Here's a nice sweater," said Dave, playing with it. "I could use me one of these some time when it gets cold. Where do you get them?"

"Any store," I told him.

"It's a fucking old used sweater," said Jim.

"Nice color," said Dave. "What color of shade is this?"

"Charcoal grey," I said.

"That is a real uptown shade for a sweater on the site, yo Jimbo?"

Then Dave looked at me because I was staring at him.

"What's on your mind, my friend?" he asked me.

What was on my mind was what this story is about, but before I could answer we heard a man scream in the hall. Jim pulled the door open, and there was one of his neighbors, in a vested suit and carrying an attaché. He blushed.

"I . . . I thought I saw a mouse," he announced.

"Well, now, that mouse belongs to Waterloo the cat," said Dave, coming up to the door.

The man said, "Thank you"—as upper-middle New Yorkers will when they don't know what just happened—and moved on.

"See, Waterloo," Dave asked it, "the cat?"

Waterloo, now guarding the kitchen with grim eyes and ruthless tail, didn't turn.

"Everybody out," said Jim. "I got a date coming."

Dave and I ambled the three blocks to my building, and I took him up onto the roof to watch the sun go down, Dave blithely chugging his Scotch.

"What are you planning to do with yourself?" he asked me, and I told him; and "What part of the south are you from?" I asked him, and he told me. There was some more of that, back and forth, then silence. Dave kept passing me the bottle, and I would take a sip, and he would take a slug. We were looking down on the street and up at the darkening sky, out of conversation with nowhere to go. But some men are comfortable having nothing to say or hear, and Dave was one of those.

I remember thinking then that I was twenty-five, and had thus far done nothing worth mentioning. I was going to have to do something about that.

We drank and listened to the town. Even on the hottest days there's a wonderful wind up on my roof, fifteen floors above the street.

Dave stretched and leaned against the railing, handing me the bottle. Blue T-shirt over a white T-shirt. He nodded at me very solemnly. "Johnny Boy'll be back soon," he said. "I can always tell, somehow."

I was a bit startled, and stuttered, saying, "It must be refreshing to have the place to yourself, though."

He thought about it. "I don't think it is," he said. "Because when he's there I always know where my morning coffee's coming from. Johnny Boy goes around the corner for it. He gets up before me, and does his shower, and then out he goes. So when I'm just coming out of the bathroom, he's got all the stuff set up. Buttered roll, you know, or a Danish. He likes to surprise me. And he gets all fussed about the sugars. I like to look over and see him fussing with the sugars for my cup of coffee."

I was staring at him again but he was looking away, didn't see.

"I like to have him around," he said. "Guess I'm just used to his ways."

I nodded.

"He has to do this now and again. The ladies just love that young lad and he feels obliged to respond. I've no quarrel with that. Every lad should have his day off."

He passed me the bottle.

"His day off," I asked, "from what?"

"From being serious. Thinking about how it feels."

"How what feels?"

He shrugged. "Your brother should be telling you, not me."

"How it feels to be really close friends?"

He looked evenly at me. "Well, we've grown to depend on each other. Is that what you'd call really close friends?"

I tried to pass him the bottle, but he went on, ignoring it.

"We can swing into this balance sometimes. You know? Swing right into it. Then it's hard to swing out again. Very hard to do that, very close friends.

Now, maybe I don't like to see him go off with the
ladies all the time, but he's got a right. He wants to
show me what he can do. Show himself, too. He
may well be there with some sugar right now. Right
as we speak, here. And he's pleasuring her so nice,
you know, just laying there, nothing doing but pleasure." He reached over and took the bottle from me.
"And he's thinking, What if someone could pleasure
me that way? If I was laying there. That's how it
starts, you know. I believe so. Who do I know could
pleasure me so? Who could I ask?" He hefted the
bottle and took a long one.

I was staring at him again, speechless. And he
nodded at me, and gestured in some odd way, and
smiled, and shook his head. See, you had to be
there; we need the visuals, the two T-shirts and the
bottle of Dewar's and the endlessly kind wisdom in
his eyes.

"So he asked you," I said.

Dave shook his head. "That's a tall order for a lad,
asking like so. I had to figure it out and help him
along. Mind, I was not needful to plow Johnny Boy
for myself. I started in to pleasuring him because it
was the best way to hold him, you know. And I was
needful to hold him, that's true. Needful of his
ways." He smiled. "Well," he said, and that gesture
again: Think nothing of it? Let's discuss? None of
the above? "Well . . . tell you the truth, I was not all
so sure how I was to proceed. I waited till we were
in bed one night, in that darkness, you know, with
the traffic going by, and sirens, and the sign lights
going on and off at the deli. And I got him to talking
about things, and one thing that we talked on led to

◆ 29 ◆

another thing. And finally I got to ask him to roll over for me, if he would be so kind, and he gave me no quarrel about it." Another swig of scotch. "He gave me no quarrel." He regarded me. "You know why?"

I shook my head.

"Because I believe my young lad Johnny Boy was brought here to be my buddy. My really close friend, like you're saying. And I was brought here to be his, you know." Another swig. "It sometimes happens. As long as you're very tender about it, everything is okeydokes."

I flashed just then on a wise old queen of my acquaintance who habitually hired street trash to perform his sex for him. Describing the comely clarity of one kid in particular, he said, "He's the sort of boy who was *put on earth* to wear a Mexican lace shirt and black Speedo shorts, and have them *ripped off him* by reckless *muscle* hunks!" I flashed on that, for some reason.

And I had been right about those two all along; I know everything. But that's not what the story's about, yet.

Dave shrugged. "What the hell," he said. "If that's what he wants. I just got to see him happy. And that's why he'll always come back. I got a hold on him." He extended the bottle. "Really close friends."

"What is it like when he comes back?" I asked, taking the scotch. "Is he embarrassed?"

"Hell, no! He comes in like a barn dance! Wants to tell me how it was."

"You don't mind that?"

"Mind?" He smiled. "He looks so happy talking about his ladies, now what kind of buddy would I be to mind?"

"Isn't there any. . . I mean, he walks out on you and then just—"

"He doesn't walk out on me, my friend the kid brother. He just takes a little side trip."

"Doesn't he do . . . I mean, just some punctuation . . ."

"Yeah, some punctuation here," Dave said, laughing.

". . . some token gesture, to say he's glad to see you?"

Dave was humming.

"To say he's back?"

"Well . . . he always shakes my hand." He nodded. "Does it real special, too. A long, solid shake like we just been through a war together. You know why? Because he knows, a way back of all this, that I liked what he was so I went after him. He knows. That'll occur from time to time, men going after lads like Johnny Boy. And he knows that the thing I went after him for isn't in the fucking. Do you know that? I'll tell you what it is."

This is what the story is about.

"It's in the feeling. The feeling that we have together." He passed me the bottle. "Like we're walking along the street about eveningtime there with a good dinner inside us, and we both know that when we get home we're going to talk things over and then I'm going to pleasure him, put a hold on my Johnny Boy. And nobody knows that but us. It's in

the feeling, because we know it and they don't.
See?"

"Yeah."

"That's why," he said. "Why one guy may just go
after another. For the feeling."

"Is anyone after Jim?" I asked. "That you know
of?"

"How much truth do you want, my young
friend?"

"How much have you got?"

"Listen." He set the bottle down. "What it is. You
got to be just a little afraid for someone to come after
you. That's the kind of thing it is. And Jimbo ain't
afraid of anything."

"That's his problem," I said.

He looked at me for quite some time.

"No, it ain't. It's just how he is. And I'm how I
am. And you. Like that, down the line." He kicked a
foot in between the railings, pulled himself up, and
gazed up at the sky, dark now, and the city heavy
below. We didn't speak for a while, and I heard the
darkness moving around us.

"He'll be home soon," said Dave. "I know that
much."

I thought of him aiming the cat for Jim, and talking to the man with the attaché in the hall.

"I know his ways."

I thought of the wise old queen gloating over the
stagey savaging of his gutter Ganymede, and of
Dave singing for Johnny Boy and talking with him to
set aside the cares of the day, and asking him to roll
over if he would be so kind.

"Shake his hand. Going to ask him how he feels."

I thought of my book contract, and the place of the visual in contemporary society. I thought of very close friendships, having a hold put on you. Then I thought of what I was planning to do with myself— but (as Immanuel Kant once said) every story is about love. It's in the feeling.

Dave finished off the bottle.

"Maybe tonight," he said.

"Johnny Boy," he said.

"To be home with me," he said.

"Coming home tonight now, don't you think?" he said.

"Dave, I wouldn't be at all surprised."

Do-It-Yourself S & M

■■■■■

WELL, THE BOYS AND I ARE
sitting around Dennis Savage's
place, talking S & M. As with most New
Yorkers, none of us is an expert but we all have firm
opinions. One of the group points out that while S &
M's rituals tend to the piquant, at least its platonic
essence favors devastating hunks. Another (whom I
have long suspected of harboring atrocious fantasies) observes that S & M has more sheer style
than alternate love modes, recalling for proof a
movie he saw in which a weight lifter made passion-
ately tender love to a bound boy and, at climax,
strangled him. A third is amused to note that S & M
originated gay's unique gift to the world, fisting—
the equivalent of Italy's opera and Finland's sauna.

Also on hand is a man I loathe, an activist who
lives and breathes Movement. But which one? He
isn't as much in favor of anything as he is against
everything. Besides, he is one of the least charismatic people I've ever met, the Fearless Leader as

schmengie; and shouldn't our heroes be men of style and vigor? Most social or political movements take their tone from the most admirable—at least the most striking—characters available. (Think of the champs and exemplars who instructed the spirit of '76—Washington, Jefferson, Adams, Franklin, Tom Paine.) Gay liberation is the only movement I can think of that often throws its worst people to the top.

Like this guy. In his veins flows dialectic, not blood; and when he talks love he means murder. Murder for you and love for him. After years of attacking that excrescence of gay life, Fire Island Pines, he finally decided to see it for himself. No sooner had he stepped off the ferry than he screamed that he had found Paradise and ran amok, chasing anything that moved. At the sight of his furiously hungry eyes, his K mart *pour le sport* attire, and his fish-white belly, the houseboys ran for their lives, locked themselves in their houses, and wouldn't reappear till the activist was back on the boat.

Of course, now that he's in the city, the activist has retrieved his cool, replete with abrasive, ecumenical putdowns and plans to rule the world. At Dennis Savage's, he outlined the utopian gay future, which included among other benefits "coupling by assignment," racial quotas for everything, and sumptuary laws beyond a Methodist minister's meanest dreams. Dennis Savage and I shared a profound look at this, but his other guests were blithely intrigued, for this was the mid-1970s, and we thought we had the world wired down. We took the activists about as seriously as we took Methodist ministers.

"Will we be able to put in for certain preferences?" the activist is asked.

"Yes," another agrees. "Like the ads: 'Applicant favors sizable S with full toy shop. Must be non-smoker and love screwball comedy.' "

"Smoking will be prohibited in any case," says the activist. "And screwball comedy is a sentimental fascism."

"Well, can I still have an S?"

Dennis Savage gets restive. This was not one of his better parties—short on connection but deep in lecture, a compound of closed systems, like a night of anonymous bathhouse encounters. Dennis Savage likes interlock, a density of communion and a streak of culture. Surveying this soiree of jerks, he becomes touchy, railing against everything like a sit-com mother-in-law. "S & M!" he scoffs. "It's a hoax. It's a mess of paradoxes."

He notes them, to murmurs of dissent, under the activist's beady eye: "S & M teaches us the ultimate hunk—doesn't it?—in those cartoons . . . Tom of Finland, Etienne, A. Jay. But let's look in the pages of *Drummer*, let's examine their real-life counterparts—skinny sillies scowling in a pantry! S & M assures us that its erotic transaction is the most intense in the gay world. Am I right? And what is it made of? Cheesy intimidation. Aggression. Name-calling. Is this love? Is this our revolution?"

The activist nods, smiling. It's sure news that the Movement won't tolerate S & M, comes the day. "And as for style," Dennis Savage continues, "it may be style to you, but all I see is dreary routine."

"You've never been there!" cried one of the group. "S & M is a frenzy! Why, people have killed each other in mid-session! You call that routine?"

"You must admit," said another, "that the S & M scene would make a wonderful movie."

"Actually," replied Dennis Savage, "I don't think it would make a competent Looney Tune."

Cries and whispers followed, then laughter, then the various exits, for it was getting on. The activist, however, showed no signs of leaving, and when he visited the bathroom—drink in hand, be it said—Dennis Savage held a war council.

"Help me get rid of him," he begged. "Throw a drink in his face or something."

"He's *your* guest, boyo."

"But he's after my bones!"

"So tell him to get lost."

He groaned. "You don't know these political types. They think it's homophobic to say no."

"Yeah. To *them*."

"I'll be your best friend," he pleaded, tautologically.

"Tell you what. I'll go down to my place and get my antique Hindu beheading sword. Out I go. You tell him I'm your jealous lover, and when I come back I'll charge him and he'll run out."

"What if he doesn't?" He grabbed my arm. "No, do it. It'll be fun, anyway."

I keep this curved sword, a present from my dad, hanging on my wall. It is carved in intaglio, long, dull, and mean. Sometimes I answer the door with it, held at the ready, and so I reentered Dennis Savage's apartment; but the activist had gone. Too bad. I was looking forward to playing the bravo.

"Boy, did he race out of here," Dennis Savage told me as I hunted down a last glass of wine. "I told him you're the most notorious S in the East Fifties."

"Did he believe you?" I asked, sipping and thrilled. "Maybe I should investigate the scene."

"I can see you getting into S & M. First, you'd assemble collateral reading matter, from Dante to William Burroughs. Then you'd make lists: The Ideology of S & M. The Iconography of S & M. The Ontology of S & M, above all, surely."

"Don't call me Shirley."

"Footnotes, anyone?"

I fondle the sword. "I believe I'll cut off your lips."

"Listen, there are only three questions to ask before getting into S & M, only three. One: How would I look in leather? Two: Am I willing to keep late hours—because, you know, S & M gives no matinees. Three: Am I the goon or the milquetoast?"

"I suspect you are a *trompe l'oeil* troll."

"That's all S & M is, really: costume, schedule, role. Is it compulsion? Liberation? Romance? No. What is it? Presentation."

"What isn't?" I ask.

"And you know why? Because there is no S & M. Everyone's an M. Everyone wants to be loved. *Possessed.* See? That is the dream of this presentation—'Take me away from all this. Take me out of myself! Rebear me into life!'"

"So there *is* an S in S & M, then—the bearer."

"Can you name?" he says, so wily. "Can you, now: a *genuine* S in the *world*?"

We have to rank out this cynic. Mind, race!

"Well?" he goes, so wry, so Ivy League.

I'm crazed. I can focus on nothing. I am back in seventh grade, when Mr. Van Santvoord swooped down on me crying, "Who kills Hamlet?" and I couldn't even recall who wrote it.

"Not a single name?" Dennis Savage taunts.

Yes, wait! "Mitch O'Connell."

"Mitch O'Connell is a sweetheart! He wouldn't squash a bug. And here I thought you would cite me some angry avatar . . ."

"S & M isn't about anger."

He waves this nonsense away. "Mitch is a lover, not a fighter. He dreams of April and tulips and scented encounters sealed with a puppy's kiss. Where do you get S & M in that?"

"S & M has love in it."

"Oh, sure. There's nothing as tender as a tit clamp. And cock weights are charity, loyalty. Yes! Yes!" he cries, like Fats Waller. "Push your beau down the stairs—it's true romance! Run him through the meat grinder—it's love, it's love!"

"In San Francisco, they would say that you sound like an old biddy who thinks there are fairies at the bottom of her garden."

"I happen to know that in your *whole life* you spent exactly ten days in San Francisco—most of them in record stores. So don't tell *me!*"

Well, it is true that no one would take Mitch O'Connell for an S at first acquaintance. He could perhaps play the role in some movie: dark, intense, taciturn. At times, he smoldered. But a collegiate spring in his ambitions typed him among the bourgeoisie, and the man was a flagrant romantic. He had It, but It wasn't easy to pin down, for he carried himself a bit off-kilter, as if he were trying to be blond, carefree, and gregarious. Still, he had *vast* shoulders and the boldest eyes ever seen, virtually navy blue. People kept looking at him; but he never looked back.

What did he want and what would he get? Well, you'll see.

But how did he find it? Through a natural mastery of S & M techniques.

And I don't mean as an M.

This will take us back to The Pines, summer of '73, when I rented a room for four weeks with, among others, Mitch O'Connell. The others came out only on weekends; I was temporarily permanent. Also in The Pines that month was my friend J. D. (for John David—he's a southerner, and you know those boys take their middle names everywhere they go). J. D. and I would sit on a bench in the harbor making fierce and facetious commentary as the boats pulled in. Friday afternoon was our gala, as the great and near-great collected, including our respective house-mates, who would greet us with city dish before trooping off to organize dinner, eat, nap, and dance. Those were the days, weren't they?

On this certain evening I wish to tell of, Mitch O'Connell arrived with an uncharacteristic aplomb. He was standing on the top deck of the ferry glow-ing, grinning, swaggering without having to move. He wore black running shorts and a gondolier's shirt and it seemed the whole boat was wondering who he was.

So were J. D. and I. "Is that Mitch O'Connell?" he asked. "He looks ten years younger or something!"

"He could be a movie star."

"He's dashing!"

"He's high as a kite on the—"

"He must be in love," J. D. whispered, and promptly clamped a fist in his mouth, amazed at the bitter beauty that stirs a sullen world. Bitter: for not all postulants are taken into the order.

"He is in love," I said, surprised that I hadn't realized it before. "He's in love with Bill Apgar."

"That little Californian boy?" J. D. drummed on his thighs in excitement. He loves a good story, as long as there's plenty of sex in it and a happy ending. "Lots of flash and no reality whatsoever," he once told me, describing the Perfect Party. But that's the way he likes everything. "Bill Apgar," he now observed, "is just right for Mitch O'Connell. He's *just right!*"

"Will you please stop hitting my arm?"

"Oh, think of them at beach parade tomorrow! Mitch's hulking, tempest-tossed dark ways next to the bright-eyed blondie boy! I *thoroughly approve* of this story!"

"If you hit me once more—"

"Look!"

At Mitch O'Connell, he meant, as Mitch disembarked. He gave us a frisky salute as he passed but did not stop to talk.

"Did you *see* that?" J. D. whispered, so loudly that some of the arriving passengers turned to stare at us. "Did you see how he *walked*? He was . . . *striding!*"

He was moving like the protagonist of the kind of

stories J. D. likes, like a man on a date with the love
of his life. Now everything fell into place. Bill Apgar
was also one of my housemates, and what I had
taken for weekend blather and roughhouse I suddenly saw as the outline of a heavy flirtation. As
Mitch vanished down the boardwalk, I told J. D. of
their pensive stares across the breakfast table, of
their moonlit walks, of how, when you came upon
them talking in the living room, you felt as if you
were barging in on the second act of a thriller. I told
how Mitch called Bill "Billy" (no one else did), as if
staking a claim on him; and how Bill reveled in the
nickname. It *was* love. But something was missing—
the happy ending, perhaps even the sex. Mitch's
eyes glared at times; Bill's wavered. They had
moved from the flirtation stage not into forthright
romance but some densely ambivalent mystery.

Two boats later, Bill himself arrived. Though he
was still in his early twenties, he had just sold a
screenplay for an unholy fortune, and his weekdays
were consumed with the doing of lunches and the
taking of meetings. He stopped to chat with us,
flushed and exhausted by success; I helpfully
hummed "The Lady's in Love With You," but no
one got it. Mitch was not mentioned.

"Do you think?" J. D. asked as Bill ambled off.
"Are they really and truly . . ."

"Lovers?"

J. D. screamed.

"Oddly enough," I said, "I doubt they've as much
as kissed."

"Is it *possible*?"

"Bill is afraid."

"Of what?"

Trying to verbalize an answer, I paused, and J. D. pummeled my arm again.

"Hey!"

"Of what?" J. D. repeated. "Of being fucked?"

"Maybe of being loved."

J. D. liked that at first; then it frightened him and he ran away. The story was getting too good: too much reality whatsoever.

Of course the setting itself, The Pines, only intensifies the passions of story, of any story. And The Pines, in the 1973 of no-fault sexuality, always tried to be as unreal, as fantastic, as possible. The heavy drug intake dulled the perspective, but the scenery, natural and human, beguiled and stimulated; and the recklessly appetitive prowling blew wide the vistas of Stonewall. How many thousands of men rode the ferry in those days believing, like Mitch O'Connell perhaps, that this would be the weekend that changed their lives?

It was nearly twilight. I lurked around the harbor some, pestered two housemates in the Pines Pantry till they asked me to go away, and finally passed on to the house, where I found Mitch and Billy wildly smooching on the couch like two frat brothers after a hell night.

Bill tried to leap up as I came in—he had had plenty of warning, given the noisy Pines decks—but Mitch held him fast. Stuck for a lead, I broke into a vocal of "The Lonely Goatherd" with creative dance steps. Bill struggled out of Mitch's grasp and put the dining table between them.

"I have nowhere to go," I told them. "My sidekick deserted me, my housemates threw me out of the grocery, and I'll lose my reputation if I'm found on the beach after sundown."

Mitch was moody, Bill all for company. He made me a Bloody Mary. He got out the cheese and crackers. He talked Hollywood and status games. He said they all play roles out there. Mitch said nothing. After a few minutes of this, I left: no place to go was better than that place just then. But Bill came running out after me.

"Please stay," he said.

"I'm not wanted."

"I want you. Anyway, this isn't the right moment for Mitch and me to be alone."

"Are you mad? Are you *wild*? You two had *Butterfield 8* working when I came in. What do you want, witnesses?"

He looked away. "No, yes, I . . . I just . . . did *you* ever . . ."

"Did I what?"

He took a deep breath. "It's overwhelming me. Why does it have to happen so fast?"

"He likes you. If you like him, say yes. If you don't, say no."

"Oh, it's that simple?"

"So far."

"You old grads of the Movement think the whole world boils down to whom you're going to sleep with tonight, don't you? Your whole revolution is nothing but sex. What about the other things in life?"

"They're all there. Our whole revolution is more comprehensive than you've been told. Whom have you been listening to? Some activist?"

He just looked at me.

"Activists don't make the revolution," I told him. "We do. *Chacun à son gout.*"

"Would you please come back in there and tell that to Mitch?"

"You're a nice kid. I wish you success in love, a great career, and a fast metabolism. But when it comes to kids, I prefer to seduce and abandon, not give courtship counseling. So huh?"

He thought, nodded, and started back inside.

I grabbed his arm. "I'm sorry. But don't call me old. And let me tell you something. No one can help you out in something like this. It's your story; you write it. Besides . . . generally it *is* simply a question of you like him or you don't. Yes or no."

Just then the rest of the house came rollicking down the boardwalk with the weekend provisions and we all repaired inside for a Fire Island cocktails, cooking, and dinner session, rich with subtext. After a while, Mitch stopped sulking and opened up some; by the third round of vodka he was giddy, making grimly robust jokes and sticking very, very close to Bill. I wondered how much of this was getting through to the others. They were not a particularly observant bunch, but let's face it, this was theatre. Still, much of gay life is theatre. Much of life, period.

Bill's performance seemed somewhat undirected. He was sort of unhappily amiable, possibly dreading the hour when the rest of us would go dancing and he would be left alone with Mitch for Act Three.

But two things happened. First, Bill got up during dessert, said he had to go visiting, and left. Second, Mitch went into his room without a word. And he was *mad*.

By then, everyone knew something about it. Everyone looked at everyone else and wondered. But The Life goes on, and what everyone mainly did was get into dancing uniform. It was plain that year: the basic white T-shirt and your second-best jeans. An early entrance into the dance hall was also favored that summer, at least by my housemates, serious dancers rather than event-attenders, who tend to arrive very late and thus Make an Entrance.

So off we went, clump after clump of us sneakering along the firm sand near the waterline in the midnight darkness, sure of ourselves, confident of our freedom. Why not? It looked easy then. Every so often, however, it felt hard to live up to the demands of that avidly bewitching style. It felt less like freedom, more like a mission. That night, I impulsively turned back on the verge of the Grove; The Life was too much with me. My housemates scarcely noticed, for I had been dragging behind them. Oh, perhaps for quite some time, in all—more than even I knew. Another tune I could most appropriately have broken into was "There's Gotta Be Something Better Than This."

I, too, dreaded having to play a scene with Mitch, and I paused outside our house, though all the lights were out. I virtually crept up our walk, scuttled into my room, and eased onto my bed, my head spinning from the predinner drinking. I lay there, pondering, organizing, making lists in my head.

Then it happened.

Footsteps on the deck. Lights on. Something's moving. Pause. More movement from somewhere deep in the house. Then:

"I'm glad you're here." Bill.

"And I'm glad you're here." Mitch.

"Are . . . are you sore at me?"

"No." Thoughtful. "No, Billy, I'm not sore at you."

"You sound . . . Aren't you cold without a shirt?" Indefinable noises.

"Why are you putting a chair against the door?" Bill.

"So you can't get away."

Silence. I should say something, no? I could stir, or cough. I could sing the rest of "The Lonely Goatherd," perhaps launch into "An Ordinary Couple." But I never liked that one.

"Please don't be hard with me, Mitch. It's not what you think. I had to—"

"What do I think?"

"I wanted to go over it in my mind. See—"

"What do I think, Billy?"

"Can we talk about it? I didn't go visiting. I took a walk. Now I . . . I came back to tell you something. Don't be hard, now, okay?"

"Too late. You came back too late. I've been doing some thinking, too. Come here, Billy."

"Okay, except you . . . you look . . . hard . . ."

"There's a good reason for that."

"What . . . what are you going to do? Just tell me, okay?"

"I'm going to beat you up."

Nothing. Then Bill: "Any special reason why?"

"Did you hear me say 'come here' to you?"

I imagined J. D. asking, "What were they *wearing*?" and I ached to look, but I didn't dare move. Would you rush the stage to interfere with the actors' business?

"Mitch, you have every right to be sore, but if you just listen to— No, Mitch, wait!"

At a horse race you can leap and yell. Watching television you can make remarks. If the dam bursts you can run. I had to sit there motionless through these excruciating silences, eyeless in Babylon.

"Please listen to me!"

"You have this coming, so just take it nice and easy. You're such a cute little kid, aren't you? So beatable, now. So right." Scraping noises. Something heavy. Was Mitch moving the table? "Nothing you can do about it, Billy. Come here to me now."

"Mitch!"

"Billy . . ."

A chair went over.

"Oh, Mitch, please—

"Here we go now, Billy."

"Stop using my name! You . . . you said you wanted to be my friend!"

The table again.

"Just let me get my hands on you and I'll show you what a friend I can be."

That's what Bill's been afraid of all along, I

thought. But this was not the ideal time for a psychoanalytic reading of the case. Bill was sobbing. "Why are you hurting my feelings?" he wailed. Because you hurt his, I noted silently. "I wanted you to like me. Don't . . . not like this, Mitch, please!"

Oh? Some other way would be acceptable? He's tormenting you and you're loving it; so whom do I root for?

Bill spoke again, suddenly calm: "You don't have to move any more furniture. I'm going to come over to you and I'll . . . you can do what you want to me. I just wish you'd hear me out first. Then if you want to hurt me, you can. I can't stop you, anyway. You can wait a few minutes. Okay, Mitch? Okay?"

Silence. Was Bill "coming over"? Who in this scene is the bearer into life?

"You peeked, didn't you?" said Dennis Savage, when I told him the tale. "This is where you peeked."

Peeked? I was afraid to breathe. I was also consumed with admiration for this couple's instincts for S & M stylistics. No training, no arrangements, no practice. Just get in there and do it. Now Bill was whispering to Mitch. Damn! Key dish forever lost. Clearly, he *was* afraid of something, and Mitch demanded that he not be for the sake of romance—and if that isn't S & M, I don't know what is. In the gay utopia, when we couple by assignment, we'll be at the mercy of the activists. But for now we can always get locked in a room with Mitch O'Connell.

"I'll do anything you want."

Which of them said that? I was so rapt in thought

that I didn't hear this till it was an echo in the air, and I could no longer place the voice.

"*Now* you peeked," says Dennis Savage.

"No. I lay doggo, guilty, thrilled. *Who* will do anything? Only a gay. Wives won't swallow; husbands won't spank. But a gay who Won't loses love. What difference who actually said it? We all say it, or hope to. Bill was sobbing again; his sobs filled the house. Enough. Out I came, sweater in hand.

They were standing in the middle of the room, swaying in each other's arms, heart to heart. I doubt they were even aware that I passed them. I walked onto the black beach and fretted.

"That's your idea of S & M?" Dennis Savage asks. "Two cream puffs kissing?"

"On one hand," I tell him, "I'm concerned about your health. On the other hand, how do I know this antique Hindu beheading sword works till I chop-test it on your neck?"

"Now, that's S & M," he avers. "There it is: talk. Just talk."

"You think Mitch wouldn't have given Bill a beating if the kid didn't know how to handle him?"

We'll never know. Walking along the water's edge that night, I thought that everything I'd heard of S & M paled before the confrontation of Mitch and Bill. It was the *measured* nature of their text that got me, the calculation of anger and fear and need, the ritually repeated "Billy" and the maneuvering of roles, each an aggressor and a victim at once. But then that's one of the things that makes gay romance unique:

two bearers, in place of straight's bearer and receiver. Perhaps it was the incongruity of Mitch's attack that most impressed me, the dense love mixed into the violence. Or maybe it was because I couldn't *see* it; maybe S & M is never as good as it sounds.

Out on the sand that night, reviewing the event, I decided that I knew nothing of S & M. But I know hot dish when I have it. I ran off to J. D.'s house to share it. His mates were advocates of the late entrance and were still engaged in working out a fastidious improvisation of costume. J. D. was all set to go, in a cowboy's shirt, a fisherman's sweater, and a painter's pants. "Who are you?" I would have said, but before I had a chance to, he cried, "What were they *wearing*?" Costume, schedule, role.

"Jeans," I told him. "Bill was in one of those washed-out Lacostes he always wears. Mitch had—"

"And were they . . ."

"What?"

"For the first time? The last time?"

"This could be the start of something big."

Waiting for his housemates to assemble and depart, he was getting in a last-minute munch. The two of us looked up to admire them as they came out of their rooms, plumed and painted like Regency rakes.

"I'm going to dance for my life tonight," said one of them.

J. D. ate some peanut butter off a knife. "What if Mitch had . . . done it?" he said.

"Done what?" asked another housemate, adjusting his cap in a mirror; he was going as an American sailor.

"Beaten up his boyfriend," I said.

"Making up is hard to do," the sailor replied; the thought seemed to come easy to him.

"What happens to them now?" J. D. asked.

"Plenty of sex, I expect, and a happy ending."

Ecstatically floored, he was silent.

"All right," one of his housemates called out, "let's *get* there!"

"Let's *show* them!"

"We're going to *do this thing!*"

I couldn't go back to my house, so I decided I'd better go dancing after all. As we walked, J. D. was silent at first; then he hit me for more details of Mitch and . . . Billy.

"When you came out . . . who was. . . ?"

"Both."

He sucked in his breath. "And was it. . . ?"

"To die," I told him. "To *die.*"

"But after you left . . . do you really think they. . . ?"

I shrugged. "It was the moment, wasn't it?"

"Don't you wish?" he murmured. Then he turned to the ocean and screamed at the top of his lungs, "Don't you *wish?*"

I speak fluent gay, but I swear sometimes I haven't the vaguest idea what we're saying to each other.

The Ghost of Champ McQuest

━▞▞▞▞▞━

> *Faithful, indeed, is the spirit*
> *that remembers*
> *After such years of change*
> *and suffering!*
>
> —*Emily Brontë,*
> *"Remembrance," 1846*

DENNIS SAVAGE GROANED when I told him I had invited Tom Adverse for a midweek overnighter at our Pines house.

"That dreary lump!"

"He'll repair the decking for us and blot up the leaks in the roof. And I'll bet he can fix the upstairs john so we don't have to jiggle it every—"

"He has the eyes . . ." Dennis Savage begins wearily, his head all a-shake, *must* he explain, *why* will I never see reason? "The eyes," he repeats, "of those psychotic hustlers who keep tuning out and going blank on you because as long as they hold you at a distance you don't really seem human. So they don't have to feel conflicted when they pull out the knife to kill the faggot."

"Tom isn't dangerous around gays. He only gets into fights with straight men. And women, sometimes. I mean—"

"Where do you find them?"

"You introduced me to him. You said he gives a great massage."

That stops him. Ah, he remembers, nods. "A great massage, yes. Except for the jokes he tells over your shoulder. 'How many niggers does it take to start a Cadillac?'"

"He's got a racist, reactionary, and intolerant streak that is extremely unappealing, I admit. But what else would he be? He comes from a small town in North Carolina, goes right into the Marines after high school, survives Vietnam, supports himself by oddjobbing from hustling to housepainting, and spends his off hours failing to understand women and fending off their jealous boyfriends in bars. You must admit, it's a fascinating tale. He can't enjoy what he should have and he doesn't want anything else. He's all puzzled up."

"He's a vicious loon," says Dennis Savage.

"No. He's a big, sexy, kind man who's had a lot of bad breaks. *And* he's the only straight anyone ever met who had such a bad time in his world that he only feels comfortable in ours. If there were such a thing as homophilia, he'd get a medal for it. Don't you agree?"

"He's a lurid baboon," says Dennis Savage.

"Come on, he's a good guy."

"A *good guy*? He's so wacko, they're thinking of changing the word 'crazy' to his name!"

"They were getting up a list of the five most intolerant people in the history of the world. They had Hitler, Savonarola, Nero, Pope George Ringo I—and in fifth place, it was a toss-up between Caligula and you."

"He's a demented bore," says Dennis Savage.

More precisely, Tom Adverse was the Cherry Grove Carpenter, for those of you who con the folklore back into the early 1970s. Hammering and sawing away on roofs and decks in direly cut-off jeans, Tom Adverse was not only an amenity of the gay part of Fire Island but a regular stop on the new-comer's tour. Day-trippers to The Pines couldn't call their visit official till they had marched over the sands to scan the Cherry Grove Carpenter.

And scan they must, for Tom was truly a sight, dev-astating at first glance and mesmerizing on reconnais-sance. Still, he can't have been enjoying himself. He posed for mail-order porn, yet he was reportedly un-available. He did give massages, in those same car-penter's cutoffs, yet they were just that: massages. He had the winged shoulders, louche navel, and ruthless nipples of the absolute dreamboy, yet he had no atti-tude, no fire, no certainty of self. He palled around with quick, fierce gays, yet to most questions he gave dead eyes and said, tonelessly, "Uh-huh." There were a lot of things he didn't like to talk about. He preferred to play tambourine while the gay boys danced. The whole place drank him in; he didn't seem to notice.

Then he tried porn posing, strictly for the money: but look at his eyes in those pictures. They're sad. The only sad eyes I've ever seen in porn, a sorry hot.

So what did he love? Carpentry. Painting. Making and repairing. He felt alive in such work, placed, needed. Posing in the nude was giving too much away, at that to strangers who would plunder him of something he didn't know he had. Building and fixing was good work, doing oneself proud. And his rural right-wing style wasn't all racist jokes and Rambo politics. Once I was talking to him at the Pines ferry when a vastly noted New York fashion designer vastly noted Tom and approached with an offer. Normally this very wealthy and influential personage had only to ring out his name for men of all sizes to fall in with his schemes. Tom just looked at him.

"I know who you are," he said calmly. "You get young kids out here who don't know any better and you give them drugs to warp their heads around. Then you mess them up with sex stuff. So you can get away from me before I teach you one good lesson."

The fashion designer could indeed get away, and very immediately did.

Never till remember rest you will I.

*—allegedly recorded
during a "spiritual visitation,"
Denver, 1962.*

I suppose Dennis Savage was right to question Tom's suitability as a guest in our house, with his uh-huh and dead looks. But it was an odd house to begin with, known as Chinatown for no reason that anyone could name, and, this summer, veritably full of unsuitables—Lionel, for instance, one of my best friends but entirely too intelligent for anyone's good. Some people get 800 on their physics boards; Lionel got the Nobel Peace Prize. It was Lionel's resolute caprice to be attracted only to the dimmest, most impenetrable men. "I'm in love with that number," he would murmur in a bar. "He looks so *stoopid.*" Lionel's number of the hour was Bert, so stoopid he spoke like a Valley Girl. When you first met him, you assumed he was doing a Valley Girl imitation. No, he simply spoke like a Valley Girl. I found it amusing, though it drove Dennis Savage crazy.

It was 1979. I had just turned thirty and was only now seriously considering the prospect of Growing Older, with all the loss and vitiation that it promises; today, of course, I look back on this time as my salad days. Dennis Savage's lover, Little Kiwi, had joined us but recently (alas, with his incalculably batty dog, Bauhaus), our supreme hunk-in-residence, Carlo, was still fancy-free and keen with dish on the giddy ways of the Circuit, and we all knew we hadn't yet learned everything there is to learn. We were young. We were healthy. We were having a grand time. The only person I knew of in our generation who had died was Jeff Willis, of my class at Friends Academy, killed in a car accident in his freshman year at Duke.

It is a quirk of the Island that while all houses in Cherry Grove run on the same rhythm—i.e., retirement torpor—each Pines house sets a unique pace. Some are as Arranged as Neapolitan marriages, others rather libertarian, some crowded with berserk guests, others strictly limited to the shareholders. Ours, set up by Dennis Savage, was classic Pines, slow to start in the morning, thinly lively by lunch, building to a heavily socialized dinner. However, there we diverged from the norm, which called for naps, drugging up, and the walk along the beach to dance at the Ice Palace. Lionel, Bert, and Carlo danced, but without artificial stimulation; and the rest of us usually hung around for games and assorted nonsense. Dennis Savage and I were playing out a craze for the old word game Jotto, and Little Kiwi was obsessed with mastering the Polaroid camera Dennis Savage had bought him, and with the construction of plastic models of dinosaurs, a group of which he had set up on the little table out on the deck, dubbed The Wonderful Museum of Terror Lizards. Never one to waste a passion, Little Kiwi would inveigle drop-ins and bystanders into posing with his models so he could photograph them.

Tom Adverse fit into our routine with his typical lifeless aplomb. "I could buff this," he would observe, running his hand pensively, caressingly, over the faded paint on the deck railing, or—looking over the kitchen end of the living room—"You ought to let me put in one of those spigots that come out with instant boiling water."

Cooking was another of his fields. Apparently he fended off gay hunger by busying himself with kitchen matters—it gave him a chance to turn his back, politely, on the roiling, wishful needs of men he could like but never love. Thus, hearing Dennis Savage, Lionel, and me arguing over whose turn it was to prepare dinner, Tom said, "Well, you know I could fix some four-happiness rice pastry for dessert."

Whereupon Little Kiwi snapped his picture.

"Do you like four-happiness rice pastry?" he asked Little Kiwi.

"Mostly I just know Rice Krinkles."

"Uh-huh," said Tom, not as much replying as punctuating the exchange.

Vietnam was another of Tom's topics, though the subject seldom came up in the house. Not that that mattered, since Tom never heard what anyone was saying in the first place. His every utterance was an outburst, a non sequitur, a frame without the picture. You would come upon him hammering away at something on the deck. You would offer a pleasantry or two about nothing in particular. And he would look up from his work and say, "On a scale of one to ten, I give *Apocalypse Now* a four."

Little Kiwi enjoyed Tom's line of speech for its sheer surprise. But after a while even he began eyeing Tom askance, because no matter how much you put in, nothing ever came out. I truly believe Tom was starved for friendship, grateful for any attention (as long as it didn't bear a sexual price tag), literally *relieved* to be asked among us. Yet he seemed unable to respond to people, almost preschizoid in his absentee companionship. So Tom fit in as he always did: by not fitting in. It's hard to complain about a man that terrific looking (though Dennis Savage found a way), and he did make himself useful around the house, tinkering and repairing. Besides, trying to cheer Tom up, to make him feel *connected*, was my good deed for the week.

Everyone helped, except Tom. The more welcoming you behaved, the weirder he got. Coming downstairs in the bright midmorning after his first night with us, he went right to the kitchen to make breakfast for the house.

"Carlo will love this," I said, noting the full complement of eggs, bacon, toast, three kinds of jam, and coffee that Tom was whipping up. He was even heating the milk. "One thing Carlo believes in is the full dinner pail."

"Uh-huh," says Tom. "I saw a ghost last night."

"A . . . ghost?"

"That's right."

And he goes right on with his work.

"A real ghost?" I pursued.

"I don't know how one of those things would be real or not," he replied, setting up the plates. "But it was a ghost."

He ladled out the food and brought two heaping plates outside. I took the milk and coffee.

"How do you say 'Come and get it' around here?" he asked me.

I shrugged. "Everyone just shows up, sooner or later."

He nodded. Hot food, cold food; nothing matters.

"So," I said, working on the imported roughcut Scotch lemon marmalade, a house gift from earlier in the season, so New York and hip and A-list, so sovereign of style and playful of taste. Tom, across the table, munched his toast naked. The toast was naked, too. "So, Tom, what about this ghost?"

"Yeah."

"I mean, was it . . . wearing a sheet?"

"What're these funny animals for?"

"That's Little Kiwi's Wonderful Museum of—"

"I could paint these deck things for you. Put some orange and navy blue on these chairs, so you'll stand out from the other places here. Hot boys looking up from the water during the beach parade after lunch, they'll want to be a part of this."

Note that Tom knew and was totally comfortable with the ways of the Circuit—the only straight I've known who was. All of the few nonhomophobic straights of my acquaintance would just as soon not hear about The Life in too much detail. Some faces go white at the very mention of the word "popper." You could describe the ins and outs of a Colt orgy to Tom, down to the last balling in and creaming out, and all he'd say is "Yeah."

Dennis Savage found that odd. "Doesn't this guy ever date?" he asked. "I can buy that he's happy around gay men, for whatever virtually unbelievable reason. But if he's really straight, shouldn't there be a woman in the picture somewhere?"

"There have been several. But there's always trouble, somehow. They break up pretty fast."

We had been cleaning out the pantry. He took me by the arm, led me to the couch, sat me down, and joined me.

"Tell," he said.

"No, because you're just looking for holes to poke into his story."

"Nay, I merely love to hear you make icons of various deadbeats and zanies just because you like their looks. First there's Carlo, your typical do-nothing Circuit joyrider, building a life entirely

around the next meal, the next lay, and the next unemployment check. There are hundreds like him
around here. I could buy a party of them for pin
money. But no, after you get through recreating
him, Carlo is our King Arthur, our Gandalf, our Little Boy Blue, isn't he? Our oracle! Our *guru*! And
then we have . . . *Tom*!"

Who was standing at the doorway to the deck,
now sporting the famous cutoff jeans, his face its
usual blank. "I was going to fix lunch," he said.
"Some chickens in the fridge. Could you stand to
take them barbecue, or were you saving them for
some other deal?"

"No, chicken is fine."

"Build a fire," he said, backing up, "out here on
the—"

"Just don't step on my diplodocus," came Little
Kiwi's voice, along with the click of the Polaroid.
"Bauhaus, let's make some more candids."

Bauhaus barked.

"Oooh rillly," said Lionel's boyfriend Bert, coming
up from the beach with Lionel. "Prehistoric *Cit-ty*!"

"Lionel, could you please stand there a second so
I can take your picture? No, closer to the bron-
tosaurus."

"Like *tot-tal* behemoth," Bert observed, coming inside.

"Bert almost killed a palaeosaur," Lionel announced.

"Nöe, I did-dn't," as they swept through the
house.

Carlo came down and sat on the couch with us.

"Everything's happening at once," he said, grin-

ning. "This place is full of loving, dancing gentlemen trying to figure what they're supposed to be
doing with their own history."

"The first ten years of Stonewall," I crowed to
Dennis Savage, "in a sentence!"

"I'll get you later," he said, rising.

"Crazy house," said Carlo.

"Look out for my iguanodon," Little Kiwi cried
from outside.

"Saw something odd here last night," said Carlo.
"Upstairs there. Wonder if you saw it ever."

"If I had to cite all the odd things I've seen in
Pines houses over the years . . . You know, this is
one of the Island's historic sites. It's had everything
from visiting movie stars to a suicide."

"Yeah, well, now it's got a ghost, too. You know
what I mean?"

"Uh-oh."

"Or what should I call it? Something creepy coming around at night. Unless the kid himself there is
doing tricks with his camera."

"What exactly did you see?"

He thought about it. "Kind of hard to say it exactly. It's more of a feeling that something's there
than a sight to see. There's some light to it, sort of,
like a million tiny candles moving together. And you
hear something, like very slow words. Like different
people taking turns on a sentence. Couldn't quite
make it out."

"You weren't afraid?"

"Happens too fast to be afraid. Got up to take a
whizz and this thing comes down the hall, right past

me. I just wondered if anyone else has checked in with you on this matter ever."

"Oddly enough . . . uh, this couldn't by any chance be some elaborate joke, could it? I mean, I love the million tiny candles and the sound effects are intriguing, but you realize of course that there are no such things as ghosts."

Carlo smiled. "I always think so. But I did see something last night in this house like I'm telling you about."

"Tom said something about a ghost, too. I just thought maybe you and he . . ." Carlo and I looked out through the sliding doors giving onto the deck, where Little Kiwi was holding forth on the size of the teeth in the stegosaurus, demonstrating on his model as Tom blankly stared, socially detained but emotionally touring, off on a tear among his private demons. "No," I said, "that's impossible. Tom is incapable of making anything up. What he is is what you get."

Carlo shook his head. "He's hiding plenty of stuff. Rough stuff inside there. He only shows you the smooth."

"Oh, certainly. I just mean that he can't create anything. There's no art in Tom Adverse."

"Forty years old," Carlo mused, "and he's still got a twenty-eight-inch waist. How does a guy that fine-looking get so wrecked inside?"

Tom suddenly wandered in—he's vague but he's abrupt—to ask where the charcoal was. Carlo had an appointment in another house, Lionel and Bert went back to the beach, Little Kiwi came inside to try "some shadow poses," and so the house reshuffled its hands, set up for the next play as surely as the stage of a repertory theatre. I could say that I was so busy with one thing and another (not to mention the Jotto championship, which Dennis Savage and I played as if for our lives) that I didn't bother with the ghost reports. I could say that. But then, how does one cope with ghost reports in the first place? What agency does one alert? What steps can one take on one's own?

Besides, there are no ghosts. There are only scientific explanations for alleged sightings. I reckoned the explanation would come along in due course, so I thought no more of the matter till late that night.

I had been putting together a party tape out of an antique miscellany—the overture to *The Boy Friend*, dated ballads by Bing Crosby, Julie Andrews, Diahann Carroll, and Danny Meehan, the Warner Brothers symphonies of Erich Korngold, a bit of *My Fair Lady* in Swedish, and so on, the whole tracked over with dialogue from old movies. I made such tapes for a living when I first came to New York, and though I had long retired from the field, I occasionally revved something up for an old friend, for the fun of it. When I began, this night, I was surrounded by company, because a thunderstorm had struck and dancing was out. Lionel was playing cribbage with Dennis Savage and (for narrative honesty demands a fair report) was wiping up the floor with him. Bert was getting his culture in, catching up on some old *Target* magazines someone had left behind. Little Kiwi was constructing a triceratops. Carlo was assisting Little Kiwi. Tom was sitting quietly in his usual daze.

Even a sixty-minute tape can take hours to complete, what with the split-second expertise needed to splice a conniption from Joan Crawford in her *Mildred Pierce* period into, if possible, Judy Garland's "Over the Rainbow," or to jump from Ella Fitzgerald's "No Strings" into Fred Astaire's in midchorus without cheating the beat. So, long before I was finished, the company had begun to scatter to their beds, and by the time I hit the finale—Bobby Short's "I'll See You Again"—only Carlo was left, idly rummaging through the *Target* books to see if he could find someone he hadn't had.

Time for a little talk.

"Carlo," I said, in the murmur of late-night Pines for the dishing of persons but inches away, "do you think Tom is straight?"

"He surely is. But he's nice, for a gringo."

"You don't find an interior contradiction in a Pines-loving, massage-giving, former porn-posing man who doesn't date women and doesn't know men?"

Carlo shrugged. "There's contradictions all over the place. Who's *not* a contradiction, when you look close enough?"

"You aren't. I'm not."

He grinned. "Ain't we got fun?"

"Did you ever run into Tom along the Circuit?"

"Sure. He's been around about as long as any of us."

"Well, did you ever try to set something up?"

He shook his head. "You look at a guy like that and you think, Hey, that's damn hot cake, now how about a slice? But wait a bit here. Never saw a man

◆ 66 ◆

could talk to you for so long without knowing you're there. His quarter's twenty cents short, right? A smart guy would not want to take that on."

"He doesn't really seem dangerous, though, does he? I mean, he's strangely vacant, all right, but—"

"No, I catch that story. I truly do. See a tough guy like that who's kind of wounded and trying to be likable, and you think, I bet there's some real tender inside him, if only I could reach it. What a lover he'd make then, right? Is that the story? Some guys really go for that. So I'll tell you—don't go messing around looking for tender in Tom Adverse to strike that vein in there. Like what I told you before about the rough and smooth—you ain't going to hit gold. You'll bust a volcano."

In slow motion, whispering, he imitated an eruption; and went to bed.

Taping had energized me too much to consider sleeping. I took a walk along the beach, did some reading, and made myself a sandwich. I was halfway through it when Lionel came down. Besides dating idiots, he also mystifies his friends by wearing very questionable outfits. At the moment, he had on a white karate gi over an elaborate jockstrap of hempen webbing, the kind of thing you normally only encountered in the fashion layouts in *After Dark*. Lionel was also, at the moment, very shaken.

"What's wrong?" I asked.

He held out a hand: wait, let me collect my thoughts, choose my words. He kept pacing and looking upstairs.

"Lovers' tiff?" I asked.

"No, I . . . I don't know how to express this. You'll . . . will you promise to take me seriously?"

A thought struck me. "You saw a ghost, right?" He stared at me.

"When Tom was the only one who saw it," I went on, "I dismissed it as Tom in a Mood. When Carlo joined in, I must admit, it was disquieting. But what the hell, what the hell. Now I *know* it's a joke! So call the pranksters downstairs and let's do a little giggling and pushing while—"

"Please don't humor me," he said. "This is not a joke and I'm not giggling. I saw something . . . phenomenological."

Now I stared at him.

"Surely not," I said.

He took another look upstairs, then sat on the couch. "I saw something," he insisted.

"Was it like a lot of little candles? Did it sound like—"

"It was silent. A sort of metaplasmic laser beam with shapes inside it . . . bumpy and . . . spinning . . ."

I know Lionel well enough to tell when he's joking around. He wasn't.

"You realize," I reminded him, "that ghosts do not exist. You realize that."

He nodded.

"I mean, there's no Santa Claus, no Shroud of Turin, and no ghosts. Right?"

He nodded.

"So—"

Bert came down the stairs so quickly he virtually leaped into Lionel's lap.

"Oooh," Bert gasped. "Like *tot-tal-ly* haunted!"

> *But, for the unquiet heart and brain*
> *A use in measured language lies;*
> *The sad mechanic exercise,*
> *Like dull narcotics numbing pain.*

—*Alfred Tennyson*,
In Memoriam, 1850

Lionel and Bert refused to go back upstairs that night, so I stayed with them, talking till all three of us fell asleep. The rest of the house was up early, and they found us strewn about the living room like dummies in the set of a war movie. So there was giggling and poking till Lionel spilled his story. Then Carlo chimed in with *his* sighting; and now the ghost became the house topic.

Dennis Savage, like me a fervent unbeliever, scoffed. But Little Kiwi immediately organized himself and Bauhaus into the Ghost Patrol and went around the house all day wearing a clove of garlic, a cross, and his Polaroid. He even made up business cards to hand out. "Remember our motto," he'd add:

> Ghost Patrol will come and so
> All the ghosts just have to go.

"You can start in my room," Lionel told him.

"Anyone who believes in this rubbish," Dennis

Savage announced from the kitchen, "gets no break-fast."

"Carlo," said Little Kiwi, "did you really see a ghost?"

"Well, I truly hell saw something."

The weather had cleared nicely, and from over-head came the noises of Tom Adverse, hammering and whistling as he patched the leaky roof.

"Rillly," observed Bert. "Why don't you get The Twisted Macho Man to like mǎybê for exam-mple scare it a–*way*?"

"Tom?" I said. "He's sort of a ghost himself."

"Oooh, *bark* me into the ca-*loset*."

"Don't worry," said Little Kiwi, adjusting his garlic. "The Ghost Patrol will exterminate this house. Remember our motto—"

"If you don't stop that," Dennis Savage began; but Little Kiwi put a finger on Dennis Savage's lips and made him blush.

"I play him," Little Kiwi told us, "like a stereo."

After breakfast, while Lionel considered com-pleting the weekend in some quieter establishment and Dennis Savage accused him of giving way to bad dreams and California brain meltdown ("Oooh, gag me," said Bert), I went outside to check up on Tom.

"How're we doing?" I called up to Tom, happily ensconced on high amid the sᵧmbols of his calling, the affable eructations of the toolbox.

"Almost done here. I'm taking it easy awhile."

"How'd you get up there without a ladder?"

"Climbed up," he said, holding out a hand to me.

If he can, I can, I told myself, pushing off the front-deck railing to join him.

"It's great up here," he told me. "You can see clear to five counties." He laughed. Another thing about Tom is that while he has a sense of humor, it's invariably the wrong one. I think he tells those atrocious racist jokes not because he believes they're funny but because he wants to see how you'll react to his having made you listen to them. Denounce his morals and he'll go Uh-huh. But if you sell out a little and forgive him with a doubting smile as you shake your head, he'll put a hand on your shoulder or chest very lightly, one of those almost meaninglessly nuanced demonstrations straights make with each other.

I think they're all starved for fun.

"Just let me finish up here," Tom said, taking a swallow of the beer he chugs while he's working, "and you'll be dry for life."

"You know, the rest of the house has been seeing what you saw. The ghost. It's . . . uncanny. I've known people who believed in ghosts, but I never knew anyone who claimed to have seen one."

"Uh-huh."

"Tom?"

"Yeah?" Smearing the tar, casing out a shingle, lining it up.

"What do you think we should do about this? I mean, some of us apparently aren't comfortable sharing quarters with . . . Well, if it were mice we could trap them. But what do we do with a visitation?"

He nods. Nails in his mouth. Hammer. One side, other side, step by step. Start a thing. Finish it.

"Tom?"

He lays in the last shingle, dumps the can of nails into the toolbox, toys with the hammer.

"I know who it is," he tells me. Why not? He doesn't care what I think. "Visiting at night here? I used to know him."

"Hey!" Little Kiwi called up to us from the poison ivy and tundra that holds the Island together between foundations. "Have you seen any ghouls around here? Bauhaus and I are the Ghost Patrol."

"Hey, Little," Tom called down. The notion of a fully grown (if boyish) man named Little Kiwi was more than he could accept. At first, Tom called Little Kiwi nothing, then compromised on the first half of his name, solo. No one, including Little Kiwi, seemed to notice. "Hey, come on up here with us."

"There's no stairs."

"Chunk up on the fence there and we'll pull you along."

"Hey, this is great," Little Kiwi ventured after Tom had helped him up. "The Ghost Patrol can really do a lookout up here."

"You can see clear to five counties," said Tom.

Little Kiwi laughed.

"Who wants a slug?" Tom asked. His term for beer.

So we all sat on the roof and slugged beer.

"Tom," said Little Kiwi, "did you see the ghost?"

"Yeah."

"Can I take your picture?"

"No, I don't want my picture taken anymore."

"Why not?"

"I guess I took too many when I was young. I'm all pictured up by now."

"I want to get a photo of the ghost. What does it look like?"

Tom went into his secret hell, but he stayed with the theme. "He's a very sad guy. Very nice guy and very sad. Good-looking. It was hard to know what to do with him because his feelings always got hurt very easily."

"Whose feelings?" Little Kiwi asked.

Yes, whose? Tom could have been describing himself.

"His name was Champ McQuest, and this was something like 1972. Maybe 1973. Champ McQuest."

Little Kiwi, not following the computation, looked at me.

"He's recalling an old friend," I said.

"He was so sad," said Tom, "that no one could cheer him up. I gave him a massage for free once, to make him happy." Tom shook his head. "Not even that."

"Then what happened?" asked Little Kiwi.

"He died out on drugs. That stuff's so mean. He just got out of control with it."

"That happened a lot then," I put in.

Tom nodded. "Everything was an experiment. Because you didn't know what the end was. But it was the nicest guys who got wrecked the worst. You remember that, Little. The *tough* guys are still standing when the dust clears."

"I'm afraid to be tough."

"Champ had a lot of friends. Everybody loved

him. But no one could figure out what was hurting him. Now he's trying to tell us something. A message from the past."

"What?" I said. "You think that's—"

"I know it." He looked at us, one after the other. "I knew him close and I know he's what's been coming around at nights here."

"Why would he tell *us* anything?" I reasoned. "He's trying to get to you, isn't he? Maybe there's something the two of you didn't finish . . . Jesus, look at me talking as if there really were a—"

"What are you three hayseeds doing up there?" Dennis Savage called. "Half the house is in a state of panic, I don't know where our next dinner is coming from, and you're on the roof guzzling beer. And Little Kiwi, I told you to lose that garbage around your neck."

"Come up and make me," said Little Kiwi, aiming and snapping his camera.

"Little's getting tough," said Tom.

"I'll make you but plenty when you come down! And stop taking those pictures!"

"In one minute," said Little Kiwi, "this candid photograph will be developed, and then I'll send it to the Curiosity Section of the *New York Times*."

"The world's nuts," said Dennis Savage, stomping off. "But come dinnertime, let no one complain to me because there's nothing to eat."

"There have to be ghosts," Little Kiwi mused, "or there couldn't be Ghost Patrol."

"What is Champ McQuest trying to say to you, Tom?" I asked.

Tom was quiet for a bit. Then: "He was a very sad guy."

They're out there whether you like it or not.

—A crank on a local television news show, Philadelphia, 1977

Wise old queens know everything, and it was to a wise old queen that I took The Problem late that afternoon. Not that I fancied asking him how one exorcises a ghost. But this man had been all over the scene for a good thirty years; he was *old* gay, older than clones and discos and politics. He was not a Circuit rider, but a considerable fortune put him at the very helm of the New York section of Stonewall while protecting his crony ties with the Big Boys at City Hall. He gave some of the greatest parties ever given, yet—and this is considered questionable—he was never to be glimpsed in the center of his dos, prancing and quipping, but far to the edge, talking to a friend or silent and watching. Some men know everyone; this man would have thought them parvenus. This man knew everyone he felt like knowing. There was a good chance that he had known Champ McQuest.

He is not a showy man. He prances and quips in private, for his personal pleasure. His Pines house is far to the east, on the ocean along the most chic strip of the choice quartier: but this is no palazzo. He doesn't even have a pool—he uses the Atlantic Ocean. He lives simply, easily, securely. When he throws a party he goes for it; when he lives he just lives.

He was one of my first clients in my party-tape era, eventually my best one, because his tape commissions turned into a sly challenge match. Not realizing how varied, extensive, and bizarre my record collection is, he kept asking for more and yet more recondite compounds. "Intimate, Brahmsian, a lot 'cello," he'd say, or "Honky-tonk, Sophie Tucker and ragtime—make it all sound like a battered upright piano with a broken middle C." I never failed him, and finally he asked me not only to tape a soiree but attend it, perhaps hoping that I'd at least insult the dress code or fake the politesse. I did neither, and we became friends. I relate all this to underline how necessary it is to understand your associates, for only then can you be sure what you can ask of them, and what they can give you.

Of course he had known Champ McQuest.

"One of many such," he said. "Those chillingly handsome young men who fell into the city in droves in those first years after the Riot. The gates were pulled down," he recalled, with a somewhat regretful smile. "The citadel was opened up. Champ was not the handsomest or the youngest, but he may well have been the nicest."

We were sitting on his back deck, looking at the ocean. This far east, there were few ˙ sunbathers; even the beach parade, a routine of Pines afternoons, tended to give out and turn back several houses to the west of us. Two boys were wrestling in the sand. A jogger robustly pumped along the water's edge. A straight couple laden with grocery bags trudged toward Water Island.

"Young men, young men, young men," he sighed. "Some of them place themselves well, others put on stomachs and tend bar to East Siders slumming in Chelsea, and a few fall into very wrong hands. Handsome young men. I've wondered what life might have been like if I'd been born when they were. Born, I mean, into this demotic everything-is-possible Stonewall thing, where you go to a gym and grow a mustache for love instead of paying for it. I never mind paying. That's what money is for. But if I had been *younger* . . ." He slurred out the word with a trace of wonder, as if the concept could scarcely be imagined, much less debated. "If I had been young when everyone else was young . . . and if I had not been rich and powerful." He hugged himself, shrugging playfully. "Well. Would *I* have gone to the weight rooms and worn jeans and frequented orgies just on the basis of who I was or pretended to be? Would I have delicious companionship *just because I showed up*? I love to ask. But I don't quite see it. All that effort, all that . . . *handsome* running around. It's so much easier to buy love than hunt for it. And then . . . even if you find it . . . don't you have to *deserve* it? You have to be as worthy as your partner, don't you? You have to be a *handsome young man*! Much, much more fun to buy your love, wouldn't you?"

"But can you buy love?" I asked. "Or just sex?"

"Writers are so naïve. You can buy anything, in fact. You can buy murder, don't doubt me. Don't. Don't."

The two boys on the beach, spent by their wrestling, lay side by side in the sun. One put his hand on the other's head.

"Anyway," he went on, "you can't necessarily have your love for free, either, so where are you then? Champ, now, dear Champ was certainly one of the elect. Yet he was always falling for men who didn't respond. *He* had no love. And my. *My*, how it rent him. The *passion* of a boy in love with a boy! The incredible *dis*regard for the *stand*ard *cau*tions!"

"Why did he die?"

"He was too sweet to live. He was too sensitive to survive. He fell prey to overwhelming despairs. Choose one. Freshen your drink?"

The two boys on the beach ran into the ocean and started wrestling again.

"You mustn't get into a state about Champ McQuest," the wise old queen warned me. "There were so many such. So many handsome young men who never even made it to bartender. And Champ was *born* to doom. Who knew *anyone at all* as glum as he? Did you? Tom Jones in the Dostoyevski edition, that was Champ McQuest."

"What did he die of, though?"

"Oh, he was one of the overdoses, technically. There was quite a lot of that at the time. Many of them simply lay there and gave out the soul, but some actually *did themselves in*. One went out a window shouting the name of the model agency that had dropped him for galloping debauchery. Alas, he had defied the cautions."

"And Champ?"

"Hm . . . can one recall a specific event, some *triggering* thing? He had such a greed for agonies, poor boy. It happened in your house, didn't it?"

I was speechless.

"Aren't you in the house they call Chinatown? Way over on The Other Side by the cruising park? It used to have a myriad of Oriental gewgaws hanging from the eaves over the deck. Wind chimes and fairy bells and a whole orchestra of gongs. If the breeze was right you could hear 'Limehouse Blues.' But you stalwart sprouts of Stonewall have taken all that down, haven't you? All the . . . decoration. You want to be your own decorations."

"Champ McQuest died in our house? Jesus, I knew there had been a suicide, but I—"

"Oh, I shouldn't call that a suicide. I shouldn't. Such a *deliberate* word, don't you? There comes a time in certain lives when one is too miserable to live, so one simply dies. *How* one dies is of rather small moment. Champ was very mixed up, and very unhappy, and very drugged. So it all came together on him one night, and the next day he was no longer with us. You know, I think . . . I just *think* I have something you should see. Sip your wine and gaze upon the sempiternal sea while I make sure it's out here."

He went into the house. While he was gone, the two boys came out of the ocean arm in arm, grabbed their towels, and dried each other off. They stood for a while, looking at each other.

"Well, we're in luck," said the wise old queen, returning with a small black rectangular box. "I must say, I *thought* I'd taken it out here."

I would have said something, but my attention was held by the two boys from the beach, who were coming up the walkway onto the wise old queen's deck.

"Russ and Billy," said the wise old queen.

They called to him, waved at me, and went into the house.

"Believe it or not, I don't do anything with them. I just like to watch them together. Why? Who can tell us why? Maybe even money is not enough. Maybe the reason some homos stay straight is out of *fear* of the *dream*. They fear to be . . . all homoed up into starving wraiths who get nothing. Take your wine along, I've this to show you now."

The box held videotape.

"Russ and Billy will be napping, luckily. I wouldn't want them to see this. It's strong material. What we used to call 'private films.' Of course, everything's transferred to video now. What pleasing novelty to see dear old friends back among us from the past. But don't expect state-of-the-art . . ."

Waves of static gave way to what looked like a piece of cardboard bearing the ballpointed legend, "Sailor Dick and Pants-Down Johnny."

"A certain half-baked Seventh Avenue *tycoon* who must remain nameless or I might vomit used to hire boys to make these . . . what to call them, my dear? Noose operas? Where it looks as if one boy is getting hung by another?"

"Hanged," I told him. "Not hung."

"Is there a difference?"

"Porn stars are hung. People are hanged."

"Ah, there's Champ. How tired he looks. I wouldn't appear in a piece this tawdry to save my life. Of course, they're totally fake and harmless, and the money was terribly good. Still . . ."

Champ was pretty much what I had expected, a solemnly nice-looking chap who seemed very uncomfortable to be where he was, in a spotlit corner of a dark room, sitting in a chair. The raspy voice of an unseen man directed him in a stripping scene, item by item. "Leave your socks on," the voice ordered. "Now let's see a little action."

"That's our friend from Seventh Avenue," said the wise old queen. "He liked to *superintend* his shows through a microphone, right into the sound track. Everyone else was making silents. Not he. Lavish productions, spare no expense."

"Don't rush it, baby," the voice grated out. "Take your time and you'll get your dough."

"Rather Brechtian, wouldn't you?" said the wise old queen. "All these directorial impositions *during* the show?"

Champ stopped masturbating and said something toward the camera. He seemed hostile, but he wasn't miked, and I missed it.

"Silly name, isn't it, Champ McQuest? It was originally something extraordinarily simple. David Jones? Donald Jones? There was so much of that then. So many David Joneses coming to the city to turn into Pants-Down Johnny."

"Or Sailor Dick."

"No, the sailor is an unusual item. He looks like a pro to me."

That he was, as I soon saw: sturdy, self-possessed, edgily efficient, and incongruously mustached in his navy whites. He hulked into view through a doorway and stood there, a pose in the shadows. The brutal voice told Champ to undress the sailor, step by step as before, and go down on him. They obeyed the command in the awkward simulation of hot that bedeviled early porn; and the technical setup was so poor that most of the action spilled out of the light into darkness. It was hard to see, much less believe.

"Paramount is eating its heart out," said the wise old queen.

"Fix the lights," the voice muttered to someone, and the beam slowly and effortfully reached out to the two actors. As the light hit him, the sailor gazed up, straight into the camera, and it struck me that he looked just like . . .

"Sweet Jesus!"

"A friend of yours?"

"It's Tom Adverse."

"Ah."

"You must know him—the Cherry Grove Carpenter."

"I've never been to the Grove," said the wise old queen, airily. "Is it nice?"

"Okay," said the voice. "Take him over now. Real slow. Slower. Keep him calm."

The camera swung over to another spotlight, this one trained on a length of rope dangling from the ceiling and noosed at the end. Tom brought Champ over to it, and the two of them waited, apparently for instructions. But we heard nothing.

"A penny for his thoughts, wouldn't you?" said the wise old queen.

"Okay." The voice had returned. "Now loosen up his neck muscles so he'll respond to the rope when he drops. Easy does it. Got to soothe him up for this."

Whoever he was, the man running this show suddenly symbolized everything I loathed in that early era of Stonewall, all the selfish money and back-alley egomania that still helps keep our world disjointed, all a-spin upon itself. "God, what a voice," I said.

"Yes, he should have sung opera."

"Loosen him up, come on. Think about how nice it'll be to do him now. He's almost ready. Turn him around to show us. Yeah. Stand over to the right a little so . . . yeah, so we can see what you got. Beautiful, baby. Nobody does it like you." A beat, then: "Look at them, huh?"

Champ said something to the voice, again off-mike. He spoke to Tom, too, and Tom looked inquiringly at the voice. It told them, "No play, no pay, baby. That's what it is."

Champ and Tom had a few more words, but the voice cut in with, "Noose that boy up and hang him," and Tom threw his left arm around Champ's middle and reached for the rope with his right.

"Jesus."

"They're standing on the floor, you know," said the wise old queen. "Nothing can happen."

"I know, but . . . I think Champ has a crush on Tom."

"*Had* a crush."

To myself I said, Don't be too sure.

Champ was fighting like a tiger, but Tom easily overmatched him. Within a moment he had looped the rope over his head and zipped it up. In the shadows let me come and sing to you.

"Lovely," said the voice.

"It's so beautiful when they struggle," came a second voice.

"Poor Champ," said the wise old queen.

Tom was holding Champ from behind, holding him tight and talking into his ear. Champ was shaking, but after a bit he suddenly grew quiet. I could hear the voices breathing. What was Tom telling Champ—"Work with me till we finish this gig and we'll get our money and split"? Would they go out to celebrate? Was this as far as Tom ever went, stylized snuff duets?

Champ broke free of Tom's grip, but Tom reached for him and Champ turned and impulsively threw his arms around him.

Surprised, Tom thrust Champ away with an odd look on his face. Champ tugged at the rope. Tom stopped him and with a single movement pulled the noose open and slipped it off.

Champ turned away from Tom.

Tom looked at the camera.

"Tasty boys," said the voice, and the screen immediately went dead.

"Isn't it savory," said the wise old queen, "that Russ and Billy will never know about such things?"

> *One must not forgive. One must understand.*
>
> —Cosima Liszt von Bülow, 1870

When I got back to the house, it was nearly dark. Dennis Savage and Lionel were in the kitchen, arguing over whether or not to put garlic in the salad. Bert was napping on the couch.

Little Kiwi, on the stairway, beckoned me upstairs in elaborate pantomime. He and Carlo joined me in my room.

Door closed, Little Kiwi said, "We have a plan. We're going to lay for the ghost tonight. Carlo is part of the Ghost Patrol, and you can be, too."

"Look . . ."

"We're going to lay for the ghost."

Carlo grinned at my questioning glance. "He learned a new expression."

"Carlo taught me. Don't you want to help us trap the ghost? We're all going to stay up, and when it comes out, I'm going to take its picture. Ghosts die when you photograph them, you know."

"Why don't we just wait out the weekend," I suggested, "and let it vanish the way it came?"

"We're going to lay for it."

I looked in on Tom. He was lying faceup on his bed staring at the ceiling.

"You okay, Tom?"

"Uh-huh."

"Want to talk?"

"Thought I'd get some sack time in. I'm kind of beat."

"Okay."

As I turned to go, he said, "You could tell those guys they shouldn't fool around with it. It's more serious than that."

I waited.

"I haven't been out here in a long time," he said. "I didn't want to come particularly."

Tom, I saw you and Champ McQuest in a private film.

"It's just that nothing's going on in New York now. No work for me. Thought I'd take a vacation here. It doesn't seem the same, though. I feel cold."

He pulled the spare blanket over himself.

"Everyone's been nice to me. I really appreciate it."

What happened after the film was over? What did you say to each other? Everybody loved him but you, right? Or did you love him gringo-style, without touching? Come ye out, Pants-Down Johnnies, in Tom Adverse's Club Stonewall, where you can have anything you want. Except Tom Adverse.

"A while along, it's almost like you don't have as many friends as you once did."

"Hey!" said Little Kiwi, leading in Carlo and Bauhaus. "This is the night, so everyone should get ready."

"You be nice and tough, Little."

Of course, you can't be both nice *and* tough, but, typically oblivious, Little Kiwi sat on the bed, patting Tom's chest and heartening him for the work ahead.

"Uh-huh," said Tom.

Carlo glanced at me, everything in his eyes: poor busted guy.

"I suppose you heard we're going to lay for the ghost. Behind a barricade!"

Tom put his hand on Little Kiwi's shoulder. "It's more serious than that."

One cannot understand. One must simply forgive.

—*The Cocktail Dandy, 1988*

It was another of those nights, boys and girls—no rain, now, but everyone sticking close to home as I fiddled with my tapes and the others sported about. We sat in on a television movie, held a game of Risk (everyone played except Tom), and still no one headed upstairs.

Apparently we were staying up to see the ghost.

It got so late that Dennis Savage and I had to rustle up an antipasto plate to keep everyone fit and happy. "Like, *tot-tal* sąlämi," said Bert, tucking in. Then we heard Bauhaus whining upstairs and Little Kiwi gave Carlo an Extremely Meaningful Glance and slithered away.

"I should know better than to ask this," said Dennis Savage, "but what's Bauhaus doing in the bedroom?"

"The kid himself leashed him up there," Carlo explained, "as part of his Ghost Patrol."

"Oh, for heaven's sake!"

Tom went outside, I assumed for a cigarette. House rules banned smoking indoors.

"I think this joke is getting out of control," said Dennis Savage.

"It's no joke," Lionel told him.

"Like, it was rillly a *hor-ror* show!" Bert agreed.

"It was marsh gas," said Dennis Savage.

"In a second-floor hallway?" Lionel challenged.

Beeping like the old RKO radio tower, Little Kiwi, upstairs, yelped out, "Ghost Patrol calling Carlo Smith. Come in, Carlo Smith."

Carlo grinned. "Got to go," he said, getting up. "Duty's calling."

Yes, I'd guessed right. Tom was standing on the deck looking at the ocean, the white gnat of a lit cigarette the only motion in the picture. A pose in the shadows.

"This jive about ghosts," Dennis Savage warned us, "is offensive to Stonewall pride. Are we not men?"

"Sometimes it can be very difficult to believe in anything," I said. "Some people can scarcely deal with the most ordinary things in life, no? Until we are all direct and articulate with each other . . . until we can face each other fairly, how can we possibly approach the metaphysical?"

Dennis Savage stared at me. Lionel mimed the tugging of a sage's grey beard. Bert said, "Oooh, *school.*"

"I mean," I went on, "how can we even discuss the existence of supernatural phenomena when some of us can't even believe in . . . Where'd Tom go?"

The porch was empty.

"Believe in what?" Lionel asked.

A crash overhead.

"Little Kiwi," Dennis Savage called out. "Would you come down here, please?"

"In a minute!"

"*Love.*"

"What's going on up there?" Dennis Savage cried.

"Ghost Patrol! Remember our motto—"

"It's the most commonplace thing, all about us. It's the very essence of our revolution. Yet some of us can't . . . see it."

"The two of you goons get down here pronto and stop wrecking the house!"

Upstairs, Little Kiwi complained to Carlo, "He never lets me have any fun," and there was another crash, followed by a thud.

"I'm going up there," said Dennis Savage, rising.

"You'll be sorry," Lionel told him.

The lights went out upstairs. Dennis Savage paused. In the silence, we heard Little Kiwi giggling.

"I'm telling you," Lionel insisted, "there's something in this house."

"Oh, please," said Dennis Savage, and up he went.

I excused myself and went outside, following the cigarette light to Tom, brooding down near the water. He nodded at me, but said nothing. After a while, I asked him, "What makes you think it's Champ McQuest?"

Nothing.

"Talk to me, Tom."

"It was fine of you to ask me out here, I know that. I want to be nice when people do a friendly thing. But I think I better go back to the big city tomorrow, get me off your hands."

"Come on to the house. You'll feel better inside the party."

"If you get the chance to be nice to someone, you should take it. That's a lesson I learned."

"Didn't you say one has to be tough?"

"There are people to be tough with and some to be nice with. That's the lesson that I mean."

"Come on back, Tom."

"Yeah. Okay."

He threw the cigarette into the water.

"God fucking damn it to hell," he said as we walked back. "Jesus shitfaced baboon sucking *damn* it all fuck!"

Nothing specific. A mood piece.

Then Tom halted. "I don't want to go back there," he told me. "You know somewhere else I can stay?"

"What's the matter?"

He turned back to the ocean. "I've been making so many mistakes that I just can't rectify. No *way*. You know that feeling?"

"Who doesn't?"

He was turning from the ocean to the house and back, a man without a place. Suddenly he stopped moving. "Why'd the house go dark?" he asked.

I looked back. All the lights were out.

"I think they're trying to lure the ghost out."

"Man, they shouldn't be doing that."

"Listen, Tom, what exactly did you see when . . . what did the ghost look like?"

He thought about it. From the look of him, I expected no more than an uh-huh, but then he told me, "It looks like a movie."

Just at that moment the house lit up to shouts, screams, and the barking of Bauhaus, and Tom and I ran up onto the deck and inside. Everyone was on the second floor, amid a barricade of chairs. Little Kiwi was studying one of his Polaroid three-by-threes. Carlo was flat on his back on the rug. Dennis Savage, his face as white as Mr. Softee, staggered over and grabbed me by the arms.

"I *saw* it!" he cried. "I saw a *ghost!*"

"It came through so fiercely it knocked Carlo over," Lionel reported.

"Like, shove me down the sli-yed!"

"Oh, no!" Little Kiwi wailed. "There's no picture in my photograph!"

He held up his Polaroid print: empty black.

"Maybe the flashcube didn't—"

"Ghosts probably don't—"

"Everyöne was like môving so—"

"Where is it now?" I asked.

"It went out the window," said Lionel. "Just . . . zoom."

Tom was not, as I had assumed, behind me. "Tom?" I called.

The reply was a fabulous series of crashes from the porch.

"My dinosaurs!" Little Kiwi shouted.

I raced downstairs and outside. The whole porch was a wreck. Tom was on his knees, in a stupor, slowly picking up the pieces of Little Kiwi's model collection.

"Tom?"

He shook his head.

"Are you okay?"

He laid some plastic parts on the deck table and looked at me.

"It's all right," said Tom. "He said it's all right."

I felt the others piling out behind me.

"Tom," said Little Kiwi, "you didn't knock down my dinosaurs, did you?"

"He said it wasn't me. He won't be back again. He wanted to make sure I . . . he talked to me . . ."

Tom knelt again and picked up the iguanodon.

"It's all right now. He talked to me."

Carlo righted a fallen deck chair; next door, two men had come out on their balcony to investigate.

"He talked to me."

Tom began to weep: this big, beautiful, kind man with a broken middle C.

"He said . . . he said . . ."

"What, Tom?"

"He said, 'Remember me.'"

It was not a message from the past, then, but for the future.

Tom held out his arms, showing us the wrecked patio. "I'm sorry," he said, the tears running down his cheeks. "I did this to you."

"You didn't do this," said Carlo, coming up to Tom. He put his arms around him, and this time Tom accepted the embrace.

("Does this mean there really are ghosts?" Dennis Savage murmured in my ear.

"*I* didn't see one," I whispered.)

"It's all right," said Tom, very gently breaking away from Carlo. "Okay?"

He put the iguanodon on the table.

"Okay, now? Is it okay?"

Yes, Tom. It is okay.

The Boffer

I CHERISHED MY TOYS. I shielded them, hoarded them. I kept my toys neat and slick and whole and true, and by the time I finished college and came to New York, my toys were still alive and perfect, in closets in my parents' house or on shelves in their garage. My toys. And when I took my present apartment at Fifty-third and Third, I brought some of them along—the Meccano construction set my dad lugged home from France in 1955; Plasticville: The City in a Box; my Sneaky Pete Complete Home Magician Outfit; and about a ton of Lego.

The Lego I eventually passed on to my little cousin Scott, and it gave him such a kick that I added Plasticville. The day I came over with it, I showed him how to set it up, snapping the building walls into right angles, aligning the fences, dotting the crisp lanes with mailboxes, benches, and lampposts. A serene American village then lay before us, with a church, a K mart, a barn, a school, and

93

houses. An informal civics class. See? They get the kids when they're too young to know any better; they recruit them, make them straight for life in a village with a church and a K mart.

At least it didn't work with me. The Meccano set still rests under my bed on Fifty-third Street, but the Sneaky Pete Complete Home Magician Outfit I had to give to Little Kiwi, to distract him from his obsession with *A Chorus Line*.

Dennis Savage blamed me for this, of course. I had taken Little Kiwi to the theatre for his birthday one Wednesday afternoon, and he was so entranced with the show that he went out the next day and came back with a *Chorus Line* cast album, coffee mug, and T-shirt. The record he played day and night, the mug he not only used for everything from water to ice cream but carried around with him like a shaman's fetish, and the T-shirt he wore incessantly till Dennis Savage wrested it off him and scrubbed it in the sink. (At that, Little Kiwi couldn't wait till it had dried and put it on half wet.) This is not even to mention the *Chorus Line* ·scenes and numbers he insistently favored us with. At the nine thousandth haunting repetition of "Kiss today goodbye," Dennis Savage groaned and told me, "You started this. Do something."

I started this because I sometimes think it the truest act of friendship to introduce someone to something instructive or delightful that might—who knows?—change his life. Still, I did something. I gave Little Kiwi my Sneaky Pete Complete Home Magician Outfit: and *A Chorus Line* dissolved before our eyes. In a trice—in a bath towel, actually, which

he wore as a cape—Little Kiwi reinvented himself as
La Dolce Pita the Magnificent, complete with his assistant, Ferdinand (the inevitable Bauhaus, Little
Kiwi's dowdy dog, half German shepherd, half
weasel, and half kraken; and I know that's three
halves, but you don't know Bauhaus). Visiting Dennis Savage became recreationally hazardous. Without even waiting for a lull in the conversation, La
Dolce Pita the Magnificent would run through the
Sneaky Pete program, beefed up by card tricks with
a deck he found in a joke shop, all this to the tune of
Johann Strauss's "Roses From the South" on the stereo. Those who have taken these journeys with me
in the past will not need to be told that La Dolce Pita
was somewhat less than magnificent in his command of the magician's arts.

"The Disappearing Coin!" Little Kiwi announced
one evening, flourishing the oval yellow tray with
the secret compartment. I was a whiz at this in my
youth: one deposits a coin in the tray, covers it, deftly pulls a lever that whisks the coin slot to the side
and a second slot, empty, in its place, and presto!
the coin has seemed to vanish. Reverse the action,
and the coin reappears.

"If some gentleman in the audience would provide
a sovereign," La Dolce Pita requested, with an opulent wave of his hand. "Never you mind," he went
on, in the administrative croon of the hopelessly
tenth-rate performer, "for though the coin will truly
disappear, La Dolce Pita the Magnificent will restore
it with a murmur of the magic code."

There was a lot doing at Dennis Savage's that late
autumn day, for he had received another round-

robin letter from his Hamilton alumni group. The men whom Dennis Savage had been close to in his college days had doggedly stayed in touch all these years, though all but he had married and most were raising kids and many had moved to distant quarters of the map. The wives took turns garnering everyone's news by phone and then sent out a kind of homemade newspaper to all the gang every six months or so, with news stories, burlesque gossip columns, photos, and even editorials on the state of the nation from a post-yuppie platform.

I found all this rather touching, even if it tested one's patience to have to attend to Dennis Savage's moony nostalgia for the days when he was embosomed in the tersely supportive confraternity of the collegiate male. He would cite names that had no meaning to me beyond the haze of data generally attached to the whole four years—the road trips with Henry Christian, Budge Lewis, and Pete Hedstrom; the two-man volleyball with Jojo Baker; the bull sessions with Cal Colson and Warren Acker—and mainly, the sheer ground-zero miracle of knowing, trading confidences with, and having a violently secret crush on Chad Jeffers, Dennis Savage's best friend. Now, this name stood out. This name had meaning. One had only to breathe these three blessed syllables to provoke from Dennis Savage a litany of such plangent, mesmerized eyewash that he'd come off like a Cherry Grove queen returning from a day in The Pines to throw himself across his bed with a terminal case of Houseboy Attitude Breakdown.

Ah, these scars of our college days, the mark they

leave on the gay soul! The beauty! The purity! One never quite recovers. For of course the world after college is unbeautiful, impure. I myself regarded college as an idiotic detour on my way to here, but I could share Dennis Savage's enthusiasm. It was always a big event when one of these alumni newsletters arrived, and Dennis Savage and I were far more involved in digesting the latest one than in taking in La Dolce Pita's performance.

"Just a simple coin, such as may be found in any fine gentleman's pocket."

"It says here," I noted, "that Warren and Janey Acker just had their sixth child."

"Three boys and three girls," Dennis Savage rejoined. "One gender after the other."

"So neat, so sure, so Hamilton."

"Any coin will do, but a quarter works best."

"Did you see about Pete Hedstrom living in San Francisco? Is that a message, do you suppose?"

"Never," said Dennis Savage. "That's his hometown."

"Everything is magic, if you only know. The coin is there, the coin is gone, the coin is there."

"Is Budge Lewis's real name Budge? Or is it short for one of those fancy WASP surname-first names like—"

"Roses From the South" suddenly cut off and we looked across the room to find Little Kiwi at the stereo, holding up the playing arm and glaring at us.

"Look, can I please have a quarter?" he cried.

Bauhaus growled.

Digging into his pocket, Dennis Savage muttered,

"What do I get for a quarter?" and Little Kiwi went on with his act as Dennis Savage handed me a letter.

"Wait till you see this," he said.

"You view the coin. I cover it. Now the magic code word . . . *Robitussin.*" As I read the letter, Little Kiwi fiddled with the lever. "And presto!"

"Bravo!" said Dennis Savage, and I clapped mechanically, the two of us too intent on the letter, handwritten by Mary Beth (Mrs. Henry) Christian, to look up.

"Oh, *no!*" Little Kiwi wailed. "It still doesn't work." The coin had not disappeared. Better yet, Little Kiwi promptly dropped the tray, and about two dollars' worth of nickels and dimes fell out. "So *that's* where they went!" he said. "They don't make these tricks right."

"Jesus Christ," I said, "an alumni reunion!"

Dennis Savage nodded. "The Colsons just moved to New York. It's a housewarming party, obviously, but apparently everyone's going to be there."

"Everyone?"

"That's what Mary Beth says."

"Including Chad Jeffers?"

"Now La Dolce Pita the Magnificent, assisted by Ferdinand, will present the notorious card stunt known to an elite few as The Bashful Deuce. Notice the colorful way I shuffle the deck to assure complete honesty."

The cards flew all over the room.

There was silence for a bit, then I said, "*Including* Chad Jeffers?" and Little Kiwi said, "Oh, gee," and Dennis Savage said, "You know, I haven't seen him in over fifteen years."

"Seen who?" asked Little Kiwi, picking up the cards.

"Maybe it's a cute idea to have an eighteenth anniversary reunion party instead of a twentieth," Dennis Savage went on. "Maybe they should have done something like this long before. Maybe every so often I think of the way things were back then and all. And I miss that life. No maybe about it. I traded it all for the Eagle and the Saint and the Pines and the meat rack and the Everard and the backroom bars and a few other things I haven't dared mention to you—"

"If you mean that orgy in Burke Fuller's loft when a Colt model took a bath in motor oil and you licked him dry, Lionel told me all about it."

"—and I've never been sorry," he continued, closing his eyes briefly in a kind of visual scream but holding to his rhythm. "I've never been sorry for that trade. They were straight and I wasn't, and the wisest thing I ever did was to admit that and get on with my real life instead of trying to live like them."

"So?"

"So why should I go to their party? The lone bachelor amid the marrieds and the dates. I'd feel like a fool. I'd look like a . . ."

"A queer?" I asked.

Little Kiwi was looking at us from the floor, attending, taking in this new thing.

"Don't you want to see them again?" I said.

"Oh, yes. You don't know how much. I suppose in a way I've been hoping that something like this would come up. But now that it has, I'm afraid of it. Aren't I?" He shifted position on the couch. In the avid stillness of the listening room this seemed almost violent, and Bauhaus growled. "That's how it feels, anyway. Like fear."

"Fear of what?"

"I have no idea. But it's there." He shrugged. "It would be great to go, though, wouldn't it? And yes, I imagine Chad Jeffers will be there. Boston's not that far away, and he was always a real gung ho about alumni stuff. If he goes to every homecoming, he'll certainly come to this. Clapping the guys on the back. Dredging up the old sagas. All that. Oh, he'll be there. He's so good at this kind of thing."

There was that look again, and that mooing tone, and Dennis Savage was going into his nostalgia trance.

"And then someone will tell one of those dumb old jokes again, and Chad will smile and his eyes will crinkle up."

"What is crinkle?" asked Little Kiwi.

"Oh . . . it's this odd face he gets sometimes when he's really happy. It was the most devastating thing, and I'll bet you he isn't aware of it even now. It happens when he smiles. His eyes narrow and the edges get squishy, as if they had been made by a cookie cutter. It's very boyish, and he's such a . . . a manly guy that the combination of . . . well, you just . . ."

"Quietly dream of him for eighteen years?" I said.

He slowly shook his head. "These crushes we get on our straight friends have to be laid aside when we come into Stonewall. It's like having tantrums when you're eight or pimples when you're fifteen. You outgrow it."

◆ 100 ◆

Like my toys.

"This all sounds very sensible," I said. "If you ask me, you have a very adult take on this and there's no reason why you shouldn't go to the party."

"Little Kiwi," said Dennis Savage, "what are you doing?"

Little Kiwi was staring at us, grinning and squinting at the same time. It made him look like a jack-o'-lantern.

"I'm trying to crinkle like Chad Jeffers."

"It's not something you can put on," I told him. "Your features have to do it naturally."

"In the world of magic," he told me, "everything is possible. There is always a trick you can do."

"Actually, he had a lot of boyish qualities," Dennis Savage went on. "He'd look like a Cub Scout if you taught him something. He used to come to my room to listen to *Tosca*, and he'd get so serious and happy about it, you know, when I'd explain what was happening on stage. He really liked that. He liked to learn. I think that was the bond between us, in fact."

"That boring old Leinsdorf recording of *Tosca* was your bond? Maybe if you'd played Callas for him you could have gotten him into bed."

"I didn't want to get him into bed. One didn't think of those things then. This was an enchanted time, the vale of innocence. We weren't trying to plunder each other, don't you see that? We were all in love, but it wasn't erotic love. It was some sort of ideal love, very trusting and delicate."

I glanced at Little Kiwi and he said, "Get her."

"Oh, for heaven's sake," said Dennis Savage.

"Can't you imagine anything but cruising and dancing? Is that all there is?"

"I'm just trying to imagine you teaching somebody."

"I *am* a teacher, as you well know, you festive pigpen! What do you think I do all day while you're out boulevarding around the town?"

"Oh, yes."

"Don't 'Oh, yes' me, you tank-town swell!"

"So are you going to this reunion shindig or not?"

"You just *bet* I'm going!"

"Can we come, too?" asked Little Kiwi.

Startled in the midst of his offended reverie, Dennis Savage surveyed us: me in jeans and a spaghetti-stained T-shirt, Little Kiwi in his bath-towel cape; and let us not omit quaint Bauhaus, just then dancing around the room on his behind to ease an itch.

"Well," said Dennis Savage, "that . . . would be complicated."

"A Stonewall loyalist would take his buddies," I observed.

"And I want to see the eyes of Chad Jeffers," Little Kiwi put in, "when they crinkle. I might be able to use that in my magic act."

"Yes, well . . . we have to consider whether we would all be comfortable in the admittedly narrow environment of a—"

"You're ashamed of us," I said.

"It's very difficult to be a stranger at a party like this. It's hard to break in."

"Not if you're connected," I told him. "Introduce us around, set us up right, and presto—"

"The magic is made!" said Little Kiwi. "Everything is magic."

"Everything is friendship," I corrected.

"Everything is straights," Dennis Savage reminded me, "at a party like this one. Do you really want to try to reenter that world, you, even for a night? Really?"

"I do," said Little Kiwi. "I'll knock them over with my tricks."

Dennis Savage winced, but he pressed on, certain that reason would discourage us. "It's a closed society," he explained. "I see it as a memory open only to those who were there originally. With all those code words and legends and nicknames, you know."

"Nicknames, huh? What's yours?"

"The Boffer."

Jolted, I said nothing. Little Kiwi asked, "What does that mean?"

"You can't go to this party," Dennis Savage almost pleaded. "I'm afraid to go myself. I just don't think I can handle—"

"The Boffer," I said. "Well, now, The Boffer."

"Just to be there again is trouble enough, surely, but—"

"It's an honorable name," I said.

"What does it mean," Little Kiwi asked, "if you're The Boffer?"

"It means he goes on road trips," I said, "and he calls the Mount Holyoke girls 'Hokes' and gives pointers to the freshmen. It means he teaches Chad Jeffers how to boff a sweet young thing, and how to know about boffing, and how to be a boffer. It's sacred brotherhood stuff. It's the boffing science on the theme of the virgin Hoke. It's fucking."

Little Kiwi's mouth was open, and Dennis Savage said to me, "And you still want to go to this party?"

"More than ever. And I know why you don't want us there—may I? You're afraid Chad Jeffers will figure out that you're . . . light in your loafers . . . is that the expression he'd—"

"Blackmail," Dennis Savage said, his tone pure outraged innocence but his eyes cloudy with ambivalence. "This is blackmail."

"Everyone will be there with his wife, right? His true partner. Does it not behoove a Stonewaller to bring *his* partners? His lover and best friend? That's what we have for families and that's what you should bring."

"You should bring your magician," Little Kiwi put in, "to regale the guests with the Chamber of Disguise where I put objects into this little house and they vanish."

"I remember that one," I said. "There's a mirror inside that conceals the back half of the chamber. You put objects in *behind* it and they seem to disappear."

"You shouldn't tell about the tricks," said Little Kiwi. "As one magician to another."

"Oh, hell," said Dennis Savage.

"If you *talk* about the secrets too much," Little Kiwi observed, "they lose their secret qualities."

"Hell, of *course* you can come."

"You can know too much about magic, you know."

"I doubt I could get through it without you. You *have* to come. I was just playing around."

I question that.

"I just don't think you'll enjoy it, that's all. It's such a . . . a reversion into old business."

"Oh, I'll enjoy it, my dear old Boffer," I told him. "Old business is true business. Hidden objects must be retrieved from the Chamber of Disguise."

"And I, La Dolce Pita the Magnificent, must demonstrate the truth of magic, assisted by Ferdinand."

"The dog," said Dennis Savage, with penetrating finality, "stays home."

And Bauhaus growled.

This was not a simple matter of getting dressed, grabbing a cab, and showing up. Phone calls and letters passed among the Hamilton folk, as the party took shape and Mr. and Mrs. Cal Colson confirmed the date and old grads from Portland to Atlanta made their travel plans. Here was a Heavy Party. To top it off, Dennis Savage and I took Little Kiwi to Lord and Taylor for a new sports jacket on the afternoon of the do. Little Kiwi crinkled at the salesman while trying it on, and the salesman pretended not to notice; but he and two colleagues were buzzing like bees in a petunia patch as we left.

"What do you think they were thinking about us?" asked Dennis Savage after we got out of the store. "Those salesmen."

"They thought we were some sort of gay ménage," I answered. "What do you think people take us for, palling around like this?"

He said nothing.

"What do you think people will take us for," I

gently added, "at the Hamilton party? A law firm? An archaeological dig?"

"They'll know what we are," he said, firming up his jawline. "They will know and they should know."

"And what will they say? After we leave, of course, like those salesmen."

"After we leave? Who cares what happens after we leave?"

At home, we separated in the elevator, but I went up to his place for dinner. He seemed remarkably calm, considering how close he was to bumping up against his dearest legends. How many of us, boys and girls, get to greet our own history? Now, it is true that half the party—the wives—would be strangers. But the other half—the Hamilton alumni—would be men who had known Dennis Savage intimately when he was dwelling behind the mirror, when he couldn't be seen. Now they would see him. He must have had highly mixed feelings about all this, but he wasn't showing us a thing: just a man in an apartment, a decent hand at dinner, a sharp dresser, a good friend, wise enough to know that no one, whatever his genetic advantages and luck, gets all that he wants out of life, and that we all pay a price for that which we do get. He knows this and I know this, and we can live with it. And that might very well explain why we get on so well.

"Why do I just have jackets?" Little Kiwi complained, coming into the living room ready to go. "Why can't I ever have a suit?"

"You look so nice like this," said Dennis Savage, straightening Little Kiwi's tie. "What do you need a suit for?"

"For when I go on the stage, as La Dolce Pita the Magnificent."

Bauhaus barked.

"Plus Ferdinand."

"That's a little rich for the contemporary marquee," I observed. "Why don't you take a trimmer stage name? Something like . . . The Boffer?"

Dennis Savage knifed me with a look.

"I guess we'll be hearing a lot of that tonight, won't we?" I continued. "There we are, making our entrance—and all those wild and crazy Hamiltonians will rush up and cry, 'Say, it's The Boffer!' and 'Hey, Boffer!' and 'How're they hanging, Boffer?'"

Little Kiwi giggled. "The Boffer," he said.

"Then comes the moment of moments. All is still. The crowd piously parts. And across the crowded room on this enchanted evening, you will see a . . . no, not a stranger, but a comrade, a vision, a ghost of your sweet youth of bracingly platonic rhapsody: Chad Jeffers, younger than springtime. He wafts toward you . . ."

"Crinkling," said Little Kiwi.

"Crinkling all the way, yes. Then he leans over and murmurs into your ear, 'Hey, there, my . . . Boffer.'"

Dennis Savage smiled. He would not be needled this night. "He never called me The Boffer. He called me something else."

"What?"

He shrugged.

"Shall I guess? Groucho, perhaps? So fitting."

"Daddy-o?" asked Little Kiwi.

"Attila the Nun? It's chic and it's true."

"Everybody hush," said Dennis Savage, "and let's go."

"I guess we'll hear it soon enough, anyway," I said.

"Doubtful," he said, getting his coat. "It was a private nickname. He only used it when we were alone."

"Listening to Erich Leinsdorf murder *Tosca*."

Riding down in the elevator, Little Kiwi said, "When I go on the stage, I'm going to wear a three-piece suit."

"Why do you always have some bizarre project going on?" Dennis Savage asked. "Don't you like your life?"

"How would *you* like to be your houseboy?"

"It's a responsible position," Dennis Savage reasoned, his voice quiet, his mind elsewhere. "The free time . . ."

"It's woman's work! I should have a real job."

Finally hearing Little Kiwi, and realizing what upheaval this complaint portended, Dennis Savage looked alarmed and turned to me—but this is a story for later. I put on my innocent face and whistled a happy tune as the elevator door opened, and we headed out for the party.

First of all, the Colsons had a terrific apartment, one of those room-after-room things on West Ninety-second Street; and the rooms were *big*. I know three people whose combined apartments would fit inside the Colsons' powder room. No doormen, true. But the expanse of sheer place that confronted us as we entered the apartment was as daunting as welcoming, at least to those of us who dwell in the dollhouse accommodations of the post-war high rise.

We scarcely had time to take this in before The Receiving Line was giving greeting. The Line was all women, and we weren't inside for more than three seconds before Little Kiwi had his trick deck out and was asking the girls to pick a card.

("I frisked him before we left, I swear," Dennis Savage whispered to me.

"He probably had it planted in his overcoat.")

"I'm Mary Beth Christian," an attractive, slim yet motherly woman was telling Little Kiwi.

"Linda Baker," said another, more amply curved, somewhat severe of mien, just as attractive.

"Terry Finn," said a third, a delightful post-tom-boy deb with a halo of blond curls.

Little Kiwi was shaking hands with them. "I'm Virgil Brown," he said. "But basically I'm known as The Little Boffer."

Their smiles froze, but they took it in stride, as bourgeois maidens are taught to do, especially when Receiving. Then Dennis Savage and I grabbed their attention and thus we moved into the party, Little Kiwi trying one last "Pick a card" as I hustled him forward.

"Just keep moving, Little Boffer," I told him.

We were in the center of a very fully done room— icy glass tables to the left of us, truculent couches to the right of us, and all about us vases of a very precise shade of antique green. This always means trouble. Naturally we had arrived somewhat late, as if prancing into a dance hall last and most awaited, *grandioso, chic deluxe,* and the rooms were spilling with Hamiltonians, strollers and couples and groups and whole coteries. And, pretty much as I had pictured it, a gang of males rushed upon Dennis Savage crying out, "It's The Boffer!"

He shuddered with a glad, stinging thrill as they surrounded him, shaking and clasping and pushing him in that way they have, that old-boy style. He nodded and reached for them, as if he were going home again even as he knew one cannot. They were crashing all over the place at the dead center of the party, he and his old boys, and their wives were coming up, drawn by the hoopla. Dennis Savage was encircled, and terrified, and content.

Or did I read it wrong? He was swimming smoothly in this sea of bright shadows—and I was watching carefully to see how much they liked him: they were wild. Little Kiwi was taking it in quizzically. This was a side of Dennis Savage he had never seen, opened to his gaze not by action but by reflection, in the excitement of the men roaring and pawing at him, in their attempt to share with him a relapse into the boisterous, bracing freedom of their youth.

Dennis Savage was calming them, and laughing, and nodding; they were strident, insistent. Then someone came up to him out of nowhere and said, "Hey," so softly that I had to read his lips. But Dennis Savage heard him, and turned, and there was Chad Jeffers.

Yes, he was terribly handsome, and shockingly young looking, one of those do-or-die, take-no-prisoners preppies who somehow never lose that sense of having been rejected for the role of Prince because they are too nice, too real.

"There he is," I told Little Kiwi.

Rather, I told the place where Little Kiwi had been. He had slipped away. Trying to keep an eye on Dennis Savage, I surveyed the room—ah, there he is, shuffling cards and effervescing at Linda Baker, who severely took a card, gave it back to him, and when he had reshuffled the deck and produced a card, severely shook her head. Wrong card. Well, all that's harmless enough. Dennis Savage was shaking Chad Jeffers's hand in a grip of death, and that can be harmful: because the grip must yield after the time passes and the boys separate to find themselves as men. You can keep your toys under your bed, perhaps, but you can't shake hands again, not with your enemy.

You may wonder at my choice of word. Well, you'll see what I mean presently.

You can imagine that I watched Dennis Savage's reunion with Chad Jeffers as a camera turns. I wanted to measure this data securely. But there was little to see. They were at ease with each other, focused on their conversation but, very clearly, free of those overtones of injured affections that long-lost friends sometimes give off when they speak. I imagined them tracking down old capers and catching up on recent curriculum vitae. I tried murmuring unlikely dialogue to the rhythm of their talk: "'Remember the night we gave Doofus McWasp an apple-pie bed?' 'Hey, and the time we road-tripped those two

Smithies all the way to Canada and *really* ran out of gas? What a high!'"

Little Kiwi joined them. I continued to improvise as Dennis Savage introduced him: "'This is my hot little fuck buddy, bet you wished you had one, right, Chad?'"

As Chad shook hands with Little Kiwi: "'Can I borrow him, Boffer? It's perfectly safe, in the Hamilton way. I use three condoms, one on top another, each made of sheep entrails and individually packed in your choice of spermicidal creams, jams, jellies, pastes, and . . .'"

A dark-haired woman had pulled up next to me to listen. She was smiling. "You're not from Hamilton, are you?" she said, as a merry wife of Windsor might tell Khomeini, "You're not an old Etonian."

"Hi, there," I replied, feeling a blush make a jerk of me.

"Nor I," she said. "Susan Drinker, outsider."

"Bud Mordden, best friend," I replied as we shook hands.

"I married into this pep rally. What's your excuse? Something unseemly, I hope."

"Some people think so."

"That's my husband," she told me, pointing at a former stalwart lad now settling into the flabby grandee phase of the respectably accoutered straight. Family, career, and a house in one of the more ruthless suburbs of Boston. "Jensen Drinker," Susan went on, "president for life of the singing group known to glory as the Six Hamiltones." Jensen was speaking in a very confidential way to a small bevy of alumni. He was holding a pitch pipe and what looked like a college yearbook, and they had all changed into blue blazers. "I believe they are popularly known as the *Sex* Hamiltones. We can only guess why."

Did she just wink at me?

"Let's really get down," she sighed, sinking into a couch, indicating the place next to her with a toss of her head. "One thing you have to say for the University of Pennsylvania. *Their* alumni don't drag innocent wives away from their children, especially on the littlest one's birthday. Oh, she sounded very brave about it on the phone this afternoon, but she'll be weeping at dinner and her two brothers will bully her and make it worse."

"Did you go to Penn?"

"Class of '75."

"Egad," I said. "Class of '69." I held out my hand again, and as she took it, she said, "Buster, you just made the team. What do you say we kibosh the Hamiltones's act with a fast chorus of . . . What *is* the Penn song?"

"'Drink a Highball at Nightfall.'"

"Sounds really barfy. Teach it to me."

Three lines into it, the two of us giggling like freshmen cutting an orientation tour, Little Kiwi came up with his magical deck of cards and launched one of his tricks at Susan Drinker.

"Now *this*," she averred, "is really cute. This makes the party. Did he go to Penn, too?"

"I went to the Lake-of-the-Woods region on a fishing trip," said Little Kiwi, carefully shuffling his cards. "But I didn't like the food. I told my pop I wasn't going to fit in, but he made me go, anyway." Somewhat tentatively, he pulled out a card to show Susan Drinker. "Was this your original card?"

"Yes," she said, sporting that smile again. It said, People are interesting because sooner or later everyone's bizarre.

"I *knew* I could do it!" Little Kiwi exulted. Then he looked at the card. "No, that wasn't it."

Susan shrugged, still smiling.

"Why can't I do it right?"

"He's sort of a Peter Pan figure," she told me. "He should fit right in at this party, because this is a night for all the little boys who never grew up. Why *are* you all here?"

"We're friends of that fellow there," I said, pointing out Dennis Savage. "The one talking to—"

"Golden Boy. I can't remember the names of all these historical personages, but I know what each of them represents. To Jensen, anyway." She laughed. "What do they look like to you?"

I grunted.

"Ask Peter Pan to sit with us and we'll sing him a chorus of the good old Penn song." We made room, and Little Kiwi sat between us. "My ten-year-old is going to look like him in about ten years, and he's going to break hearts like a highwayman. And he plays beautiful piano. Men never realize what that does to a woman."

"Why don't you tell *me* that?" Little Kiwi asked her. "I can talk, too, you know."

She quietly sang to him:

> Drink a highball at nightfall,
> Be good fellows while you may;
> For tomorrow may bring sorrow . . .

"That's silly, isn't it?" she said. "This notion that everything after college is a letdown. It's just silly. I didn't like college. All that homework. The catty sororities and the frat boys using you to prove themselves. I couldn't wait to be married. I live in a house with people I love, instead of a rathole of a dormitory. My chores mean something to me—to me, not some professor. Everything I put into my life comes back a hundredfold. Little things and big things. I remember the day my daughter first walked by herself as vividly as I see you two now. Her brothers witnessed the whole bit; and they were so excited."

"Do you make grilled cheese and tomato sandwiches?" asked Little Kiwi.

"'For tomorrow may bring sorrow,'" she repeated. "How does the next line go?"

I told her: "'So tonight, let's all be gay.'"

"Brace yourselves," said Dennis Savage, looming over us. "The Six Hamiltones are going to sing."

We scarcely had time to connect Dennis Savage and Susan Drinker and get him ensconced on the couch with us before Jensen Drinker was calling for silence and attention. As the party wafted back into chairs and against the walls, he welcomed us, joked at us, and marshaled our reserves of sentimental recollection. He held up an old yearbook so we could look back at the Six Hamiltones in their and our youth, so we could split the difference between then and now and feel . . . perhaps not younger, but less adult, less wise, less finished. A buzz ran through the room as old hands murmured, "The *Sex* Hamiltones" to each other. We laughed, relaxed.

Throwing off your bad, mean wisdoms is a hard trick; but the trick was taking.

As the blazer men slid into their first selection, "Hello, Young Lovers," I tried not to harp on the thought that, had they been gay, they could hardly have brought the original sextet back for an encore twenty years later. Some of them would be dead.

Dennis Savage was thinking no such thoughts. He was misted in a dream. Susan Drinker was smiling her smile and watching her husband lead the music. Little Kiwi whispered, "This is nice."

Three songs then followed, to warm, even thrilled applause, all favorites from the Hamiltones' old repertory. However, for their final number, they offered a contemporary song in a new arrangement especially for us, here, tonight. So memory renews itself. Maybe. And at the first strains of "Kiss today good-bye," Little Kiwi was up and moving, and by the line "The gift was ours to borrow," he was standing right up there with the Hamiltones, his tenorino lightly tracing the melody as confidently as if he had always lived in the castle, as if there were no enemy.

"Well, now," Susan Drinker whispered to me, "this is one for the yearbooks."

The Hamiltones took it so calmly it might have been part of the staging. The man behind Little Kiwi even put one hand on this young stranger's shoulder, as if to portray the serenity, the sweet clarity of the moment when everyone is happy and well liked.

And Dennis Savage, jolted from his dream, looked upon this picture like Cortés upon his peak in Darien. Like Diogenes finding an honest man. Like a lover seeing love.

But Chad Jeffers was staring at Dennis Savage like someone who just figured something out and dearly wishes he hadn't.

After the singing, the party restruck its cymbals. Everyone rose and refilled his glass and started grouping up again, but I stayed on the couch talking to Susan Drinker till Jensen called her over for something or other. As she left, she made an "I wish he wouldn't" suburban grimace at me. It made her look like a six-year-old fresh from a mud pie session. Then Chad Jeffers pulled up so quickly that I was staring at him before I realized who he was.

And he was talking.

Sitting next to me on the couch. You know: any chum of my chum is My Chum.

Oh, he raved on about the Hamiltones, and asked me what I did, and told me how much he missed the Old Days. He mentioned the playings of *Tosca* in Dennis Savage's room. Pausing now and again to look comely, confidential, sternly bemused, he leaped from topic to topic as a hunter crosses a woodland rapids stone by stone. He always counted Dennis Savage as one of his best friends, even through all the years of separation, because Dennis Savage is *so* smart. Really such a . . . such a *smart* guy. And knowing smart people is the best thing for you, isn't it? The best way to live. The best friends to have.

"Friendship," he said "amplifies our opinions."

Another pause. We approach a difficult stone, slippery, distant, perilous.

Of course, we all have opinions of each other, he

was telling me. Everyone is very judgmental in our society. Some of us are merry; some are earnest. But all of Know What We Know, don't we?

Who's talking here? you ask. Who's judging? Who's on the couch with a very dazzling Golden Boy, his head swimming with the novelty of place, the excitement of encounters, and, very possibly, the vertigo of the brimming cup?

Who was crinkling? Not Chad Jeffers. Golden Boy is concerned about something. Golden Boy is going to tell me what it is. But Golden Boy doesn't know quite how to manage it. Golden Boy's head must be swimming, too. Two men at this party are very wet just now. But watch the cautious passage atop the stones: from *Tosca* to opinions and smarts, back to *Tosca*, thence to opera to I like opera, don't you? and Oh, you do? because I have this wonderful friend, single, pretty, who'd love to meet you, would you like me to give you her number or no, I could give her yours how about?

And the hunter has made it to the far bank of the rapids.

Now, years ago, when various relatives would do this to me, I had an answer all ready: "Anyone you'd have access to, I'm not interested in." The rudeness deters them from ever doing this again, and also bounces their boring straight fascism back in their surprised asshole faces. Okay, that's very satisfying—and how can it be wrong if it feels so good? Besides, if I were straight, it still would have been true. Eventually, however, I began to feel I was letting my side down by not dealing with the question directly. The issue was not (only) They are trying to manipulate me. The issue was I am gay. So I developed a new answer, and I revived it in conversation with Chad Jeffers.

Let's do this again: *Tosca*, amplifies, pretty friend, can I phone number . . . and I said:

"No, but does she have a brother?"

I believe that's what Chad Jeffers was waiting to hear. His eyes lidded over—the opposite of crinkling, no doubt—and his head hung heavy, and he gasped. I'm wrong, aren't I?, to play Show Them How It Feels with Dennis Savage's special friend at Dennis Savage's alumni reunion. But hypocrisy shatters the soul.

"Anything else you'd like to ask?" I said. "Because I need another drink."

I was already rising, but Chad Jeffers got up with me, his hand on my arm.

"I'm sorry if I . . . intruded," he said. "The . . . young man . . . with the card deck. He came with you tonight. Is he your . . . Is he?"

"Friend. My friend."

"Yes." Chad Jeffers nodded. "Quite a fine fellow. He was up there singing with the—"

"Sex Hamiltones."

Chad Jeffers laughed. "He also . . . the young man . . . knows Dennis Savage. I mean . . . doesn't he?"

Over Chad Jeffers's shoulder I saw Dennis Savage watching us. I believe he had been doing so for some time. He looked somewhere between thoughtful and worried.

"What are you asking me?" I said. "What are you trying to hear?"

"The truth," he said, all wide-shouldered and up-jawed. "I want to hear the truth."

"Mister," I replied, "you caught me on just the right drink."

"No," said Dennis Savage.

"You snuck up on us," I reproached him.

"The truth, that's all," said Chad Jeffers softly.

"This is my scene," said Dennis Savage.

Now Chad Jeffers took Dennis Savage's arm.

"It's my fault," said Chad Jeffers.

"You're both blitzed," said Dennis Savage.

"I am *not* blitzed!" I told him.

"What does 'blitzed' mean?" asked Chad Jeffers.

"Drunk."

He thought it over. "Nor am *I* blitzed!" He shook off Dennis Savage's touching hand. "You're gay, aren't you? That young fellow is your . . . your confidant."

"Look—"

"He *is* blitzed," I said.

"I am *not* . . . I simply require some information."

"Tell him nothing!" I muttered.

"Will the two of you please sit down? You're spinning on your pins."

"No, the room is spinning," said Chad Jeffers. He sat down.

"I'm not sitting next to him," I said.

Dennis Savage pushed me down on the couch next to Chad Jeffers.

"Starting tomorrow," I added.

"I'm sorry if I pried," said Chad Jeffers. "I just think friends should trust each other."

"Friends," I offered, "should respect each other's privacy."

"Look who's talking," said Dennis Savage.

Little Kiwi was suddenly looming over me with those cards. "This time," he said, "I've really got it. Okay. First you—"

Dennis Savage closed up Little Kiwi's outfanned deck, brushed the hair back from his forehead, and said, "Would you please go get our coats?"

"Not yet!" said Little Kiwi.

"Yes, yet. And you," Dennis Savage told me, "should be ashamed of yourself."

"Not yet."

"What did he do?" asked Susan Drinker, who must have come up with Little Kiwi.

I tried to stand, but Dennis Savage pushed me down again. Maybe I fell.

"A controlled substance," said Susan. "Tang in the punch."

"Everyone's gay," said Chad Jeffers.

After a moment Susan said, "Well, you'd better make an appointment with Nurse Renfrew, so Doctor can see you and cure your ills."

"I don't have ills," said Chad Jeffers.

"Oh, Nurse Renfrew!" Susan and Dennis Savage called out at the same time.

Nobody laughed.

I guess I was blitzed. Chad Jeffers was even more so. I looked at my watch—we had been at the party over six hours. All that drinking on an empty stomach, fatal every time. Pushing forty and I still can't hold my juice. Don't tell my father.

"'For tomorrow,'" Susan told Little Kiwi when he brought our overcoats, "'may bring sorrow.'"

"Not at our house," he told her, distributing the coats. "I saved these really radical chocolates from the dish that turns around." He put a hand in his pocket and pulled one out. "Oh, they got a little—"

"I just bought that jacket!" said Dennis Savage. "It isn't even paid for yet!"

"He buys clothes for his friend," said Chad Jeffers. "A sports car. A co-op." He looked up at Dennis Savage. "Is that right or not?"

I said, "Everyone's blitzed on this couch."

"What do you want?" Dennis Savage asked Chad Jeffers. "Tell me and I'll give it to you. Because what you want I swear I don't know. I swear it here. Speak. I listen. I'm still your friend. So what is this about? What have you been looking at? Did something catch your eye or were you out hunting? Just tell me. Because I don't know what this is about. And I'd love to. The two of you stumbling around here, like potty old Latin professors battling over the possibility of a sixth declension. And the term is not 'confidant,' it's 'lover.' This man is my lover."

"They didn't really melt yet," said Little Kiwi. "They just started to squish together a little, so—"

"Come on, confidant, help Uncle Bud to his feet."

"Well, it's been terribly *entre nous*," said Susan as we shook hands. "We'll do this again."

Chad Jeffers hung back, still on the couch, staring at us a trifle glassily.

Little Kiwi smooched her hand like a Parisian bon vivant.

"Lord," she said.

She gave me another wink of her bright, sharp eye, and we were off and away and, in due course, home. Little Kiwi went on up to see to the copiously invalid Bauhaus, while Dennis Savage insisted on accompanying me to my apartment: because otherwise I would pass out in the hall.

This was a bald libel. On the contrary, I was just getting my second wind. I put on the Gieseking recording of Debussy's *Children's Corner Suite, moltissimo pianissimo,* and steeled myself to talking it out. Anyway, I had a feeling he had more on his mind than keeping me from disgracing us in the hall.

"It was a good party," I began. "Wasn't it?"

"The best of its kind, I'd say."

"Though I was getting awfully tired of all those blue eyes. Chad Jeffers figured it out, didn't he?"

"He was bound to. The men who liked you the most when you were innocent have the most to lose when you grow smart."

"Don't be wise so late at night," I told him.

"I thought I was afraid of what he would think of me when he found out. When I first heard of this reunion, that's . . . what I feared. His opinion of me. Just as I was afraid of their opinion way back when I pretended I was one of them. When I did what they did."

He crossed over to the stereo, carefully picked up the playing arm, and switched off the turntable. No Gieseking. Something important to say.

"As soon as I walked in," he said, "I realized that their opinion couldn't possibly matter anymore. Oh, I . . . yes . . . I liked hearing them go through the old routines. That Boffer stuff. I always liked that. Sure I did. And the Hamiltones, too. And those absurd old songs that used to matter so much to me, God knows why. But in the end this is nothing.

There's no *here* in it. I'm not like them," he said, looking right at me. "I never could be, whatever I thought once. And if I'd gone on trying to be like them, I would have wrecked myself." Right at me, still, this, because he knows that I understand him and that this aperçu matters greatly to the likes of us. "Those straights can go back to that time because that *was* their time. That . . . that Arcadia of self-righteous adolescence. Gays can't go back. Everything in gay moves forward, do you realize that? It's getting out of school so you can reach the city and find your people. Working for political rights, looking for love, hoping for a cure." He touched wood: my desk. "Am I right?"

I nodded. "'And point me toward tomorrow.'"

"Tomorrow—when I was to have had dinner with Chad Jeffers," said Dennis Savage. He sighed. "Well. Something tells me that has been indefinitely canceled. By gentlemen's agreement."

"What would that have been like?, I wonder."

"It would have been an awkward fit, trying to keep his bourgeois order in kilter with my subversive surmises."

"So you admit you want to take over the world."

"I admit I'm trying to claim my place in it." He got his coat. "It *was* a good party, you know. It just wasn't the right party for us."

"The Boffer passes judgment."

"Can you make it into bed by yourself, you backbench tosspot, or am I going to find you sprawled on the floor in the morning?"

"Just for that, I hope Chad Jeffers shows up to claim his dinner tomorrow."

It was I who showed up for dinner, because Dennis Savage is not only a reliable cook but a generous one, even to drop-ins from the sixth floor in their stay-at-home rags. His apartment was in its full swell of life when I arrived: Little Kiwi, in his bathtowel cape, was running through his magic act to the strains of "Roses From the South"; Bauhaus, his snout caught in the paper packaging material from the *Chorus Line* CD, was scrounging around near the bathroom; and the master was in the kitchen, happily preparing his celebrated (not to say infamous; to which he would snap back, "Then why do you have to *say* it?") Stuffed Chicken with Wild Rice and Mushrooms.

"I hope I don't look as bad as I feel," I told him, parking myself in the kitchen doorway.

He gave me a quick once-over and grinned. "You'll live."

"You always look most content when you're making food, do you know that? Maybe you should have been a chef instead of a schoolteacher."

"I'll admit that I really blew it on career choice," he mused, stirring the mushrooms. "But I believe I did everything else right."

"Well, you certainly know how to run an apartment. This one comes complete with dinner and a show."

"Was that the buzzer?"

"Sometimes, when I'm sitting in my hobbit cave downstairs, surrounded by books and records and gloating in the stillness, I wonder why I never have

to give a guest refreshment or keep him entertained."

"Everyone's afraid of your apartment," he said.
"People have been killed there."

Little Kiwi joined us, bearing the Mysterious Talking Dice. "Watch this, now."

"Little Kiwi," said Dennis Savage, "did I just hear
the buzzer?"

"Yep. Now, watch closely, as La Dolce Pita con-
fers with the Mysterious—"

"Well, who was it?"

"Chad Jeffers. He's coming up."

The doorbell rang.

"Oh, *shit*," Dennis Savage observed in a kind of
murmured shout. "Look at this place! Look at . . .
everyone. This is like a . . ."

"A homosexual be-in," I said.

"What do we do?" asked Little Kiwi, missing the
implications but enjoying the excitement.

Dennis Savage took the mushrooms off the fire,
wiped his hands, strode through the living room,
and opened the door.

It was Chad Jeffers, all right, a blatant contrast to
the scene in his neat suit and splendid chesterfield.
He and Dennis Savage stood in the doorway for a
long moment.

"Can I come in?" Chad Jeffers said.

"Sure," said Little Kiwi, coming up. "You're just
in time for the Mysterious Talking Dice."

Chad Jeffers stepped in and took in the room, its
things and people and Bauhaus, still poking about in
his *Chorus Line* logo muzzle.

I shut the stereo off.

Chad Jeffers turned to Dennis Savage. "I guess I'm supposed to say that this isn't going to be easy, or something like that. But it's going to be very easy. I should have done this a long time ago."

Dennis Savage was still holding the door open, his body rigid but his face a blank.

Chad Jeffers nodded at the door. "Maybe you'd better close that," he said. Dennis Savage looked at him as if thinking it over, shut the door, and slowly turned back to Chad Jeffers.

"You get used to certain things," said Chad Jeffers. "You expect a way of living from other people and from yourself. It feels right. So when other people don't agree with you, you think they're wrong. You just do. If they're strangers, they're just stupid or crazy. But if they're people you're close to, you resent them. It's complicated. I feel it better than I understand it. My brother Brian—you met him that time you spent Thanksgiving at my folks'. My older brother. I guess . . . you remember him. Because . . . anyway, we were very close when we were growing up. Those old-fashioned kid things like camping trips and . . . we did all that together. And he . . . well, he told me a lot of things. When I got into trouble at school, you know, or how to get around, like, with the girls, making those right moves. See, we had that. We sort of grew apart after college. Living in different parts of the world, and other things. Things that have nothing to do with . . . with like the fact that he's gay. But the gay part is . . . hard. You must *really* hate hearing that, I know."

His voice was grinding a bit, as if he was trying to

show us how rough it feels—not only to hear it but to have to say it.

"But it's the truth. It's not what people expect, and when you give them this instead, it's very hard to take. You try to like work around it, see if you can keep all the rest of it together. You say, Okay, the gay stuff can be a secret. And I know that some of you . . . I mean, some of your people . . . they play it that way, don't they? But Brian is a very football-player kind of guy. He doesn't believe in secrets. That's the way he is, and, I'll tell you, I've always looked up to that. I knew that whatever shit anybody was handing out, anywhere—our father, or at school, *anywhere* . . . I could always count on Brian to clear it up for me.

"So of course he had to clear this gay thing up for me, too. That's Brian, see? He insisted that we talk about it, and that . . . that is the hard part. He said I ought to understand it, and look, I don't *want* to understand it. Why can't I just accept it? Brian says that with just anybody on the street I can accept it, but with my brother I have to understand it."

He looked around at all of us.

"Well, let me tell you, it made a lot of trouble between us, and it got mixed up with everything else there can be in your family, all those feelings that you want to accept without understanding them. I always get afraid that if I understand one thing, I'm going to get mixed up in all of it. That's why I say it's complicated. No one wants to confront all that . . . feeling in there. Nobody else has to, why should you? Like which kid got the better deal. It's not good to go into that, not good for anyone. My whole family knows that I was the favorite child—"

"Me, too," said Little Kiwi.

"—but that doesn't mean that Brian and I should sit down with our parents and talk it over, does it? It's not what people expect. It's just not what they expect. And Brian's always pounding at me about his lifestyle, which is none of my business. And other people do it, too—suddenly this . . . this event is happening to the rest of us. I can accept it, I know I can. And you're probably saying, Big deal, who cares what he can accept? I'm just telling you this, so you'll know. You'll know that one thing drags in another. All hard things. Because . . . because like how come the guy who took me on fishing trips and showed me how to smooth it out on dates and stand up to authority assholes and . . . yes, and play opera records for me and coach me for my chemistry exams which if I couldn't pass them I was going to get the ax from college . . . How come those guys can get so . . . different from me? I don't know what side I'm supposed to be on anymore. I told you saying this is easy. I've wanted to say it for years. But the feelings behind it are hard. It's not what I want, to have to know so much. And that's why I said . . ." Pausing, he gave a little shrug. ". . . Well, whatever it was I said last night. I apologize to all of you. I just didn't expect to have to relate to all those feelings at that party. I just wanted to go back to . . . to . . . before everything got complicated."

There he halted, staring at Dennis Savage for the longest freeze-frame I've ever seen.

Then he said, "Can we shake hands?"

And they did, and Chad Jeffers shook hands with us, too, and Little Kiwi liked it so much he shook hands twice, and it turned out that Chad Jeffers had come to dinner after all, so that's what happened. We had a fine time. Little Kiwi enlivened dessert by putting on his complete magic show, and a few of the tricks almost worked. Chad Jeffers hoped to encourage the budding performer by asking for revelatory explanations, but La Dolce Pita only smiled—for, as he himself has said, if you talk about the secrets, they lose their secret qualities.

I believe this was the true reunion party, most literally a reunion, a rejoining of splintered interests. And I believe that Dennis Savage and Chad Jeffers felt their bond more keenly this night than ever they had in their rash, free youth at college, because they knew better now what their bond was made of. You can grow up and move on and forget almost everyone you knew, but the truest friends are those who teach us something that matters greatly, even something with hard feelings in it: and those friends stay essential to us for life, not only part of our past but of our future as well. Our teachers are always with us.

So I was not surprised to detect a trace of moisture in Dennis Savage's eyes when Chad Jeffers got on his overcoat and said good-bye. He gave Dennis Savage a whack on the shoulder and told him to take good care, and when he was halfway through the door he stopped and turned back and nodded.

Then he crinkled and said, "So long, Denny."

Away he went: and Dennis Savage's college days were over.

"Is that the name?" asked Little Kiwi once the door closed. "That only Chad Jeffers called you?"

"Did you really help him with his chemistry?" I put in. "You who don't even know how much lime to cut into a Perrier?"

Dennis Savage sighed heavily. "He's out the door but two seconds and the fun begins. This is where you mock my most intimate and beautiful memories, isn't it? Humiliate my quaint paeans to boyhood. Expose secrets that I never entirely understood in the first place. Loot my pathetic treasury of recollections. Right? Am I right? Fine. Go right ahead. Won't you please be my guest?"

"Oh," I said. "Not this time, Denny."

I Read My Nephew Stories

▰▰▰▰▰

OKAY, WHAT AM I DOING on a beach in Massachusetts?

Simple: my brother Ned ran away from home when he was fifteen.

I bet you didn't know I had a brother who ran away from home—also an aunt who committed suicide, a great-uncle who went to prison, and a cousin who dropped out and moved to India. I'm still trying to get the rights to our saga back from the O'Neill estate.

Anyway, Ned not only ran away from home but never came back, which had my younger brothers and me agog, but which my other older brother Jim called A Very Outstanding Event. Jim and Ned stayed in contact, and I would receive periodic, laconic reports. Now Ned was doing bits at Cinecittà, now he was a reporter for the Paris *Herald Tribune*. Presenting the news was Ned's forte, it seemed, for he stayed with it. He even did it on television.

Better, he came home to do it on American televi-

sion. Better . . . *Huh.* It seemed unnaturally forgiving, like Samuel Beckett coming home to Dublin,
licking his lips at the sight of the Martello Tower, and
crying out, "Champion!" Jim and I met Ned for lunch
one day at Clarke's; Ned was up for a transfer from
New Orleans to New York. So many distances, voy-
ages, in some people's lives. You notice this particularly if, like me, you stay in one place for entire
epochs, enthusiastically resisting all opportunities to
travel, even just to Brooklyn for dinner.

Ned didn't land the New York job. He ended up
in Boston, which he said he preferred. To what, I
wonder? New York? Paris? His past? He was married and had a little boy; and that got me amazed.
Here was a man, flesh of my flesh, only three years
older than I, who had already set upon his course of
leaving his mark upon the world—and I was still
worrying over whether I would ever come upon a
copy of the Capitol *Pal Joey* with the original cover.
We were brothers, but we weren't entirely related, if
you see what I mean.

It turned out that even a Boston television anchorman has to come to New York periodically for Meetings, and lunch with Ned and Jim became a regular
feature of my life. At one of these, looking toward
the summer, Ned invited us up to stay with him on
Martha's Vineyard. Jim said no, but I was curious. I
wanted to see what else I wasn't entirely related to,
Ned's wife and son. I had a good time and went
again the next year, and it became an annual visit—
more than a visit, a tithe. After three or four of these
trips, I felt certain that if I tried to stick out a summer without visiting the Neds, they would hale me

into court. I had become a participant in their season, a member of my own family.

A certain weekend would be assigned me, set aside, built around the things I was likely to do and say. Ned was a man of Significant Draw, and the trip's logistics were Advantageous. Zesty, highly inflected metropolitan types, doing this important favor for a friend of a friend of a friend, would pick me up in front of my building, the car packed with cold collation, ambition, and wit. Crowded cars, rigid stages. This is traveling. I hate it but—sometimes—I do it. There was usually one guy too many (besides me), and someone would get stuck with a liverwurst sandwich, and one of the women would want to stop when no one else did, and one of the men would drop a truly ghastly ethnic slur of some kind (no one would say anything, but the silence was a hiss). Then, too, the car trip from Manhattan to outer New England must vie with the Damascus-Peking caravan line for density of tedium. Still, eventually I would land at the ferry slip, thinking of some story I might get out of the car people. Soon enough I would be standing on the top of the boat, and I would see my brother and sister-in-law standing with my nephew. I would wave. My brother, whom I understood very well in our youth but now think of as This Guy I Know, or Mr. Mordden, or even (Hey) Mister, waves back. He is jaunty, confident, always taller than I remember. He's going to age poisonously well. He's even getting just a bit gray; good career move. My sister-in-law points me out to the little boy, and he'll gaze at me with wonder and suspicion and bashful delight.

So that's what I'm doing on a beach in Massachusetts: sitting in their kitchen at the "breakfast bar," finishing my morning coffee.

Curtain up, and my sister-in-law says, "I wish you and your brother got along better."

"We get along quite well for two people so near yet so far, don't you think?"

"I mean, I wish you acted as if you liked each other. I know you do like each other, of course." She rinses out the name mugs: Ned, Ellen, Toby. How come they can find a Toby and I can't find an Ethan? "It's just so nice to see him . . . relating?" A paper towel to dry the mugs. My sister-in-law is very neat; her theory of eating implements is, they're either in use or in the cupboards. None of that wet stuff hanging in the porte cochere, or whatever they call those plastic racks next to the sink. You wash it, you dry it. You're brothers, you relate.

"Ned really isn't a big relater," I say. "I expect the television camera has spoiled him. He's gotten so used to addressing a population, he probably doesn't know how to talk to one person anymore."

My brother, I gather, is a very hot item among analysts of the 18-to-49 female demographics, but we never mention this to him because he has a fierce aplomb, always did. No wonder he left home without explaining why. Frankly, I don't think he ever did know how to talk to one person; anchormanning is perfect casting for him.

Still, he has a perfect marriage: his wife likes everything about him and his son is so young that his occasional testy rebellions pass for standard-make puerile mischief. I think there may be a problem on the brew there, but my sister-in-law sees the three of them as a gang of fun-loving pals. She is very proud of Ned's fame, too. She sends me his clippings. She used to accompany these with warm little notes, trying to explain why she is doing this. Then I told her that in publishing, where time is the first concern, we just write FYI ("For your information") on something and send it off. Amused, she has made it a household joke: she will hand me a bowl of rice pudding, indicate the whipped cream with a spy's nod, and murmur, "FYI, friend?"

Anyway, I already know why she is doing this: loyalty and love. She's terrific, but she feels too hard. "You know," she begins, "last night . . ." She looks away, looks back at me.

"Okay, yes," I say, "but please don't cry."

I always know when she will. It's not really crying; she leaks for joy. It's like those sudden, momentary thundershowers in London, when you look up and see the sun right through the rain. It'll be over shortly. But you still get wet.

"It was just so nice," she says, "to be all together. And Toby loves it when you read to him. He won't let anyone else, you know. We have so much trouble getting him to bed in the city. It's different when you're here."

"It's always different where I am. It's in my contract."

"Now, don't make a joke of it. It was so sweet. And I know you know that, so don't look away, either. You and Toby look so cute together, too. And you read so well." She is leaking.

"Toby and I aren't that great a team," I put in. "He's very tough for six. I only read to him so he won't grouch at me."

"Oh, that's not true." She gazes happily around the tidy summer kitchen: the mounted utensils, the standing machines, Toby's watercolors on the wall, Smurf stickers on the fridge, all their little heads carefully cut off. "Grouch at you? It's family! We've got to be our own best friends!"

"I wish you wouldn't enthuse just after breakfast."

"When he has a nightmare . . . of course, he doesn't often. But when he does, do you know he speaks your name? As if he's worried about you? I've heard him."

"Toby speaks my name?"

"Not Toby. Your brother."

Alarmed, I head for the beach. There's not much else to do out here but eat, sleep, and bake on the sand. You'd think an anchorman would be at a loss here: nothing but individuals to swank around for, at, with. What a waste of an act.

And God knows, Ned's got one. The first time we were alone together as adults—at lunch at my neighborhood joint, the Mayfair, at Fifty-third and First—he broke a copious silence by telling me a sure way to fascinate a woman: immediately after, read her a story. He recommended *The Velveteen Rabbit*. He said the combination of the aggressiveness of cock and the sweetness of the fairy tale overwhelms them. Wrong. It isn't the combination—it's the paradox of the aggressive and the sweet working for and against each other.

But he's definitely onto something here. Sometimes I try to visualize Ellen lying next to him, listening to him read *The Velveteen Rabbit*. I can see it. I can see it more easily than I can see myself on this patch of beach among—forgive me, Ellen—strangers. Still, I'm a game guest. I bring a quart of Johnnie Walker Red. I make my own bed, first thing up, even before the toothpaste. I spell them in looking after Toby. I take us all out to dinner on my last night. And I read my nephew stories.

It started by chance. One evening after dinner, three or four years ago, I happened to pick up an ancient Oz book lying next to me on the couch. As I leafed through it, Toby came up and said, "Mine." His father looked over from six newspapers, including the *Manchester Guardian*. "No, Toby, that's mine," he said. But my name was written on the front free endpaper.

"Read," Toby urged me.

I demurred with some evasion and he hit me.

"Better read to him," my newscaster brother said, not unamused.

I did read to him, and he listened carefully. All three of them do; and they watch me as they listen. It's like reading one's work in a bookstore. They even unplug the phone. After a while, Toby puts his head in my lap, and after a longer while he falls asleep. Then I carry him upstairs and his parents follow, his mother to dote and his father to stand in the doorway, framed in the light from the hall as if he had moved from the news to a suspense series. It's film noir; it's coming too close. Sometimes Toby murmurs reproachful excerpts as I put him to bed— "Why didn't you tell me the secret?" or "You are not playing fairly." Surely these are not meant for me, precisely. Not precisely. By then, my brother has moved into the room to put his arms around my sister-in-law from behind. These soft noises there, as I tuck Toby in. He likes to be tightly wrapped, like a present. Then I turn to face them, hugged together as they are, and for a moment I fear they won't let me out of the room.

The beach is always quiet here, nearly deserted on weekdays. I open my spiral notebook and pursue the tale of the moment—about, as usual, things I have seen, done, said. I have got to try writing *fiction:* about the encounter of Nabokov and Tolstoy in heaven, perhaps "The Goblin Who Missed Thanksgiving." I do not want to write anymore about people I know, people with feelings that I have been tricked into sharing. I should write books like those I read to Toby, set in fabulous places among bizarre creatures. You can say anything you want to in such tales and no reader will wonder who you are. You could be the Velveteen Rabbit.

My sister-in-law comes along after a bit with Toby and several tons of beach equipment. There are flagstaffs to stick in the sand and pails of two sorts, the metal kind decorated with merry scenes and the plastic kind with a side pocket for the toting of a shovel. There are rubber balls, a Slinky all coiled up in itself, picture books, drawing tablets, and remnants of a hundred miniature zoos, forts, shopping centers, and such, the pieces recombined in Toby's imagination to form the characters of some dire cosmopolitan epic.

I burrow deep into my notebook as my sister-in-law pulls out the old Modern Library Giant edition of *Ulysses*, the orange jacket encased in plastic. She maintains the reading level of an academic, but is hurt if you ask why she doesn't do something besides be married to my brother. Or she would be hurt if I dared ask. I've delved into *Ulysses* so often I recently took it up in Italian to keep the quest venturesome. (*Ulisse*, translated with astonishing resourcefulness by Giulio de Angelis. It comes complete with notes and commentary, just as I do.) Yet my sister-in-law knows it better than I, can even recite the chapter titles in order. She holds absolutely still when she reads.

Toby ignores us, digging, patting, piling. A grand, circular moat. A lump of sand in the center. Flags at the perimeter. Soldiers, rustics, exotic animals, and Hollywood extraterrestrials lining up to get in. Toby growls to himself as he works, like a dog fussing at a sock. "I'm making a sand tower," he announces at one point.

When my sister-in-law excuses herself to ready dinner, Toby and I dart suspicious glances at each other. He waits till she disappears over the dunes, then says, "Do you want to help me dribble?"

"Sure."

He hands me a pail and leads the way to the sea. "Look out for octopus," he warns.

He's going to grouch at me, I know. He always does.

"You fill it with water," he says. "It has to be just right. Not like that!"

He keeps pushing me.

"Like this," he shows.

It takes me eight dips to satisfy him; apparently the water has to fill the pail tight to the rim without spilling. How often in this life one must negotiate a walk along the blade when the topic at hand is absolutely nothing at all. How often one plays one's life for trivial stakes. With certain people, everything matters.

"Now, watch," says Toby.

This is dribbling: you ease the bottom end of the pail upward, leading the water to plop onto the sand, creating a mason's effect on the walls of your fortress. You decorate your power.

"Now you," says Toby, with a sense of challenge.

"Why don't you show me? I don't have the feel of it yet."

Growling, he grabs my pail and throws it off to the side. "I didn't like that water," he explains.

I return to my story, a sad tale of growing up and pulling away in a small southern town. Toby busies himself with his dribbling.

In the city, the scene is fury, speed, and ice, sheer ice. Holding your own, you may accidentally alienate one of the four or five most influential people in your professional or social or romantic life, and you may spend years working off the blunder. But on the beach, nothing happens, and everything is forgivable. The happy time crawls past. You can't go wrong.

"Hey, Toby," I ask, "what's on for dinner?"

Toby looks out at the sea. "No, there won't be any dinner for us at all. Can birds swim?"

"Why won't there be dinner?"

"My daddy is mad at Mommy and they aren't

going to feed us. I heard them crashing last night, so that means they're mad at someone. Do they like you?"

"Your mother does."

"Is she your sister?"

"No. Your dad is my brother."

"I don't think he likes us."

Toby's dog comes snorting up the beach from the west: a large, wirehaired terrier who moves with the frozen despair of an old man and the mild curiosity of a baby, named, by the child, with a child's logic, Tober.

"Get away, Tober!" Toby screeches. "Get away, you sneaky hound!"

The dog gently investigates the sea, sniffing at the waves. Toby's father, my brother Ned, cannot be far away. He is always walking the dog, possibly to see what stir he can inspire with his fame.

Possibly.

This is a sophisticated beach, the cream of Boston hip (if there be such a thing). He would be in no danger from autograph crazies. But people would surely recognize him—"as seen on television," the ultimate American credential—and buzz like wasps in a pancake house.

I see my brother in the distance, walking slowly around the curl of a dune, his hands in the pockets of his shorts, the long-thighed light brown kind you only see on straight men, brothers and fathers.

Tober noses up to Toby, who stares at him for a bit, then gives him a push.

"You aren't very nice to your pet," I venture.

"He comes around too much. And he snapped at

the doorman. They bought a muzzle for him. But you know what? I hid it in my toy chest. Sometimes I wear it in my room. Tober isn't really mine, anyway. He only likes my father."

My brother is almost upon us now.

"Hey, Tober," I call out. "Here, Tobes."

Tober looks at me, starts over, halts. It's not always easy to know what you're supposed to do in this family.

Toby eyes the beast with disgust. "Make him nap," he says.

And Ned arrives.

"How are you coming, my friend?" my brother asks me. He doesn't act like a newscaster, but like a man who might know a few.

"I'm doing just fine."

"Good man. Toby, did you remember to put water in Tober's dish this morning?"

This means Toby didn't, but the boy has unconcernedly returned to his sand tower. "He didn't look thirsty."

"I hate to think that a poor dumb animal is going without water because a little boy was too lazy to bother with him."

Toby and I glance at the dog, quietly settled on his haunches, looking far out to sea. A handsome, suave animal, not the kind to dance on your leg or suddenly begin howling when company comes, like a certain dog I know.

"He was naughty yesterday," says Toby. "So I'm not giving him water for a month."

Toby's father kneels to reason with his son.

"Toby," he begins, "you can't punish a living creature by depriving it of food."

Toby looks down, but resolutely. "You took my allowance away," he says.

"That's just money."

"I was going to buy candy with it. Candy is food."

Toby's father grasps Toby's little child's shoulders and tells him, in the voice that tolerantly introduces those irritating responsible opinions of the opposing viewpoint, "Listen here, Toby, have I ever deprived you of nourishment? Have you ever gone hungry?"

"Yes."

"No, you haven't."

"Last week," Toby insists, "you didn't take me to the puppet play."

"That was nearly six months ago, first off, and second, if you remember, you weren't taken to the puppet show because you got chocolate all over the television."

Patricide.

"Toby," he goes on, "look at me when I talk to you."

My family is made of those who demand to be looked at when they talk to you and those who look away when they hear. My brother started as a looker away; now he has to be looked at. No wonder he became a newscaster. An entire city must look at him when he talks. I visualize his television audience sitting before their sets in high chairs, wearing bibs discolored by strained prunes. Their faces are sad as they are reproached and reasoned with.

"Hey," I put in. "Why don't you tell Toby about the time I pushed you off the roof?"

My brother ignores this; Toby looks up.

"I think you'd better take Tober up to the house," my brother goes on, "and see if—"

"What roof? Our roof? Did he push you off that high?"

"Toby—"

Toby looks at me. "When did you push him? Was I there?"

"No. But I was thinking of you at the time."

"What's that supposed to mean?" my brother asks me. "We were kids then."

"I knew you'd have a child someday. I did it for him."

"Thanks a lot."

"He broke his arm," I tell Toby. "I broke your father's arm. He had to wear a cast for a month, and they threw him off the football team." I ask my brother, "Remember?"

"All right now, Toby, you march straight up to the house and assume some responsiblity for Tober. He's your dog."

Toby claps his hands like a pasha, and Tober meticulously gets to his feet, capping the motion with an elegant stretch of his spine, from rigid neck to apologetic haunches. With half this finesse, Bauhaus would be almost acceptable.

"Tober, come here!" Toby screams. "You mental case!"

"Not so loud," my brother directs. "Go on up, now."

"Keep watch on my sand tower," Toby warns us. "Don't let the other people come and wreck it."

"There are no other people," my brother tells

him—one of those apparently aimless statements, mere punctuation from the sound of them, that, on the contrary, burst from the heart. Who but a fifteen-year-old runaway would get so much out of the statement "There are no other people"?

As Toby and the dog proceed up the beach back to the house, I appear engrossed in my work. I am writing gibberish in order to look inaccessible; a useless defense against a man who remembers what you were like when you were eight.

"Ellen says you brought her a present," my brother offers. No one is inaccessible to a newsman. Impenetrable, maybe: but approachable, absolutely.

"I got both of you a present."

"A mayonnaise jar, was it? Sounds very handy."

"It doesn't just hold mayonnaise. It helps make it. The recipe is printed on the glass. Bloomingdale's."

"She really likes you, you know."

Out come the weapons. We estimate our worth in the quality of the people who like us—as witness the hearty bantering that goes on on news shows between the features and the commercial breaks. A Boston friend taped some of my brother's programs for me, and on one of them it seems to me—it *seems*—as if the other newspeople turn their backs on him and cut him out of their banter, leaving him to shift his papers and chuckle at imaginary colleagues out of camera range.

"Toby says you aren't going to give us dinner," I say as my brother kicks shells and pebbles down at the waterline. "He heard you and Ellen quarreling."

"Toby's doing a very awkward time nowadays. You shouldn't encourage him. It's hard enough to keep him in line without you telling him stories about brothers throwing each other off roofs."

"Why not? You did it to me and I did it to you. It was the great moment of my childhood. I wanted to share it with him."

My brother works his way onto the crest of the tide flat, kicking gusts of sand as he travels. "You know how easily he gets stirred up," he goes on.

"It's funny how cool you were as a child, and how high-strung Toby is. I wouldn't think it would run in your family."

"He's just a kid so far." My brother is kicking up whole wads of sand now, aimlessly, business on his mind. "What'll you do with that writing piece when it's done? Does it go in *The New Yorker?*"

"Why are you stamping around in the sand like that?"

He shrugged. "High spirits. Why even ask?"

"Because you've even kicked Toby's sand tower to bits."

My brother sees what he has done.

"I'd hate to be in your sneakers when Toby gets back and sees what you did," I exult. "He takes his beach sports very seriously."

"So do you."

I have to laugh at that. "I envy Toby his enthusiasms," I say. "He gets such a thrill out of everything, whether he loves them or despises them. He *feels.* Were we ever like that? Puppet plays and candy?"

"I wasn't," my brother says.

"How come you ran away from us?" I suddenly ask. "Do you expect Toby to run away from you?"

He is speechless.

Barking and shouting from across the dunes signal the return of Toby and Tober. They race down to us like a circus on a four-a-day booking. Toby is heading for the water, but his father catches him as he passes, pulls him up, and tosses him into the air as easily as if he were confetti. Toby says, "Daddy!" with delight as he comes down; only this, but this is enough.

I pet the panting dog.

"Toby," says the newscaster. "Listen to bad news. I wrecked your sand castle. Accidentally. I was kicking at the sand without thinking. I'm sorry."

Openmouthed, Toby turns to me.

"I didn't do it," I warn him.

"What if you get a spanking now?" Toby asks, turning to his father, looking up to find him, taking hold of his hand. "Or no dinner?"

"We don't punish anyone for accidents, Toby," his father lectures. "You know that."

"Yes," Toby agrees. "I have to go finger-paint."

"Okay." His father turns to me. "Okay, my friend?" Why do I have to render an opinion? My brother slaps Toby's behind lightly and the child runs up the beach, Tober dragging decorously after him.

Okay, he says. Look, don't waste a smile on me— but my brother does, a television smile suited to a quaint human-interest feature, perhaps a convention of street-food aficionados in south Boston. "See you at dinner," he says.

I go back to writing my story. Bits of the day flip into the text, a field expedient. Bits of every day; it makes people nervous. "You snitched!" a bag lady cried at me once, on Park Avenue.

"No, I didn't," I said; but I was thinking of some story.

"You told how I made a commotion with a cigarillo in the no-smoking section of the Carnegie Cinema show!"

"Never."

"No?"

"No," I repeated.

She shrugged, looked away, and coughed. "So what happens next?"

On the beach, next is always a meal. You pay out a certain number of minutes and then comes food, the four of us at table, all eyes aimed at some imagined central point of contact. But I ask you: Who imagines? Who directs the aim? When we gather at the board, I babble, dispersing the attacks. I am like a bag lady in the scattered energy of my references. I speak of Louise Brooks, of *The Egoist,* of Schubert's song cycles. They nod. They ask Intelligent Questions. They feel they must encourage me, my sister-in-law because anyone she is related to becomes wonderful by rules of love loyalty, and my brother because it is not entirely useless, in his line of work, to be connected to a writer, even a brutally honest one. Still, he'll never quite be able to see me as anything but an infant rebel, reckless, bold for his years, but ultimately ineffectual. He treats me as someone who may have to be soothed, even humored, perhaps disarmed, at any moment.

This only exacerbates my defiance, of course. From the moment I enter the house my brother lives in—to my sister-in-law's welcoming half-smile, as warm as one blanket too many on a surprisingly balmy November night—I am at war.

My brother cuts greens for his Caesar salad, which, for some reason, is genuinely cordon bleu. But then Ned was always a stickler for High Style in everything he did. I hear, from secure sources, that back in Boston notables of the local great world stare over his shoulder as he prepares it. Oh, it looks simple. Who can't make a salad? They can't—not like his salad, anyway. Theirs is correct; his is superb. They come back again and again to watch him and he pays them no heed. He acts as if no one should be able to do what he does.

From Toby's room comes the festive din of the Walt Disney versions of *Snow White, Pinocchio,* and *Alice in Wonderland,* on a tape I made for him last year. Occasionally, Toby sings along. I idly glance in at the door. Toby and Tober are sitting on the floor, engrossed in the act of listening; both of them are wearing cowboy hats and neckerchiefs.

When I return to the kitchen, my sister-in-law hands me a glass of white wine. I take it outside to watch the sun burn red over the water. I try to think of my latest story and all this real life. How inconvenient that work merges with truth. I was planning to model myself on Evelyn Waugh, not Thomas Mann. Yet even Waugh turned Mann in the end. Writers have a hundred dodges but a thousand revelations. Every so often, some of my friends ask pettishly why I never write about them. "But I do," I respond, as nicely as possible.

Then they grow uneasy.

Amazingly enough, I enjoy these summer visits up here, so far off my proper turf. I like the break it makes in my city rhythm, the sense the place gives me of owing nothing to everybody—professionally, of course. If only I owed nothing to absolutely anyone socially, emotionally, and historically, I would be white clean free.

A family forms around me as I sit on the deck. Something licks the back of my hand: Tober, a relief from the incessantly dilating Bauhaus. My sister-in-law joins us. A breeze animates the scene. Now Toby is here, querulously asking about the parentage of Donald Duck's three nephews. He knows they have none, but he wants to see what he will be told. His father comes out, balancing his hand on Toby's head as the twilight deepens.

I do not need to look at them to know how it appears. She is gazing upon my brother and he is gazing down at the boy and the boy is gazing at all of us, one after the other. For a moment, I luxuriate in the sentimentality of knowing that, whatever else happens, he will be raised in love. How terrifyingly important that is. Then I feel manipulated by this frenzy of feeling and swear to avenge the dishonor by styling all three of them as villains in my most scabrous stories.

My brother takes my wineglass to refill it, and Toby sits next to me, holding a juice drink poured to resemble a cocktail. "Now you could tell me more," says Toby, "about when you pushed my father off the roof."

"I don't think I ought to."

"Why?"

"That's a good question."

"Then why did you tell me before, on the beach?"

"That's an even better one."

"Tell me a story, anyway."

"Once upon a time," I begin—for these are the easiest stories to invent and the most comfortable to tell, set hundreds of years ago among perfect strangers—"there was a little boy who lived all by himself in a great sand tower in the middle of a forest."

"What was his name?" Toby asks.

"He had none. He had lived all alone as long as he could remember, so he had never needed a name. One day, a knight rode by on a beautiful black horse, and the knight was encased from head to foot in resplendent silver armor."

"What was the horse's name?" Toby asks.

"Toby, you shouldn't interrupt the storyteller," his mother gently chides, her doting look slipping from him to me and back.

"The knight's armor shone so brilliantly in the sunlight that the little boy, looking down from the window at the very top of his tower, could actually see himself. It was the first time he had ever done so, for there were no mirrors in his tower. None whatsoever. There was nothing to look into, no reflection—"

"Did he have Cinemax?" Toby asks, absently yawning.

"Hush. Now, the little boy was surprised to see the knight. But he was even more surprised to see himself. And from his window high above the forest he called down to the knight, 'Who are you?'"

"Here you go, my friend," says my brother, returning with refills of the drinks.

"But the knight thought the little boy was speaking to his own reflection, and so he said nothing. The little boy was consumed with wonder, for he suddenly realized that he must be lonely in his tower. He longed to go down and say hello to the knight and find out some things about the world. But there was no way down through the tower. Nor was there any way for the knight to climb up to him. The little boy felt very sad."

Toby stretches out with his head in my lap.

"The knight was sad, too, for he had been wandering in the forest for many days, having lost his way. He feared he might wander forever, for this forest was so big that no one who strayed into it from outside ever found his way out. But there was nothing for the knight to do but move on, and he spurred his horse to pursue his journey. The little boy again cried out, 'Who are you?' But this time the knight happened to be passing behind a great oak tree, which hid his armor from sight and thus cut off the boy's reflection. So the knight assumed he was being addressed this time, and he thought he should answer the question. He should tell the little boy who he is . . ."

Toby has fallen asleep.

"This tyke is all tuckered out," I tell his parents. "He didn't even wait for dinner."

"Did . . . did Ned read to you?" my sister-in-law asks. "When you were boys?"

"He didn't have to. I wasn't grouchy."

"Did he?"

She is looking at him and he is looking at her.

"Well, my mother didn't, and my dad was away a

lot . . ." Now they are looking at me. "I suppose somebody had to do the reading."

She takes his hand. "*Did* he?"

"Please don't leak."

"Don't . . . what?"

"When the little boy asked the knight who he was," says my brother, "what did the knight answer?"

I look at him for a moment. "He answered, 'I have the same name as you.'"

My brother frowns. "Unusual repartee."

Toby stirs in my arms.

"I have the same name," I observe, "as all of you."

My sister-in-law smiles. But my brother, puzzled once too often this day, looks at me as if he does not know who I am.

Beach Blanket Mah-Jongg

DENNIS SAVAGE FINALLY broke down and bought a VCR, and Little Kiwi was in heaven with a new toy. As winter dwindled into the coolly clever, touchy, mercurial season that we New Yorkers call spring, Little Kiwi began assembling what he touted as "this superscope collection of classic cinema." However, the titles he collected ran to the likes of *Abbott and Costello in the Foreign Legion*, *The Nutty Professor*, and eight versions of *Heidi*. At that, Little Kiwi somehow never mastered the fine art of taping by timer. On a number of occasions, he herded Dennis Savage, Carlo, and me into the living room for, in his words, "the local world premiere screening" of some hapless old movie, only to unveil, to his flushed befuddlement, *Strike it Rich!* or *Modern Farmer* reruns—even, most useless of all among the likes of us, *Sermonette*.

Carlo didn't mind; he thinks anything a sexy man does is sexy. I was wry about it; you have to be wry at just about everything Little Kiwi does. But Dennis Savage, who has become as much Little Kiwi's father as his lover, would get up and patiently go over VCR mechanics again, which made me twice as wry because Dennis Savage knows less about machines than Little Kiwi does.

"Instead of giggling and fooling," Dennis Savage told Carlo and me, "why don't you help him get his movie collection together?"

"Make up a list," I advised Little Kiwi. "Put down all the films you'd like to tape and hunt them down. Structure your project."

"A list!" Little Kiwi thrilled; he always finds the glamour in the mundane. He immediately got a pad and pencil to start his list, and the rest of us fed him suggestions.

"The Broadway Melody," I offered.

"The Grapes of Wrath," Dennis Savage added.

"The Boys in the Sand," Carlo recalled.

"And *Tigers in Connecticut!*" said Little Kiwi.

The company was baffled. Even Bauhaus, Little Kiwi's incompetent dog, appeared bemused.

"That one where Katharine Hepburn has a tiger and she loves Cary Grant," Little Kiwi explained. "So then she wrecks his dinosaur."

"Bringing Up Baby," said Dennis Savage.

"And it isn't tigers," I added, "it's leopards."

"That one goes *right* on my list!" Little Kiwi cried. "This is a pad of classics, you know." Enthused by a thought, he told Carlo, "And guess what else!"

Carlo just looked at him, his thoughts unreportable even to an all-male readership.

Little Kiwi turned to me. "How about *Cabaret Lady?*"

"What's that?" I asked. "A Lotte Lenya musical?"
"No, Hildegard Dietrich."
"*Blonde Venus,*" said Dennis Savage.
"And it's Marlene—"
"Oh, this is a swank list, my boys," said Little Kiwi.

Little Kiwi got so caught up in the provisioning of his library of classics that from time to time he would venture downstairs and knock on my door, eager to have someone come up and admire his latest acquisition. It was still spring, those two or three days that New Yorkers get between the chill and the boil. Dennis Savage wouldn't be free from schoolteaching till late June, and I was handy and agreeable and only two floors of apartment building away. Actually, it was fun watching Little Kiwi show off his technical dexterity. When he tried to fast-forward, the sound would mute; when he pressed the mute button, the tape would rewind; when he summoned rewind, the television would go off.

One day, as I sat at my desk wondering if I should take an eighth work break without having done any work, I realized that Little Kiwi hadn't been dropping in lately. Who's he been showing his tapes to? I thought. About three days later, I found out: I heard a knock, opened the door, and laid eyes on an unknown teenager, younger and shorter and fairer than Little Kiwi.

"Virgil," he said, "wants you to come up and see our show."

Startled, I stared.

"I'm Cosgrove," he explained.

He led the way up to Dennis Savage's, and after a while I began to feel like the head of a day-care center. Apparently Little Kiwi and Cosgrove had put together an entire mixed-bill program: main features, coming attractions, cartoon, newsreel, and second feature. There were still kinks in the system—the coming attractions bit was simply network hype for *Dallas* and the "newsreel" was a slice of the evening news, mostly of commercials. At least the cartoon was a Mickey Mouse, though Bauhaus got frightened and had to be locked in the bedroom.

"This is just like a Saturday kiddy matinee," Little Kiwi was raving. "Isn't it?"

I said, "It's very nostalgic."

Cosgrove was looking at me as if wondering if they even had movies when I was a kiddy, much less Saturday matinees, and I was looking at him as if ready to haul out his blanket and woolly panda for nap hour, when Dennis Savage staggered in from another day of improving the minds of the American young.

"Those cretins," he muttered.

"Which?" I asked. "These or yours?"

"Oh, they're all mine," he sighed. "Hello, Cosgrove."

"Hello."

Dennis Savage shot me a look of amusement, which I shot right back, and Carlo dropped in, so Little Kiwi went into the kitchen to make everyone grilled cheese and tomato sandwiches, Cosgrove assisting. Every so often, Little Kiwi's voice would float into the living room, with "Slice them real crunchy now, Cosgrove" or a "Cosgrove, let's serve half-sour pickles as a side order today."

"Sounds like Little Kiwi's found an even littler Kiwi," I said.

"One of the neighborhood kids," said Dennis Savage, unpacking his valise. "He dropped out of school and his parents more or less threw him out. Or so they tell me." He was shifting papers about, showing us the official kit of his hard work. He seemed distracted. "One of those gay stories, I guess."

"Are those book reports and Latin tests?" Carlo asked Dennis Savage. "You would surely have flunked me if you were my teacher, wouldn't you? You would have stood me in the corner."

A rare half-smile elegiacally unfolded the line of Dennis Savage's mouth. Usually, he's either chuckling or grouching. Especially grouching.

"Go easy on me," said Dennis Savage. "It's been a heavy day."

"Now I'd be pounding the erasers," Carlo went on. "Sharpening the chalk sticks. I'd always be in dutch."

Cascades of giggles from the kitchen.

"If this were 1955," Dennis Savage opined, "that kid would have to straighten out with a wife and a job and make a whole new generation miserable. But Stonewall City has places for boys who are always in trouble."

"Yeah," I said. "He gets to adopt a buddy and revel in a VCR."

Dennis Savage nodded, sorted his papers,

shrugged. "They're quite inseparable. The kid does everything but sleep here."

Carlo shifted position and I cleared my throat. We traded glances. Then we grinned at Dennis Savage. As the Germans say, *Luftpause.*

"What's with you two?" asked Dennis Savage. "Are you totally zonked out from a hard day of loafing and goofing off?"

"He doesn't get it," Carlo told me.

"Give him time," I said. "He's totally zonked out from a hard day of reading and writing and 'rithmetic."

"Taught to the tune," Carlo agreed dreamily, "of a—"

"Give me time for what?"

Carlo and I performed a mock innocent-guilty whistle.

"All right, you jokers. What's the game?"

" 'The kid does everything but sleep here,' " Carlo said. "It sounds so truly innocent."

"Two dear little play pals," I chimed in, "with their VCR and their alphabet blocks."

Finally catching up to us, Dennis Savage expostulated with the strenuous resistance of the sighted blind. "You think those two kids are . . . You dare to suggest that Little Kiwi would cheat on me with some . . . some—"

"Some beautiful blond kid?" I said. "Why not?"

"Terrific! Just terrific! You see a perfectly innocent little friendship and all you can do is . . . ravage it with Circuit innuendo. Dishqueens of the world, unite!"

Carlo and I bowed to each other like mandarins.

"It's not funny!"

"Jesus, can't you take a joke?"

Dennis Savage was calming down. "It's not fit comic material," he huffed. "You should tread gently in the sacred wood."

At which Carlo and I laughed so hard we had to hold our stomachs; and Cosgrove, helping Little Kiwi serve the food, eyed us with bewilderment. Little Kiwi, inured to such exhibits, ignored us, and we quieted down, but then Cosgrove tucked his napkin into his shirt collar like a five-year-old, and Carlo and I had to look away to keep our faces straight.

Summer beckoned to us from the Island of Fire, but Little Kiwi moped at the notion of having to abandon his beloved VCR. Finally Dennis Savage agreed to drag the equipment out for the season, and Little Kiwi was in heaven again.

Cosgrove was still around—more than ever, if possible. It was not clear where he went and what he did when he was elsewhere, but he, too, was certainly in heaven when he was in the company of our gang, the typical bourgeois youngster who has evaded a reproving family for a troop of males who accept him as he is. This is called Why Boys Leave Home.

Cosgrove's attachment to Little Kiwi was virtually absolute, and Little Kiwi liked it that way. Once Little Kiwi had hung back in the shadow of Dennis Savage; suddenly Little Kiwi had a shadow of his own, to instruct in the ways of the great world. "Cosgrove, do you think that's a good tie for the eighties?" he would say; and Cosgrove would immediately lose the tie. Or "Cosgrove, your grilled cheese isn't quite as *grilled* as it should be"; and Cosgrove would beg to put the sandwich back on the fire.

Cosgrove even functioned as Little Kiwi's secretary. One evening just before Memorial Day we were sitting around at Dennis Savage's as Little Kiwi updated his list of classic films. He paced the room like a tycoon giving heavy meeting while Cosgrove, with the pad, watched him like a hungry puppy.

"A nifty video collection," said Carlo, "should have lots of horror movies."

"*Razor Fingers With Main Street!*" cried Cosgrove.

"*Knife Man,*" Little Kiwi corrected, "*on Main Street.*"

"*A Nightmare on Elm Street 2,*" said Dennis Savage. Cosgrove noted it down.

"And what about that one where the guy goes downtown," said Little Kiwi, "and then everybody does things to him?"

"Yes!" said Cosgrove. "*The Statue Boy in Soho!*"

"No, Cosgrove," said Little Kiwi. "*Soho Nights.*"

Carlo and I looked questioningly at Dennis Savage.

"*After Hours,*" said Dennis Savage, patiently.

I chuckled.

"While you're at it," said Dennis Savage, "why don't you get my favorite—"

"*The Breakfast Lunch!*" cried Little Kiwi, jumping up.

"No, *Don't Play the Music!*" said Cosgrove, bounding around him.

Carlo and I looked at Dennis Savage. "My favorite is *Love Me Tonight*. And that's *The Breakfast Club* and *Can't Stop*—"

"How do you know what they mean?" asked Carlo.

Dennis Savage shrugged. "I've been watching television and going to the movies with them. I know what they've seen."

"Is *Love Me Tonight* your favorite?" I asked. "You have good taste."

"I always go for the good things," he said. "Don't you know that by now?"

"Cosgrove," said Little Kiwi, "maybe I should alphabetize our list."

"Oh, could I do that?" Cosgrove threw a look of such opulent need at Little Kiwi that Carlo and I furtively nodded at each other, as if swopping answers on an SAT exam. I'm positive Dennis Savage saw us. But he made no remark.

"Do you think it *is* a joke?" I asked Carlo. "About Little Kiwi and Cosgrove? I mean, isn't it—"

"They are truly close now," said Carlo, looking it over in his mind. He likes to pretend he misses everything but who's hot, yet he's as observant as a writer. He doesn't see things; but he sees people like nobody's business. "When two sexy little boys are close, well . . ."

"Well?"

He nodded. "Don't they fuck?"

"Who would be top man in that combination? Aren't they both natural catchers?"

I had decided to paint my kitchen; I think it very restful. Carlo, who had found himself hungry and came over to see about some lunch, ate a red delicious apple and watched.

"Everyone's a natural catcher with someone who's a pitcher," said Carlo. "But two catchers always figure out who's the most natural catcher, and the other guy gets to do the pitching."

"Actually, they could go to bed without fucking, couldn't they? Princeton rub, and so on. Would that count as adultery?"

"Well, I truly think Little Kiwi is fucking that Little Cosgrove."

Shocked, I stopped painting.

"Just like so?" I said. "You describe the infidelity of the era as if it were the tricking of a pair of exchange students in the NYU student union."

"Somebody's got to cheat sometime," he said. "Otherwise, you'd have nothing but people who love each other."

"Somewhere in Stonewall," I said, "I got the idea that *that* was the idea."

He tossed the apple core into the garbage. "Fruit is a good dessert," he said. "Instead of jello."

"What do you think Dennis Savage would say if he knew Little Kiwi was cheating on him with Cosgrove?"

Carlo looked at me as if I had asked him what a condom is. "How could he not know?"

I put down my brush.

"Just a minute there," I said. "Are you telling me that you believe that Little Kiwi is doing the sidestep with Cosgrove *and* that Dennis Savage accepts it?"

He looked at me for a bit. "So what do you believe?"

"I believe Dennis Savage and Little Kiwi are as attached to each other today as they were when they met nine years ago."

"In their feelings, yes, I truly know that. But in bed, too, all this time? Is that what you believe? And with Dennis Savage away all day, and those two alone up there, watching the videos and getting very serious about making little bowls of tuna salad just right. You don't believe there comes a moment in there when those two little boy bodies suddenly can't concentrate on anything but the sound of the other one's breathing, like that, and then the next thing, which is they take turns slowfucking each other?"

"Little Kiwi isn't a little boy anymore. He's twenty-seven."

"Even better," said Carlo. "He'll know how."

I left the kitchen, shaking my head. "I just can't feature Little Kiwi suddenly turning into a couch artist after having been so reticent all these years. He still blushes when someone cruises him too blatantly on the street."

Carlo was staring at the lipstick office tower that replaced the brownstones that used to command the corner of Fifty-fourth and Third. "Look at all those people in there," he said. "Office workers. Do you think they wish they were like us? When they see us fooling around while they're working?"

"Carlo, what would you do if you were Dennis Savage and you knew that Little Kiwi was sidelining with Cosgrove?"

He smiled. "I'd let him get it out of his system. A boy that nice deserves a chance to prove that he can be top, too. Everybody needs a Cosgrove sometime."

"What does a Cosgrove need?"

"He's a beautiful young dude, isn't he? The squirmy kind. If he was my type, I'd surely gobble him up. Anyway, you know how young kids are. They hang around waiting for someone to show them how, don't they?"

"Well, I'm just amazed," I said. "I'm fabulously amazed."

"Young kids need a lot of attention. They really need to be hugged and spanked and screwed pretty nearly every day. I wouldn't have the energy. Maybe that's why I like big guys. They sort of take care of themselves." He settled into my desk chair. "Let them do the spanking and such. A really big guy is so good at that, somehow. So very truly good at that sort of thing, you know."

"I've been your friend for some fifteen years now," I told him. "And you still shock me."

"A really big nice guy," he said. "To hold me when I'm sleeping."

◼▨

I let Dennis Savage and his Dingdong School get themselves settled in at The Pines before I came out for my visit. If Dennis Savage has had a chance to miss me a little, he doesn't get grouchy as easily as he does in town. Besides, I was running a deadline.

So it was late June before I got out there, and I felt full of the devil, as I always do when I touch base with the only part of the world that is so gay that, for once, straights are the neighborhood problem. For a joke, I left my bag where the boardwalk gave onto Dennis Savage's house and sleeked inside to materialize as if by magic. One of my Pines routines.

No one was in sight, though it was near cocktail time; yet I thought I heard an odd sound somewhere about, as if someone were calling for help from very far away. Following the sound to the doorway of the guest room where I usually stay, I saw Cosgrove on his back, his legs dangling over Dennis Savage's shoulders, the pair of them gone from the world in the dangerous clarity of Buddy Position Number One.

Silently I backed away, left the house, and took my bag back to the harbor. I let a few ferries dock, traded a pot or two of dish with comrades, and finally heaved myself back into gear and returned, whistling, coughing, and stamping the last few feet like the country dolt in an antique melodrama.

Dennis Savage was occupied in the kitchen area. Overhead, I heard the shower going.

"Well, well, well," he said.

"Well enough," I told him.

"Deep as a well."

"Oh, was it?"

"I thought meat loaf and those roast potatoes you love that no one can make as good as your mother."

"I have to admit," says I, setting down my bag, "she is unrivaled in her specialties. Everyone should have a few, don't you think? Specialties, I mean."

The shower was turned off.

"How's the city coming along?" he asked.

"Well, it's still there." I fixed myself a drink. "So are you, I see."

He laughed.

"You usually say, 'What's that supposed to mean?'"

"I'm feeling frivolous today," he replied, washing vegetables and briskly drying them. "I'm running on mellow."

Nothing from me.

"What, no banter on that? No saucy sortie?"

"I haven't seen you this jolly in quite some time. What's your secret, old pal?"

He was about to answer, but stopped as Cosgrove came along the second-floor walkway wearing a bathrobe so oversize that it looked as if the Ringling Brothers had sold him last year's tent.

"Hey, big shot," I said to Dennis Savage.

He was watching Cosgrove come down the stairs; and Cosgrove was subdued.

"What's your secret, big shot? I want to be jolly, too."

"Did Virgil come on the ferryboat with you?" Cosgrove asked me.

"He isn't here, then, is he?"

"He had a job interview," said Dennis Savage. "To be a receptionist at a women's magazine. Apparently they have a policy of hiring—"

Halfway along the stairs, Cosgrove lost his footing and slammed down to the floor on his ass; and I was so tense I laughed.

"I'm sorry," I said, racing over to him. "I'm terribly sorry, Cosgrove."

"I'm okay," he said, just sitting there.

"Anyway, Little Kiwi didn't come out with me. I didn't even—"

"His interview," said Dennis Savage, "was for four-thirty, so he probably—"

Cosgrove burst into tears.

"Oh, Jesus," said Dennis Savage.

"No, I'm okay," Cosgrove repeated as I picked him up and held him. Carlo's cure. "I just got hurt a little on my bum-bum."

At which I could not restrain another shock of giddy laughter even as I patted his back.

"Where did you get that bathrobe?" I asked him, to stir the place up a bit, steer past the trouble.

"It's mine," said Dennis Savage.

"You're not this big, are you?"

"Who says I'm not?"

"Okay, okay," I told him. "Don't flash your eyes at me."

Footsteps on the walk heralded Little Kiwi's arrival, and Bauhaus, who would probably have dozed through the Battle of Stalingrad, suddenly decided to seem useful and barked once from the porch.

"Hey, I think I just got a new position," said Little Kiwi. "And Cosgrove," he added, opening his bag, "look at what I brought out for us for Sunday night: that superclassic gangster flick with James Cagney and Jean Harlow—"

"*Machine Guns and Mothers!*" Cosgrove exulted.

"*The Roaring Twenties?*" Dennis Savage guessed.

"*The Mean Old Slums!*" Cosgrove decided.

"No, Cosgrove—"

"The Public Enemy," I said quietly, gazing at Dennis Savage.

I don't know why I felt so scandalized—even betrayed—by finding Dennis Savage and Cosgrove together. I should have been prepared for it by Carlo's theory, which runs, roughly, "Gay men are always going to think of something hot to do, then they'll go do it." Anyway, surely it's Dennis Savage's relationship to worry about, not mine.

However, I've grown terribly used to this coterie we have, used to playing uncle to Little Kiwi and big little brother to Carlo and whatever I am to Dennis Savage, for which no word has yet been coined. I just don't want anything shaking up the procedures here.

Things calmed down considerably by dinnertime. Dennis Savage does make a first-rate meat loaf (one of his few accomplishments) and the mustard-dill sauce that accompanies it is to die. Now that my folks have moved to California, it's thoughtful of Dennis Savage to complement the entrée with my mother's celebrated roast potatoes, an arcane delicacy of Luzerne County, Pennsylvania. (He came out for a summer day of R & R when my parents were still living on Long Island, in 1972, and was so taken with the potatoes that he asked for the recipe. Mother shared it, but reluctantly, and she retaliated by calling him "David Savage" for the rest of the evening. It made him sound like a Broadway chorus boy.) Wafted on a wave of vodka, I forgave everybody, and doted upon the "kids," merrily lapping up the meat loaf, potatoes, and broccoli as kids do, utterly unconcerned with the relish and gusto of the gourmand. Good food is not delight; good food is to eat. They even raced off before dessert—raspberry sherbet topped with fresh blueberries and drenched in Grand Marnier—to prepare for the evening's entertainment. Little Kiwi and Cosgrove don't just show a movie: they *present* it, like the proprietors of a jazz-age picture palace.

Dennis Savage and I, in sweaters, took our coffee onto the porch and gazed at the ocean.

"How did you know?" he asked me, after a while.

"I saw what you did. I sneaked in to surprise you and . . ."

"You got surprised."

"It's none of my business," I said. "I have no right to an opinion," I said. "I'm a little threatened and that makes me judgmental, so I'm sorry," I said.

"It just happened," he told me. "You should know that. One time," he said. "One slip, that's all. There is no affair. No . . . ongoing calculation. I lost control and I feel terrible about it, but that . . . incredible little boy came up from the beach in those little swimming togs of his and he . . . I just . . . I went for him. Do you know how many, many moments it's been now, having that little darling around and not being allowed to make myself at home? I can't have him, I can't ask him to leave, and I can't loan him out, can I? He's always there. He's going to be near me, right here like this. Go hale me up for rape. Any jury would let me off."

"Was it really rape?"

"You know it wasn't."

"What are you going to tell Little Kiwi?"

He said nothing.

"Yes, good," I said. "One of those old-fashioned relationships. Just like our parents."

He said nothing.

"Maybe it's for the best," I observed. "Why ask for trouble? Forget it. Time will pass. Things happen, this and many other things. Little Kiwi counts his offenses, too, God knows. Then one day you and Cosgrove will be together again with no one else around and *pow*."

He said nothing.

"Just to satisfy my innocent writer's curiosity, would you be willing to tell me how it was? Because you always go for the good things, I know."

He said nothing.

"*That* good, huh?"

He turned to me, tears running down his cheeks.

"Oh, Christ," I said, my hand on his shoulder. "What the hell is going on around here? Where is everybody going?"

"Okay, it's all set up!" cried Little Kiwi, bouncing in with Cosgrove at his heels, as Dennis Savage furtively wiped his eyes.

"Friday night at our free movie show!" Cosgrove added.

"Guess what we've got for our surprise feature!"

"*Gentlemen Prefer Blondes?*" I asked. "*Dr. Jekyll and Mr. Hyde? My Little Chickadee? Love From a Stranger? Nothing Sacred?*"

"*Strange Interlude*," Dennis Savage pleaded. "*An Innocent Affair.*"

"Oh, no," I corrected. "*Greed. Golden Boy. A Fool There Was.*"

"*Charade,*" Dennis Savage insisted.

"*Idiot's Delight,*" I went on.

"*The Night of the Hunter,*" he said reproachfully. He meant me. "*The Informer.*"

Little Kiwi and Cosgrove were staring at us like chipmunks who come home from a day of frolic to find all their acorns have been stolen.

"Or your favorite," I noted, sure of my climax. "*Love Me Tonight.*"

"No," said Little Kiwi, bewildered. "It's *The Awful Truth.*"

"Ah," I said. "*My* favorite."

"Curtain," said Dennis Savage. "*Please.* Okay?"

The Right Boy for Cosgrove

"Look, I'm telling you," Dennis Savage is telling me, "Cosgrove has simply got to be farmed out. I'm sorry, but someone's got to take him out of here. I can't have this . . . this apprentice sweetheart underfoot all the time."

Not to mention on the end of your cock, I thought; but I said nothing, for Dennis Savage's moment of weakness was to be our secret, his and mine. No one must know of his adultery—better, no one must know of adultery, no matter whose or why, tomorrow and tomorrow and tomorrow. Not even Carlo, who would forgive Hitler an act of sensual self-enhancement if his partner was hot enough. Not even Little Kiwi—especially not Little Kiwi—the victim of the adultery but also the person responsible for it, as the one who brought the young man known as Cosgrove into our circle.

In the event, Little Kiwi agreed that Cosgrove ought to find a place of his own. "He's been living in our socks, almost," Little Kiwi observed.

174

"He likes it here," said Carlo, biting into a Granny Smith apple, his latest food discovery. (He likes to sample the stuff in your fridge, and sometimes it changes his life. One dinnertime Dennis Savage and Little Kiwi came out, amid a great deal of hushings and fa la, with a chocolate soufflé for dessert; but Carlo said, "Can I have one of those tart green apples that Bud buys?" and Dennis Savage was ready for the straitjacket.) "That cute little Cosgrove," Carlo concluded, "has a hateful family and no other home but this."

"That's just it," said Dennis Savage. "We have to get him one. He needs a place to move to. His parents have virtually thrown him out. He doesn't have a job. But he's marketable, let's face it. All we have to do is find him a good home."

There was a pause as we faced it. I felt Dennis Savage looking at me, then Little Kiwi looking along, and at length Carlo joined them. All three were grinning. A home for Cosgrove.

"Nothing doing, you bum Samaritans," I cried. "What is this, the Fresh Air Fund?"

"He could be very agreeable, running your errands," said Dennis Savage.

"I'm not taking your refuse."

"He loves your Victrola," Little Kiwi urged.

"That's his problem."

"He's a beautiful little honeystuff," said Carlo, and we other three looked away in bemusement, the usual condition when you pal around with Carlo. "One solid paddling every morning, and he'd—"

"I don't want a roommate," I said, with intense conviction.

"All right," said Dennis Savage, "all right," wav-

ing a soothing hand. "All right, but he's got to go.
He has to . . . find someone to live with." He
shrugged. "My nuclear family is big enough as it
is."

He was looking out the window, but his feelings
swept the room, and for the tiniest moment something very crucial and abstract became almost intelligible; I couldn't grasp what the something was. It
moved so quickly that you'd have missed it if you
blinked.

Little Kiwi missed it. "Just when I taught Cosgrove," he sighed, "how to make Baked Beans à la
Whorehouse."

I guffawed and Carlo chuckled.

"It's a gourmet delight," Little Kiwi told us, somewhat hotly, "whether you're laughing or not."

"Oh," I said, "I'm definitely laughing."

"What goes in that?" asked Carlo, trying to look
serious.

Still at the window, Dennis Savage turned back to
us. "He opens a can of B & M beans and puts raisins
in them."

"And minced onions," Little Kiwi added. "That's
what puts the crunch in Baked Beans à la
Whorehouse."

"Why à la *Whorehouse*?" I asked.

"He named it for the night we met," said Dennis
Savage. "At *The Best Little Whorehouse in Texas*. The
show."

"Boy, that was a long time ago," said Little Kiwi.

Dennis Savage nodded. "Nine years."

"Cosgrove," I noted, "was only eight then. A
child."

Again I sensed an unnamed feeling doing a riff on itself. Something in the room with us.

"Why don't you give one of those Pines dating dinners?" Carlo asked. "We'll bring over all the eligible bachelors and set Cosgrove up."

"How are you going to explain that to Cosgrove?" I countered. "You might scare him into—"

"We don't tell Cosgrove," said Dennis Savage. "We just give the dinner."

"Then how will he know he's supposed to charm everyone? Put his better foot forward?"

Carlo smiled. "Do you really think a kid that sweet has to do something to make guys wild for him?"

"You aren't wild for him, I notice."

"Little kids aren't my type. You know that."

◼◼◼

"Kids aren't his type," I said to Dennis Savage later, when we were alone.

"Well, they aren't. He likes to get on top of dark, shaggy monsters. What do you like to get on top of?"

"I had a feeling we'd get to me sooner or later."

"Well, it *is* rather notable that this perfectly cute little . . . honeystuff—"

"You get so urbane when you quote Carlo."

"The Voltaire of the Circuit," he dryly notes. "So this kid becomes available and our Cocktail Dandy, who maintains no other berth that I know of, refuses to—"

"Why don't you let me be the judge of what is honeystuff and what isn't?"

"You listen to me," he begins, getting into his Uncle Know-it-All frame of mind. "He's a very strange character. Okay. But somewhere in there is a nice kid who got strange because of what his family did to him. He's not smart. He's wild and he's young and he hasn't been around much. But he's waiting to fall very loyally in love with the first man who's willing to be kind to him. And he'll . . . be kind to you in return. Couldn't you use some of that, now?"

Keep talking, my friend. Let's do a little scene here.

"I've seen his sort before," he goes on. "They just want to fit in somehow. If they're actors, they fall in love with their director. If they're writers, they fall in love with their editor."

"I never did."

He puts his hand across my mouth. "And if they're houseboys, they fall in love with their host. Remember that old man and that incredible hunk at the Pines ferryslip?"

I sometimes think that Dennis Savage and I are coasting on dire memories more than we are living in the present. Things seen, heard, or read will set off a chain of reminiscence—and suddenly we are twenty-two or so and it's the early 1970s and no one has to pay a price for being alive.

"Remember?" he urges.

I nod.

"It was just after they had redone the Sandpiper, and we were waiting for Lionel's ferry. You had some atrocious jingle you wanted to sing him."

"'Cock full of nuts is that heavenly coffee,'" I sing.

He reacts exactly as he did back then, with that bossy rationalism that Little Kiwi finds sportive, Carlo finds picturesque, and I find endearing. "A cock," he declares, "*cannot* be *full* of nuts."

"Cock next to nuts?"

"*As you recall*, one of those dreary old fat queens was going back to town and he had what was obviously a hired cohort with him. Describe the cohort."

The tester tested. Sartor resartus.

"Tall," I say. "Straight dark hair. Twenty-five. Boyishly handsome. Very gymmed. Very style. Very smooth and opulent. An extraordinarily true man."

"And what was he doing?"

"He was holding the old man, and caressing him, and asking him to stay on the Island."

"Now the old man."

"He was . . . appreciative. He offered to stay, but then the hunk said no, you have affairs to settle in the great city."

"And what did they pass to each other?" he pursues.

"What is this, my SATs? Little endearments. Rash glances. It was a bit much, truth to tell."

"Truth to tell, you were mesmerized. If they hadn't been so intent on each other, the hunk would have punched you out for Aggravated Eavesdropping."

"*You* went out for a snow cone, I suppose."

"I was as dazzled as you were." He rose, crossed the room, looked out the window again. "I want to know the same things. But I always believed in them. You have to be shown over and over, don't you?"

"Shown what?"

"That the hunk-host partnership can be as magical, as real, as any. That a beautiful man can show an unbeautiful man attention, and suddenly, one day—"

"The beautiful man runs off with the household cash."

"*One day it's love*, you unsavory gasbag. It's love, can you bear it? Now, will you please take Cosgrove?"

"No, I'll take the hunk from The Pines that day at the ferry."

Still at the window, he is contemplative. Maybe the tiniest shrug.

"This is where you really shaft me, right?" I say.

After a while, he says, "This is where I vividly recall seeing those two men embracing right in front of everyone. Because their emotional bond was so strong that they had to celebrate it."

"They were celebrating a business deal."

"That gorgeous hunk *loved* that old man!" he insists, advancing on me. "He loved him! Can't you see anything, at long last?"

"Where are they now?" is what I see to say.

So he stands stock-still in the middle of the room, then he nods and demonstrates a quaint little shudder. "'Where are they now?' Right. And that's it for love and Cosgrove."

"Well, that's it, I would say, for the promotion of love and Cosgrove. You can't arrange these things, you know."

"Now you'll run to Carlo, and the two of you will pick it apart and decide that Cosgrove isn't *man* enough for the likes of you. Isn't that how the two of you operate?"

"Terrific: Dueling Types. The kid versus the clone. Why don't you just leave Carlo and me out of this and get your dinner together and give Cosgrove to someone who can appreciate his type?"

"Because I feel guilty." He sits next to me on the couch. "All he wants is to move in here and become Little Kiwi's little brother. And I'm going to sit him at a table with a lot of intimidatingly worldly men and tell them, 'Hello, this is Cosgrove Replevin and one of you gets to—' "

"*Replevin?*"

"That's his last name."

"Replevin . . ."

"So who should give the dinner? Kern Loften? He loves making couples. Perhaps because he never—"

"Jesus, I thought you were joking."

He shook his head. He not only *was* serious, he *looked* serious. "Cosgrove has to go."

"Cosgrove Replevin."

"It's your last chance, Bud. Take him or someone else will."

"Round up the hungry parties," I tell him. "I'm staying innocent on this one."

◼◼

So the dinner was on, and Cosgrove had to go. As the days passed, Little Kiwi began to wane in his support of the project. Coming home from a literary lunch, I found him moping on the sidewalk in front of our building, the tethered Bauhaus, Little Kiwi's thuggish dog, lying on his back in a trance.

"All set for the big dinner?" I asked him.

He eyed me as Isaac should have eyed Abraham. "If Cosgrove knew, I don't think he'd be glad about this."

"You're the one who wanted to find him a home."

"I didn't know we were going to auction him off like a slave of olden times," he said, dragging after me into the lobby. As we rode up to Dennis Savage's, he was silent, almost sulky. It isn't easy to have to yield up a disciple.

"Look at you in a suit," said Dennis Savage to me as we came in.

Little Kiwi handed him Bauhaus's leash and marched without a word into the bedroom.

Dennis Savage shrugged.

"So who's on tap for the gala?" I asked.

As he recited names and eligibility credentials, I thought back to similar dinners he and I and others have given over the years. And yes, sometimes they do take, not unlike a bitter medicine: because sometimes somebody gets the idea that this year it's Love or Die. But, as I say, you can't arrange these things. Chemistry observes its own schedule.

"You're still determined not to tell Cosgrove?" I asked.

"I didn't tell you when I gave *your* setup dinner, did I?"

I was startled speechless.

"When was that?" I got out, at length.

"The summer of 1977." He was smiling, enjoying my surprise. "You don't remember, do you?"

Bauhaus, haunted by a vision, ran snapping at Dennis Savage's home entertainment center, jumped at the television, fell backwards, and slunk off to the kitchen with a resounding fart.

"While you're getting rid of Cosgrove," I suggested, "why don't you throw in Bauhaus for a package deal? A boy and his dog."

"It was at Lionel's house. When he was still in the Grove."

"No wonder I don't remember it. I usually block out Grove dinners."

"The median income was one hundred thousand dollars," he said. "They were all witty, spry, and nice. A very contempo crowd." He was virtually reciting; he might have been saving this up for years.

"You did this for me?"

Bauhaus stole back into the living room, panting.

"You got drunk," said Dennis Savage, "and started fights with everyone. Lionel was beside himself. You pushed Bill Swanson into a cake."

"Probably for some very good reason."

"He said he didn't like *A Little Night Music.*"

"*See?*"

Bauhaus stared at the television screen.

"Nothing's on," I told him.

"Such fine men, too," Dennis Savage went on. I was not going to brisk my way through this one. "Fine young stalwarts of Stonewall, even if it was in the Grove."

Little Kiwi came out of the bedroom, his attire changed from dog-walking pullover and chinos to go-everywhere shorts and a *Me and My Girl* sweatshirt.

"It's cold in here," he said.

"No, it isn't," said Dennis Savage.

"Thank you for giving me that dinner," I said.

"You're welcome, ten years later."

"How come no one around here calls me Virgil, when I ask so nice?" Little Kiwi cried. "Why doesn't anyone listen to me ever?"

Cosgrove arrived, and Little Kiwi sat him down before the television, where the two of them and Bauhaus screened *Alien*, Little Kiwi morose, Cosgrove, obeying his chief, carefully subdued, and Bauhaus whining during all the alien's raids.

"Everywhere you go," I noted, "some monster's coming to get you."

Little Kiwi, his face a mask drawn too tightly around the mouth, put an arm around Cosgrove; it was not an affectionate but a defensive gesture. No one, it said, is taking this treasure away from me.

I went into the kitchen, where Dennis Savage was sprucing up an old beef stew with last-minute infusions of coriander and plum jam. This is what I call "Bloomingdale's cooking."

"Little Kiwi's in a really sour mood," I said.

"He'll get over it."

"I'm not sure he will."

"Don't give me grief."

He poured a bit of red wine into the stew pot.

"I smell bay leaves and lima beans," I said.

"You smell the rapture of the visuals and the tremor of the stories, and the holly and the ivy and the running of the deer. But can I tell you?"

"Why not, after such a poetic outburst?"

"I'm handling this operation. Okay?"

"Okay, captain."

"So do me a favor—*help* us land this kid some-where. Don't hinder. Please?"

"You talk about him as if he were a subversive you're trying to deport."

At one of those "something's happening" shifts in the atmosphere, he and I turned. Little Kiwi stood in the doorway. "Can I take Cosgrove to buy a new bathing suit?" he asked.

"It's almost dinnertime," said Dennis Savage.

"Yes, but this is *very* important."

Dennis Savage contemplated his lover for a bit. "It's not that important," he said finally.

Little Kiwi stamped back into the living room.

Dennis Savage poured a bit more wine into the stew. He put the wine down. He waited. He corked the wine. He started to put it away, dropped it on the counter, retrieved it, and put it in the fridge.

"What's the matter?" I asked. Something in the room again. Some feeling, some idea.

"Here," he said, offering me a spoon of stew gravy. I tasted it. "Nifty," I told him. "I love lima beans in stew."

"Cooking is one of my virtues," he said. "Big, simple meals."

"Little, simple kids."

He covered the stewpot.

"What was all that with the wine bottle?" I asked him. "What's going on?"

He didn't say anything for a while. Then: "On top of all this, I have to give a banquet and feel guilty, and that kid will still be around unless we set him up with a Tibetan monk."

Now it was Cosgrove in the doorway, staring at us for who knows how long before.

"I'm hungry," he said, oh so quietly, to us.

▰▰▰

Kern Loften threw the utmost in Pines glamour at our disposal for the Cosgrove husband-hunting dinner, and between him and Dennis Savage a *carte des invités* was assembled to rival the elite at Catherine the Great's coming out ball. One odd note in all this: Little Kiwi brightened up suddenly, without explanation, as if he had decided to walk along with us. Cosgrove, as always, seemed to have no opinion. As long as he was among friends, he was happy.

The natural condition of gay. All friends. So, good; fine. The day of the dinner approached without incident, though we celebrated the avid intention of the feast by riding the hydroplane out to the beach, at my insistence. (The train is filled with straights, and the bus has become unreliable.) Dennis Savage doesn't like spending the money, but I like saving the time. Then, too, Cosgrove couldn't afford his ferry fare, much less a ride on the wind. We compromised: Dennis Savage paid for Cosgrove, and I paid for Little Kiwi. That's what I call an uncopious compromise.

But that's family life; even when you're in the process of cutting loose an excrescent relation. Dennis Savage had promised to supply dessert and salad—unnecessary, for Kern Loften is virtually made of parties—and he spent all the Saturday of the Cosgrove dinner working up to the dressing of the Caesar and the baking of the pies, fastidious, imperious, and audacious.

"Will there be hand-baked croutons," I asked, watching him at work, "or cheesy consumer-ready boxed croutons for this restorative yet divisive banquet?"

"There will be a cheesy author, and in about three seconds I'm going to—"

Footsteps on the deck dissuaded him, and a friend, grade six, materialized. On a scale of one to ten, grade nine is "I always wanted him," grade seven is "I feel better when he's around," grade four is "Intolerable after an hour," and grade two is "May he be refused admission to a disco in Fort Lee, New Jersey, on grounds of looks, style, and happiness quotient." Grade six is "I don't particularly care, but he's too nice to snub," so Dennis Savage and I gave him refreshment and fielded his questions till a clamor of giggles out on the deck warned us of the official closing of the beach for that day: Little Kiwi and Cosgrove had come home. By house rules, they were supposed to wash the sand off their bodies with the usual Pines hose, leave their beach toys on the deck, and come into the living quarters like gentlemen of quality. But by habit their return usually comprised a hose war, playing bullfight with Bauhaus, the knocking over of all the deck furniture, and the sneaking of various scrofulous beach toys into the house. This day, we got an extra: a chorus of one of Little Kiwi's new songs, "The Ballad of Fauntleroy." It's one of his weakest compositions, but Cosgrove loves it. Conversation in the house faltered as the two of them, wearing swimming trunks and canteens, paraded in in full chorus:

Fauntleroy was a funny clown,
Went to school with his panties down;
Out of luck in an old dump truck,
So they call him Fauntleroy!

"Little Kiwi," said Dennis Savage patiently, "the pails stay outside."

"Yes, but this time it's our unparalleled shell collection," Little Kiwi replied, mounting the stairs. He gestured: "Cosgrove, if you please."

Cosgrove, who apparently had been rehearsed, solemnly held up a shell for us to admire.

"Yes," I said. "That's a shell, all right."

Our guest, grade six, entranced by Cosgrove, asked, "Do you . . . do you know the names of all your shells?"

Cosgrove said, "This one's Herbert."

"Come now, Cosgrove," said Little Kiwi, moving on, "we really ought to change for dinner."

"Can I wear your dark blue sweater?" Cosgrove asked him. "With my khakis?"

"That's an important combination," said Little Kiwi, leading Cosgrove along the second-floor walkway. "But only if you'll be a good boy at the dinner."

"I'll be very good," Cosgrove promised as the two of them went into the bedroom.

"Tell me," said our guest, with the oddest smile on his face. "Is someone around here married?"

Someone was going to be, as the local intelligence ran. But I couldn't help noticing how enthusiastically Little Kiwi pressed his Kazootie Koolers upon us at cocktail hour. Dennis Savage, intent on his pies, missed a nuance here; I thought the usually abstemious Cosgrove was imbibing rather resolutely, a questionable act for a young man on the verge of his engagement party, even if he supposedly didn't know that's what it was. Questionable, too, was Cosgrove's intake of wine at the dinner itself. At the slightest provocation, Little Kiwi would suggest, "Let's drink to that, Cosgrove!" and Cosgrove drank.

What about the flowers? you ask. The decor, the tone, the stirrings of the place. Well, it was the usual Kern Loften A-list do; I'll let him identify the flowers. I'd call the decor late-middle beachfront attitude palazzo soothed by a pride of bodybuilders who act as if helping get you through the night is their essential deed. I don't know where Kern finds them. Anyway, there we were: four lawyers and doctors or so, three physiques of death, a writer, a schoolteacher, two little kids, Carlo, and Kern Loften; and Cosgrove got blitzed from all of Little Kiwi's "Let's drink to that" toasts and began to chortle, waver, and fade. He was leaning on Carlo's shoulder, calling him Mr. Smith in a dreamy manner, and Carlo, who does not comprehend such behavior but thinks it's probably hot if you like little kids, patted his head as if he were a poodle. Finally, Cosgrove's eyes closed and he went slack in his chair, so Carlo picked him up and laid him on the couch.

"So much for the *jeune premier*," said Kern with a merry shrug.

"He had a very heavy day," said Little Kiwi.

"Of what?" Dennis Savage asked.

"Of being asked to go away," said Little Kiwi. "Of everybody doesn't like him enough."

"What delicious pie," said a lawyer.

"Sweet," said a doctor, "yet I seem to taste no sugar."

"As sweet as sweet can be," said Little Kiwi, furious. "As very sweet as they make them. If only certain people knew that at the table."

Cosgrove was asleep, and the party went on without him. It was a fine party. The intellectuals poured forth, the sensualists listened well, and the friends did a little emotional squeezing. Then it was over, and everyone went his way. Cosgrove had not been connected. In fact, Cosgrove had totally passed out. I thought he'd have to stay over at Kern's till Carlo offered to take the boy home.

"That's fine with me," said Dennis Savage.

Little Kiwi was sitting at the table, the last diner, holding his arms around his chest defiantly.

"That's fine with you, too, isn't it?" I asked Little Kiwi.

His eyes tightened aggressively, but his face tried to stay impassive. This is like Joan of Arc trying to stay peaceful. I wanted to tell him what I knew, and how much I sympathized with him; but that sympathy was disloyal to Dennis Savage. Cosgrove had to go.

Kern, Dennis Savage, and I went on cleaning up, and still Little Kiwi held his post. I believe he was on strike of a certain kind, telling us in his immobility that he hated us, at least for tonight. I busied myself with the tape deck, sifting through Kern's old party reels, some of which I, in my penniless youth, had effected. Dennis Savage and Kern were clearing the table.

"I," said Little Kiwi, "am not moving from this peculiar spot."

Dennis Savage's eyes tensed, but Kern, sponging up the bits, laughed and said, "Well, you're such a nice-looking youth that you can do whatever you want around here."

Dennis Savage gave Little Kiwi a searching look but went on with the cleaning up, helped here and there by one of the bodybuilders. Finally the dinner was over and everyone was long gone, and nothing had been accomplished. This sometimes happens, even with the dearest intentions. Little Kiwi left the table and we all went home, where Dennis Savage fiddled with the pie tins and I made a drink and Little Kiwi scoured the house. Then he announced, "Cosgrove isn't here."

For which he got nothing. Not just silence: *nothing*.

"Carlo was supposed to take him home," Little Kiwi went on. "This is home."

"Maybe he's at Carlo's home," I said.

"Why would he be there?"

A fair question.

"I'm going to go find him," said Little Kiwi—but Dennis Savage put a hand on his shoulder and looked at him.

"Well," I said, "we probably should figure this out." The two of them glaring at each other. "Where Cosgrove is just now."

"So go find out," said Dennis Savage, turning away.

Carlo's house is way on the other side of The Pines, on the sea to the west, filled with suave, rich, grey-haired men on weekends and empty on weekdays. It was silent and dim, but Little Kiwi purposefully pushed in and I followed. He stood there for a moment, listening. Then he walked to Carlo's bedroom.

And there he froze.

I waited for a bit; I don't know why. The whole caper was running past me, somehow, like those ideas, those feelings, that flew by me in rooms filled with my friends, ideas of déjà vu mixed with feelings of the avant-garde. When I drew up to Little Kiwi, over his shoulder I saw Cosgrove lying in bed next to Carlo, the boy's arms wound tightly around the man. Cosgrove was sleeping, but Carlo was awake. Wasn't he? It was hard to be sure in that odd light. He was looking at us, I believe. And we looked at him, certainly, for quite some time. Then Carlo did something I found unforgivable yet beautiful: he ran his hand through Cosgrove's hair. Cosgrove said, "Please." And Carlo said, "Yes."

Just that.

I couldn't tell whether Carlo was smiling or just being there, just having screwed Cosgrove, just knowing who Little Kiwi is and who I am, just being able to point to us if he is ever challenged to produce friends.

Cosgrove said, "Please," again.

I gently pulled Little Kiwi back through the house to the boardwalk, both of us silent.

Until Little Kiwi said, "Everybody takes advantage of Cosgrove."

"'Out of luck in an old dump truck.'"

"You can just see how much he needs love, and that's how they lure him into the trap."

We walked on.

"And you know how handsome he is," Little Kiwi added. "So they're going to start grabbing for him. They think he's some little punk, so it doesn't matter what they do to him. But I know that he has feelings just like the rest of us, and you have to be very careful with Cosgrove."

"Were you very careful when you fucked him?" I asked.

Yes, he was shocked, but he kept his cool. We were passing the harbor, to some the most romantic part of The Pines, a great horseshoe of welcome scooped out of the sand, where boatloads of mythical figures would sail up before one, standing there on a Friday evening on the verge of perhaps the major weekend of one's life. To others, the harbor is the scandal of The Pines, the straight section, where abrasive owners of little cabin cruisers would rend the serenity of a Saturday trading atrocious gobbling noises; and where the mainland kids invaded in the evenings.

I have very mixed feelings about the harbor. Sometimes I try to believe that it is merely one of the places I have frequented over the years, like D'Agostino's or my roof. A location, no more. But this is hard to believe. The Pines harbor is where, in my twenties, I first realized that in coming out of my former life of lies and excuses, I had caught a fabulous adventure by the tail, its danger no less intoxicating than its exuberance. This is what my friends and I call "the rapture," and I feel it acutely every time I pass the harbor, even if only on an errand to the grocery—even now, in the midst of trying to trick A-list dish out of Little Kiwi, wretch that I am, sleuth and storyteller that I call myself.

"I knew that Cosgrove was unsure," said Little Kiwi. "I had to be protective of him. That's what I knew."

The thing about Little Kiwi is, he cannot lie.

"Poor little Cosgrove is not what you think. He's very unknowing. And he always says please."

"Did he say, 'Please love me'?"

"He said he would die if I didn't take care of him. I couldn't just shove him away, then, could I? When he was holding on to me, and he even cried?"

I cleared my throat. "So, did you in fact—"

"And poor Cosgrove is so dandy when you're nice to him. You and Dennis Savage don't know that, because you never are. You just laugh at him."

"But did you and Cosgrove finally—"

"Oh, it did him no good, did it, at the dinner? All those rich men around the table. It was like a meeting of a fancy club."

"Well, he got blitzed rather quickly, didn't he?"

Little Kiwi said nothing.

"And not," I went on, "by chance."

After a bit, he said, "I had to do something. You guys were turning the whole place back on us. You were giving us plenty of worry." He shook his head. "I told Cosgrove to drink a lot so we could push them all away." He sighed. "My poor little Cosgrove."

We walked on some more. Then: "So did you," I asked, "or didn't you?"

Long pause. Long, long, long pause; and we were almost home.

"Well, everyone's so mean to him but me. I was the one who had to make him happy, because he's my pal. So what else could I do?"

"So *what* . . . did . . . you . . . do?"

"Well, he wouldn't let go of holding me, and he kept saying please. And Cosgrove is so little when you hold him like that, and he gets scared so easily. So then . . ."

"So then *what* then?"

He thought about it for a long time. "I made him happy," he replied.

That is all he would say on the matter, and all I was ever to hear, but now I knew two secrets about Cosgrove, one from Dennis Savage and one from Little Kiwi. And by then we were back and Dennis Savage said, "Well?"

"When Carlo offered to take Cosgrove home," I told him, "that's exactly what he meant."

"You've got to be kidding."

"It's all over but the retrospectives."

"Carlo and *Cosgrove*?"

"Why not? I've known stranger pairings to occur in the misty elegy of a Pines nighttime."

Dennis Savage suddenly got busy poking around in the fridge.

"I don't feel so good," said Little Kiwi quietly, sitting alone in the center of the couch. "Something didn't happen right."

"What didn't happen?" asked Dennis Savage.

"Cosgrove went to the dinner," Little Kiwi began,

tripping over his thoughts the way little kids do when they don't know how to center an all-pervasive complaint. "He went to it, and then he was afraid and went to sleep."

"Afraid of what?" I asked.

"Everyone's bigger than Cosgrove. He isn't smart enough yet. I was going to teach him. Now he'll always be afraid. Poor little Cosgrove."

"Poor little Cosgrove?" I said. "He just got a date with the hottest man in town. He's surrounded by loving friends." Then: "*Deeply* loving," I added, tossing it to Dennis Savage.

"I don't know that he is that well loved," said Dennis Savage, facing me down this time.

"He's not," said Little Kiwi. "He's lonely in the crowd." A tear ran down his cheek. "What will Carlo do to him? I know that Carlo is kind, but he's a big fellow and Cosgrove is very delicate." Another tear appeared. "He doesn't know anything. He's just Cosgrove."

"Not anymore he isn't," I said. "He's one of us now. He's a buddy, staying over in the best little whorehouse in The Pines."

"I'm mad at everyone," Little Kiwi blurted out. "My feelings got hurt!"

Dennis Savage pulled him up, held him for a moment, then let him go. "Get on upstairs," he said, putting his hand lightly on Little Kiwi's head, right there on top. "I'll be up in a jiffy."

"All right," said Little Kiwi, wiping his eyes as he started for the stairs.

"Boy," I said to Dennis Savage, as that oddly confidential but remote feeling pestered me again, begged me to know what it meant to me and my friends. "Back there, an age ago, when you first came to New York, did you have any idea all this was going to happen? I mean, that all this was possible?" Now, the feeling nudged me; yes, it urged; forward, it says. I wonder if at just that moment Dennis Savage felt it, too—he was looking at me in an indefinably certain way, as if he had just forgot something terribly important, or just remembered it.

"Could we have French toast for breakfast tomorrow?" said Little Kiwi as he trudged upstairs. "With powdered sugar on mine?"

"Have we ever refused you anything?" Dennis Savage replied.

"You didn't let me wear my mesh T in the parade last year," Little Kiwi told him.

"That parade is perilous enough without you in your mesh T."

"When I was very young," said Little Kiwi, pausing as he reached the second-floor walkway, "I asked my parents that since there was a Mother's Day and a Father's Day, how come there was no Little Kiwi Day? And they said that every day is Little Kiwi Day."

"Well, today," I announced, "is Cosgrove Day."

"Now they tell me," Little Kiwi said tragically. And he went into the bedroom.

"Poor kid," I said. "He lost his devotee."

"Everyone's been losing out on something in this adventure," said Dennis Savage. "Except you, as usual."

"I have nothing to lose."

"Stop rehearsing Cocktail Dandy lines on me." He

started upstairs. "Go take a walk in the misty elegy of the Pines nighttime. That always revives you."

"I was planning to, actually."

He stopped halfway up. "What was it like at Carlo's?"

"Scary." I pulled on a hooded sweatshirt. "Cosgrove was saying please."

"He always says that."

I looked at him. "Always?"

"I mean, he said it to me that time."

"Did he, now?"

"It'd be funny if Cosgrove couldn't walk around for the next few days after . . . you know, after Carlo. He'll be limping around with his legs crossed and falling all over the place."

"We could rent him a golf cart to ride around on."

"Tell me something. What exactly did you see there?"

"Two people becoming."

"Becoming what?"

The feeling roved through the room. I felt it very powerfully. I felt haunted. I felt inflamed. I felt daring and reckless, like a child playing war games with, yes, nothing to lose. I felt so free I could have been generous to my worst enemy that night. I felt grateful that there were still things to be comprehended, even discovered.

"Becoming what?" he repeated.

I shrugged. "I'll tell you when the story is over."

He went upstairs and I took a walk.

▰

Strolling the beach at night does revive me; I suppose I feel stimulated by the dense rustling of the curtain as it falls on another day in the life of the gayest address in the world. Maybe I just need the solitude, the peace. Heaven knows, it's quiet there on the edge of the sea. A good place to think about your feelings.

The lights were on around the pool at Carlo's house, and I caught the firefly of a toke moving softly in the dark. It was Carlo, surely, smoking the day's last joint, and I walked up to his deck. This is what is known as the *scène à faire*, the obligatory confrontation in the well-made play. All the world's a stage, and this is the end of the story.

"Well," he said, "I truly thought you might be along soon enough."

"I know two secrets."

"Yeah, you're always around when someone's life is falling into little bits, aren't you?"

"How's Cosgrove doing?"

He exhaled deeply and proffered me the roach. I shook my head.

"You always have to do everything your own way," he said. "Beautiful kid's up for grabs, you don't want him. Someone's smoking, you don't smoke. The trouble calms down, you're collecting secrets."

"Don't blame me. I'm not a snoop, I'm a confidant."

"You're a snoop."

"I've been a good friend to you," I said. "Haven't I?"

He relit the reefer and took another puff.

"I just noticed something," he said. "So here's another secret for your collection. Unless you already made your quota for the day."

"Carlo, I'm not a snoop."

"Did you ever wonder what guys are really after when they have sex with someone new? A hot time, you'll say. Sure. Some guys, now, that's very true of them. They want pleasure. Sex is a pleasurable thing. That's very true of sex. But some other guys want something besides that. What do you believe they want?"

"Tell me."

"They want a friend, some guys, now. They want a friend so bad they don't even care is the sex good or not, precisely. Not as long as they can know that other guy as close as it gets, know him to death." He stabbed the cigarette out. "But then there's another kind of guy here, and what he wants is to be taken care of. That's what I just noticed. You'll say, sure, that's what kids are like." He shook his head. "No, sir, my friend. I've seen kids'll top you so hot they make Big Steve look like a seven dwarf or something the like. Some little twerp thing. No, there's kids who don't need a friend, don't need someone taking care. It's not kids versus men. It's not the size of a man anymore now, it's the shape of his feelings."

"Was Cosgrove afraid of you?"

"Secrets," he breathed out. He waited a bit, looking around at the night. Moody man. Then he said, "What do you mean, afraid of me?"

"I mean, he's very nearly a virgin, after all."

"The hell you say." He laughed softly. "Let me tell you about was he afraid of me. Let me tell about that. I've never been with a real little kid before, so I played like Big Steve does. You know that scene, on the lap and so on? I toyed around with him, and I whispered sweet talk in his ear, like Big Steve loves to do. He's really good at that . . . cajoling stuff. He can make you anything he wants, turn you into something he thinks will look real cute on you. I asked that Cosgrove, Has he been a good boy? He said yes, he was always good. And I said, What about how you drank more than your share tonight and got pissed and went to sleep? And he admitted he was not a good little boy tonight. So I asked him what he thought we should do about that, especially because he has such a beautiful little butt which is all ready to take a very heavy whipping."

"I don't want to be shocked any more tonight."

"Well, now we truly see that some secrets are too much even for the secret man himself. But there's one thing for you to know about now, and that's what this Cosgrove here wants out of sex."

"Then you can tell me what you want out of it."

"That's *just* the kind of fucking thing you always have to do, huh?" he shouted, grabbing the front of my sweatshirt. "When do we hear about *your* secrets, you son of a bitch?" He pushed me back so hard I lost my balance and fell off the bench. "How about I pound you pretty good now, and you can figure out what that means, huh?" he growled.

"Didn't you get enough of that already," I said, getting up, "with Cosgrove?"

With a coarse shout, he jumped up and shoved me against the deck railing, looming over me as he forced my head back. His breathing sounded like an avalanche. I tried to ease him off me, but he wouldn't yield. Carlo has a violent streak, I know, but he only gets into fights when he has been attacked.

Physically, I mean.

We were locked there for quite some time, not moving, silent, just looking at each other, as his hostility—not his anger—died away. Finally he let go of me, stepped back, nodded his head once, twice, put his hand on my back, gently pressed me over to the bench, and sat me down. He sat next to me, looking away, back toward the house. I was shaking, I have to report, but that strange nameless feeling slipped alongside us, both of us, and put an arm around my shoulder.

"I'll feel like heck about this tomorrow," he said. "But right now I'm not going to apologize. You have been a good friend and all, and I shouldn't have done that. Except you . . . you truly have to stop doing this."

Now he looked at me.

"Yes, you have to. You go around and watch everyone and you know too much and it gets on everyone's nerves. Because no one gets to watch you. You don't want anyone knowing about you. So you and me, we're very much alike in that, see? Very much alike."

He was silent for a while.

Then he said, "You remember when I was hustling for Dave Direnzi, way back a time there? You and Dennis Savage got all on my case how I was taking a chance with doom and like that, but my unemployment ran out and I needed the money. And most of the guys I did the calls with, they didn't want much from me. Anyway, you gave me some advice, at least, just in case. Remember?"

I didn't do anything in response. I wasn't remembering; I was looking forward.

"This was it: If the door opens, and there's two of them, get careful. If there's three of them, get worried. And if there's three of them and they're grinning, run like hell. You remember that?"

I remembered.

"Okay, I went to this one gig, and just as the door opens this flashpop goes off right in my face and there's this old guy with a camera. And behind him is this huge black muscle dude, not a stitch on his build. And in the corner there I see a young guy in a sailor suit. And everyone's grinning."

He laughed quietly.

"So what did I do, huh?"

He laughed again, a warm rolling sound.

"I ran like hell."

That feeling put an arm around my shoulder again, and now so did Carlo.

"I'm ready to apologize for what happened before," he said—but just then Cosgrove came out of the house, holding a blanket around himself. He stood on the porch, watching us, then approached.

"He calls me Mr. Smith," said Carlo.

Without a word, Cosgrove folded himself into Carlo's lap and Carlo held him.

"This young boy is one of the ones who wants to be taken care of. Maybe it's time for me to try some of that. I've been playing around for so long. Now I'm forty, and maybe I should get serious about this. Sometimes when we're all together, I believe I am thinking of something. Something real important. I'm never sure what it's about."

So Carlo feels it, too.

"Maybe this is what it's about, here." Carlo stroked Cosgrove's hair and the two of them turned to me.

"See, it's us watching you now," said Carlo.

In the pool lights their eyes blazed like the fierce embers of a fire that won't go out no matter what you do to it. They had become, Carlo turning from boy to man, Cosgrove from orphan to son. One day it's love; and so the story ends.

"He's not afraid," said Carlo.

Cosgrove took one of Carlo's hands and opened it up.

"He has nothing to be afraid about," said Carlo.

Cosgrove placed his little hand inside Carlo's great paw and folded it around his own.

"He's not the one around here who's afraid of me," said Carlo, pulling the boy close so the two of them could tremble together and feel that keen, brash moment at the start of love when the heart speeds.

I left them then.

Because of course Carlo is right: Cosgrove isn't the one around here who's afraid of him.

I am.

The Dinner Party

━━━━━

IT IS A TRUTH UNIVERSALLY
acknowledged that a gay man in
possession of a fortune must be in want of
an oceanfront house in The Pines. And I *told* Colin:
east of the co-ops is the chic quartier. But no. No, he
found what he wanted so far west that when we're
still, we can hear people coughing in Hoboken. But
we are seldom still this weekend, for the usual Pines
reasons—a lot of guests, a lot of dropping in, a big
dinner planned, and there has been another death.
Greg was diagnosed, went right home, and decided
to choose in a no-choice situation. Heroin overdose.

Are you with me so far?

Greg's family hadn't known he was gay, I was
told—but isn't this just another of those euphemistic
concepts designed to protect straights from seeing
the world too well? A markedly unwise and unob-
servant family might honestly mistake your sexuality
even into your late teens. But Greg was twenty-nine
or thirty and uncloseted. He never spoke of his life

205

to his parents or siblings, apparently—but surely by this time they must have Known. They just didn't Speak of It.

This left them with little to say at the funeral, when they met the people of Greg's life. Straight sons are survived by a wife and kids, not by a porn star, an opera impresario, an ad man, and an airline pilot.

Guillermo, Luke, Stephen, and Cliff.

They had all (or mostly) been boyfriends—Stephen and Greg, Cliff and Guillermo, Guillermo and Luke. Eventually the five of them passed into a second honeymoon of casually devoted friendship, a state unique to gay—penetration without sex, you might say, penetration of the feelings. They were always together, dancing, planning a surprise party, dining at the Tiffany Coffee Shop after the gym, breezing into The Pines atop a ferry—Stephen and Cliff waving, Luke grinning, Guillermo solemnly charismatic, Greg drumming restlessly on the boat's wooden ribbing. It was not my circle, particularly, but I went to college with Luke and was an old Eagle buddy of Cliff's. A fellow traveler, they called this, back when the subversives were political rather than sexual.

In a dream, my fourth-grade class, at a carnival, beckons me to come along, flourishing cotton candy and Pokerino prizes. I hang back; someone behind me needs help. I turn: and everyone I have known for the last fifteen years is lying in a heap of corpses. We are all children in this dream.

A porn star and an opera impresario, you say? An ad man and an airline pilot? And Greg himself was a professional sweetheart, a "houseboy." It's a questionable coterie, no? What is a striped-tie-and-vest ad exec doing in the company of a man whose work clothes are chest hair? What did the opera maven and the pilot talk about? Ah, but was not this very sophistication of identities one of Stonewall's revolutions? Have we not made the received bourgeois discretions of status and culture irrelevant? Sex outranks status. Friendship purifies culture.

And these men were good at what they did. Greg took his liaisons so seriously that he held his employers' hands as they strolled the boardwalk. He wasn't, he felt, hired for ecstasy, but for affection. Guillermo may have been the best-known pornothespian of the late 1970s, strenuously pacific, opulently brooding, known to the many under a Colt code name I daren't reveal because he'd get mad and brood at me. Luke rose to dominate the American opera scene, most adept at casting. Once I challenged him to cite ideal casts for the three most obscure operas I could think of, Casella's *La Donna Serpente*, Delibes's *Jean de Nivelle*, and Auber's *Gustave III*. Luke not only did it, he cast *Gustav* entirely with artists of the Prague National Theatre, for a *bonne bouche* of expertise. Then I hit him with a fourth challenge, describing an unperformable grand opera by D'Indy that doesn't exist.

Luke knew it didn't. His eyes narrowed as he leaned in, the scent of the kill strong in the room. "No one living can sing those roles," he said, "so I'll cast from the Golden Age." Out came Melba, Ponselle, Nourrit, the de Reszkes—a night, in all, of some twenty stars. I was about to crow, "You left out the Page"—those old grand operas always sport a trouser part for a page—when he said, "I'll have to cut the Page's scene. Even Marietta Alboni couldn't get through that."

Because they were a circle, a set quintet, I gave them nicknames. Guillermo was El Macho Muchacho. Greg was The Boy. Stephen was Eyes—his were green, and a man once told him, "I'd love to take a dip in your eyes." Luke was Il Divo. I could never reckon one for Cliff, but he came up with one for me: The Human Typewriter, because he knew the source material for some of my stories and was amused that I plunked things and people in from anywhere. He said everything I see and hear goes right to the typesetter.

It's time he went, anyway. I've been saving him up, because I'm a little apprehensive of him, of his slashing moral clarity, I guess, or the questioning fervor of his conversation—brunch with Cliff is as exhausting as the Royal Shakespeare *Nicholas Nickleby*. Or perhaps it's just the way he slams out when he doesn't like what he hears.

Cliff was not only good but downright radiant at what he did—flight, friendship, education. He flew planes, befriended gay men, and educated the ones he loved. He was a gay success story, a Washington Stater who came east and made the scene in all its appetite, intellect, style. His thrift-shop special, screw-you attire was a fashion defeating Fashion. His rash wisdom was mission irresistible. The first time he and I talked at length, I told him I didn't like the word "homophobe" because the stem had been incorrectly applied in the word's invention. "Homo," from *homos*, denotes "same." A homophobe hates what he is. Thus, a homophobic lawyer would hate not gays but lawyers.

Cliff and I were sitting, this particular night, on a couch at a party, his thigh pressing mine, his arm around my shoulder. He had this way of . . . what? Militantly relating.

"You will use this word," he told me, "because it's our word. So we defy them, see?"

"Them?" I asked.

"Breeders."

He's the only man I've known who used the word consistently.

"Writers are useful," he said. "Publicizing the lingo, doing it along."

"I don't want to be useful," I said, "except to myself."

Wryly pensive, he replied, "In revolutionary times, everyone contributes. Everyone inside."

"Inside what?"

He smiled, but his eyes were blazing. "Give your hand here, ace," he said.

"Why?"

He took it, clapping it between his two, and he laughed, watching me, as he pulled it around into a stalwart shake.

"I want to be your friend," he said. "Inside the ghetto."

This was 1976, the age of High Attitude, and I had never met anyone who behaved like this. Under the abrasive gambado, Cliff was ruminative, intellectual, a historicist. Others said, first thing, "How are you?" Cliff said, "What have you done this year?"

He would look at you as if reading the caption under your likeness in some chronicle. "One day," he constantly predicted, "they'll write about all this."

He saw *long*. He lived as if inhabiting an era, a locale, an ideology. A little smoother, gentler, he would have been a star; he acted as if a man with energy and dedications shouldn't be handsome, as if perceptions made hot unnecessary.

It was shocking, then, to wander down a hallway at the Everard baths and realize that the Swedish lifeguard who just stalked past you had, three brunches ago, discussed *The Soft Machine*, *Intolerance*, and antihumanist tendencies on the *New York Times'* editorial page. It was Cliff, of course. His head was so intense that he looked different silent and undressed. He was better than handsome or sexy: he was exciting. I accepted his not saying hello; one didn't observe punctilio in a bathhouse. But then Cliff sidled up behind me, to point out an absorbing hunk often seen in the Eagle but never elsewhere.

"Off his turf," Cliff murmured. "Uncertain, disconnected. What mores obtain here? Is he supposed to have sex? Is he not supposed to have sex?"

Indeed, the Eagle avatar did look confused.

And Cliff, who is simply not afraid of anything, called out, "Hey, buddy!" And he said, "This is where," and the Eagle guy went into Cliff's room and Cliff had him shouting for joy, and a small crowd pulled up to know more about this, and the Eagle guy came out literally staggering, goofy with pleasure. Then Cliff stood in his doorway and said, "Big cock, slow fuck, deep intention." He laughed at the way everyone stared at him. "It's slick," he said, I swear to you.

So he was a star, in the end. But primarily he was a comrade, tending his relationships, heartening his mates with his copious, impatient affections, holding them when they ached and congratulating them when they prospered, lending them money and giving them holiday dinners and musing fondly on their capers. He kept them warm. One flaw: he was not always gentle enough; but he could only be gentle with the wounded. He complimented his friends by treating them like soldiers, barking when they broke formation. "Solidarity," he would urge, even before there was a Poland.

The left-out gay writers who have to publish in porn slicks or local newspapers of occult circulation try to cheer themselves up by hating what they think of as the Pines School of Fiction: all about good-looking men finding themselves, so to say. And yes, I can see why tales of men getting men threaten them, because they don't get anything. (A homophobe hates what he is.) However, the primary theme of my particular Pines fiction has been friendship. Not sex: a kind of eroticized affection. Not cruisers: buddies. Men such as Cliff, Guillermo, Luke, Stephen, and Greg. This is where, I swear to you; and knowing of such men and their sense of fraternity must be even more threatening to the left-outs than a simple Pines travelogue, because good friendship is harder to find than good sex. And you can live without sex, but you can't live without friends.

And this: I've known men who made wonderful lovers but terrible friends. But I never met a wonderful friend who couldn't also be a wonderful lover.

I tell what is.

So it's the last weekend before Labor Day, big dinner promising, and I'm staying at Colin's for a change of company while Dennis Savage enjoys a last chance to entertain some deserving city-bound friends. It's Saturday, and I still can't get the hang of Colin's coffee-brewing machine. Or anyone's. At home, I make it cup by cup, fresh-ground, hand-poured water, the works. On Thursday here, I didn't put enough water in. On Friday I didn't put any coffee in—and Colin, viewing this pot of hot water and intent on soothing anxious guests, observed, "That'll be very handy for tea," which no one in the house drinks. Today I must have pushed the wrong button—everything that Colin owns has eighty buttons, a timer, and a musical attachment that plays, for instance, "Nessun dorma"—because the machine uttered atrocious noises, shuddered, then was still: and *nothing* came out.

Colin appears, sees me glaring at his coffee machine, and says, "You know, I can always get a new machine."

He is what is softly known as "well off." I try to redeem myself by vacuuming the living room for the big dinner tonight, but Colin has to explain how the vacuum works.

"You never used a vacuum before?" he asks, incredulous. Think of the dinner parties I must have given, with more dust than *The Grapes of Wrath.* "Didn't your maid ever cancel on you?"

"What maid?"

He passes over this lurid confession in a soigné

manner, and, to the barking of his malamute and Akita, Luke and Guillermo arrive. (Actually, the Akita, Nijinska, does most of the barking. The malamute, Dame Margot, barks here and there out of formality, but, fed up with Nijinska's commotions, often growls at or even nips the Akita, as if to say, Enough is enough. We call her Miss Manners.) Luke is playful; Guillermo, off sure turf, is wary. Colin is festive and impeccable. Now Stephen breezes up from the beach, signaling more barking from Nijinska and some heavy chiding of Nijinska by Dame Margot.

The gang's almost all here. Ensconced in the living room with notebook and pen, I simply wave at everyone and pass up the usual convening chat by the pool. Anyway, I know (and dislike) what they're talking about: reincarnation. I suppose that belief in an afterlife makes it easier for them to bear a world in which important people are missing. Important to us. This is the last weekend before Labor Day, nearly the end of the summer, but it feels much more final than that, like the end of an age.

Of course, the summer doesn't end all at once for everybody. Colin comes out whenever he wants, because he owns his house, and even some renters take leases that last till Columbus Day. There's always someone left after everyone else has gone. But the essence of a Pines summer—the Rhine music, so to say, if gay life were *Der Ring des Nibelungen*—is the bonding of the crew as a whole, the circles of friends intermingling, corroborating the theory of erotic platonism, even if only by a hello as merry strangers pass on the boardwalk. The summer needs everybody, to claim this place for us, not just porn stars and houseboys but opera impresarios and airline pilots.

Cliff suddenly plops down next to me. He has crept through the house and, tousling my hair, too roughly as always, nods toward the voices down at the pool and says, "The Human Typewriter furtively delineating. Round up the usual suspects."

"Hey, Cliff."

"So many breeders on the walks. Why do they have to go where we are? Why don't we make it uncomfortable for them, like they do for us?"

"Did you hear about Big Steve? He goes out after dark and when he meets straights, he throws them off the walk. Almost all his old boyfriends are ill or dead, and he's so angry he—"

"Good man. Give it to them back."

"I talked him out of it. It's good therapy, but he'll get into police trouble."

Cliff nodded. "Still. Get some action going, maybe, and Big Steve would be prime soldier stuff. That boy must be the biggest thing in New York, huh? I was always a little afraid of him."

"You're not afraid of anything," I told him.

Given pause, he quietly regarded me.

"The Human Typewriter," I went on, "sees and knows." On my fingers, I ticked off the storyteller's four essentials: "Experience, observation, retention, imagination."

He shook his head, half-smiling.

"The day you're afraid of something," I concluded, "will be the end of the world."

He nodded again, his mind speeding through

agendas—emotional, cultural, sociological. "Get some action going," he murmured. "Do some fight, some taking. Even it up." He turned to me, his eyes keen as searchlights. "They talk about boycotts. What if we boycotted the closet? We all know a few sneaks." His term for closet gays. "Across the country, right?, everyone writes letters to parents, bosses, friends. Reveal those suckers. Push them out. What are the breeders going to do, ace, fire twenty million men? Disown twenty million sons? Make them see us, ace. Make them know."

"Pretty heavy artillery."

"What are they waiting for?" he asked. "How can they stand living like that, sneaks? Do they think they're going to be spared the roundups because they're such good liars? What you are is what you see."

"That's just it—what you are is what *they* see. The sneaks will be spared. They *will*. Because it isn't homosexuals the straights hate. It's gays. They don't mind if you have a secret. They don't have to deal with secrets. Secrets aren't there. It's that hammering home of the truth that enrages them, the *exploding* of the secrets."

"So why? Tell me why."

"Apparently their whole civilization stands or falls on the fucking of women."

"Jewcatchers," he says. "That's what the closet creeps are. In Berlin in the 1940s, because some Jews were still hiding out, the Nazis had platoons of Jews temporarily free of the Hitler death camp. Why?"

He points a finger at me, warning, showing, this is the world. A little history for me here.

"This is why: they stroll through Berlin looking for old friends, for non-Aryan faces. And they follow them home and alert the SS. Because the Nazis can't rest as long as a single Jew is still alive. The *hatred*, ace! It's as if nothing matters to them as much as this one thing, this murderous hatred of . . . what? Of *what*? Of people who are very different from them and almost exactly like them. Can you comprehend this hatred? Can you understand a Jewcatcher?"

"We'd be Jewcatchers if we blew the whistle on all the closet gays, wouldn't we?"

"Roy Cohn, ace. There was the king of Jew-catchers. A gay man, listen to me. Yet he helps Mc-Carthy root through the government for gays to hound." Hating what you are. "Aside from count-less other crimes." He closes his eyes. Being Cliff is hard. It's endless. "Ace, the greed of these people. The implacable hunger to destroy what they can't own. The unlimited debauchery of the closet, the breeders' conspiracy of silence, the . . . this Gulag guardhouse of fat-cat ghouls. But he died gay, didn't he, that Cohn bastard?"

He wants me to see the history, comprehend the grid of patterns. In cafés, discos, bars, I would spot this athlete of ideas lecturing to boys who just wanted to party for their lives. Do you see it, you must read, let's consider, get off the drugs, stop dancing. If he couldn't talk you around, he'd reform you with love, and if that didn't work, he'd get mad and beat you up. It worked with everyone but Greg.

"What do you think Roy Cohn will be in the next life?" I ask. I'm joking, but even Cliff has been toy-ing with the possibility that dead souls return. He is not remotely convinced, but some of his friends are, for they need something to believe in besides Cliff— he is somewhat beyond love, beyond touch and sentiment and kidding around. He can be unforgiving, like the Old Testament God; and asks too much of them, like the New One. He mustn't be loved, only feared and admired. Greg once told me that life with Cliff was like being found innocent at a show trial.

Colin comes in to ask about lunch. He fends off Cliff's controversies with a disquisition upon the versatility of the Cuisinart. I don't know what his politics are; but he doesn't like anger in any cause. I got in trouble with him some years ago for blowing up at dinner.

Colin proceeds into the kitchen and Guillermo comes in to change his outfit and make his standard lunch, an arcane preparation of Bumblebee solid white in water. Guillermo changes his clothes every time he does something: there's one kind of Speedos for sunning, another for beach parade, one fashion of tank top for napping, another for tea. Luke and Stephen amble in, and after a moment's hesitation, Guillermo decides to fix his lunch in the running shorts he bought at a boutique in the harbor on the way here.

"I think they will match the blue T," he says, heading upstairs to change.

"When the going gets tough," Luke remarks, "the tough go shopping."

Cliff, encased in thought, is an age away, assembling analytical contributions: Socrates, the Taiping Rebellion, pink triangles.

Now Stephen joins us, completing the set; and

dead Greg comes with him, for their affair was the longest and deepest transaction in this circle, the sexiest of the romances. Stephen sits, listening to Luke and me trade opera quips, then says, "Everything just goes right on."

We turn to him, Cliff with the grip of a hunter at point.

"I mean," Stephen explains, "just because someone dies, that doesn't . . . the whole world doesn't keel over. Nobody stops doing anything. We pick up where we were, same difference. So we go to the funeral and we stay alive."

Luke cleared his throat opera-style, a lengthy, grinding rasp like the windup before the pitch. Some high notes coming up.

"We stay alive," Stephen repeated. "Sure. No matter how many of us die, nothing is going to change. Well, so rip out a few pages in your address book, that's all. So what? And you know what they're saying? They're saying the ones who get sick had the best sex. That's what they're saying."

"Leave it to The Pines," I sigh, "to come up with plague prestige."

"Sex doesn't give you AIDS," said Cliff. "Breeders give you AIDS."

Went the day well? After lunch, Cliff and Stephen returned to their houses, Luke and Guillermo sunned at the pool—Guillermo turning at precisely regular intervals—and Colin and I went to the harbor to assemble the dinner. The guest of honor owns an art gallery in Soho, *the* art gallery in Soho, really;

he also owns Soho. He and Colin are not close friends, not playfellows, confidants, comrades, God forbid buddies of a shared Stonewall mission, the chosen people without a God. We chose ourselves. Yes: so why is Colin going to such trouble over this party? We ransack the grocery, denude the liquor store of choice wine; there will be Tabasco chicken wings in sour-cream–bleu-cheese sauce for cocktails, the thinnest veal cutlet the world has ever seen with tortellini in a prosciutto sauce, plus condiments in fetching little crocks and two astonishing desserts. This is world without end, but what world? This is metropolitan life: only gays would take it along to the beach. Colin and I even sock in a little container of nasturtiums, a flower you can eat. It goes on one of the desserts.

There are a lot of straights about, I notice, as we regroup with our bags at the harbor. Are they going to take The Pines away from us if we don't Big Steve them down? I look at the gays standing there with us, chatting, meeting the ferry, heading for the grocery. A lot of muscle there; but what do they do when some mainland straight kid mutters "faggot" as he passes? What's muscle for?

Who was it who said, "Extremism in defense of liberty is no vice"? Oscar Wilde? Eric Blore? Richard Locke?

Another dream: I am lying wounded in the middle of Third Avenue, and a troop of straight doctors, thin-lipped and as savorless as dishwater, line up to cut me open and rip out my vital organs. As I scream for help, they brandish their accessories— scalpels, clamps, catheters, bedpans. The first one kneels. It is George Will. Following a drawing in a textbook, he drags an electric can opener down my torso from neck to waist.

The house is silent when we return, but for momentary elation from the dogs. Luke and Guillermo are off visiting.

"I don't know why I'm doing this," says Colin as we unload, referring to if not answering the question I myself have raised. "Every time I give a dinner, somebody loses his temper." He describes the last three parties, all superbly planned fiestas and all, in the end, drunken brawls. The trouble with Pines dinners is, they start so damn late. What do you expect at a ten o'clock starting time but maniacs and bums, pugnacious on booze and frantic with hunger?

We unload. Colin starts cooking and I walk the dogs along the beach, the Akita straining on her leash to attack every dog we see. The wind has come up and almost everybody has gone inside. I run the dogs along the water's edge. I worry. A lot of that lately. At the access to Colin's beach walkway—PRIVATE, DO NOT ENTER—I turn and survey the view. I have seen amazing things here over the years; I am postulant, celebrant, town scribe. I told what was. If Stonewall were a sentence, this summer is punctuation. Comma, semicolon, period? Maybe it is world *with* end.

Amazing things. You mean, the poignantly restitutive sight of a talismanic hunk with heebie-jeebie tits and junk of death tersely encountering an elegiacal youth of bracing attributes? No, I mean a flea circus. *Yes*, I mean: of course, I mean. But I've been trying to tell you about something else in story after story; is it taking? I've been trying to tell you that a man-to-man system that doesn't fear sex creates the ultimate in man-to-man friendships. This is what I mean by penetration.

No, *this* is what I mean:

About ten years ago, I took a share in a muscle house, as The Pines terms it: seven tremendous men, a fair passel of free weights, and me. My lease gave me weekdays only, so I seldom saw anyone until August, when everybody started taking vacations. Used to treating me as a sort of flesh-and-blood nonperson, like Oakland without a *there* there, two of my housemates came back from the beach assuming they had the house to themselves. In fact, I had been there all day, away when they were around and vice versa, and now I was in the bathroom shaving while they were in their bedroom changing clothes, with nothing to separate us but what the construction business calls a party wall. Thus I overheard—virtually was drawn into—the end of a long conversation between two men who, it appeared, had had a lot of sex but little personal contact. Not lovers, fuckers. But listen, as I did, to how easily sex slides into friendship.

(I wonder if the heightened sense of comraderie that suffuses The Pines derives from the pervasive lack of privacy. No, that's absurd.)

The two boyfriends in the bedroom were not, from the sound of them, equals on any level. One was older, tougher, smarter; the other, one of those young, know-nothing charmers that the gay world can't seem to get enough of. The youngster was speaking of the family farm in Iowa that he might return to. He said the city was "a hard place," that he didn't know what he was doing "here."

The older man told the boy what indeed he was doing, why *here* existed in the first place, and I heard what amounted to a commentary on, a crusade for, and the national anthem of gay life all at once. Standing at the sink, razor in hand, half here and half there, I stared at the mirror as the man went on with his exhortation. He said he would help the boy with his rent, help him get a job, help him. *Help him,* the italics are mine. And the boy said, "Why would you do that for me?" And the man said, "What do you think I've been stuffing your ass for? For the fun of it? What do you think we've been doing?"

"I . . . I don't know what there is," the boy replied. "I guess I didn't hear the choices."

There was a long pause, then the man said, "It's because I like you. That's what the choice is."

Another pause; and I heard the pair of them head downstairs. A bit later I came out, too, and found them in the kitchen making salami-and-cheese sandwiches. They were much as I had pictured them, the boy clean-cut trash with a delicate mouth and the man a Viking with self-reproaching eyes. They smiled at me, and the boy said, "I'm Greg and this is . . . this is my friend, Cliff."

Watching Colin prepare the dinner, I wondered why someone—Colin, I, anyone—would go to this trouble just because somebody owned the hottest gallery in Vanity Fair. Well, who knows what else

we have in our here, what inducements and loyalties a Cliff would find hard to respect?

I kept us supplied with Finlandia on the rocks, savored with cuttings from the special lemon-lime
hybrids Colin has flown in from northern California,
whence he derives. Lifestyles of the rich and famous. Step by step, the menu comes alive, the hour
grows apace, the Finlandia flows . . . and by dinnertime I'm a bit hazy on data. Even a Human Typewriter occasionally jams.

I do remember the arrival of the art gallery owner,
an enraged schmuck with a suave facade, sweeping
in with entourage of aged-queen sidekick and pleasant young boyfriend. The two older men were already so wet they could have been served in glasses.

I remember Luke and Guillermo walking in
straight from tea, Cliff and Stephen following a minute later.

I remember the art gallery guy putting down
everything within reach, including Guillermo—
something about "Well, if you like meat on the
hoof"—and his hand waving, waving.

I remember going into the kitchen and telling Stephen, "These people are dreadful."

I think I remember Cliff looking more pensive
than usual, as if he were in caucus with the
querulous presences of history, propelling him on to
sanctions, rebuttals, orations. Anything, Cliff, but
compromise. I remember tensions rising during
cocktails; I remember the sour-cream–bleu-cheese
sauce. And I remember the art gallery guy, at the
dinner table, going into a eulogy of Roy Cohn, how

misunderstood he was, how fair and smart and delightful.

I was in the kitchen. I glanced at Colin, obliviously ladling out tortellini. I heard a skirmish, gasps, a clatter. Looking around the corner into the dining room, I saw Cliff strangling the art gallery guy. Strangling him. I don't remember what everyone else was doing, name by name. I expect some were clearly upset, some went on with what they were doing, and a very few sought to do something about it—as with AIDS, as we do, as we all, as it is. I believe Stephen got to Cliff and smoothed him off: held him and talked to him and made him stop. Cliffed him, you might say. How many times Cliff had got his friends out of trouble like that. There was a lot of yelling then, and Colin materialized, looking stunned with a platter of the most incredibly thin-sliced veal cutlets, and a certain amount of walking out and door slamming followed. The dogs picked up on the tension, and when I tried to calm the Akita she bucked her head and snapped at me, sending me reeling. Stephen said, "You're bleeding," and I went down to the bathroom to find a cut near my eye.

I'm hazy on the details thereafter. I recall staying up to listen to CDs of *Die Frau Ohne Schatten* with Stephen and the art gallery guy's boyfriend. Everyone else had left or gone to bed.

I do remember saying, "We never served the nasturtiums," as I saw Stephen and the boyfriend to the door; then I bundled up to taste some night air before I hit the hay.

The wind was rolling furiously in, great black waves beating the beach, the clouds so rocky they thudded. I was cold in a sweater and sweatshirt; it might have been winter. I was shaking, and I kept thinking, At least it wasn't me.

I sat down at the edge of Colin's steps and waited for The Midnight Rambler, a stranger who, on weekends, uses Colin's walk instead of the public right-of-way, blithely strolling along the decking, sometimes closing an open door, latching the front gate behind him, and marching off into The Pines, somehow never arousing the dogs.

Maybe he'll try it tonight. It's so dark he won't see me, and if he's straight, I, like Big Steve, will toss him off the deck. This is private property. This is Inside.

Now Nijinska barks, and someone does come along, but behind me, from Inside: Cliff. He sits and puts an arm around my shoulder. He grips me, he Cliffs.

"How's your eye?" he asks.

"Okay. I can feel a bump there."

He samples it.

"You're going to have a black eye," he says. "We'll do some ice on it."

"I don't want to do ice on it."

His mustache tickles my ear: "What are you going to tell people when they ask where you got that bruise? 'An Akita punched my lights out'?"

He shoves me a little because I won't laugh.

"Who're you mad at, ace?" he asks.

"Not you."

"Take it easy," he says, "and you'll live longer. Came back to apologize to Colin, and the whole house is dead here." Then he says, "Listen to the wind. When I was a kid, I thought wind was the voice of God. So many nights sitting like this, or on the deck of someone's bedroom, huh? I'd listen for the messages. Accusations. Warnings. Best wishes on a memorable occasion. I don't understand the right language, though, sure. Back when All This got started, I would listen really careful, because I thought . . . well, there ought to be some interpretation in it, you know? *Purport.* Maybe no purport a gay man wanted to hear. Nothing we'd like, right? But something to know. Something that I could hear most clear here in this place. Something in the wind out there, ace."

"Go on," I said, for he had stopped.

He patted my head. "I will," he replied. But he was silent.

We listened to the wind.

"I will," he repeated.

I don't understand the right language, either.

"It was bad enough at first," he finally went on, "because it was so obvious that there was a plague on and no one was doing anything about it. And there we are trying to figure out what the victims have in common, to know who's going to get it next. It's from drugs, it's poppers, it's from rimming, it's in the quiche, it's attitude. Maybe it's in the wind. Then it's got half the guys you know, so how come you're healthy?"

He found a rock in the sand below the walk and pitched it into the black night.

"Neat scheme, wasn't it?" he said. "Infect a few faggots and let their baths and bars and beds do the rest. Excellent mischief, huh? By the time they realize what's happening, they'll all be poisoned, the whole degenerate Stonewall gang of them. Then we pull out the deterrent vaccine and say, 'Oh, look what we just found. Too bad about the queers, but now those perverts are going to be buried up good and tight, sir, yes *sir*! Won't be no Stonewall trouble around here again, sir, no *sir*!'"

Another rock flies in the dark, this one all the way to the water.

"I used to think it was who's going to get it and who isn't," he told me. "Now I think it's who dies first and who dies later."

Just like the *Ring*: everyone is dispensed with. "Good weather," I said, "for *Götterdämmerung*."

He pulled the hood of my sweatshirt over my head, surveyed me, nodded. He likes it when his friends turn into little kids who need soothing. Greg was more a kid at thirty than most ten-year-olds are.

"What should we do?" he said. "We ought to leave something behind. We were going to change the world and all we're doing is leaving it."

"Why don't you write down how you feel?" I asked.

"That's your cure for everything, isn't it? Getting published?"

"If we all write about what we did, and how we felt, who we were . . . we *will* leave something behind. They can't kill books. Even the Nazis couldn't."

"Can a book change the world?" he asked. "Change a guy's life, now?"

I threw a rock at the wind, me.

"What changes lives?" he asked. "I tried to change Greg, you know. Listen to this—I was going to make him a better man. Get him off the stuff, make him believe he had things he could do."

I pulled the hood off my head.

"Do you ever change a life?" he wondered, putting up my hood again.

Two rocks, one each.

"Do you remember," he asks, "that beautiful black muscleboy that Carson Jennings brought here? Way back in . . . must have been 1975 or nearly so. Just picked him up off the street and out he comes here. What was his name, remember? Very sweet man, never opened his mouth. Incredible bod, real big stuff. If you went over there when Carson was in the city, that boy would come over to you and just start making love. He'd be cleaning the pool or something, and he'd see you and smile and just give it to you. Never said a word the whole time. Very thoughtful, any way you liked it."

"His name," I said, "was Roy Deevers."

"He remembers! Good man."

"The reason he never spoke was, when he did, everyone laughed at him."

"How would you know this?"

"He told me. Can I take my hood down?"

"No. So the boy was doing a happy summer on the beach, and sooner or later Carson would close up the house and dump him back on Forty-second Street or wherever he came from. This is changing a life, watch. Because there are halfway houses, right? Community setups? There's placement, sociology, education, all this. Easy to do if you're connected. That's how it works, being connected. Too bad I'm connected with just what I need, but it's in San Francisco. Friend of mine runs a halfway house there. Ran it, I mean." He pauses. "And he changed plenty of lives, I know that. So all we need is the money to get this boy out to San."

"And you can't get it from Carson, because he doesn't want you interfering with his summer-houseboy routine."

"Stet." Let it stand, meaning That's correct. Publishing term.

"I taught you that," I said.

"Everyone teaches and everyone learns. That's friendship, ace."

The Pines-hating leftouts must be screaming by now, because the thing they can't abide is to hear that the love they couldn't get in touch with actually exists.

Scream, you fuckers.

"Changing a life," Cliff went on. "Everyone chipped in five bucks and I got the black kid on a flight as a standby and I took him to my friend's place and I told him to stop screwing everyone he met."

Rocks. Wind. Death by catastrophe as the world looks on.

"How'd he do?" I asked.

"Terrific. I changed a life. He got on to painting apartments. Union and everything. He lived out good."

"Stet."

"Did you ever go over there? To Carson's? For a date with that kid?"

"No. Just dinner."

"Why not?"

"Because that parade of horny Carsonians was racist and exploitative."

"What are you, ace, a saint?"

"In some ways."

"That boy was filled with love. Sharing it with everyone was his way of communicating."

"Cliff, my ace, you are dead wrong. He wasn't sharing love—he was putting out because he thought he had to if he wanted to stay in paradise."

Cliff threw a rock. "Anyway," he said, "I changed his life, right?"

"You changed a lot of lives," I said. "Anyone else, I'd bet, was fishing for this. But you're so busy taking care of everybody you probably never noticed how much care you took. And nobody knows you. They don't know you at all, because there's so much of you. In the baths, they thought you were some hotshot top. At the Firehouse, you were the Great American Organizer. In San Francisco, you're a chance not to loathe New York. At the airline, you're straight. With Stephen and Luke and Guillermo and Greg . . . you're the reason the center holds. Held."

Lighten up, boy.

"At brunches, you're a matinee idol, a little on the robust side, perhaps. But at dinner tonight . . ."

I stopped, out of breath. Jesus, that man is handsome.

"At dinner you were a hero," I went on. "I admire what you did. I've always admired you. When I first came to New York, I was afraid that all the gays were going to be like the ones in *The Boys in the*

Band, full of self-hatred and cultivating phobias. You know what I saw instead?"

He is smiling. "What, chief?"

"You. And the people you knew. They came in every kind going—queens and clones and uptowners and villagers." I wrote in the air: "The ambitious and the slack"; he grabbed my hand and held it for a while. Stop writing, Human Typewriter.

"Okay," he says.

Okay. "That was a whole world," I went on, sensing some distraction in him, something on his mind that he means to hide. My observation chills me, for even here in the darkness his sorrow glows, rigid, unsharable, uncharacteristically not okay. My retention will hold the visual, my imagination fear the worst. That may be one of my problems. Take it easy and you'll live longer.

"A whole world," he says. "I am thinking of that world, ace."

"Your friends all took their sexuality for granted, is the thing," I tell him. "It wasn't a cross to be borne, but their gift. They were great examples for someone like me."

"Where are all the self-hating gays now?" he wonders.

"They're writing book reviews."

"Bet you Colin doesn't admire what I did."

"Colin has a different take on everything," I told him. "He's of the great world. We're ghetto boys. Inside."

"*Inside*."

"Nobody knows you."

"Right you are, ace." He patted my head, his sorrow a flame. It lit up the beach. I took his hand, and he looked away, toward the Grove—which is also toward Washington State, where Cliff, incredibly, was once a kid who needed help himself, band-aids and love and a paper route—and he asked me, "How come I never scored you, chief?"

"You mean," I said, "how come I never scored you. Because I wasn't good enough. You only go with the best."

Now there was a great space of nothing, and finally he nodded. "Maybe just as well, my good friend," he said. "Because I've got it too, now, and who knows if I wouldn't have given it to you?"

He gently pulled my hood back and put his hands on my shoulders. "I haven't told anyone yet, because . . . I don't know why. Because nobody knows me, maybe. They need me to keep them tough. Stephen was fit for the white coats the night we heard about Greg, you know. He kept asking me why I wasn't there to stop him before . . . stop him in time. Got me so mad I belted him. That's all I do now, get mad. I've had pneumonia already, and now I've got KS. I'm not ready to tell them. I don't want anyone to forget me. I don't want the world to go on as if I hadn't been here."

"Cliff," I began, but he clamped his hand over my mouth.

"Don't sympathize, ace." He shook his head. "Don't be kind to me, don't. Better not test me. This would be the wrong time."

Listen, the wind.

"I thought we were going to achieve a new evolutionary state," he said. "If this was a heart attack or a car jumped me, I could take it, right? Sure. Because everyone else would be left to remember me. But if we all go, who's going to be there to know we were here?"

"I'll be there," said a man standing before us, an outline in the ink. "I promise I'll remember."

"Who goes there?" I said.

"Do you two live here?" he asked, approaching. "I've been wondering who does."

The Midnight Rambler!

"My friend Colin lives here," I said, "and he's very annoyed with you. Why do you use his house for access?"

"I have dinner with my ex-lover and his wife in the Grove every Saturday night. How else can I get home?"

The stranger was close enough now to glimpse. Thirty-five or so, a woozy preppy with a southern accent.

"Aren't you Cliff Dickenson?" he said.

"Yeah. How would you know that?"

"Everyone knows you."

Cliff shook his head. "Nobody knows me."

Staggering a bit, the stranger very gently touched Cliff's face. "If you're Cliff Dickenson," he said, "how on earth can you be crying?"

"Because I'm going to die."

We were still sitting on the walk, looking up at the stranger like boarding school truants being chastised by an indulgent junior master, and he said, "There was one night in the Eagle. You were standing with an unbelievably beautiful man. Laughing. And then you were quiet. Just looking at him. And he opened up the buttons of your shirt, very slowly. One button after another, right there in the bar. He ran his hand down your chest. And I thought if I could know you, I would give ten years of my life. Just to be your friend."

Cliff whispered, "*Is that what I'm going to be remembered for?*"

The wind tore at us and the ocean thundered. It was like the moment just before a hailstorm, when the sky blots out black and God hates you. It was like earthquake fever, when animals craze and the earth, not yet shuddering, is furtively lurking, ready, avid.

Cliff began to sob, and it was like the end of the world.

The Tale of the Changeling

▰▰▰▰▰

LATE OCTOBER NOW, ON
the mild side, a drizzly Tuesday. I
had to come up with a costume and was
rummaging through my closets for something picturesque yet flattering when Dennis Savage came
down for a grouch session. He was on sabbatical this
term of the school year, so he was around all day;
but so was Cosgrove, it seems. Thus the grouching.

I had been wrong about Cosgrove and Carlo. That
was not love: that was Carlo's soft heart accommodating Cosgrove's need. Technically the kid was
still living in Carlo's apartment, but Dennis Savage's
place remained Cosgrove's headquarters, just as before.

"I hate to tell you," Dennis Savage let slip, "but I
don't even like him. Call me a scandal, do your
worst, I don't care. You think he's a cute little
number, right? Well, he's a little fiend. A tyke
thug."

"He was a little honeystuff, if I recall it correctly,

235

when you were trying to park him on me a short while ago at your Pines bride-finding ball."

He takes a deep breath and nods. "Oh, yes. Yes, you're quite right. I was totally wrong about him. But it took a while for me to absorb the depth of menace in that kid. To see through his disguise. He looks like a homeless orphan, but in fact . . ."

I was trying to assemble the parts of my old Boy Scout regalia. I had the shirt, the shorts, and the neckerchief; I couldn't find the doodad that goes on the kerchief. What do they call those things?

"What are you doing?" Dennis Savage asks. "Planning to disrupt another Jamboree?"

"I'm trying to decide on a getup for this Halloween weekend thing in Woodstock. Saturday night is a costume party."

"First, that's not a costume, that's a uniform, and second, you couldn't get into that today with a six-foot shoehorn."

"If you're so smart, why aren't you rich?"

"Why don't you go as a corpse? A real one?"

"Boy, Cosgrove really brings out your sweet side."

"He fucks from the bottom up."

I looked over at him from my hunt for the thing that holds the kerchief straight.

"Yes, I thought that would get you. A new story, right? Yes, he's a born catcher—but even so it's as if *he* were in charge. In his sad, scared little way he's always looking for an angle. A hook. So no wonder he tired of Carlo—there's nothing to hook on to, is there? But, oh, here's a nice den of bachelors or whatever you call us, and some of them are lovers and some of them are friends, and let's just see, shall we? What can we get out of them? Everyone's going to feel sorry for me, right? Poor little me, never hurt a thing, secretly vicious and crazed, but they won't figure that out for months and months . . . oh, *now* what?"

"Well, I've got a few cowboy shirts, the string tie and the hat and the boots. With a pair of jeans I could—"

"That's Village prowling attire, not a Halloween costume."

"Straights think it's a costume. Remember, this is a publishing party—mixed grill. They're not too up on Village prowling attire. Anyway, I can't find the Boy Scout tie thing, so I'll go as a cowboy, *force majeure*. What are you going to do about Cosgrove?"

"I'm going to throw him out of my house."

I looked at him.

"Let him do it to Carlo. Not to me. No more of this from him."

"Do you think Virgil is going to stand by and let you toss that kid into the streets?"

"I'm not tossing him into anything, because he isn't my responsibility to begin with. His parents are the ones who did the tossing—though, for all we know, they're roaming the town right now with lantern and bloodhounds crying for their lost boy. And ho, do my ears delude me or did I hear you call somebody Virgil? *Virgil?*"

I was looking for my boots in the coat closet. "You may as well face it," I told him. "He's not your private little nonesuch anymore. He's not a little anything. He's twenty-eight and he wants a job and he's got his own little something in tow. He may have more whimsy and frolic in him than all of E. F. Benson put together, but he has other things, too. And you can't stifle them. You're going to have to let him be what he is."

"Or else what?"

"Or else your relationship is going to become very troubled." I found the boots and took them to the bed. "He came down here a few days ago and asked if he and I could have, as he said, 'a man-to-man talk.' The gist of it was that he wants me to call him by his real name from now on, and would I please help him to convince you to do the same?"

"*Never*," he seethed.

"Maybe you should try for a compromise," I suggested, trying on the cowboy drag. "He'll let you call him Little Kiwi and you'll let Cosgrove stay."

"You still don't realize what I'm up against, do you? Cosgrove is not the innocent victim he pretends to be. He's the Eve Harrington of Fifty-third Street. Besides, no one who is truly innocent is that expert in bed at the age of eighteen."

"How good can he be?"

"He's not good, exactly. He's *hungry*. It's like making love to a black hole. Debauchery is his . . . his language. The medical problems alone are bound to be overwhelming, somewhere in the near future. I mean—imagine what he was doing before he met us. Imagine with *whom*. And the emotional problems are intolerable. He's a *bad influence*, like some . . . some kid from across the tracks in a fifties movie. A rotten apple. He's corrupting Little Kiwi."

"Oh—"

"I'm telling you! You should see the two of them, singing that idiotic song, like . . . like demons plotting a raid."

"You mean 'The Ballad of Fauntleroy'? It's just a—"

"They sing it deliberately to annoy me. Whenever I leave the room, they drop whatever they're doing and start in, verse after verse of that unseemly nonsense. Grinning at each other and . . . dancing . . ."

"What?"

He nodded. "They dance to it. It's like a Black Mass or something. And when they get to the choruses, they put their heads together and lean forward to make their voices go down to bass. It's *indescribably* repulsive."

"Maybe it's a new form of safe sex."

"That shirt's a little tight on you," he gloated. "Cowboy Bud's been hitting the chuck wagon a little heavy."

"It'll pass."

"You should hear the new lyrics they've been putting in. 'Fauntleroy, he was home all day,'" he quoted, "'laid a kid, then he let him lay.' What the hell is that supposed to be? What . . . what could be running through their minds when they sing that? And why do they have to put their heads together and drop their voices? It's so—yes, *you* think it's funny, thanks a lot! You don't have to live with it. Why can't I just have a lover? Why do I have to have a lover who is also a performer?"

"All gays are performers. But is it possible that this tirade is a mere projection of guilt?"

"What guilt?"

"Yours," I said, tugging on a boot, "for taking a taste of Cosgrove. His being around so much magnifies your sense of self-reproach, no? Hem-hem, my dear. George Cukor said that Clark Gable had him fired from *Gone With the Wind* because Cukor recalled Gable from his first days in Hollywood, hustling the gay Circuit for money and notice. Now you want to fire Cosgrove for nearly the same reason. It's understandable, but is it fair?" I rose. "What do you think?"

"Oh, look, it's John Wesley Mordden," he said, somewhat unenthusiastically. "Head for the hills, the savage is loose."

"Well, I've got my costume set, anyway. I'll go back with you and show off to the two buckaroos upstairs."

"That'll make their week."

"Are you going to spend your whole vacation like this? Maybe you should go away somewhere. You haven't traveled for fun since—"

"I'll tell you where I'd like to go: back in time."

We walked the two flights, and even before we reached the hallway we could hear a chorus section of "The Ballad of Fauntleroy" through Dennis Savage's door:

> Fauntleroy,
> Home all day,
> Laid a kid
> Then he let him lay.

Imagining the two boys head to head in the center of the living room, ooching down to deepen their voices, perhaps dancing a bit as well, I tried to look nonchalant. But Dennis Savage's jaw was set as he pulled out his keys.

Even before he had clicked the metal home, the singing cut off, and when we got inside, the two were across the room from each other, sitting and reading. Virgil, bless his heart, held *The World According to Garp*. Cosgrove was deep in the *New York Times*.

"Little Kiwi, I told you to lose that disgusting song."

The couple stared at each other.

"What song?" asked Cosgrove, the third man, with an edge.

"Cosgrove," said Dennis Savage, "go home."

"This is his home," said Virgil.

"This is my home," Dennis Savage snapped back. "Cosgrove, out. Go back to Carlo."

Cosgrove shot an imploring look at Virgil.

"I had some good news to tell you," said Virgil, putting down his book. "I thought you could be in a good mood. The magazine called and they said the guy they hired didn't work out and I could have it instead."

"Have what?" Dennis Savage asked; but his features jiggled a bit and I saw that he already knew.

"The job, remember? That I had that interview in the summer for? They said I can start right after Thanksgiving."

"I'm going to get a job, too," Cosgrove vowed.

"Are you still here?" Dennis Savage cried, wheeling on him.

"Please don't be mad at me," Cosgrove pleaded,

getting up. "I am always trying to be nice. Please let me be nice."

"Don't pull that stuff on me!"

"It isn't stuff!" Little Kiwi cried. "It's Cosgrove!"

"Little Kiwi—"

"And stop calling me that! My name is Virgil Brown!"

Cosgrove got behind Virgil, watching Dennis Savage as if ready to dodge a flying chair.

"Why don't I take Cosgrove down to Carlo's?" I said. "I haven't been out yet today, anyway. We can settle this later."

"Now," said Dennis Savage, his eyes boiling.

"I'm going with Cosgrove," Virgil said.

"The hell you are!"

"I won't stay with you if you treat me like this," Virgil told him. "I can go to Carlo's, too."

"Virgil," I put in, "you'd best remain here and straighten it out about your job. Congratulations; and you two have a lot to talk about." I asked Dennis Savage, "Okay?"

"Who the fuck are you to call him Virgil?"

Cosgrove ran for the door, hauled it open, and fled.

"Cosgrove!" Virgil shouted, and began to follow, but Dennis Savage grabbed him by the arm and threw him back on the couch.

"You go fix it up with that little monster," Dennis Savage told me. "I'll handle this one."

"You're the monster," Virgil told him.

As I wasn't moving, Dennis Savage turned to me. "Please," he said.

Fourth man. Carlo, no doubt, completes the

quintet. He's the oldest of us all, did you know that? "Just as long as you're always trying to be nice," I warned Dennis Savage as I left.

Cosgrove, in the hall, was frantically pushing the elevator button. When he saw me, he cried, "Don't do anything else to me, you can see I'm going now!"

"Just take it easy. No one's after you."

We rode down in silence, Cosgrove glaring at me, till the fifth floor, when one of my neighbors joined us.

"Can't the Tenants' Committee do anything about that street trash that's always hanging around?" she asked me. "You never see a policeman anymore."

"We're meeting with the precinct captain next week," I told her.

"Everyone's mean to me," Cosgrove put in.

She glanced at him; then, back to business: "You have those meetings every year and it doesn't do a bit of good. Pushers, dopers, vagrants, and faggots, they must think they own the—"

"Cosgrove!"

No sooner had the door opened than he pushed past us and ran for the street. I caught up with him a few doors east, but he pulled away from me and kept running—and not in the direction of Carlo's. Hunched under the umbrella line, weaving furiously through the heavy weekday afternoon pedestrian traffic, he lost me in no time. I hadn't realized how upset he was. I had also forgot that my costume made me look a little, uh, sightly in the middle of midtown. To the grins of passersby I went back upstairs.

Frost greeted me at Dennis Savage's; these two were calm but unmollified.

"Where's Cosgrove?" Virgil asked.

"He didn't want any company," I said. True enough, however evasive.

"I apologized," Dennis Savage told me, in the tone you'd use for "I confessed under torture by sadistic Mongolian devil midgets."

"Not to me, yet."

"You're both monsters," said Virgil.

"I told him we can go on a trip," Dennis Savage explained.

"But he won't take Cosgrove."

"A new idea," said Dennis Savage. "That's what you have to have every so often. You need a sudden shift of tactic, right?"

Virgil shrugged. "I don't care."

"We're losing something here," Dennis Savage went on. "We're getting confused. Where's our list of goals, you know, to write down and shoot for, like on those long yellow pads?"

"When do I get apologized to?" I asked.

"Oh, please. Once you lead a sit-down strike at the Valley Forge Boy Scout Jamboree with someone, you're brothers for life. You never have to apologize to him no matter what you do."

"Do you by any chance remember what they call those things we put on our kerchiefs, to hold them in place?"

"At this point, I don't even remember what they call Valley Forge."

"I don't want just any old trip," Virgil grumbled.

"How about coming with me to London?" I asked.

Gasps, thrills, fears, and silence.

"Well, why not? My trip's all set and the timing is perfect—mid-November. You won't have any trouble slithering in on my dates at this time of year, and we'll be back just before Thanksgiving, so Virgil can start his job right on schedule."

The two of them treated each other to bellicose looks but said nothing.

"It's a bargain with the hotel tie-in," I went on. "And just think, Virgil's never been to Europe. It's a new idea."

"I want to see the Colossus of Rhodes," said Virgil.

"*Finito.* But you can see Westminster Abbey, Big Ben's tower, and St. Paul's."

"What are they like?" asked Virgil, weakening.

"Fabulous."

"I'm willing," said Dennis Savage. "Anything to escape this glut of arguments."

"Can we really just *go* to London?" Virgil asked. "Like that?"

"Why not?"

"One of us needs a passport," said Dennis Savage.

"This time of year, it'll come in a week. You can apply right at the post office. A mere block away."

"London!" Virgil marveled. "A mere block away! Do you have a map of London?"

"I've several."

"Can I see one? Right now?"

"Sure as Bob's your uncle."

As we left, Dennis Savage appeared to be tidying up in a desultory manner, but he wore the face of a man new-made. I paused at the door and caught his eye; he said nothing, but his face read "I apologize."

True, the Question of Cosgrove was as yet unsettled. The boy did not go back to Carlo's—nor, especially, Dennis Savage's—but he stayed in contact with Virgil. Dennis Savage told me the phone sometimes went dead when he answered its ring; this was almost certainly Cosgrove fishing for Virgil. Dennis Savage also suspected that Virgil was sneaking meetings with Cosgrove and giving him money out of his allowance. Most unpleasant was the realization that I had exacerbated the trouble by letting Cosgrove slip away from me. Virgil must have thought me the blackest of scoundrels. But the subject was so tense as it was that nobody wanted to bring it up again, and we all kept our counsel.

Friday night before Halloween I packed up and went upstairs for a bit of visit before going down to wait for my ride to the publishing-world weekend party in Woodstock. Carlo was there, in a thoughtful mood, darkening what was, as so often those days, a gloomy place. Even Bauhaus, snarling to himself in a corner, seemed peckish, his growls perfunctory and his eyes half-closed.

"Next thing," I told them, "you should pull down the blinds and cover the mirrors and stalk around with veils over your faces like the women in *Vanessa*."

"There's romance blues in this house," said Carlo. "It happens when love loses its mystery."

"How would you know?" Dennis Savage asked

him, almost piteously. "All you've ever had are flings."

Virgil was looking at me, rather militantly for him. "See what everyone is like now, because a certain person went away?"

"Listen, guys," I said, "we all better air our feelings and find some solutions, or we won't be happy again. I've never seen you like this. Like a bunch of sulky children."

"And the dinner," Carlo observed, "was very mediocre. BLTs and potato chips."

"Sandwich platter," I replied, "in The House of Mary Gourmet? Then is there truly trouble in paradise!"

"You're not supposed to make Mary jokes during Stonewall," Virgil told me.

So Carlo winked and said, "Virgil's getting into New Age."

Dennis Savage, who bristled, glowered, or passed a sarcastic noise at every mention of this name, muttered something about not having been raised to be a short-order cook.

Then there was silence.

I cleared my throat. "Okay, gang," I began. "I'm going to start it off and Carlo can be referee and you two just better get this Cosgrove thing wired down so we can all go back to being glad about each other and supportive and so on. Now—"

"How about if you let Cosgrove be your houseboy?" said Carlo. "Then he can be real close to the kid himself here and we wouldn't have to worry about where he is."

"That's a *wonderful* idea!" said Virgil.

"That's a quite terrible idea, actually," I said, "because—"

"See, I tried to take him in," Carlo went on, "but
he truly didn't like it around my place."

"—goes against the sacred beauty of the libertarian bachelor plane of existence, besides which—"

"It's feasible," said Dennis Savage.

"I think Cosgrove would forgive you," Virgil told
him, "if you let him visit anytime."

"—would really throw my work routine out of—"

"Does anyone know where he is now?" Carlo
asked.

"I have a theory that some of us do," said Dennis
Savage, eyeing Virgil.

"—not to mention, of course, that I am allergic to
being in rooms with people in them for more than
an hour or two, three at most, and—"

"Well, *someone* had to make sure that nothing happened to him," said Virgil, facing Dennis Savage
down. "He only just turned eighteen and he's very
sensitive."

"Oh, he's legal now?" said Carlo. "That's outstanding."

"—couldn't possibly agree to any arrangement
that would so to say encircle my—"

"Oh, please shut up," Dennis Savage told me.
"It's the only way out for everyone."

"We're trying to be nice," Virgil told me.

"I'm afraid to be nice," I concluded. "And anyway
I have to go downstairs and wait for my ride."

"La, the merry dance of New York," said Dennis
Savage.

"This is much better," observed Virgil as I went

for my bag. "I don't like it when everyone's mad and Cosgrove is in distress."

"You were worried about that Cosgrove, huh?" said Carlo.

"It's a dirty job," muttered Dennis Savage, "but someone's got to do it."

"I call it a good thing," said Carlo, "to see someone worried about his pal. Come here, Virgil." They were sitting next to each other on the couch; he meant, Come closer to me so I can hold you. Resting contentedly in Carlo's arms, Virgil said, "I just want to make sure he's all right."

"Yeah, I know that," Carlo replied. "You have a real good heart deep in there, and you know what? That's why everybody loves you."

"But how come nobody loves my Cosgrove? He has a good heart, too."

"Well, yeah," Carlo drawled out. "Yeah, okay. But that Cosgrove . . . well, he's run into a spell of bad luck, I guess."

A shadow crossed Virgil's face then, because he knew that Cosgrove was pledged to sorrow far more deeply than this. "I just . . ." Virgil began, and gulped, and was quiet, and Carlo shook his head and held him tightly and said, "You truly goddamn very sweet little kid."

I was at the door, staring, and Dennis Savage said, not unkindly, "So go."

Something fancy happened downstairs as well. It was warm for the end of October, and a great many people were out, rushing and strolling and lurking,

including the usual complement of midevening hustlers, though the plague and its concomitant closing
of most of the local buy-a-kid bars had thinned the
ranks to a large degree. Glancing down the block to
the east, I saw Cosgrove in front of the antique armor boutique.

He was looking at me.

Just then an atrocious fat geezer came up to him
and started talking. Cosgrove made some brief reply, refusing to look at the man, but the stranger
went on with what was obviously a john's sweet-
talk spiel.

Cosgrove shook his head.

The man went on, unperturbed, smooth, rehearsed by experience, and Cosgrove moved away a
few paces, toward me.

The man hesitated, started back to Second Avenue, paused, looked around, and followed Cosgrove.

Again Cosgrove bore the man's come-on in irritated silence, then said something sharply and
moved away again. By now he was almost up to the
garage of my building, about thirty feet from me.

Still the man pursued him.

So I picked up my bag and went over to them. I
told Cosgrove, "Pack it up, 'cause you're all covered
for tonight. Deep-pocket appointment in Yorkville.
Real pretty gig." I don't know the lingo, but I can
invent.

"I was just telling this fine young lad," the man
told me, with oily geniality and a shabby smile,
"about my place on Park Avenue."

I gave him a B-movie once-over and said, "Beat it,
scum."

Luckily, he did.

I put down my bag and waited till he was out of hearing. "Cosgrove," I asked, not gently, "what do you think you're doing?"

He looked down, hands in his pockets. "Just waiting," he said.

"Waiting for what? Money and death? Have you been selling yourself on the street?"

"What do you care?"

Good question. "What do you think Virgil would say if he knew?"

Better question; and Cosgrove was silent.

"He's working his tail off to fix things up for you," I pointed out, "and meanwhile you're turning into street grunge. Nice timing."

Cosgrove looked at me, soft anger there, and despair, and a flash of hope.

"Where have you been staying at night, Cosgrove? Tell me. I won't get mad. Just tell me what you've been doing."

He started to weep. Wiping his eyes, he said, "I had such a nice time in the summer at the beach with everyone. I wanted to go on like that. I don't do anything wrong. Why are people always so mean to me?"

"Hey, Mordden, get your bod in the truck!" somebody yelled, and a horn sounded, and someone else called, "You're missing the trivia championship of the age!"

My ride to Woodstock. Cynically cheery faces at the windows, Cosgrove gazing wonderingly at the car, my bag in hand: the weekend begins.

What would you do? I took Cosgrove to Woodstock.

Even in a packed car, no one seemed put out or even surprised at the extra man. Straights of the publishing world, from senior editors down to assistants in the sub-rights department, generally take gay in their stride, perhaps enjoy it as another aspect of the rebellious glamour of fast-track New York. Granted, the attitude varies from house to house. The corporation-oriented places that emphasize textbook publishing and the tight-assed trade houses that cultivate an air of Ivy League old-boy conservatism both frown on rebellion and glamour, all the more so in combination. But my houses of choice admire originality and eccentricity, and their people are quite used to the sudden appearance of an attractive young man with no word of explanation beyond his name. Of course: this would be the current . . . beau, date, companion. The *trick*. But perhaps that last word should be made outcast; it reaffirms the myth that gays fuck rather than love. You're not supposed to make Mary jokes during Stonewall. In any case, Cosgrove was not my trick but my emergency, charge, friend in need. My charity.

Cosgrove was quiet, afraid to make the move or say the thing that, life had taught him, suddenly and mysteriously turns people against you. Breadsticks and fruit were as plentiful as shop gossip and jokes as we headed for the West Side Highway, yet Cosgrove didn't dare partake of any of it. He was listening, watching the faces to guess how they would treat him; and he was hungry, clearly, because he so carefully tried not to look at the food. I handed him two Granny Smith apples and a box of breadsticks while holding my own in another of those trivia challenge contests we of the great world obsessively hold, trying not to think of what Cosgrove had been doing in the last few days. We were one married couple, two women, and two men; we represented Knopf, Random House, and two magazines; we quizzed Hollywood, Modern European History, and Famous Murder Cases; we piled smarts upon knowledge and wrapped them in put-down drollery; we were good company. But Cosgrove was still, all the way to Woodstock, no doubt in the hope that if he did absolutely nothing, nothing bad would happen.

The merrily neutral acceptance of Cosgrove continued through our arrival, to his shyly growing delight. He stayed close to me, which tells us how unsure he is of strangers: for was I not as mean to him as anyone, laughing at his faux pas and standing by when Dennis Savage threw him out of our lives? Dinner was a big do-as-you-please buffet in a basement rec room, something like the opening night of the opera season blended into a freshman mixer. Cosgrove's eyes searched the room, but he never circulated, and I felt that if I let my hand dangle he would have grasped it like a child on his first day in school.

Everyone was nice to Cosgrove, though no one attempted to trade more than a line or two with him. Discretion? Thoughtfulness? Miriam Sonkin, however, decided to dote on Cosgrove, in her ambiguous, stepmotherly way. The maximum leader of the

party, organizer and maintainer of many such expe-
ditions, Miriam has an eye for all kinds of people—
but I believe pretty kids with an air of worry most
comfortably fascinate her.

Cosgrove was careful with Miriam; but then so am
I. He quickly warmed to the attention and didn't
hang back when I suggested he refill his plate at the
buffet table. While he was there, someone spoke to
him and he responded, and soon he was in lively
conversation with some PR people from Simon and
Schuster. I recalled Eliza Doolittle running her
gauntlet at the embassy ball in *My Fair Lady*.

Miriam was humming, any old notes, ironically
intoned.

"Do tell," I dared her.

"No, you. Who is he and what is he like?"

"You just met him." Keep it light, lots of foot-
work. "What's your impression?"

"I want the long view."

"What he's like . . . is raw and wounded. Who he
is . . ." I gave her a smile and a shrug. Two for
nothing. "He's nobody's boy."

"Wounded. Raw." She sighed, mock-sighed,
surely; but who knows? "These are a few of my favorite things."

"I can cover Cosgrove's share in the—"

"Already covered," with a forgiving flat of her
hand. "Someone didn't show, can we talk? We collected more than we needed, anyway. You don't
mind if I put you in the faggot suite, do you? The
only other gay couple is—"

"Don't use that word to me."

Startled, she blinked in retreat, bit her lip as she

regrouped, and stormed forth with, "My brother is gay, my ex-husband is gay, and half my friends are gay. If I can't say 'faggot'—"

"You can't."

Maybe a little humor? "Don't crab my act, buster. I'm breaking par tonight. I'm hot."

"If you were Jewish and I called you a kike, wouldn't you mind it, no matter how sure I was that I'm not a bigot?"

Another hesitation. Maybe we'll fight about it. "I am Jewish," she says, challenging me not to be appeased.

No way, ma'am. "Then you know exactly what I mean."

◼◼

Perhaps I should say something about this party. It is not typical of the publishing world, or of any world I know of. Weekends around New York tend to run on more intimate connections, and publishing socializes in one-on-one lunches, Friday afternoon booze rodeos at a favorite café handy to the office, and Christmas parties, as a rule. Grandly organized weekends like this one, especially thus centering on a camp holiday such as Halloween, are usually the notion of someone who is eager to attain to a reputation as top madcap and is fearful that no one else's invitation will fulfill it. So Miriam, a major editor in a minor house, gives her own party—fifty bucks a person for expenses, transportation mildly guaranteed, prizes for the costume party Saturday night— at a surprisingly sizable old house in Woodstock, the inherited property of a friend of Miriam's who likes noise and fun every so often.

This is a party for in-house staff rather than for authors, middle-level people at that and not the fabled great of the book world who steal each other's writers over a nosh at the Russian Tea Room. Miriam's guests are young enough to believe in crazy silly weekends built around charades and costumes and free enough to spare the time. Perhaps this is what makes the party typical: the very ambition to pull off a party of this size is New York, as is the availability of a crowd sharp and fast enough to finagle the details of an end-of-the-world costume and to fill out a tournament-level charades match.

I don't like party games. The simple instituting of teams and rules and time limits reminds me, horribly, of the Boy Scouts; I have only to take part in anything involving the supervised activity of a group for my hands to begin tying imaginary sheepshanks and my throat to choke on the memory of campfire Spam. Old pressures die never; and look, I didn't move to the City to recall the collectivist energies of the Country. Monopoly, where it's every man for himself, is so much more civilized than, for instance, Capture the Flag.

Still, I must admit that Miriam's friends play a wonderfully wild-and-mad, anything-goes charades. Each player puts down on a slip of paper a title, name, or quotation for someone on the other team to try to communicate—yeah, you know all about that, right? But my contribution was Rimsky-Korsakof's opera *Skazaniye o Nyevidimom Gradye Kityezhe i dyevye Fyevronii*. I expected a cry of Foul! from whoever got saddled with this impossible challenge, but no: the player studied the paper, nodded, and set to—and he was gamely plowing through when time was called on him. This is what I call zoom. Most players dispatch their assignments in seconds—this, mind you, in a game that bans the aid of category definitions as amateur style. No mimes of "movie," "book," or whatever for this crowd: you check your slip, call out "Time!" and start in. Now this (for those of you from other places) is New York.

Not everybody plays. Bands of kibitzers gravitated to far corners of the basement hall, and a few people served as spectators for the game and, led by Miriam, cheered us on impartially. Cosgrove chose to play, encouraged by the friendly atmosphere. I fretted. I was certain he could never master the intricate deployment of wit, speed, and body language dell'arte called for: and true enough, when it was his turn at bat—on a quotation from Lord Chesterfield's letters to his son—he had his team completely mystified. Nor was he adept at reading anything in his teammates' mime. But he did realize, quickly enough, that a goodly number of the slips of paper posed movie titles, and he began to punctuate the turns by calling out anything that came to mind, such as "Movie! *Close Encounters in the Third World!*" or "Movie! *Hitler on the Roof!*" This scattershot approach will get one nowhere, right? But then someone on Cosgrove's team was struggling badly, unable to get a single word out of his band. With time running out—this was a "sudden death" round, and you lose five points if you don't get your message across within forty seconds—Cosgrove's

teammate had taken to repeating an obnoxious pantomime over and over, walking and insistently
pointing at his feet.

"Legs?"

"'Cripple Creek Something Blues'?"

"Play: *On Your Toes*?"

"Movie!" Cosgrove happily shouted, "*So Wales
Was My Valley!*"

The actor of the turn stood stock-still, then beckoned wildly to Cosgrove.

"Movie: *How Green Was My Valley*," someone corrected, and the points were saved—the bit with the
feet and the walking was supposed to suggest
"grass," hence *Green*. Cosgrove, quite accidentally,
had made the touchdown, and I watched his eyes
grow wide as his teammates clapped his shoulder
and shook his hand.

Poor guy, I thought. If you hold your self-esteem
hostage to such idle compliments, you will never
know peace.

I was afraid, too, that his success would make
Cosgrove tipsy and lead him into some indiscretion.
But something happened first. The *How Green Was
My Valley* actor was one half of the only other gay
couple at the party, and as he went back to his chair,
he affectionately ran his hand along the back of the
neck of his lover; and his lover, smiling but not looking at him, grabbed his hand and held it for a moment. Most of us scarcely took notice, but Cosgrove
was so transfixed by this little byplay that he said
very little for the rest of the game.

This gay couple, I should warn you, is another of
those "ideal" combinations, both of them hand-

some, firmly built, intelligent, polite, strong and tender, young but on the rise, uncloseted junior editors working in separate houses. I think they're a pain in the ass—like Lanning Kean, the kid down the street from us, who always got straight A's when I barely skidded through math. "Why can't you be like Lanning?" Mother would fume; and of course telling her that she is a rag and Lanning a brownie, though good for the soul, cannot defeat the sensation of Overwhelming Reproachful Comparison. Miriam's gay couple, Jack and Peter, always make me feel like a rolodex in a gay dating service.

Jack and Peter rather impressed Cosgrove. Like Lanning Kean, they went to bed like good little brownies sometime around midnight, while the rest of us continued to play. The wine flowed, sweet music soothed us, and Cosgrove was drowsy long before he and I climbed to the faggot suite.

We can say it. They can't.

Jack and Peter were asleep in their bed; we two undressed in darkness. By now Cosgrove was so tired he could barely stand, yet he stared at Jack and Peter for a long moment, as if trying to place the playful hand-squeeze from the charades game in this utterly pastoral scene, two lambkins intertwined in a misty spring on some farm where no one eats mutton. I was already in bed, and Cosgrove joined me as coolly as a mandarin taking a bow. He knows his business, I thought to myself, as he calmly folded about me, one arm under the pillow and the other around my chest.

"Can they hear us?" he whispered.

"No, they're asleep."

"You know what? I want to be just like them when I'm grown up. Do you think that can happen?"

"I think wanting it is halfway there."

He dropped off then, but came to after a bit and asked, "What do you want to be?"

"Well . . . I'm already grown up."

"Yes," he agreed. Then: "What are you?"

He fell asleep again, this time for the night, so I didn't trouble to respond.

Saturday, almost unnaturally warm, brought on a kind of free-lance field day, with touch football, nature walks, and hide-and-seek. A far cry from a weekend in The Pines, but then this is Straightville. Clothes matter, so Peter lent Cosgrove a black turtleneck and sunshades to go over his corduroy pants from the day before and give him something of a Look. Jack topped it with a Greek fisherman's cap.

"He looks good enough to eat," Miriam told me as the company sashayed into the sun after breakfast. "*Is* he?" she insisted.

"As you asking or telling?"

"You know I don't like mysteries. At least share what you talk about at night."

"He tells me what he'll be when he grows up."

She performed one of those slow polysyllabic laughs that Irene Dunne specialized in. "Gay men always think no one knows anything about them."

Cosgrove ran by us, shouting for joy. He had already lost the hat and the glasses.

"No one of you possibly could know us," I told

Miriam. "We're still working on knowing ourselves."

"What's there to know? We're all the same. There is only one life. When you're young, you run through it yelling because you're loaded with sex and friends. When you're forty-eight, scarred by a couple of tough romances and terrified your building will co-op and dump you out, you stalk, *stalk* through your life." She snorted. "So for God's sake, give me a hug, you!"

Lunch was a hamburger cookout, and if they had held an eating contest, Cosgrove would have taken it. I've never seen anyone so devoted to baked beans. However, he had plenty of opportunity to run it all off in the hide-and-seek that followed. I enjoyed it; it must have been well over twenty years since I had uttered the words "Not it." In the event, It was a cumbersome art director who had the air of resenting everything about the weekend, especially including hide-and-seek. Cosgrove and I smuggled ourselves high up in an apple tree, and when It came upon us, in sight but out of tag reach, he looked like L. B. Mayer screening Joan Crawford's porn loop.

"You're supposed to hide," he told us. "Not *do* things!"

The straights' reply to Stonewall.

Meanwhile, in the near distance, we heard one of the other players cry out, "Allee allee, olsen gee; everybody tagged is free!" Giggles and catcalls resounded as It turned to see all his prisoners running loose.

"You goofball!" said Cosgrove.

Whereupon It grabbed a loose branch and began banging the trunk of our tree in irate frustration.

"Neutrality! Neutrality!" said Miriam, coming up from the house in something like a bridal gown, veil and all. "It's the Red Cross." She took us all in. "Whatever is this man doing?" she asked me.

It complained, "How am I supposed to get them way up there?"

I whistled "Here Comes the Bride," and Miriam responded, modeling her wedding dress. "My motto," she explained, "is 'Be prepared.'" Like a number of straight women who chum around with gay men, Miriam both fears and apes the queen. "You never know what will happen," she concluded.

Two players came sailing by, taunting It, and he ran off in pursuit. "I only hope to give," said Miriam, watching It's progress through the trees, "the truest party ever given."

"I love it," said Cosgrove. "I don't ever want to leave."

"You don't ever have to," she replied very simply.

"Why *are* you dressed like that, anyway?" I asked.

"It's Halloween. I came out to bring you all inside. To save you from things that go bump in the night."

In fact, it was getting dark. We had literally whiled the day away. Miriam held out her arms to us. "Come!" she called. "This is our time!"

She was speaking to us but she was looking at Cosgrove, and he scrambled down the tree and ran into her arms with that peremptory desperation that always shocks the unready. But Miriam loved it; she seemed to understand, all at once, his grief and anxiety, and to want to assuage them.

"Now this is what I believe is a hug," she said.

Nowhere in this weekend was the difference between straight and gay as evident as in the parade of the costumes. Gays spend all of their lives in costume, from the disguises of childhood and the closeted to the dress codes of the ghetto. One's costumes are, in effect, an objective correlative of the role or roles one chooses to play. To straights, clothes are at most an expedient, a convenience, perhaps a sensation: but always supplementary and occasional, varying with the personality rather than attempting to identify it. To straights, costumes are a treat. To gays, costumes are life.

Cosgrove, of course, had no costume. Even if he had had a chance to appoint one, I doubt he could have done so, for Cosgrove was of neither the straight nor the gay world, culturally an orphan. He did not feel left out at the costume ball, however, for Miriam let him and two other noncontenders judge the contest, and the responsibility entranced him. He got a little carried away, asking a Fairy Princess to "turn around all over" and telling Kharis the Mummy to "do a funny dance." But everyone seemed to be taking him for a charming eccentric; and heaven knows they've all had to put up with far more questionable behavior from men they took to be tricks.

The costume ball peaked in an impromptu theatrical, under Miriam's direction. Each of us was assigned to extemporize scenes in the role suggested by our dress. Naturally, Kharis the Mummy was after the Fairy Princess, who blundered, at Miriam's suggestion, into his tomb. We also had a Robot, Jimmy Carter, Snow White, and miscellaneous monsters, and I as Cowboy eventually rounded everyone up and knelt to do homage to the Fairy Princess, while Peter, who for some reason came as Charles Evans Hughes, passed judgment in his Supreme Court robes.

It was fun, though it lacked the demented verve of comparable exhibitions by Stonewall's thespians. Cosgrove, nonetheless, was thrilled. He clapped and cheered like a suburbanite at *Cats*.

"Why do we have to go back?" he asked me when the music came on and the gang took to the dance floor.

"We don't live here."

That's easy for me to say, he thinks: I *do* live somewhere. Where does Cosgrove live? He looks at me with the wheedling eroticism of Cosgrove the intruder, Cosgrove the hungry, the devious, compulsively begging men to use him in the absurd hope that sex will connect him. It will: but not to what he needs. He wants to be Jack, permanently emPetered, enfolded. He uses sex because love doesn't work for him. It comes too slow, or not at all. It fails to shelter him.

I should reassure him; I have been thinking of what we can all do to rescue him.

"Cosgrove," I say, taking him by the shoulders. "Don't be afraid. You have friends. We won't let you down."

He watches me. Has he heard this before: before he was let down by friends?

"Can we go back to the beach?" he asks.

He doesn't mean physically, but emotionally: can we treat him like a member of the family again?

"Yes," I tell him.

"How?" he poses.

He's not that stupid. Nothing is automatic. Everything must be arranged and agreed upon by all parties.

"We're just going to have to find a way."

"Please," he says. He always says please.

And I think, after all these years, of the narrator of the clown dog story, and I see a version of him in Cosgrove, and I have no choice but to put my arms around him and pronounce the most meaningless two words in English, "There, there." Why *there*? What's there?

Miriam is; she misses nothing, especially the sight of two men who can't figure out what they mean to each other. The party has gone quite well, all told, but it has climaxed. Tomorrow will be a series of farewells, of guests breaking free of Miriam's hold and, for all the good times, probably not returning for another of these so very elaborate endeavors. Sometimes even charm, wit, and good intentions are not enough, and the fun simply dies on you.

"It's all over," Miriam comments, "but the toast and coffee in the morning."

"Every story ends," I tell her.

"What about the story of nobody's boy?" she asks, scanning Cosgrove's face. "How does that end?"

"Is that me?" Cosgrove asks.

"Just the question I ask myself," says Miriam. "Almost every day now. 'Is that me?'"

"I know a story," says Cosgrove.

"When you're young," says Miriam, "you never have to ask. You don't think of it."

"Once there was a mother and father," Cosgrove begins, "and they had a baby boy. But there was magic, and the Elf King put an elf baby in its place and took the human baby to live with the elf people. And the elf baby seemed just, just, just like the human baby, and ate the same foods and watched television. But the human mother and father were not sure. The mother said to the father, Something is wrong with him, and the father said, He is not what we wanted. He doesn't please us right."

Cosgrove looked at us.

"Even though he did everything to be good. He was out playing, and they said, No, no, no, you clean up your room, you are selfish. So he was inside cleaning everything right up, and they said, No, no, no, you have no friends, you don't act right. And they were mean to him, like making him eat foods he hated and saying he was stupid and probably not even human."

Cosgrove looked at us.

"But the elf child knew that the other children in the family were not good, even though they were always getting presents. The elf child gave presents to his mother and father more than the human children did, because he *had* to, so they would think he was human, too. He gave better presents every time. He gave them high castles to live safe in, and fire that would never go out, and dreams that come true. But the mother and father never cared about it. All they knew was, he was not what they liked. So he ran away and begged the Elf King to take him back where he belonged. But the Elf King said, No, no, no, you must be with humans and give them more presents."

Cosgrove looked at us.

"But no matter what, the boy couldn't make the humans like him. They always figured out that he was an elf, and they would never let him in, because they were frightened of elf stuff. So one day the boy gave them other presents. You know what he gave them now? He gave them clothes that itch and you can never take them off, and scare-you noises coming from secret places, and candy that when you eat it it's like broken glass in your mouth and your blood pours down your chin and everyone screams when you look at them."

Miriam shook her head. "If he does that, the Elf King will swoop down and take him away and shut him up where no one will ever see him again. He has to learn how to live with humankind." She looked at me. "And with straights," she said. "Right?"

Cosgrove looked down, his hands in his pockets. "Maybe he doesn't care after all this," he said. "Because how come he has to give presents and never get any back?"

Everyone else had gone to bed. Alone in the great room, we shuffled about in some halfhearted tidying and then dragged upstairs. Miriam kissed us both good night.

Once again, Jack and Peter, so beautifully inter-
locked they might have been poured from a mold,
held Cosgrove's gaze. And again, Cosgrove slid into
bed and fitted up against me as if we had been, like
Jack and Peter, doing this for years. For a long while
we lay thus, listening to each other breathe, then
Cosgrove whispered, "Would you please pet me a
little?"

"Pet you?"

"You know."

We played together then, Stonewall-style with a
postmodernist edge, circling around the scary parts
in our morbid new Precautions for this age of Love
Is Death. Even so, cut off from each other at our
most intimate, the physical remains the essential
communication of our fraternity, the door through
which friends long to pass. How else shall we know
each other? Compassion, you may say.

But this was compassion.

I didn't care to have Cosgrove till I cared what
would happen to him. Selfishly, I suffered a rage of
distaste for him because his reckless adventures had
compromised my ability to know him: selfishly, because these adventures were the dues Cosgrove
feared he must pay, the changeling's attempts to become human, his presents. I squeezed him, all of
him, arms and legs, so tightly I thought he'd cry out;
I wanted to squeeze the recklessness out of him. But
all he said was "Please." I loved him furiously. I
hated him dearly, for comprehending the perfect
lovers Jack and Peter while having helped to destroy
the perfect safety of such love. I was in bed with the
Plague—poor thing; it can't help itself. It doesn't
love to kill you. It just kills you.

And Cosgrove, beside me, was laughing so quietly that I didn't realize what I had heard till some moments later.

Of course, none of my friends knew that Cosgrove had come with me to Woodstock, and there was great relief when the two of us turned up at Dennis Savage's on Sunday afternoon. Virgil, unable to reach Cosgrove through whatever code procedures they had set up, had been frantic with worry, and Dennis Savage, as The Man Who Sent Cosgrove Away, had been paying for Virgil's discomfort with his own. So, then: a knock, we enter into a moment of dumbstruck catharsis, and Virgil explodes with greeting of Cosgrove and Dennis Savage apologizes to him and Cosgrove, barely able to believe this change of fortune, is telling of his Halloween weekend.

And "Look what we got a copy of," Virgil cries as he shows his buddy the latest videotape, *The Wizard of Oz.*

"It's magic," Cosgrove rhapsodizes.

"It's also missing a chunk of the beginning," Dennis Savage puts in, "because someone in this room decided he couldn't do without a tape of *Pee-wee's Playhouse.*"

"I was just experimenting," says Virgil, blushing.

"Virgil," says Cosgrove, "we had a show last night, and a costume party. I was one of the judges of the contest."

"Was our Cowboy Bud cited?" Dennis Savage asks. Now that he's off the hook he has to catch up on his baiting and teasing.

"I was cited," I say, "for having the worst friends in town. Now come downstairs and give me your ear."

"Sit quietly and watch a movie, children," Dennis Savage tells them at the door. "And no singing."

"If you tell me what is right to do," Cosgrove promises, "I will always do it."

"Cosgrove will be good," Virgil adds.

Dennis Savage has misgivings, but away we go to figure out what to do.

Yes, yes, yes, got it all figured. Cosgrove stays with Carlo till the London trip. Then he house-sits for Dennis Savage and the Katzenjammer dog. We come back and spang! Cosgrove can move in with me.

"Suddenly this?" says Dennis Savage.

But there's magic. We help him get a job, an apartment. One of those share-a-place services.

"Reality says no," he tells me. "What job could that little dope hold down? And somehow I don't see him persuading anyone legitimate to let him live in. The kid's a ditz. He'll just get in trouble again."

No, no, no, we'll help him.

"A terminal ditz—and sorry, but what about the medical problem? For all you know, he may be infected."

We'll work it out. Some dream that comes true.

"What is it? What's happened to you?"

His hand on my shoulder, yes; but no, don't be sage and understanding because you don't know about feeling so sorry for someone that it changes your outlook. I didn't know about it myself. What I knew about was, for instance, someone brings his new boyfriend to a party and you think, Oh, I want that, and somewhere in there the boyfriend is telling you about his job as a waiter and he can't direct a story and he's not articulate and you wonder if he's just being social to please his lover, but what you are *really* aware of is how he leans in *very* close when he talks to you and tut-tut, mon vieux are we slavering and making a fool of ourselves and will our appetites be dish of the week tonight? We all know about that. What we don't know about is being touched sufficiently by someone's pain to want to gentle it.

And suddenly I remember what the Boy Scouts call the kerchief clasp: a woggle!

"He's not a stray puppy," Dennis Savage is warning me. "He needs a great deal more than eats and a mat."

"There is only one life," I tell him. "He needs what everyone needs. One thing. One word. You say the word."

"You're the one who never says it, man of the world."

"Hush, I use it all the time."

"You write it. You don't say it."

"I'm getting to it."

The Woggle

$\blacktriangleright\blacktriangleright\blacktriangleright\blacktriangleright\blacktriangleright$

VIRGIL WAS SO EXCITED about the London trip that he was packed a good two weeks before we left. Reading in histories and appreciations of the city, tackling Evelyn Waugh and Simon Gray, listening to tapes of Flanders and Swann and music-hall records, studying guidebooks, tracing walking tours on maps, and memorizing key routes on the underground public transportation system, he attacked this novel adventure—as he does them all—with a rash savor.

Well he might. He had never been out of the country before, had scarcely been anywhere but Cleveland and New York. Dennis Savage, however, one of those well-traveled people who become tirelessly sedentary on the grounds that they've Done It All, fell in with my travel plans out of sheer desperation.

"A new idea," he kept saying. "What I need is a new idea."

Taking Virgil to London was it, then: so I called my travel agent and plonked them into my reservations, not only for the same hotel and plane but even in the two seats next to mine for the flights over and back. This is one advantage of traveling in November rather than in the summer's high season. Another advantage is the proliferation of theatre in London's autumn. Summer theatregoers can only pick up the tail end of the previous season. It's a has-been *cartellone*. The pre-Christmas visitor, however, gets to sample a pride of new works, some of which will close before one's theatre-buff friends can get to them in the spring, thus driving them crazy and adding to the fun.

I logged all my London sightseeing decades ago. Nowadays it is enough simply to traverse the streets of this amazing city, or to cross the Thames on Waterloo Bridge and glimpse Big Ben, the Houses of Parliament, and the Abbey to the west, and St. Paul's and (on the rare clear day) the Tower to the east. The London of Christopher Marlowe and William Shakespeare vanished in the Great Fire of 1666 and in any case would have lain eastward, beyond the range of the West End of playhouses, restaurants, and hotels that my tour centers on. But Dennis Savage and Virgil were coming as neophytes, to do what newcomers do and undergo the rites of debutant tourism.

Dennis Savage was not looking forward to it. Grumping and grousing, he counted the days till takeoff as if he were going to the hospital instead of to London. Two or three times a day he would stomp down to my place, leaving Virgil to pore over his touring kit alone.

"Trenovant," Dennis Savage exclaimed, crashing in on the eve of our departure. "Trenovant, okay? That's the latest from our little Brit in residence. If he waves that map at me once more—"

"If you feel that way," I said, "why did you agree to go in the first place?"

He threw himself on my disreputable couch, upholstered in blankets and pillows to keep the stuffing from dripping out through the lining's thousand tears. I feel like that couch myself, sometimes.

"Why?" I repeated. "No one was holding a gun to your head."

He just looked at me.

"It's a new idea," I said. "Right?"

He shrugged. "I'll tell you what I'm hoping: that he'll be so exhausted and homesick after the week is up that he'll be relieved to get back to . . . I don't know . . ."

"Life with you?"

Nothing from him, and a face like a blasted wall.

"You know," I ventured, "lately we've been getting signals of grave misgivings upstairs."

"Well, he's growing up on me. That's the trouble."

"Most people look forward to a trip like this, you realize."

"He's a confident young man. Remember when he was a shy waif?"

"I secured us tickets to the big shows by phone on my plastic—*Follies, Kiss Me, Kate*, the National Theatre *A View From the Bridge*, and the new Maggie

Smith–Peter Shaffer comedy. I figure that's all you'll want to see in a week. I'll do the rest of it on my—"

"He's finally figured out," Dennis Savage growled, "that everybody, but *everybody*," he went on, "loves him at first sight," he concluded. "And you know what?" he asked. "He likes it. He knows it and he likes it."

"What's got into you?"

"*He* did, for a fact. Last night. His first time."

Possibly not counting Cosgrove.

"Had you ever wondered about that?" he said. "So now we know."

"How'd you enjoy it?"

"I hate getting done. I've always hated it."

"Okay. How'd *he* enjoy it?"

"He's out of control. He's all over the place now. Take your eye off him for a minute, he's going for it somewhere. He used to be afraid to walk the streets of this town, took me years to train him how to keep an eye on the scene, watch out for trouble. If he can't be alert, let him pretend to be, right? So he pretended. The wide-eyed kid who sees nothing. Oh, and that worked fine for a few years. Now you know what he does? He cruises. He's wide-eyed all right."

"Come on."

"He watches men, just as we do. A few weeks ago, when I was coming back from the grocery, I spotted him about thirty yards ahead of me. I was just catching up to him when a man came out of the hardware store—big fellow, the rangy, lean type. I didn't see his face, but he was wearing bright red corduroy pants, and he had the most incredible butt, the sort that was put on earth to be admired in corduroy pants. And our little boy there, he just stared at this man, drinking him in as they walked together a few paces in front of me."

Shaking his head ruefully, he paused there, letting his headline news sink in: UNSPOILED KID TURNS INTO RAVING WHOREMASTER LIKE ALL THE REST OF US.

"Just think of it," he went on after a while. "How long before one of those corduroy dreamboats turns around and sees him and picks him up?"

"So he'll cheat on you. Everyone cheats sometime."

"Yeah, he'll cheat. He'll cheat again. Then he'll happen upon a devastato with a great job and a house in the country and pots of money and charm of death, and Little Whatshisname will ask himself, What do I need with that broken-down Dennis Savage when I can start all over again with the real thing? Because, in case you haven't noticed, the world is full of incredibly nice, alarmingly handsome men."

"Why are you suddenly doing this? Why *now*, I mean? If he was going to leave you, he could have done so long before. New York has been nice and handsome for quite some time."

"He needed me before. He . . . he wanted raising. I was his teacher. Now it's been nine years. For every couple, gay and straight, that's the danger time."

"I just don't see Virgil picking up street meat. Everything with him is social. If he was to leave you, he'd choose someone like Carlo or Lionel or even Big Steve."

"Never. They're like uncles to him. He'd as soon go with . . . with Cosgrove or someone."

We are all fools.

"No," he went on, "I think he's ripe for the romance of the surprise encounter. He's finally reached that epiphany of Stonewall that we all had a hundred years ago, when you realize that the world is full of marvelous men and all you have to do is jump out and connect with one." He sighed. "'Only connect,'" he added, quoting E. M. Forster. "That's the whole opera, right?, right there. Isn't it? That's all that matters to anyone."

I said nothing.

"You know I'm right. A feeling comes over you every so often that you've got to put your arms around a certain man and be held back—held tight, I'm saying—and feel the hardness of him, and the hair of his head, leaning against your head. And you can't do it with just anyone, oh, no. A *certain* man, waiting somewhere out in the world for you to come and take hold of him like an apple on the bough. Ah, but what if you never find the man I so pathetically and embarrassingly describe? What then? Can I tell you? This then: nothing that you do in your entire life is ever going to matter, not hardly at all."

He got up as if to leave but he just stood there. "Trenovant," he said at last. "He wants to rename Bauhaus Trenovant. Do you know what Trenovant is?"

"The legendary ancient name of London, if you believe the tale that it was founded by survivors of fallen Troy. Totally spurious, of course. One of those majestic bygones that cities sometimes dress their histories in.''

He nodded. "I figured you'd know all about it.''

Well, I do know a lot; but I am yet capable of surprise. I had remarked Virgil's steady maturing as a man of the world, an authentic gay New Yorker. Still, his childlike love of games and frolics had never deserted him, and it obscured the densely gathering articulations of his coming of age. Brought up short by Dennis Savage's talk, I stopped to take a clean new look at Virgil—perhaps as a parent does, one day well along in the course of life, to see the dear pieces of the child all fallen away in the bursting forth of the adult. For years I had taken Virgil for granted as a member of my family. Now I actually felt proud of him. I had helped raise him, after all. There was something of me in him.

My family: an odd notion for an outsider to accept, no doubt. And even some of our own initiates, boys and girls, might take us three for no more than a house party, two queens and their weekend guest. Certainly a lot of my tales deal with people being taken for something they aren't. I wonder what the craggy-featured, Scots-accented British Airways steward took us for as he flirted shamelessly with Virgil, even *over* Dennis Savage and me, because Virgil had insisted on taking the window seat so he could mark his first view of London from the air. It is widely known that a substantial fraction of the airline steward, uh, community is gay; why is that? A bartender once told me that the salient one-up of his

profession was "You get to see everyone and everyone gets to see you." This is true of stewards, certainly. But you know what?

It's also true of writers.

Virgil accepted the steward's attentions with a
mild amusement, and as soon as the man passed on
to take the other drink orders, our little tourist tried
to imitate his speech. Virgil was juggling two
guidebooks and three maps, wearing a headset,
chattering about the quickest route between
Trafalgar Square and our hotel, and balancing the
expediency in concentrating on different sections of
town on different days or on steaming through the
place in a mad medley—all this, remember, put
forth in the sketchiest of haggis twangs.

He's a silly boy, but he has great charm. And he
does command, in astonishing quantity, one of the
most significant virtues: loyalty.

Dennis Savage was patiently floating along with
Virgil's lecture, putting in his oar at the odd moment. I sometimes think that he gets along so well
with Virgil because he doesn't have to work as hard
with him as with our more intellectual friends. Like
Carlo, Virgil needn't be constantly entertained or
amazed; he brings his own theatre with him. I was
scribbling away in the aisle seat as the merry partners plotted their sightseeing campaigns, and so the
time passed, broken by the dinner break, the movie
show (*The Untouchables*), and the continued flattery
of the Scots steward. We had taken a late-night
flight, and long before the film was over, most of the
passengers were asleep, some stretching across
three seats, empty in the calm of off-season. I can't

sleep on planes, but Dennis Savage made some fitful stabs at a doze, and Virgil, depleted by excitement, went out like Samuel Pepys's candle. I had put my notebook down to do some thinking, and the steward, passing, paused to look upon us and smile.

I smiled back.

"Can I gaet ye anythin', ser?" he asked.

"Another of those little bottles of white wine," I replied, "would do me nicely."

"Wus it the dry German ur the French?" he said, admiring Virgil.

"The German."

"Yur brother is fast asleep, I sae," the steward noted, his voice lowered. "It's a peaceful picture."

"Wait till he hits London. It'll be about as peaceful as the Blitz."

"I'd be glad to know him then," said the steward, and I half expected him to slip me his phone number to give to Virgil. But he went off to the galley, and Dennis Savage, his eyes still closed, snorted.

"Do you believe that?" I whispered.

"'Your brother,' huh? Your lover. Your project. Your hustler . . . What do they call hustlers in England?"

"Rent-boys."

"Your rent-boy." He opened his eyes and looked over at Virgil, deep in dreams. Looked, I dare say, for quite some time. As the steward came down the aisle with my wine, Dennis Savage closed his eyes again, murmuring, "Tell him it only works in bright red corduroy pants."

◆◆◆

Upon arrival we took a cab to the hotel and moved in. I conquer jet lag with extra infusions of

Shaklee Vita-Lea multiples and an iron will. Besides, I had the rest of my theatre tickets to buy. But Dennis Savage proposed a nap.

"I'm tired," he told us. "I'm done in. I'm dead or dying."

"How can you be tired?" Virgil asked. "London is outside."

"How can I be tired? How about an eight-hour plane trip, not to mention getting out to the airport and hanging around waiting for our flight?"

"But all you did was sit there. You didn't do push-ups in the aisle or anything."

Dennis Savage was already pulling down the bed-clothes.

"Well, *I'm* going to see London," said Virgil; and away we went. We walked down prim little Gower Street to the Shaftesbury Theatre, where I had to pick up the *Follies* tickets I had ordered by phone. Here the southwestern tip of Bloomsbury opens up on a more metropolitan London. Here, suddenly, were men in business suits, scorning overcoats despite the nippy weather, and the unique black taxi-cabs and the red double-decker buses. The streets grew broader, the buildings soared, the town began to clatter, dashing and seemly as it is. And Virgil stood stock-still and took it all in.

"Are you going to be okay?" I asked him. "You won't get lost, will you?"

"Are you kidding?" he said, brandishing his nine-teen maps at me.

I might have said something about . . . well, I don't know. When are you coming back? Will we see you for dinner? But he is a man now and needs no looking after. Just as I was about to enter the

Shaftesbury Theatre, I turned back—oh, just in case, you know—and saw Virgil authoritatively pointing a passerby off toward Oxford Street. Apparently the man had asked him for directions to somewhere.

Apparently Virgil, now, could give them.

Well, I proceeded from the *Follies* box office to the Cambridge Theatre (for Lulu in *Peter Pan*), just reopening in a new coat of white paint after three years in the dark. The Cambridge is my favorite London theatre because the unsuspecting can never find it. Most London playhouses are named for where they are: the Piccadilly, the Aldwych, the Strand, the Savoy, the Haymarket. The Cambridge is named for where it isn't: Cambridge Circus. The Palace, where *Les Misérables* is playing, is in Cambridge Circus. The Cambridge itself is two blocks away in Seven Dials, a crossroads of seven streets. This reminds us that things are not invariably sensible or fair. We need to be reminded, especially as we near our forties.

I went on gathering tickets into the late afternoon. This is always a choice time for me, as my trip takes on its shape and color. This tour took in the World War II musical *Girlfriends*, the drag artiste Dame Edna Everage in her one-man show, *Back With a Vengeance!*, *King Lear* and *Antony and Cleopatra* at the National Theatre, the new Simon Gray play *Melon*, with Alan Bates. Thus a world opens up in a week—history, parody, wit, poetry. Of course, just being in London opens up a New Yorker's perspective—somewhat, I think, as age enlightens youth. One cannot help but learn here, in the very shadow of the history of Western democratic civilization; and

the intelligence and politeness of the people is quite
a lesson after the lawless rages of New York.
London does not teem with madmen on a spree,
with desperadoes hungry for an order of mugging to
go, with crowds of the homeless, tossed into the
gutter as if they were literally human garbage. Nor
does London challenge you with bizarre, un-
provoked assaults from waiters, bank clerks, and
such, as New York insistently does.

All this is London. But there is something more,
and very important: the people you run into are not
only courteous and sensible but *pleasant*. Dealing
with them even in the most impersonal and formal
capacity gives one a lift, adds a sweet breeze to a
warm day. Shocked, a New Yorker finds himself
easing up his defensive postures and enjoying his
encounters with strangers.

It's a high. It's like dropping ten years from your
age or lucking into a dynamite apartment. The difference between New York and London is like the
difference between being alone and being in love.

My ticket buying kept me so busy that I didn't
have time to go back to the hotel. I had dinner out,
took in *Peter Pan* with a house full of children, and,
just beginning to fade from fatigue, went home and
crashed. So I didn't catch up with Dennis Savage
and Virgil till the next morning. Our typically English hotel offered the typical bed and breakfast, and
when I entered the dining room I found Virgil conversing with a middle-aged Australian couple. He
was telling them all about England in a wildly coun-
terfeit English accent, something like David Frost
trying to talk with Piccadilly Circus in his mouth. On

the table close to Virgil stood a little metal copy of the red London Transport bus, the first of what was to prove a caravan's worth of souvenirs.

I joined this improbable trio, saying as little as possible: who wants to crab an act as fetching as Virgil's? Certainly the Australian couple were enjoying his company. The man sat on the quiet side, with a touch of wry, but his wife avidly pumped Virgil for sightseeing tips, and she virtually had to tear herself away from the table when her husband rose to go.

"I say," Virgil observed in his voice of a thousand monocles as they left, "a rather posh couple, any-road, don't you think?"

"So what did you do yesterday?" I asked, working on my typically English runny eggs and raw bacon.

"Oh, I saw everything!" he cried, losing the accent. "I was on the tops of buses and I went into Westminster Abbey and across the river on some bridges! Guess what I found! Refrigerator magnets of London street signs! I got you one that says Covent Garden, because of opera."

"Was Dennis Savage in on any of this?"

"That old fogy. He was still sleeping when I got back, so I went to a pub for a pint of the best and some—"

"You went to a pub? By yourself?"

"Sure, my dear chap, old bean. I found some really nice people, too. They have neat names here, you know . . . Simon, Rupert. And Gillian, of course. She's Rupert's bird. Topping sort. I wish we had food like that at home, like this stew you get inside a pie. Only they don't give you any napkins. Rupert and Gillian are going to invite us to tea."

"Wait a minute. You just walked into a pub and
. . . I can recall when you were afraid to go into a
bar. Suddenly you're having tea with Rupert and
Gillian? *How?* I want how."

"Well, Gillian said how cute my little bus was, especially in a pub just like that, and then she thought
I might be American, so I—"

"She *thought* you *might be*—"

"Well, I gave them a little of the old-boy pi-jaw,
don't you know."

"Listen, you—"

"All the comforts of home," said Dennis Savage,
sitting down. "Everybody's fighting." He noticed
the bus with a silent groan but pressed on. "What's
in store for us today, skipper?" he asked Virgil.

"Knightsbridge, Harrod's, the Royal Albert Hall,
and the Albert Memorial in the morning," Virgil told
him, pulling out a map as Hannibal might have
shown his elephants their route to Rome. "Lunch.
Then—"

"Are you along with us on this?" Dennis Savage
asked me.

"No, I've got a matinee at the National, and the
traditional Checking Out of the Record Stores."

"There's a Tower Records," Virgil informed me,
"in Piccadilly Circus."

"So I've noticed."

"If Bud doesn't have to go," Dennis Savage asked
Virgil, "why do I?" But he paled at Virgil's look of
bewildered disappointment. "I'm joking, of course."

"We'd better get started," said Virgil, grabbing his
bus. "This is going to be a crowded day."

"Don't forget we've got *Kiss Me, Kate* tonight," I said.

"At the historic Old Vic," Virgil rejoined.

"If I live that long," Dennis Savage put in.

That last little exchange might be our trip in miniature, with our boy centering on the theatres, Virgil on tourism, and Dennis Savage on sheer survival. And I have an illustration to fix this paradigm in its visual truth, from that same afternoon, when I was walking back across Waterloo Bridge after my National *Antony and Cleopatra*. I had reached the traffic light at the Strand end of the bridge, and a man approaching me on the walkway called out, "Some bloke's tryin' to twig ya, mate." He pointed at a bus. I turned just in time to see Virgil waving at me in a grin of innocent devilry in a window of the upper deck, Dennis Savage asleep next to him, his head a-loll against the glass.

■≣

"You aren't traveling hard enough," I told Dennis Savage later in my hotel room. "You're sleeping your way through London."

"I don't even know why I came."

"Perhaps to shake up the settled routine of your existence with a little adventure."

"This is too much adventure. He's had me in and out of every attraction between William the Conqueror's bedpan and Virginia Woolf's outhouse." Sitting on the edge of my bed, he threw himself back to stare at the ceiling. "What am I supposed to be getting out of all this? St. Paul's was so thronged with tourists it was more like a D'Agostino's than a

church. And Poet's Corner—what a thrill. A bunch
of tombs and plaques. He was falling all over himself and he doesn't know who half the people
were."

"Why do you keep calling him He? Is it too much
for you to ante up with his name?"

Slowly he pulled himself back up. "What is this,"
he asked, "the Face the Music Hour? Whose side are
you on?"

"Ours."

"Oh, you very clever, feeling man. With a best
friend like you, who needs mid-life crisis?"

"Is *that* what this is?"

"I'm tired," he said. "I'm old. I've lost my looks. I
made crucial mistakes. I'm not content. I didn't get
to do what I wanted to do."

"What did you want to do?"

He looked at me for a bit. "Carlo's had a nice life,"
he observed. "Wouldn't you say?"

I didn't say.

"True, he has reduced all human existence to one
essential act," Dennis Savage admitted. "But within
that limited compass, he did hit all the points, didn't
he? Or even Big Steve. It's a simple way of life, I
grant you—he doesn't go to brunches, or the theatre, or London. He goes to the gym. But he gets up
when he likes, and he works when he likes, and he
dresses as he likes. And when he walks down the
street in summertime, lovely boys tremble with a
terrible joy at the sight of him. Even now, and how
old is he? Forty-five? And while we're on the subject—stop me if I advance overmuch upon our inti-

macy—why aren't *you* miserable by now, like most
of us?"

"Maybe I did what I wanted to do."

He gave me a shrug.

"What, no riposte?" I said. "You must really be
down."

"I really am."

He got up.

"I really, really am."

"Maybe a change in wardrobe would cheer you
up. What do you look good in?"

"Winter."

"Has it occurred to you that you'll only make
things worse by going around in this . . . the stupor
of doom? Why don't you fight back?"

"What is there to fight? What's there?"

"Inside you, I mean."

"No." He shook his head. "It's inside him. It isn't
happening to me. It's happening to him. So let it
happen."

"You don't want to try outwitting it? Forestalling
it?"

"Oh, please," he said as he passed through the
doorway. "You are what you are."

Still, Dennis Savage did seem to energize his manner after that, if only for the sake of style. He was
always an arbiter of gay manners, one way or another, and disdained defeatism as surely as an incorrectly soiled T-shirt or balcony seats. "How many
times have I told you?" he would tell me. "You
don't go to the Village in a suit."

"I came from the opera," I explain.

A hand weighs on my shoulder, the hand of probity; and I looked up to him then, because he knew more than I did. Also, he's taller than I.

"You're supposed to go home and change first," he would say.

I try not to give the past more than a backward glance, for it can be dangerous to recall days when one had few cares, no stomach, and all the time in the world. But this London trip kept forcing a retrospective mood on me, as if we had come to a watershed of some kind.

I ignored it. I banded with my two friends to see the town. We became tourists, disintegrated from the place we were in and thus made to become complete unto ourselves.

It was easy to do. Gay men do it, in fact, every day of their lives. No gay can ever be a part of his nation unless he gives away something of himself, his self-esteem, perhaps. We are always disintegrated from the status quo, always complete unto ourselves. In the straight world—in the world—we are tourists till we close Them off behind our doors.

At least New York is filled with us. London's gays blend into the scene. One notes none of the gym development and dress code of gay America—virtually no visibility of subculture, unless one counts the posters and stills for the film *Maurice*, playing at the Cannon Shaftesbury, which we often passed on our way back to our hotel.

Only connect.

Virgil invariably stopped to examine the *Maurice* pictures and ask about them. As so often with him, he knew none of the background—E. M. Forster as closeted novelist with the closeted novel, this same *Maurice*, that only came to light after his death. Yet Virgil sensed something extraordinarily relevant in the logo shot of the confidingly secretive Maurice, in the photographs of Maurice and his . . . chums. In a city devoid of bomber jackets and loaded glances, a picture of two men lying asleep in each other's arms was a high-concept visual.

"I'm going to have to see that movie," Virgil told us as we hustled him up the road. It was a Saturday, two days before our flight home, and we had stuffed the day with events. I squeezed a used-bookstore rampage between two shows; Dennis Savage and Virgil had taken a bus tour to Windsor Castle and Oxford University. We met in Chinatown for a late dinner and were taking a slow walk through the West End to our hotel. A light fog had set in; strangers would not approach but suddenly materialize before you—cause for terror in New York but a bemusing novelty in London, the most graceful city in the world. Venice is more colorful, Paris more elegant, Vienna more beautiful. But London has an ease, a logic, a sense of fairness, that has no rival.

I don't know how much of this struck my friends as we strolled the last few blocks home, the two flanking me, Dennis Savage's steady tread to my left and Virgil, watching, pausing, and absorbing, to my right. But I definitely sensed, from both of them, the blithely stimulated romanticism of the true traveler, who comes into the exploit for its own sake, not to find anything in particular: just to look. You cannot learn without first observing.

It has been a success, perhaps, I told myself.

When we got our keys at the porter's desk, there was a message for Virgil.

"Who's Rupert Duttson?" asked Dennis Savage, looking over Virgil's shoulder.

It was Virgil's pub companions, inviting us to tea tomorrow at four o'clock.

"Nifty," I said. "London's dead on Sundays, anyway."

"Rosebery Avenue," said Virgil, reading from his paper, his eyes aglow as he savored the single r: another place to look up on his maps. "It says we have to take the Number 38 bus from the southeast corner of Bloomsbury Square."

"We'll just cab it," said Dennis Savage.

"It's more scenic on the bus," said Virgil.

The bus it was; you have to get up on the top deck of things and *observe*. I went down the hall to their room the next afternoon to fetch them. We were to leave London the following morning, and there were signs of incipient departure, most directly in the full-scale display of Virgil's souvenirs. These now included, besides the bus and street sign magnets, a little black taxicab, an underground map mug, a Prince Charles–Princess Di dessert plate, an Old Vic T-shirt, a *Follies* sweatshirt, teaspoons adorned, at the handles, with miniatures of Big Ben and the Nelson column, metal mockups of the Tower beefeater, a bobby, and a Buckingham Palace guard, matchboxes decorated with postcard views of Great Britain, and a tiny Union Jack.

"Wrap up a set of spoons, please, shopkeeper," I said, "and a box of soldiers. You take VISA?"

"Very funny," said Virgil.

Dennis Savage was chuckling.

"Nice to hear you laugh, pardner," I told him.

"Guess where we went," said Virgil.

"The only thing you haven't seen that's open today is the British Museum."

"Which has not, despite the song, lost its charm," Dennis Savage put in. "Now let's go to our first authentic English tea party, and that's the trip, and then we're all going home."

"Don't rush me," said Virgil, fussing at his exhibit. "My spoons are crooked."

"Many replies come to mind," said Dennis Savage, getting him into his coat. "Many replies of a drastically soigné nature. But we're on vacation from all that."

"Teatime, everyone," I called out at the door.

"I can get my own coat on," Virgil complained.

"Yes," Dennis Savage agreed. "But it's more fun this way."

"Come on, Dick Whittington," I said as we gained the hallway. "We're going to Islington."

One odd thing about London is that while no one lives in the city center—as we may in Manhattan—everyone ends up with a house rather than a flat. It's like one's Brooklyn friends, with English accents. Rupert and Gillian's house was small, but it was a house; and they had an instructively wide circle of acquaintances. The party took in a baby and a grandmother. The baby was Otto and the grandmother was hard of hearing.

("All she needs is an ear trumpet," Dennis Savage whispered to me, "and the curtain could rise on a veddy English play, old sport.")

Virgil greeted his hosts as if he'd known them all his life, a swank of bravado they clearly were not used to. But I must say he was right in there, taking stage, as they say in the theatre. Dennis Savage and I were so busy balancing our teacups and sandwich plates—not to mention trying to eat cake with our hands, in the English teatime manner—that it was quite some portion of the party before we could take part. By then, of course, Virgil had established himself as Our American Cousin, fascinating the company with accounts of life in the United States.

"The main thing," said Virgil, "is that there's a constant supply of napkins."

"Eh?" cried the grandmother.

"And the streets are bigger and the heat never goes off. And we dress warmer than you outside."

"Yes, I must say," Rupert agreed. "You can always tell an American in winter by the astonishing amount of sweaters and scarves they wear."

Simon arrived with Graeme, clearly—to the practiced eye—his lover. This unelaborate mixing of straight, gay, and family was utterly unlike what I'm used to in New York, where gays party either among themselves and trusted fellow travelers in a distinctly gay atmosphere, or among outsiders on the outsiders' terms. Seldom if ever in New York have I seen a gathering that merely included gays yet *took gay for granted* as naturally as it accepted a baby and a grandmother. But then, one expects it of travel to develop a long-term view of one's home life, to see one's routine with extraordinary eyes. A good voyage sends one back a little wiser, maybe a little younger as well, with a renewed sense of mission.

Of course, one has to have a mission in the first place.

Speaking of that: no one did speak of missions at this tea. In New York, one's profession is a key tack of conversation. In London, it isn't done to ask for or volunteer such information. Work is a private matter, a clue to self not to be exposed to strangers. Work is like sex. I wonder if Rupert and Gillian— even Simon and Graeme—ever realized that their three American visitors were gay.

"One thing we never get enough of back home," Virgil was saying, "is cucumber sandwiches," biting into what was probably his first ever.

"Yes, it's right out of *The Importance of Being Earnest*," said Dennis Savage.

Our hosts appeared impassive.

"Eh?" added the grandmother.

"What do you put in them?" asked Virgil. "Besides the cucumbers."

"Cream cheese," Simon replied.

"I'm going to give a tea with cucumber sandwiches when we get home," said Virgil, "and have a sensation."

"I expect you must be eager to get back into the swim of your own pond," said Gillian.

"Oh, I could stay here forever," Virgil told her. "And I know where all the buses go already."

"Fancy."

"Yes, they are. Our buses are so dumb-looking."

He plopped down on the couch next to the grand-mother. "I wish I were English."

That one she heard. "He's a very nice lad," she said. "Got his tie on and all."

"I'm growing up now," said Virgil. "I don't need anyone to show me how to do things. I even got my passport all by myself, and when it came in the mail, I was very excited. It's a nice picture, too. You know what? I'm going to visit here again next year. Could I come back to another tea with you?"

Startled by this very American informality, this very un-English confidence, our hosts paused before uttering firmly polite responses. And immediately, the entire room froze upon us. Only the most ex-quisite calibrations could have measured the change in atmosphere, but we had unmistakably crossed a line, been forward, mugged the protocol. This was not merely a faux pas, but a menace of who could say what further enormities? A man who would in-vite himself into your home is capable of anything.

Dennis Savage, lost in thought, missed it all; and Virgil had no idea he had committed an outrage. So I led off in making our farewells, and we went back to the hotel to pack and laze around till bedtime. No, I beg your pardon: Virgil wanted to do some last-chance exploring, so Dennis Savage and I went up to his room to split the end of my scotch.

"Interesting party, what?" I said.

"Oh, yes. Yes. Handsome people, aren't they? The women are so beautifully featured. They all look like musical comedy heroines. Yet one sort of has the feeling that they're finding you wanting in some way."

He seemed distracted, as so often on this trip, dealing out the aperçus as if they were cards for a hand he had no desire to play.

"Have you noticed," he asked, with a fearsome smile, "how young everyone is? Gillian, and Roderick, and Egbert, and Athelstane, and the kids ganging up in the street, and the businessmen with the furled umbrellas in those wonderful striped suits. The last bus Virgil forced me into, I looked around and lo, I was the oldest thing on it, I swear. Young is what it is. *Everyone* is young *everywhere* you go. I can remember what it was like to be twenty-two, and walk into a bar, and believe I could get just about anyone there if I hit the right approach. Remember twenty-two? Remember how that felt? Everyone moved about you, everyone after something they maybe couldn't get; and you're so still, right in the center of it all. Twenty-two, that was. And now . . . well . . . I'm the one doing the moving and the looking and the needing. I'm the one after something."

"I shouldn't have taken you to *Follies*. All this jeering at yourself for not having borne the years well, or made a righter choice . . ."

"Okay, pal." He held out his empty glass. "Fill 'er up. Right in the center of it."

"Easy, boy."

" 'How about a country house?' " he asked, quoting *Follies*.

"Unaccustomed as you are to private drinking."

"Sure. Easy." He took a huge swig of liquor. "Simon was very nice-looking, wasn't he? Tall, probably very slim under the sweater. Smooth, I bet. It's supposed to be impossible to tell who's hairy and who isn't. I can always tell. I'm never . . . But you don't care about that, do you? Simon. Aren't they cute, with those names? Did you notice that deftly sculpted mouth? Do you think Little Virgil noticed?"

"Not likely. He treated them all as an audience, not—"

"Simon and Graeme. You could hold a twenty-two contest and it'd be a draw, wouldn't it? Everyone's being young together nowadays. You know—and this may surprise you, in light of the extremely inelegant performance I've been giving of late—I intend to be utterly accepting when Little Kiwi takes off. Yes, I . . . refuse to yell at him, or keep him tied up in some evil place, a slave of love . . . or what? *Blackmail* him with medical juju? It's vicious, but it works. I could tell him I've got plague and if he'd only see me through it, I'll make him my heir. I could play that one for an extra year, couldn't I? It's a really mean stunt, true, but . . . in fact . . . I'm going, when the time comes, to accept it, and bless him, and shake his hand . . ."

"Enough of this."

"Everyone hates self-pity except the people who need it."

"You don't need it."

"Oh, you don't know . . ." Shuddering, he began to weep, as he did on The Night of Cosgrove out at The Pines. "You don't know what I need."

I took the glass from him and placed it on the table and sat next to him on the bed and put my arms around him and he held on to me for a bit and then he said, "Oh, this is such a concessive cliché," and tried to free himself, but I held on to him. So he stayed put till we heard Virgil's key nudging the lock, whereupon we sprang apart like adulterers in a Whitehall sex farce.

Virgil, getting out of his coat, sensed trouble. First he checked his souvenir counter. Then he went up to Dennis Savage.

"What do you want?" Dennis Savage asked him. "What can I give you? A rent-boy in a leather jacket and bright red corduroy pants? How about a steward with a Scots accent and veined forearms?" Tenderly, he brushed Virgil's hair back. "A piece of candy? A suit? You want a suit?"

"What have you been doing to him?" Virgil asked me.

"What do you want?" Dennis Savage repeated.

"I want to go to *Maurice*. I came back to get you two."

"It's playing in New York."

"I want to see it here."

"Anything. Anything at all."

So we went to *Maurice*; we had nothing better to do, anyway. We got there a little late, but English movie shows always start with commercials; the film itself began just as we had settled down in the top of the balcony, and all three of us connected with it immediately. It is a "beautiful" work, in the classic sense: visually sensitive, enacted with elegance, a radiant presentation. More important, it is agelessly relevant, though set in an older England of murderously homophobic prohibitions. In brief, two friends, both homosexual, choose different paths. One, in terror of prison, swears off his feelings and plays the straight man; the other, after wrestling vastly with his devils, blissfully abandons himself to his real nature in the arms of what the British call "a bit of rough," the gamekeeper on his friend's estate.

Antique stuff, you say? Yet men face this same choice today, take either of the two paths. All gays are born actors, selecting the role they feel most secure in. Your first sixteen years or so comprise the audition, as you juggle your self-enlightenment with what the world will tolerate. You are too young to make sound judgments; but you have learned to act, to judge each scene as you enter it, to finesse the cast and work the house. Sometime later—for a few, as early as in high school or college; for many, one marriage or so after that—you take on your life's role, portraying what the world expects of you or defying the world. Of course, even free-choice gays can choose to maintain a portrayal, to favor certain personae in our dress and speech, to join or boycott the elect covens, to dwell in the ghetto or balance the gay life with the larger culture. But these *are* free choices, whereas deciding whether to be what you are or what They are is fraught with terrible pressures and penalties—and never, before *Maurice*, did a work of art present this so clearly. Never have I felt so truly the sheer tedium of dishonesty, the rapture of the truth.

The movie ends suddenly, and I was still absorbing its lesson as the credits rolled along. But Virgil was so stunned by what he had seen that he refused to move, even to speak. Dennis Savage kept looking from him to me and back. I was standing in the aisle; the houselights were coming on. The theatre was going to close for the day.

And Virgil shook his head.

"What's the matter?" Dennis Savage asked him.

I hadn't seen him like this in years, with the absolutely crushed expression of the orphan who is once again passed over on Adoption Day.

"I thought you were all grown-up now," I said, coming over to reason with him from the row ahead. "Grown-ups don't get blown away by movies. They go out for coffee and discuss them. So come on and we'll try that."

But Virgil wouldn't budge.

"If we do this much longer," Dennis Savage put in, "we'll miss our plane."

"We were so glad about you," I told Virgil, "the way you took charge and led the expedition." Dennis Savage shot me a look. "Some of us, anyway."

"Can't you tell me what's wrong?" Dennis Savage asked, sitting down next to him.

No, Virgil didn't reply.

The theatre had completely emptied. It was just the three of us up in our corner, and I began to worry that we might get locked up in the building all night. Or surely some employee had to make certain that everyone was out. Indeed, the man who had taken our tickets now appeared before us. "Sorry, gentlemen," he announced, "but we're shutting the house."

"See?" Dennis Savage told Virgil. "You're interfering with this man's job. It's late, and he can't leave till we do. You don't want to keep him from his family, do you? So late on a Sunday night?"

"What if he calls the police?" I added. "The reckless English press will drag our names through the muck."

"What's the trouble, then, eh?" said the usher, coming up the aisle to us.

"My friend was so deeply affected by *Maurice*," Dennis Savage explained, "that he can't seem to . . . carry on with . . ."

The usher looked at Virgil for a bit. "'Ere, that's no way," he said. "Goin' on about it like that. It's just a movie, in't it?"

Interesting to note, as soon as the usher went beyond the set idioms of his job, he slipped into his more natural and less polished sounds. In England, speech is class, and class is strictly observed. I imagine the guy couldn't have got hired without this diplomatic effacement of his inflection. Not that anyone handing him a ticket to tear really cares what he is when he's at home. It's all a matter of style, of acknowledging the received values.

"I've seen plenty o'people come chargin' out of a movie," the usher told us. "Mad as hornets they'd be, too, some of 'em. But I never seen a one stop movin'."

"He's mortified by the theme of the movie," I ventured. "What does *Maurice* tell us, after all? It says that presentation is everything, that people—*all* people—get through life by portraying some ideal of themselves."

"No and no." Dennis Savage shook his head. "And thrice no. This film warns us that, however deliriously beautiful sex may be, friendship is more valuable. This is why we pity the closeted man in the movie—not because he's missing out on a night at Boybar, but because he's cut himself off from being able to enjoy the affection and support of his best friend."

"That's all very well, gentlemen," said the usher. "But, if you'll pardon me, the significance of this film is to the gay men in the 'ouse. It says to them, When you're with the main part of the world, you will always be alone. Isolated, like. But when you're with your gay mates, you'll be safe. Now, that may be right and that may be wrong. I don't know. But that's what it says, clear as I can make out."

"I think so, too," said Virgil. "But I want to know one thing. Did Maurice and the gamekeeper stay together, despite the demands of intolerant society? I mean, did one of them ever leave later on?"

"I'm very certain," said the usher, "that they lived 'appily ever after."

And so, trying to smile through his worries, Virgil let the usher lead us to the exit, and not many hours later we were aboard British Airways Flight 177 from Heathrow to Kennedy. It was an autumnal flight, as this is an autumnal story, reflecting on the past and trying to ascertain what point one has reached on what course of action.

In other words: What have I accomplished? There comes a day when one must ask.

There are hard stories and soft stories. The hard ones I define as strongly plotted, based on actions; the soft ones are largely interior, based on feelings. Perhaps I owe my readers an apology for closing this book with a soft story—but this is the third and, I am very nearly positive, final volume of tales on my

New York adventures, and a certain amount of intellection must be allowed.

Certainly that was the atmosphere among my intrepid cohort on the trip homeward. All three of us were quiet, considering the possibilities of stabilization or meltdown, holding on or packing up. There are no permanent solutions, no absolute states. We were confounded.

Virgil had laid in so many trinkets that I had to take some of them in my valise. He wanted to set them up in the living room all at once, in another of those incomprehensible rituals he's forever instituting, so when we reached Fifty-third Street I went to their place first.

Carlo was there, watching television with Cosgrove, and they gave us, respectively, broad and tremulous smiles of welcome. Strange: I had almost forgotten them for the last week.

"Virgil," said Cosgrove, "did you bring me something from the United Kingdom?"

"Did you go to all the play shows, Bud?" said Carlo, switching off the television.

"I took very good care of your house," Cosgrove told Dennis Savage. "Mr. Smith and I made dinner every night and we always cleaned up after."

"He's going to be the top houseboy of the East Fifties," said Carlo.

"I'm a good boy now," Cosgrove agreed.

We travelers didn't say much. We were running on London time, five hours later than New York, and thus had reached the end of our waking hours while our fellow citizens were enjoying the middle of their evening. I gave Virgil his souvenirs and was about to drag myself downstairs when Carlo said, "Now we all have to go and help Cosgrove start his new job."

Cosgrove, standing apart from us all, put his hands in his pockets and looked down at the floor. I remembered his Story. Dennis Savage, his eyes flickering with fatigue, managed a grin. Virgil was brisk and Carlo fleet, gathering up Cosgrove, my bags, and me in a sneaky whirl, and the whole pack of us trooped downstairs to my apartment.

Inside me, voices protested that my right of free choice was being overwhelmed by an officious do-gooder faction. The sanctity of the one-person household was under attack. I was so upset that I couldn't hold my key straight when we reached my door.

"Look," I began; but Carlo calmly took my key and let us all in. Plenty of sex and a happy ending, you know.

"Oh, you'll have a lot of tidying to do here, Cosgrove," says Virgil as the lights go on.

"Don't break anything," I beg. "You can't do it with just anyone. I don't want to be a woggle."

"He's going to be a good boy," Carlo promises me.

"Four against one," I cry. "No fair."

"Just throw his bags anywhere," Dennis Savage tells Cosgrove.

Could I be dreaming this? I've had such dreams before. Sometimes I'm atop a falling building, sometimes I'm going under in an avalanche, and sometimes I'm being assigned a live-in houseboy.

"That little Cosgrove's going to take care of you,"

says Carlo, having a wonderful time, putting a hold on me.

"His veal marengo!" Dennis Savage raves. "His cassoulet!"

"I fix an afternoon tray," Cosgrove tells me, "of cheese and potato chips."

"Kiss today hello," says Dennis Savage. That's what the choice is.

He always goes for the good things; this is my turn, now. The theme demands it. Mission accomplished. I am the bearer, the actor. I say, "The Cambridge Theatre is in Seven Dials, not Cambridge Circus."

"He's babbling," observes Dennis Savage. "The horrid zany. Somebody slap him."

I sink into my desk chair. All this reality. "How can you do this to me?"

"With a certain giddy pleasure, actually," Dennis Savage replies. "Because this ties up everyone's problem, and you can live happily ever after."

"This doesn't tie anything up. Nothing is resolved!"

"Well," he shrugs. "Such is life."

"Oh, suddenly you're in a good mood?"

"I've got all the future to be morose in, haven't I? And some recent moviegoing to think about. Maybe we're not all as grown-up as we think we are."

"Cosgrove," says Virgil, "you're going to be happy ever after."

"Am I?" Cosgrove goes up to Virgil like a felon suing the governor for a pardon. "How do you know that?"

"Because all your friends are here now. Every-body *loves* you, Cosgrove."

"But I don't know if that's true!"

Virgil takes Cosgrove by the shoulders. "I know it's true, Cosgrove. I was always planning to watch out for you."

Pulling Cosgrove to him, Virgil slips his arms around him, and Cosgrove holds on to Virgil.

"Look at those two kids playing Lover Man," says Carlo. "With those little waists and their smooth boyskin."

Cosgrove's eyes are wet when the two break apart, and he whispers, "Everybody loves me."

The phone rang.

As I reached for it, Dennis Savage stopped me and beckoned to Cosgrove. "Let the houseboy do his job," he ordered.

"I'll get it!" shouted Cosgrove, rushing over. As he picked up, he said, "This is Mr. Bud's resi-dence."

"Oh, for heaven's sake!"

"Why, this is Cosgrove . . . the houseboy . . . Yes . . . No, because . . . because I have a smooth boywaist."

I grabbed for the phone, but Carlo held me down in the chair. "Let him do it."

"It might be somebody important!"

"Cosgrove will handle it," said Virgil.

"Well," Cosgrove was saying, "you know he was in London, England, and then he came back . . . I know, but I always have to find out who it is first. I want to do a good job, so nothing bad happens any-more. I don't want to be street grunge . . . Yes, for a while, but there were certain things I wouldn't do even when they threatened to beat me up. I was like a secret to them. But I knew who my friends were. The Elf King left me with a terrible family, but I escaped and came here. I don't have to be a secret anymore. And Miriam said if I don't behave that the Elf King will . . . he will . . ."

Cosgrove is turned away from us, but Virgil knows all about his little comrade and whispers, "You mustn't cry on the job, Cosgrove."

"I'm not crying," says Cosgrove, crying, as he extends the receiver to me. I take it in one hand and gently pull Cosgrove closer with the other. I am thinking of Cliff just now.

"Yes?" into the phone.

"What on earth is going on over there?"

"Hello, Mother."

"What was that young man talking about?"

"He was trying to tell you that . . . that everybody loves him."

Cosgrove burst into sobs at this, and I put my arms around him, and Dennis Savage had to get on the phone and keep Mother busy with the first thing that came into his head, a recollection of the time he and I subverted an all-Jamboree Capture the Flag and were thrown out of the Boy Scouts, woggles and all. Virgil and Carlo pressed close for family support as I realized, startled, furious and full of joy, that I am back where I started, as the middle boy of five brothers: except Carlo and Dennis Savage are kinder to me than Ned and Jim were and I promise not to bully Virgil and Cosgrove the way I did Andrew and Tony. One other difference from the old-style family: no parents. No authority figures saying no. Now the parents are overthrown; we are our own authority.

On the strength of this new union, I told Cosgrove that we would all take care of him, that he was home and free. He held on to me, but his head was shaking, because he has vast doubts that anyone will take care of him for long. True, he has been disheartened by past dealings with incorrect company, by a shortage of Cliffs. But I am determined that my family find a place for the elf child, because I have not forgotten how lonely it felt to be one myself, when I was very young and didn't know the way to Stonewall City.

I've a feeling I'm not in Pennsylvania anymore. And as for what now transpires, I leave you to reckon, boys and girls, for this is the utmost of my report.

ETHAN MORDDEN was born in Heavensville, Pennsylvania, and was raised there, in Venice, Italy, and on Long Island. He is the author of twenty-four books, including the celebrated "Buddies" books, *The Hollywood Studios*, *Opera in the Twentieth Century*, and *Medium Cool: The Movies of the 1960s*.